THE MOON PROMISE

BY

QUENTIN GRADY

This is a work of fiction. Names, characters, places, and incidents are either products of the author's imagination or are used fictitiously. Any resemblance to actual events and locales or persons, living or dead, is entirely coincidental.

ISBN-13: 978-0-989366-6-1
ISBN-10: 0989836665

CONTENTS

PREFACE

The Moon Promise is a work of fiction. This second book of *The Ghost Eagle* series builds upon the characters and their stories revealed in the first book. It takes place in 1754 in the vast wilderness areas of Lake Erie, Lake Ontario, the rivers and major tributaries of New York, Pennsylvania, and the Saint Lawrence River in Canada. The story unfolds against the backdrop of the French and Indian War (1754–63), sometimes referred to as the Canadian-American War. The first year of this war goes well for the French as they sweep the English military presence from the lands west of the Allegheny River, but in subsequent years the English navy dominates and cuts off aid and resupply to Quebec and Montréal. In 1754, that was not yet the case, but the historical figures and the fictional characters see it coming. This drives their behavior and plans, which are often at cross-purposes.

Henri Gerrard has survived his trials from Book 1 and brings all those "learned abilities" with him into Book 2.

As an author, I have my plot plans and narratives pre-determined, but in fiction, as in life, the characters grow and evolve, and often they will not do what the author wants; that is to say, they will not "act out of character." It is rather spooky when this happens, while also highly compelling for me when it does. For example, in Book 1, with Henri and the cave scene, I did not plan for it to turn out the way it did. The result affected me profoundly. I could not write for almost two weeks afterward. And as with real people when tragedy strikes, that occurrence at the end of Book 1 haunts Henri in good and bad ways and drives how he will react to situations in the future.

Villains, too, are often warped by life experiences, making them heinous and unpredictable. Often, they try to excel in their wicked natures because of a belief or a desire to achieve some pinnacle. When a villain goes "off script," so to speak, then the reactions of the characters become spontaneous. Um, particularly that of demons!

At certain points in this story, I did not know where a scene was going, or who was going to live or die. But in the end, the story continues into

Book 3, *The Falcon Queen*, which is already being written. At least the ship has a future, yes?

The Prologue of this book is a little longer than usual, as it completes the tale of the Druid priest, Daeniel, whose legend and story began in the first book of the series, *The Ghost Eagle*.

As with the first book, there is a glossary of names at the end. And the illustrations are all in the front. For e-book readers, you can get copies of the maps and illustrations on my web page and my Facebook page, if you prefer to print out copies to keep handy while you read.

(www.ghosteaglepublishing.com)

So here's to you, all my excellent, valuable fans and readers. Thanks for all your positive reviews and comments.

Enjoy!
Quentin Grady

ILLUSTRATIONS

Wilderness Forts and Villages, 1754
City of Montréal, 1754
North American Cities and Forts, 1754
Illustrations and cover art and design by Yoko Matsuoka.
http://www.m-y-designs.com/

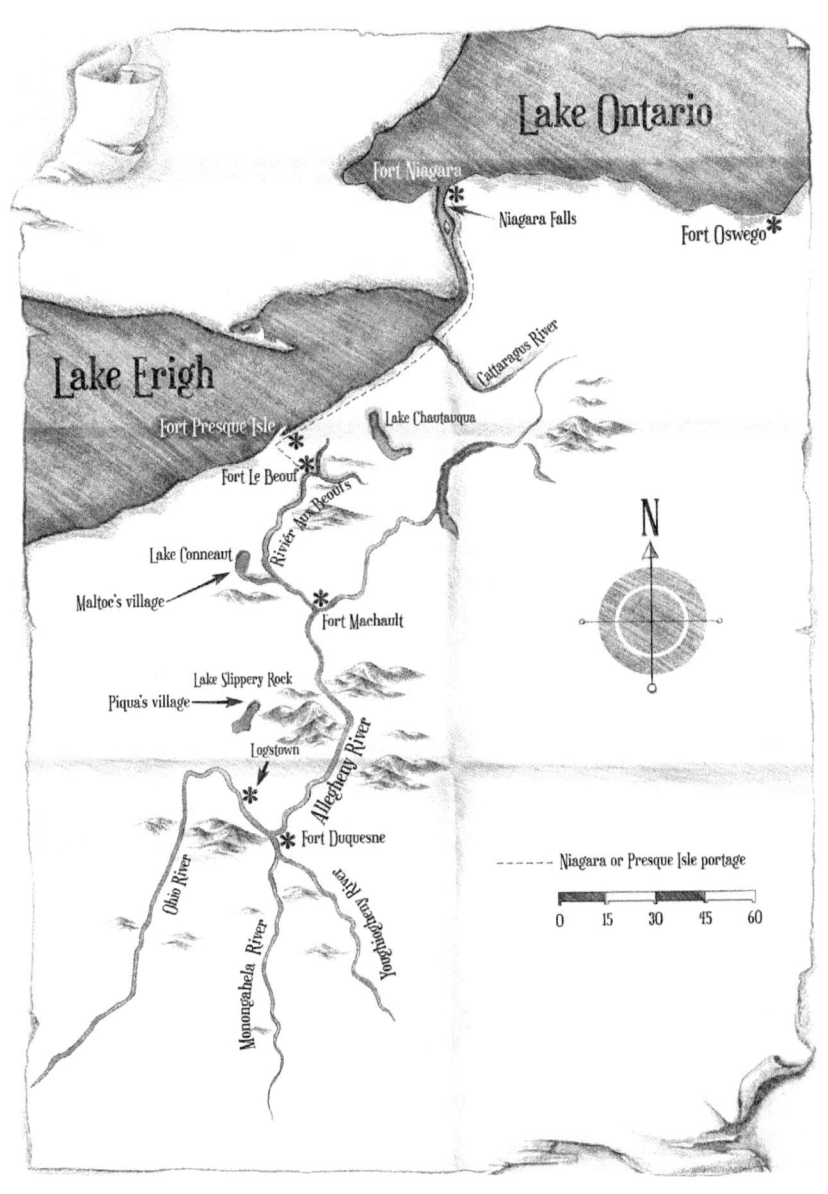

Lake Ontario

Fort Niagara

Niagara Falls

Fort Oswego

Cattaraugus River

Lake Erigh

Fort Presque Isle

Lake Chautauqua

Fort Le Beouf

Rivèr Aux Beouf's

Lake Conneaut

Maltoe's village

Fort Machault

N

Lake Slippery Rock

Piqua's village

Logstown

Allegheny River

Ohio River

Fort Duquesne

Monongahela River

Youghiogheny River

- - - - - Niagara or Presque Isle portage

0   15   30   45   60

WILDERNESS FORTS AND VILLAGES, 1754

IX

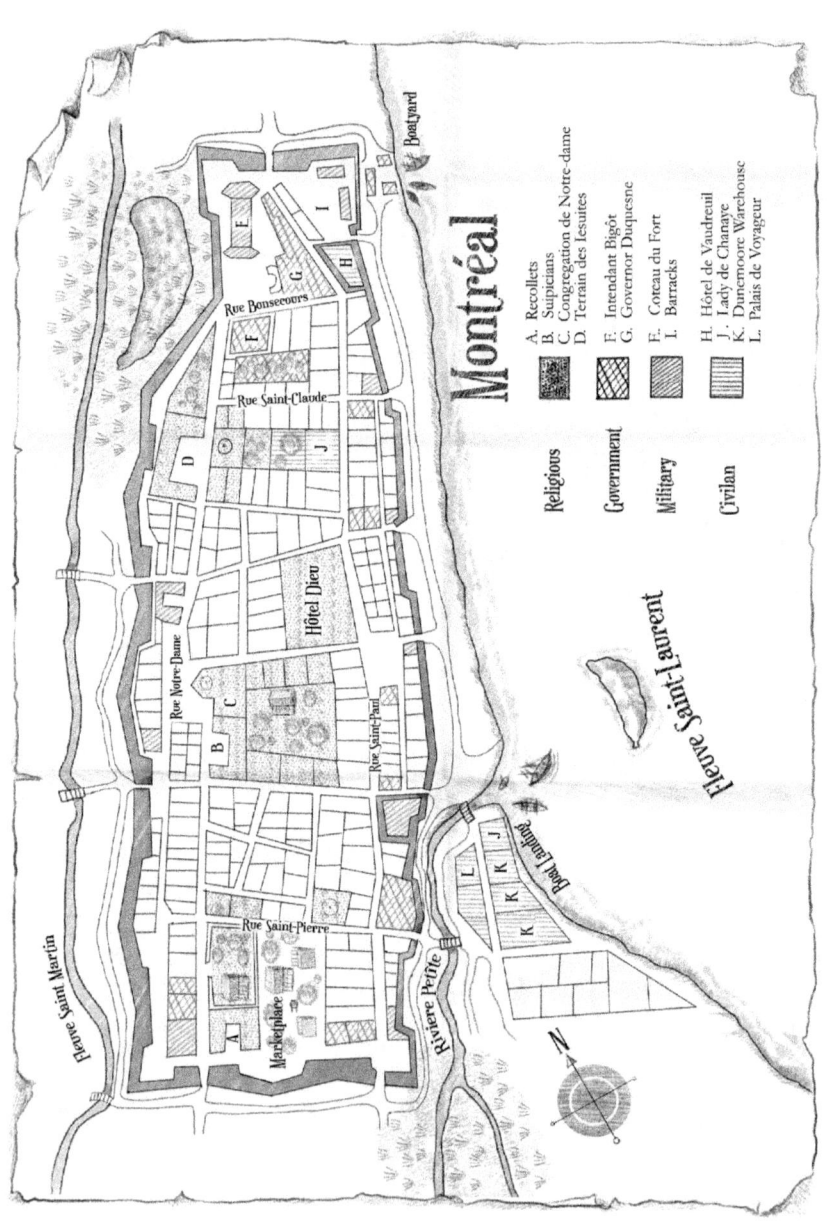

Montréal

Religious
A. Recollets
B. Sulpicians
C. Congregation de Notre-dame
D. Terrain des Iesuites

Government
F. Intendant Bigôt
G. Governor Duquesne

Military
F. Coteau du Fort
I. Barracks

Civilan
H. Hôtel de Vaudreuil
J. Lady de Chanaye
K. Dunemoore Warehouse
L. Palais de Voyageur

Boatyard

Rue Bonsecours

Rue Saint-Claude

Hôtel Dieu

Rue Notre-Dame

Rue Saint-Paul

Rue Saint-Pierre

Marketplace

Fleuve Saint Martin

Rivière Petite

Fleuve Saint-Laurent

Bord L'Eau

N

CITY OF MONTRÉAL, 1754

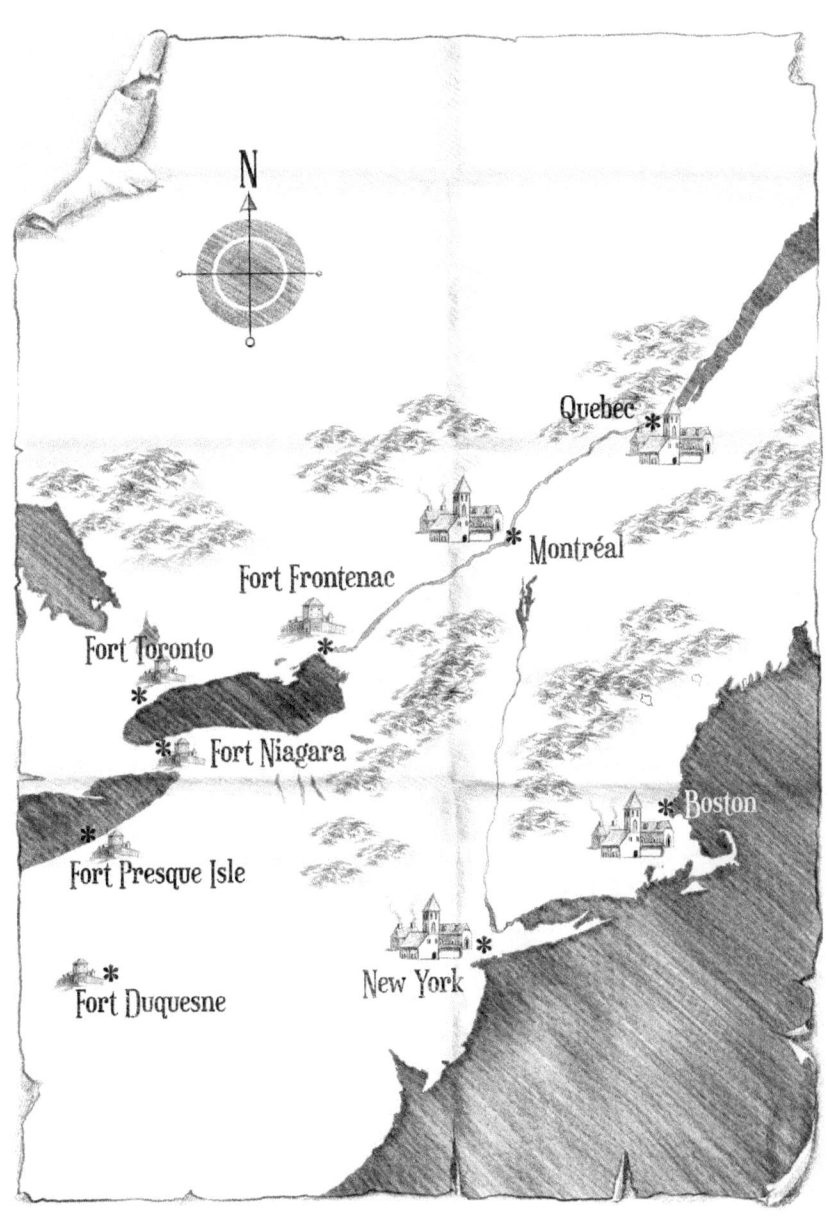

NORTH AMERICAN CITIES AND FORTS, 1754

PROLOGUE
NORTH AMERICAN WILDERNESS
NOVEMBER 988
A Place That Cannot Be Found

As the morning mists lifted, the Northmen were greeted by a great silence once again. Daeniel saw the now-usual frowns of uncertainty on their faces. It had been over a month since they'd left Greenland. They had seen no evidence of people after making landfall on this new western shore, lands so apparently deserted they seemed sinister. The Vikings beached the ship only long enough to collect wood for their firepots and then backed out to anchor the dragon knarr offshore during the night.

Daeniel worried the Norse were losing their nerve, hard as that was to believe. He did not want to turn around...not after coming so far.

"There must be a coastal village here somewhere. There must be people. This land is simply too vast not to have people, yes?"

"Greenland had no people, Druid, until we landed there, and we've come much farther than that," the Norse captain grunted in response. "Row!" he shouted to his men.

Seconds later, the oars dipped and pulled. The Norse began another day of exploration. Many more would follow.

Three uneventful weeks passed before they turned west as the coast eased in that direction. The captain assumed it was just another large bay. He had begun to feel apprehensive and had tried not to show it, and not because of the dangers of this voyage.

We should have seen large animals by now; even if it is winter. The foreign shoreline was far, far away from his home, well beyond any tale or myth from their sagas. *Maybe the gods did not intend for us to come here?*

Daeniel continued to try and bolster the captain's mood. "It's good land. We've seen numerous rivers."

"Small rivers. Greenland was friendlier."

"Greenland is made of ice. Here, at least, they have trees! And if there

1

is a village it…it may contain plunder!"

"Plunder?" The captain frowned at Daeniel, only a little amused. "What plunder? Dried fish?"

Yet, despite his skepticism, the captain really did wish to keep going. He desperately desired something to show for this extraordinary voyage, something to commemorate going beyond Iceland and again beyond Erik's Island, as Greenland was called. This was, as the Druid said, new land, forested land. As a Norse high lord, the discovery belonged to him. But it would be worthless if he could not get anyone else to follow him back a second time. He needed something more to establish the value of this place, not just an unbelievable story; something—anything—for validation, furs, weapons, or some kind of metal objects would prove helpful. A slave maybe? But after sailing these coastlines south and west for weeks, it remained unchanging; there was nothing to see beyond occasional seabirds. A cold land filled with stark, leafless trees under gray winter skies.

They had rowed onward for eight more days, staying close to the northern shore of the bay…if it was a bay. The captain had now sailed his sea-battered knarr further than he ever intended. Their provisions were dangerously low, and he was sick of fish and seal. They'd been lucky the weather had not worsened; a condition that could change overnight and turn deadly. And the winter days were growing shorter. Even his usually stoic warrior crew was now grumbling at their oars. The captain's initial boldness and courage presently seemed foolish. As the captain walked the length of the ship in restless deliberation, he sensed the eyes of his men following him. He could almost hear their thoughts. What's the point of this? There is nothing here. Why go any further?

Still, the decision to give up was not one to boast about later, particularly when the trials of the return winter voyage would be harsh. Without a trophy, he needed a face-saving reason to stop.

Well, at least the sun is out today, he thought.

The captain looked out across the water, shading his eyes, searching the horizon for any fishing vessels. A poor prize to be sure, but it would be something. Then, in that bright morning sunrise, as the morning mists cleared, the captain discerned a shoreline a few miles across the water from him.

"Taste the water!" he shouted.

A bucket was lowered.

"It's fresh," a crewman confirmed.

"This is no bay," the captain whispered to himself.

He ran to the bow and climbed to the top of the dragon's head. He extended an arm at an angle halfway between amidships and the bow, selecting and pointing at the tallest of the trees he saw on the other bank.

"Row hard!" he shouted. Then he began to count.

The captain knew exactly how fast his ship would move with a hard steady row on calm waters. As the vessel moved forward, he kept pointing at the tree. It was a long count before his arm extended fully to the left and the tree was directly across from him.

"Rest your oars!"

As Daeniel watched, he knew what the captain was doing. It was simple mathematica; a geometric measure of distance and time. The captain now knew the distance to the other shore and how long it would take him to reach it if he chose to do so. If the channel remained straight, then it would eventually narrow.

But the captain's short burst of optimism vanished. Directly ahead, he saw the beginnings of icy fingers stretching out from the shore. *Damn! The shallower water is already icing up.* The decision of when to stop had now been made by the winter. It was time to turn around. "We go no further, Druid," he announced loudly. "I've only come this far because of curiosity. This isn't a bay. It's a river, a big one. If there be people in these lands, they will live that way,"—he pointed straight ahead—"upriver, along these banks."

The captain turned to his helmsman. "Steer to shore! Druid, we've arrived, at least for you. This is where you get off."

"Get off? But we've seen no people yet," Daeniel protested.

The captain faced him with his fists on his hips. "That's true. But this was what you wanted, yes?"

"Yes, but here? There are no people here!"

"Look out over the water. See that? That is the other bank of this river. Keep going up this river, and you will soon reach its mouth. On foot, you can probably get there in three, maybe four days."

"On foot!" Daeniel blanched. He had known this day would come, but now…right now? The realization that he would be leaving the knarr was terrifying. "But, captain, if your measurements are true, you could sail to the mouth in half a day!"

"Druid, this river is already freezing. It could freeze over in half a day! Then we would be trapped. Even if you had more gold to offer, I can go no further. You wanted a place 'that cannot be found,' well, this is about as bleak and desolate as anyplace I've ever seen. But take heart, there are surely enough fucking trees. You won't have trouble collecting deadwood to make a fire. And all these trees should green up nicely in the spring. You just need to survive until then." He laughed. "Anyway, you can drink water from the river now. We will give you as much food as you can carry, plus snare lines and hooks to fish, some weapons too, and a firestone. Stay near the shore and walk toward the sunset. Fisher folk usually dwell by rivers at the place where it empties into the sea."

"But what if there are no fisher folk?"

The captain smiled sardonically. "Then, Druid, you will become lord of the largest kingdom in the world."

Minutes later, the dragon ship's prow pushed into the soft mud and coarse sand of the riverbank. The stern swung slightly.

"See how the current moves the stern? That's the river. As I said, go that way, upriver."

The Norse captain had Daeniel carried ashore to keep the Druid's feet dry. Another man carried over a heavy pack of food and supplies, a few knives, and a short sword.

"Just think, take but a few steps west from this spot and you have achieved greatness. Nay, even one step will be a great accomplishment beyond anything we Norse have ever dared! We will sing your tale around our fires and tell others how we saw you do this! Of course, no one will believe us."

Some of the crew laughed and others cheered at the thought of going home. They waved at Daeniel and whistled with approval. The rowers pushed hard on the oars to back the vessel away from the riverbank. As the bow swung downriver, the center sail was raised. It bulged with air.

Through cupped hands, the captain shouted at him from the stern. "Fare thee well, Daeniel! May the gods of Valhalla be with you!"

Daeniel stood shivering on the shoreline and watched the tiny ship sail out of sight. When it was gone, the enormity of his impending loneliness descended like an icy fog. Daeniel took one step and looked down at his feet.

"You were right, Captain. I am a hero. But who will ever know?"

For a person fearful of water, the Druid had now traveled farther than any seafaring man from Roman lands. But if he did not find the courage to face this situation bravely, he would die…and soon.

He sat down on his pack and prayed.

"Goddess, help me to see your vision and fulfill the reason why I have come."

Instinctively, his hand dropped to his waist to feel the bulky pouch of dirt holding the jaw and hand bones of the vulnax, the scarring wraith, a thing from the ancient graves of the Old Ones, unwittingly disturbed, unleashed by Lord Vaelblez's mercenaries, who freed something that should not have been freed. The rest of its human body was entombed back in Francia.

The sack was always disturbingly warm to the touch, and a constant reminder of the evil presence he carried with him. As a measure of how perverse this predicament had become for Daeniel, right now that warmth seemed both ominous and reassuring; it had become his only connection to home.

If the Norse can bring me here, the wraith can find me here.

Daeniel had said these words to himself countless times during the crossing. Until he sealed these few remaining bones of the wraith in a new grave under the signs of the four Great Houses, it could attack him in his dreams. He was safe for now, but only as long as the grave back in Francia remained sealed, and it was likely only a matter of time until it was plundered. If that happened before he had sealed these other bones in a new grave, the wraith would find and attack him in his sleep, slashing him into insanity and a sure grotesque death. He'd dwelled on these consequences for too long as the knarr traveled the stormy seas. He was resolved to make a new grave or die trying.

After praying, he filled the empty water bladder from the river and took a long drink. It was clean, fresh, and chilling. There was plenty of daylight left. He pulled the pack over his shoulders, arranged the knives and sword, turned, and marched forward into the leafless forest. Keeping the water on his left, he moved upriver, as the captain had encouraged. The pack seemed to grow heavier from his exertions, and soon he was panting. He could tell his feet would blister before the day was over. But without any heavy foliage on the branches of the trees, he made steady progress pushing through them. Before long, he was sweating in spite of the cold November air.

The empty forest was so quiet that he hummed a marching song the warrior Franks would sing when going into battle. He didn't know if his goal was a hundred feet or a hundred miles, but as the hours passed, he felt he had made progress traveling…somewhere…west, at least. Unexpectedly, he spotted animal tracks in the earth and smiled. Small paw prints, something he could snare. It was a good sign.

He came upon his first obstacle as the land sloped upward before him. He heard the sounds of rushing water and halted at the top of a twenty-foot cliff face overlooking a tributary of the river. The rapids before the small waterfall flowed from his right, coming down from the north. Having no choice, he followed this smaller river to the north until he located a place shallow enough, with stepping rocks, where he could cross. Fording rivers and streams was something he'd done all his life, but he was proud when he reached the other side of this one.

"The first river crossing in this new land," he said to himself, smiling. "I should keep count."

Each step was an accomplishment. This feeling of success lasted only a few minutes. As he pushed farther into the trees, he found the ford connected to something that made his heart pound in a mix of panic, fear, excitement, and relief.

"Goddess, protect me!"

Daeniel had come upon the miraculous sight of a trail spreading from west to east. It had not been traveled recently. The moist earth bore no sign of footprints. He gazed down the path toward the west. There was nothing moving in any direction, or anywhere in the adjoining forest.

"At least it's going in the right direction."

Without hesitation, he started down the trail. He contemplated what he should do when meeting the people who surely used this trail. He would be a stranger to them. Would they welcome him? He could not speak their language. He wondered what they would look like, what level of culture they had achieved. They could be primitive, of course. But he'd seen some primitive tribes to the east of Germania and had survived those encounters.

People are people...though I should probably appear unarmed.

With that thought, he slipped his pack to the ground and pushed the short sword and the longer dagger deep within the pack of supplies he had been provided. He was stunned to find a two-foot throwing ax tucked in among the other supplies. Other than a dagger he used more as a tool, Daeniel was not inclined to brandish weapons of any sort. And he certainly did not want these new people thinking him a warrior. He would need their help.

"The ax and sword would be good for trade."

His conclusion would prove prophetic.

As night approached, he came across a cave, collected some wood and dead leaves, made a fire, cooked the odorous salted seal meat, which almost made him vomit, curled into a ball between the pack and fire, and slept fitfully. He would sleep along this trail for the next three nights, and over the next few days he managed to set and snare some squirrel-like animals that tasted wonderful.

On the afternoon of the fifth day, an icy snow began to fall, a stinging sleet driven by winds. Head down, hugging his robes around him for warmth, halfway across a clearing in the woods, he heard a noise and looked up.

Standing not ten paces away were six men and three women. Behind them, a tall palisade of logs. Down slope to the left, he saw the frozen waters of the river. He also saw what looked like fishing baskets and a dozen boats lying upside down on logs in a line by the shore.

Fisher folk!

Curious children soon joined the adults to stare in amazement at this man, strangely dressed, a face heavily tattooed with blue lines, who had appeared from the winter forest like an apparition.

Equally stunned, Daeniel held out his hands, palms up, to show he was unarmed. These men, however, were armed with long spears that boasted three pointed tips, a type used for fishing, perhaps? Such spears could kill, of that the Druid was certain. These people were not much taller than him. Their skin was highly tanned, and their black hair braided in various ways and accented with feathers. Even brows arched over dark curious eyes. Bone ornaments dangled from their ears, noses, and in necklaces. The women had shells woven among their braids. They were all completely covered in leather clothing, neatly stitched with leather cord, and some of the women had added bead stones and colored shells in patterns on their dresses. They wore high leather boot-like footwear that laced up nearly to the knee.

"Hello."

Hearing his deep voice, the entire group of people flinched and looked at one another, reassuring themselves that no one had been hurt.

Daeniel smiled. One of the smaller children smiled back.

They called themselves the Sinangerey. Daeniel would stay with them through the winter and early spring, quickly learning their language. The tribal shaman first saw him as an enemy, a dangerous rival, but Daeniel was generous with his healing knowledge and turned the healer into his friend. His own pharmacopeia had been depleted in the sea journey with the Norse. He needed to learn the local cures. The shaman began instructing him on native herbs, roots, and curative potions. As soon as Daeniel had learned enough of the language to converse intelligently, the Sinangerey elders inundated him with questions about where he had come from. They believed the sunrise seas were endless, and explained that many of their people had sailed that way, only never to return. Their mythologies were rigid in defining the world and its origin. Daeniel's appearance represented a threatening revision to those beliefs. He sensed telling these superstitious people the truth could result in his death, so he invented fictions that somewhat matched their legends and beliefs and mixed his lies with small truths: That he came from an island across the water. That it was covered in ice most of the year. That he was also a shaman of his people. That he was searching for people who knew how to cut stone.

The Sinangerey nodded. All this was plausible enough. And they wanted it to be true.

There wasn't much to do in the winter, which had descended within days of his arrival, covering the lands with prodigious amounts of snow. Daeniel became hugely popular in the hide-covered roundhouse at the center of the village. Most nights, the Sinangerey would sit in a circle while he talked with the elders, half of the tribe crowding into the structure. He would entertain them with fanciful stories, and amuse the children with simple slight-of-hand tricks. At other times, he would have more serious discussions with the elders about where he wanted to go and why.

"I carry a spirit with me," Daeniel explained, "that must be buried in a certain way beneath large cut stones. If I do not do this, the spirit will harm me. At the same time, it guards me as I travel," he added as a warning. "It is inside my pack."

He did not want the Sinangerey poking through his things.

The Sinangerey had harvested large stores of corn, beans, and squash to augment larders full of dried fish and smoked meats. Daeniel had never seen or tasted corn before and found it to be delicious and filling. The long winter nights passed slowly and peacefully. Daeniel was given a small hut of his own, and the Sinangerey made certain he never slept alone; to his great surprise, some even offered their wives for his enjoyment. The elders shared their knowledge of other tribes, most of whom were considered fierce enemies, but they said that far to the west it was rumored there was a tribe who built huge mounds of earth and suggested perhaps they would know how to move and cut large stones. They agreed to guide him to a familial tribe, also in the west, who was not an enemy.

In the spring, Daeniel bid farewell to these people, amid the hugs and tears of the women, several of whom appeared happily pregnant with his children. In private, to honor and thank the chief of the Sinangerey, he made a gift of the throwing ax, along with a tale that it had been in his family for hundreds of seasons, its origin a mystery. Daeniel demonstrated its cutting power, cleaving a three-inch limb of wood with one swing.

The chief held the ax reverently, awe and gratitude on his face. "You are forever welcome here."

In addition to learning the Sinangerey spoken language over the winter, what would prove even more valuable than that was the signing language they had taught him, a common widespread form of communication all the tribes used.

With the chief's two sons as his escort, they walked west for two moons. The green forests, flowers, and other growing things were in full bloom. Lakes, rivers, and waterfalls were everywhere.

The lands were untouched by war, teeming with life. It was magnificent. Daeniel saw animals everywhere, large horned beasts, similar to deer, huge shaggy creatures called buffalo, new breeds of wolves, bears, predator cats, plump birds, and water creatures. He learned much about woodland lore during these travels, memorizing numerous survival skills.

Daeniel also learned most tribes were not friendly toward strangers, and if he offended them in some way, the torture he would endure before death would be inventive and hideously painful. His escorts smiled as they described with enthusiasm some of the worst of these grisly activities.

Eventually, Daeniel was introduced to a people similar in appearance to the Sinangerey. They also grew crops but relied more on hunting animals for meat to survive. They were immediately frightened by the white skin they saw beneath Daeniel's tattoos, which, coincidentally, matched the legend of a ghost demon in their mythologies. He was later told by these people that had he not been accompanied by the chief's sons, he would have been killed.

He retold his fictions of where he came from and that he was a wandering shaman, looking for people who could move and cut stone. He would live with this new tribe until midsummer, teaching, learning, healing, sharing stories, and memorizing new medicinal cures. They told him of another tribe of people south of the large lakes who knew those who could build the structures he spoke of. Once again, Daeniel made the gift of a weapon—this time the dagger—to the chief, who provided Daeniel with an escort around a lake so huge it looked like a sea. The Druid would do this once more, and it would take almost another year until he came to live among the people who built ritualistic mounds. They called themselves the Mound Builders.

Over two years had elapsed since he left the Northmen, and word of a powerful shaman with white skin had spread far enough that his fame preceded him. Stories claimed him to be a peaceful but powerful sorcerer with great knowledge to share: That he carried hard, shiny stones to make fire. That he could count beyond his fingers and toes, a useless talent but impressive. And that he had names for all of the shiny spirit lights of the night sky. If such a powerful sorcerer could be made a member of a tribe, that tribe's power and prestige would increase immensely. Tribes competed for his presence, sending emissaries, hoping to influence his travel. So when it came to pass, the chief of the Mound Builders welcomed Daeniel with great celebration. After sitting with the elders, Daeniel explained what he hoped to build. Their answer was immediate.

"For what you desire to build, the ones you seek are the Chunkee. They do not build mounds as we do, they build mountains. They live two moons to the sunset," the chief told him. "But winter is upon us. It is too dangerous for you to travel more this season. The Chunkee are fierce and do not like strangers. They might ambush, kill, and eat you. We will take you in the spring. Stay with us now, sit by our fires, keep warm, share tales with us, and enjoy our hospitality."

Only two moons away! That was close. Daeniel wanted to leave immediately, but he had learned such courtesies were rarely given to strangers, and once given, could not be refused without good reason. That he was in a hurry was not a good reason.

A feast was held in his honor that first night. The food was delicious and the hospitality was indeed generous. Again, he was assailed with endless questions, which he answered thoughtfully and carefully, although each answer generally seemed only to generate two more questions.

In the midst of Daeniel's undesired celebrity, his eyes were drawn to a graceful woman serving food. She was young, exceptionally beautiful, and unusually tall compared to the other women, with a longer nose and fuller lips. Small gold owl feathers adorned glistening black hair hanging down to her waist. Some of her hair was braided and tied back with loops of beaded leather. Multiple necklaces of shiny white shells hung around her neck. A bone ornament of a crescent moon dangled from her nose. The people regarded her with deference when she passed near them. She held her chin high even as she bent to serve the tribal elders.

She's someone important, he thought

Daeniel followed her movements, hoping to attract her eye, but she avoided his gaze. Her face remained expressionless.

The chief noticed Daeniel's interest and smiled. *Our plan is working,* his eyes communicated silently to one of the other elders.

"What is her name?" Daeniel asked.

The conversation nearby immediately became subdued. The elders smiled. The chief gestured and nodded at the woman in question. She knelt on the other side of the central fire, directly across from them.

"You must ask her yourself. This is our custom. If she wants to answer you, she will."

Custom? I must be careful, Daeniel thought.

He saw the smiles and nods of approval appear around the fire.

This could be the chief's daughter.

But it was too late. Daeniel had to say something. He cleared his throat

nervously and directed his attention across the fire. "I would be honored
to know your name."

She lifted her chin and looked directly at Daeniel, her eyes reflecting
the firelight. For several seconds, she did not speak, but continued to stare
into his eyes as if taking his measure.

"I am called Red Moonglow."

Her voice had a melodic, scratchy quality. Daeniel thought her words
sounded accented compared to the other tribal members. He could not recall
ever seeing such large, expressive eyes among the natives of this land. They
were deep copper-red in color, in contrast to the darker brown of the other
women. And now that she looked at him, they did not blink, and he found
he could not look away.

To his relief, she spoke again. "What is your name?"

Daeniel noticed the chief smiling. Everyone in the hushed room was
nodding and watching him.

"My name is Daeniel."

Red Moonglow repeated his name aloud. She smiled briefly, rose up,
walked around the fire, and knelt next to him. She held out a basket of
small, round corn cakes.

She smells of flowers, Daeniel thought. He became acutely aware of
the heat radiating from her body.

Daeniel had eaten these tasty cakes before. He took two of them, thanked
her, popped them both into his mouth, and nodded approvingly at the taste.

Red Moonglow's eyes widened, and then she smiled warmly, stood up
next to him, and turned in a slow circle to look upon the faces of all those
in the room. Then, without saying a word, she dropped her gaze and left the
roundhouse. And with her exit, the room filled with animated conversation
and excited voices. From the few phrases he overheard, Daeniel was able to
understand that this woman, this Red Moonglow, had bestowed some type
of honor on him simply by the act of sharing names, followed by serving
him food.

The next day, the chief would explain that after the asking and sharing
of names, the expected response from Daeniel was to select one corn cake
when it was offered, but not to eat it. This would indicate appreciation with
polite curiosity, leaving room for further interaction if both people were
attracted to one another.

Daeniel had taken two cakes and eaten them both—immediately—in front of the entire tribe!

He would soon learn the significance of that.

As an honored guest, Daeniel was given a bed that night in the chief's own large circular lodge. He was tired from a long day of travel and the heavy feasting. The chief pointed to a bed on the far side of the lodge and encouraged him to rest. Daeniel removed his outer clothes, with the exception of his loincloth, and lay down on a soft bed of furs, a first in many months, exhaling loudly at that wonderful comfort. He was asleep within minutes.

He awoke with a start some time later. He half sat up, unaware of how long he'd been asleep. The interior of the lodge was dark, save for the yellow-red light from slow-burning embers deep in the fire pit at the center of the lodge. He could just make out the bulging shadowed outline of the chief and his wife lying across from him beneath their furs on the other side of the room. The lodge was quiet except for some wind noise outside.

Daeniel lay back down on his side and, while staring at the fire pit, began to drowse. A smell of flowers lingered in the air. He thought of Red Moonglow's large coppery eyes, how they sparkled with the firelight.

I can still smell her, Daeniel thought. *How remarkable. It's like she's right here ... He felt dizzy. Am I dreaming? Was there some strong potion in those cakes?* He felt himself stiffening and smiled. *Too bad she's not here right now.*

As if in answer to a wish, Daeniel felt a light touch on his cheek. Reflexively, he lurched to a sitting position. The dream had become real. Red Moonglow knelt at his other side.

His mouth slackened in surprise.

"What are you doing?" he whispered.

She placed a hand over his mouth, shaking her head. She spoke in rushed, tiny whispers, telling him to be quiet. He glanced nervously at the chief. The man was snoring on his side, with his back to them, only five paces away. Daeniel's conscience warned him that this was trouble.

Red Moonglow's hands touched Daeniel everywhere. She untied the leather straps at the shoulders of her dress. It slid smoothly and silently to the ground. In the dim firelight, her nakedness was both highlighted and shadowed.

Again, Daeniel was captivated by her entrancing gaze. *She must be a sorceress. Her eyes have cast a spell on me*, he thought…followed by an afterthought. *And I don't really care.* He wanted her. He sat up.

Red Moonglow placed her hand on his chest and gently forced him back down. Her hands swept aside the interfering loincloth.

Daeniel reached up and cautiously cupped one of her breasts. It was gloriously hot.

Red Moonglow smiled and slowly stretched a leg over him until she covered his body completely. She rubbed her nose under his chin. With one fluid movement, she pulled the furs over them and slid down his body to absorb his hardness inside her.

"Ohh, Goddess!" he hissed.

Their quiet lovemaking went on for a long time, multiple times. During an interlude, Daeniel slipped languidly into another deep slumber and when he awoke, Red Moonglow was gone. The light from the fire pit had diminished to a point where it created no more shadows; the first glimmers of a new day were seeping beneath the skins of the door. Daeniel closed his eyes and speculated what would happen now.

I've slept with the daughter of the chief…in his lodge, he thought glumly. If I am lucky, I will be killed outright without the customary torture first.

Daeniel had had no shortage of women to sleep with since his first night with the Sinangerey. All of these tribal people, while incredibly cruel and torturous to their enemies, were equally generous and affectionate to their friends.

The Druid strongly endeavored never to insult, intrude upon beliefs, or frighten anyone he met. And it had worked. He was still alive and nearing his goal…until now.

Stupid! Stupid! Stupid!

Becoming involved with a woman had never been part of Daeniel's plan. In fact, he had never been overly infatuated with women his entire life. He enjoyed them well enough, but he found alchemy, the healing arts, languages, the observation and interpretation of the stars, and other natural wisdoms far more compelling. Women tended to compete for his time and attention. Without meaning to, he had lost his senses and possibly his heart to Red Moonglow in only one night. His impropriety was beyond rude, and he doubted her father would understand.

And you took her in his lodge. Fool! Daeniel decided that openly admitting his terrible offense to the chief before he heard it from Red Moonglow, or anyone else, might evoke the man's mercy, if he was lucky.

Goddess, help me.

He dressed and sat down to wait for the chief and his wife to awaken, which occurred only minutes later.

The wife sat up first, smiled amiably, and nudged the chief, who responded in kind.

"Ahh! Daeniel. Did you sleep well?"

Daeniel stood and bowed his head in shame.

"Yes, very well. But I am afraid I have offended you."

A look of surprise came to their faces.

"Offended? How?"

"I shared my bed with Red Moonglow."

The chief blinked a few times, looked at his wife, and then back at Daeniel. "Red Moonglow came here? Last night?"

He pointed at the ground for emphasis. "Right here?" He pointed at Daeniel's bed. "And coupled with you there?"

"I-I've dishonored your hospitality…I am deeply sorry …"

The faces of the chief and his wife broke into expressions of joy. They stood up, hugged one another, and laughed excitedly. The chief grabbed Daeniel by both shoulders.

"My friend, this day could not have a better beginning!"

Daeniel was stunned. "I don't understand."

"Red Moonglow is not my daughter. She is a high priestess of the Chunkee people. But even better…she is the sister of the chief of the Chunkee. All the lake and river tribes know you are trying to reach the Chunkee. They have heard of your powers. The Chunkee were impatient for your arrival, so Red Moonglow was sent here with her warrior escort to await you. We were asked to arrange an introduction, which I planned to do today. Except, at the feast, you asked her name…in front of everyone!"

But you told me to do that, Daeniel thought but did not say.

With great excitement and some amusement, they expounded further.

Daeniel learned that the entire courtship ritual—the introductions, the proposal for Red Moonglow's hand, and her acceptance—had been completed during the feast.

"Red Moonglow stood and looked at all the witnesses to indicate she had accepted your proposal. She only needed to take you to bed to complete the next step. And that could occur anytime within a few days of the proposal. That part of the ritual is the woman's decision alone. The briefest wait of two days is considered respectable. Usually, if the man and woman are familiar with one another, all the steps take about ten days."

Daeniel saw a glimmer of hope. "But it has not been ten days."

"No, it has not. But after the feast, the invitation to couple with Red Moonglow was the only remaining step. And you did, right here, last night! I only wish you had been noisier." He started laughing again. "We could have joined with you."

Daeniel was stunned. "I…I don't know what to say."

"The Mound Builders have now done a great favor for the Chunkee, and they are the most powerful people. I am not certain something this important has ever proceeded so quickly."

The chief looked at his wife, who nodded in agreement.

"All that remains is for Red Moonglow to announce to all the witnesses that the ritual steps are complete, and that she has coupled with you. Of course, you must announce to everyone the coupling was satisfactory for you too. It was…was it not?"

"Of course," Daeniel answered in a daze, before he had a sudden thought. *Wait…what happens if I say it wasn't…?*

"Well then, Daeniel, be joyful! Don't you see? Everyone will be very happy."

Hard as he'd tried to stay focused on his goal, and as close as he was to achieving it, what had occurred with Red Moonglow struck him like lightning from above. It had to be fate, something the Goddess wanted. He was a chip of wood in the rapids of a river…and would go wherever this was going, at least for now.

"The next step is to have you join the Eagle clan of the Mound Builders."

"What? Join the what?"

"The clan of the chief. My clan. The Eagle clan," the chief said proudly. "It is necessary for the binding. It is our custom. You come from across the Great Waters. You have no clan, and you must be a member of a tribe and a clan to be bound to a woman. Is this not the custom where you are from?"

"Yes," said Daeniel reluctantly. *I am Wood Chip of the River Rapids clan*, Daeniel thought.

That day there were a series of minor rituals in preparation for Daeniel's marriage with Red Moonglow. Daeniel did not see her at all throughout the day as he was led, pushed, or pulled from one ritual to another.

First, he was stripped and his genitals were examined…by hand…by five female elders of the tribe, who happily, through toothless smiles, declared him worthy to be a member of the tribe. Next, he inhaled pungent smoke from a pipe, sitting alongside three tribal shamans, and learned to chant an important prayer to their deity. The smoke gave him a painful headache. Then a group of younger women brought him new clothes to wear since his were foreign and "…*smells of ground animal scat.*"

This appeared promising at first. But when he was naked for the second time, they led him into the river and bathed him by scrubbing sand all over his skin. He had to remind them three times his tattoos could *not* be scrubbed off before they stopped trying.

When redressed in the traditional garb of a Mound Builder, he was officially adopted by the Eagle clan. Daeniel was publicly declared to be the son of the chief.

"I have named you White Eagle. As your new father, it was my privilege to name you. Eagle, after the clan name, and because your skin is white!"

Pleased with himself, the chief smiled.

"Of course."

"I think your name was a most clever inspiration, yes?"

"A work of genius," Daeniel answered dryly.

The time of the formal wedding ceremony was arranged in conjunction with the sunset. Daeniel had to admit the crisp autumn air, the cloudless twilight, and the blazing mix of red-orange and yellow sunset colors made a dramatic backdrop. Along with many other senior members of the tribe, Daeniel stood atop the Head of the Snake Mound, which seemed purposed for this type of ceremony. Red Moonglow was carried by four women in a shoulder chair all the way along the winding body of the snake to the top of the mound at the head. Behind her came six heavily armed warriors, her Chunkee escort.

The rest of the Mound Builder members gathered around the bottom of the head, carrying torches. It was far more ceremonial behavior than Daeniel had observed in any of the tribal peoples since arriving on these shores.

It spoke to the Chunkee tribe's power and the sophisticated influence it exerted on its closest neighbors. If the Chunkee wanted Red Moonglow to marry Daeniel, how could such authority ever be challenged…short of death?

When Red Moonglow was lowered to the ground, Daeniel was captivated again by her beauty and seductive gaze. She was wearing a heavily ornamented beige leather robe fringed with ermine and covered with mysterious, beaded designs of red, blue, yellow, black, and white. She was naked beneath it, except for a decorated rectangular piece of fringed leather, belted around her waist that hung to her knees. Her hair was braided, piled high on her head, and decorated with colorful shells, stones, and feathers. Multiple necklaces of bones, larger shells, colored stones, and feathers hung around her neck to drape enticingly over her breasts.

As she neared, she smiled at Daeniel as if he were the only person present.

Goddess! Daeniel had never seen anyone look so beautiful. He reached out to touch her.

She shook her head. *Not yet!*

The Mound Builder shaman gestured for Daeniel and Red Moonglow to stand close before one another, inches apart. Daeniel could feel himself becoming erect.

Red Moonglow glanced down and stifled a laugh.

The shaman recited the steps of the marriage ritual loudly, announcing the completion of each one to the assembled people.

"Red Moonglow, did you invite White Eagle to couple with you?"

"Yes. Last night we coupled. And it was satisfactory."

"White Eagle. Did you find the coupling with Red Moonglow satisfactory?"

Daeniel did not answer right away.

I truly love you, he thought, surprised he felt this way after so many years alone. The silence quickly became awkward.

"White Eagle?"

"What?" Daeniel responded as if he were coming out of a trance.

"Oh! Yes! I found coupling with Red Moonglow…to be the most joyous experience of my life."

A roaring cheer of celebration rose from the crowd.

Daeniel completed his journey to the Chunkee nation the next spring. As they neared their destination, the paths quickly became broader roads, flat and dusty, well-worn signs of continuous use by people. They traversed huge farming areas. He noted they grew the standard crops of corn, squash, wild grains, and sunflowers. There were villages too, each with a tall center post with curious symbols he would later learn were astronomical in nature. It took three days to pass through these large farming areas and villages.

Finally, they reached an enormous capital city of tens of thousands of people situated on another great river. It was very organized, laid out along the four sacred directions, with a sensible pattern of crisscrossing roads. He saw thousands of thatched houses, dozens of mounds, more of the spirit poles, a multitude of private and public buildings, some of them several stories tall, and a scattering of temples. It seemed they walked another five miles before the roads converged and they entered a central plaza, with an edifice of even larger structures, high earthen mounds, and a stair-stepped pyramid-like structure. The rectangular open area took ten minutes to walk across, and which was almost as wide. By then, a huge crowd of people were following them.

As they approached the far end of the plaza, it seemed like a hundred of the apparent high rulers of the city were waiting atop the first step of the pyramid. The dress of one of them was more colorful and decorated with longer feather plumes and more bone necklaces than the rest.

The chief, Red Moonglow's brother, Daeniel thought.

Red Moonglow and Daeniel were welcomed by her brother who took hold of Daeniel's shoulders and welcomed them in a loud voice for all to hear.

Then began a great celebration. The shamans of the Chunkee from every village had all gathered to meet this famous holy man from across the Great Waters of the Sunrise. Even before the evening feast had begun, they pressed to know more about him.

They explained that Red Moonglow was given her name because she had been born on a night when the moon glowed dark red in the sky. They asked Daeniel if he knew the reason for that. Without thinking of the consequence of his answer, Daeniel simply said yes. He saw their combined look of shocked surprise. He immediately regretted speaking so quickly.

"Tell us the reason," demanded the high shaman.

Daeniel exhaled with frustration. *Too late*, he thought. "Our legends claim the moon goddess rests in the earth's shadow on such nights and glows red...with desire."

Not quite right, he thought. But it would have to do.

Red Moonglow nodded solemnly. "He is indeed the one I was destined to marry," she asserted strongly to her brother and the assembled elders. "We have coupled. I carry his child."

"We have more questions," said the high shaman in an urgent tone.

Red Moonglow's brother stood. "No. We will talk more of such things another day. Today we celebrate the return of my sister and honor her new husband."

They would remain in the city until summer's eve. His son was born on the seasonal change. And on a day Daeniel had decided was the happiest in his life, something equally astonishing occurred. A Chunkee shaman, from a village far in the west, arrived at the city escorting a strange man, a man reputed to have crossed another great water, except this one at the end of the sunset lands.

The man was introduced to Daeniel and bowed deeply.

"My name is Shou Yelu," he said with his head still bowed. Then he stood straight and smiled broadly at Daeniel. "Together, we may have traveled farther than anyone else in the whole world."

This man had distinctive facial features Daeniel had seen only one time before, when he visited the ruins of Rome and met another foreigner of similar resemblance. This man was from a place of legend, a place called Khitai. The world was indeed round, though they were probably the only two men who had experienced this.

Daeniel gripped him by the shoulders in welcome and laughed with childish excitement.

Shou Yelu reacted in kind.

The two men would converse continuously for the next two weeks. Shou Yelu explained how Emperor Shengzong of Liao in Khitai had decided to sail north and east on the great seas in search of new lands. Eight large ships were embarked. All but one were lost in terrible polar storms, and the last was dashed upon the rocks three months later on the western shore of this new vastness. Shou Yelu was the only one to survive. He could not return the way he came. So he had decided to explore this new land, and perhaps try to reach the other great water.

They would become lifelong friends. Together, Daeniel and Shou would answer the continuous stream of questions posed by the Chunkee shamans who grew less friendly after each session. Red Moonglow saw the animosity and signs of deadly jealousy forming among the medicine men. *We must leave*, she decided.

"Daeniel, have you forgotten your quest?" she asked one day. "Do you still seek to create a new grave for the spirit you carry?"

Daeniel had not forgotten. He glanced at the pack and pouch lying in a corner of their home. The thought of the vulnax and the curse seemed outwardly less important in this new life he had found, but deep within he knew otherwise. He nodded reluctantly.

"My brother has agreed to give us stone cutters. We will go back to the Mound Builders for their help and find a place to make this grave. And then we will form our own village, far enough away from the Chunkee shamans to escape their growing wrath."

"Away from here?" Daeniel protested this idea. "But I like it here. And these are your people!"

"If we do not leave, and leave soon, you and Shou, and our son, will be killed."

His wife's wisdom far surpassed her eighteen summers.

With the blessing of the Chunkee chief, an entourage of nearly two hundred artisans, warriors, farmers, and their families, they marched back into the lands of the Mound Builders, who were delighted to help Daeniel locate a place where he could establish a village of his own.

They picked a place near another great river located among the Mound Builder lands, where they would be surrounded by friends. While the palisade of logs was built, and the farmers planted crops, Daeniel, Red Moonglow, Shou Yelu, and the Mound Builder shamans next identified a spot they all agreed would be a good place for a grave. It would take until the spring of the following year for the stone cutters to find appropriate stone and transport the great pieces to the place where the tomb would be built.

With Daeniel's direction, the sigils of the Great Houses were cut into the faces of the pillars and the stones were raised. On summer's eve, amid the torches of those assembled, Daeniel dug a hole and placed the jaw and hand bones of the vulnax wraith into a hole at the center of the grave. He spoke the words in the old Celtic tongue, the Frankish tongue, and in Latin. Then he repeated all of the hex words in the Chunkee tongue for those who were present. Not until that moment did everyone finally realize the grim import of what Daeniel was doing. Their faces now fixated where the bones had been buried.

Seeing their fear, Daeniel decided to repeat the final words of the hex.

"Malus spiritus be condemned to shadow!
Sealed forever beneath the stone crests!
And as these four houses stand,
So shall it be!"

Daeniel turned to look at all of them. "You are bound to keep the secrecy of this tomb. If this spirit ever becomes free, it will seek you out, or it will seek out your descendants."

Angry voices arose from those present, some men cursing Daeniel for involving them in the ceremony. Red Moonglow raised her arms, silencing the protests.

"If the grave is not disturbed, all of you are safe! Let us bury this place under the earth to hide it forever. We will surround it with many young trees, vines and brambles too."

With the help of the Mound Builders, they concealed the tomb inside a twelve-foot mound of earth and planted seedlings as suggested. But after that, all of the Chunkee artisans and the majority of the warriors left the new village, voicing their desire to be far away from Daeniel and the terrible curse he'd invoked.

As the village palisade emptied to a handful of people, mostly farmers, those remaining met in the central roundhouse.

"Without warriors, we are vulnerable to attack," a despondent Shou complained. "Maybe we should return to the Eagle clan's village as well."

"No," Red Moonglow objected. "Instead, we will create a village no one would dare attack. A place where shamans can gather from across the lands to learn and share their knowledge. A village that will be friends with any other people, and yet one that is protected by strong totem spirits and guarded by a legendary evil one. This we all know to be true."

Heads were nodding. She continued.

"The strongest magic of three different lands is right here, right now. I am Red Moonglow, high priestess of the Chunkee. White Eagle is high shaman of the lands from across the Great Waters of the Sunrise. Shou is high shaman of the lands from across the Great Waters of the Sunset."

Red Moonglow nodded at Daeniel to say something.

Daeniel had also been dismayed by the sudden Chunkee desertions. He had thought Shou may be right until he heard Red Moonglow's words. He gave her a brief smile of approval and took her place at the center of the roundhouse.

"Those that have left will never escape the curse, no matter where they go. To be safe," Daeniel declared, "we need to create a home of our own. A home not protected by warriors, but by magic.

"We will be a place known for its powerful magic, a place of healing, a place of teaching, with a knowledge of the spirit lights in the sky. And we will share this knowledge with other shamans who visit us. This is a good place. We have food and strong walls to sleep behind. We are already among our friends, the Mound Builders. This place is the home of our people."

"What is the name of our people," someone shouted from the assembly.

If I am White Eagle, this will be our nest, Daeniel thought.

"We will call ourselves the Aerie."

The Aerie people prospered. Their village grew. Some of the artisans even returned and created new homes for themselves. As intended, Daeniel and Shou established a place of learning, for between these two men they had a world of knowledge to share. Together, at Red Moonglow's urging, they invented a new language.

"Call these the words of magic, unlike any others," she suggested. "Then no one else can claim the words as their own. The language will be unique to the Aerie shamans alone."

Daeniel and Shou would instruct apprentices, who had been sent by many other tribes, bidding them explore other lands and cultures and to return with new lore, new magic, and healings to add to the great knowledge of the Aerie. These apprentices became known as Shamans Who Wander, protected by their reputation alone, therefore welcomed wherever they went, a wandering messenger from their gods, holy men. In a few seasons, Daeniel became regarded as the high shaman of the Aerie, the Andrototekan, as Shou conceived the title, at Red Moonglow's urging.

Red Moonglow would give Daeniel five sons.

Shou Yelu gave up his quest to seek the waters of the sunrise and married. His wife would birth three sons and four daughters.

Together, they taught their sons as much as they could remember and encouraged them to wander further and learn even more. Red Moonglow instructed the girls.

Twenty-five seasons later, for the first time since leaving the Francia lands, Daeniel felt safe and at peace. He thought it odd it had taken so many years for this sentiment to suddenly manifest within him. Maybe it was because Red Moonglow had made love with him that morning as the sun was rising, and it had been as good as their first time.

He walked outside the palisade, in the comforting coolness of the morning, with the warm promise of a new day, and Daeniel the Druid raised his hands and eyes toward the sky and thanked the Goddess for her love and protection. As he gazed into her deep blue face, he saw a great white eagle circling above him, whom he had joined with before.

"Hello, old friend."

An apprentice had brought a medicine from the desert lands that allowed a shaman to join with the spirit of an animal. Daeniel found that to be an amazing and versatile gift.

Daeniel reflected. He'd crossed the icy cold seas, found love, and managed to seal the scarring wraith after all. *Yet, even these new sealing stones could be disturbed*, Daeniel thought.

But first they will have to be found.

Daeniel assumed it must be men who disturbed the sealing stones. He never imagined it would be a river.

And while the prosperity of the Aerie people lasted a long time, it did not last forever. They would eventually become too proud, too arrogant, and war would find them. It would be a war of annihilation, an evil war, as all wars are evil.

The vulnax wraith had waited patiently…and the seal was broken.

CHAPTER 1
LAKE ONTARIO
JULY 1754
Le Boucher de Nuit

In the morning, at the first glow of sunrise, Helmut Colbért started west again. The surface of Lake Ontario was glassy calm from lack of any wind. The three-man Oneida war canoe glided soundlessly across the water, except for the rhythmic wet dipping sound of his paddle. The canoe left a wide triangular wake of ripples behind Colbért, as if he traveled on a country pond.

He proceeded steadily and considered his options upon reaching the next fort. Presumably, Fort Niagara was a much larger version of Fort Frontenac, but that didn't tell him much. He needed to know how many troops, how many civilians, and how much daily activity took place to provide diversions for his movements. With too many unknowns to contemplate, he concentrated instead on what was possible. First, if his luck continued, all of his intended victims might be there. So when he entered the fort, he'd remain unobtrusive and not announce his arrival to the fort commander.

As with his past victims, he desired they be unaware of his presence until he struck, until it was too late—his single greatest advantage. Second, they would not know him even if he stood right next to them. But he would know them instantly; Philippe Gerrard, his bastard son, Henri, and the bastard's mother, Sister Michelle, had all been well described to him. And they enjoyed some celebrity, most people would know them, so said the *voyageurs* he'd met.

Third, he expected little trouble from any of them, except, perhaps, the woodsman. Once he located their presence, he would kill the woodsman first. A quick slash of his stiletto to the neck just below the ear. Stoop and roll to the opposite side as he spins to counter, parry this with another deep slash high on the inner thigh. Roll to his feet, back away a few steps, and enjoy the bleeding until his eyes go dull.

Au revoir, Monsieur Woodsman.

In Paris, the gendarmerie called Colbért *le boucher de nuit,* the Night Butcher. The thought of his *nom de guerre* always evoked a feeling of pride in the assassin. He endeavored to live up to this reputation, butchering his victims with his knives in hideous ways whenever possible. But here in the wilderness of New France, savage butchery seemed commonplace.

Ironic that I need civilization for my talents to be appreciated, he mused. *I must perpetrate something unforgettable before I leave. Something that will be remembered...even here.*

A reverie of grotesque ideas occupied Colbért while he canoed toward the mouth of the Niagara River. He was less than a quarter mile out from the beach and kept careful watch for any signs of the fierce peoples who occupied the shorelands. If they attacked in force like before, it was unlikely he would survive. A week earlier, the four Hurons escorting him from Fort Frontenac had all been killed in a lake battle with an Oneida war party... well, one Huron he'd killed himself. But he was not overly concerned by his prospects. The night visitor from his dreams repeatedly assured him he was safe.

It was prickly to have this haunting spirit inside his head. *The night visitor.* Colbért could not think what else to call...*it.* Not that he ever talked about *it* with anyone, except, of course, with the Marquis de Propei, who had provided the introduction to this...*ghost*? It was a vivid, threatening presence in his dreams, but whose presence diminished to only a hint of a whisper in the daylight, more like an intuition, sometimes saying what he wanted to hear, or whispering reassurance to bolster his resolve. But most importantly, it was always right in its advice. That made it real to Colbért and made its pervasive menace tolerable.

The voice had manifested after his first meeting with the Marquis at the restaurant, before he left Paris. It provoked a dull headache as a constant reminder of its presence. But, after so many months, he'd gotten used to that too.

His recent journey from Montréal began six weeks ago. Three weeks earlier, he had stopped at Fort Frontenac to hire the Huron guides; two weeks later, the attack on the lake occurred where he lost his guides and supplies. It had been a day since he left the mutilated corpse of the Oneida woman hanging between two trees. Starving and alone in the forest, he had attacked a native family at night, killing her husband first, then the month-old baby, and then raped and tortured the wife for hours before she also succumbed. He recalled the muffled gurgling sounds she made as he'd strangled her. He licked his lips. She'd lasted much longer than the most hardened Parisian whore.

Tough people, he thought.

Based on what he was told when they started the circuit of this lake, he guessed the vaunted French fort on the Niagara River had to now be less than a day away. He had eaten all the food he found carried by the dead Oneida brave and his wife and was back to drinking lake water as before. The assassin wondered how he had managed to get himself lost in the middle of a wilderness, starving, alone, when a handful of months earlier he was being toasted in the finest restaurants in Paris as Gaspard de Propei, the Marquis' heir. Yet here he was, heading for this next island of people among the endless trees.

You will be rewarded, the thought came suddenly, as if the night visitor was sitting close by, sharing the trials and dangers of this journey with him.

While he was to kill Philippe Gerrard in vengeance for the slaying of the Marquis' son, Colbért needed only to kill Philippe Gerrard's bastard son, Henri, and the bastard's mother, Sister Michelle, to secure his title as heir to the Marquis de Propei. He was a professional assassin, used to attacking from the shadows, but in this circumstance he needed to kill them all in front of witnesses. And he could do this with impunity, a new experience for him.

As an aristocrat and a *shérif* for King Louis, positions dubiously obtained, he could not be challenged for enforcing the King's justice. *Le boucher de nuit* could kill anyone he wanted, if they had been labeled a traitor to the crown, which all of them were.

Indeed, the world he knew had turned upside down.

Before midday, he saw the outline of the fort looming on the coast ahead. He smiled brightly and paddled his canoe closer to the shore beneath the great stone castle house perched high on a cliff overlooking Lake Ontario. He hailed the guards on the wall, and a sentry waved him forward.

The boat landing teemed with soldiers and cargo handlers, not an inch of space was available, so Colbért pulled his canoe up among the garbage wash and refuse near a makeshift pier. The assassin expected his arrival to be confronted, and while a few of the day laborers and *coureurs de bois*

lifted their heads and gazed at him with mild interest, the arrival of a solitary man was largely ignored. He retrieved his belongings, abandoned the
damaged canoe, and sauntered through the small boat-landing gate. The
laconic sentries hardly looked at him as they batted insects away from their
sweaty faces. He slipped into the myriad of activities occurring inside the
fort and paused in the middle of the marshalling yard, turning in a circle
to assess his next move.

God! This place looks to be a bigger shithole than the last one!

Fort Niagara was huge compared to Fort Frontenac, and the army engineers were busy making it much, much bigger. For certain, he could remain
undetected in these crowds if he did nothing to draw undue attention. He
managed to beg a meal from a trio of soldiers for a few écus, and learned
that Philippe Gerrard was not present at the fort. He frowned at this news.
They suggested he confer with the fort's Jesuit monsignor.

"Father Beauharnois can probably answer all your questions."

"And where can I find this…priest?" The word *priest* sounded like
pustule on Colbért's lips.

"Over there." Private Bouchet pointed with his boning knife at a large
group of women and children gathered around the water well, near the
center of the fort.

"*Merci.* I will be sure to inform the commandant of your cooperation."

Colbért left them and walked toward the throng of people.

Private Bouchet watched the stranger wend his way through the crowd.

"Sergeant, why did you poke me in the ribs like that?"

"Next time, don't be so fucking helpful. You don't know who he is.
He's no fur trader, that's certain. Did you see the blood stains all over that
silk shirt under his coat? He's tried to wash them. How did he get them?
He speaks like a noble. And that alone always means trouble." The sergeant
looked down at his half-empty ration pot. His stomach growled. "And we
won't be letting him or anyone else eat from our pot again."

Father Antoine Beauharnois was overjoyed with the multitude of converts he had made since the arrival of more troops for the spring campaign
against the English. In the army's wake, droves of Indians from every
direction had descended on the fort to trade and petition for gifts, hoping
for a share of the new wealth arriving in an almost never-ending line of lake

bateaux carrying supplies for the army. The natives would kneel, bow their heads in humility, be baptized, and receive a gratuity of some sort. Most of them had gone through the same ritual numerous times. But Father Antoine had become lost in the fervor of his missionary duties and temporarily turned a blind eye to the charade.

The Jesuit was handing out round loaves of bread as Colbért approached, alternately blessing each of the children as they ran off with their boon.

Colbért waited patiently while the women and children hastened away upon seeing him.

"*S'il vous plaît?*"

The priest turned. His smile vanished as he took in the man's appearance. His nose wrinkled at the foul smell.

"How may I help you, Monsieur?" the priest asked warily.

Helmut had grown a mustache during the sea voyage to New France as part of his new identity; Seigneur Gaspard de Propei, heir to the Marquis de Propei. Unused to this facial hair, he had developed an unconscious habit of slowly stroking it with his thumb and forefinger when he concentrated.

Like a spider combing its mandibles, the thought came abruptly. The priest's adverse reaction was plain to Colbért.

"Please forgive the way I look. I am on government business. I carry urgent dispatches for Colonel Contrecoeur and came by way of canoe along the south shore of the lake. My party was attacked by hostiles. I alone escaped."

"You transited the southern shore of Lake Ontario?" the Jesuit replied, astonished. "Past the English? Past Fort Oswego?"

Colbért nodded. "But not alone. Unfortunately, we were ambushed. My Huron escort was slain by the Oneida savages."

"You are lucky to be alive, Monsieur. And had you been captured… well, God indeed has protected you."

"God…has blessed me in so many ways."

Father Antoine thought he heard sarcasm in the stranger's reply. "So you are a courier?" The stranger was not wearing anything close to the uniform of a military messenger.

"Yes, of a sort."

"Where is your courier packet, Monsieur?"

The assassin noticed the scrutiny of the three soldiers who'd given him food. Other people, curious, gathered near the priest. Colbért glanced around guardedly and took a step closer before answering.

The Jesuit frowned and leaned away as the stench intensified.

"I need to be cautious. My pack was destroyed in the ambush," Colbért replied, quick and quiet. "I memorized my missive as a precaution against such a circumstance."

The stranger's eyes were almost black and very menacing. Father Beauharnois involuntarily shrank away a step. *He is lying.* But whether the man was a *courier* or not, this was a matter for Commandant Pouchot.

"Well, you are too late, Monsieur. Colonel Contrecoeur marched many weeks ago. He is at Fort Duquesne. But I am sure Captain Pouchot, Fort Niagara's commandant, can offer his assistance. Allow me to escort you. Come this way."

Helmut Colbért debated whether it would be prudent to engage the fort commandant in conversation about his mission at this point; now that it was rumored Philippe Gerrard was not present.

"Tell me, Father …?"

"Beauharnois. Antoine Beauharnois."

"Yes…Father Beauharnois. Are you familiar with a man called Philippe Gerrard?"

A chill passed through the Jesuit. He stopped walking and turned.

"*Votre nom, Monsieur*?"

"I am Seigneur Gaspard de Propei, *shérif* for King Louie and a *capitaine de policiére* for Intendant Bigôt."

Father Beauharnois blinked. *My God!* He perfectly matched the description in Archbishop Nicolet's letter. *How could I be so stupid!* The Jesuit wasn't sure what to do.

"Uh, Philippe Gerrard, you say? There is no man at this fort by that name," he answered quickly. *This is true*, he thought, *since Philippe had left days ago.*

Colbért smiled. *The priest has been warned, probably by his sniveling archbishop.*

"How unfortunate. Maybe someone else could help me find this man? This is an urgent matter," Colbért added. "I carry a message for him from Montréal."

"There is no one at Fort Niagara with that name," the Jesuit insisted.

The assassin heard an edge of fear in the priest's voice. "I'm certain a Jesuit would never lie to a *shérif* of the King." He probed in earnest. "*Was* there a man here by that name?"

Father Beauharnois ignored the question. "I believe the fort commander can better assist you."

Colbért suspected the priest and the fort authorities would disregard the credentials he carried and collaborate to delay him. He decided to use silver to loosen other tongues. *Someone* would tell him where the trader was.

"I am sorry you could not be of more help, Father. I will seek my answers elsewhere."

The assassin began walking away.

Father Beauharnois followed a few steps. "Wait, Seigneur. The commandant must …"

But the man had moved on and was now quickly engaging some fur traders in conversation.

It took the assassin only a few écus and a few minutes to confirm that Philippe Gerrard was not in the fort, and that he was taking dispatches to forts further down the portage. Neither was Sister Michelle and the bastard son, Henri, present. They had somehow been captured by the savages. While that was irritating, they were probably dead by now. He would concentrate on the woodsman.

He's probably a week's march ahead of me, Colbért concluded. *How many fucking forts could there be?*

Helmut left the fort by the small, less-guarded river gate, the same one he'd entered. The landing area was overflowing with noise and people. A breeze carried the smell of sewage. There were makeshift tents, canoes, and a few filthy *voyageurs* sitting around, just the type of men he was looking for. A bargain was quickly made. Helmut paid in silver. With the help of his new guides, he easily purchased supplies intended for the army.

Before an hour had passed, Helmut Colbért had set out for his next destination, another fort at a place called Presque Isle.

Father Beauharnois spent almost an hour getting past the sentries posted in the crowded antechamber to gain an audience with Captain Pouchot. The Jesuit blurted out a convoluted explanation before Pouchot could ask any questions and finished with a plea.

"We must hurry, Captain!"

The aggravated commandant simply shook his head. "Father, do you see what's in progress here? I don't have any time for you…for this!"

The Jesuit glanced at the faces of the other officers in the room and elevated his voice. "Captain, Gaspard de Propei claims to be a courier with dispatches for Colonel Contrecoeur. Doesn't that make him worth detaining, at least until a proper military escort can be assigned? What if he is killed?"

Captain Pouchot's lieutenants now looked concerned. The commandant's face turned red and sullen and then he sighed with resignation.

"Very well, Father. I need to inspect progress on the walls anyway."

They walked around the fort interior for almost an hour, the commandant talking with his engineers, Beauharnois snagging *voyageurs* at random before finding someone who'd seen the stranger.

The *voyageur* pointed upriver. "He hired two men to take him up the portage."

Alarmed, Father Beauharnois confronted Captain Pouchot. "We've waited too long! Now do you see? Someone must be sent to pursue him!"

Commandant Pouchot took off his hat and wiped the sweat from his forehead and brim.

"Father Beauharnois, I don't *see* anything! In the future, I would prefer you petition one of my aides and waste his time instead of mine!"

The irate captain stomped away before the Jesuit could protest further.

Holy Father, what am I to do? He followed the commandant halfway back to the castle and stopped with his hands fisted on his hips near the well, ignoring the children pulling on his robes. His eyes shifted to the Dunemoore Company trading post.

Moments later, the Jesuit entered the main door. The room was packed with soldiers and civilians, all vying to purchase equipment and supplies. Okeanneh was assisting Claude Guillot and two other *coureurs de bois* with the bartering.

"Monsieur Guillot," he shouted. "A word with you, *s'il vous plaît.*"

Huddled together at one side of the noisy room, the clerk explained to the priest that most of the company's *coureurs de bois* had been hired as scouts for the army.

Guillot was happy. "We are overwhelmed with the demands for business." He gestured with his arms at the crowd of customers in the store.

The Jesuit tapped his lips. He knew if he said anything to *this* particular clerk, the whole fort would know by nightfall that a *shérif* of the crown was looking for Philippe Gerrard, which could cause all sorts of problems. His mind raced.

Guillot became curious. "What is so important, anyway?"

Father Beauharnois noticed Philippe's wife, Okeanneh, moving across the room. She stretched her arms high above her head to retrieve a stack of blankets from a shelf, drawing the lewd stares of the men in the room.

"Okeanneh," the priest hailed over the din.

Heads turned and seeing the Jesuit's black robes, the room quieted.

"Okeanneh," the priest said in a more subdued voice, after gaining her attention. "May I speak with you…alone?" He spoke in Ottawa, her native tongue.

Okeanneh regarded the priest with annoyance, but, noticing the curious looks on the faces of the other white men, she nodded curtly and moved toward the forge area. The noisy bartering at the store resumed with their departure.

In the dusty but quiet forge room, Father Beauharnois quickly explained the circumstances, describing as much as he knew about Gaspard de Propei.

"This man intends to harm Philippe."

"How can this be true?"

"He is a *shérif,* a man authorized by our King to arrest Philippe."

"Why?"

"I…I am not sure," Father Beauharnois stuttered, abruptly realizing he didn't know why. "But if Philippe resists, he could be killed!"

"Killed? Philippe killed?!"

"Yes."

"*No!*" Okeanneh balled her fists and struck the priest angrily. "Snow Hair is of your clan, your village! *You* would not let this happen!"

Ow. That hurt. Father Antoine rubbed his shoulder. "Okeanneh, our laws are different from yours," he stammered.

"No! Michel and Louie are with him! His soldier friends are with him!"

"Okeanneh, this *shérif* has power. The soldiers are required to help him. Maybe the Dunemoore Company will send some of its *coureurs de bois* to…?"

The Jesuit was stunned to realize he had just contemplated a *murder*!

Holy Father, forgive me. Beauharnois crossed himself, sank wearily onto a stool, and shook his head. *I seem to be doing that often.*

Okeanneh remained standing with her arms crossed, glaring at him.

Even if Gaspard de Propei was captured, what would we do with him? One by one, the priest eliminated ideas. According to Archbishop Nicolet, the agent carried written authority from Intendant Bigôt to act as a *capitaine de policiére.* In that capacity, the commanders on the frontier could at most only delay the man's travel. *This is up to Philippe Gerrard to resolve…but he must be warned.* How? How? Then he brightened.

"I will go," he said. "I will warn Philippe."

"You? You are not a warrior!"

Father Beauharnois shifted to French.

"I have letters from Archbishop Nicolet telling me to detain this man," he stated more to himself than to her. "Yes, yes. That should be enough to get the military to do as I ask…at least until they are given countermanding orders. And that will take time."

"I do not understand …"

Father Beauharnois held the wood cross of his prayer beads before her.

"You see, Jesus can help us, through the power of His Church. The Church will make the army help!"

The priest became lost in the righteousness of his bold idea. It sounded almost heroic. Suddenly, he frowned. He could not leave Fort Niagara. There was simply too much he was responsible for here: the mission, the hospital, the spiritual well-being of the citizens, his converts. Archbishop Nicolet's missive said to *assist* in delaying Gaspard de Propei should he arrive, not *chase* after him.

The Jesuit slumped on the stool, dejected, and just as quickly reversed his decision. "I cannot go."

Okeanneh had seen the powerful influence this white shaman exercised over the French soldiers. Still, the white priests were not warriors. She made her decision.

"I will go."

"You?! But this man is very dangerous." Beauharnois shook his head. *I must make her stay here. Philippe would go mad me if anything happens to her.*

"No, child. You must stay here…in case Philippe returns!"

Father Beauharnois could see she was not convinced. He took a different approach, though he wasn't proud of it.

"Philippe might return with Sister Michelle. And if you are not here… well …"

Okeanneh bristled at the mention of the white woman. She would find Philippe no matter what the priest said.

"I am going!"

The signal cannon atop the castle boomed. Captain Pouchot moved several paces from the castle door and looked up.

"Shout it out," he yelled to the sentry through cupped hands.

"Indians, sir! Three canoes from the east!"

The commandant was surprised. East? That was Oneida land.

"Did you say *east*?"

The sentry pointed eastward. "Yes, sir!"

Captain Pouchot quickly assessed the implications. *Three canoes? Not enough for an attack. Maybe to trade?* Still, armed Oneida should never be presumed friendly.

"Sergeant Major Gabriel, bring a platoon, fully armed, to the boat landing! Quickly now!"

As they passed the front of the fort facing the lake, the Oneida chief saw all the activity along the walls of the stone lodge. Soldiers and *coureurs de bois* were gathering at the boat landing.

"Do not raise your weapons," the chief reminded the other braves.

The three Oneida canoes beached at the landing. The braves got out and pulled their vessels securely ashore.

The Oneida chief quickly identified the leader of the soldiers standing in front of the others. He approached Captain Pouchot, stopping three paces away. From a pack he was carrying, the chief withdrew a shredded, bloody leather dress. He tossed it to the ground between them.

Captain Pouchot looked from the bloody rag to the Oneida. There were seven in all, dressed in clothing decorated with colored beads, quills, and dyed hair, the type of dress worn on special occasions meant to impress an observer. But these were warriors, heavily tattooed, armed, and with menacing expressions that said they were ready to fight. Pouchot sensed anger, but it was not directed at him.

The commandant turned to his interpreter. "What the hell is this all about?"

The interpreter and the chief exchanged questions and answers for a few seconds.

"His name is Tall Mountain Among Trees, high chief of the Oswego Oneida."

"Welcome, Tall Mountain Among Trees," Captain Pouchot said quickly. He held out his hands, palms up, and made a curt nod to the chief.

"What does he want?"

"He says he has come to claim the man who killed his daughter, her husband, and his granddaughter."

Captain Pouchot was confused. "Claim what?"

Tall Mountain Among Trees began talking loudly and gesturing.

The interpreter continued. "The bloody rag is his daughter's dress. He claims someone from this fort tortured and killed her."

"Someone from this fort?" Captain Pouchot was incredulous. "That's not possible. No one from here would venture into Oneida lands."

Though he did not understand French, Tall Mountain Among Trees recognized the denial. He spoke and gestured further.

"He is adamant, Captain. He claims the man is in this fort."

"How does he know that?"

In response to the question, Tall Mountain Among Trees pointed to a damaged canoe lying amidst the driftwood to one side of the landing.

Captain Pouchot walked over to the canoe. He examined its markings. They closely matched the other three Oneida war canoes.

"Where did this come from?" the commandant shouted to the crowd of soldiers and civilians thronging the landing.

"It belonged to the *shérif*," replied a voice from the crowd.

"Who speaks?"

The crowd parted to reveal the same *voyageur* who had spoken to Captain Pouchot and Father Beauharnois earlier that day.

"I did, Commandant. The *shérif* arrived in this canoe and hired two men to guide him up the portage."

Captain Pouchot pointed emphatically. "*This* canoe? You're certain it was *this* canoe?"

"I saw him too, Captain," said a soldier. "I was on watch atop the castle when he arrived. He was coming from the east. I challenged him. He said his name was Gaspard de Propei."

Captain Pouchot noticed one of the Oneida braves translating the substance of this to the chief.

Tall Mountain Among Trees spoke and gestured.

"He asks we bring this man to him."

Captain Pouchot held out his open palms to show his sincerity and shook his head. "Tell the chief, the man he seeks has already left the fort."

And thank God for that, Pouchot didn't say. The last thing he wanted was any kind of provocation of the Oneida, not with the Seneca already provoked by the army.

"This man has marched into the Seneca lands. Tell him I will send soldiers to find him."

The interpreter explained this to the Oneida chief. An awkward silence followed before Tall Mountain Among Trees stepped to within a pace of Captain Pouchot. The Oneida chief carefully studied the face of the French officer.

"I am trying to see your honor," the chief said, "to see if you speak true. We do not war with the French. But a white man tortured my daughter to her death. What would you do, if she were your daughter?"

Captain Pouchot listened to the translation solemnly. Beneath the fierce features and the tattoos, he saw the anger and terrible grief of a father. The officer removed his hat and placed a hand over his heart.

"If she were my daughter, I would not stop searching until I took my revenge on the one who murdered her. I will help you in obtaining justice."

Tall Mountain Among Trees gripped the French officer by both shoulders and nodded solemnly.

Chapter 2
Piqua's Village
July 1754
Sister Michelle

The hungry, bloodied remnants of Maltoc's once-proud people straggled into the Seneca Wolf clan palisade on a morning marked by high humidity and an ominous stillness. There were nine in total, three children under twelve, one baby, three old grandmothers, and two mothers, all of them starving and exhausted by their journey of survival. The piping screams of the baby raised the anxiety of everyone in the camp. The six-month-old boy had red burns and blisters over half of his body.

The people of the Wolf clan surrounded the skinny villagers, offering food, water, comfort, and affection. Many had relatives among Maltoc's clan. Mothers were reunited with daughters they hadn't seen in many seasons. Some of the old women and sick children collapsed in exhaustion after the week-long journey by foot, exposed to the cold at night, with little food to eat.

"Queee! Queee!" screamed a Wolf clan mother when she learned her youngest daughter had been killed in the attack. Soon, the village resounded in screams, as others learned of a similar fate to their relatives.

Piqua and his elders gathered around cousins scowling at the incredible sight. The Hawk clan village was destroyed? How could this be? That village had been among the strongest of the Seneca settlements.

"Who did this?" Piqua demanded.

"The Erigh," a grandmother cried. "The People of the Panther attacked us. Hundreds of them. They had thunder guns."

"Thunder guns?"

"The Erigh have soldier cannon?" Piqua's braves were disbelieving. Warriors hooted with concern.

But the Erigh are a defeated people! Piqua thought. *How did they manage this?*

"Where is Maltoc?" Piqua asked the group.

"We do not know," an old woman replied. "He was not at the village when they attacked."

Piqua asked more questions and learned that many thunder guns were used. The Erigh set fire to the lodges and the palisade. Women and children were killed by the great explosions and fires. But when the Erigh had entered the village, the slaughter began in earnest. Few escaped.

"There is a red skull on a post in front of our gates," the old woman wailed.

Alarmed, Piqua looked questioningly at Ootego, the Wolf clan shaman.

"It is a death hex," Ootego said grimly. "Chittaqua's sorcery. It means the Hawk clan is dead forever."

This boded ill for everyone. Piqua knew Maltoc would go to war immediately. But who would Maltoc attack first? This ghostly band of Erigh warriors with the thunder guns? How did the Erigh get such weapons? Maybe it was not the Erigh who attacked. Maybe the attackers were French *coureurs de bois*. Maltoc has ambushed them often enough to warrant revenge. What if, in his rage, Maltoc attacked the French soldiers, and the French begin to war on all the Seneca in retaliation? The Wolf clan village could be next!

Seven elders and six lodge chiefs gathered in the ceremonial roundhouse. Piqua related everything he had learned and asked for opinions. Everyone talked at once, most clamoring for revenge.

Piqua pointed to the oldest member of the clan and asked him to step into the circle at the center and speak first.

One by one, the elders spoke and made recommendations. We should arm and defend our walls, said one. Kill all our captured Erigh slaves, urged a third. Leave no evidence of our alliance with Maltoc. The debate went quickly. Against such powerful forces, there were few options for a single clan.

Dissatisfied, Piqua decided to send additional scouts to monitor the movements of the French soldiers, but the French and English were not to be harassed or attacked.

"What of Snow Hair's woman?"

Piqua nodded thoughtfully. A good question by a wise elder. Iron Pots had been found dead after lying with Snow Hair's woman. Killed by deadly medicine, by magic, by a shaman. Ootego claimed Iron Pots had been killed by Chittaqua, the powerful Erigh sorcerer who seemed to be everywhere. Was Snow Hair also behind the attack on Maltoc? If he was, then Snow Hair and his allies would be searching for his woman. The Wolf clan was not safe. Maybe they should kill the white woman and leave her body in the forest for the scavengers to eat?

Ootego stood in the circle to talk. "Too many know Snow Hair's woman is here. Snow Hair will come to get her soon. He will bring soldiers and *coureurs de bois* with him. I say, do not fight them. I say, we make a trade. Iron Pots promised muskets for the woman. But Iron Pots is dead. Make Snow Hair trade muskets for his woman."

Many hooted in support of this idea. Piqua nodded. With war spreading rapidly, the Hawk clan needed such powerful weapons.

"Ootego's words are wise. Snow Hair will make a trade for his woman. Maybe even for thunder guns. The white woman must not be harmed," Piqua declared.

When the Hawk clan survivors arrived at the village, Michelle lingered near the edge of the crowd and listened carefully. She had learned enough of the Seneca language to pick out key words from the general babble of the women. There had been an attack on the Hawk clan village!

Through eavesdropping months earlier, Michelle discovered Henri had been taken to the Hawk clan and was alive. And now this dreadful news! She waited until she could question one of them alone, without provoking any of the village women who guarded her. She saw her chance when food was brought to the exhausted survivors.

Michelle knelt by an old grandmother lying on a blanket, sweating with fever contracted during their flight. She carefully lifted the woman's head and helped her drink some water from a wooden bowl. The old woman gulped ravenously, nodded, and smiled in appreciation. Michelle rolled an animal skin and slipped it under her head. She covered the woman's gaunt, bruised body with a blanket. She felt the woman's brow with one hand. The fever was raging.

"I bring you willow bark tea," Michelle promised.

The woman patted Michelle's hand gratefully.

"Grandmother, you see white boy in your village?" Michelle whispered in the few halting words of Seneca she had learned.

The woman looked puzzled.

"A white boy," Michelle repeated, rubbing her own skin for emphasis, "did you see him?"

"Ahh, yes! Tamaqua's boy," the old lady said. "He escaped almost one moon ago."

Escaped! Michelle seized on this information, elated. Oh, thank God! But to where?

The old woman saw the white woman's tears, the look of relief. She realized suddenly who Michelle was.

"Your son?" She pointed a finger at Michelle's chest.

"Yes." Michelle nodded. "My son."

"Your son is brave. He killed a bear!"

"A bear?"

Michelle wanted to know more, but she saw the fat sisters she lived with already glancing in her direction and frowning.

"Thank you, Grandmother."

Michelle left the old woman's side and scurried back to her lodge. Out of the others' sight, she knelt in prayer to give thanks. Three months and more had passed since they had first been taken captive by the Seneca. Almost a year since Philippe Gerrard had liberated Henri from Saint Ouen's Church in Rouen, France, thus thwarting more imprisonment by her crazed stepfather, the Marquis de Propei.

If Henri had now escaped the Hawk clan as well and lived, maybe she was destined to survive after all.

Pierre Dunemoore had visited several clan villages off and on for two months, seemingly trading for furs, but always watching for signs of Michelle or Henri. If the village was Seneca and there was a white woman or a white boy present, chances were he would have found them by now. But after two frustrating months, he'd not heard even a rumor of a white captive, except for one at Maltoc's village. But Maltoc's village was far to the north. Philippe would likely check that one himself.

Then, late in June, Colonel Contrecoeur asked Pierre Dunemoore to travel eighteen miles downriver to the heavily defended palisade of a Seneca chief named Monakaduto, also called Half-King because he was one of two sachems who ruled this enclave on the river. Several tribes occupied Logstown because of its ideal location for fur trading. English and French traders were also known to stop by from time to time. The colonel wanted Pierre to gather what intelligence he could on the Seneca's mood concerning Fort Duquesne and gather what they might know about the English militia approaching from the south.

Colonel Contrecoeur knew he was asking the Scotsman to do something dangerous; particularly now, when the English were so near, and considering how the trade alliance the English enjoyed with the Iroquois might be extended into a war alliance at any time.

"We will only learn the depth of their alliance if and when the Iroquois begin killing us. I need this information, but you could be walking into an ambush. I will give you some volunteers as an escort, but it may not be enough. The danger cannot be underestimated."

Pierre smiled. "I am happy tah dah' it, Colonel. As long as there's profit in it for my company. Of course, I am a loyal citizen, but I am also a man o' commerce," he added plainly. The Scotsman winked.

"I must go back upriver to Fort Machault to inspect its new fortifications," Contrecoeur said. "If what you learn is valuable, bring news to me there, and we can celebrate the opening of another Dunemoore Company trading post, yes?"

"Ahhh, yes, Colonel. Spoken like a warrior o' trade! Ya' learn quickly!"

Pierre Dunemoore marched into Half-King's Logstown with fourteen *coureurs de bois* and his escort of four French soldiers. They carried many gifts.

Monakaduto faced the approaching French soldiers with a metal tomahawk in one hand and his brand new English musket cradled on the other arm.

The sachem was the most distinctive warrior in the group of over fifty braves confronting Pierre Dunemoore's smaller band of visitors. He wore a cape of beautiful gray owl feathers and was unusually tall for an Indian. The highly polished, black, English riding boots he wore only accentuated his height.

And the sachem was scowling.

Pierre Dunemoore was instantly wary.

For months, Half-King's scouts had been reporting the French army's steady construction of the new fort at the three-river confluence. The sachem was incensed by all the new forts, but this new one was biggest of them all, and the French had already placed many thunder guns on its walls.

The English traders at Logstown had been urging him to attack Pierre's group as they made their way downriver from the new fort, but the Seneca chief ignored them. Though his own inclination was for war, he trusted the English little more than he trusted the French.

As the French drew closer, Half-King thought the leader looked familiar. Then he noticed the great war ax draped over Pierre's shoulder. Only one white man carried such a weapon.

Pierre Dunemoore, known as Animal Scalp to the natives, had worn his jet black toupee of wolf skin on his head. He had borrowed some pomade and even greased a hair part into the silky pelt. It looked almost real, or at least he thought so.

"Ho, Monakaduto! I am honored to stand before the greatest warrior among the Seneca. I bring you greetings from the white chief in Montréal."

"Ho, Animal Scalp!"

As was expected, Pierre stooped and opened a canvas satchel full of gifts. He quickly spread them on a blanket. Three shiny, engraved skinning knives with bone handles. A two-pound sack of sugar, flints, shot, powder, a polished dragoon pistol, a thick bolt of bright red cloth, and a bowl of colored beads.

The Scotsman bowed. "Fine gifts for a great chief."

Half-King was impressed, particularly with the pistol. Two new weapons in the same day! But he pretended indifference. Animal Scalp had not yet said what he wanted. And white men always wanted something.

"It has been three winters since I have seen Animal Scalp at this village," the war chief replied in unfriendly tones. "Many promises have been broken. Many of my people have been killed."

Pierre spotted some English traders skulking in the background. *Bloody hell!*

As if a signal had been given, the Seneca braves began spreading out from both sides of their chief and slowly encircled Pierre and his eighteen companions.

One of the *coureurs de bois* became nervous and grumbled a warning.

Pierre sensed the panic in his men; a few gripped their weapons menacingly.

"Easy boys," Pierre said. He wasn't as worried about the Seneca as much as he was the English. "Mind your manners. We're guests here." He turned back to the chief. "I have two more gifts for ya'."

Pierre withdrew a shaving mirror from his backpack and a thick steel needle used to thread leather and held them out to the curious chief. The needle was far superior to ones made of antler bone and an extremely rare object on the frontier. Even among the English traders, a metal needle was a prize.

Half-King grunted with approval. He nodded and accepted the two gifts. Then he stepped forward to the blanket and picked up the dragoon pistol and one of the ornately engraved knives. With a wave of his hand, some of the braves rushed to scoop up articles. With the weapons now taken, the Seneca chief next waved the villagers forward. A small mob of ecstatic Seneca women surged and fought over the remainder of the gifts.

Pierre and the Seneca waited until the commotion subsided before continuing the parley.

"So many gifts, Animal Scalp," Half-King observed. "It is said the French can afford to be generous, now that they march with many soldiers on Seneca lands."

"My gifts are nah' from the French soldiers. The gifts are from me. Will ya' share a pipe with me?"

Half-King saw the English traders listening attentively to the exchange. He recalled the pathetic excuses they'd given him for the humiliating surrender of their soldiers at the three-river junction.

Maybe the English are hiding more lies than the French, Half-King thought suspiciously.

"We will talk in my lodge," he told the Scotsman.

Pierre and his men had settled on a plan before they arrived. While the private discussions took place with Half-King, the other *coureurs de bois* were to roam Logstown village, under the guise of trading, and discreetly ask questions about a captive white woman and boy. Meanwhile, Pierre would try to enlist Half-King's help in the search. But after two hours of delicate flattery, Half-King would still only talk about the injustices perpetrated by the French.

Pierre finally got the sachem to admit to knowledge of the Seneca attack on the Erigh at Fort Niagara.

"The snows of winter were still deep then. My people were not involved."

"The forest says two clans of the Seneca were involved."

Half-King could not comprehend Animal Scalp's unswerving interest in such a minor matter. Is this the only reason for his visit? The high chief studied Pierre discreetly. They had known each other for years. Animal Scalp was one of the few white men who had never lied to him.

"This attack happened long ago. Why is Animal Scalp so interested?"

"A woman and a boy were captured in the attack."

"Your woman?"

"No. Snow Hair's woman."

Half-King's chin lifted perceptibly. He now understood many things. The reason for the risky attack became clear. Snow Hair had killed Iron Pots' brother. Iron Pots had gotten Maltoc to steal Snow Hair's wife, even though this dangerous, foolish action threatened the delicate neutral balance existing between the Iroquois and the competing white tribes. And recently Iron Pots was found dead, killed by the Erigh shaman, Chittaqua. Chittaqua was Snow Hair's friend.

Yes, many things were clear to Monakaduto now.

"You talk of ambush as if only the Seneca are guilty. Snow Hair ambushed and killed Whiskey Man, my daughter's husband."

Pierre had hoped to avoid discussing this. "Yes, though he claims it was tah' take back furs stolen from him."

Half-King scoffed. "Furs given to me as a gift by the French soldier chief!"

Pierre lowered his gaze as if shamed by what had taken place. "The ambush was a mistake," he said sincerely, "and it happened two seasons ago."

Unknown to Pierre, Half-King had intensely despised his daughter's English husband. He had only allowed the marriage because of his daughter's relentless whining. He was secretly happy Whiskey Man had been killed, although he grieved with Iron Pots publicly and had sworn revenge.

The sachem took another long draught on the pipe and handed it back to Pierre.

"The attack on the Erigh at Fort Niagara rests with Maltoc's clan alone. I was not aware of it," Half-King said. "The Wolf clan may have been involved because many of their families are married."

Pierre had not known about the Wolf clan. But what Half-King revealed next was astounding news.

"But Maltoc should not have attacked so close to the French fort. He knows that now. The Hawk clan village was attacked by the Erigh. Maltoc's clan was destroyed."

Pierre Dunemoore was stunned. *Maltoc's clan...destroyed by the Erigh?* That seemed impossible.

"I dinnah' know Maltoc's village had been attacked," Pierre responded truthfully.

It was Half-King's turn to be surprised. The French soldiers did not know about this? He'd only learned about the attack the day before. Thunder guns were used, which implied an attack by the French, contrary to the rumors of this being an Erigh attack. Did the Erigh act alone then? Half-King didn't know. He decided to send runners and learn the truth of this.

"Why are the French soldiers making the fort at three rivers larger and stronger?" Half-King accused abruptly, changing the subject. "These are not the actions of a friend."

Pierre decided now was not the time to ask about Michelle and Henri. With Maltoc's village destroyed, he hoped they both were with the Wolf clan, because that's where he was going next.

"The English were building a fort," Pierre answered. "The French soldiers stopped them."

"So the French soldiers can go home now, yes?"

Pierre shook his head. "The chief of the French in Montréal thinks if we leave, the English will come back and build a new fort. The English want to stop us from trading with the Seneca and other tribes. Our chief in Montréal will not allow this to happen. We know the English are coming with a great force of men even now."

"The English only march to Onondaga to ask the Iroquois to fight the French. When did the French chief last visit the Onondaga council?"

Pierre knew the answer to the question was *never*.

Half-King knew it too.

"We have no treaty with the Iroquois. But my war chief at the three-rivers fort would like to parley with Monakaduto."

"Tell your war chief I am here, at this place, where the Seneca have been for many winters. Tell your war chief he can come to parley with me here."

"I promise I will urge him to smoke a pipe of peace with you."

"Urge him to leave our lands!"

Pierre had learned a lot. With the initial parley over, Pierre went to the front gate of Logstown looking for his men. He found the *coureurs de bois* leaning against the palisade.

"Sister Michelle is with Piqua's clan," one of them said.

Pierre nodded, excited. "What about Henri?"

The man became thin-lipped and serious. "He was with the Hawk clan. The Seneca claim the Erigh attacked and burned Maltoc's village two weeks ago."

"Half-King said the same thing. Gather the men. We're goin' tah' Piqua's village."

Pierre Dunemoore knew the trails leading to the village of the Wolf clan well. Overland, it took them only four days to reach it, but when they arrived, he learned messengers from Logstown had arrived a day ahead of them. The *coureurs de bois* were expected.

Piqua, leader of the Wolf clan, was not as physically impressive as Half-King but Pierre knew him to be more superstitious and therefore more dangerous than the diplomatic high chief. If the Wolf clan had been involved in the Hawk clan's raid, then he assumed they would not easily give up Sister Michelle and Henri, if indeed they were captive here.

"Ho, Piqua," Pierre greeted the sachem. Pierre was exhausted from the relentless pace of march that had allowed only a few hours' sleep each night. He planned to use the same strategy as he had used at Logstown: offer gifts first, then ask questions.

"Ho, Animal Scalp."

Pierre spread a blanket and arrayed gifts similar to the ones he had given at Logstown, only this time for Piqua's benefit, he added two three-gallon kegs of whiskey instead of the dragoon pistols.

Piqua smiled happily and retrieved the two kegs before signaling the rest of his warriors and villagers to take what they wanted. The sachem invited Pierre to his lodge where he greedily began drinking one keg so rapidly he became incoherent and drunk before Pierre could get past the cordialities to ask him any meaningful questions. Within an hour, the Wolf clan chief passed out in a stupor.

Since the sun was setting and Pierre was exhausted, he fell to sleep on an adjoining bed of furs.

The next morning, while his host was sleeping off the effects of the alcohol, Pierre walked around the compound, making ridiculous trades with the village women while he searched for one white woman. He knew she had brown hair and white skin, but little else about her appearance.

The Wolf clan village was larger than he expected. To draw the women to him, Pierre held streams of brightly colored ribbons high in the air above his head and let the women and children laugh and jump to reach them. Even the Huron and Ottawa slaves fought for a short strand of the red and yellow streamers.

Sister Michelle was not among them.

Pierre examined the faces of the throng of women crushing about him in a screeching, arguing mass. They were all Indian. As his disappointment grew, he noticed a woman sitting in front of a lodge thirty paces a way. She was all alone, her presence conspicuous in being apart from the rest of the village. And she was unmistakably white!

"Oh, blessed Mother," Pierre whispered thankfully. It had to be her. It had to be Sister Michelle!

"Take hold of these ribbons," he shouted to another coureur de bois.

Pierre slipped out of the crowd.

"Keep them occupied," he told the coureur de bois.

Slowly, Pierre sidled his way to a place near where Michelle was sitting. He positioned himself close enough that he could glance at her without fully turning his body in her direction.

In spite of his obvious nearness, she ignored him.

Sister Michelle's hair was tied back in braids like the other Seneca women. She wore the same deerskin dress the others wore, although hers looked much more ragged. Her body rocked gently in the rhythm of her task, rolling the heavy round stone in a wooden bowl, grinding the chestnuts into a powdery meal, stopping periodically to pick out the husks.

"Sister Michelle," Pierre called softly. "Are ya' Sister Michelle?"

Michelle froze. Her head turned suspiciously toward the stranger, but she didn't answer. She was exceedingly skinny, and a crazed glint was in her stare. He whispered more urgently.

"Are ya' Sister Michelle? Answer me, please! We dinnah' have much time."

Michelle wondered if this was another trick. She'd been given to one English trader for a night of abuse and rape. She did not want to experience that again. But this man spoke French with a curious accent and had called her by name.

To Pierre's delight, the woman nodded slowly.

"Oui, mon nom est Michelle."

The voice Pierre heard was devoid of emotion.

"Oh, glorious Mother o' Christ," the Scotsman said with glee. "Mademoiselle, my name is Pierre Dunemoore. I am Philippe's partner."

"Philippe?"

Her voice quavered. She began to stand.

"No, Mademoiselle! No! Dinnah' get up! Dinnah' look at me. Go back tah' what ya' were doin' and listen."

Some of the villagers were already glancing in Pierre's direction. He smiled and waved his arms.

"Go on with ya'," he shouted, encouraging them to keep assailing the coureur de bois and his magic sack of presents.

"We've come to rescue ya', Sister, but we kinnah' do it today," he told Michelle quickly. "Bless the saints, ya' are alive. We've been searching for ya' for months." Pierre faced the mob of villagers while he talked. "Can ya' hear me, Sister?"

"Yes, I hear you."

"I've nah' enough men tah' force your release this time. But it will nah' be much longer. And Philippe will be with me when I return."

Michelle's head was spinning at the thought of rescue, but the mention of Philippe was alarming.

"No. Do not bring Philippe. The Seneca plan to kill him," she whispered frantically to his back.

Pierre glanced over his shoulder. Tears were streaming down her face.

"Sister, shhhh. Quiet! Please!"

"No, you don't understand. They expect Philippe to come here for me.

They are waiting for him!"

"Sister, dinnah' talk so loud. They will hear ..."

But it was too late. Three of the village women ran over to them.

"Aieeeyaaa!" One sister struck Michelle and kicked her into the lodge entrance. The other two scowled angrily at the Scotsman. One began threatening him with a knife.

"Henri," Michelle shouted out to Pierre. "Tell Philippe, Henri has—"

Thwock!

Pierre winced, knowing they'd hit her on the head with something hard. Michelle started screaming, and the beating continued. He considered trying to take her then and there. But they were at the back of the village, nearly two hundred paces from the main gate. More of the village women and a few of the braves were already being drawn to the commotion.

Pierre reluctantly moved away from the lodge until he was among the milling villagers again. He started offering more gifts, but signaled his men to begin moving slowly toward the main gate. When everyone else had exited, Pierre told his *coureurs de bois* to rip open and scatter the few remaining sacks of trade articles near the front gate of the palisade.

Mirrors, more ribbons, knives, steel pots and pans, whole bolts of cloth, colored beads, metal bowls and spoons were tossed in every direction.

The Seneca thought the *coureurs de bois* had lost their minds.

In the resulting melee, Pierre and his men retreated from the encampment unopposed.

"Hurry, lads, hurry," Pierre urged.

"Retreat in a skirmish line," the sergeant ordered his three soldiers.

"*Oui*, that sounds good. Do tha'!"

The two soldiers at the forefront, stopped, turned, and knelt on either side of the trail, pointing their muskets back toward the village while the rest ran by. They waited till the others were out of sight before following. As they ran to catch up, they passed the position of the other two soldiers, formerly in the lead. The retreat continued, the soldiers taking turns guarding the rear. They didn't stop to rest until nightfall.

That night, while he lay awake in the darkness of the forest, Pierre recalled Michelle's screams and frowned. She had been trying to tell him something about Henri.

The boy must be alive, Pierre decided. She would not have been so eager to convey the news of Henri's death.

As if reading Pierre's thoughts, one of the coureur de bois spoke in the darkness. "She's a brave woman."

"Aye, she is tha'," Pierre answered. "And we are goin' back tah' get her," he vowed.

The warrior dragged the white woman by one arm and dropped her at Piqua's feet.

"She was talking to Animal Scalp."

That's why they'd left so suddenly, Piqua decided. He scowled at the pathetic woman and kicked her in the ribs.

Michelle shrieked and curled into a ball.

Piqua was uncertain what to do. Now, the French would know the Wolf clan kept a white woman slave. And they had many soldiers only a few days away. There was friendship between Snow Hair and Animal Scalp. A friendship that might bring evil on the clan of the Wolf as it had the clan of the Hawk. Maybe the French will not make war. Like Ootego suggested, maybe Snow Hair will come to trade for his woman.

The chief grabbed Michelle's hair, bent her head backward, and brought his face close to hers.

"What did you say to him?" Piqua growled.

Michelle trembled. "I asked his name," she whimpered.

"Liar," Piqua said. He struck her with a closed fist.

Painful sparks exploded in Michelle's head. She collapsed limply to the ground. For a few frightening seconds, her skin tingled as if it were on fire. Blood dripped from her left ear. And then a merciful blackness descended.

"Aieyaaa," Piqua said with disgust at seeing her stop moving. "Keep her out of sight," he told the fat sisters.

Pierre Dunemoore reached Fort Machault after another grueling forced march of four straight days and much of each night. He found Captain Benoit in command when he arrived.

The Scotsman gripped his friend by the shoulders as they greeted one another. "She's alive, Jean-Claude! Sister Michelle is alive! I saw her. I talked tah' her!"

Captain Benoit couldn't believe it. "Then you've seen a miracle."

"She's at the Wolf clan village. I spoke tah' her! I promised we'd return."

"And Henri?"

"Henri's nah' with her," Pierre replied with less enthusiasm. "But I believe Michelle thinks he's alive too."

"Colonel Contrecoeur anxiously awaits your story."

"Oh, there's more good news! Half-King claims the Erigh attacked and burned down Maltoc's village," Pierre whooped. "The bloody Erigh raided his camp while he was gone and burned down his fuckin' palisade and all the lodges. Maltoc's clan is nah' more!"

"We've already heard about that. So here's the bad news. Whoever did this used cannon…French cannon. And Maltoc is loose on the frontier with most of his warriors. It's only good news as long as the Seneca don't think the French army killed his people. And even if he learns otherwise, he will likely war on us anyway."

CHAPTER 3
FORT NIAGARA
JULY 1754
Henri Gerrard

Chittaqua's dream that night was as strong and frightening as any he'd experienced, with the exception of the dream of the demon from the island of stones—and that had not been a dream. From within a deep sleep, the high shaman of the Erigh people stared inland, away from the lake. His vision had expanded. The trees fell away from sight, the hills and valleys of the land became ghostly, barely visible outlines he could see through or around as he chose to. Things far away could be seen closely, simply with the desire it should be so. It was like the whimsical hallucinations of dreams, expect this one was not produced by any special medicines. This one seemed induced by an overwhelming fear for his life and that of Henri's.

He glanced quickly at Snow Hair's son. The boy was sleeping peacefully a few feet away. The fire had expired to a few glowing embers. There was no moon. The night was black. The sky was filled with abundant spirit lights, large and small.

Chittaqua looked up, captivated by their splendor for a time. And then he looked down from where he was perched to see his own body lying still, as if in death. Chittaqua was one with the white eagle. It spread its wings and soared into the sky. It banked sharply to the right and headed toward a specific place high above the portage. There were numerous dwindling campfires along the road leading to Fort Presque Isle, but one place in particular emanated evil, a complete blackness devoid of light or any reflections, so much so, it stood out like a blot against the forest's natural background of shadows. He flew as close to the blackness as he dared and landed in a tree high above the ground to wait for sunrise to dispel the darkness. And with that thought, the first glimmers of red appeared. Within moments, morning light permitted him to discern bodies surrounding the fire pit. But one place near the fire remained opaque. It was the evil presence that haunted his dreams. It had been moving across the water and lands for a long, long time; a vile, unmerciful thing. And it was hunting Henri for some reason. He could discern the blackness of its spirit, and this familiarity brought with it the knowledge it could be defeated. From that he gathered his courage and resolve.

The demon-like being was unaware of the eagle's presence, at least for now.

The Erigh shaman abruptly sat up, wide-awake from his dreaming, as if he'd not been asleep at all. The lake's water stirred at the touch of a light breeze. Waves were lapping gently against the shore. The orb of the sun was only halfway above the horizon. Henri was still asleep to his right. For a few moments, he stared out across the lake and wondered how he had joined with the eagle without the use of any medicines. Then again, he had not chosen to do this. It had just happened. It had chosen him.

I will dwell on the eagle's intentions later, he thought. He had the survival of the Erigh people to worry about and fulfillment of the promise to rescue Snow Hair's son. Chittaqua took hold of the pouch of dirt and bones to make certain it was still secure. He could feel the outline of the silver talisman inside. An idea came to mind…what if this demon from the island of stones had possessed this man, this evil one moving across the lands hunting Henri? Had this man also come from across the Great Waters …?

These are problems for the white man, he thought with irritation.

A heaviness came over him after such deliberations; conclusions he did not want to face, decisions he did not want to make. The shaman bowed his head and rubbed the weariness from eyes. He took a deep breath and prodded Henri with his foot.

"Wake up. We must go."

Chittaqua dressed and arranged Henri's clothing in the style of the Erigh. He tucked Henri's blond hair beneath a beaver-skin hat, leaving the feather braided into the blond hair exposed to one side. The boy's face was heavily bruised from the trials of his escape from the Seneca and would be for weeks to come. The nose broken from his fight with the Seneca brave was apparent. While the boy howled, Chittaqua had straightened it as best he could, but it would be crooked for the rest of the boy's life.

The shaman evaluated the boy's appearance and grimaced. "You will get questions, but it is enough."

"Questions about what?"

"About who you are. We will make up some answers as we walk to the fort."

"Why?"

"Come. You want to get to Fort Niagara, yes? More walking. Less questions."

Chittaqua led Henri out of the trees onto the wheel-rutted portage. For a few moments, he looked down the road in the direction of Fort Presque Isle. He did not sense any danger as he thought he had in his dream. The evil one was moving away…for now.

He pointed to their left.

"We go this way."

They marched along on the firmer ground to the side of the portage, which in a few places had expanded to a morass almost twenty-feet wide from the extensive wagons passing back and forth. But it had not rained for days and the surface was hardening again.

Within the hour, they began to encounter people. Chittaqua cautioned Henri not to speak to anyone beyond greetings. Not many of the soldiers or civilians traveling the Niagara portage to the west were inclined to speak to them. The men plodded forward, already drained of their strength by the heaviness of the wilderness supply loads they were carrying or pulling. But sometimes a soldier would smile in greeting.

Then they passed a group that did not look well at all.

"They have a bad smell," Henri said.

It was a malady. In addition to smelling it, Chittaqua could see it too. The soldiers' and *voyageurs'* faces were pale, their eyes hollow. They walked listlessly. Some dragged their weapons behind them. He recognized the symptoms.

"They are sick. They drank bad water possessed by a demon. Once inside the body, this demon hides and casts out the body's water, and it will not let you eat. Look."

Chittaqua pointed at a groaning soldier who was noisily relieving his bowels in the bushes.

"Many of these men will die. Accept no food or water from people who look like this," he warned. "Or this demon will attack you too."

When they encountered a group of *coureurs de bois* next, Henri raised a hand to hail them.

"No!" Chittaqua said quickly. "One of these men could be your enemy. Do not speak to them."

Henri was puzzled by the shaman's heightened concern. These men spoke French, and he wanted to talk with them. He didn't care how sick they were. It was hard to believe one of them might want to harm him.

"Why? You said they will not even know who I am."

"And so it should remain. Until the fort."

"I am French. So are they!"

"And which of these men do you know to be your friend?"

Henri recalled his father's warning when meeting strangers in the wilderness, which was Chittaqua's point. Reluctantly, he heeded the medicine man's caution.

After midday, they arrived at the outer environs of Fort Niagara. The small village encampment had expanded enormously since Chittaqua left two moons earlier. It was nearly four times the original size and was no longer organized along tribal or clan lines as it once had been. They began to wander among the maze of teepees, hide-covered wooden lodges, lean-tos, and a few canvas-covered carts. The entire area reeked with the odors from cooking fires and, in some places, excrement. Men and women from a dozen different tribes and an equal number of half-breed *coureurs de bois* gawked at them curiously as they walked by.

"Where did all these people come from?" Henri asked.

Chittaqua frowned and admitted he did not know.

They wound their way through the sights and foul smells. Chittaqua was disturbed by much of what he saw. But few people seemed interested in their passage, and that at least was good.

Henri had never seen so many Indians in one place. Some glared at him suspiciously; others seemed friendly and hailed them in languages he didn't understand. Some of the braves were nearly naked, their head shaved, their hair cut into a single, long scalp lock. Others had full heads of long hair adorned with feathers, and some wore brightly colored hats. He saw chest shields made of bone. He saw beautiful leather clothing adorned with red, yellow, and blue-colored beads. Some women dressed in leather buckskins, bleached pure white. As they penetrated the camp, small children began to trail behind them. A few started tugging at their clothes, laughing and babbling.

It seemed to Henri they were going to wander back and forth endlessly in the dusty heat of the afternoon, when Chittaqua finally stopped.

"Ahhh," he exclaimed. He had discovered the small rectangle of seven Erigh lodges comprising the surviving members of his clan. His wife, Juniata, was sitting on her heels in front of his lodge diligently crushing cornmeal in a large clay pot.

Juniata raised and lowered the wooden pestle in the ages-old rhythm. Fatiguing work, she stopped to wipe the perspiration from her brow and noticed the shadow of two figures stopped in front of her some six paces away.

"Aieeee!" she shouted and ran into Chittaqua's arms and hugged her husband around the neck. Tears began streaming down her cheeks.

Chittaqua hugged his wife tightly. Juniata's body felt strong, warm, and comforting.

"Not so much noise," he urged. He did not want the news of his arrival to reach too many ears. Not yet.

Henri shifted on his feet, self-consciously straightening his belt and arranging his clothing. He took off his hat and ran a hand through his hair. During the nights in the wilderness, Henri had learned how to cut and re-stitch his leather clothing to make it flexible but waterproof. Chittaqua had taught him how to pierce and thread the bear claws into a necklace, which now draped proudly across his chest. After washing the grime and gore from his hair, using the foamy mash from a plant root, the shaman ceremoniously braided an eagle feather into Henri's clean blond locks, then added colored stones so the feather would lie flat over his right ear. Chittaqua had told him the feather would signify to other braves he was a tested warrior. In the calm surface of a spring pool, Henri had proudly examined his reflection. He knew the proper way a brave wore his knives and other weapons. Chittaqua also had Henri move the Seneca scalp to the front of his belt, where it was certain to be seen by others.

"Who is this?" Juniata asked.

Chittaqua answered with pride, "Snow Hair's son."

Juniata was speechless. She smiled and approached him slowly, peering into the mottled and bruised face and eyes. Indeed it was Philippe's son! But the physical changes were remarkable. The youthfulness was gone. He was so much taller. The nose broken, the face lined with small scars and browned by the sun. There was no fat on the boy's body, and no fear in the cool blue eyes gazing back at Juniata with friendly curiosity. The boy had a natural strength in his stance, a slight tilt to his shoulders. One of Henri's hands rested casually on the butt of the skinning knife tucked at his waist.

"Welcome home," she greeted.

The Erigh woman opened her arms and embraced him. She felt Henri momentarily stiffen before he relaxed. She leaned back and smiled warmly.

"Look how strong you've become. You are a young warrior," Juniata cooed, stroked his hair, and enjoyed the boy's sudden embarrassment.

"I am thankful to visit your lodge," Henri stammered in the Erigh tongue.

Juniata's mouth opened in amazement and she glanced at Chittaqua. She squeezed Henri's arms and replied in Erigh.

"And I am very happy you visit us!"

"He is still learning to speak our tongue," Chittaqua said. "But he learns quickly."

Chittaqua urged them both inside the lodge. So far, none of his people had noticed his arrival. There was too much activity and noise in the camp. He wanted to keep their arrival quiet for as long as possible.

"Where are Chesanin and Achipan?"

Juniata knew her husband would not like hearing this. "They are at the fort. They carry earth for the soldiers to build higher walls."

"Why?"

Juniata bowed her head. "We get our food from the fort. There are no animals left in the forests. Even the fish from the river become fewer. The soldiers give us food in return for work."

"Our people will die if we remain at this place." Chittaqua felt a tired anger stir in his chest.

"Our men made war on the Seneca," Juniata added with more optimism. "They were victorious!"

The shaman felt a rush of emotion. First pride, then anger he'd not been with them, and finally fear of the reprisals from the French and the Seneca. If he'd remained at the village, he would have stopped them from this meaningless attack. Thus making it clear to him why the spirits arranged he be somewhere else.

I am glad I was not here, he decided. "How many returned?"

"Not many. The younger braves remained at Fort Presque Isle. Some are becoming scouts for the army."

Henri could tell the shaman was upset with something Juniata was saying, but they were speaking too fast for him to understand.

"Chittaqua! We should go to the fort," Henri urged.

"Tomorrow," Chittaqua replied.

"But others should be told I am here. Maybe my father is back."

Chittaqua glanced quickly at Juniata. She shook her head.

"Your father is not in the fort. You are safe here. Remember, his enemies are looking for you. Tomorrow we will go to the fort and see if it is safe for you to live among your people. And you will decide then. But I am tired. You are tired. We will eat and rest here first."

Henri looked toward the fort; it was so close. He could walk there in less than an hour. And he was anxious for news about his mother.

"The night will be here soon," Chittaqua added. He placed a hand on the boy's shoulder. "Eat and rest. Tomorrow morning we will go to the fort together."

Juniata quickly offered Henri a bowl of warm corn mixed with beans and bits of deer meat. The aroma sparked his hunger and convinced him to stay.

Chittaqua's right. One more night won't make much difference, Henri decided.

He'd started devouring the bowl of gluey corn stew when Chittaqua's sons appeared inside the lodge, filthy from carrying baskets of dirt all day.

They were excited to see their father and hugged him, but looked suspiciously at the white boy.

Henri matched their gazes with wariness.

"Sit," Juniata said.

Chesanin and Achipan dropped to a cross-legged position on Chittaqua's left and right. Juniata sat next to Henri.

"This is Henri, Snow Hair's son."

The twins continued to stare at the white boy, uncertain about his presence as a guest in their lodge. Juniata handed food to her sons, who began to eat without making conversation.

The shaman sensed Henri's nervousness. His sons were the same age as the Seneca boys who had so cruelly tormented him when he was in captivity.

Henri was expecting some type of harassment.

"I am going to tell my sons about your journey so they will know you better," Chittaqua told Henri. "But I will speak in our tongue."

Henri recognized several words as Chittaqua chronicled what had occurred since he was captured. After a few minutes, the shaman paused. Chesanin and Achipan looked at Henri with growing respect. Chittaqua gestured subtly to his son. *Go ahead, ask him.*

"Are those the claws of the bear?" Chesanin asked in French, pointing at Henri's necklace.

Henri stopped eating and glanced down at the necklace decorating his chest. He nodded.

"You fought and killed the bear?"

Henri nodded again. "Yes. But not by myself."

"My father claims you traveled with a wolf," Achipan said.

The twins saw Henri's wince.

"His name was Roland," Henri replied. "He was my friend."

Chittaqua and Juniata observed the boys' conversation. Henri unexpectedly gave Chesanin his Seneca skinning knife as a gift. Chesanin responded by giving Henri a copper bracelet. A friendship was forged.

"He learns quickly," Juniata observed.

"Like his father," Chittaqua said. "He thinks to live among the white men at the fort."

"I would think so too."

Chittaqua shook his head. "He will no longer like what he sees in the fort. You and the other women must build him a small lodge of his own, so he can live among us."

"Will he want to?"

"He will want to stay with his people." Chittaqua yawned and rested his head against the center pole. "Treat him like a son," he told her. "He is now of our clan."

The next morning, Henri Gerrard was packed and waiting outside before the sun had fully risen. He and Chittaqua made their way through the teeming jumble of teepees, huts, and lodges covering the ground all the way to the portage road. Many of the temporary hovels pressed against the main wagon trail, which meandered through the menagerie of humanity like some refuse-choked river. Once on the road, the shaman concentrated on avoiding the waist-deep ruts filled with a foul mixture of mud and human excrement.

"None of this was here before," Henri said, gesturing at the treeless field in front of the walls. "Where did all these people come from?"

Chittaqua only frowned and grunted in response.

They kept to one side since the road was busy, crowded with wagons, carts, and pack-carrying *voyageurs*. On the road before the main gate, a horse-mounted army sergeant swore and kicked at the beggars to keep the road clear for traffic. People moved in both directions. Fort Niagara itself offered the biggest surprise.

The scale of the fort's expanded construction loomed larger the closer they got to the enormous main gate. The former wooden stockade had been torn down completely, replaced by sloping earthworks, crowned with pointed timbers, notched at regular intervals with cannon emplacements. A broad thirty-pace-wide trench had been dug all along the front. Anyone approaching the wall would have to traverse a pit tactically situated to bring an aggressor under heavy fire from at least two separate battlements. New bastions in the shape of arrowheads were being created atop earthworks thrusting out like a trident from the fort. The new earthworks were covered by endless lines of filthy laborers, vagrants, and Indians, young and old, men and women, many toting baskets of black dirt, dumping their loads, adding to the height, while others tamped down the piles with heavy rocks. French artisans, mostly carpenters and stonemasons, worked at specific points fashioning the custom cannon placements.

The waterfront to their left had also expanded. Henri saw numerous supply bateaux and even a small two-mast lake sloop moored at a second pier constructed on top of thick wooden pilings driven into the silt in front of the old boat landing outside the western wall.

A tether line holding six huge dogs with curled tails was secured to a stake in the ground. The dogs' coats were thick with long strands of brown fur. Their eyes were shockingly light blue, almost white. Later, he would learn they were usually used to pull sledges or sleds in the winter. He watched as one of the friendly dogs barked at a coureur de bois who walked close by. Its tail wagging happily, it was looking for someone to pet or scratch its ears. The trader smiled and did what the dog wanted. In trade, the animal stood on its hind legs and placed heavy front paws on the man's shoulders to lick his laughing face.

Henri looked away. The scene reminded him too much of Roland.

Guards had been placed around the dismantled cannon being unloaded from the boats. Three long lines of bulbous, log-shaped black iron snouts of various calibers were arrayed in the marshalling yard. They were tended to by a crew of wheelwrights setting them up for transport, either up onto Fort Niagara's walls or for overland shipment to the barrier forts on the frontier.

"Oho," Henri said, delighted. "Chittaqua! Look at all the cannon!"

Chittaqua scowled. He had never seen so many thunder guns, nor had he ever seen so large a fort. A tenseness rose in his back. The change was too great. Like a rare, great shaking of the earth. Nothing would ever be the same. And there would be no going back.

The shaman recalled the words spoken by the French officer who'd originally asked permission to build a "trading lodge" at this place.

"And this is the white man's 'trading lodge'?"

Henri heard the shaman's bitter tone.

"What's wrong?"

"Come."

Up on the walls, soldiers walked the new battlements in clean gray uniforms, carrying muskets topped by gleaming baïonnettes and paying little attention to the jumbled mass of people, cargo, and animals moving in and out of the gate. The sentries on the towers were more concerned with watching the forest line, which had been cut clear of trees on all sides and now extended more than three hundred paces beyond the original field of fire, to make it difficult for enemy sappers to dig tunnels close to the walls.

Chittaqua and Henri entered Fort Niagara without challenge. Henri could barely contain his excitement. But nothing seemed like he remembered. The fort's interior was a mixed commotion of noisy construction: the clanging hammers of blacksmiths, the rip saws of timber jacks, shouting and swearing, and individual voices clamoring to be heard above the din. Chittaqua led Henri directly to les Négociants Dunemoore's trading post. A freshly painted red-and-blue sign hung above the door. The entrance was thronged with customers going in and out. Henri's gaze shifted to his left and right, hoping to see a familiar face, but he saw only strangers.

They struggled past the scowling *coureurs de bois* into the main trading room and found it overcrowded with people and piles of supplies. Henri's nose was assaulted by a mixed smell of rancid animal pelts and the sharp aroma of human sweat. Pungent clouds of tobacco smoke hung in the air. Bargaining was occurring at three different counter tables. He looked wistfully at the faces of the traders and faced the possibility he might not see his father. As he searched the room, his eyes were drawn to a beautiful Indian woman standing behind one table. She was haggling with two *coureurs de bois*. When she momentarily glanced in their direction, an expression of surprise and curiosity crossed her face.

Chittaqua! Okeanneh was stunned to see the shaman had returned. *Who is the boy?*

Chittaqua was equally surprised to see Okeanneh.

The shaman touched Henri and pointed to a place at one side of the room where they would wait.

Okeanneh finished her present bargaining quickly, agreeing to a price that, moments earlier, was not good enough. The two men picked up their dry goods and moved to the front door, eyeing Chittaqua suspiciously.

Okeanneh ignored the requests of the next man in line and came out from behind the table to greet Chittaqua.

Henri continued to gawk. Except for Madeleine, a girl he'd known in France at Saint Ouen's Church, he'd never seen such a beautiful woman before. Chittaqua began talking to the woman in a native tongue. Their tone was subdued, but Henri sensed tension in their voices.

"Where is Snow Hair?"

"He left."

"His wounds were healed?"

"No. I asked him to, but he would not stay."

"Did he go with the soldiers?"

Okeanneh shook her head. "He was riding a horse. He seeks the white woman," she added tersely. "She has poisoned his heart."

The shaman scowled. "You know little of what is in Snow Hair's heart, or who his enemies are, or where his destiny lies," Chittaqua responded. "Do not—"

"He is my husband," Okeanneh hissed. "I am going to find him." After

Father Beauharnois had told her of the danger Philippe was in, the only reason she had not set out at once was Anamosa. "No one will take him from me!"

Chittaqua turned so she could see Henri.

"This is Snow Hair's son. His name is Henri. You must welcome him."

Okeanneh bristled and gazed at the blond hair and ice-blue eyes. *So it's true*, she thought morosely.

Even through the bruises, Henri's resemblance to Philippe was remarkable. Oddly, his dress was more that of a young Erigh brave than any of the white boys she'd seen walking around the fort.

The boy was staring at her.

He is my husband's son, Okeanneh reminded herself. "Bonjour," she greeted him.

"Bonjour, Mademoiselle," Henri answered politely.

She placed a hand to her chest. "I am Okeanneh."

"Henri Gerrard," he responded touching his own chest the same way.

Okeanneh reached out and impulsively brushed away some cockleburs that had collected in his hair and on the shoulder of his leather jersey.

Henri liked this attention but was uncertain how to react. *Should I embrace her?* Standing so close to her was strangely provoking.

"This is your father's lodge," she said. "It is your home."

"I know. I used to live here. Where is my father?"

Okeanneh's face flashed briefly with irritation before it softened.

"He has gone with the French soldiers…to look for your mother."

"Where?"

"Far from here. Many days' march."

"Is my mother alive?"

Okeanneh did *not* want to talk about the boy's mother, but she could not resist the longing in Henri's eyes.

"The Seneca keep many captives. She is probably alive."

The relief on Henri's face was immediate.

Chittaqua interrupted. "Stay here. I go to speak with the chief of the fort. Do not go anywhere."

"I want to go with you!"

"Wait here until I come back."

Henri nodded reluctantly.

When the shaman left the trading lodge, Okeanneh touched Henri's shoulder.

"Do you like tea?"

"Yes." He'd not had any in several months.

She pointed to a seat near a table in the corner.

Henri sat down to wait but quickly became restless and got up to walk around the trading post. Bartering continued loudly at the other two counters by men he assumed worked for his father. Occasionally, one of them would glance at him with curiosity. One of the clerks he recognized as Claude Guillot, but he resisted the urge to talk. He looked beyond the bargainers at the surroundings. On one small table was a great pile of hard tack. A rope was strung across the ceiling with dozens of metal tomahawks hanging from it. Eight shiny new muskets were racked one on top of the other on the back wall. Piled next to the trading tables were sacks of corn flower, bundles of root fibers tied in ugly bouquets, and bolts of brightly colored cloth. Powder horns and sacks of lead shot hung from pegs on the front walls. Huge skinning knives in beautifully beaded sheaths were arranged on a display board. Towering bales filled with skins taken from beaver, fox, ermine, and mink dominated all other sights and smells.

Henri moved behind the canvas separating the front room from the back to look around the sleeping area. His father's bed remained in the same place as before, across from the hearth separated by a wall from the other bed. Both beds were clean and neatly covered with gray blankets. A heavy roll of fur lay at the foot of each. Two huge casks stood side by side near the rear window. The lid was half open on one. He sniffed and smelled a briny odor.

Henri's mouth watered.

Pickled corn!

Henri reached in, pulled one out, and crunched it between his teeth. The taste was tart, sour, and wonderful. Shifting his gaze, he noticed someone lying on a bed to the side of the fireplace. It was a small girl. Henri felt nervous, as if he were trespassing somehow. He went back out to the table in the front and sat down.

Okeanneh returned bringing a tin pot full of hot tea, a bowl filled with hard biscuits, bread, and cheese.

"I must help with the trading," she said after placing the food on the table.

"*Merci.*"

Henri hadn't tasted tea since before he was captured. It was delicious. He gulped it hungrily while he gobbled down the food he had been served.

At the conclusion of each trade, Okeanneh would let the customers out, then bar the door to stop others from coming in. Soon, only Claude Guillot was left in the store. But Okeanneh wanted to talk with Henri alone.

Claude Guillot eyed the boy with the bruised and swollen face sitting at the table on the other side of the room.

"Who is he?" he whispered.

"No more trading," she answered without explaining.

"No more trading?" Claude was surprised. He didn't think it was Okeanneh's place to make this decision, but he knew it would be unwise to challenge her.

"Go outside and eat with your friends. I will open the door again in a little while."

Claude squinted at the boy sitting in the shadows eating ravenously.

He is dressed like an Indian. The face looked slightly familiar. *But who could it be?*

Claude nodded a greeting before he left the post, but the boy was concentrating on his food and did not look at him.

Okeanneh lowered the bar on the door and returned to the table.

"Where did Chittaqua find you?"

Henri quickly related the tale of his capture and escape.

Okeanneh listened attentively. Henri's gestures and words looked and sounded like Philippe, so much so, hard as she tried not to, she was entranced with him. The story of Henri's escape was courageous enough to become a song among her people. It evoked feelings of compassion that warred with her resentment: *He is the son of your rival.*

Henri finished his tale along with the food and drink.

"Your ancestors protect you. Not many young braves are taken captive by the Seneca and return to tell about it." Okeanneh stood. "I must open the door again," she said reluctantly.

When she threw over the wooden bar, an old Indian woman pushed her way in and began haggling with Okeanneh even as she entered.

With the food gone, Henri decided to wait outside.

Okeanneh watched him leave, wondering what the boy's arrival would mean for her.

Henri breathed deeply. The sunlight and fresh air felt good after the smelly stuffiness of the trading lodge. A quick search of the long and broad marshalling yard revealed no sign of Chittaqua. But there were plenty of other things to see. He adjusted his bow across his back and strolled to the gate to observe the commotion. He examined the face of every soldier or white man walking by, but, outside of Claude Guillot, he did not recognize a single person. Remembering Chittaqua's warning, he walked back to the area near the front of the trading lodge and waited to one side of the door.

The present fort bore little resemblance to the one in his memory, except for a few of the interior buildings. Of course, the great stone castle looked the same, but it also looked smaller sitting to the rear of the expanded grounds.

Sights and sounds of construction were all around him. Stone cutters sawed and hammered huge wedges into great rocks that hissed with strain before they split with a loud crack. Lines of men heaved baskets of raw earth hand over hand up the slopes of the battlements. Others mixed great vats of mortar. Amidst it all, hooting native women begged or offered things to trade to any of the soldiers or *coureurs de bois* who made the mistake of standing still as they crossed the fort's interior. The soldiers on the ground inside the gate were sitting or leaning against the timbers. Some of them were asleep. Henri recalled how Captain Benoit had severely reprimanded a guard for sleeping at his post. But in all the activity, no one took any notice of this man at all.

Henri walked to one of the walls to watch a stone mason and was reminded of the men he had known at Saint Ouen's Church.

"Move," an annoyed voice said.

Henri turned. A worker, covered from head to foot in gray dust, looked at him with irritation. He'd been standing in front of a ladder blocking the man's way. Henri moved, then looked for a place where he could sit that would be out of the way. To his right was a large pile of rocks and boulder rubble several feet in height. He climbed up to the top and found he could see the entire yard.

No one will be bumping into me up here, he decided.

He reached inside his shirt and withdrew a long stick of stiff venison Juniata had given him. He sucked and chewed on the meat, wincing at the sour salty taste.

New shouts of excitement in the center of the parade ground drew his attention. Children of all ages began to throng around two Jesuit priests as they exited the chapel a hundred paces away, directly across from where Henri sat. He recognized one of them instantly.

Father Beauharnois. Henri smiled. *At least I know him!*

The two priests were holding leather pouches high above their heads.

"From the Lord God," the younger priest declared as he showered the air with bits of clear rock candy.

More than thirty children roiled, pushed, and shoved each other to grab as much as they could. Within moments some of the smaller ones were crying, a few were knocked down, one was bleeding.

One of the stonemasons nearby elbowed his apprentice. "Look! Monseigneur Beauharnois is feeding his new converts."

"I'll wager it's leftovers from what he and his priests couldn't eat," answered the other man.

Henri listened then frowned. The children were skinny with a look of starvation, like most of the Indian children he'd seen outside the fort.

The mob of children became increasingly frantic, punching and scratching at each other. Workers on the wall stopped to watch the turmoil. A few of the carters laughed and whistled their approval. Seemingly oblivious to the harm he was creating, Father Beauharnois continued to shout Latin blessings as he tossed confectioneries in a circle, heedless to the escalating viciousness of the fights breaking out all around him.

The excited shouts and screams of the other children had awakened Anamosa. She knew exactly what it meant. After peeking out the door and seeing the priest tossing sugar rock, she ran from the trading post, ignoring Okeanneh's protests. Anamosa got as close to the priests as she dared. The smaller children had retreated, leaving the fighting to the older, bigger boys. But Anamosa was determined. Jumping up and down, she waved her hands in the air, hoping to be seen.

"Me! Me! Me!"

Henri saw the small girl hanging back from the melee. She had long black braided hair decorated with tiny pink shells. Her voice was overwhelmed by the noise, but she continued to jump and wave her hands at the priests. He hoped they saw her.

One of the boys directly in front of the monsignor's assistant had blood streaming from his nose.

"Monseigneur, look!" the younger Jesuit said. "Maybe we should stop. They are hurting one another."

"Nonsense. There is plenty to go around. Throw it farther. Spread them out."

The monsignor continued to fling the confections. "God's blessings, my children. Receive God's blessings."

The assistant saw a little girl standing alone some thirty feet away from the laughter, snarls, and shrieks of the other children. She was jumping, waving, and stepping closer at the same time.

Can't have her coming into the middle of this, the priest decided.

The priest reached into the bag and felt around until he located a smaller pouch of candy he knew was there. He had been saving this for himself but felt inspired to toss it to the small girl. He threw the small sack in a high arc toward the girl's outstretched hands. She stretched, caught it off balance, and fell backward on her rump. The priest smiled.

Shrieking with delight, Anamosa stood and held her prize aloft, triumphant. Some of the older boys swarmed toward her.

Henri sensed trouble. Impulsively, he jumped down from the pile of rocks. Nearby there was a wooden pole the stonecutters used as a fulcrum to lift the stones after they were cut. Henri grabbed it and sprinted toward the girl.

Anamosa had started to run back toward the trading lodge with her prize but was overtaken by the largest of the boys. He slammed her on the back of head with the flat of his hand. She flew forward, fell face first into the dust, and screamed.

The boy struggled to tear the sack of candy from Anamosa's hands, but Anamosa spit, bit, and kicked ferociously. A second boy reached her. Between the two of them, they twisted the prize from her fingers. The older boy held the sack up victoriously.

"Hey!"

The boy turned.

Henri delivered one end of the pole to the larger boy's gut then whacked him on the backside, driving him to the ground. Stunned by the unexpected onslaught, the second boy backed away. Henri picked up the bag of candy and gave it back to the astonished little girl who retreated to the arms of her angry and equally astonished mother. Okeanneh, recognizing Anamosa's scream, had come running and had witnessed Henri's gallant rescue.

The background noise in the fort dropped dramatically as workers stopped to watch the unfolding drama.

Henri recognized Martin Herault, the baker's son, who he had knocked to the ground. Soon, seven more boys were facing Henri in the middle of the yard.

Martin got back to his feet and scowled angrily at the bruised and unfamiliar face standing in front of him. "I'll break your skull," he snarled. He signaled to his friends. All seven advanced on the single opponent, expecting to see him retreat.

Henri balanced the pole in both hands and took a deep breath. "*Hooo-keee-yi-yi-yi*," he screamed.

The dreaded Seneca war cry startled them. Henri waded into the group, cracking heads and legs with the staff. He managed to temporarily knock four of the boys to their knees before the others converged and wrestled the hard wood pole from his grip. The boys closed in on Henri, now deprived of his weapon, ready to deliver humiliating punishment. But Henri was strong and sinewy from months of captivity and hard marching. He struck his attackers more often and harder than they struck him. Two received bloody noses with the first punches and stopped fighting altogether.

The soldiers and workers whooped and hollered encouragement from the wall.

"Go get 'em boy!"

"Kick 'em in the balls!"

Henri knew he couldn't keep them all at bay without the staff. Breaking free, he grabbed it up once more and dropped back several paces. His attackers regrouped, picking up rocks and sticks of their own. Their numbers had grown to ten.

"Stop this immediately," bellowed Father Beauharnois. "In the name of Jesus, I order you to…my God! *Henri*? Henri Gerrard? Is that you?"

Everyone ignored the Jesuit. Soldiers at the gate were now wide-awake, sentries on the wall no longer looked at the tree line. Instead, they cheered, finding the singular ferocity of the blond-haired youth impressive and were greatly interested how he would fare against the increasing odds.

Henri didn't hear the protesting cries of the priests or the urging shouts of the soldiers; he heard only a pulsating roaring in his ears.

"Come on," Henri challenged loudly. "Come on!"

The boys advanced warily, spreading out again in a semicircle. Henri thrust the tip of the staff at one and swung at another. He scored stinging hits, but the boys split and moved, slowly surrounding him.

I need a wall at my back, he thought. He knew the trading post was behind him.

But as he backed away, those in front and to the side, stopped and straightened from their fighting crouches. Sensing movement behind him, Henri whirled around.

Chesanin and Achipan were standing behind him to his left and right. Each held a rock. They were covered with mud. Chesanin smiled. Achipan nodded.

Henri turned back, threw down the staff, and grinned at the leader.

"Come get me now, Martin," he dared the other boy, gesturing with his hands.

Henri Gerrard? Martin Herault straightened as it dawned on him who it was he was fighting.

"Cease this disorder!"

An officer and half a dozen soldiers burst upon the scene, separating the combatants. Loud groans and whistles rose from the disappointed workers and soldiers.

"Disperse immediately," the officer ordered the surrounding crowds. "Disperse or you shall be barred from the fort."

The fort contained only a two-man jail. No one was worried about being arrested. Being barred from the fort, however, could have dire consequences. People quickly started moving away.

Captain Pouchot arrived at the scene accompanied by a frowning Chittaqua. The shaman had hoped to arrange a private meeting between the fort commandant and Henri, thereby limiting the notoriety concerning their return.

"Is *that* Philippe Gerrard's son?" the officer asked an aide.

"Yes, sir. The blond one."

Some of the remaining onlookers overheard the question and examined the white boy more closely. Surprised murmurs could be heard. *That's Henri Gerrard! Henri Gerrard is back!*

"Come here, young sir."

Henri approached the fort commandant. He could tell Chittaqua was not pleased.

The commandant held out his hand. "It appears you took quite a beating from someone. But welcome home."

Henri avoided Chittaqua's eyes. "Thank you, sir."

Father Beauharnois joined the reunion and a smile beamed from his face. "You're dressed like an Erigh savage. A necklace of claws. The bow. The feathers. Very quaint. Come hug your priest, boy."

Henri glared at the Jesuit. "Chittaqua is not a savage!"

The boy's indignation surprised Captain Pouchot.

"Of course not," Father Beauharnois replied quickly. He glanced at Chittaqua. "I did not mean to imply …"

"It was Chittaqua who found me in the wilderness. I would have never gotten back were it not for him. Most of these people are starving," Henri said, directing his anger at the Jesuit. "You should not throw food among the young ones. It was a cruel thing to do."

Bravo, Captain Pouchot thought.

"Of course it was, Henri," Father Beauharnois replied apologetically. "You are right. I did something stupid."

"Yes, yes, yes. The monsignor is indeed stupid. You are forgiven, Monseigneur." The commandant did not really care. "Young sir, the whole fort rejoices with your safe return. But please accompany me to the castle. You possess valuable intelligence on the Seneca that I must learn. Is that all right with you?"

Henri glanced at Chittaqua. The shaman nodded.

"As you wish."

Captain Pouchot grinned at his aide. "Sergeant Major Gabriel, please provide an escort of honor. Come, come. We have hot food and drink inside. I look forward to some enjoyable conversation."

"I want Chittaqua to come with me."

"Certainly." Pouchot gestured for the shaman to follow.

"You do indeed dress like a proud Erigh warrior," the commandant said. "I will have scribes make a record of everything that occurred since your capture. I am sorry your mother and father are not here to greet you. But take heart in the fact you have returned against enormous odds. Maybe they will too, eh?"

"I only got back because of this man," Henri repeated.

"I understand." The commandant turned and addressed Chittaqua. "I am certain Philippe Gerrard would extend his personal gratitude for the safe return of his son."

Chittaqua nodded but said nothing.

The trio entered the stone house and went into the commandant's offices. A smiling Sergeant Major Gabriel soon followed with a maid and a tray of hot soup, bread, and wine.

"Enjoy yourself," urged the commandant. "There are a few matters I must attend to. I will return shortly."

"I'm sorry I got into a fight," Henri told the shaman when the officer left.

His face reflected both his shame and justification.

"But they were *hurting* that girl."

Chittaqua was not thinking about the fight at all. One whole wall of the commandant's office, from ceiling to floor, had been converted into a book case. The shaman pointed and looked at Henri.

"*Books*?"

"Yes. Those are books." Henri picked one out at random, opened it, and pointed to each word as he read a few sentences. He paused. "You see?"

Chittaqua selected another volume and felt its weight. He handled the book as if it were a delicate treasure, something fragile, easily broken. Carefully opening the book, he turned a few pages, marveling at line after line of the mysterious marks he saw. Chittaqua pointed at a word and looked at Henri.

Henri peered at the page. "That word is *magnificent*. This next one is *ocean*. That's our word for it. You know? It's the name of the great water you sometimes talk about."

The Erigh high shaman saw it clearly. It was so simple. *Books!* The real source of the white man's power. It was the first thing he'd seen from the white man that was not intended for killing.

He decided Chesanin and Achipan must learn to make these…words. He slowly ran his fingers across an entire row of gilded bindings.

Magic!

CHAPTER 4
RIVIÈRE AUX BOEUFS
JULY 1754
Peter Blue Jacket

When the rumors of the attack on Maltoc's village first reached the ears of Peter Blue Jacket, he was sitting among the elders of the Mohawk council at a special gathering held near the headwaters of the Allegheny River to discuss the enormous French fort being built at three rivers. The council met close to this fort to hear opinions from various Mohawk and Seneca tribal elders and clan leaders about this latest in a series of war-like events between the French and English.

The Seneca and the Mohawk were the most powerful tribes in the Iroquois confederation. The Mohawk controlled the eastern lands, the Seneca the west; at least, that was the generally accepted view of the other four nation-tribes of the Iroquois. The Mohawk were close friends of the English. For that matter, the Seneca were equally inclined toward the English. Except, the French were building forts all over the Seneca lands, and the English seemed more ready to run away than fight. Four French forts had been raised on Seneca lands in less than one season. Half-King—most important among the Seneca, but absent at this council—grudgingly showed a neutral face to the French; his people could not bear the fight against the French alone. But the Seneca high chief's indignation regarding these transgressions was well-known.

A few days into the meeting, the Seneca sent word to the council of the attack on the Hawk clan village by the Erigh tribe. The council reacted with disbelief. The pathetic remnants of the Erigh tribe were camped by Fort Niagara. They could barely feed themselves. Mostly boys and old men, they were simply not strong enough to attack anyone, least of all the palisade of Maltoc, the fiercest of the Seneca clan chiefs. But what gave the Mohawk-Seneca council pause was the report the Erigh had used thunder guns in their attack.

"This is not possible!" Peter Blue Jacket spoke first and loudly.

Peter, however, was only a council messenger and could voice his opinions only if invited to do so by an elder. But he could not accept this exaggeration and remain silent. "Only the French and English soldiers have thunder guns," he continued.

The council chief, Tiyanoga of the Mohawk, gestured for Peter to sit back down, then pointed to the first elder. The man stood and walked into the circle.

"If thunder guns were used, and if not by the Erigh, who dares to attack the Seneca with the white man's weapons? And why? And if it was the Erigh, where would they get such powerful weapons if not from the French?"

At this, murmurs rippled through those present. The council chief held up a hand to quiet the discussion.

The Mohawk and Seneca speakers each took a turn in the circle. They had many questions but few answers.

Facts were discussed first. The French had marched deep into Iroquois lands without asking for parley or permission. Shots were being exchanged daily in isolated meetings between the French and English fur traders. The French continued to build large, powerful forts armed with thunder guns. It was inevitable; the white soldiers would soon clash in a major battle. The French emissary to the English was murdered in a recent ambush. Open war between the English and French loomed larger every day.

The greater Iroquois Council of Fifty was steadfast in their desire to remain neutral for as long as possible. Let the white men fight until the likely victor could be identified. Once the outcome was certain, only then would the Iroquois council commit the might of the six nations to the winning side.

"Our best future comes if the white men slaughter each other," one elder said. "Even then, what will happen to these forts?"

Finally, Tiyanoga, the council chief, rose to stand in the circle. "The Mohawk and Seneca are brothers. Thunder guns have destroyed a Seneca village. So I ask you…has war been thrust upon us already?"

Opinions burst forth. Peter Blue Jacket listened carefully. Some council members were inclined to war, others were not so sure. In the end, most elders were disinclined. The English and French were still giving gifts and lying with more vigor than ever before. But if thunder guns were used to attack the Seneca, where would these terrible weapons be pointed next?

And who would fire them?

"And what of Chittaqua, the Andrototekan, the great sorcerer of the Erigh?" the oldest and wisest of the elders asked. "What part does his magic play in this?"

Heads nodded solemnly all around the council lodge. A disturbing question indeed.

There was great need for this council at the Allegheny to know exactly what had happened at the Conneaut lake village and who was involved before any unified decision could be reached.

"We will send Peter Blue Jacket back to the Seneca lands to learn the truth," Tiyanoga declared. "Until he returns, the Mohawk should prepare for war in support of our Seneca brothers."

Hoots of agreement filled the council lodge.

If Peter used the shortest trails, he estimated it might still take him a week. Or maybe less? He planned to run overland to the southern point of Lake Chautauqua, canoe to the northern shore, and run west overland to the Rivière aux Boeufs. From there, it would not take long to reach the Conneaut village by various rivers. But along the way, a chance encounter followed by an enormous discovery changed everything.

Philippe was forced to wait several days for Major Péan to write new dispatches to Colonel Contrecoeur. He wandered among the Fort Presque Isle villages, the *voyageur* carts, and the barracks, asking questions of anyone who had traveled the lands west or south of the fort. Had anyone seen or heard a rumor of a white woman or a boy captive with the Seneca? And what had occurred when the Erigh attacked the Conneaut lake village? What he learned was mostly rumors and exaggerations from the various traders and half-breeds lingering near Fort Presque Isle. Fortuitously, Three Finger Knife, heralding himself as the Erigh war chief, was passing through, heading back to Fort Niagara. He was eager to discuss the attack. He told Philippe two things: the destruction to Maltoc's village was total, and there were no whites found among the dead.

"I scouted the village for three days before we attacked. I saw no sign of any whites living there. Maltoc and the majority of his braves were away during the attack."

"Where were they?"

Three Finger Knife shook his head. "My scouts claim they were searching in the east. For who or what, I know not."

Philippe gazed grimly at the trees. "If Maltoc is alive, his Seneca will be warring. They will kill anyone they meet."

"They have already made kills near this fort."

Philippe's brow furrowed at the thought. "And what of Chittaqua?"

"No one has seen him in over a moon," the war chief replied. "But he would be pleased by our victory."

Philippe didn't think Chittaqua would see it as a victory, just the opposite, but he didn't say so.

"The rumors claim the Erigh used cannon. Is that true?"

Three Finger Knife smiled but avoided answering the question. "Good fortune to you, Snow Hair," he said before walking away.

Philippe was now more eager than ever to get to Fort Le Boeuf. After some unpleasantness with Major Péan concerning who had charge of his horse, he continued his courier ride.

Trying to make up for lost time, he galloped south on the expanded army road. Suddenly, the horse stepped into a stump hole filled with water. The animal's right front leg plunged into the two-foot-deep depression. Carried by momentum, the *coureur de bois* was thrown forward in the air in a complete summersault before landing flat on his back. The horse flipped rump-over-head; its foreleg shattering with a sickening snap. The animal whinnied in terrible pain before landing with a heavy thud.

Winded and dazed by the fall, Philippe sat up, wondering what the hell had happened. He wasn't seriously hurt, except for another new lump on his head. He glanced back at the horse. It was down with a broken leg. He was suddenly reminded of the unexpected pain in his own leg when he had camped a week ago on the Niagara portage. That pain was the most searing sensation he'd ever experienced. He was still provoked with uncertainty over what had caused it. The surgeon traveling with him at the time said it was invented by his mind, that he'd seen it before in other soldiers, veterans mentally shocked by memory of a battle so terrible, they sometimes relived the event. But Philippe didn't think that was what had happened to him. This had been no nightmare. This pain had been too real, too specific to the exact spot of the previous wound, incurred when he had first set off to rescue Henri and Michelle after they had been taken captive by the Seneca. The barest touch to the skin had been like a hot piercing blade. Yet, oddly, if he did not touch the scar, there was no pain at all. It seemed it would never end. Then as suddenly as it began, it stopped—nothing, no pain—like it had not happened at all. No, this was no mental shock from some perverse memory. He had hideous vivid memories far worse than the break to his leg, painful as that was. And he'd been wide-awake while this happened. He wasn't sure what this was, but he worried it would abruptly happen again, endangering the lives of people around him.

He cautiously felt his arms and shins, praying he'd not broken anything new. All seemed well. Using the stock of his musket lying nearby, the *coureur de bois* hoisted himself off the ground and staggered back to his injured animal. The animal's right foreleg was twisted and hanging limply, bones piercing the skin. It was snorting and breathing heavily in torment. He grimaced with compassion, knelt at the horse's side, and gently patted its flank.

"Easy boy. Easy."

He stroked its neck and shoulder, speaking to it soothingly, to calm its fear before doing what he knew he had to do. When its labored breathing slowed, he loaded his musket with extra powder and double shot. He placed the muzzle behind the animal's ear and pulled the trigger.

In the morning stillness of the forest, the sound from the musket was loud enough to stun his hearing for a few moments. A large white cloud of acrid, powdery smoke hung in the air.

Philippe had stooped to collect his heavy backpack and other weapons from the saddle when he heard the sound of bushes moving behind him. He spun around, his skinning knife in one hand, a tomahawk in the other. A man was standing only a few paces away. He also carried weapons, but his posture was not menacing.

There could be others, Philippe cautioned himself.

He slowly gripped the tomahawk, readying to make a throw. At this range he could not miss. He glanced beyond his target to the forest edge, looking for signs of movement. If this was a war party of Seneca, things would get deadly quickly. The dragoon pistol was still in the saddle bag of the horse. His bow was not strung.

But the man raised a hand in greeting. "Oho, Snow Hair."

Philippe blinked and squinted at the face, which now looked familiar. He wore a mix of Indian and *coureur de bois* clothing.

"Peter? Peter Blue Jacket?"

"*Oui*." The Mohawk set down his musket and held up both palms. "I am alone. I heard the musket shot."

Philippe relaxed and straightened. "Where are you going?"

"To Maltoc's village. They say it was attacked."

Philippe nodded. "By the Erigh."

Quickly, they traded facts and rumors.

"I'm told the Erigh had thunder guns?" Peter Blue Jacket inquired.

"I've been told the same thing. But I don't know where they would get such cannon. The army did not give any to the Erigh…but there are a lot of arms on the move. Some could have been stolen."

"Then the French did not support this?"

Philippe was well aware of Peter's role as an Iroquois council messenger. The two men had been thrust by this coincidental meeting in the wilderness into speaking for two of the three great powers: Philippe speaking for the French.

"Why would the French start a war with the Seneca? We have *nothing* to gain by that…or by threatening the council. *You*, of all the Iroquois, know this. Our enemy is the English, not the Iroquois. You spy for the council. That's why you are so far west, yes?"

"And what of Maltoc?"

"Why do you ask me? All I know is that his warriors were not present when the attack occurred. That they are warring. Many white traders have been killed and tortured all over these lands." Philippe paused so his next words would make a point. "I warn you. The French army will *not* tolerate this. And there are a great number of French soldiers here now—with many thunder guns. Maltoc, acting alone, could do something to force the French to war."

There was another awkward pause in the conversation. Philippe waited. It was Peter's turn to speak first.

"And where are you going?"

"To Fort Le Boeuf."

Peter Blue Jacket wanted to ask about Snow Hair's woman and son, but decided it would not be a good idea. He looked at the dead horse.

"A totem animal should not die like this."

Philippe sensed Peter knew more than he had volunteered. "What will you tell Maltoc when you find him?"

"What would you have me tell Maltoc?"

"Tell him if the French army is provoked into war with the Iroquois, the Seneca villages in the west will be attacked first."

As a friendly gesture, Peter Blue Jacket helped Snow Hair drag the horse off the army road and fill in the hole with rocks and dirt. They shook hands and parted respectfully, but Peter clearly heard the potent warning from the *coureur de bois*. And that was a problem. Events were moving too quickly. He was running out of time.

When Maltoc and his braves first returned from searching for Snow Hair's son and found their village and palisade in ruins, some ran about wildly, screaming with anger, others stood motionless, bewildered, and stunned. All of the bodies were dead. If there had been wounded, they were slain. There found no wandering survivors.

The attackers were gone. The Seneca pursued immediately, not only for revenge, but also in the hopes the Erigh had taken captives. Maltoc led his men in a marauding rampage, following the trail of the attackers north, searching for someone they could torture in revenge. The trail led them to the French Presque Isle fort. And there the Seneca stopped, staying inside the tree line, unwilling to carry their anger to the walls of such a strong fortification, not until they knew the truth of this. Why the trail led to this fort was confusing. The attackers had clearly been Erigh. The markings on the arrows and spears they found littering the inside of the Seneca compound were unmistakable. The Erigh hex sign and the putrefying corpse of a brave dangling by his wrists from leather straps above the main entrance to the palisade further confirmed the Erigh as their enemy. And yet, thunder guns had been used, many thunder guns. Only the French had thunder guns.

Two Seneca were sent to the fort and asked to make trades. The soldiers at the gate were suspicious and did not let them enter, but the braves chanced to glance within the large marshalling yard. They did not see any Erigh dwelling inside the fort.

Hearing this, Maltoc captured *voyageurs* hunting in the forests near Fort Presque Isle. The few they chose to question before cruelly killing them confirmed what he now suspected. An Erigh war party had passed by Fort Presque Isle. They'd boasted of their attack on the Seneca. They boasted they had acted alone. French soldiers were not involved. But the Erigh were nowhere to be found. Maltoc had to assume they'd returned to Fort Niagara. He chose not to pursue them further, not yet. The Hawk clan must first restore their home.

Days later, the Seneca returned to the Conneaut lake village, hungry and tired, filled with disappointment and rage. Chasing away the carrion birds, Maltoc abruptly recognized the black, swollen face of the corpse hanging above the main gate. It was the husband of his sister. The man's body was heavily mutilated, either through torture or by hungry carrion birds. The sachem jumped in the air and slashed the bindings with his skinning knife. The bloated corpse collapsed in a rattling heap of rotted flesh and bones. The half-eaten skull rolled off to one side. Maggots and insects poured from an eye socket.

Maltoc chopped down the nearby hex sign and smashed the red skull to bits.

With a sullen expression, the Hawk clan shaman watched his chief's rage. A red skull hex was not so easily reversed, particularly one made by Chittaqua. The medicine man blamed Maltoc for all this misfortune. But he held his tongue. It no longer mattered. Their clan was defeated.

Small animals ran in all directions as the Seneca braves entered the burned-out encampment for a thorough search. Maltoc stumbled through the ashes, scowling at the rotting bodies and terrible stench of the dead, his unfulfilled desire for vengeance leaving him feeling sick and feverish. He came upon the decayed remains of a woman and her child. They lay huddled together, a spear had pierced both bodies, pinning them to the ground. He dropped to his knees and raised his arms to the sky. The wrenching howl from the clan chief was heard by everyone. But his was not the only voice wailing with sadness. Every one of the Seneca warriors had suffered terrible losses.

Maltoc stood and pulled the bone-tipped weapon free. The markings were Erigh.

The Erigh are old men and boys, he raged silently. *How could they possibly have caused such death?*

Searching further, the clan chief found the body of another woman he recognized by her colorful necklaces. It was his sister, a knife still gripped in one of her hands, evidence she had fought back before her skull was crushed by a tomahawk. There was little left of her to be buried. What was not consumed by fire was carried off by scavengers. His wife. His daughter. Now, his only sister.

Maltoc was alone.

The Erigh did not *act alone. They had help…help from the white man.*

Treachery *always* led back to the white man. He flung the Erigh spear outside the burned stumps of the palisade.

"The white man did this!" he exclaimed loudly to his warriors. "Only the white man has thunder guns. The French helped the Erigh!"

For the next two days, the Seneca warriors tended to the dead, digging graves outside the scorched palisade. They sorted and buried the bodies in families, in those instances where the bodies could be identified, along with their personal items.

Amazingly, a few survivors of the attack returned, three women and six children, which brought a measure of great joy to a few of the braves. Then a dozen other solitary men and women arrived, strangers, having heard of the attack, looking to see if there was anything of value to recover. After surviving a near-death encounter by the Seneca warriors who thought them to be Erigh, they appealed to Maltoc that they be allowed to join his clan.

This sudden influx of people gave the sachem new ideas. He decided they could stay and refused to listen to others' protests.

"We have beans, corn, and squash ripening in our fields that will need harvesting soon. We must rebuild the palisade and set up new long houses before winter comes. We need more men and women to join our clan."

"And what of the Erigh?" one of the braves complained.

"We will have our vengeance," he replied hotly. "But if everything here dies, so does the Hawk clan! Our vengeance will be meaningless."

Maltoc ordered his warriors to raise a new camp of hunting tepees and lean-tos beyond the crop fields and told them to hunt for food. He had the male newcomers begin rebuilding inside the palisade and sent the women to tend the crops.

"It's a beginning," he told his shaman.

The skeptical medicine man did not reply. *We have two moons before the harvest must be complete*, he thought. *There are not enough of us.*

After each day of successful hunting, the Seneca braves would gather around the fire pits at night and argue among themselves in whispers. Thirty-two grim men huddled around muddy cooking fires, amid a grimy collection of hastily constructed lean-tos. Should they war on the white man, join other clans, or rebuild their village? They knew time was short. To rebuild and harvest crops would take all of their combined efforts if they wanted to survive the winter. But most of them had lost their entire family and only wanted revenge. Yet, every few days, one or two survivors would return: a wife, mother or a sister, two small children, and one of the braves would hoot with happiness. But these numbers were only a handful compared to the hundreds who'd once occupied the strong enclave.

Maltoc became withdrawn and retreated to one side of the camp. He wanted to be left alone, to be by himself, to deliberate their fate. He walked through their crop fields again. He saw the corn, beans, and squash growing healthy and plump. This food must be harvested before winter. Without a harvest, his people would die of starvation when the snows came. But who would harvest the crops? The women were all dead or scattered. He could send warriors out to find the survivors. Some were said to have gone to the Wolf clan. Or, failing that, tell them to find new wives and return. That would take time. The work on the new palisade had begun, but it would not be complete before the snows. There were two new longhouses started that would need more than three hands, at least. There was not time to complete such tasks before the winter snows.

Maltoc saw the grim expression of his shaman, a man usually outspoken, now strangely quiet. *He knows this too.*

The sachem brooded. The majority of his warriors wanted revenge. He had only to tell them where to march and who to kill. Attack the Erigh at Niagara or wait until the spring?

Without food and shelter, we may not be here in the spring.

Maltoc's rage sparked hotly at this thought. He did not want to wait! He wanted to attack! To kill! But if too many braves were lost, it could mean the end of his clan. Rebuild the village or make war? Survive in shame or die like warriors? Accept defeat or take revenge? His passion for vengeance and his desire to ensure his people survived agitated his mind. He prayed to Tahiawagi to give him a sign. He ate little, slept little, and talked little.

After leaving Snow Hair on the Fort Le Boeuf army road, Peter Blue Jacket continued on his intended path to the Conneaut lake village. While he walked, his thoughts dwelled on the council elders waiting at the headwaters of the Allegheny. He contemplated what the council might conclude when he eventually repeated Snow Hair's words. He knew the Iroquois elders well. He sat with them often. He knew their moods, their intelligence, those who would argue for peace, and those who were war sachems. He could almost hear their voices and guess at their opinions as they discussed the fate of the Seneca Hawk clan. Snow Hair was a highly respected *coureur de bois*, a man of honor. If he gave a warning to the council, they must regard it seriously. As a group, the council was experienced, brave, and wise. They would stop short of voting for any war-like action against the French—at least, not yet.

But if the stories of the Erigh attack were as bad as Peter Blue Jacket had heard, and he took this report back to the council, they might also anticipate Maltoc's malice and come to an agreement on a message for Peter Blue Jacket to carry to Half-King, high war chief of the Seneca at Logstown.

Maltoc is rogue.

The underlying meaning of this message would be clear, but the council would not say it outright: *Do something about Maltoc.*

Half-King, however, was already leaning toward war against the French. This invasion had been on Seneca kinds.

The only thing that restrains Half-King now is his desire not to act out of unity with the council, Peter thought. *And he will not kill one of his own war chiefs for avenging an attack on his clan village.*

As he thought about it, Peter knew there was simply no time to carry Snow Hair's warning back to the council and return. Events were moving too swiftly. He must find a way to subdue, divert, or delay Maltoc's killing rage before it was too late.

Yet what if it were me? What if it were my village, my people? I would laugh at the council's words—call them all cowards and old women. If this had happened to me, many would die for this. And if this caused a war between the French and the Iroquois, so much the better.

The Mohawk shook his head wearily. He would have to worry about his own life. If he wasn't careful, Maltoc might take a tomahawk to his head for mentioning the Onondaga council, or any suggestion about not seeking vengeance.

They might be waiting to ambush on these trails even now, he thought suddenly.

With that prudent thought, he left the main trail, going west in order to move more discreetly. He found a less-used path that ran south alongside a small lake. Halfway down this trail, he saw clear signs of wagon wheels in the soft earth. They led directly into the water of the lake.

Peter moved to the water's edge and stared into the murky depths. He counted at least three sets of wheels.

Without hesitation, he stripped off all his clothes and waded into the water. As the depth reached his neck, he stretched out a leg and felt the long, smooth, tubular shape of a cannon barrel. He took a deep breath and dove into the dark water, exploring further with his hands. After several dives, he discovered three cannon all close to one another. He stuck his hand in the muzzle of one of them. It was the size of his fist.

The Mohawk swam back to shore, quickly got dressed, and chopped a mark high in a tree where the wheel tracks departed from the lakeside trail.

Then the Mohawk spent several hours eliminating any sign of wagon wheels along this trail as he continued his walk. Eventually, the path intersected with another trail leading west again. It would take longer to reach the Conneaut village by this route, but it was far less traveled.

This lucky discovery was huge. Cannon *had* been used. They were small, but if aimed correctly, deadly. Whoever used them had hid them there. They would likely come back for them.

Peter's face broke into a rare smile. *Unless someone else takes them first.*

Peter Blue Jacket had expected the story of the attack on Maltoc's palisade to be exaggerated as it had been repeated from mouth to mouth. When he arrived at the Conneaut lake village, any remaining skepticism vanished. He gaped at the extent of the destruction of the log palisade. Not a single lodge remained untouched, although a few showed signs of being rebuilt. There were huge shell holes everywhere, ample evidence of cannon fire. He saw arrows and spears too. And they had Erigh markings. But the dead had all been collected and presumably buried.

The Mohawk spy left the village and the lingering smell of death and headed toward columns of smoke he saw rising in the sky nearby. They seemed to be coming from somewhere beyond the Seneca crop fields.

CHAPTER 5
RIVIÈRE AUX BOEUFS
JULY 1754
"All the soldiers in the fort must die!"

One morning, Maltoc heard a familiar voice.

"Oho, Maltoc," Peter Blue Jacket hailed loudly as he approached the Seneca camp.

The Hawk clan warriors quickly surrounded the Mohawk, weapons ready, their expressions full of anger and suspicion.

Maltoc looked up from the boulder he sat upon, where he'd been staring off into the distance. Recognizing the man, he rose to greet the Mohawk visitor.

"Oho, old friend." Maltoc gestured for his warriors to lower their weapons. "Welcome to the Hawk clan."

Peter Blue Jacket was shocked by the squalor within Maltoc's makeshift village. Animal bones, refuse, garbage, and the smell of human excrement assaulted his senses. The Seneca braves looked hungry, some appeared sick, but he saw scalps too, as if they'd been conducting raids in the surrounding countryside.

"I bring greetings from the council. Your people have suffered greatly. My heart is wounded to see this."

Maltoc's anger surged to the surface. "My village was attacked while my warriors and I were absent. The cowards responsible will soon pay for their boldness."

"I want to hear the truth of this attack, to see if our Seneca brothers want the help of the Mohawk and Oneida."

For the first time in weeks, Maltoc's twisted expression relaxed. The offer was generous and totally unexpected. He imagined several new possibilities.

"Come, friend, sit by my fire. We will smoke and talk together, as we used to inside my lodge."

The two men went inside the simple hunting tepee. They talked quietly for hours and on into the night. Peter Blue Jacket asked numerous questions and offered his opinion on future events. The use of cannon in the attack on the Seneca village was disturbing, yet evidence of cannon and the Erigh weapons were plain to see.

"I have questioned others during my travel here," the Mohawk said. "They say the Erigh acted alone. And yet, the Erigh are weak. They must have had help."

Maltoc nodded. "The French are to blame!"

Peter Blue Jacket knew the French wanted the Iroquois as allies against the English. They would never attack any of the council tribes.

"None of the French soldiers I met on my way here admitted to any knowledge of this attack. Not one of them."

Maltoc scowled. "They are liars. Thunder guns were used! You've seen it with your own eyes."

And, there it was again. Maltoc's village was attacked with cannon. And Peter knew where those cannon were. But who fired them? And where did the ammunition come from?

A tense quiet ensued as they both brooded.

It was clear to Peter Blue Jacket that Maltoc had decided to attack the French soldiers. And the sachem would not be dissuaded. He must use the chief's anger and still avoid a war between the French and the Iroquois. The cannon were the key. And with that thought, a plan unfolded in his mind.

"I passed Snow Hair on the trail. He was heading to the fort called Le Boeuf. He is looking for his wife and son. What became of them?"

Maltoc's eyes widened. *Of course!* How had he not seen this?

Now, it all made sense.

"It was *Snow Hair* who provided the thunder guns to the Erigh. Snow Hair helped *Chittaqua!*" The war chief stabbed his knife into the ground next to him.

Peter Blue Jacket pretended surprise. "Snow Hair?" He noticed a gleam in the sachem's eyes. He'd seen such raging madness before.

"Snow Hair," Maltoc said the name with venom.

Maltoc knew the hearts of the Mohawk and Oneida were quick to anger. The Seneca had been attacked; they would expect the Seneca to take revenge. He was compelled to make this decision. "The Hawk clan will make war."

"I need only one victory," Maltoc said, now thinking out loud. He nodded vigorously at the glorious images this logic suggested.

Peter Blue Jacket prodded him. "One victory?"

"Yes, only one."

Maltoc decided a great victory would help to establish his leadership as war chief. Joined in alliance with English soldiers, Maltoc was certain the bravest warriors would flock to him. With their strength added to his, he would expand the war and spill the blood of their enemies until it washed through the forests like a river. When the victory was achieved, his palisade would fill with new people. But he had to do this quickly. And what better victory could there be, he decided, than one where he could also take revenge on two of his greatest enemies: Snow Hair and Chittaqua.

"If Snow Hair is at the weakest of the French forts, we will go there now!"

His decision to fight drove the weariness from the sachem's expression. Suddenly, he was very hungry.

Three days later, Maltoc's war party slipped among the trees nearest Fort Le Boeuf. His men were painted, shaved, and armed with every kind of weapon they could carry. Having lost their families most didn't care if they lived or died. They only wanted vengeance for the destruction of their home and the death of their loved ones. Vengeance, most of all, against the white man.

Snow Hair has powerful totems, but so do I, Maltoc thought.

The sachem knew his warriors would fight fearlessly but could also throw away their lives carelessly. Dying bravely was an honor. But Maltoc needed a victory. He did not want a disaster. Not if he wanted others to join him. He had learned from one of his scouts, a section of Fort Le Boeuf's wall had been taken down for some reason. As he gazed from the tree line, he was pleased to see this was true.

Maltoc wanted to massacre all of the inhabitants, to capture the enormous store of weapons certain to be inside. The thought of possessing some of the fort's great thunder guns was very exciting.

Then I will be as powerful as the white soldiers, he envisioned. *Warriors will run day and night to join with me.*

But the clan could not linger long in the woods nearby the fort; *coureurs de bois* and army scouts moved in and out of the fort, hunting and trading. They must attack before the soldiers learned of their presence.

Maltoc circled the fort with Painted Snake and quickly evaluated the fort's construction. Mounds of dirt as high as a man's head extended outward like fingers in four different directions. Each of these fingerlike mounds had a chest-high palisade of timbers erected on the top with customary loopholes cut for musketry. But, like he'd been told, there was one place where the wall had been shortened, cut in half for a distance of ten paces.

They captured a half-breed trader, who had left the fort alone to head up the portage trail. Before they killed him, they learned only ten hands of soldiers moved about inside.

"More than us, but not many more," Maltoc told Painted Snake. "The white man's palisade is built to favor the thunder guns. But they can only kill things far away. They are difficult to aim down at an enemy. We can climb the shorter stockade and run up the mound closest to the gap in the wall and enter the fort in force. If we run fast, most of us will get inside. Once inside, our tomahawks will kill the clumsy soldiers."

Painted Snake nodded in agreement. "*If* they don't see us first. Maybe we should attack during the night."

Maltoc considered this counsel wise. He retreated deep into the trees with his men and began describing the plan of attack. He drew a picture of the fortification in the dirt.

"You must not stop to fire. Run quietly like a deer until you get inside the fort. Logs stick out of the earth below the top of the mounds. They will stop any bullets from the soldier's guns above you, if you are seen. Once you reach the wall, they cannot aim the thunder guns. The climb will be easy."

The sachem straightened and regarded Peter Blue Jacket with expectation.

"I must not take part in this," the Mohawk spy said before he was asked. "But I will inform the Mohawk council of your victory."

Privately, Peter Blue Jacket thought Maltoc's attack on the French to be madness. But successful or not, the reason for the attack could be used in negotiations with the English or the French. And if they were lucky, the renegade sachem would be killed. But there was also a chance they might win.

Maltoc addressed his men sternly.

"All the soldiers in the fort must die. The fort will burn as our village was burned. And the song of our victory will be sung at the council of

Onondaga."

Some of the braves hooted.

"No," he commanded. "Now is not the time for celebration. Now is the time for the quiet walk of the lion before it attacks."

Maltoc led his men back to the trees opposite the open field of fire surrounding Fort Le Boeuf. The sun would set in two more hours. He planned to attack as soon as it was dark. After leaving the bulk of his forces among the denser woods, Maltoc and Painted Snake circled the tree line for a hundred paces so they could keep watch on the main gate. The two Seneca had settled down amid the trees when a soldier and a *coureur de bois* stumbled onto them from behind by accident. The two white men were returning from hunting, a gutted deer carcass hanging from a pole carried between their shoulders.

Maltoc and Painted Snake attacked them with their tomahawks. The men were killed but not before the soldier had fired his dragoon pistol. The shot missed, but the explosive sound was unmistakable.

"We go," Maltoc told his companion. They began to quickly circle back to where the rest of his men waited.

The commander of Fort Le Boeuf, Captain Prideaux, finished donning his battle dress after reaching the top of the wall. He swept the area with his watch glass. The information the sentries had given him was sketchy. Men were seen moving among the trees. Who, what, or how many they didn't know. The commandant was not expecting trouble, but neither had the English before Captain Benoit took the three-river junction.

"Corporal! Wake all the men in the barracks," he ordered. "Order them to arms. Even the sick ones. Engineer Seratard! Supervise your men and move those two cannon closer to the gap in the wall."

Half of Captain Prideaux's hundred-man garrison was sick with the shits. He regretted his decision of a week earlier to allow the ambitious battlements engineer to chop a hole in his palisade in order to create a cantilevered cannon emplacement above the first two lunettes. The engineer said it would only take three days. Prideaux looked at the completed piece of fortification lying in the center of the marshalling grounds. It was supposed to have been hoisted into its new position two days ago!

The commandant searched the tree line again. "I see nothing moving out there."

"That doesn't mean no one's there," Philippe Gerrard warned him. The *coureur de bois* had just reached the commandant's side. "I told you the Seneca were warring."

Philippe had planned to travel on to Fort Machault the next morning. From the trader and soldiers at Fort Le Boeuf, he'd heard a rumor a white boy had escaped from Maltoc's village before the Erigh attack.

He was both happy and upset to hear this story. Henri may have escaped, but if he was alive, he could be wandering anywhere in this wilderness. Philippe originally planned to prowl the trails leading to and from the Conneaut village, disregarding the danger, when another trader told him of a white woman said to be held captive at the Wolf clan village. *Michelle*, he thought. *It has to be. The Seneca would have split up the captives.* Between the two of them, Philippe decided Michelle was more at peril. He had changed his plans to go to Piqua's village instead.

"It might be the hunters we sent out this morning," Prideaux suggested tentatively.

"Pray you're right, Captain," Philippe replied. "Pray you're right." But his gut didn't think so.

"The Seneca wouldn't dare attack this fort…would they? We're too strong…aren't we?"

Philippe pointed out the obvious. "Captain, you have a fucking *hole* in your wall."

Captain Prideaux turned and shouted down to his sergeant forming up the men in the yard below.

"Sergeant, take one platoon and sweep the tree line. See what's out there."

"I'll go with them," Philippe said. He climbed down the ladder.

Out in the trees, the Seneca saw a line of soldiers stream out from the fort's main gate.

"Snow Hair," Maltoc hissed.

Painted Snake counted the soldiers.

"Maltoc! There are only a few men on the wall. Most are outside the fort. We should attack the gap now," he urged.

The Seneca chief pulled his eyes away from Snow Hair and watched the gap in the wall for signs of men. There were none. Painted Snake was right, but he had only seconds to decide. Maltoc turned his attention back to Snow Hair and the soldiers advancing on the tree line a hundred paces to his left.

The sachem waited to give the order. If the soldiers marching toward him got too close, they would not retreat, but would instead drop to one knee and fire on his men. Maltoc wanted them to come close enough so he could use the time it took for the soldiers to run back to the gate to allow his men to storm the wall through the gap. Unfortunately, they would not have time to reload after firing their muskets.

The Seneca chief communicated by hand signal for half of his war party to prepare to fire on the soldiers.

The army had cut down the trees for a hundred paces in every direction, so the enemy would be exposed when they attacked.

Philippe knew a walking advance across the open field was suicide.

"Sergeant, an enemy could be waiting in the trees! If we are going to advance, order your men to break ranks and run for cover in the trees."

Another voice hailed them. "Sergeant!"

They stopped and looked back at Captain Prideaux. The commandant was waving his arms frantically and pointing at the trees to their left.

"There! There!"

"*Merde*! Sergeant, we are exposed!" Philippe pulled on the soldier's sleeve urgently. "Pull your men back to the fort! Now!"

"Withdraw on the run," the sergeant yelled.

When Maltoc saw the soldiers turn he signaled to his men. *Now*!

The Seneca fired a volley. Numerous musket balls struck the mass of soldiers retreating to the gates.

Soldiers began to drop. Some of the veteran's turned, dropped to one knee, and fired at the telltale powder smoke coming from the tree line.

The marksmanship of the soldiers was dismaying to Maltoc. Four of his warriors fell dead. The sachem ordered the frontal attack to begin, and the majority of the war party burst from the trees intent on storming the gap in the wall.

Maltoc took Painted Snake and six other braves and moved sideways through the trees as the main attack was pressed. He saw the first of his warriors climbing the timbers closest to the gap. One fell, shot through the head.

The soldier who bent over the wall to make the shot fell from it with an arrow through his neck. Maltoc looked at the main gate. The soldiers were crowded at the gate in a mass. Something was blocking their way!

"We attack...there!" the sachem screamed and pointed.

Philippe climbed over the top of the soldiers who had piled up at the gate. One had fallen, which had started an avalanche of bodies as the others behind him also tripped and fell. The long muskets tangled in their clothing and more than one soldier screamed, stabbed by the sharp *baïonnettes*.

Philippe struggled past the mass, wanting to get to the wall without delay. He had already deduced the Seneca strategy was aimed at the fort's obvious weakness. He cursed loudly when he saw the heads of the first warriors appear at the gap. Without immediate reinforcements on the wall, the Seneca strategy might succeed.

"Captain Prideaux! There!" Philippe pointed urgently.

Philippe heard the roar of war whoops and screams behind him. He turned to see a second group of Seneca descending at a run on the half-open main gates. The sergeant ordered some of the men crowded outside the gate to turn and fire, but the Seneca fired first. Bodies exploded in a spray of blood, flesh, and bones as the musket balls whizzed and sliced through torsos, heads, and arms.

Screams erupted. The dead and wounded fell against the men still struggling to unravel themselves from the pile of bodies.

The sergeant fired his pistol at the nearest of the Seneca who attempted to come through the gate.

The brave clutched the wound in his throat and pitched backwards across the other bodies.

Philippe looked over his shoulder as he ran toward the gap. The knives and tomahawks of the ferocious Seneca warriors were cutting the platoon to pieces. He glanced up at Captain Prideaux and saw the inexperienced officer running back and forth along the battlements shouting senseless orders.

"Captain Prideaux!" Philippe cupped his hands to be heard over the sounds of the battle. "Use your sick inside the lunettes," he screamed.

Up on the battlements, Engineer Seratard had properly positioned the cannon, but the unarmed soldiers had abandoned him when they jumped to the ground to retrieve their weapons. The engineer dutifully loaded the powder and shot. Behind him, two Seneca were climbing the last few timbers of the shortened wall.

"Seratard! Behind you!" Philippe Gerrard yelled as he climbed the nearest ladder.

Engineer Seratard turned. One of the wild-looking savages had raised an ax above his head. The snarling man was only a few paces away.

The engineer had once sighted a range, but he had never actually fired cannon in battle. But he *was* holding the firing brand. With a flick of his wrist, he touched the powder hole of the four-pounder. The blast was enormous and dwarfed all other sounds of battle. The Seneca brave in front of the muzzle disintegrated into a chunky red mist that splattered down the battlements. Part of an arm struck the brave behind him. He was thrown backward between the lunettes and fell to the ground on his back, dazed but unhurt.

The fiery discharge of cannon ball smashed into the timbers of the palisade splintering two and igniting two others. The wood burst into flames. The unsecured cannon recoiled from the blast and threw itself backwards off the platform, directly on top of a soldier kneeling to fire at one of the Seneca storming the main gate. There was a loud crunching sound.

Engineer Seratard could not believe the awesome effect the cannon had on the body of the warrior.

"Amazing," he whispered. Then a musket ball tore into his chest. His dead body pitched over the edge of the battlement.

Captain Prideaux had reached the gap with five of his men when the next Seneca brave climbed around the flaming timbers. He swung his sword in a high arc and chopped at the spear. More Seneca climbed into the fort.

Philippe Gerrard reached Prideaux's side and shot his pistol into the face of the nearest brave. Spears were thrown in response. Three of Prideaux's soldiers fell. Philippe attacked with tomahawk and skinning knife. They managed to beat back the Seneca but ten more were already climbing. He glanced back at the main gate. The soldiers there were falling back too. They had to gain the upper hand at one of these fronts or be overrun.

"The lunettes," Philippe shouted at Captain Prideaux.

Without waiting for the officer to respond, Philippe slipped over the edge of the battlement and dropped to the ground. A dangerous bolt of pain shot up his left leg. He limped quickly into the hospital inside the nearest lunette. The sick men inside raised their weapons to fire before realizing it wasn't an Indian.

Philippe pointed with his knife. "Raise the gun ports and fire," he screamed.

For a moment, no one moved. Philippe shoved one of the sick men out of the way and pulled on a chain that dropped a wooden shutter on the outside of the lunette.

On the other side of the earthen wall, a Seneca brave peered into the dark hole that suddenly opened in the grassy face of the mound right next to him.

Philippe tried to skewer the Seneca with his knife. The man backed up in surprise out of reach. But the demonstration was enough. The other soldiers pulled open the fifteen firing ports. The musket barrels poked through. The combined volley of musket fire was like a cannon broadside from a ship.

Philippe dashed from the first lunette barracks and ran across the gap to the other, opposite the first. On his way, he could see five more of the Seneca were completely inside the fort. After the initial clumsy musket fire, the fighting was hand to hand. Captain Prideaux was fighting bravely, swinging his sword in vicious arcs, but Philippe could see the soldiers were withering before the determined assault. The battle was now a matter of attrition.

It took Philippe less time to demonstrate to those in the other barracks, since no one was standing in front of the lunette gun ports. In addition, the soldiers had a clear shot at the Seneca crouched beneath the musket holes thirty paces away. When the firing started from the other side, the remaining braves tried to retreat but were cut down in the murderous cross fire.

Through the limited view of the firing port, Philippe watched the brutal decimation take place as Engineer Seratard had predicted it would. It seemed almost too easy.

Maltoc had been using his war ax with devastating effect and had fatally wounded six soldiers. His other warriors seemed ready to overwhelm the defenders at the gap now that the cannon were abandoned. They had killed almost fifteen French soldiers at the gates. He'd lost eight of his braves at his last count.

The thunderous sound of the mass of musket fire momentarily startled both the soldiers and their attackers at the main gates of the fort. A strange silence ensued after the unexpected surge of musket fire coming from *outside* the walls. Maltoc no longer heard the war cries of his other men.

More soldiers, he thought.

An instinct sharpened by years of fighting told the normally fearless sachem they were now in mortal peril. He motioned his remaining four men to retreat out the gates. A giant of a soldier stabbed a *baïonnette* at his belly. Maltoc used his tomahawk to parry the blow to his right, then swung the heavy weapon overhead, striking the soldier between the neck and shoulder.

Philippe Gerrard rushed from the lunette and saw Maltoc and his remaining braves pulling back. He charged. The sachem barely avoided the slashing knife of the *coureur de bois* by throwing himself backward on the ground. Painted Snake stopped the next killing slash with his tomahawk. Maltoc rolled to his feet like a cat.

Painted Snake perfectly matched Philippe's next five strikes, taking the blows, steel on steel, on the head of his weapon. Sparks could be seen after each resounding clang. But it was a defensive posture and one he could not hope to maintain. As soon as he saw Maltoc was safely outside the gate, Painted Snake leaped over the dead bodies to follow his war chief.

Philippe tripped over a body and was thrown off balance. He grabbed the nearest musket and thrust it into the back of a brave following Painted Snake. It cut into the base of the man's neck and into the vertebrae. The Seneca died instantly.

Maltoc and three Seneca were getting away, but Philippe felt his exhaustion overtake him. His injured leg was throbbing. Instead of pursuing them further, he sagged back against the gate and slid to the ground. Breathing heavily, he wondered if he had the strength to get up again.

"Move!" a soldier shouted. "You are in the way!"

Philippe crawled on all fours so the soldiers could swing the gate shut behind him.

A silence settled over the fort, broken only by a few residual musket shots and the poignant pain-filled moans of wounded and dying men. The battle was over.

"Cease fire," Captain Prideaux shouted hoarsely from the wall.

The order was dutifully repeated by the few remaining sergeants and corporals throughout the redoubt. Soldiers not wounded, ran about, frenzied, ministering to their friends. Some called for a priest. Any Seneca found wounded but alive was immediately executed.

On shaky legs, Captain Prideaux climbed down a ladder from the upper battlements as the main gates groaned shut. He listened to the crossbeam drop into place with a reassuring thud. Fort Le Boeuf was secure once more—*except for the hole in the wall*, he thought ruefully. The body of his dead engineer, Seratard, lay on the ground nearby.

The men inside the lunette barracks fired at one another randomly without looking out the gun ports to see what they were shooting, thinking the return fire was still coming from the Indians.

"Hold your fire," Captain Prideaux yelled in a trembling voice.

"Someone tell the men in barracks to cease fire!"

A corporal ran to do his commandant's bidding. The commander shouted more orders to his surgeons and the stretcher bearers. Then his legs began trembling heavily.

Captain Prideaux spotted the blood-smeared, smiling face of Philippe Gerrard.

"Monsieur Gerrard," the commandant exclaimed as he sagged to the ground next to the *coureur de bois*. "I thank God you were with me here today, or it would have gone badly for us."

Philippe placed a hand on the commandant's shoulder and addressed the officer by his first name. "Camille, without you in command, the battle would have been lost. You have a victory!"

CHAPTER 6
FORT PRESQUE ISLE
JULY 1754
Helmut Colbért

As usual, when the dispatch rider arrived at Fort Presque Isle, the unoccupied officers followed him into the commandant's office, anxious to hear the news. Among those who entered was Gaspard de Propei, who'd been making endless requests of the commandant for further escort into the frontier. So far, the commandant had rebuffed his request.

Major Michel Péan broke the wax seal and quickly read the latest dispatch from Fort Le Boeuf. An expression of surprise spread across his face. He looked at the grime-covered rider.

"This says the Seneca attacked Fort Le Boeuf."

"Yes, sir," the rider affirmed. "They attacked without warning and were repulsed. The garrison suffered heavy casualties. Captain Prideaux begs you send him reinforcements without delay."

"It doesn't make sense. Why would the Seneca attack one of our forts?"

"A new alliance with the English," suggested one of his officers.

"Because of the Erigh attack," offered another.

"In response to our building forts without their permission," said a third.

Major Péan decided any or all of those premises could be true. Not that it mattered much to him anymore.

Major Péan had received orders from army headquarters directing him to turn over command of Fort Presque Isle to his second and return to Montréal. Major Péan was pleased to receive this order. He suspected Intendant Bigôt had persuaded General Duquesne to replace him with someone else now that the three-river junction was occupied, and the new fort was being built.

"Lieutenant, assemble the garrison in the marshalling yard immediately," Péan ordered. He decided to send a full company of infantry to Fort Le Boeuf, plus a battery of the new cannon.

When the officers filed from his offices, he noticed Gaspard de Propei lingering behind.

"Monsieur Propei, I see you wear your customary face of annoyance."

"Since you are sending a company of infantry to the next fort, I expect to accompany them."

Major Péan inhaled deeply. As before, the man's tone was more like a demand. He'd been ignoring the *faux shérif*'s persistent request for an escort for nearly a week, and with nothing else to do, he was curious to know more about the Marquis de Propei's seemingly compulsive interest in Philippe Gerrard. Michel Péan didn't believe it was only because the *coureur de bois* was a criminal wanted by the King. How ridiculous. Send a *shérif* all the way to New France for one man? No, it had to be something more. Péan had challenged him, but Gaspard de Propei declined to answer. So he'd kept the surly man waiting, expecting the *shérif* would give in or he would eventually figure out his motives. But Gaspard de Propei was impatient and offered money, which changed everything, of course. It had been the substance of their conversations for the last three days.

All that changed again with the dispatch from Fort Le Boeuf.

"Monsieur Propei, I have decided to grant your request for an escort at the price of one thousand livres."

The assassin barely kept his anger in check.

"I offered that amount three days ago."

Major Péan shrugged.

"Today, I feel generous. Of course, I expect to have your signature on a draft for this amount before you depart. I will see to the preparation of the draft, as a courtesy to your station. I presume you have such funds reserved with someone in Montréal or Quebec, yes?"

Colbért preened. "Intendant Bigôt."

"Very impressive."

"Have someone find me when the document is ready." Colbért turned to leave.

"Monsieur Propei, one more thing."

The assassin stiffened and slowly turned.

The commandant was cognizant of the man's menace. The officer's hand instinctively rested on the handle of his sword. His eyes shifted momentarily to the guards standing outside his open door.

"I remain perplexed by your obsession with Philippe Gerrard. I will be returning to Montréal even as you march deeper into the wilderness. I suggest, Monsieur, you pay close attention to the ground upon which you march and consider the denseness of the forests to either side. Remember, the savages are warring. With every step, you retain less privilege. When you go south of Fort Presque Isle there are *no* rules, Monsieur. They end here, with me. By the time you reach Fort Le Boeuf, you will simply be someone interfering in the interests of many other people. Therefore, I would advocate you find a way to induce Philippe Gerrard to come to Montréal, where all kinds of civilized rules may work in your favor. And since I will be in Montréal, I will be in a position to work on your behalf…for a fee, of course."

Colbért stared at the officer. This was unexpected.

By the time the assassin had reached the wilderness forts, he clearly understood his new weaknesses. His skills depended on a familiarity of a city-society, or even a farming countryside. Usually, his kills occurred in the final few seconds after a week or more of proper planning, which was not possible here. He would have left Fort Presque Isle days ago except… leave to go where? There were simply no cities out here.

Only these vast enigmatic forests.

And yet Colbért felt stronger with each passing day, as if—in his weakness—he drew power from something else. It was an odd sensation, but he was certain this was the right place to be. Even the voice of his dreams seemed satisfied with his progress.

Now, hearing the major's unsolicited advice, Helmut Colbért decided his good fortune still held. It was, actually, an excellent idea. Make Philippe Gerrard chase after him! There was only one problem.

How? he wondered. *What would make this woodsman come after me?*

Perhaps some type of personal insult? *Too weak*, he judged. But what? The answer was not apparent, but he expected it would be revealed to him, eventually.

He tilted his head in respect to the officer. "I look forward to when next we meet in Montréal, Major."

Philippe Gerrard arrived at Fort Machault delighted to find Pierre Dunemoore already there. They quickly traded information regarding Michelle.

"Ya' kinnah' dah' this alone. Even with our *coureur de bois,* we'll need more men. Piqua's village is large, probably more than a hundred braves."

"Can we get soldiers?"

"Maybe. Fortunately, Colonel Contrecoeur is inspecting this fort. And he is anxious to talk with ya'."

"I bring a report on the attack at Fort Le Boeuf."

"Aye. We were informed by other Seneca it was Maltoc's clan. Acting alone?"

"They got the worst of the attack…but they nearly succeeded."

Sergeant Major Routier approached the *coureurs de bois.* "Colonel Contrecoeur wants to see you both immediately."

The construction of the commandant's office at Fort Machault had been completed that morning. The walls were bare and made of split pine, as was much of the floor. The room was permeated with the pungent odor of pine resin.

Philippe Gerrard delivered the dispatch pouch and became the center of attention for nearly an hour. He sat at a rough hewn oak table fresh from the carpenter's saw, directly across from Colonel Contrecoeur. Captain Jean-Claude Benoit sat on one side, Pierre Dunemoore on the other. Two scribes sat at a separate, smaller table, scribbling rapidly as Philippe described the Seneca attack on Fort Le Boeuf.

The discussion paused. Colonel Contrecoeur's gaze shifted toward a window as he contemplated the army's appropriate reaction to this news.

Philippe became impatient. "Pierre has located Sister Michelle. She's being held at a Seneca village west of here."

Contrecoeur returned his attention to the *coureur de bois.* "And I presume you want troops to go to her rescue?"

It was the officer's tone of voice that made Philippe's jaw tighten. It suggested Contrecoeur thought the idea absurd.

"Yes." Philippe's voice was flat, almost challenging. "I have—"

"I am grateful for your service to the army, Monsieur," Contrecoeur interrupted. "But understand, the action you contemplate, if accompanied by French troops in light of recent events at Fort Le Boeuf, might be construed as retaliation against the Seneca. So far, the attack at Fort Le Boeuf looks like the action of one rogue clan chief. Or so it was asserted by Half-King. Somehow, the Erigh attackers on the Seneca village to the north got hold of French cannon and used them in this attack. And someone with the knowledge of such weapons helped them do it."

Philippe frowned angrily. "Are you suggesting I had something to do with that?"

"No, Monsieur. Only that these cannon have not been found. I would ask your help in finding them. The other Seneca clans in the area have shown no inclination toward hostility, not yet anyway. But they are asking the same questions of me I would ask if I were them…if we did not shell Maltoc's village, who did? And if we do not have these cannon, where are they?"

"After I bring Sister Michelle back from Piqua's village, after I find my son, I will help you find these cannon, Colonel. But I am fetching her first."

"As commander of the French forces on the edge of war with the English, I must consider the potential effects of any action taken by my troops."

Tense silence filled the room before Philippe spoke again.

"Are you saying you will not help me?"

"Well…I think the government of New France is obligated to assist in the rescue of any French woman held by the savages." The commandant began to quickly pen an authorization for men and supplies as he continued talking. "After all, what purpose does an army have if not to protect its citizens, yes?"

Contrecoeur blew on the ink, stood, and held out the authorization. "Captain Benoit, I presume you desire to command this detachment?"

Captain Benoit accepted the document and read the orders. He had been prepared to accompany Philippe, even if it meant his court-martial. He smiled broadly and saluted. "With your permission, Colonel."

Pierre elbowed Philippe, who was still smoldering. "See? Ya' worry too much, laddie."

"He should have just said yes without the speech," Philippe replied under his breath.

Contrecoeur approached the blond-haired *coureur de bois* with his hands clasped behind his back. He studied Philippe's face.

"Monsieur Gerrard, you seem to have cultivated the patronage of a number of important persons in New France, among them Archbishop André Nicolet and the Governor. But you have enemies too. There is a man named Gaspard de Propei who carries the title of King's *shérif*. He seems most obsessed with arresting you."

"Men like him have come looking for me before."

"*Not* like this man. And it would be well for you to remember that before you make a tragic mistake. I have left orders which prohibit this *shérif* from traveling anywhere into the frontier without my explicit permission. Yet he may find a way to reach Fort Niagara and beyond, contrary to my orders. I warn you, Monsieur, his credentials as the King's *shérif* are quite authentic. There is only so much the military can do in this matter."

"Then I hope to meet him soon," Philippe answered coldly.

"Boldly said. Maybe even foolishly. It might be better to avoid him altogether if possible, Monsieur. With the warrants he carries, he can shoot you right in front of me and there would be nothing I could do about it."

Philippe stiffened. "Colonel, you presume he would see me first. This is my land."

Colonel Contrecoeur smiled indulgently. "On that assertion, there is no dispute. But if you kill this *shérif* in front of me, I am ordered by the King of France to kill you, or arrest you...and *then* execute you. Of course, that presumes I *see* you slay this *shérif*, yes? Much occurs in this vast land of yours that goes unnoticed and things get lost or missing. Take, for instance, cannon."

Later that same day, Philippe, Pierre, five Dunemoore Company *coureur de bois* and twenty-one soldiers under the command of Captain Benoit prepared to leave Fort Machault to begin the journey to rescue Sister Michelle from the Seneca.

While these men gathered weapons and supplies and packed them into canoes on the bank of the Allegheny River, a singular half-breed Mohawk beached his canoe and walked through the main gate of the fort. He was immediately surrounded by a ring of *baïonnettes*.

"My name is Peter Blue Jacket," he announced to the scowling sentries in perfect French. "I come from the Mohawk council to see Colonel Contrecoeur. I have information concerning French cannon."

CHAPTER 7
MONTRÉAL
AUGUST 1754
Lady de Chanaye

Lady Corrinne de Chanaye smiled with surprise when Mathilde presented the sealed missive from Fort Niagara. *From Philippe!* After several other disconcerting letters she'd received from her various spies, good news would be welcome. But the smile quickly faded as she read the pages.

Corrinne walked disconsolately to her boudoir's window seat. She hesitated before sitting; the broad sill seeming dangerous. Her fears were recent and uncharacteristic. But the memory of the searing pain in her neck was still fresh in her mind, even though the frightening incident had occurred over a month ago. Since then, she had been seen by two of New France's best physicians, who came upriver from Quebec. Both came to the same conclusion. *Nothing.* Neither could find anything wrong.

"A temporary spasm," offered the more experienced man, "brought on by weariness and dehydration. You should drink more water and get more rest."

Idiots, Corrinne thought angrily. *That had been no spasm.* Though she considered herself a woman of the sciences, she could not explain it either. It had felt like an attack…an attack by something she could not see, which was even more disconcerting as it suggested the problem was an invention of her imagination. She had not mentioned her suspicions to the physicians.

But on that night, a month ago, the repeated stabbing jolts of pain to her neck and shoulders had been so excruciating that she'd lost control of her bowels. Then, at its worst, it had stopped. Inexplicably, the pain vanished. There were no wounds, no cuts, no bruises, no mark or scars, no soreness afterwards. But it most certainly had been real. It was not her imagination. And it had left her exhausted, frightened, and sobbing like a small child in Mathilde's comforting arms.

Corrinne had never experienced that type of fear in her life. Even after so many weeks, she remained terrified it might occur again, without warning.

So, on that beautiful warm morning in Montréal, she stood for a few moments before the window seat and chided herself for her childlike apprehension. She took a deep breath, said a prayer, closed her eyes, and sat down. It took a minute before her breathing calmed. She would remain there the rest of the morning with an embroidered pillow propped on her lap.

The window was ajar. Fresh river air breezed into the room, and soon her preoccupation with the bizarre attack diminished. The terrors of that night were displaced by real morning anxieties, the challenges of the day ahead. This was a different type of headache, but it was genuine and logic could be applied to determine its cause and find a solution, if she could get her rather annoying emotions to cooperate, of course.

Clutching the pages of Philippe's letter in her hand, Corrinne leaned her head against the cool window jamb and gazed moodily at the shimmering waters of the Saint Lawrence. The year was not at all going the way she had planned, and she was not used to her plans being hindered. She'd thought all the barriers to her desired goals had been removed. She had expected Philippe to be back in Montréal in the spring, like he did every year. But the spring and early summer months had been filled with a series of troubling events. First, Philippe did not return to Montréal. Instead, she received a distressing letter from Claude Guillot, her agent at Fort Niagara. Sister Michelle and Henri had been abducted by savages, and Philippe had been nearly crippled attempting their rescue!

His left leg was severely broken. *But do not be troubled*, the company clerk had written. Philippe was being attended by an Erigh medicine man. He was healing.

A medicine man? She would have to be patient for a few more months, she had told herself. Until he could walk again.

Then *Shérif* Gaspard de Propei, purported nephew and heir of the Marquis de Propei, arrived in Montréal intent on arranging Philippe's death. From what she had gathered through her agents in France and through small pieces that Philippe had mentioned to her over the years, Philippe had fled France that first time—thirteen years ago—after killing the Marquis' son, who had been trying to rape Michelle. And the Marquis was not one to let his son's death go unanswered. When this *shérif* appeared, Corrinne could clearly see the stain of the Marquis' vengeance on the warrant for Philippe's arrest. This man was a serious problem. But Corrinne had deadly friends and deadly ways to deal with serious problems. That is, if Philippe didn't deal with him first. While she was sorting out a solution for this *serious* problem, Monsieur de Propei had abruptly disappeared from the city.

Then, yesterday, two missives from Claude Guillot arrived. This first one informed her that Philippe had marched off into the wilderness to search for Sister Michelle and Henri.

"Impossible," she'd shouted at the letter. "Philippe's fucking *leg* is severely broken!"

The next one in the stack described the arrival of Gaspard de Propei at Fort Niagara.

Then the new letter of that morning. And glory of glories, it was from Philippe himself. Surely it was time for some news that would elevate her mood. But Philippe's letter only filled her with fresh uncertainties. He'd hastily penned it before he'd charged off into the deep wilderness alone.

I should have prayed for good *news*, she rued. She read the last wrinkled page again. *He is not saying good-bye*, she argued to herself. One part of her mind, the part reserved for making cold, realistic assessments, was less sympathetic. *He will attempt to rescue Sister Michelle and the boy by himself. And he will recklessly disregard any danger.*

She read the end of the letter again.

… In case I should fall, know I care for you, deeply. I would say more if my heart would permit …

She never indulged passionate thoughts about anyone. Philippe was the exception.

"'In case I should fall'! You mean in case you die! Is that supposed to leave me feeling hopeful? Oh, Philippe …"

I care for you, deeply …

It was as close as Philippe had ever come to saying he loved her. And that simply was not good enough.

"'I care for you deeply'? What does that mean, Philippe? How deep is that? As deep as your ink well? Couldn't you use your imagination? Would it hurt for you to write the word *love*? I hear it all the time," she fumed at the page. "I hear it from all sorts of men…except from *you.*"

Long ago, before going on to Montréal from Quebec, Philippe had promised to come to her aid should *ever* she need him. Corrinne had smiled. *So foolishly gallant.* Men had made promises to her before. Few were kept.

But two years after her arrival in Quebec, agents arrived from France seeking to discredit Lady de Chanaye and take her back to France. She fled to Montréal and found Philippe. The men chased after her, arriving a month apart from one another. Within a week, under some pretense, each was challenged to a duel by a tall, blond-haired woodsman. And each had died, bewildered, within minutes of drawing sword. Corrinne had witnessed the second combat, watching from the crowd, her face and identity disguised by a black veil. She screamed when the second man drew Philippe's blood. Later, she had worried as her private physician stitched the shoulder wound closed. And later, she'd offered Philippe anything in payment for what he'd done.

"Anything," she had whispered, thinking her intentions clear and irresistible.

"One does not take payment for keeping a promise," Philippe had responded.

What an idiot, she thought recalling the incident. *Didn't he realize what I'd offered?*

Corrinne sniffed and looked at the river. "Probably not. If I stood pink and naked in front of him with my arms held wide open in invitation, he'd worry I would catch a cold…probably run off to bring me a blanket."

But not on the night she'd dined with Philippe and Captain LaTour, late last year, after his return from France with his son. That night had been different. When she'd gotten drunk, and Philippe carried her to bed, she sensed his desire. When she'd embraced and kissed him, he became aroused. He had leaned into her…kissed her back. She knew the signs in men. In another few seconds, she could have guided his hands to her breasts and slipped her hands inside his pants. But then…she'd passed out.

Christ! Of all nights to get intoxicated. Cursed wine. The squawks of sea birds carried past the window. *Another beautiful day.* She was feeling wistful.

If the winters in Montréal were harsh, the summers made up for it with their loveliness. Yet Montréal was but a stop on the way to a final destination. Corrinne de Chanaye had plenty of money, most of it safely stored in banks in the English colonies, away from the prying eyes of Intendant Bigôt and the thieving, corrupt bureaucrats of New France. She had been ready to leave for years. But she would not leave unless Philippe came with her.

And Philippe had given no indication he wanted to leave. Not yet.

Of course, there's Okeanneh.

A very beautiful Indian woman by all accounts, but Corrinne dismissed Okeanneh as a minor dalliance. Michelle was another matter. Philippe had gone back to France to rescue Henri, and to Corrinne's surprise, he'd brought back a woman—the boy's mother. Michelle arrived as *Sister* Michelle, a nun *bona fide.*

And Henri is just another virgin birth, no doubt, she thought mockingly.

According to Claude Guillot at Fort Niagara, Sister Michelle was very decent, very compassionate, and very brave. Nothing sexual was occurring between Philippe and Michelle. Philippe spent most of his time with his son. This left her only with Okeanneh as a rival.

Then in July, Corrinne's agents in France sent an astonishing report: *Sister Michelle* was the *daughter* of the Marquis de Propei. Another woman beset by evil men.

How ironic. The Marquis wants Philippe dead. Sister Michelle too. But if something happens to Sister Michelle, Henri becomes the Marquis' direct heir. And Henri is Philippe's son! This Marquis could not be happy about that, Corrinne mused, before that very thought stole her breath.

Corrinne straightened in the window seat. "Gaspard de Propei did not come here only to slay Philippe," she said aloud. "The Marquis sent him to kill Michelle and Henri, too!"

Lady de Chanaye left the window seat and went to her writing table. She took up a quill to pen the logic to herself.

Assuming Philippe manages to free Michelle and Henri from the savages, Gaspard de Propei will be waiting for him...somewhere. And Francois Bigôt has vested this man with police powers. If Philippe kills Monsieur de Propei, Intendant Bigôt will eventually arrest Philippe and will probably hang him. If Monsieur de Propei arrests Philippe...no, it is more likely he will try to kill him, but if not, Philippe is turned over to Intendant Bigôt and Philippe still hangs for treason. Can Gaspard de Propei murder the nun and boy without consequence? Not easily. He will need help. He will go to Francois Bigôt. What does Intendant Bigôt get? He always gets something. But what? Money probably...always a good choice.

A new, disturbing thought occurred to Corrinne.

Bigôt might use this threat to Philippe as leverage over me.

Corrinne shook her head slowly. She set aside her quill and concentrated. She talked to her image in the writing table mirror.

"Well? What do you think?"

You have all the information you need, the image told her. *The solution is there. Take your time to see it. What does each person want most? Including you.*

Corrinne closed her eyes and let ideas swirl and merge. Before long, the pieces fell into place. The answer unfolded like the petals of a beautiful flower, at the center of which was a person she'd never met.

Henri Gerrard.

The solution was dangerous, but it was definite. Corrinne would have to risk everything. She stood and stretched with pleasure.

"Why do I suddenly feel so happy?" She opened the door to her boudoir. "Mathilde!"

The matron appeared moments later. "Yes, Mistress?"

"I want to dress now. Afternoon dress, *s'il vous plaît*. Darker colors without ornament, I think, yet it must emphasize my bosom. I have men to distract today."

As the maid fluttered around her, Corrinne felt eager. The old abbot in the Parisian orphanage she had grown up in would have been impressed with her logic. She had the funds necessary to balance the risk financially, but her solution would require the help of Financier Jean-Baptiste de Machault. Fortunately, she'd also received letters from him regarding their earlier plot to siphon away the wealth of the Marquis de Propei. She had only to answer his latest missive and inform Machault of the new variation she intended for their plans. Of course, the profit for the financier would be much greater.

When dressed, Corrinne took a seat again at her writing table to pen the letter to Machault.

It's already August, she thought. *If this letter leaves before the week is out, it would still be the end of October before I receive his reply at the earliest. By then, I will have made my bed, whether Machault agrees or disagrees.*

"Well," she told the image in the mirror. "Then I must assume he will agree and my plan will simply have to work."

CHAPTER 8
FORT NIAGARA
AUGUST 1754
The Artist

Charles VanderMeer applied the last blended shades of greens, blues, and browns to the oil paintings, hoping to capture the rapidly changing landscape surrounding Fort Niagara. He had set up four easels between the cannon on the rooftop deck of the great stone castle. He'd now labored for three days, jumping from one painting to the next to record the spectacle of activity.

The artist was so intent on his work, he did not notice Captain Pouchot appear behind him on the gun deck. The commandant watched his crews working on the battlements with pride. From this rooftop vantage point, he could better appreciate the expansiveness of these new fortifications. He envisioned the completed work and thrilled at how formidable the battlements would appear to an enemy. The breastworks were being expanded and even included a moat and drawbridge.

I should have some of my lancers armor up as mounted knights...maybe hold a mock jousting tournament. That would give the savages something to ponder, eh? The fort commandant was in a good mood.

The earthen walls of the ramparts were fifteen feet high, twenty feet thick, and acutely sloped. Two horizontal lines of pointed tree trunks protruded at an angle, running parallel from each other, eight feet apart, positioned to inhibit frontal assaults. The whole fortification was set in the shape of an inverted triangle, with Lake Ontario to the north and the Niagara River to the west. The main earthworks faced southeast and were further buttressed by a trio of triangular lunettes, giving the front of the fort the defensive shape of a trident. All the walls had cannon, the batteries tactically sighted. If any frontal position or lunette was overrun by enemy attack, it could be fired upon from positions directly behind it.

Pouchot casually examined each of the scenes the artist was painting, impressed by the liberal use of colors. Accurate, but, in his opinion, the paintings tended to diminish the intimidating nature of the bastion.

"I think your artist's eye imposes a false poetic scene, Master Artist."

The artist turned with a start, his brush halted in mid-stroke. "Captain Pouchot! I did not hear your approach."

Nothing irritated Charles VanderMeer more than for someone to watch him paint. He would not express this to the captain, however. The artist set aside his palette, praying the interruption would be brief.

"Your mix of colors makes the fort less foreboding, I think."

"I am hoping to capture the heroic nature of the structure being created here. There is artistry in this work. Perhaps someone else can paint the aftermath of an assault…blood, death, and destruction, something more aligned with what you desire."

Pouchot laughed. "There's nothing heroic about slogging about in mud and horse shit. You paint all my sentries in dress uniforms, yet the only thing uniform about them is the muskets they carry."

"Captain, I presume you would want the King to see a picture of your command as you prefer it to appear if the King paid a visit. And what of the historians? Do you want them to surmise the army of New France was only slightly more civilized than the savages?"

Captain Pouchot stiffened at the mention of the King. He'd forgotten the artist was here at the direction of King Louis himself. Men who had any direct connection to the King made Pouchot nervous. An inadvertent remark meant as a jest, said in front of the wrong person, could have adverse repercussions.

"Of course, you are right, Monsieur VanderMeer," he placated. "I do not want to seem unsophisticated. I only wish your romantic illustrations were true. Look at the saintly countenance you've given the natives."

The captain was correct on that particular point. But to get a truthful representation would require VanderMeer to study the facial features and musculature of the natives at much closer proximity. The thought was unappealing to him.

"I paint them as converts to Christianity. According to Monseigneur Beauharnois, he has converted most of them already. I should think one of them, at least, would have saintly virtues, no?"

"Virtues? *Most* of them have probably murdered a Frenchmen or two in the past year." Pouchot snorted. "And now I am forced to dine with them, not that we can call it *dining* out here. And as for their celebrated conversion to Christianity, most haven't the foggiest idea what they are converting to, nor do they care. The heathen will say or do anything we ask, as long as gifts are forthcoming and our brandy keeps flowing. You'll see what I mean for yourself, tonight."

VanderMeer swallowed apprehensively. "The savages will be eating with us tonight?"

Captain Pouchot enjoyed the queasy look on the artist's face. He wondered if Indians scared the artist. *Of course, they do*, Pouchot decided, amused. *That's why VanderMeer has not strayed outside the castle since his arrival. That's why he paints up here in the clouds.*

"Yes, the Indians will dine with us. Tonight!" the commandant answered and pointed. "Down there in the marshalling yard."

Prior to this conversation, Pouchot hadn't planned on inviting any of the local sachems to dinner, but the Dutch artist struck him as soft and effeminate. Such an episode might be entertaining and would provide a break from his boredom.

"But don't worry. We will be inside the compound. There will be plenty of guards," he assured.

"Yes...yes, of course," VanderMeer whispered, suddenly finding it hard to swallow.

Captain Pouchot decided he would invite Three Finger Knife, the new war chief of the Erigh tribe. *Who else? Ah, yes, Chittaqua.* The Erigh sachem had only just returned with the Gerrard boy. Pouchot wanted to learn more about his travels to the south. The story the boy told had been amazing. He doubted if the dour-looking Chittaqua would be half as entertaining. Still, according to the Jesuits, Chittaqua was supposed to be some kind of powerful sorcerer.

"Monseigneur Beauharnois will be joining us. As you know, he is a respected scholar. I think you will find his conversation most diverting."

Maybe I can get the sorcerer to sit between the two of them, Pouchot speculated. *That should spice up the evening. Then again...maybe that would not be prudent.*

Pleased with the prospect of an amusing evening, Captain Pouchot decided to leave the fidgety artist to contemplate his paintings. He tilted his head deferentially.

"Until this evening, Monsieur."

The table was set outside the stone castle in the center of the fort's drilling grounds. It was a beautiful night with warm, low breezes. The tables were arranged in a U with wooden benches for the officers and guests. Candle lanterns were arrayed every six feet behind the chairs. Captain Pouchot presided at the center table with Father Beauharnois and Three Finger Knife to his immediate right. Charles VanderMeer and Chittaqua on his left. The remainder of the guests consisted of ten other officers, two minor clan chiefs, several *coureurs de bois*, and a few bourgeois French civilians.

"To all my distinguished guests," Pouchot began with a toast, "my table is set for your pleasure. Please remain until your stomachs are full and your senses sated with wine."

Charles VanderMeer found the table manners of everyone crude and disgusting, including the French officers. Ironically, the only exception was Chittaqua. The shaman barely ate, preferring to glare moodily at the others.

The cooks brought out fresh bread, cheeses, casseroles of beans and corn, three huge rounds of seasoned roast beef, and a chicken bouillon spiced with onion leeks, parsley, and cloves. To the artist's surprise, table manners of the others aside, the meal was quite delicious. But the liberal servings of wine were probably not a good idea. Before an hour had passed, the behavior of the dinner guests became more than disgusting.

"Oho!"

Erigh war chief Three Finger Knife lifted a bowl of soup to his mouth and quaffed it in one gulp, liberal amounts running over the sides of his chin and splashing on his neighbors. He looked down the table toward VanderMeer and made exaggerated smacking sounds with his lips, rolling his eyes with pleasure.

"Mmmmm, good!"

The Dutchman correctly interpreted this to be a compliment to the host. There was not much conversation during the eating. Most of the Indians ate as if they were starving. Only a few decided to use the spoons, knives, and forks provided. VanderMeer was surprised to see Captain Pouchot amused by the whole spectacle. It was obvious he had contrived the contrasting seating arrangements.

He turned his attention back to the food. There was a gull pie cooked in a pastry crust that reminded the artist of Cornish game hens. Dessert was purported to be extremely precious chocolate-filled biscuits.

Two fiddlers began to play a lively song. By this time, Three Finger Knife had consumed too much brandy and wine, and the sachem and two of the *coureurs de bois* got up and began dancing in front of the tables, whooping and hollering, occasionally falling into some of those still seated.

"Well done!" shouted the commandant with approval, slapping his hand on the tabletop to the beat of the music.

"Want more to drink?" one of the *coureurs de bois* asked. He dumped the contents of his cup on Three Finger Knife's head.

Monseigneur Beauharnois stood and attempted to bring the primitive dancing under control.

"Stop this fiddling! Cease this disgusting behavior!"

Three Finger Knife swayed drunkenly for a few moments, trying to focus his eyes on the priest, unsuccessfully. The vertigo made him nauseous. He belched loudly and vomited the bouillon, brandy, and pie all over the table, some of it splashing on the front of the priest's clothing.

"You will burn in hell!" Beauharnois screamed with horrified outrage.

The Indian burped more on the priest's shoes.

Captain Pouchot was overcome by a fit of choking laughter. But several other French officers were clearly displeased. Charles VanderMeer saw the tension rise dramatically. The Jesuit continued to yell acrimoniously at the Indian. The artist was petrified violence might occur.

Three Finger Knife fell backward on the ground.

Chuckling, Captain Pouchot signaled one of the cooks' helpers to assist the Jesuit in cleaning himself.

"*S'il vous plaît,* Monseigneur. It was simply an accident," Pouchot said good-naturedly.

VanderMeer decided to leave and slipped his legs over the bench. His foot struck a sack sitting on the ground, knocking it over, causing something to slip out. There was a clinking sound and a silver amulet appeared. In the torchlight, he saw that it was etched, which immediately drew his attention. Without considering the identity of the owner, the artist reached down and carefully picked it up. As with any type of jewelry, the artist wanted to peer at it more closely.

Fascinating!

It was a beautiful piece. To his surprise, there was something oddly familiar about the engravings he saw…engravings of a cross, a war ax, a lion, and the moon. The talisman was unsophisticated but exquisitely crafted. He carefully put the piece back into the pouch.

Chittaqua approached, noticing the artist fingering items inside his medicine bag. He quickly gathered up the talisman, cinched the small pouch together, and glared at the white man. The bones of an ancient evil lay in his pouch, guarded by that talisman that the artist had just now been studying.

"Oh! Please forgive me, sir," VanderMeer said, holding up his hands. "I meant no offense. You see, I am a jeweler. The engravings on the silver piece looked interesting. I thought I'd seen them before," he continued meekly. "Forgive my bad manners."

Chittaqua's expression gradually changed.

The commandant recovered his composure long enough to hear VanderMeer's muted apology, but had not heard the reason why.

"Hah! That sorcerer does not consider you bad-mannered, Monsieur. If he did, you would be dead by now," he teased.

To the commandant's delight, the artist's expression became pinched.

Chittaqua partially withdrew the amulet from the sack and held it out to VanderMeer. "You have seen this? You know these marks?"

VanderMeer was eager to appease the offended man.

"Well, yes. I think so. The engravings are a cross, the moon, an ax, a lion. Um, yes Monsieur…is *Monsieur*…proper?"

Chittaqua's gaze grew more intense, his voice more insistent. "You know these marks? What they mean?"

"Perhaps. But I cannot recall from memory. It must have been in one of my reference books in Montréal."

"Books?" *Again, books!*

"Yes. May I examine that again? *Merci.*"

Chittaqua nodded. Keeping the pouch right next to it, he laid the talisman on the table. *The bones of the wraith must not be disturbed*, Chittaqua thought.

VanderMeer moved one of the standing lanterns closer. With more torchlight, he noticed the center stone was cut in facets. *My goodness!*

This is a gemstone! But how does a cut gemstone end up with a savage ...?

He pulled his jeweler's glass from his vest and looked more closely. The jewel was flawless. He decided to keep this fact to himself.

"Remarkable. The moon, ax, cross, and a lion—but possibly a griffin. Yes, I remember seeing them now. The design of the cross is Celtic."

VanderMeer paused.

"But I must be mistaken. This amulet has obviously been made here. My books contain only renderings of things made in the Christian nations."

"Books?" Chittaqua repeated, his expression now almost reverent.

"Uh, yes. In books. Where did this come from?"

"I made it."

"*You* engraved these?"

Chittaqua nodded.

VanderMeer was surprised and glanced at the amulet again. "But why?"

"A ring carries these marks," Chittaqua said.

"A ring you say! Now *that* I would very much like to see." VanderMeer was excited at the prospect.

Three Finger Knife returned and grabbed the mug of brandy VanderMeer had scarcely touched. He quaffed it in one noisy gulp then used his tongue to flick at the triangular piece of animal bone suspended from one nostril, vainly trying to suck at some of his vomit clinging to it.

Revolted, VanderMeer shrank away from the table.

Relishing the artist's reaction, Three Finger Knife smiled maliciously and grabbed one of the terrified man's arms.

"Mmmmm...yum, yum!"

"Let me go," VanderMeer squeaked, but he was powerless in the iron grip of the larger man.

"I think our guest is still hungry." Captain Pouchot roared with laughter.

Three Finger Knife generously covered VanderMeer's arm with juices he scooped from the gull pie, then looked at VanderMeer and licked his lips with the obvious but fake intention of devouring the artist's palette arm.

"Stop it!" VanderMeer squeaked, struggling in vain to free himself.

The other *coureurs de bois* laughed uproariously.

Chittaqua stood and fixed his gaze on Three Finger Knife. The shaman's eyes glittered with an angry light. This half-breed war chief may have brought victory to the Erigh people, but there were consequences. Attacking the Seneca would hasten the Erigh toward an uncertain destiny, a destiny Chittaqua could not see, a destiny that could bring complete annihilation to the Erigh.

Now this new Erigh war chief dances and smells like the white man, bringing more shame to the clan, giving the white man more reasons to treat the Erigh people like scavengers.

Chittaqua pointed an eagle's talon at Three Finger Knife and spoke in a loud, menacing voice.

"Carrion eater!"

Everyone at the table was startled into silence.

Three Finger Knife dropped the artist's arm as if it were a hot coal. He cowered back in fear.

Chittaqua suddenly loomed over the table and seemed to swell in height and girth. His eyes were crazed. His voice was full of doom. It was a frightening visage to behold, be they Indian or white man. He shook the eagle talon at the man more strongly and spoke again in the Erigh tongue.

"Carrion eater!
Leave these lands before the rising moon,
Or your skin will drip with pus.
You will forever eat your scat,
And drink your water.
Walk no longer among us.
Be gone!*"*

Three Finger Knife had been cursed. Pale with fear, he slid slowly back from the tables on his rump, then turned over to crawl on his hands and knees for ten paces before he stood and ran quickly from the fort. It was the last time anyone ever saw the half-breed.

For several seconds after Three Finger Knife ran from the group, there was only silence. Everyone was too stunned to react. The more experienced *coureurs de bois* understood the language and the import of the words. Some of the French officers were unnerved by Chittaqua's malevolent tone. A few crossed themselves or made a circular sign with their fingers to ward away evil.

His clothes still reeking with vomit, Monseigneur Beauharnois was aware that some form of sorcery had been performed right before him.

"Chittaqua, I pray you! Speak no blasphemy here."

The Jesuit held up his crucifix and lapsed into Latin chants, blessing everyone repeatedly, pronouncing benedictions one after another, attempting to overturn whatever the shaman had invoked.

As Monseigneur Beauharnois' chanting became prolonged, Captain Pouchot lost his good humor. He slammed down his flagon.

"Must we endure this too?" the commandant exclaimed, disgusted. He did not care for sorcery. He did not like curses thrown about his dinner table. And he certainly did not want Father Beauharnois to call for a novena!

"*S'il vous plaît*, everyone be seated. There is dessert to enjoy."

Chittaqua's grimness had not abated. VanderMeer had never witnessed anything so frightening in his life.

"Forgive me, Commandant, but I must retire," the artist said.

"Nonsense, Monsieur VanderMeer. Be seated. The bad manners are over! You need to acquire tolerance where the natives are concerned. They have no appreciation for etiquette."

"Nevertheless, with your indulgence, I will retire. Please excuse me."

Without waiting for acknowledgement, the Dutchman began walking briskly toward the stone castle. He had not gone twenty paces before Chittaqua's imposing figure unexpectedly moved in front of him. The artist froze in alarm.

Chittaqua leaned in and peered closely at his face. "You say *books*! Books have these marks? Show me these books."

It was not a request. The tone was not unfriendly but insistent. VanderMeer was nervous. Then an idea occurred to him.

"Honorable chief, I have been asked by my King to paint what I see in this land. Will you sit and allow me to paint you?"

Chittaqua was puzzled. Why would this white man want to put paint on him?

VanderMeer pulled a folded piece of paper from his pocket. In the reflecting light of the lanterns, Chittaqua discerned a charcoal sketch of some soldiers.

"Paint," the artist asserted, moving his hand as if sketching.

"But with colors."

The shaman didn't quite understand, but the white man's words sounded like a bargain.

"You show me books?"

"If I have them with me, then yes, I will show you books."

Chittaqua nodded with satisfaction. "Tomorrow,"—he pointed toward les Négociants Dunemoore's buildings—"we talk there."

The next morning, Henri Gerrard was loping back and forth in front of the trading post with Anamosa on his shoulders, pretending to be a horse, delighting in the giggles he provoked in her.

"Excuse me, young sir."

Henri stopped and looked at the strangely attired man. He set Anamosa down.

"Yes?"

A slender man was carrying an arrangement of wooden poles plus a large square piece of white canvas stretched over a wooden frame. Leather canvas cases and a whole basket full of pigments, brushes, a palette, spatulas, and oil pots hung from straps around his neck and shoulders. He was also wearing a paint-speckled black frock that draped down to his knees.

His fashion reminded Henri of the street mimes he'd watched from Saint Ouen's towers in Rouen.

"I am looking for an Indian, uh, person, they call Chittaqua," the man inquired, his voice tentative but friendly.

Strangers can be enemies, Chittaqua had warned. But this man simply looked too ridiculous to be dangerous.

"Oh, apologies for my rudeness," the man continued at seeing Henri's hesitation. "My name is Charles VanderMeer. I am an artist. Chittaqua is, uh, expecting me…at least, I think he is."

"My name is Henri. I will find Chittaqua for you. Wait in there." He gestured at the trading post door.

"Inside? Ah, yes. *Merci.*"

Henri decided to go out to the village and tell Chittaqua about this man. He spread his arms wide to the blue-eyed girl who gazed at him adoringly.

"Come on, Ana. You can ride me again."

She giggled, delighted.

VanderMeer struggled to get all his things through the door at the same time. The wood poles clacked together like oversized rattles.

Okeanneh was bending over a large bundle of fur goods and turned in surprise at the unexpected noise. She straightened and looked suspiciously at the oddly dressed white man.

For a few seconds, Charles VanderMeer was speechless. He had never seen a woman of such raw, earthy beauty. Her lustrous black hair was tied back in a long tail with multiple braids, the braids twined with pink and white shells, and a long piece of fur from some animal and two feathers from a large bird lying flat and pointing downward. The glorious amber color of her eyes was unique and mesmerizing. He wondered if he could mix shades necessary to capture such a color.

Okeanneh had seen men stare like this before. "What do you want?"

The way she looked at him made VanderMeer feel self-conscious.

"*Bonjour,* Mademoiselle," the artist stammered. "I was told I could find Chittaqua here. I am to meet with him."

Okeanneh sniffed. *He smells queerly,* she thought. *Like pine sap.*

"Chittaqua does not live here," she replied brusquely. "His lodge is outside the fort."

Her accented French was charming. VanderMeer marveled at her attire, a mixture of highly decorative Indian dress and articles of a French woman's undergarments. Okeanneh had discovered a trunk of women's clothing in the shipment of store goods from Montréal. Assuming the puny white woman wore such things, she wanted to learn how, hoping to please Philippe. She first tried the highly curled wigs and found that they smelled bad. She had tried on different parts of the dresses, but could only guess at how to wear the puzzling hoops, petticoats, and loose billowy pants. They seemed impractical.

That particular morning, she'd put on a bone-reinforced corset. It seemed to give her back support, so she decided that was its purpose. The corset, light blue in color, was improperly laced and her breasts bulged over the front, giving her figure a voluptuous appearance. Over the corset, she wore a loose tunic with lacings up the side and front. This left her arms free to lift heavy bundles above her head to place on high shelves. The tunic was cinched at the waist with a leather belt and was trimmed with leather and fur tassels and some simple beadwork. She wore doeskin leggings that hung over the top of calf-high boots. The polished gold medallion of Saint

Denis dangled from her neck. It caught and reflected the light anytime she shifted position.

VanderMeer found the woman's appearance striking. She possessed that special haughty expression he'd seen often in the eyes and posture of more than one of the royals who had sat for him. *Those eyes*! Expressive… deep…amber. Cat-like. Probing. He tried not to stare, for too long, anyway. He cautioned himself not to give offense. He wanted this woman to like him. It would be enjoyable to sketch her. *I wonder if she'd let me?*

She could see him looking at her closely and frowned.

"Chittaqua asked me to meet him *here*," the artist said quickly, seeing her displeasure.

She stared at him ambivalently and did not reply.

"I said, Chittaqua asked me to meet him here," the artist repeated politely. When she still did not reply, he became uncomfortable. "Mademoiselle…shall I wait outside?"

Okeanneh shook her head. "No. You stay."

"*Merci*, Mademoiselle. Um, may I know your name?"

"Okeanneh." She pointed to a chair by the long table. "Sit there."

"*Merci*, Okeanneh." *What a marvelous name*, he thought.

VanderMeer carefully took a seat near a table piled high with trade goods and tried to be unobtrusive.

Okeanneh resumed the work she was engaged in when VanderMeer entered, untying large bundles of animal pelts, inspecting them for signs of vermin, carefully trimming the more ragged edges, sorting them according to type, size, and quality. Occasionally, someone from the fort would come in to trade or make a purchase.

The artist was impressed at the deft way she handled these transactions; her experience was obvious. The smelly *coureurs de bois* traders doffed their hats, posturing like young boys while she complimented them on the lush, soft quality of their catch of furs, or how physically fit they looked. A few of them she touched on the shoulder and smiled warmly at; one or two lucky ones she kissed on each cheek in the French custom. Those men would beam and strut like roosters afterwards. He also noted how respectfully the civilian-clothed buyers treated her, how she could wither any of them with a look if an unfair price was offered, and how she invited a few favorites to sit at the long trading table where she would give them tea, the most favored ones some extremely precious coffee.

From time to time, Okeanneh paused and glanced over at the strange little man, curious what he wanted with Chittaqua. She could feel his eyes follow her as she moved around. His smile and gaze was respectful in an appraising way. Not with desire, as some of the soldiers did, nor proud or challenging. He was clearly not a threat, but his prying interest made her a little nervous, nevertheless. And she was pleased when Chittaqua suddenly appeared at the door leading from the forge area.

"Ah, Monsieur Chittaqua," VanderMeer said, rising immediately.

The shaman nodded once at the artist and gestured. "Come."

"Come with you? Oh, yes."

Noisily, VanderMeer gathered his things and followed the shaman into the adjoining forge area.

Okeanneh abruptly urged the other visitors outside. She threw the bolt on the front door to the store and followed them into the forge.

From his medicine bag, Chittaqua brought out a large intricately carved wooden amulet. He handed it to VanderMeer and cleared the forging tools off the work table.

Okeanneh stayed quietly to one side, to listen in on their conversation.

Chittaqua withdrew another pouch from the medicine bag and pulled out a silver amulet placing it also on the table top, keeping the dirt-filled pouch within inches away. "They are the same," he stated. "You, look closer."

Charles VanderMeer nodded. He'd noted how carefully the shaman held the silver talisman.

Be careful, something within warned the artist. *This has great value to him.*

VanderMeer arranged the silver and wood pieces side by side. The symbols were essentially identical…and, again, he thought how oddly familiar they were. *I've seen these before …?*

"They are more beautiful than I first thought. And you say there is also a ring?"

"Philippe Gerrard. These marks,"—Chittaqua pointed a finger insistently—"they are the same?"

"Philippe Gerrard?"

"In your *book*? These marks?"

The medicine man's eyes were absolutely intimidating.

"A moment, Monsieur. A moment, *s'il vous plaît*."

VanderMeer turned the wooden carving over in his hand, fascinated. The native symbols around the outside edges were intricate and beautiful. He looked back and forth between the wood and silver pieces.

"Whoever made these is a great artist. The workmanship is remarkable."

"These marks?" Chittaqua repeated with impatience and pointed again.

"Yes, indeed, I have seen these marks, probably in one of my books. I cannot recall if the engravings are part of a brooch, or a necklace, or a…"

VanderMeer had a startling thought. *These symbols are remarkably similar to the symbols on the back of Archbishop Nicolet's crucifix! But how can that be …*

"The marks are the same?" Chittaqua's voice was higher.

"Apologies, Monsieur." Charles VanderMeer was surprised by this unexpected coincidence. *The archbishop's crucifix, this talisman, Philippe Gerrard's ring…they all have these symbols. How is this possible?*

"The marks are the same?" Chittaqua's voice became insistent and louder.

"Remarkably…yes, I think they are," VanderMeer replied. Recovering his composure, the artist prattled on happily, as if addressing one of his customers.

"Oh, yes. Exactly, I think. You see? This standing lion? Very unusual. Very old. Not a griffin after all, as I originally thought. And this cross. See the ornate weave? See how the crossbeam is crafted? That is a Taranis symbol, I presume. This design is very old indeed and definitely Celtic. Now this intricate circle had me puzzled, but seeing this up close, I suspect it's a Celtic moon symbol. And this is certainly a war ax. See the curved nature of the blade? Germanic or Norse influences. Many of the families in Gaul used an ax in their coat of arms. Based on the age of all these symbols, the ring you speak of…you say it's Philippe Gerrard's? Well…it may date to…well, it must be very, very old…it may even date back to a time before the Crusades."

As usual, VanderMeer had spoken in conclusions. When he looked up, he saw a different kind of intensity on Chittaqua's face.

"Oh, my! Forgive me, Monsieur. How rude of me. You have no idea of what I speak."

But Chittaqua was exhilarated. *Old, very old, he said! Snow Hair must*

*meet this man. He must hear this. Only then will the ring's message be
known. And the demon's cruel purpose be revealed.*

"These books," Chittaqua said hopefully. "Here?"

The artist shook his head. "No, not here. There are too many. My books
are in Montréal."

And unfortunately, so is my sketch of the Archbishop's crucifix. VanderMeer's brow pinched in disappointment. "You say these same symbols
are on Philippe Gerrard's ring?"

Chittaqua nodded. He breathed heavily with frustration. He looked out
the smoke hole at the shaft of sunlight.

The shaman decided to tell the white man of the legend and the curse.
Seeing Okeanneh lingering nearby, he pointed at the forge doorway.

She frowned but left them alone.

Chittaqua did not understand how these ancient things were connected.
But this man, this white *picture maker*, being here, now, at this place…this
was supposed to happen! A sudden shower of red sparks surged from the
forge as if in response to his thoughts. Chittaqua thought about the promises
he'd exchanged with Philippe that had involved the ring and talisman. He
could see the ring's influence in this now. The promises were not important—they never were. What *was* important were the symbols he'd cut in
the silver talisman. Chittaqua had learned by painful experience that it was
dangerous for the symbols to be separated too far from the bones. But he
had no more time for pursuing this legend, this curse. The Erigh people
were dying. He was their chief, their shaman. He had to lead them from
this place of death.

The prolonged silence and the shaman's dark brooding became awkward for the artist.

"Monsieur Chittaqua, have I offended you?"

Chittaqua met his gaze. "No." *He is the one*, Chittaqua decided. *My
part in this is almost finished.* He would give the mystery over to this white
man. Picture Maker had revealed much without knowing its importance. But
there was much more to be revealed. Picture Maker must be convinced first.

"There is more to tell you."

The shaman took a seat, placed the silver talisman back inside the pouch,
then spread open the top of the pouch with his fingers to make the inside
visible. He gestured for Picture Maker to sit in the other chair.

VanderMeer sat down, leaned forward, and looked closely into the pouch of dirt. Beneath the amulet, he saw teeth. Human teeth. And a jawbone. Alarmed, he drew back.

"What is this?" VanderMeer asked.

Chittaqua poked his fingers through the dirt until the jawbone was completely visible.

"Listen to my words."

He spoke slowly to make his French as clear as possible, gesturing with his hands, occasionally touching his heart or head for emphasis as he talked.

"These bones, this dirt, come from a grave mound, on an island, in a river far from here." He pointed to the talisman. "There are four standing stones at this grave, each carved with a mark. One stone, one mark. Just like these marks. The legend of this place is older than the memory of my people. We have forgotten how the grave was made. We have forgotten who pushed up the stones or why. It is an old place, a secret place. But every season, the river floods increase, destroying the island. The stones are falling over. Soon, the river will cover everything with mud and water. So I took these bones and dirt and put them in this pouch with the talisman, with the marks of the stones. I hoped to one day make a new grave for the spirit buried there. These bones and talisman must *always* be together!"

Chittaqua gripped his hands around the pouch and paused. He looked pointedly in the Picture Maker's eyes so he would not forget this.

"These things must *never* be apart!"

VanderMeer nodded quickly. "I understand." Yet he did *not* understand, not exactly. He was having difficulty grasping the significance of this revelation.

Chittaqua pressed on more strongly.

"The marks on those stones guarding these bones are the same as *these marks*,"—he pointed to the symbols on the talisman—"and the same as the marks on Snow Hair's ring. The ring is from Snow Hair's *clan*. I think the legend of these stones is a *white man's* legend. You said these marks are in your books. Snow Hair must talk with you and learn of this. It has great importance."

As the shaman talked, Charles VanderMeer suddenly began to understand. His mouth slackened in wonder. If what this...this *medicine man* said was true, it was not just coincidence—it was a miracle. *But wait—it must be a coincidence, yes? How could it possibly be anything else?* the artist thought. *Indeed, a very extraordinary coincidence.*

"Who is Snow Hair?"

"Okeanneh's husband. Philippe Gerrard. The ring belongs to Philippe Gerrard."

"I would very much like to talk with Philippe Gerrard, but I am returning to Montréal soon."

Chittaqua nodded. "Montréal," he repeated carefully. "The great walled village across the lake. Snow Hair will come to see you there. He must see the marks in your books."

"Yes, of course he can."

Chittaqua took hold of the artist's hands and wrapped them around the pouch. "These things must not be parted," he warned again gravely.

VanderMeer swallowed hard, nodded, and promised.

"Sir, I understand. I promise to take good care of them."

Chittaqua felt as if a great weight had been lifted from him. He stood. "Now you make picture."

VanderMeer saw the shaman's grim expression relax. He swallowed nervously. "Thank you." He began setting up his easel.

Chittaqua opened the door to the trading room and gestured for Okeanneh to return. She moved with speed and threw the bolt on the trading-room door.

Sunlight beamed through the smoke hole in the roof. The room became more illuminated, as if a cloud had finally gone.

"Oh, that light is very warm, very good. This will do nicely," Vander-Meer said. "Yes, yes. Stand over here, Monsieur Chittaqua, near the light."

The artist placed the shaman so the sunlight would highlight the colors of his clothing.

Chittaqua was uncomfortable with the man's touch but found no intended insult in the Picture Maker's behavior.

The artist stood back and evaluated Chittaqua's pose.

"You should wear the amulet," he told the shaman and brought the pouch to him.

Chittaqua withdrew the amulet and slipped it around his neck, after placing the pouch with the bones and dirt between his feet. But this simple precaution gave him great pause and new disturbing thoughts. *What if the white man does not heed my words? What if he separates the bones from the talisman?*

VanderMeer rubbed his chin. "Something is missing. We need more… do you have anything to wear that has even more color?"

Okeanneh went to the shaman's medicine bag and retrieved the Andro-totekan's spirit cloak.

"He should wear this."

She draped the cloak around Chittaqua's shoulders and bowed her head in respect to him.

"What an astonishing garment! Yes, that is perfect! Now," VanderMeer encouraged, "look out this window, as if you are gazing at a mountain far away in the distance."

"Perfect. Now, please, Monsieur, remain still."

VanderMeer opened up a small portable table with a Y-shaped support stand, and spread out his jars of oils and various *dirts*, as he called them. He also laid open a heavy neckerchief, which contained dozens of semiprecious stones of various colors. Anticipating he would need to match their color, he inspected a few of them in the beam of sunlight and nodded, satisfied.

"Good. Yes. This will all do nicely."

With his painting stones, oils, and easel set, VanderMeer selected a brush, took a deep breath and calmed himself, focusing his concentration. The artist studied the shaman carefully before beginning. He would have only this day, maybe only a few hours, to complete the beginning of the work. He wanted to memorize his first impressions, capture the man's visage in his mind, in case he had to finish the painting alone later.

Many of VanderMeer's paints contained pulverized glass, which induced a healthy glow in the hues. Each of his paintings was built upon an under-lying quality, some basic nature of the subject, the reflection of the person's soul—at least, he tried to make it so. Chittaqua's face and eyes seemed an amalgam of sadness and wisdom, natural, genuine, unaffected by ego. And yet the shaman held himself proudly, as if in defiance of some heaviness of the heart. Such honesty would drive the selection of colors, the accents and highlights VanderMeer would emphasize. He loved to paint this way. It was instinctive. He realized this painting could potentially be one of his most meaningful works from New France. When he was ready, he asked questions of himself that he always asked.

How do I feel about him? What does he say to me? Who do I see? What shall be the emotion? The artist reflected for a few moments. *A heroic soul... humble but courageous?*

He smiled. *Yes,* heroic. *That's it.*

And he began.

Okeanneh watched over the artist's shoulder for a time, until she sensed he was not pleased by her nearness. But she was amazed at how quickly and accurately he was capturing Chittaqua's image, almost like that of a metal mirror, only with the intensified coloring, the painting seemed to reveal the deeper passion in the shaman's expression.

She touched the artist's shoulder lightly.

VanderMeer was startled. "Mademoiselle?"

"You do that for me," she asked, pointing at the painting.

"You want me to paint you too?"

Okeanneh nodded. *"Oui!"*

The request was unexpected, but VanderMeer bowed his head. "I would be deeply honored."

Okeanneh smiled and asked tentatively. "And you paint my love face, and give it to Snow Hair? As a gift from me?"

Her beauty had blossomed further with that smile and with her simple words. If a goddess from Olympus asked him to do the same thing, it could not have provoked a more rewarding emotion.

"It will be my great, great privilege to do as you've requested."

She looked puzzled.

VanderMeer smiled. "Yes, Mademoiselle, yes. I will give it to Monsieur Gerrard as a present from you."

"Good! I must go back to the trading room, but I will return."

Okeanneh kissed both of the man's cheeks in the French way, showing her appreciation.

A stunned Charles VanderMeer watched her leave the forge room.

But another surprise, much greater and not very pleasant, would come to the artist before the day was over.

The artist reluctantly stopped painting three hours later when he lost the bright light of the sun. He would have to finish the work over the next two days and doubted he would have Chittaqua's further cooperation. Anticipating this, he'd spent most of his time on the color, shadow, skin texture, age lines, and other qualities of the Indian's face, using the more simple strokes and generalizations to portray the shapes and color of the rest of the body, elements of his posture, plus the drape and folds of the shaman's clothing. Other than the face, he could detail the rest from memory.

VanderMeer bowed deeply before the shaman. "I am most honored you have permitted me this time."

Chittaqua relaxed but his mind still dwelled on the bones. *What if the demon gets free?* He had now brooded about these concerns for hours. *The Picture Maker must somehow be made to understand the terrible thing he will carry.* Chittaqua had to be sure. And there was only one way to do that. *The white man must be made to see.*

The shaman stepped around the easel to glance at the work briefly. Surprised at the stranger he saw, he pointed at himself.

"I look like that?"

"W-well, it's not finished yet," VanderMeer stammered. "But I am done for this day. The light is …" He gestured at the smoke hole. "*Is* there a chance you might consider—"

"Good," Chittaqua replied quickly. "We must do something new."

"Something…*new*?"

Just then, Okeanneh returned carrying a tray of tea, cups, and a basket of fresh bread.

"Aaaah! Mademoiselle, you have read my mind."

She looked at him quizzically.

He tipped his head. "*Merci*, Mademoiselle. The bread smells wonderful."

As VanderMeer gulped down hot tea and delicious bread, he watched the shaman go to the far side of the forge and, taking up a straw broom, sweep away a thick layer of sooty dirt on the floor. Then he lifted a hatched door in the floor that would otherwise cover a shallow stone vault. From this hidden space, he withdrew a small ingot of silver.

Again, Chittaqua gestured to Okeanneh that she should leave the forge area.

She frowned and turned to the artist.

"You find me soon to do this, yes?"

VanderMeer nodded his head rapidly. "*Oui*, Mademoiselle. Maybe even tomorrow."

The smile she gave the artist almost melted his heart.

After Okeanneh exited, Chittaqua lowered the heavy bars on both doors leading into the forge, one from the trading room and one from the marshalling grounds outside. Next, he added wood to the glowing embers in the firing hearth, plus several handfuls of small black coal, and started pumping the bellows.

VanderMeer wasn't sure if he should stay or leave, but began packing away his paints, enclosing his latest painting inside a hollow leather carrying case to protect it. When he was ready to leave, he turned toward Chittaqua only to find the shaman facing him a few steps away. The talisman was out of the pouch. Chittaqua held it close to the artist's face.

"We must make another one of these," the shaman announced.

"*Another ...?*"

Chittaqua pointed at the purple center stone. "Do you have a spirit stone?"

"A *spirit* stone?"

"A stone must be at the center of the talisman. It must be a stone *you* carry, that is a part of your spirit." Chittaqua pointed at the bulging kerchief full of painting stones he'd seen the artist use. Like one of those, you have one stone that carries your spirit before all the others. My heart tells me you do."

Indeed, the Dutch artist had such a stone, though he wondered how the shaman had known such a thing. But it wasn't a simple painting stone. It was an eight-carat emerald, a flawless gem, cut traditionally. He'd done the work himself. Offered enormous sums of money by people over the years desiring to own such a rarity, Charles VanderMeer found he could not part with it. In fact, he could not bear being parted from it at all and had the piece sewn into a secret pocket in the crotch of his pants; such pockets he would personally create in any new trousers he wore.

"Yes, Monsieur Chittaqua. I have such a stone."

Chittaqua nodded vigorously. With the Picture Maker looking on, the shaman emptied the teapot and refilled it with hot water from the forge water bucket. To that, he added the tiniest pinch of the Apache medicine. Mixing it thoroughly, he took a sip to test its potency, nodded, and poured a small portion into a cup for the artist.

"And what is this? You want me to drink this? Is it a new blend of tea?"

Chittaqua nodded solemnly. "Yes…it is a tea."

VanderMeer took a deep breath. "Very well."

Within a few minutes, the effects of the medicine gripped the artist's thoughts and perceptions.

Something popped in the firing hearth. It emitted some sparks.

"Look at all those amazing colors!" VanderMeer began smiling. He now responded easily to any suggestion or request Chittaqua made of him.

For the next six hours, working side by side, the two artists would heat, fashion, hammer, and engrave another talisman, a virtual duplicate of Chittaqua's, only more polished, more precise in its detail now that VanderMeer did most of the work, using his skills as a jeweler. At its center, VanderMeer carefully set his large green emerald, his *spirit* stone.

The Dutch artist thought the finished piece was truly wonderful, one of his best works. He had been a little uncertain whether placing his treasured emerald in such a setting was a wise thing to do, but the amulet was a beautiful piece, and he had never planned to sell it anyway. *Better than hiding a stone of such color and quality in my crotch.*

When the new talisman was complete, Chittaqua opened the door leading into the marshalling yard and walked out a few steps until he located the moon. It was only an hour after sunset. A three-quarter moon had barely risen above the horizon. With no explanation to the bewildered artist leaning against the open door, the Andrototekan elevated the talisman above his head and offered it to the moon's spirit in a hushed voice, repeating the sacred words several times.

"*Loh cai teem!*" Guide to the truth!

Then he returned to the forge and dropped the bar on the door again.

VanderMeer followed Chittaqua, lightheaded from the incredibly potent tea the shaman kept giving him.

"Are we finished?"

"No." He led them back to the forge table and placed the emerald amulet atop the pouch and bones. "Give me your hand."

The artist extended his left hand without hesitation.

And without hesitation, Chittaqua took a knife and made a small cut in Picture Maker's palm, not very long or deep, but enough so the blood would flow.

While the white man howled with pain like a small child, Chittaqua made a similar cut in his palm, then gripped the other freshly cut palm tightly. He held the original talisman in his other hand, above the emerald talisman lying on the pouch.

"Quiet!"

VanderMeer was going to protest, but he suddenly realized the cut didn't actually hurt. *Remarkable. It must be the tea. I must ask him where I can find more of those herbs.*

Chittaqua began to chant enigmatic words in a low, rhythmic tone, repeating them several times.

"*Ha teh ko ha sen kah.*" One light, one life. "*Ha teh ko ha sen kah.*"

The mix of Chittaqua's blood and that of the Picture Maker's dribbled over Chittaqua's talisman onto the new piece and into the dirt in the pouch. It was a blood ritual for sharing magic. "*Ha teh ko ha sen kah.*" One light, one life. "*Ha teh ko ha sen kah.*"

All at once, he stopped.

"It is done," he told Picture Maker.

"Well, then I guess I should be going …"

"No." He handed Picture Maker a cup of tea. "Drink more."

"More?" But VanderMeer drank the tea.

In the darkness of the forge, as the night deepened outside, Chittaqua indicated to Picture Maker he should sit cross-legged on the floor.

Dizzy, yet obedient, the artist did as he was told. Looking at his palm, he wondered why the small cut still did not hurt. In fact, abruptly, it was as if he stood on one side of the room, watching himself. And VanderMeer found his *own* reaction to these bizarre occurrences and his meek participation equally amazing. *I should be petrified.* But inexplicably, his mood was tranquil and accommodating. In addition, all the colors he saw were brighter, smells were stronger, and he could see… *Like an owl*, he decided. Not to forget how his skill at working the silver and crafting jewelry seemed to have increased tenfold.

Chittaqua handed Picture Maker the emerald talisman. "Hold this before you, hold it to your chest, like this, like a war shield," he said.

VanderMeer timidly asked why, but the shaman was already moving a few steps away.

Chittaqua set the pouch of bones and dirt on the floor of the forge between them and lifted his talisman from the bag. Then he sat down, cross-legged, and looked over at Picture Maker, who had a blinking, confused expression on his face.

The Erigh shaman was not entirely certain what would happen when he did what he was about to do…but either way, they would both witness the truth of this.

"Picture Maker. Do *not* let go of your talisman," he warned.

VanderMeer nodded his head, intentionally mimicking Chittaqua's low and serious voice. "I understand. I must *not* let go of my talisman." Then he smiled.

To the artist's continued wonder and amusement, the Indian medicine man began to push himself backwards across the floor with his heels, away from the pouch of dirt, pausing with each movement. He was about to ask if he should do the same thing when he noticed sinuous streams of creamy white smoke begin to ooze from the pouch in several directions.

"Oh! What an amazing illusion," VanderMeer said, awed. "How do you do this?"

The artist set aside his emerald talisman, intending to crawl over to the pouch to see the trick up close.

"*No!*"

VanderMeer felt a slashing pain in both of his hands, as if they'd been suddenly set on fire. He screamed in agony. An instant later, Chittaqua's body knocked him backward.

The shaman placed his body over the two of them while an angry buzzing thing dipped and circled, looking for a way to slash again. But Chittaqua's talisman kept *it* just a few feet away.

One talisman alone is not strong enough for both of us! The shaman looked around wildly for the emerald talisman.

"My hands! My hands! Do not touch my hands!" VanderMeer screamed. "What is happening?"

Chittaqua saw the other talisman just to the right. Fortunately, he could reach out and pick it up. He placed the talisman on the Picture Maker's chest. The angry buzz became less pronounced, the shapeless white smoke becoming less dense.

"*Do not move!*"

Chittaqua started to slide toward the pouch while Picture Maker watched on in terror.

VanderMeer lifted his hands, so they would not touch anything, a grimace stained his face.

The closer the shaman got to the pouch, the less visible the demon became. When it was gone completely, Chittaqua drew a line on the ground for later reference and moved quickly the last several feet to place his talisman back in the pouch.

Afterwards, Chittaqua lay flat on his back, panting.

"Monsieur Chittaqua?" VanderMeer asked, his voice high-pitched. "What in the name of *Christ* just happened?"

Chittaqua pushed himself to a seated position. At least he knew the Picture Maker's talisman would protect him. *But will it keep the demon inside the pouch?* He stood, went over to the artist, and retrieved the emerald talisman.

"Do your hands hurt?"

"No, Monsieur. The pain is gone. My hands are fine. But what in God's name was that?"

While VanderMeer protested loudly and made fear-induced whimpers, Chittaqua removed his talisman from the pouch, replacing it with the Picture Maker's. Then he backed slowly across the forge room, pushing the Picture Maker behind him.

Nothing happened.

Chittaqua nodded with relief. He picked up the pouch and set it on the forge table. He pointed to a chair and told the Picture Maker to sit.

"I have more to tell you. Our oldest legends speak of a man from across the Great Waters—"

"Stop, Monsieur! Please! I beg you!" VanderMeer held up a hand and spoke in a pleading tone. "I would like some water to drink first. *Not* your tea! And I think I have soiled my pants."

CHAPTER 9
FORT NIAGARA
AUGUST 1754
The Journey of the Aerie

Okeanneh posed for the Picture Maker the next morning, almost in the exact same spot as Chittaqua had the previous day. But the man who was so friendly with her the day before, now seemed anxious. He smiled only briefly and, before starting, scanned the forge intently, as if in search of something hidden.

Finally, he took a high stool from the trading room and directed her pose, similar to what he did with Chittaqua.

He complimented her clothing, asked her to move various pieces in a certain way, arranged her braided hair to hang across one shoulder, and removed one of the necklaces, saying, "The shells are much too large." All his smiles were brief and, while polite, he hardly spoke at all. His mood only lifted after he started painting, particularly when he brought the hand-carried roundish board he called a *palette* close to her face. This action provoked the genuine smile she'd seen the day before.

"To permit me to better capture the color of your lovely eyes," he told her as he mixed the various paints with dabs of his brush. "Now, if you please, look out that window and pretend you see your husband coming back to you."

Two hours later, he abruptly announced. "You may look if you wish."

Okeanneh stepped around the easel and was astonished by her portrait. Her face was finished, but the clothing and body was only partially complete.

"I look like that?"

VanderMeer smiled at hearing the vulnerable question he'd heard so many times before.

"I assure you, Mademoiselle, you are indeed this beautiful, and much, much more so. I will finish your clothing later. Your face is the most important part. Do you like it?"

Okeanneh looked at it in wonder. She patted her chest lightly with one hand. "You…this…my heart beats fast."

VanderMeer had never been given a more endearing compliment by anyone who ever sat for him.

"I paint what I see, though my skills may have fallen short this time." He had said this to so many others, but this was the first time it felt true.

Okeanneh did not understand that last part of his reply, but she smiled broadly at the first. She kissed both of his hands, paused for a moment, and kissed him directly on the lips.

"My husband says this kissing should only be done with those you like very much," she explained. "And you have made me happy."

No one had *ever* kissed his hands before! VanderMeer laughed nervously and wiped his face with a paint rag to remove a stray tear, leaving a streak of yellow across his nose by accident. "I am honored."

"I am leaving today."

"Leaving? To go where?"

"To find my husband. He is in the river lands. An enemy is looking for him. I will kill this man when I meet him. My husband will return in one moon. Will this be ready?"

These lands must be possessed! VanderMeer decided with alarm. *My arm is nearly cannibalized at dinner. I am given a tea that makes me as irrational as a small child. I set my most prized gem in a primitive amulet and receive a curse for doing it. I am strapped to a…thing…from some primitive sorcerer, the kind who carry ancient bones around in pouches of dirt, and which I am now given to carry with me until I solve some grisly Carolingian riddle to get free of it. Now, this beautiful woman is setting off to kill someone she's never met?*

Charles VanderMeer had studied the works of Newton and Leibniz, of Halley, of Huygens and Pitot, of Diderot, of Voltaire and Rousseau. But after what had happened to him while visiting New France, and, in particular, the last few days, the artist resolved to leave Fort Niagara that day, to go home, all the way home, back to Amsterdam. He would have started already but for his promise to paint Okeanneh. He decided not to tell her where he was going.

Who knows how she might react.

"Mademoiselle, when I see your husband again, I will give him this painting myself. I will tell him this is your *love face*."

When the sun was high, Okeanneh went to the Erigh lodges among the sprawling village south of Fort Niagara, straight to Chittaqua's lodge.

"I am leaving to find Snow Hair," Okeanneh announced.

"Why?" Chittaqua asked.

"I will help him fight this evil one."

Henri knew many of the Erigh words now. His eyes widened. *Fight an evil one?*

"I would like to leave Anamosa with Juniata until I return."

Chittaqua nodded. "She is welcome as my daughter. When do you leave?"

"Today. Soon."

"Snow Hair walks among the new forts. He will be at the one farthest away."

"Then I will prepare."

Okeanneh slipped out the door. Henri rose to follow her.

"Wait," Chittaqua said quickly.

Henri frowned.

"Sit." The shaman laid a square piece of beaver skin between them. He took the carving of the wooden amulet from his medicine bag and placed it on the pelt, then set the silver one next to it.

"You know what these mean."

"I've seen them before."

Henri had only seen the curious silver talisman once when they were camped by the lake. It had been inside a pouch in the medicine bag. Henri had not forgotten Chittaqua's angry reaction when he touched it. The markings between the silver and wooden ones were similar. Henri considered them just a part of the copious magical charms Chittaqua usually carried.

Chittaqua pointed. "You know these marks?"

Henri looked closer. "A cross. An ax. A lion." He pointed at the circle and shook his head. "This one?"

"The moon." Chittaqua seemed pleased. "Have you seen your father's ring?"

"I've seen it."

"These marks match the marks on his ring. The ring is very old, Snow Hair says. Old things contain magic. Old things have wisdom to share."

"Do these marks mean something?"

The shaman sat back. "Yes, but the meaning is in a *book*," he continued.

"A book?"

"The man who makes pictures in the fort…he has pictures of these marks in a *book* at the great French village on the river. Snow Hair must be told about this. If not by me, then by you. Your father must go to the Picture Maker at the great village. See his *book*," Chittaqua said fervently.

"Why did you make these marks on your talisman?"

Chittaqua thought about his answer.

"It is a count of four promises."

"Four promises?"

Chittaqua explained the events since Henri's capture, the reasons for his father's offer, why Chittaqua could not accept the ring as payment for finding Henri, the covenant, how it sealed the fate of the two clans. How such a destiny had resulted in their meeting by the lake.

"My father owes you four favors?"

"One for each mark. Even after my death. Our clans are bound by this.

"But this is a good thing," he assured him.

"Do Chesanin and Achipan know?"

Chittaqua nodded.

Henri touched the silver talisman. It felt warm. The wooden one did not.

"If my father has promised, then I will promise too."

The shaman smiled with approval.

"Good. We will seal the promise tonight, when the moon is high in the sky."

Anamosa knew something was wrong when her mother led her to the lodges outside the fort.

Juniata and Chittaqua watched as Okeanneh knelt in front of Anamosa.

"I must go away for a while, little one. You will stay with Juniata until I get back."

"No!" Large tears rolled down Anamosa's golden cheeks.

Henri did not understand all the Ottawa words, but he could see Anamosa's terrible anxiety.

"You will be safe with me," Juniata tried to assure her, holding out her arms in welcome.

"No, Mama! *No*," Anamosa pleaded. She wrapped her arms around one of Okeanneh's legs.

Henri came forward and stooped next to her. "Anamosa?" He touched her shoulder gently.

Anamosa turned her teary, red eyes to Henri.

"I will take care of you," he told her.

For a moment, Anamosa looked at Henri, saw his smile, his open arms.

To Okeanneh's surprise, Anamosa let go of her leg and slipped her arms around Henri's neck. The little girl placed her head on his shoulder.

Other than Philippe and Pierre, Okeanneh would have stuck a knife in any white man who dared take hold of her daughter. But now there was Henri, too. She watched Anamosa gather comfort in Henri's arms. It was the second time Philippe's son had come to Anamosa's aid.

He would trade his life for her, she realized.

Okeanneh smoothed Anamosa hair. "You see, Henri will be with you."

"Ahh-ree," Anamosa said, correcting her mother.

Okeanneh smiled. "Ahh-ree," she repeated and put her arms around Henri and Anamosa to hug them both tightly.

"I will be back in two moons," she whispered to Henri.

Anamosa began sobbing again.

Okeanneh stood and, in a smooth movement, lifted and shrugged the heavy backpack across her shoulders. It contained almost a hundred pounds of supplies, weapons, and clothing. In case she found Philippe without food or weapons, she had packed enough for them both.

Henri stood holding Anamosa in his arms. Okeanneh looked longingly at her daughter.

"She will be safe with us," Juniata said. "Go find your husband."

Okeanneh moved close and rubbed her nose on Henri's cheek. "You are holding my heart," she said, looking into his eyes.

"I know." Henri's eyes shone. "Tell my father…tell him, I am well."

As sunset approached, the Erigh elders prepared the sweat lodge for use. Juniata and the other women began stoking the fire to heat the stones.

Chittaqua held his arms toward the full moon beginning to rise above the horizon.

"The moon spirit rises. Tonight, I will call to the ghosts of our ancestors."

Chittaqua ducked into his lodge to prepare for the ceremony. This particular naming ritual had not been performed in many seasons.

Henri waited nervously with Chesanin and Achipan.

"He said we become warriors tonight!" Chesanin told Henri.

"What will happen?"

"You will see," said Achipan. "We will become as brothers."

"We will be painted and dance," Chesanin added. "And receive our totems!"

Receive totems? That sounded sinister, but if Chesanin and Achipan could do it, Henri decided he could too.

Twilight colors merged as darkness overtook the shadows cast by the trees and lodges. The evening air was cool on the skin. The moon was not quite full, but bright enough to allow the boys to discern the small animal carvings on the wooden poles that had been placed near the entrance to the sweat lodge.

When the last reds of sunset faded to dark purple, Chittaqua emerged from the darkness. His body was painted black with white stripes, creating a skeletal image. The sockets of his eyes were painted red. Bone ornaments hung from his ears, wrists, waist, and ankles. When he moved through the crowd, people heard snicks, clacks, and rattles. In his left hand, he carried a skull. The top had been removed and inside burned a small flame feeding on animal fat and hair. He held the talons of an eagle in his right hand.

When the shaman stopped, he raised his arms, turning to briefly face each of the four directions, and began chanting in a loud, deep monotone.

Henri glanced nervously at the twins. They claimed to have seen the ceremony only once and had told Henri what little they remembered, what to expect. Like them, Henri had removed all of his clothing except for a loincloth. The shaman's sons seemed proud, undaunted, so he did his best to keep his apprehension hidden.

At seeing the pile of bonfire logs and other preparations made by the Erigh, curious villagers started to gather from every part of the huge encampment. Word was spreading, something important was happening. Chittaqua, the Andrototekan, may be making predictions.

The shaman lifted and tied back the skin on the sweat lodge door then approached the three boys solemnly. He pointed at them and pointed toward the entrance.

The boys entered one at a time, with Henri in the middle. The women had moved hot stones into the fire trench minutes before, and the interior already smelled hot and dry, like a cooking hearth. There was a small ceremonial fire in the center, barely enough to give light, a small pile of dry wood sat to one side. Moonlight beamed through the flue hole above their heads. A wisp of smoke rising from the fire moved sinuously in the moonlight. The shaman positioned his face to catch the shaft of silver blue light.

Chittaqua pointed to where each boy should sit until they were arranged in a square. He set the skull of the mountain lion in front of his crossed legs. A tiny flame guttered at the bottom of the skull, enough to make the eye sockets glow in the darkened lodge.

For Henri's sake, Chittaqua decided to speak in French as much as possible, except for the more important ceremonial words, which had no equal translation.

"Prepare your hearts," he whispered. He withdrew several items from the medicine bag lying at his side.

Chittaqua handed each boy a folded edible leaf. In the center of each, he'd placed a tiny pinch of a pale fungus he had carefully measured out earlier. The shaman placed the leaf in his mouth and chewed slowly, bidding the boys follow his example.

Outside, a single drum began thumping.

In a few minutes, Henri began to feel dizzy. His heart started pounding. He glanced at Chesanin and Achipan. They remained motionless and composed.

More drums joined the first in a steady beat.

To Henri, everything suddenly seemed to be moving slower. The flame in the skull swayed back and forth. Its yellow-brownish color darkened to a rich orange. In contrast, the skull became whiter and glistened in the moonlight coming through the smoke hole. Chittaqua's body was outlined in a purple aura. Each time the shaman's hands moved, tiny sparks of light seemed to shoot from his fingertips. Henri looked up. A rainbow of colors played off the smoke swirling above his head.

From the looks of wonder on the boys' faces, Chittaqua could tell the medicine was working. Joined by reed whistles, the drumbeats became louder.

"The spirits of our fathers are among us," Chittaqua declared in a hushed voice. "Stand and receive your guide, your totem."

Chittaqua took bowls of red, blue, and yellow pigment. With his fingers, he painted the totem symbols on the chest and arms of each boy.

"Chesanin, you have the joy and courage of a hunter. Receive the spirit of the lion.

"Achipan, you are to learn the holy ways. A shaman's totem comes from the sky. Receive the hawk."

Turning to Henri, he was certain the wolf was the proper selection. But together, they had conquered the bear. He felt the boy should receive that sign as well.

"Henri, you have the wisdom and courage of the wolf and the strength of the bear. Together, they shall walk beside you."

Chittaqua painted the sign of the wolf over Henri's heart, and the symbol for the bear on each of his shoulders. The greasy pigments felt warm on Henri's skin. Paint dribbled down to his wrists and legs.

Behind the boys, long sticks clattered in the fire trench as the cooler stones were removed to be replaced by hissing new ones.

The shaman spoke slowly, looking from one boy to the next.

"Hear the words of the ancient ones. Heed their message. Use the strength of your totems to call upon them. Take strength from the ghosts who dance among us."

The shaft of moonlight shifted. The shaman was bathed in a gentle patina of silver light. An eerie quiet descended.

The strong medicine had a lesser effect on the shaman than it had on the boys, but he was not completely immune to the illusions it induced: images in the smoke, the sweet smells of flowers, animal sounds, the bitter taste of roots. He would usually explain to those being initiated they were only signs of a particular spirit totem, the way they sometimes speak.

But that night something would occur that he'd never seen before.

Chittaqua watched as another burst of tiny orange embers rose from the small fire and floated in gentle spirals toward the flue. Near the opening at the top, two embers appeared to stop and began to move together. They doubled in size, and doubled again, the orange tones taking a more reddish tinge.

Like eyes, Chittaqua thought. A foul smell descended. He glanced at the boys. They gazed straight ahead and seemed not to notice. The orbs dropped, spiraling slowly toward Henri. The shaman quickly placed the silver talisman in front of Henri.

The red-orange sparks paused, the light sputtered, then rose quickly again to disappear through the smoke-hole opening at the top of the sweat lodge.

The evil has marked Henri!

Chittaqua's breathing became labored.

As the medicine's influence began to wane, Chittaqua's agitation was eventually noticed by the boys, who looked at one another expectantly. The skull on the ground between them had lost its shimmering aura. In fact, all of the swirling colors above their heads had disappeared.

A gentle gust of wind blew beneath the deer hide covering the door. Henri shivered. Now he was cold. His skin puckered. The hot stones in the fire trench had also been withdrawn.

Chittaqua saw clarity return to their eyes. Chesanin and Achipan had not been touched, but Henri was now in greater danger.

The shaman spoke to them again.

"You are but a part of a greater spirit, a greater light. Your lives will rise like a wave to rush toward the shore before returning to the greater whole. You have little time to leave your mark on the sand, and only a few of us will travel so far. Embrace the trail blocked by fallen trees. It will lead you to new wonders. Swim against a river's strength, as only dying fish swim with the stream. Embrace your passions now, or your memories will be but sad shadows as the sun declines. Guard your heart as you would a child. Teach it not to hate, not even the white man, or your heart will become what you hate most. For we are all part of one tribe."

The shaman peered deeply into the eyes of each boy.

"Chesanin! The lion has accepted you. Learn the ways of the white man and become a great hunter among them. Your brother Henri will be your guide.

"Achipan! The hawk waits to lift your heart and eyes. Learn and remember the legends of your ancestors. Live among the shamans in the tribes beyond the lakes. Learn the prayers and the stories and return to teach the children.

"Henri! Your courage comes from the wolf, but your strength is from the bear. You are joined with two totems and two peoples. You will someday speak for both."

Chittaqua reached into his medicine bag and took out his spirit cloak, spreading it between them. He placed the wood and silver talismans in the center. Then he took the eagle talon and used its sharp point to reopen a small cut on his palm, the one he had made with the Picture Maker the night before. He repeated this action on the palms of each boy and had them lay their hands on top of his. Drops of blood dribbled over the edges of their palms to fall onto the objects.

And it was done.

"You are all my sons. You are brothers."

Chittaqua lifted his eyes toward the moonlight then began another prayer in the French tongue, looking back and forth from Henri, to Achipan, to Chesanin as he spoke.

"As I might have been,
All I could be or desire,
In my legends or my failures,
From my passions or my angers,
In the whispers of my life or my secrets,
What was to be said or experienced,
The things left undone or now will never be,
Now, all that remains as a reminder
Are you."

Chittaqua squeezed the boys' hands.

"My meaning goes forward with you or ends forever!
Journey together, my sons,
Wonder at the spirit lights,
Seek your passion, teach,

And remember."

He placed his bloody palm against the forehead of each boy.

"You forever share a common spirit and destiny. Rise. Go before your people and shout your name."

It was the first time Chittaqua had asked any of them to speak since entering the sweat lodge. They emerged from the lodge one by one.

"I am Chesanin, the Lion!"

"I am Achipan, the Hawk!"

"I am Henri, the Wolf-Bear!"

The Andrototekan came last.

A sudden tingling swept over Henri's body. He indeed felt changed, different, and proud.

"Walk as warriors among your clan," Chittaqua shouted, so everyone outside the lodge would hear.

The three painted and blood-spattered boys were greeted by hooting and shouts of joy. The tempo and strength of the drums and whistles intensified. The bonfire was fed more wood to burn. There were few pleasant diversions amid the sickness and starvation of the vast, muddled encampment. The morose inhabitants were drawn to the resonant thumping of drums and the exciting flames, compelled to join the Erigh, to take part in the dancing. Hundreds of people from a dozen different tribes, half-breeds, some *coureurs de bois,* and even a few soldiers found joy in the celebration of youth-become-man. The festivity around the huge center fire lasted until the moon reached its zenith.

Henri was now an Erigh warrior. These were his people, his bothers.

Holding the smiling Anamosa in his arms he danced, spun, and howled until he dropped from exhaustion. He'd never been so happy in his life.

Chittaqua slipped away to his own lodge. With Juniata's help, he washed away the paint and sweat. The Erigh tribe's time at the fort had come to an end. He would lead his people from this place. There was no reason to stay. He no longer carried the burden from the island of stones. The evil spirit now belonged to Picture Maker. This was a white man's curse, a white man's demon. Only a white man could defeat it…or, in ignorance, be consumed by it.

Now that Henri had been marked, it became more important Snow Hair seek Picture Maker to learn the secret of the curse. For now, Chittaqua would find a way to protect Snow Hair's son. His sleep was restless that night.

At first light the next morning, the Erigh shaman called his people to assemble and announced they would be leaving the fort to find a new permanent home in the sunset lands. They would build a new village near the lake of the Michigan and Ottawa. Joyous hooting began. Such was their happiness and anxiousness to leave, the Erigh broke camp immediately. Before midday, the last remaining survivors of the Erigh nation left Fort Niagara.

They would never return.

Henri Gerrard also left the fort to walk with his tribe, undecided about which path he should follow. Once they reached the Niagara portage, he hesitated and looked to the right, up the road leading toward Fort Niagara. He could go with the Erigh, or he could stay at the fort. Chittaqua had made it clear, Henri, alone, must choose the path he would take from now on. Henri had spent fear-filled months trying to reach Fort Niagara. But, after all the trials he'd endured to get there, he strangely felt like an outsider. The fort did not feel like his home. The people there were little more than acquaintances. There, his only connection to his father was Okeanneh. And now she was gone too.

"Ahh-ree!"

Henri looked down into Anamosa's glorious blue eyes. He smiled as she held out her arms to him. He knelt.

"I still have Anamosa! And *you* are my favorite girl," Henri said, rubbing his nose on hers.

Anamosa giggled as he placed her on his shoulders.

Wolf-Bear turned away from the fort and walked with his people.

The remaining souls of the Erigh tribe completed the short and arduous journey from Fort Niagara to Fort Presque Isle in nine days. With Maltoc warring, Chittaqua allowed them little time to rest. As long as there was light enough to see, they marched. No one complained. Arriving at the Indian encampment at Fort Presque Isle, they found a confusion of tribes and clans, much like what they'd left behind at Fort Niagara, only smaller. Chittaqua ordered a temporary camp built on the westernmost edge. To the surprise of the Erigh, there was a small enclave of Seneca living in squalid hovels in the camp, survivors of Maltoc's village that had not gone to the Wolf clan. They consisted mostly of women and children. Many were sick, all were starving.

When the Erigh finished setting up their teepees, they gathered around their chief and shaman, eager to know his intentions. Chittaqua held up his arms.

"This night, when the moon is highest, we celebrate as People of the Panther."

Hoots of joy arose from the villagers. They had beaten the Seneca. They were free of the French. Their dignity was restored.

The Eagle clan of the Erigh stoked a massive celebration fire built from fifteen-foot-long tree trunks. The drums and singing heard that night carried far into the surrounding wilderness and to the walls of Fort Presque Isle. It was the war song of the People of the Panther, the only tribe of the lakes who had dared to attack the Iroquois and lived to celebrate their victory.

On the fort's walls, the French sentries listened apprehensively to the low, resounding drum beats and the repetitive chanting. As the fierce orange glow from the Pyrrhic fire reflected on their faces, they were reminded again this was not their land. The white man was an unwelcome stranger here, safe only as long as he stayed within the walls of his fort.

With joy and excitement, Henri Gerrard once again spun in circles and danced around the mesmerizing fire, hooting and shouting. Sitting atop his shoulders, Anamosa squealed with delight.

The Erigh camped for only two days by Fort Presque Isle, gathering food and other supplies for a longer, sustained journey to the west. Chittaqua knew it would be dangerous for them to stay much longer. Despite the nearness to Fort Presque Isle, other clans of Seneca might attack at any time. The further west the Erigh journeyed into tribal lands rival to the Iroquois, the more difficult it would be for the Seneca to follow. If they went far enough, the Seneca would not follow at all.

There were uncertain times ahead. Chittaqua's dreams were more vivid than ever. He was embodied in the white eagle almost every night now. And in his dreams, he had begun to see a woman in his destiny, a snow-haired woman. It seemed right this should be so. The woman appeared to him surrounded by an aura of light, purple, like the stone in his talisman. Good feelings emanated from her spirit, but he had the ominous perception he would never meet her. Who she was or what this vision portended he could not say. But he felt his part in these events was now rushing to a conclusion.

On the second night of encampment at Fort Presque Isle, Chittaqua called Henri and his sons together.

"Tomorrow each of you will follow a new path. Tomorrow, you walk as braves, equal in all matters. I will not travel with you," Chittaqua announced, surprising them all. "I must perform another task."

"What task?" Chesanin asked.

"I have a new path."

"Am I going with you?" Henri pressed.

"No."

"But the clan …?" Achipan protested.

Chittaqua raised his hands to quiet them. He looked from face to face, then spoke to them with passion.

"You are children of the light,
Your song rises with the sun.
When I sleep,
My dreams will be your dreams.
When the day warms my face,
I see the sun smiling on you.
I carry your songs in my heart,
And you will carry mine."

Chittaqua was awake before dawn, restless in his sleep as usual, less certain of the choices he'd made the day before. He left the teepee and walked around in the dark, gazed at the stars, prayed to the Great Spirit, while he asked and answered his own questions. Was he making the right decision to leave his people? The Erigh no longer needed the Andrototekan to go west. They would be safe now. Chittaqua had a different destiny.

At first light, the shaman began shouting at the tents, urging the Erigh to prepare for the march. It would only take an hour for the tribe to drop their lodge poles and convert the teepees into dragging trams. When the clan was ready, Chittaqua called his people together.

"People of the Panther, I have been your shaman for many seasons. But now I must walk another path and you must finish the journey without me to your new home."

Hoots of concern rose immediately.

"My people, the Erigh must dwell at our ancient home, by the lake of the Michigan, near the Ottawa people. You must not stop until you reach that place."

The shaman gestured for Achipan to stand in front of them.

"Achipan will speak as your shaman."

One of the elders spoke. "Chittaqua! Achipan is but a child! The Erigh are but a shadow of what we once were. But without *you*, we are not a people."

Chittaqua rebuked the man.

"*Ho*! Have you forgotten the trials you endured? Do the Erigh not stand here proud and free? Did we not dance with the panther under the moon in celebration? Is this the legendary bravery of the People of the Panther? We stood against the might of the Iroquois for uncounted winters! Do not the Seneca quake with fear when we dance with our ghosts? Ho! Chittaqua is not the Erigh! Chittaqua is a shaman. And this shaman tells the People of the Panther to heed his words. Journey without delay to a place where you can grow strong again while other tribes wither and die. Look around you. Open your eyes to the truth! This place belongs to the white man, now and *forever*!"

A morning that started out so happy had turned sad. The people tied the last of their belongings to the trams. The elders came to Chittaqua as a group, trying one last time to change his decision to stay behind. But the Andrototekan was resolved. With Chittaqua's farewell, one by one, the Erigh trams moved reluctantly toward the west, leaving drag marks behind them in the dirt.

"I do not feel worthy," Achipan said, standing before his father.

Chittaqua grasped Achipan's shoulders. "I was no older than you when I became a shaman. You are my son. It is *your* time now. Be strong for our people. They will come to respect you."

Achipan's eyes were wet.

"Speak my name to the shamans of the tribes on the grassy plains. There is one among them who knows me. When he hears my name spoken, he will come to find you, and teach you in the ways of the dance." He touched a finger to Achipan's forehead. "I will speak to you here, in your dreams." He touched a spot over the youth's heart. "And I will be with you here."

They embraced one another tightly.

"Now, be proud. Lead your people. Give them wise counsel. Never let them see your doubt or fear, and they *will* follow you."

Juniata wept. Achipan hugged his mother and Chesanin. He hesitated in front of Henri, and then embraced him too. Without looking back, he trotted off to reach the front of the procession.

Runners from various tribes ran to report on the westward march of the Erigh. In ten days, all the major councils would hear of it. They would also hear that Chittaqua, the Andrototekan, did not go with his people. He was staying behind for some unknown reason. And that concerned the councils even more.

The Erigh people were never heard from again. They would slowly fragment into smaller groups, intermarry, and merge with other tribes. Their winter songs would fade from memory.

Juniata, Chesanin, Henri, and Anamosa sadly watched the trams go by until the last family stopped to turn and wave before vanishing among the trees.

Henri put Anamosa up on his shoulders. Determined as he was, Henri was not going any further west. His glowing sense of kinship with the Erigh that had begun when leaving Fort Niagara had waned during the march. He'd become even more uneasy by the speed of all the changes made during the last few days. He'd found new friends and became part of a clan. Then, suddenly, his adopted people were gone. The optimism of yesterday was now replaced by a hollow, lonely feeling. Henri's thoughts turned to his mother, wondering again if she was alive. Not that he wanted to go back to Niagara. What he wanted, instead, was to go down the portage to Fort Le Boeuf, and if his father wasn't there, then on to Fort Machault.

Chittaqua saw the cheerless faces of the remainder of his family. "This camp by the fort will be a good place for us to live for now. We must build lodges amid the log cabins of the *coureurs de bois* and the other white men who live here."

Henri was confused. "Why are we staying here?"

"You will see. Others come to join us. They will be here soon. Chesanin, you must hunt for us. Henri, get us supplies from the trading post at the fort. They will not refuse you. Juniata, we need to build new lodges." He held up three fingers. "I will cut the saplings."

By the end of the day, Chesanin managed to find and kill another buck, to the surprise of Presque Isle's *coureurs de bois* who claimed the nearby forests had been hunted out and were devoid of any game. Henri returned from the fort, pushing a barrow full of food and supplies, as Chittaqua predicted, given to him freely by the clerk at the Dunemoore Company trading post, who was stunned at seeing Philippe's missing son. Juniata and Chittaqua erected the wooden framework for one new lodge and partially erected two others. Anamosa collected and stacked firewood. They had food, supplies, and after covering the completed framework with birch bark and hides, they had a place for everyone to sleep comfortably.

The next morning, Henri, Chesanin, Juniata, and Anamosa approached the emaciated Seneca at the camp center. An old woman screeched with recognition at seeing Henri and jumped up.

Henri greeted her glumly. "Oh, God! Tamaqua."

"You know her?" Chesanin asked with astonishment.

"Yes. Her name is Tamaqua," he replied with no enthusiasm. "She...I was given to her during my time with the Seneca."

"Two Totem, *aieee*," Tamaqua screeched. She tried to hug Henri. "Care for me! Two Totem must care for old Tamaqua!"

Henri held her unwanted affection at arm's length.

Chesanin was perplexed. "She was your enemy?"

"She was."

Tamaqua fell to her knees and started pleading.

"She asks you to take her into your lodge," Juniata interpreted. She watched Henri struggle with this idea.

Henri frowned and finally touched her shoulder. "Tamaqua. Come." To his irritation, Tamaqua kept trying to embrace him as he helped her to her feet.

When Chittaqua was told of what had occurred, he was pleased. "A good sign," he told Juniata.

"Did you hear what they call him?" Juniata asked. "*Two Totem*," she said. "He is guided by the wolf and bear. It is a fitting name, is it not?"

Soon, all the other Seneca stragglers moved over to the new camp. By the next morning, construction began on three more lodges and two log cabins to accommodate the Seneca. Chittaqua tended to the sickness of the Seneca women and children, most of which could be remedied with more food and bathing to get rid of the fleas and ticks.

When the lonely soldiers and idle *coureurs de bois* in the fort learned there were females without husbands in the expanding camp, they descended on it in a drove. The starving women had little choice and chose husbands quickly. Two army privates, an Ottawa trapper, four half-breed *coureurs de bois*, and a Huron scout comprised the new *elders*.

After a few more days, the burgeoning village became populated and more stable. Chittaqua knew it was time for him to leave. In his dreams, he saw the evil one who threatened Henri lingering near one of the French forts in the south. He planned to find this *thing* and kill it.

Juniata saw her husband begin filling his traveling pack and medicine bag as she'd seen him do so many times before. But more than any other time before, her heart was filled with foreboding.

"When will I see you again?"

"Not long from now. You *will* see me again," Chittaqua assured her.

They walked outside and found Henri standing by the main campfire fully dressed and packed for travel. Chesanin was with him. They were speaking to one another in hushed voices.

"Two Totem," Chittaqua called, deciding the given name of the people in the new village appropriate.

Henri had awakened early, determined to go with Chittaqua. He saw the question in the shaman's expression.

"I am going to Fort Le Boeuf."

Chittaqua had expected this. Henri was much like his father. "You must stay here."

"I am Wolf-Bear," Henri replied, his back straight, his bearing proud. "You've given me this name. And it is my will to go to Fort Le Boeuf."

If Henri left the camp, disaster would follow, the shaman sensed this strongly. He withdrew the silver amulet from his medicine bag and held it up.

"Wolf-Bear, by the promises of your father, I ask you to stay at this place to care for Juniata and Anamosa until I return."

Henri stiffened, his face turning sullen. "The promises should not be used for such a minor purpose," he replied.

Chittaqua's brow furrowed. "And yet it will be so. Your new path begins here."

Henri angrily shrugged off his backpack. "This is not right." Without saying more, he strode off toward the beach.

Chittaqua watched Henri proudly. "You see Chesanin, he has accepted his destiny."

Chesanin was doubtful. "I think he will follow you anyway."

"No, he will not dishonor his father. And he has much to accomplish for his people."

"I think Henri will be angry and sad."

"When his heart appears heavy, send Anamosa to him. She cheers his spirit with merely a smile. You will see. It is right for him to stay here." Chittaqua slipped on his pack.

"When will I see you again?"

"Maybe one moon. You also have a destiny. *You* must learn to read the white man's books and make the white man's marks."

Chesanin did not care about destinies, nor anything about the white man. His face grew long. "Father, when I see you next...will you be alive?"

Chittaqua took hold of his son's shoulders and spoke firmly.

"Yes."

Chapter 10
Piqua's Village
August 1754
"What will you trade for her?"

Michelle understood the serious dangers of this ailment: the fever, the delirium, and the vicious diarrhea. She had endured a bout shortly after arriving at the Seneca village. It had sapped her strength. But back then, she'd not been half starved. Back then she'd been stronger and recovered after a few days.

"I must go to the latrine," she gasped to one of her captors as darkness approached. She didn't wait for permission this time before running from the lodge.

When she returned, she tried to eat some soup but could manage only a few mouthfuls before collapsing. The shivering and the cramping in her stomach steadily worsened. She cradled a waterskin in her arms, rolled into a ball, and hoped for sleep.

Pierre Dunemoore said they are coming for me, Michelle tried to console herself. *Philippe is coming for me!*

The fat sisters considered the white woman a major annoyance. She was weak, whined constantly, ate too much, could only perform simple tasks, and was always mumbling in peculiar ways. Their irritation with her had only intensified after so many months. And they would have found a way to kill her long ago were it not for Piqua, who made it clear they were responsible for the white woman's health. So when Michelle became hot, sweaty, and delirious, babbling in her sleep during the night, the oldest sister decided to cover the shivering body with a buffalo robe. It did little to help. By morning, the white woman's breathing had become ragged and strained. They started to panic. Remembering Piqua's words of warning, they begged the tribal shaman to come and see her.

Ootego examined the feverish white woman, watching her struggle for

155

each breath. She was perspiring heavily and trembling beneath the skins. This was not good. He'd seen it before. If they did not stop the water from draining from her body, she would not live more than two days. He had some medicines that could expel the demon if her strength held out. But the Seneca medicine man now wished he'd not seen her at all. Now Piqua would blame him if she died.

"The white spirit is weaker than ours," Ootego told the women as he crushed some strong smelling leaves and roots together in a bowl. "My medicine may not be strong enough to drive out the evil inside her. *You* must help her. Make a broth of these herbs. Add salt and make her drink it now, then again when the sun is highest, and again at night."

The shaman lifted the malodorous animal skins covering the white woman. His nose wrinkled. He frowned at the frail body he saw and looked at the fat sisters angrily.

"Clean her body of this foulness, and keep her clean! And make her eat! Or you will regret it!"

When eight white men appeared at the front gate of the Wolf clan palisade, a surprised Piqua charged out with over fifty of his braves. They shouted war cries and made threatening gestures with their weapons. It took discipline and assurances from Philippe and Pierre for their accompanying veteran woodsmen to remain calm in the face of this intimidation. The Seneca had an overwhelming advantage. The warriors surrounded the men and then looked to their chief for guidance.

Piqua was greatly disturbed by the unexpected appearance of *coureurs de bois* who had slipped by his scouts without being detected. If they could reach his village without being seen, what else might be lurking in the nearby forests? For days, Piqua had been plagued by nightmares of skeletal demons eating his flesh. Ootego had told the clan chief the bad dreams were an omen. White men would be coming to destroy the clan. Piqua found the shaman's interpretation unremarkable. Already, a multitude of soldiers were roaming the lands of the three rivers. Of what significance was a few more?

But when Piqua saw Snow Hair and Animal Scalp leading these white men, *that* was significant!

"You dare to approach my village like a war party? Are you my enemy?"

Piqua's agitation was genuine. Philippe tried to be cordial. "Two winters have passed since I visited the wise chief of the Wolf clan."

"I hear Snow Hair's name spoken at my campfire often. Many claim Snow Hair has done great evil to the Seneca."

"What evil does Piqua remember? You still wear the necklace I gave you in friendship."

The clan chief's hand went to his throat to touch the string of silver beads.

"Friend? Since when does a friend march with the soldiers and build a great fort at the three rivers? Who gave permission for such a fort?"

"I am not here to talk about the fort. Snow Hair has done no evil to Piqua or his clan, but it is a great evil Piqua has done to Snow Hair. You have a white woman in your camp. She is my *wife*! I am here to take her back."

Piqua quickly surveyed the men arrayed behind Snow Hair. They appeared relaxed. Most leaned on their muskets.

"Of what woman do you speak?" Piqua answered evasively, desiring to drive a hard bargain with much gain for his tribe.

"Ya' know who we're talking aboot. I've spoken with her."

The two pistols in Pierre Dunemoore's belt were cocked. He was ready to draw and fire. His rifle, also cocked, rested against his side. One arm draped across the great war ax lying on his shoulder. He was wearing the porcupine skin on his head. The shiny quills pointed in every direction, giving the appearance of a spiny toadstool. The Scotsman had painted a red stripe across the bridge of his nose and cheeks. He planned to give the impression that he was prepared for war. He called it his *medieval* face.

Piqua looked at Pierre skeptically. "When Animal Scalp stayed in my lodge, he also spoke of friendship. And now you wear paint?"

"I am Piqua's friend," Pierre replied. "But I am Snow Hair's friend too. And you have his woman. I saw her. I spoke with her," he repeated.

"I am here only to claim my wife," Philippe said in the Seneca tongue. "I have no quarrel with the Wolf clan."

"Yet it is a quarrel you provoke! Does Snow Hair think we are weak? That a handful"—he gestured with dismissal—"of *coureurs de bois* will frighten us?"

Captain Benoit dropped the cloak he'd been wearing and held up his sword. He was attired in full dress uniform. The polished saber in his right hand sparkled in the sunlight. At this signal, seven more men appeared along the tree line perimeter.

The Wolf clan braves hooted with alarm and raised their weapons at the unexpected appearance of more armed men.

Piqua's eyes darted wildly. The Seneca backed a few steps toward their gate. Piqua stood his ground.

"Easy lads," Pierre warned his men. "Rest your weapons."

"I am here to get my wife," Philippe reiterated loudly. "Only my wife!"

Piqua glared at Philippe. He did not like being threatened.

"You make demands? Are we women in your eyes, like the English? Do you expect us to cower?"

Captain Benoit raised his sword once more. Another fourteen men appeared. The perimeter grew smaller.

Piqua had not counted on a force of men so large, armed with muskets and pistols. He recalled the story of the attack on Maltoc. Thunder guns were used. Piqua knew many of his people would die if there was such a battle. He had only desired to rile Snow Hair before agreeing to an advantageous trade, but now, to save face, he must refuse to be intimidated. He raised his English musket. It was a signal. The Seneca braves aimed their bows and muskets at the forest and the eight men standing before their gate.

"*Chief* Piqua," the woodsman implored. "Let us make a trade for the woman!"

The clan chief detected desperation in Snow Hair's voice. *Good.* He sneered. "Maybe your woman is already dead. Maybe by my knife."

"Piqua of the Wolf clan!" Captain Benoit raised his voice. "If there is to be a war with the Seneca, the French soldiers at the three rivers will march here with thunder guns and will destroy *your* village first."

"*Queee!*" the Wolf clan shaman whined. "The omen," he whispered.

Piqua had seen the destructive power of thunder guns. They could splinter the thickest tree trunks with one shot. And the French fort was only a few days' march from his village.

Was any woman worth this?

Piqua spoke quietly, and two braves hurried back inside the compound.

It was a standoff. "Any ideas, Pierre?" Philippe said in a low voice.

"Easy laddie. Piqua just sent two men inside. Maybe *he* has an idea."

Philippe was not prepared for the pitiful sight of Michelle being dragged outside the palisade. She seemed barely conscious. They dropped her like a pile of rags behind Piqua.

"Merciful God! Michelle!" Philippe moved to go to her. Pierre and Jean-Claude restrained him.

"Let me go!"

"Philippe! Wait!" Pierre said urgently. "He's brought her out for a reason!"

Piqua appeared impressed by Snow Hair's reaction. *The woman has great value indeed.*

Piqua got down to business. "What will you trade for her?"

Pierre and Captain Benoit knew Piqua would demand a high price. Pierre looked at his magnificent war ax with the purple jewel in its head. Captain Benoit considered offering the beautifully engraved saber his father had carried in war and presented to him some twenty years earlier.

But neither man could match Philippe's offer.

"Me!" Philippe shouted. "Take me in trade for her." He set down his musket.

"Dinnah' be daft," Pierre roared. "Ya'll end up gettin' killed, or *worse*."

Philippe turned to his partner while he stripped off his weapons. "Take her away from here, Pierre," he said. "Get her to safety first, then come back for me."

"Philippe, I cannot bring troops back here a second time," Captain Benoit said quickly. "Don't be crazy. Let's bargain for something else!"

"Philippe! We may nah' be able tah' get back here in time tah' save ya'!"

Ten years of trading had taught Philippe valuable lessons. "Piqua knows she has great value to me. Can't you see she's sick? By the time we have returned with all the goods he'll demand, she'll be dead. Let Piqua name his price. He can keep me hostage until you bring back the goods."

Philippe patted down his body, turning anything of value over to Pierre. He noticed his ring. "Here, save this for me too."

While Pierre and Captain Benoit shouted for him to stop, the *coureur de bois* approached the stunned Seneca chief.

"Me," Philippe said, pointing at his chest, "for her." He pointed at Michelle. "Then you can bargain with Animal Scalp for me."

Piqua could not believe his good fortune. Animal Scalp would give him whatever he asked for Snow Hair. And Piqua intended to ask for a lot. The clan chief flashed his hands five times.

"Five hands of muskets," he said. It would be enough to equip all of his braves. He knew the right words. "And powder horns and shot."

Philippe and Pierre knew there were no muskets available in such quantities anywhere. And even if there were, the army would never allow the Seneca to be given such a quantity of arms.

"Agreed," Philippe said. He looked back at Pierre. "Pierre?"

The Scotsman nodded, knowing it was a lie. "Agreed."

As Philippe predicted, Piqua nodded in agreement and ordered his braves to stand clear of the captive.

Philippe quickly lifted Michelle gently in his arms. He kissed her forehead.

"Michelle? It's me! It's Philippe!" She felt light as a feather. Her skin was hot. "Oh, God, what have they done to you?"

He watched her eyes flicker and roll about uncontrollably. The pupils did not focus. She mumbled gibberish.

Philippe carried her to Pierre. "She needs a doctor."

Pierre gently took the fragile form in his arms. Philippe was right. She would be dead in a day if they didn't take her with them right now.

"I will take her tah' the forts," Pierre assured him.

Captain Benoit could not believe this bargain had been made. Colonel Contrecoeur would never agree to the muskets. And he did not expect Philippe to survive for long if they left him here.

"Philippe!" Benoit said urgently. "We've got her now. Let's make a run for it. My men are ready to fight."

Philippe's expression was odd, as if things were now as they should be.

"No fighting, Captain. I'll not chance her getting hurt anymore. This is the best way. Just make sure Michelle lives. Get out of here now, before Piqua changes his mind."

"You stay alive, laddie." Pierre was grim, his eyes moist. "I'll be comin' back for ya'."

Philippe smiled. "I know. Bring something valuable to trade for me." But they both knew next time, there would be no trading. Philippe embraced his friend, being careful not to disturb Michelle. "Now go! Go!"

The semicircle of soldiers dressed like woodsmen formed up behind Pierre as he carried Michelle back out the way they came. The Seneca braves hooted loudly as they surrounded Philippe. Captain Benoit was the last to leave. He watched them tie Philippe's hands behind his back and loop a rope around his neck. The *coureur de bois* was shoved and pulled into the interior of the palisade amid the celebration of the Seneca.

"*Adieu, mon ami.*"

Captain Benoit wrapped his cloak around his dress uniform and followed his men.

Pierre Dunemoore led the party in retreat to the northeast. They stopped only long enough to make a stretcher for Michelle. After six hours of fast marching, they rested for a short time.

"She's not getting any better," said Louie Hawkfeeder, worry evident on his face. A large man, a Dunemoore Company *coureur de bois*, he and Michel Langlois had accompanied Philippe to France on his mission to bring Michelle and her son to New France.

Pierre felt her forehead and nodded. "Well…at least she is nah gettin' any worse. She's still with us."

Michel Langlois mixed up a solution of salt and herbs he carried in a pouch. They made her drink that and as much water as she would take.

"She'll likely shit tha' out within an hour. But we'll just give her more."

"I should have brought a surgeon with us," Captain Benoit rued. "There are two surgeons at Fort Duquesne and another at Fort Le Boeuf tending to the wounded from the Seneca attack."

Pierre was definitely *not* going south. Fort Machault was closest, but she needed care from a real doctor.

"Then we'll take her tah' Fort Le Boeuf."

Captain Benoit looked doubtful. "Pierre, I can only take my men as far as Fort Machault without new orders from Colonel Contrecoeur. Can she bear the extra journey to Fort Le Boeuf?"

"Well, it's mostly by canoe," Pierre replied.

"I'll carry her all the way by myself if I have to," Louie Hawkfeeder vowed.

Michelle moved between different worlds of consciousness: flashes of strange faces, floating sensations of water, the smell of green things, and hallucinations. One moment, she saw Philippe's face and tried to warn him of the danger. She heard the terrifying screams of the savages. When she woke up, screaming from these nightmares, she was surprised to find herself in a canoe. Awakening another time, she was floating in the air surrounded by huge trees. Other times, she found herself carried in the arms of a gentle, bearded giant, who spoke comforting words to her like a father would. Then there was a man who fed her warm soup while cradling her head in his arms. Occasionally, she experienced the warmth of a fire. Each time, she struggled to remain awake, but the fever would rage and she would sweat and slip again into delirium.

Pierre and the *coureurs de bois* did everything they could to make the travel easier on Michelle. When she cried out in her sleep they would stay awake the rest of the night to hold her hand or cradle her in their arms.

Three days passed before they reached Fort Machault. They said good-bye to Captain Benoit and his men, loaded more supplies on company bateaux, and continued up the Rivière aux Boeufs.

To their relief, Sister Michelle's fevered delirium subsided one day north of Fort Machault. But she still slept most of the time and was extremely weak. It was taking too long for the canoes to stay together and to make camp. Pierre decided they could move faster as a smaller group. He chose Louie Hawkfeeder and Michel Langlois and one other man to continue with him to Fort Le Boeuf.

"It will be faster this way. The rest of you return to Fort Machault," Pierre told his *coureurs de bois*. "We'll collect you when we come back to get Philippe."

Pierre continued north with the smaller group. With each passing hour, Michelle appeared more lucid. Then, finally, she spoke a full sentence in a hoarse voice.

"Where am I?"

"Oho! Mademoiselle, remember me? Pierre Dunemoore? We've brought ya' out of the Seneca village. We're on our way to a fort."

The Scotsman signaled for the two canoes to make shore, deciding to camp, feed her, and answer her questions.

"Where's Philippe?"

"Philippe is…behind us," Pierre said guardedly. "But he'll be along soon. We'll camp for a while and eat."

CHAPTER 11
FORT LE BOEUF
AUGUST 1754
The Jesuit Coureur de Bois

Helmut Colbért arrived at Fort Le Boeuf one week after the Seneca attack with the relief company sent by Major Péan. Roaming among the wounded, it did not take long to learn Philippe Gerrard had been there during the attack, and that the *coureur de bois* scout had gone further south. The assassin went out to the river and gazed with frustration at the silent, moving water. Each mile deeper into the wilderness, the realization that he was completely out of his element became stronger. To kill Philippe Gerrard, or any of the others, he would almost need them to walk up and introduce themselves. If he took five steps beyond the tree line in any direction he would be lost; a fact amply demonstrated the last time he relieved his bowels along the portage road. Colbért found he had no idea what direction to take to get back to the column. If it weren't for a soldier firing his musket at some furry creature running across the road, he'd still be wandering around out there. He was ready to go back to Fort Presque Isle, except the voice of his dreams told him to remain.

She is coming to you, it whispered.

And so Helmut Colbért introduced himself to yet another commandant, Captain Prideaux, who assigned a tent to the aristocrat. Colbért had begun another wait, which had now lasted more than two weeks.

This place is worse than being in jail, Helmut thought. *At least in a Parisian jail, I could kill someone for sport.*

Once the gore and damage of the battle had been cleaned up, the commandant had allowed Colbért to move into the officer's quarters. Most of the officers shunned him. But Helmut didn't care. He was now an *aristocrat*, and they were commoners.

What the assassin found unbearable was the boredom, but the dream voice whispered patience. Colbért knew how to be patient. As an assassin, he'd a lot of practice being patient. So, night after night, he would linger among the soldiers and traveling *voyageurs* and listen to them talk about the latest dispatches from the other forts. One night, it was rumored the sentries were stewing some beef. Colbért hoped to eat something different from the monotonous dried meat, mashed roots, or river fish. The rainy night also brought two wet and tired *voyageurs* to the sentry tent to eat. They carried salt with them from a lick in the south. Colbért hung back in the shadows and listened to the news on the road.

For a while it was idle gossip, exaggerations, rumors of skirmishes. Colbért had heard it all before. But when the *voyageurs* began to speak of a rescued white woman, he paid close attention, his fingers unconsciously moving to stroke his mustache.

"They were camped north of Fort Machault and heading upriver. We stopped to see if they needed our help. They intended to wait another day for the woman to get stronger. And she looked real sick, I can tell you. No telling what the Seneca did to her. They say she'd been a captive since April."

"What was her name?" a voice spoke from the shadows of the tent.

The *voyageur* shivered as if something nasty had crawled across his neck. He squinted to see who had asked the question, but the tent was too dark.

"Remarkably, she was a nun. They called her *Sister* Michelle," he answered. "Why?"

A strange guttural sound came in response.

"Are you all right, Monsieur?"

"I'm fine." Colbért left the tent and marched off to his quarters, his hunger forgotten.

The assassin threw himself on his cot and debated what to do. The commandant had been given orders by Colonel Contrecoeur that *Shérif* Gaspard de Propei was not permitted travel, period. Certainly not to the south. Helmut Colbért could easily get around that. There were plenty of woodsmen to bribe. He simply couldn't decide where to go. And his night visitor had told him to wait.

She is coming! it had whispered.

Is this what his dreams meant? That the nun, this Sister Michelle, was coming here to this fort? If so, there was no need to travel farther south. And if he found a way to kill her, the woodsman would come after him for revenge. Major Péan's suggestion he retreat to Montréal now had more merit than he first realized.

The assassin had failed to notice the glaring eyes of an Indian woman sitting across the fire from him in the sentry tent. For a few days now, Okeanneh had heard men speak the name of the white man who sought her husband, the same man Father Beauharnois had warned her of. Now she could see him and was close enough to kill him.

At first light the next morning, before the sun was up, Colbért headed toward the *voyageurs'* camp to find how many days it would take for Sister Michelle to reach Fort Le Boeuf. As he walked across the marshalling yard toward the supply tents, he heard a woman scream. Colbért turned in time to avoid the vicious swing of a tomahawk at his head by an Indian woman.

The assassin spun to the right, instinct and reflexes taking over. A stiletto dropped into his hand. The angry woman recovered and attacked him again, but this time Colbért was ready. He easily parried the swing of her tomahawk and slammed the blunt, pointed hilt of his knife into the side of her skull with a loud crack. The Indian woman instantly collapsed to the ground, unconscious. Colbért desired to kill, but first he wanted to find out why she had attacked him.

A few soldiers and *coureurs de bois* gathered quickly, asking questions about what happened.

"She attacked me without provocation," Colbért declared. "You all saw this. Does anyone know why she would do that?"

"Maybe she's in love with you," someone joked.

"Did you forget to pay her?"

"Who is she?" asked a soldier.

They turned the body over.

One of the *coureurs de bois* examined her closely. "That's Okeanneh!"

"Who?"

"Okeanneh! That's Philippe Gerrard's wife. What the hell is she doing here?"

Colbért's eyes widened. "Philippe Gerrard's *wife*?"

"That's her all right."

The Night Butcher gazed avidly at the unconscious woman. His mind working, spinning, plotting what to do next. He couldn't kill her now. The commandant might arrest him, or, more likely, it would provoke an attack by the other woodsmen and soldiers who knew her. But it was obvious she knew who he was. It meant others might be lurking nearby, waiting to attack. They would know him, but Colbért would not know any of them. It was now too dangerous to wait at the fort for the nun. But if Philippe Gerrard came here, they would both be here at the same time. Then again, he still did not want to fight him here, among the woodsman's allies.

I must get him to come after me. Colbért wondered if hurting the man's wife was enough.

"Somebody call the surgeon," a soldier said. "She's not moving at all."

Acting on impulse, Colbért pushed the soldier out of the way and cut open the front of Okeanneh's leather dress with his stiletto, exposing her breasts. Intentionally laughing loudly, Colbért opened the front of his pants and started urinating on the woman's face and chest.

"What the fuck are you doing?" the soldier screamed and pushed Colbért back violently.

"She's a whore, and she tried to kill me!"

Colbért disarmed the man with one hand and threw him sideways to the ground with the other. He finished urinating on Okeanneh then kicked her hard in the side. He heard the sound of a bone cracking. Two howling *coureurs de bois* sprang forward to tackle him to the ground. He sidestepped them easily. Knives flashed out. Colbért could have killed them both in seconds, but he restrained himself. They would serve him better alive and angry.

"What happened here?" Captain Prideaux shouted as he arrived on the scene.

The soldiers quickly explained.

"Okeanneh!" The officer was appalled and knelt by the prostrate figure. "You attacked and *urinated* on Okeanneh?"

"She attacked me first for no reason. Ask any of them," Colbért responded, smugly. "She's a primitive whore, unworthy to suck my cock."

Angry voices rose in unison.

"Kill him," stated one *coureur de bois*.

"No!" Prideaux shouted. "There will be no killing here!"

The surgeon arrived.

"Take her to my quarters, attend to her wounds, and clean her up," he ordered. "Give her my bed." Captain Prideaux turned to Colbért with an expression of angry disgust on his face. "He will kill you for this."

"Who?"

"Philippe Gerrard…Okeanneh's husband."

Colbért snorted derisively. "From what I've seen of these pathetic woodsmen, I expect he won't fight much better than *she* did."

"You won't even hear him coming." This from an angry *coureur de bois*.

"Oh, no! Oh, my! Who will save me?" Colbért feigned distress in a girlish voice. "I must retire to Fort Presque Isle for my safety. Is that what you advise, Commandant?"

Captain Prideaux didn't answer. He spit on the ground and turned to follow the surgeon.

Colbért moved quickly now, almost running to his quarters to collect his pack. *She* was the woman the night visitor had spoken about. Not the nun. The coincidence was perfect. He had attacked and defiled the *coureur de bois'* wife. Publicly insulted her. And the woodsman would pursue Colbért back to France, if necessary, to get his revenge.

"Except, I will leave you a trail of crumbs to follow and wait for you in Montréal," he whispered sanguinely to himself.

When packed, he went outside the fort to the *voyageurs'* camp.

"I need two guides to escort me to Fort Presque Isle," he announced loudly. "I will pay the men in silver." He shook his coin purse. "But we must leave now."

Colbért selected two of the three men who had volunteered. Once they were alone, he gave them each twenty silver livres and watched their eyes bulge.

"I will double this amount if you get me there quickly."

About an hour north of Fort Le Boeuf, Colbért halted his guides.

"Our destination has changed. I want to go to Fort Niagara. I do not want to travel the portage roads. I want a direct path through the forests—a faster route. Do you know a way?"

The guides looked at one another and then back to Colbért. They knew exactly the path to take. It was a direct and simple route, but more difficult. And following this particular Indian hunting trail could be dangerous. The Seneca, Mohawk, and Oneida tribes used them routinely.

The older one, face marked with smallpox scars, spoke first. "Yes, there is such a trail. But you only paid us to take you to Fort Presque Isle."

Helmut snorted. "And now I will *pay* you to take me to Fort Niagara."

"It is also more dangerous," said the younger pimply one, thinking this a clever way to get more money.

"How much will you pay?" added the older guide, calculating. He knew Colbért carried more coins. Getting him off the main portage could prove profitable.

Colbért almost laughed aloud. Their underlying intentions were so obvious. He decided to make the reward something ridiculous. "I will pay you each one golden Louis d'or. Once I reach Fort Niagara, of course."

The guides glanced at one another, each wondering if the *shérif* really carried so much money.

"I want a trail to Fort Niagara the army will not traverse." He listened to their reply with an ear practiced at detecting deceit.

"The trail begins just east of this portage and runs to the northeast for five or six days, if we travel fast. We'll have to cross some hills. The trail is heavily wooded, the path is worn, well-marked, but narrow. It eventually parallels the portage to the north. The army does not use it, though they are aware of it."

That they would likely encounter tribal scouts, the older guide didn't offer. He planned to kill Colbért at the first opportunity and blame it on the Indians, so it would not matter.

"Draw a map in the dirt for me."

The guide smiled, took up a stick and drew a crude map of the lakes, the forts, the portages, and the trails in relation to one another. "I am not a map maker," he cautioned, "so the distances from one place to another are not accurate."

Colbért knew his north from south. He was satisfied the trail existed, and understood the general position of the forts and lakes to where he stood now. He committed the roughly drawn image to memory. For now, it was all he needed to know.

"Very good. Lead the way."

The guides smiled slyly at one another as they shouldered their packs, elated at their good fortune. Both expected to be wealthy before sunset.

Chittaqua arrived at Fort Le Boeuf two days after Colbért departed.

The presence of evil that he sensed was so strong, his body trembled. He expected a confrontation and was not sure he was prepared to face it. His eyes glanced to the left and right as he crossed the open ground before the main gate.

It could be anyone, he thought, *and may have even taken the form of an animal.* That frightened him even more. To his relief, nothing happened.

Upon entering the fort, he greeted a *coureur de bois* he recognized and learned two disturbing pieces of information. A man had attacked and seriously injured Okeanneh.

"Okeanneh?"

"Yes. She's over there," the man pointed at the log building in the center of the marshalling yard that housed the fort's headquarters. The *coureur de bois* continued gravely. "Word's come up the Rivière aux Boeufs. Snow Hair is a captive of the Wolf clan Seneca."

He's found the white woman, Chittaqua thought. The shaman debated what to do. The premonition of evil did not intensify. *It is near, but it is not in this fort.*

Chittaqua walked toward the building pointed out by the *coureur de bois.* There was a guard near the door. The soldier was a veteran of the Seneca attack. He leveled his musket at the approaching Indian.

"Back away, you fucking turd!"

Hearing the guard's vehement insult, Captain Prideaux came out, expecting to see Gaspard de Propei. Recognizing Chittaqua, he severely reprimanded the guard and apologized to the shaman.

"Come in, come in. She's in my bed."

Inside, an army surgeon was moving around the room. His brow elevated in surprise at seeing the heavily tattooed medicine man.

"What's he doing here?"

"This is Chittaqua. He is a high shaman of the Erigh tribe. And he knows more about healing than any man I've ever met…and more than you, for certain," Captain Prideaux told the skeptical doctor. "Stand aside."

Chittaqua knelt next to the bed and drew back the covers. Okeanneh was naked. She was breathing evenly and seemed to be in a deep sleep.

The shaman detected the smell of urine and felt the bedding, but it was not wet.

"She is unclean," he told the officers.

"A man pissed on her. The same man who attacked her."

Chittaqua closed his eyes. *The evil one attacks and defiles her. Why?*

"Where is he?"

"He's gone…maybe to Fort Presque Isle."

Chittaqua knew that was not the case. He would have encountered him on the portage coming down. But this explained the diminishing strength of its presence. The evil one was slowly moving away from this place. But to where?

"What is he going to do?" the doctor asked. "*Sing?*"

The shaman started at Okeanneh's feet and moved his hands up her body, feeling the bones, watching her reaction when he touched certain places to see if she winced with pain. When he reached the huge purple bruise on her right side, he gently probed the area and found a lump where the bone was broken. He smelled her breath but detected no odor of blood. Reaching her head, he found a large lump on the back left side. The skin was split from the swelling, but the bleeding was minimal. The lump was in a bad place. This was not good.

It is this wound that keeps her asleep, he thought. Demons that enter the head were always the most difficult to treat. They hid behind the skull bone. If she could not be awakened, Okeanneh might die of starvation. He'd seen it before; warriors clubbed senseless in battle, a horse-kick to the head, a fall from a high place. Unable to eat or drink, the person would wither away and stop breathing.

Using his thumb and forefinger, Chittaqua pushed open an eyelid and saw the pupil contract. That was good. Okeanneh's spirit fights. The demon had not taken her mind completely. He pulled the cover back over her nakedness and stood.

He asked the white shaman what medicines had been tried, if any.

Defensive and embarrassed, the surgeon shot a glance at Captain Prideaux. "I gave her water and kept her warm. She's mindless from the bash to her head. There's little else I could do. And I've not been touching her body if that's what you think," he added guiltily.

Chittaqua stared at the man for a few moments before speaking to the captain. "We must awaken her, or she will die."

"What do you suggest? Shall we shout at her?"

"I have medicines," the shaman told the captain, ignoring the surgeon.

"They are strong, but can cast out the demon in her head."

"Demon in her head," the surgeon repeated, indignant. "What's this fucking savage planning? A fucking exorcism?"

Captain Prideaux faced the surgeon and spoke tersely.

"You may leave, Doctor."

"*Leave?*"

"Yes. Now!"

"As you wish, *Captain.*"

The surgeon left the room and slammed the door behind him.

Prideaux looked at Chittaqua. "What can I do to help?"

"I will need hot water to brew a potion."

Prideaux retrieved a teapot full of warm water from the stove in the mess kitchen.

Chittaqua searched through his medicine bag and found the pouch of the herbs he wanted. He emptied half the simmering water into the teapot, crumbled the herbs in his palms above the water, and stirred the mixture thoroughly with his fingers. He poured some in a tin mug and returned to the bedside.

Together, they propped Okeanneh halfway to a sitting position. Chittaqua wet a cloth and squeezed small amounts of the brew into her mouth, so she would not choke, and continued until it was gone.

"How long?" Prideaux asked.

"Not long."

Prideaux looked down at the beautiful woman, feeling responsible for her injury, angry he'd not protected her. "Philippe will track him down and kill him," he said grimly. "And I'll help him. But I doubt Gaspard de Propei will tarry for long out here."

Hearing Prideaux's comment, Chittaqua lifted his head sharply. *That's why! The evil one goes somewhere to set a trap. It knows Snow Hair will follow.*

Thinking Chittaqua was angered, Prideaux continued. "I will send a dispatch rider to Commandant Pouchot, informing him what has happened here. And I will have guards placed around her until Philippe or Pierre return."

Chittaqua left Fort Le Boeuf after Okeanneh had awakened. She was in great pain and could not sit up without fainting from dizziness. She gestured much of what she saw was blurry. Chittaqua knew others had experienced the same after a head injury. Most times, the blurriness went away after a day or two. But it was possible the pain and dizziness Okeanneh felt could last much longer, maybe forever. It was hard to predict. What worried Chittaqua more was Okeanneh's inability to talk. She could only communicate by signing. The demon had stolen Okeanneh's voice, and the shaman was unsure how to get it back. But she was awake and comfortable, and the soldier captain had promised to care for her. It was all he could do.

Claude Guillot found Monseigneur Antoine Beauharnois inside the fort hospital examining soldiers sick with fever. He waited by the door, holding his hat in hand respectfully. The priest eventually noticed the Dunemoore Company clerk waiting for him. Claude pointed to the door, then he left to wait for the priest outside, and far enough away so no one could overhear them.

Father Antoine appeared a few minutes later. "What may I do for you, Claude, medicine or absolution?"

"A dispatch rider just brought a message from our company furrier at Fort Presque Isle. Sister Michelle was carried into Fort Le Boeuf by Pierre Dunemoore. She is very sick and was placed in the fort's headquarters by Captain Prideaux. The rider is probably delivering that same dispatch to the commandant as we speak."

Alarmed, the monsignor immediately turned to run toward the stone castle.

"Wait, Father! There's more!"

"What?!"

"Our man at Fort Le Boeuf sent a message also saying that Okeanneh tried to kill Gaspard de Propei. The attack failed and he clubbed her unconscious."

"*What?*" Father Beauharnois felt sick. This meant Okeanneh, Michelle, and this potential killer were all together at Fort Le Boeuf. "What about Philippe?"

"It's said that he traded himself to the Seneca for Michelle's release. After leaving Michelle at the fort, Pierre Dunemoore took some of our men and left to go back and get Philippe released."

For the last two months, Captain Pouchot had suddenly become the central point of information for logistics, complaints, and questions regarding this enormous campaign. He was supposed to oversee the construction of Fort Niagara's new battlements. Those had been his specific orders. Now Governor Duquesne was sending a constant stream of missives wanting to know about the Seneca attack on Fort Le Boeuf, to which Pouchot wanted to give him a succinct answer: *Ask Colonel Contrecoeur*. Why had thirty-one men succumbed to dysentery at Fort Presque Isle? *Ask Colonel Contrecoeur.* What was the condition of the battlements at Fort Machault? *Ask Colonel Contrecoeur.* Except one did not reply in that way to the Governor-General of New France.

Then came the most astonishing missive from Colonel Contrecoeur, asking Captain Pouchot to send ten of his construction artisans, with one man in charge, to Fort Presque Isle. From that fort they were to gather an additional ten men…*voyageurs, coureurs de bois, Indians, I do not care who, pay them what you have to*…the missive had said. *And proceed to the Seneca village that was recently attacked by the Erigh and help rebuild the palisade and as many of the native lodges, but no less than twenty-five, as can be done in thirty days before returning to Niagara.* The colonel went on to explain this agreement was reached with the Mohawk-Seneca council, to obtain its pardon for the misuse of French cannon in obliterating a Seneca village. In return, the council would acknowledge not a single French soldier had been involved in the attack and the French cannon would be given back, which apparently the Mohawk possessed.

"The colonel's gone mad! Now I'm to build Indian villages! And not just any village! *Maltoc's village!* That chief who recently attacked Fort Le Boeuf! Why is this peace offering given to me to orchestrate?"

He stood and glared out the window. "I am the *engineering* officer for Fort Niagara. Not…not—"

"Commandant?"

"What?" he snapped.

"Apologies, Commandant. Monseigneur Beauharnois is waiting to see you," Sergeant Gabriel announced.

Merde! Captain Pouchot groaned and nodded his assent. He sat down again, placed the dispatch pouch beside his table and massaged his temples.

"I assume you heard the news about Sister Michelle and Okeanneh."

"And *bonjour* to you too, Monseigneur."

"What do you intend to do about it?"

"Do. About. What?"

"About Gaspard de Propei! He attacked and severely injured Okeanneh!"

The commandant was angered by the priest's accusatory tone and stood up again. "I am aware of this. Captain Prideaux has the Indian woman guarded now, day and night."

"You were aware of the attack on Okeanneh? Since when?"

"Since the last dispatch from Fort Le Boeuf was delivered to me."

"And you decided not to tell me! Remember, it was *you* who did not order the arrest of Gaspard—"

"First of all, *you,* for certain, are *not* my superior officer. And secondly, Okeanneh attacked the *shérif* first. There are plenty of witnesses to this. The man defended himself. He could have killed her if wanted to. He has the authority to do that and much more."

"And she's just another savage, yes? So who cares, yes?"

"Priest, I do not have the patience for either your sarcasm or one of your rants—"

"He intends to *kill* Sister Michelle."

"That's absurd! And just how did you come to *that* outrageous conclusion?"

"And Philippe Gerrard, too!"

Captain Pouchot held up a hand. "All right, stop! Did you consume all of your altar wine this morning?"

"H-how dare you!"

"Enough, Monseigneur! Either tell me what you want, or this audience is over."

Father Antoine became flustered. "I want…I want him arrested."

"This again! Gaspard de Propei arrested? Are you mad too? He did not do anything wrong!"

The monsignor hesitated. He was at a loss for words. The commandant seized on the opportunity to bring an end to the conversation.

"Stop, before you go further! This is what I *will* do for you. When Gaspard de Propei returns to Fort Niagara, I will talk with him politely, as I would any *shérif* of the *King*…and determine the truth of your accusations."

"And then what?"

"And then I will give his pompous, royal ass a tasty dinner, my best wine, and my bed to sleep in for the night, before I bid him adieu the next morning. And while we are on this subject, let me also bid you adieu, Monseigneur, for the remainder of this day, at least. Sergeant!"

Monseigneur Beauharnois seethed with anger and indignation as he marched back to the chapel. The Church had ways to deal with the commandant's insolent rebuke. But such censure would have to come from Archbishop Nicolet, and that would take many weeks.

Hearing of Okeanneh's attack by this man, the Jesuit felt responsible. *He* had told her of Gaspard de Propei, and *he* had not been successful in dissuading her from embarking on a journey that had led to her attack. Feelings of guilt hung over him.

By invoking the name of King Louie, this false *shérif* could act on impulse. There was no time to wait.

Yet I have no authority to do anything about it, he thought glumly.

At the doorway to the chapel, he had a sudden idea. He stared down at the entry step.

But I can *stop him,* he decided. *I am responsible for the Jesuit mission in the wilderness, this hospital, the spiritual well-being of the citizens, our native converts, of which Okeanneh was one. Well, after a fashion—she does wear a medallion of Saint Denis. And Archbishop Nicolet's latest missive to me said to delay Gaspard de Propei should he arrive. So I have orders, too—and I* do *have authority.*

Of course, like before, the archbishop's missive did not order him to chase after the *shérif*—which is what he'd just decided to do.

A minor point. I do have to confront the shérif in order to delay him. Commandant Pouchot will not recognize my authority to do anything...but Captain Prideaux at Fort Le Boeuf will.

"I will go to Fort Le Boeuf," he said softly to himself. "And use the power of the Church to detain this...this murderer."

His eyes drifted across the marshalling yard to the Dunemoore Company trading post.

Moments later, the Jesuit burst into the trading lodge that was crowded with soldiers and civilians, all vying to make trades or purchase equipment and supplies. Claude Guillot and two other company *coureurs de bois* were bartering with Peter Blue Jacket and three other grim-looking Mohawk braves. Peter knew the fort monsignor and nodded politely at him.

The bartering stopped.

"Monsieur Guillot! A word with you, *s'il vous plaît.*"

After they huddled off to the side of the noisy room, the priest described the commandant's reaction to the news from Fort Le Boeuf.

Peter Blue Jacket had watched the arrival of the latest courier from Fort Le Boeuf with mild interest. He already knew most of what the dispatch pouch might carry for messages; the most important of these was the order from Colonel Contrecoeur to Captain Pouchot to have the French help rebuild Maltoc's village palisade in return for the location of the three missing French cannon. Preceded by Maltoc's attack on Fort Le Boeuf, that piece of diplomacy had been largely agreed to by the colonel based on assurances that Maltoc himself was rogue—and would be taken care of, the French thunder guns would be returned, and the tenuous peace between the Seneca and the French forts would continue, for now at least. Now he would wait to see if the men promised would be sent from Fort Niagara. The Mohawk half-breed visited Fort Niagara once every moon—more often now since hostilities were beginning among the French and English soldiers. There were no secrets kept in the Dunemoore Company trading room. Every rumor was talked about. Speculation was offered without challenge. A lot could be learned if you had access to whiskey. All Peter had to do was listen or overhear others' conversations, which was not hard to do. Officially, he was there to trade the English goods for animal furs other than beaver. More recently, with all the fortifications in progress, iron nails were as valuable as gun powder. And he always carried an ample supply—usually wearing a half dozen on his belt like small knives to advertise their availability. As usual, he traded information most of all, for the French, for the English, always for the Mohawk. But what he now overheard would be valuable to the Oneida.

Tall Mountain Among Trees was looking for this man the priest spoke of...this man called Gaspard de Propei.

He knew what the Jesuit discussed with Guillot would be important.

As soon as Claude Guillot huddled with the priest, Peter moved to place his back to the clerk's. The two men spoke loudly to one another, to be heard above the noise and voices in the room. Gibberish to anyone more than a pace away, lost among the other sounds, but Peter was close enough to hear them clearly.

Guillot was surprised at the commandant's reaction to the attack on Okeanneh.

"So, Captain Pouchot plans to do nothing? Philippe and Pierre will be walking into a trap! I should send some of our *coureurs de bois*!"

"*No*! That is what I thought of originally," the Jesuit said, "but if they killed this…this *shérif*, there will be all kinds of repercussions."

Beauharnois crossed himself at the thought.

"Then what do you want to do?" Claude Guillot said impatiently.

"This matter is up to Philippe to resolve. He must be warned, but it must be done discreetly. The *shérif* must not know. So…so I've decided to go to Fort Le Boeuf."

"You! What can you do?"

"I have letters from Archbishop Nicolet telling me to detain this *shérif*," he stated more to himself than to Guillot. "That should be enough to get Captain Prideaux to do as I ask, at least until he is given countermanding orders. That will take time. And this will all be resolved long before that happens."

Claude Guillot was now puzzled. "So what do you want from me?"

Father Beauharnois smiled and spread his arms wide.

"Everything…everything I will need for a long march into the wilderness. Things to eat, things to trade, maybe your newest map? And I plan on leaving right away, as soon as you outfit me. And after I am gone, I want *you* to carry a message to Monseigneur Cortelaine. Tell him I've left for Fort Presque Isle…to…to check on its hospital…and that he is in charge until I return. But that's *all* you tell him, Claude," he emphasized. "Nothing else. And for my sake, please do not tell anyone else what I am doing!"

The offended clerk nodded vigorously. "I understand. I am used to keeping secrets."

A few hours later, the priest was standing in front of the store, grunting from the weight of the supply pack.

Claude laughed good-naturedly. "What's wrong? Too heavy? And that's only half what a *coureur de bois* usually carries, you know."

The monsignor smiled. "Well, I guess I will just have to eat the food more quickly to lighten my load, yes? *Au revoir*, my friend."

The priest pulled a sock cap over his head, which effectively completed his disguise as a *voyageur*-trader. Wielding a polished oak walking staff that stood a head taller than him, Father Antoine Beauharnois, monsignor of the great lakes of New France, his face beaming with delight, marched proudly toward the main gates of Fort Niagara. Most of what he wore and carried was new; pots and pans, new steel tomahawks, hammers and nails, a small saw, dry food and nuts of every kind, two large waterskins, good leather boots, gloves, all compliments of the Dunemoore Company.

Unexpectedly, he encountered the commandant standing by the new earth battlements adjoining the gates. The Jesuit lifted his shoulders, dropped his gaze, and quickened his pace.

Captain Pouchot threw aside the stick he had been using to clean the mud from his polished boots. He nodded in greeting to the trader walking by. All the man's clothes looked brand new. And with all the pans and other items of metal dangling from his pack, he clanked along like a supply wagon, a comical sight to the commandant. *He seems familiar*, he thought, but only for a moment before turning his attention back to more important matters. Weeks later, Captain Pouchot would bitterly remember this chance encounter.

The Jesuit said a prayer of thanks. He'd made it past the captain without incident. As the forest closed around the portage road, he felt elated to actually be going somewhere deep into the wilderness.

I'm a Jesuit coureur de bois, he mused.

Marching was so much more interesting than boating. He would have whistled, if he knew how to whistle. The long walking stick Claude Guillot had given him was an excellent idea. Swinging the staff before him as he walked made each step feel blessed and important. He was a true journeyer, a missionary, like one of the apostles of old.

No wonder so many of the paintings of the disciples depict them carrying a walking stick, he thought. *Shepherds, too*! And he was also like a shepherd! He was doing something about an *evil animal* seeking to harm his flock.

It's almost Biblical!

Peter Blue Jacket watched the Jesuit trudge out of the fort toward the

Niagara portage. His instinct was to follow this man, but Peter and his
Mohawk companions had bartered successfully. They were now overloaded
with French trade goods.

I can journey two days for every one of the priest's, he thought.

He decided instead to visit the Oneida, to sell or trade off most of his
goods, and tell Tall Mountain Among Trees he'd located the man who killed
his daughter. Then he'd return, bringing more braves with him, bypass the
Niagara fort, and head straight for Fort Le Boeuf. With luck, he would catch
up to the priest within a week, and before any meeting between the priest
and Gaspard de Propei. It would also give him a chance to check on French
progress at Maltoc's village.

They finally encountered the hunting trail. Colbért saw it winding its
way into the distance toward the northeast. It was, indeed, clearly marked.

"This is the trail," the pimple-faced guide announced. "Maybe we should
stop to eat before we get to the hills."

"No. Not yet. Lead on."

The guides shrugged and continued walking. The *shérif* was heavily
armed. No sense in making him suspicious, the older guide thought. There
was plenty of time to take him by surprise whenever they next happened
to stop.

Helmut waited another hour to get a sense of the trail before deciding
they'd gone far enough. At the next bend, where there was a steep drop off
to the right, the practiced assassin moved quickly and silently, approaching
the younger guide from behind. He put a hand over the man's mouth and
soundlessly slit his throat, cutting with the stiletto until he felt the blade
snag on the neck bones. The dead man slid noiselessly to the ground. The
Night Butcher quickly closed the gap behind the leader.

He is right handed, Colbért reminded himself before striking the guide
at a precise spot on the head with the steel butt of his pistol. The facially
scarred man dropped like a stone. It would be a long time before he awoke.
He quickly stripped the man of his weapons.

Colbért looked around until he found a fallen tree positioned the way he
wanted and dragged the unconscious man to the trunk. He went back down
the trail to the younger guide and untied the pack from the body. He cut off
the youth's leather jersey and sliced it with his skinning knife to fashion

strapping. He tossed the body down a nearby ravine to get it off the trail and used the man's skinning knife to scrape the bloody dirt into the bushes. He returned and skillfully tied the guide, placing a noose around the wrist of the left hand, pulling the line taut behind the man's back to loop the other end of the thong around the man's throat. If his victim pulled down on his arm too strongly, he would slowly choke himself to death.

The assassin tied the man's legs at the ankles. Then groaning at its weight, he lifted one end of the log and secured the leg tether around its circumference, tying a second noose around the man's neck in similar fashion. Finally, he sliced away the clothing from the man's right arm and tightly cinched another leather strap below the bicep, but above the elbow, creating a crude but effective tourniquet. Colbért inspected all of his work to be sure he had not missed anything. He placed a rag of clothing in the man's mouth and completed the gag with a wide strip of leather.

Satisfied, he nodded.

The guide's tomahawk was made of metal and was razor sharp. *Impressive*, he thought. It would cut as easily as his stiletto. He extended the man's right arm across the log.

Thwock! The ax easily cut through the sinew and bone. The limb spun in the air, spraying blood in every direction, then fell to the ground. The fingers twitched once. He was pleased with the tourniquet. It was tight enough. Not much blood spurted from the stump, though some still dribbled.

Colbért watched with amusement as the man's eyes bulged open in agony. Mucous burst from the man's nostrils.

"*Bonjour, Monsieur,*" he greeted the guide warmly. "Did you enjoy your nap? This has been a very productive and surprising morning, don't you agree?"

Only muted groans could be heard through the gag. The mutilated arm stump swung about wildly, and the man's noose tightened. Colbért explained what would happen if the man moved too much or too quickly.

For the time being, all the assassin needed to do was wait until the injured guide capitulated. He suddenly felt hungry. He went back and retrieved the dead man's pack. He returned to the injured guide and searched through their combined belongings. He located some dried meat and some roasted nuts. One of the packs contained a bottle of red wine with a label indicating it had been pilfered from army stores.

"Ah, my friend," he told the guide, "you have anticipated my royal palate, I see. Very thoughtful of you."

Helmut Colbért leaned against one end of the log and enjoyed his meal in the cool shade of the forest. The spasmodic struggling and muffled screams of the guide slowly grew less intense. After fifteen minutes, there was only groaning.

When he was done eating, he grabbed the front of the man's shirt and pulled him to his feet. He lifted one end of the log and slid the tether free. Pulling on his well-stocked pack, he loosened the noose and allowed the left arm to relax to the side to make it easier for the man to balance. The guide cried out as the blood surged into the numbed limb. He prodded the guide's ass with the tip of a stiletto to get him walking.

"You lead," he said with a smile. "Don't forget, I am paying you handsomely for this service, yes? A golden Louis d'or awaits you!"

Just before dark, they camped for the night. Colbért noosed the man with a second strap and tied the ends to a different tree. If the guide moved in any direction too far, he would be strangled. He held the waterskin and gave the guide as much to drink as he could swallow and placed some nuts within reach.

"Those are for the morning, when you break your fast tomorrow. Sorry, no fire tonight. Now, if you allow me to sleep undisturbed, I will let you go in two more days." It was a lie, but Colbért said it as sincerely as he could. "By then, you will be very weak and not much use to me."

The guide was in constant agony and desperately wanted to believe him.

Two days later, the injured, feverish guide was stumbling with exhaustion, and steadily worsening, until Colbért had to push him roughly along the trail. The leather noose around his neck was tethered to Colbért's waist, and he trailed some five paces behind.

The mutilated man staggered against a tree and screamed curses at his tormentor. Colbért responded by turning around and prodding the guide's buttocks again with the point of a stiletto. Soon, there was little slack in the line separating the two men. Drops of blood stained the dirt from the back of the guide's pants, which mixed with the blood still dripping from his severed arm.

Along the way, the assassin had asked the guide numerous questions about the trail, the landmarks, and the hazards they expected to encounter. So far, everything the man had told him turned out to be true. He now felt convinced he could follow the well-marked trail alone. But he would wait until the man had no more usefulness.

Their progress continued to slow. Groaning and drooling, the guide stumbled along in front of him. Biting flies had covered the stump wound, only adding to the man's misery. The tourniquet above the elbow had loosened and the right side of his leather clothing had become soaked in the blood dribbling from the wound. As the trail began its incline after the first hill, the guide slipped and fell directly on his injured arm. He screamed.

That's simply too loud, Colbért decided. He stepped over the prostrate figure, pulled back on his hair, and expertly slit the man's throat with his stiletto. The body jerked convulsively, sputtering and gurgling blood as the guide exhaled his last breath.

Helmut wiped his blade on the dead man's clothes, dragged the body off the trail, and continued walking.

He proceeded, for the rest of the day, without any problems, until he suddenly encountered a split in the trail. Part of it continued straight ahead, and the other trail made a sharp turn to his left. They were both equal in width and showed the same amount of wear. The paths were distinct.

Colbért sat down, drank some water, and ate dried salted meat, thinking on what to do. The sun was setting behind him. It would be dark soon. That meant the trail to his left was going in a northerly direction. The dirt map he memorized had not shown this juncture. He drew it again with a stick to help him with this decision.

If I go north, I will eventually reach the lake and probably the portage road between Presque Isle and Niagara, he thought.

The assassin had slept in the cold for four straight nights. The insects were ferocious and much of his exposed skin was welted and itched. He was certainly well past Fort Presque Isle. Either trail should take him to Fort Niagara. The portage trail might take longer. But if he traveled the portage road, he would likely encounter other travelers with campfires, hot food, and news. Even an extra day would not matter now.

Three days after leaving Fort Niagara, Father Beauharnois reached a point on the portage road to Fort Presque Isle where a trail intersected on his left, leading away to the south. He pulled out the map given to him by Claude Guillot. He'd been looking for this trail. It was shown on the map to be a well-marked path leading directly to Fort Le Boeuf. It offered a way to get by Fort Presque Isle without being seen, so any rumor of his arrival at Fort Le Boeuf would not precede him. He wanted to surprise the *shérif,* though the priest had decided he must have soldiers with him when he did so.

This must be the trail, he thought. It looked well used.

The Jesuit wished he could ask for confirmation on the road to take, but looking in both directions, the paths were deserted. So he crossed himself and marched off into the dense wilderness.

"Thy will be done."

Helmut Colbért was starting down another slope when he heard metal-on-metal, clanking sounds. He quickly took cover to the side of the trail and watched carefully as a single man started the uphill climb.

With his head down, grunting and puffing from the weight of his heavy load, Monseigneur Beauharnois did not see the *shérif* until he was only a few paces away. The man was now standing in the center of the trail, with his hands on his hips, holding a knife in one hand.

"*You!*"

The priest recoiled in terror and fell back on his rump, holding an arm in front of his face, expecting an attack that did not come.

The assassin was puzzled. He did not know this man, but it was obvious the trader somehow knew him.

"Who are you?"

With the portage three hours behind him, Monseigneur Beauharnois knew he was beyond help and in grave danger. *Trust in God,* he told himself. He quickly fumbled with the leather lacing on the front of his coat and opened it to reveal the black robe and red piping distinguishing his office. He held out the crucifix hanging around his neck.

"I am Monseigneur Beauharnois of Fort Niagara. We've met, Monsieur Propei."

Colbért's was surprised. He looked beyond the priest, back down the trail.

"You? Where is your escort, priest?"

"Th-they will be along shortly."

The assassin snorted. "And I've been told that priests do not lie."

"I am on my way to Fort Le Boeuf. This trail is a shorter route."

"Are you sure? I've just walked it. How far is it to the portage?"

"Uh…not long. Less than half an hour, actually."

Colbért smirked. "Again, you lie to me. Why?"

"I do not owe you any explanations, Monsieur. And I will be on my way."

With his heart pounding, the monsignor stepped forward to move around the man. With his second step, the *shérif* punched him hard on the side of the head. The priest was propelled off the trail by the blow, knocked senseless.

The assassin gazed down at the man dispassionately and deliberated what to do. Encountering the meddling Jesuit had complicated matters.

I should just kill him and move on, he considered. His head suddenly burst with pain and one word filled his thoughts: *No*!

"Fuck!" When the spiking, pulsing pain subsided, Colbért grabbed the priest by the straps of his pack and dragged him deeper into the trees.

If I am getting close to Fort Niagara, he suddenly thought, *I will need information about it. And this priest will answer all my questions.*

When Father Beauharnois regained consciousness, he found himself stripped naked and lashed hand and foot between two trees. The left side of his head throbbed with intense pain. His vision was blurry.

"I am Monseigneur Beauharnois of Fort Niagara," he slurred. His own voice sounded awkward and unfamiliar. It was hard to control the movement of his tongue.

The Night Butcher had thoroughly searched the priest's pack and pockets, keeping only those things that any person would carry in the wilderness. *No sense in carrying anything priestly, eh?*

"I am Monseigneur Beauharnois of Fort Niagara," the priest still slurred, but his voice was louder this time.

Colbért got up and went over to the softly moaning priest. He grabbed the man's hair and lifted the head. "Quiet!" he said, then punched him in the testicles.

Father Beauharnois groaned loudly and spewed vomit, the intense pain taking away his ability to speak. He could hardly breathe.

Colbért waited patiently until the man's panting slowed, until low moans were the only sounds he made.

"So, priest, this is how we shall converse. I will ask you questions, and you will answer them quickly. If you do not, you will suffer more pain than you have ever imagined. Understood? Nod your head. Good. Let's begin. Why were you going to Fort Le Boeuf?"

An hour later, Colbért struggled to think of something else to ask, but learning that the commandant at Fort Niagara intended to intercept him was by far the most crucial piece of information he had obtained. He would have to find a way to disguise himself and slip past the sentries to the boat landing to buy passage with a *voyageur*. Truly, the voice of his dreams was guiding his plans. And knowing the portage was three hours away and the fort two more days hence, was encouraging too. Now, he wanted to hurry.

Colbért took up his stiletto. "Well, priest," he said. "Looks like it's time for us to dance the waltz of death."

Father Beauharnois saw blurry double images, but he recognized Colbért's foul breath.

"You will burn in hell," the Jesuit said hoarsely.

Colbért adopted a disappointed air. "Now, why would you say something like that? I had intended to make this short work. And we were getting along so well." His expression changed. The face became twisted. "You are already in hell," the Night Butcher growled. He picked up the hammer and four long spikes he'd found inside the priest's pack.

"I will prove it to you."

As he walked briskly down the trail, Colbért ate some confectioneries from a sack of hard candy he'd found buried at the bottom of the priest's backpack. Upon reaching the portage road, he decided to linger there. He needed to travel with someone into Fort Niagara. He stayed out of sight and examined any travelers heading east. The first two groups were wagons full of wounded or sickly soldiers.

But two hours later, six *coureurs de bois* with a wagonload of furs approached. He stepped out on the road and waved. They regarded him cautiously, muskets raised.

The man in front looked at him suspiciously. "What do you want?"

"My name is Helmut Colbért," he replied. It would no longer do to announce he was *Shérif* Gaspard de Propei.

"Why are you covered in blood?"

"I came down this trail from Fort Le Boeuf." He pointed. "Killed and slaughtered some small animals on the way. I'm not very good at it, obviously."

The lead *coureur de bois* looked up the trail. "That is a very dangerous path to take from Fort Le Boeuf, Monsieur."

"I know that now," Colbért agreed, assuming an air of naïveté. "I am a trade inspector and work for Intendant Bigôt. I was investigating a fur trading concession at Fort Le Boeuf. There have been rumors of, uh, illegalities. They suggested I travel back on this trail, said it was a faster way."

"Alone?"

"Yes."

"Who suggested that?"

"*S'il vous plaît*, may I first know who you are?"

The leader explained they were traders, rivals of the Dunemoore Company.

"We are on our way to Montréal."

"Ah, I see. *Merci*. It was Philippe Gerrard who suggested I take this trail."

The leader relaxed even more and traded glances with his companions.

"I suspect Monsieur Gerrard was hoping to get you killed by the savages. That's a hunting trail, used by people unfriendly to us."

"Oh, dear." Colbért continued playing the fool. "If that's true, the Dunemoore Company may have more surprises for me at Fort Niagara. How very fortunate for me to meet you. If only there was a way to get past the fort without being seen? I would gladly pay for this service…generously."

Colbért waited to see if they would take the bait.

They did.

Chapter 12
Fort Le Boeuf
August 1754
A Glint of Something Gold

M en and supplies now moved with greater frequency on the Rivière aux Boeufs. Colonel Contrecoeur's victory at the three rivers and the subsequent construction of Fort Duquesne had renewed his forces' enthusiasm. The soldiers going toward Fort Machault boasted of the victories yet to come as they rowed by Pierre's canoe going in the opposite direction.

Less than a day south of Fort Le Boeuf, the Scotsman stopped paddling and raised his hand to measure the sun. He estimated only two hours of daylight remained. Unfortunately, they would not reach the fort until the next day. He spotted men encamped on the right bank. Several canoes were beached. They were cooking meat. It smelled delicious.

"Pierre! You smell that? I've already eaten my hat," Louie Hawkfeeder complained.

"Ya' dinnah' look as if ya' missed a meal in yer life."

Michelle was exhausted. "It would help me if I could rest on the ground for a while."

Lying in the bottom of the canoe, covered with fur skins, she was amazed by her miraculous rescue. Pierre had explained how they'd gotten her out of the village, but her questions concerning the whereabouts of Philippe were evaded.

"It *does* smell good," Pierre admitted. "All right, we'll stop here. Dinnah' mention Sister Michelle's name."

"My name? Why?"

"It's dangerous for ya'. There is a man out here lookin' for Philippe… and lookin' for ya' too. It's a little hard tah' explain."

Michelle felt nauseous with alarm. She forced herself to a sitting position. "What man?" she demanded.

"A King's *shérif* named Gaspard de Propei. Claims Philippe is wanted for treason back in France."

"Oh, dear God," Michelle said softly. "The Marquis has sent an assassin."

The canoe hit the mud with a thump. The bow lifted clear of the water.

"Dinnah' worry. You're safe with us. But it will be safer still," Pierre whispered, "if ya' dinnah' mention your real name."

A deer carcass on a spit hissed and spat juices above an enormous cook fire. There was enough food for twice as many people as were present at the camp. A group of fourteen soldiers, traders, and a few Indians were gathered about. Pierre's party was greeted warmly.

The Scotsman carefully carried Michelle to a place near the fire and propped her in a sitting position against his pack. He went back to retrieve his weapons when he glanced at an Indian sitting off by himself. The man was watching Pierre with great interest.

The face seemed familiar. The Scotsman slowed to a stop. The man was heavily tattooed. A bone crescent dangled from his nose.

"Chittaqua? It is ya'! Bloody hell! I was beginning tah' thin' ya'd become one o' your ghosts."

Chittaqua stood. Pierre resisted an urge to hug the man. Chittaqua was a friend, but he was also a shaman.

"Did you find the boy?"

"Snow Hair's son is at Fort Presque Isle."

Pierre started to whirl around. "Whooo! Wooo hooo! This is a grand day indeed, my friend. See tha' woman by the fire? Tha' is Henri's mother. We rescued her a week ago at the camp o' the wolf. Come meet this woman."

Pierre waved his arms. "Louie! Look who's here."

Chittaqua noticed a glint of something gold hanging from a leather thong tied around Pierre's neck as he turned. He followed him to the cook fire.

"One more to eat with us!" Pierre announced.

The soldiers grinned at one another. "To be certain, he's welcome. He's the one who hunted and killed the deer," one of them said.

"Well in tha' case, we'll have a feast!" He bent over and touched Michelle's shoulder. "Ya' must remember Chittaqua!"

As Pierre straightened and turned, Chittaqua grabbed Philippe's ring and ripped it loose from the Scotsman's neck. The shaman examined it closely. It was the sacred totem! He was horrified.

"Where is Snow Hair?" he demanded.

The urgent sound of his voice made everyone in the camp stop talking. Pierre glanced at Michelle apprehensively. Chittaqua sensed something was wrong.

"Where is Snow Hair?" he repeated with emphasis.

Pierre grimaced. "He's being held at Piqua's camp," he said reluctantly.

"Oh, no!" Michelle's wailing sounded like a child's. "Noooo! Nooo!" She threw off her blankets and tried to get up.

Pierre knelt. "No, lassie! Don't! It was Philippe's idea. It was the only way the Seneca would let ya' go. He traded himself for ya'."

"No, no, no," she sobbed, pounding Pierre with her fists. "No, Philippe! No!"

"I'm goin' back for him. I promise. As soon as ya' are safe at the fort."

Overwhelmed with anguish, Michelle pushed hard on Pierre's chest. "They are going to kill Philippe! An Englishman named Curtiss has paid them!"

"Iron Pots is dead," Chittaqua said tersely.

"Wha'? Well, tha's bloody great news!" Pierre had not heard that before. "Ya' hear tha', lassie? Curtiss is dead. It's goin' tah' be all right."

"The Seneca will torture him. Oh, God, Philippe, why? Why?"

Michelle sagged back to the ground. She sat with her arms wrapped around her legs, and rocked back and forth. Pierre signaled for Louie to trade places with him. The burly *coureur de bois* awkwardly wrapped an arm around the shoulders of the tiny woman.

Pierre felt Chittaqua's hand on his shoulder.

"Why do *you* have Philippe's totem?"

"Wha'? The ring? Philippe told me tah' save it for him," Pierre explained. "The Seneca would ha' stolen it."

Chittaqua took the ring from Pierre and tied it around his own neck. He started walking toward his canoe.

"Where are ya' goin'?"

"To Snow Hair."

"Wait! I'll go with ya'."

"*No*. I am going to the camp of the Wolf," Chittaqua said. He pointed at Michelle. "You promised Snow Hair to take his woman to the fort. Keep your promise."

Chittaqua scooped up his medicine bag, supply pack, and weapons almost without stopping.

Pierre followed him to the river's edge. "I'll be following ya' tomorrow."

Chittaqua turned abruptly. "Do not go to the Wolf clan village," he told him, then pushed off in his canoe. "Stay beyond their cornfields. I will find you when it is time. I will bring Snow Hair to the other fort, at Venango."

The Erigh medicine man paddled out of sight. Pierre Dunemoore frowned at the departing figure. He was not easily intimidated. *But that damn man makes me feel like a young fool*, he thought with irritation. *Always has*.

Pierre walked slowly back to the glum faces surrounding the cook fire. All sense of festivity had vanished. The soldiers and *coureurs de bois* were eating quietly. Michelle was sobbing.

"We might as well eat too," he said to Louie.

"Why didn't you tell me about Philippe?" Michelle's voice was hoarse and angry.

"Because I dinnah' think ya' were strong enough tah' hear aboot it," Pierre said. "I was goin' tah' tell ya' once we reached the fort."

None of the men talked much during the meal in deference to the troubled woman's emotions. Suddenly, Pierre rapped himself on the forehead.

"Michelle! How in God's name did I forget this? Chittaqua found Henri! Henri is at Fort Presque Isle! The lad is safe!"

"Henri? Henri is safe?" she repeated in disbelief.

"Yes. Chittaqua says he's at Fort Presque Isle."

Michelle lifted her arms toward the sky. This time her tears were from relief and happiness.

The happy news broke the gloom around the fire, and boisterous conversation sprang from the men once more. Pierre felt like Father Christmas and beamed at everyone. He took a seat next to his men.

"Well, Michel, now that she is happy, and young Henri is saved, all we've got tah' dah' now is ask Piqua tah' give up Philippe without a fight, open trade concessions at all the new forts, and stop the war. Then, by next spring, we'll all be *rich*."

Two days later, Pierre Dunemoore and his men delivered Sister Michelle to Fort Le Boeuf, a day later than expected because of a hole in one of the canoes. But their good spirits were dashed upon arrival after learning about Okeanneh and seeing the results of Gaspard de Propei's treachery. They laid Sister Michelle on a new cot, next to a bed where Okeanneh already lay. With Sister Michelle's arrival, Captain Prideaux decided to move out of his rooms altogether and give over his private quarters to the women.

The Scotsman knelt between the beds and held the hands of both women, bewildered by this astonishing coincidence that held both women injured and together and at Philippe's incredible ill fortune.

Upon seeing Pierre, Okeanneh managed a smile of recognition.

Pierre gazed into her beautiful amber eyes. "Aw, lassie," he said tenderly. "I dinnah'…why …?" He was at a loss for words.

"She cannot speak," Prideaux said softly. "We think it's because of the injury to her head."

Pierre stiffened. "She kinnah' talk? Where is this bastard?"

Captain Prideaux shook his head. "We don't know. He left claiming he was going back to Presque Isle or Niagara. He might as easily have gone downriver. I've sent men in pursuit, to try and keep track of his where-abouts…so I can inform Philippe, of course. *Shérif* de Propei seemed intent on finding Philippe."

Based on the description Captain Prideaux volunteered about the mus-tached aristocrat, the Scotsman searched the faces in his memory of people in the canoes they'd rowed by on the way to Fort Le Boeuf. He could not recall seeing anyone like that.

"Where's Monsieur Gerrard?" Captain Prideaux asked.

"He's a prisoner of the Wolf clan Seneca." He explained what had happened and why. "Sister Michelle knows. I'd wait awhile before telling Okeanneh, 'til she's feelin' better. In one respect, it's fortunate they're both here together."

"How's that?" Prideaux asked.

"Well, they both care about Philippe. This way they can console and take care of each other."

CHAPTER 13
PIQUA'S VILLAGE
AUGUST 1754
The Prophecy

Chittaqua spied on Piqua's village with great concentration. The harvesting had begun. He'd scouted the area for two days, sleeping in a tree at night, carefully noting the paths the villagers used most often to come and go from the fields. He learned the forest trails, the rise and fall of the surrounding lands, the location of streams and ponds, and those places where the undergrowth in the forest made passage almost impossible. From this knowledge, he selected and memorized the trail he would take when departing, one which offered the best opportunities to deceive his pursuers and allow speed in travel.

The Seneca camp was strong, occupied by thirty-three longhouse lodges, one hundred thirty-eight braves, and twice as many women and children. The palisade surrounding it had been built alongside a small gurgling stream, making fresh water accessible and easy to carry. The defensive wall of logs was fifteen feet high and Chittaqua noted every side of the palisade was constantly manned by one or more guards. But few animals were carried in during the day by the hunters. He expected to see much more evidence of hunting for a village of this size.

He also noted with disgust, numerous animal carcasses lay rotting outside and beneath the walls where they had been thrown unceremoniously after the prime cuts of meat had been excised from the bones. Even the holy antlers of the stag deer had not been saved to make tools and religious objects. The water downstream of the encampment was polluted with excrement and other refuse, mostly used trade goods supplied by traders. The images reminded him of the white man.

Having satisfied his knowledge of what lay outside the walls of Piqua's village, he moved to inspect the interior of the palisade. Before sunrise, on the morning of the third day, when the tired sentries were cold and less

192

alert, Chittaqua dared to approach the wall near its smaller rear gate. He peered between the chinks in the timbers and observed the layout of the longhouses. They were arranged traditionally in rows of four and five lodges surrounding the larger roundhouse of the elders at the village center. Near the meeting house, he noticed a naked man hanging limply by his wrists. The man's feet were touching the ground, but the legs were bent at the knees, slack from exhaustion. The man's chin rested on his chest, his blond hair bloody. A blanket had been thrown over his shoulders. Chittaqua couldn't see the man's face but he didn't have to. It was Snow Hair.

Chittaqua had learned enough. He retreated to the forest edge to finish his preparations to enter the village. His plan was simple but dangerous. As he moved cautiously back around to the front of the palisade, he admired the large autumn fields full of corn, beans, and squash standing high and ripe, ready for harvest. As the morning progressed, dozens of women and children left the palisade to patiently tend these crops. The women sang happy songs. It was reminiscent of the peaceful times he spent as a youth before his years of wandering…so long ago.

The shaman stayed hidden beyond the edge of the forest, searching among the trees for the special herbs and plants he used to replenish the pharmacopeia in his medicine bag. There might not be time to do so later. After midday, he retreated into the forest on a specific trail. He didn't stop for a long time, purposely seeking a remote area, away from any paths made by man or animal, away from the eyes or ears of the villagers. On the way there, he detoured to the place where Iron Pots had been killed, the man who had defiled Philippe's wife when she had been held captive here. Only the skeleton remained, much of it scattered by animals.

But Chittaqua was pleased to find the skull intact. It was the part he wanted. Now he must be undisturbed to craft his magic.

The shaman reached a clearing he'd located previously. It was surrounded by some massive moss-covered boulders, beyond which stood trees thick with honeysuckle vines. The clearing was covered with a weedy grass. In the center were the blackened remains of an old fire pit, but it had not seen a fire for many moons. Off to one side stood a large basswood tree, exactly the type he needed. Chittaqua stripped off some of the bark with his knife and ran his hand across the inner surface, looking for flaws, insects, or other signs of disease. The wood felt moist and was unblemished.

Perfect, he decided.

Using his tomahawk, knives, and a lifetime of acquired skill, the shaman began to carve a mask in the malleable wood of the trunk. It had to be made to exact dimensions: three hands high and two hands wide. The wood of the trunk was firm but carved easily beneath the sharp blades of his knives. As the hours elapsed, wood shavings piled at Chittaqua's feet. The mouth, ears, and eyes took form along with a nose bent over to one side, as if previously broken.

It was late afternoon when Chittaqua stood back to inspect his work. Satisfied the image was properly made, he felled the tree and chopped the mask loose from the basswood. In another hour, he finished hollowing its oval shape until it was smooth and less than an inch in thickness. Then he pushed all the wood shavings into the center of the clearing and started a new fire in the old pit. He propped the finished mask near the fire, turning it every few minutes to make sure the wood dried evenly.

The shaman completed the face by staining it with pigments from his medicine bag. The last step would be to cut holes through the wood at the eyes and mouth, thus releasing the mask's magic, bringing its mystery to life. But he would wait to do that, just before he put it on, near the front gate of the village. Finally, he took out Iron Pot's skull and stained it red with berry juice. Then he collected his things and made his pack ready. He would leave the pack hanging in a tree and retrieve it as he retreated from the village.

The shaman began applying paint to his body, invoking the proper prayers with each step, calling the totem spirits and the ghosts of his ancestors. He prayed for the inspiration to give him the words of truth to speak, words to influence the hearts of an enemy. He must use his magic for good, make the Seneca understand. Placing the strong medicine under his tongue, Chittaqua said the ancient words to open his eyes to the other side, to allow the spirits to dwell and see through him as he conjured his magic.

Chittaqua could see and hear Snow Hair now. His friend was dying. And hearing his friend's lament, he spoke to him in a dream. *You will not die. I am here.*

The Andrototekan was ready.

As the sun moved low in the sky, a twelve-year-old girl was sent by her mother to collect some onions beginning to sprout in the meadow on the other side of the stream near the cornfield. Making a basket with her skirt, she bent over her task, humming the song of the honeybee. A shadow fell upon her from behind. She heard a strange hissing sound. She turned, gasped, and screamed in horror. The bulbs she'd collected in her dress tumbled to the ground as she ran toward the safety of the palisade and the sentries.

"A monster," the terrified girl shrieked. "A monster comes!"

The young girl ran to the center of the enclave, immediately drawing a crowd. She cried a demon had tried to eat her. The whole village was thrown into turmoil. A dozen armed warriors poured from the gate anxious to confront the adversary.

Outside of the compound, Chittaqua stabbed a six-foot pointed stick in the ground of the main pathway to the village and placed the red skull on top of it. He knew the next few minutes would be dangerous and retreated into the cornstalks. The Seneca braves spread out in front of the gate, hooting and shouting. In particular, Chittaqua watched for the appearance of a man wearing a red-tipped eagle feather, the sign of a special shaman.

Inside the village, Philippe Gerrard heard the hoots and cries of alarms. He lifted his head weakly. But elevating his head was difficult to do for very long, until it drooped again upon his chest. The torture he'd endured by Sauquita and the other braves had been relentless. Only Piqua's continued interference prevented more serious injuries beyond the partial scalping, burning, and lashing. To his puzzlement, twice a day, the Seneca women gave him food and water. The women would talk to him kindly, help him eat and drink before the torment began anew. Ironically, it was the women who beat on him the most, though everyone in the village took turns in this, even small children.

They won't let you die, he kept telling himself each time the pain became intense. *They will hurt you, but they will not kill you.*

Sweating fevers began on the seventh day, followed by a plague of diarrhea, which ran in a foul mix down his legs to pool beneath him. Body fluids and bacteria attacked his exposed skin. On the eighth day, sores erupted on his inner thighs and calves. At night, the temperature would plummet, leaving him shivering and moaning. After he had moaned long enough, one of the women would build a fire nearby and drape a blanket over his shoulders. By the morning of the ninth day, he drifted amidst periods of shivering reality and delirium. An odd numbness began to spread upward from his feet, which brought relief to the painful itching of his infected legs. After that, Philippe lost track of the time, falling in and out of consciousness, sometimes it was daylight, other times dark. The women would give him plenty of water to drink, force him to eat, and occasionally they would wash him clean. But the periodic torture never stopped. Once, he had a dream where a medicine man visited him, lifted his head by the hair and looked into his eyes. "He is dying," the shaman pronounced to the villagers. "Avoid him lest you catch one of the white man's sicknesses."

Then Philippe started vomiting. It was a bad sign. He tried not to vomit, to retain what remained of food and water in his body, but his stomach kept cramping, as if being stabbed with a knife. If the diarrhea didn't stop, Philippe knew his end was near. He might last another day, two at the most.

"If you're coming Pierre, come soon," he mumbled. "Or I am lost."

You will not die, an inner voice answered. *I am here.*

"What? Who's here?" he blurted the question through feverish lips. "Who's here?!"

Philippe heard the roar of men's voices outside the palisade. He struggled to lift his head again. It was getting dark. Already he was cold. He saw the blanket lying on the ground nearby. But there were no women around to bring it to him.

"I'm cold," he called in a weak and hoarse voice. "I'm cold!'

Piqua and his warriors formed a defensive U outside the gates and waited for the guards to return. Others had spread out in several directions to search for the source of the girl's fear. The clan chief raised his head with interest each time one of the searchers reappeared, but the scouts found nothing and returned shaking their heads.

Ootego moved closer to his clan chief. The medicine man was wearing the skin of a timber wolf on his head and a long red-tipped eagle feather in one of his braids. The shaman was confused and bewildered like everyone else, but as the darkness loomed he became impatient and anxious to return to the food his wife had prepared.

"I see no enemy," Ootego said in Piqua's ear. "The girl stood in the sun too long. Or she was simply scared by a fox. I can declare this to be so."

Piqua turned his head and scowled. "*You* can be wrong. *You* are not chief. What if the Erigh have returned?"

"The Erigh have gone into the sunset. Every clan and tribe says this."

"Then it might be the *coureurs de bois* that attacked Sauquita. And they have thunder guns! The girl must have seen something," he said, irritated with his shaman. "Keep looking," he shouted to his men.

High-pitched, eerie squeals rose from somewhere in the distance. Piqua led the way down the main trail, walking toward the sound. After fifty paces, Ootego bellowed in a fearful voice.

"Look! The red skull! It is the red skull!"

They heard the squeals again, as if someone were in pain. It was coming from within the high stalks of corn. The warriors froze. Some notched arrows in their bows.

Piqua's scowl deepened. "What trickery is this?"

His head snapped left and right, expecting to see enemies descending on them from all directions.

The high-pitched noises stopped and strange words were shouted.

"*Loh cai teem! Loh cai teem! Loh cai teem!*"

Ootego recognized the sacred words immediately. He took charge. "A sorcerer approaches," the medicine man announced. He stepped forward and waved his carved totem staff in circles above his head. "Everyone keep back. I will meet this spirit!"

"Spirit?" Piqua was skeptical.

Ootego began chanting strange words.

Piqua's growing confusion sparked his anger. He looked back and forth, first toward the cornfield, then to the queer behavior of his shaman. More surprising, Ootego's chanting was *answered* by a voice from the cornfield.

"Enough of this!" Piqua clenched his war ax and ran toward the place in the corn where the noise seemed to be coming. He avoided the red skull on the post. Some of his braves followed.

"No!" Ootego shouted. "Wait! Go no closer!"

A figure emerged from the tall green stalks. Piqua stopped a few paces away, his tomahawk high in the air, ready to strike.

"Do not touch him!" Ootego shouted.

Piqua gawked at the painted figure. He was naked except for a loincloth. He carried a long totem stick and wore a mask. The mask was a round wooden carving, color stained and decorated with two red-tipped eagle feathers and fighting bird talons. It was the face of Tahiawagi, their high deity and war god. The braves nervously formed a circle around the mysterious figure, holding their spears defensively. When he made no threatening movements, Piqua slowly lowered his ax. Ootego rushed forward.

"Do not interfere." Ootego was breathless. "He is the *Andrototekan*! A holy man!"

Ootego was excited to see the red-tipped eagle feathers dangling from the colorful mask of the apparition. This could only be Chittaqua, the Andrototekan of his youth, once briefly his teacher. But he certainly couldn't say the Erigh high shaman's name. Not here. Not now.

"He is a *holy* man," Ootego repeated with emphasis. He wondered what the Andrototekan wanted. He'd heard Chittaqua did not march into the sunset with his tribe. *But why is he here?*

The warriors turned to Piqua. With a short wave of his ax, Piqua signaled the men surrounding the painted stranger to lower their weapons. The clan chief pointed at the trees and corn.

"Search again," he ordered. "Make certain he is alone." Then he faced Ootego. "A *holy man*? What does this *holy man* want?"

Behind the mask, Chittaqua saw fear in the faces of the warriors assembled around him. It was the look of children the first time they saw bolts of sunlight burst from a storm cloud. All were frightened, except Ootego.

Chittaqua had carefully crafted his image for Ootego. His arms, chest, and stomach were covered with a white pigment, randomly spotted with red dots. His legs were tinted yellow. He knew the coloring of his body and the mask would project a special significance for the Wolf clan medicine man. Ootego would recognize it as the dress of a *ghost dancer* on a twilight journey leading to death. Legend claimed a ghost dancer on such a journey spoke directly for the spirit world and could accurately predict, but, more importantly, *influence* the future.

Chittaqua waited until a degree of calmness returned to the agitated warriors. He walked forward and stopped directly in front of the Seneca shaman.

Ootego could not believe the clan's good fortune. To have a ghost dancer visit on his twilight journey was exciting enough. But this was Chittaqua!

The Andrototekan!

For a few moments, no one spoke. Piqua's patience came to an end.

"Who are you?"

"Silence!" Ootego commanded.

Piqua's face twisted angrily at his medicine man.

Ootego was willing to risk Piqua's anger over this. This unexpected arrival of the Andrototekan provided an unprecedented opportunity for the clan to ask important questions in return for simple gifts of food, water, and a place to rest.

Ootego began to dance. The masked apparition followed his movements. The men chanted strange words, circling one another, ducking and nodding, skipping on one leg, then the other. The medicine men cracked their totem sticks together, spinning, gesturing, voices rising then falling in guttural, unnatural sounds.

Piqua and his braves could only watch in amazement.

The dancing went on for several minutes with each man becoming more animated. Among those present, only Chittaqua and Ootego knew the dance was the ritual ceremony of greeting among special shaman, between the Andrototekan and the apprentices. As it progressed, Chittaqua decided it was destiny the shaman of the Wolf clan should also be a ghost dancer. Chittaqua had personally initiated Ootego on the grass prairies of the sunset many, many seasons ago. Like other young boys, Ootego had traveled alone for months, following trails described by other shaman. The initiates came from many different tribes, walking from the grassy plains, the deep forests, the deserts, the icy cold. Each was there to endure initiation rites conducted only once every ten seasons. Some never made it to the place of ceremony, while others never made it home afterwards. This was part of the journey and a sign of their worthiness.

Ootego danced happily. Only once before had he heard an Andrototekan speak in prophecy. For two summer moons, as a boy of twelve, Ootego had braved severe physical and mental trials that ended in the death of a few. He recalled drinking the strong medicine, the endless nights of fire dancing, until, on one magical night, he had indeed conversed with the dead. He remembered how at the end of the summer, as a proud new shaman, he accepted his sacred eagle feather, its tip dyed red to signify he was one of the special priests, so few in number at any time, they totaled no more than the count of his fingers and toes.

These shamans shared a belief: One day, those pure in heart and spirit would join with the ghosts of their ancestors. They would inhabit the bodies of their youth and, in glory, live on divine lands teeming with buffalo and deer herds more countless than the spirit lights. And they would become one with the Great Spirit. But only the ghosts knew the way. The ghosts talked only with these shamans. Now, after so many seasons of turmoil and uncertainty, Ootego was proud to remember he was one of these special men.

Now the entire clan will know, Ootego thought. *And they will honor and respect me.*

Chittaqua found himself counting the number of times Ootego mispronounced the sacred words. *He is beginning to forget.* It was no surprise why so few legends and prayers survived from teacher to apprentice. And after the appearance of the white man, the number of true ghost dancers had diminished. Chittaqua suspected that by now, this number may be as low as three. He only hoped Achipan would encounter one of them on the western plains.

Chittaqua stopped dancing and pointed at the grim face of Piqua.

"I bring you truth," the apparition rasped.

Ootego threw his arms high above his head and shook his totem stick. "Stand away from the ghost," he shouted ominously. "Let him by!" He placed his mouth close to Piqua's ear and whispered with urgency. "We *must* escort him inside the gates or great evil will befall us. Only he can remove the red skull."

Piqua wasn't certain what this boded and gave a sidelong glance at his shaman. Ootego was beginning to sound foolish, but going back inside the strong walls of his village and shutting the gates was very appealing.

"We must make him welcome," Ootego warned. "Or he might send demons into your dreams."

"*Aiiieeyaaa*," Piqua responded with irritation, stepping away from Ootego as if stung by a wasp.

Whiskey, Piqua decided. *Whiskey will help me think.* With a sweep of an arm the Seneca chief gestured for the strange medicine man to enter.

Struggling in his dreamlike consciousness, Philippe heard more fearful hoots and angry shouting from the villagers.

Something has frightened them.

With great effort, the *coureur de bois* straightened his numbed legs and gripped high on the tethers tied to his wrists to keep from swaying. The day before, this action would have caused him excruciating pain. He craned his head and looked in the direction of the gate. Warriors began to file back inside the village. They seemed to be escorting someone. His vision was blurred forcing him to squint.

Is that you, Pierre?

Before anyone got close enough for his eyes to focus on, his trembling limbs could no longer take the exertion. Philippe felt himself slipping into another stupor.

I pray it's you, Pierre. I cannot hold out much longer.

Through his mask, Chittaqua saw Philippe attempt to stand at his approach only to sag limply in the tethers.

He is weak, but fights still.

But as he walked by, the shaman could also see many cuts, festering sores, a grayish pallor to the skin, vile black excrement on the ground, and a pool of vomit in the dirt. Even if he had the protective power of his ring with him, Snow Hair wouldn't survive another day like that.

"This way," Ootego said, pointing at the large ceremonial roundhouse.

Chittaqua entered, stopped to let his eyes adjust to the dim light, then saw the fire pits in the middle of the structure. He turned slowly and examined every part of the interior. The twelve-foot-high walls were liberally covered with war shields and wood carvings of various totems. As visual record of the Wolf clan's history, Chittaqua saw eleven deerskins, stretched flat over circular birch limbs, painted to illustrate clan victories from important battles fought in the past. Two of those showed triumphs over the Erigh. Dominating the room at the front, where the eyes of everyone would normally be fixed, five bleached timber wolf skulls were suspended from the roofing beams on leather tethers. They were arranged to hang in an arc, the center one two feet above the clan chief's head, a suggestion of teeth and power.

Chittaqua walked to a position three paces short of the dead embers. With his totem stick, he drew a six-foot circle in the dirt. He sat down, cross-legged at the center of the circle. He intended to sit there motionless while the room filled. Outside, the twilight shadows were gathering with the sunset.

Seneca braves filed into the roundhouse, their faces curious and suspicious. No one dared to approach the holy man too closely, hanging back instead to whisper to one another.

Chittaqua considered the Seneca to be the most ferocious and reckless of the six Iroquois tribes. And they were not given to patience for very long. A violent response to anything out of the ordinary was likely from these warriors. But he also knew from experience, matters concerning evil ghosts and dead spirits could induce great trepidation in them. His plan to rescue Snow Hair depended heavily on reinforcing those fears. His very presence, sitting motionless, saying nothing, doing nothing, asking for nothing, already raised the level of anxiety within this clan. He could see it in their faces. And he hadn't spoken yet.

Food and drink were placed near the edge of the circle. Chittaqua ignored the courtesy.

Outside, Ootego was enjoying his new status as word spread among the villagers he too was one of the legendary ghost dancers. He'd told them this before, but few had been impressed. He rekindled the rumor after the Andrototekan came inside the compound. He could feel the admiring eyes of the younger warriors and women, peering at him with new respect, desire, and envy.

With an intentionally deep voice, Ootego gave instructions to Piqua and the elders.

"My *brother* will speak to us," he proudly told them. "Be ready for prophecy. Ghosts will visit soon."

"And what of the death skull?" asked an elder.

"He will remove it when he leaves."

At least, Ootego hoped this was the case.

They'd all heard about the death skull posted outside Maltoc's village, and the ill fortune that had befallen the Hawk clan.

"I will make the Andrototekan remove the hex."

Ootego was pleased to see the elders' heads nod. Before now, the warrior-elders of the clan tended not to listen to him much.

But all of you are listening to me now, he gloated. *Aren't you?*

Not everyone was so inclined. Sauquita pushed past the slower walking warriors. He wanted to see this *holy man*. What he saw didn't impress him.

Just another painted old man, he decided, *hoping for the old ways to return.*

Sauquita wished he'd not been away hunting when this one arrived. The brooding young brave walked over and stood with his fists on his hips directly in front of Chittaqua. He glowered at the seated figure but was careful to remain outside of the circle scribed in the dirt, as Ootego had instructed.

"What do you want old man?" he whispered to the seated figure. Getting no response, he stooped so he could look directly into the eyes. "Why are you here?"

The seated figure showed no reaction. The eyes of the mask looked like two black holes.

"Do you think I am frightened of you? I am Sauquita, son of Piqua," he whispered. "Ootego tells warriors to set aside their weapons and listen to your prophecy. If you are here to preach peace with the white man, then you are my enemy. In here, I do as my father commands. But in the forests ..."

Sauquita left the sentence unfinished. This summer's events had only worsened Sauquita's resentment toward the tribal elders. Anticipating the reward that Iron Pots would give him, he had attempted to capture Snow Hair, but Snow Hair had continually eluded him. It had become personal. When his father refused to allow him to keep Snow Hair's woman, his bitterness deepened into hatred.

"You plan to speak prophecy?" Sauquita's voice was full of contempt. "I say you are here to treat us like children. To tell stories about animals. To eat from our cooking pots. To lay with our women before going on to the next village."

Sauquita saw no reaction. But the ears and eyes behind the mask were listening and watching the young brave intently. The lack of response only intensified Sauquita's anger. He moved inside the circle in order to glare directly into the dark holes of the mask.

"Beware old man," he hissed. "Make no attempt to sway the clan from our path to war, or I will follow after you leave and bring an end to your stories."

"Sauquita! What are you doing? Move away from him," Ootego scolded loudly. "This is a *holy man!*"

"Holy man?" Sauquita sneered and strutted to his place of rank, a log stump below and to the right of his father.

Ootego scowled at the young brave. Sauquita's behavior had become increasingly belligerent. He ridiculed and mocked the old ways and legends. He pressed for war against the French soldiers continuously. And Piqua made little effort to control him.

The room darkened as men and boys filled the roundhouse. Ootego ordered the four ceremonial fires arranged in a square at the room's center to be lit, illuminating the interior with a yellow glow.

The roundhouse was thirty paces in diameter, constructed from sturdy hardwood oak and ash, covered with broad sheets of birch bark. The chinks in the seams had been caulked with clay. The roof was dome-like, covered with overlapping hides and branches to form a rain-tight roof. Two holes were left open near the top center to allow smoke a place to escape.

Warrior pride is their strength and their weakness, Chittaqua reminded himself.

The shaman decided to focus his magic directly in front of Piqua, using the skulls of the wolf. Tucked behind his loincloth were two pouches of a special mixture of aromatic weed and dried cactus plants he intended to burn in the fires. It would effuse the room with a pungent, sweet odor, adding mystery to his conjuring. And if the smoke was inhaled, a warrior's mind would open to the other side. Over the years, the effect on Chittaqua had lessened, but to the uninitiated, it could be potent, provoking disturbing images. Anyone affected was highly susceptible to suggestion. Chittaqua knew it would not take much, a pinch or two of the crumbly plant if smoked in a pipe. He'd brought both pouches and planned to use it all.

The men of the clan had changed into their finest dress and spread about the room on log benches in order of seniority. Many small boys, some as young as eight or nine winters, attended the meeting, some for the first time. They sat expectantly at their fathers' feet, their excitement evident in whispers and occasional nervous laughter. The village women were not allowed to attend, but managed to observe by standing on tree stumps on the outside and peeking through the small holes they had gouged out of the clay caulking between the seams in the bark.

Ootego nodded and walked to the fires. The room quieted with anticipation. Ootego raised his arms, emitted a high-pitched wail, and discreetly tossed a small leather pouch of gun powder into one of the fires. There followed a flash, a hiss, bouncing white sparks, and billowing acrid smoke. The eyes of the young boys opened wide with wonder, nervous but greatly entertained. Warriors shifted uncomfortably in their seats.

It was a good beginning.

Drummers began a rhythmic beat. Ootego spoke in a solemn voice.

"O spirit of our fathers. Look into our hearts. Guide us to the truth."

Unexpectedly, the four adjoining fires exploded in gray black clouds of smoke filled with sizzling yellow sparks. Many in the room raised their arms to shield their eyes. Amid the confusion and surprise, Chittaqua dropped the first pouch into the flames. The fire consumed it immediately. The smoke began to curl. The drums stopped.

The apparition stood and removed his mask to reveal a white-painted face with fierce red eye sockets. The cheeks and eyes were tinted with black highlights. It was the face of death.

All in the room gasped softly.

The Andrototekan had a broken nose closely mimicking the bent nose on the mask of the god.

Chittaqua held the mask in front of his body with one hand and stepped closer to the clan chief. He stabbed his totem stick upright in the ground directly in front of Piqua and hung the mask from its top.

As the eyes of death gazed at him, Piqua swallowed, glancing nervously at Ootego.

Chittaqua turned and glared at the other men in the room. He started to smell their fear.

The fires blazed smoke and sparks a second time. The youngest boys buried their heads in their fathers' robes.

Chittaqua began speaking in a low, melodious voice.

"O people of the Wolf,
  I dwell with your fathers.
They speak to me
  and reveal to you!
Heed their words!

"I have searched the world
  for the tears of the Great Spirit,

to drink and heal the ache in my heart."

Chittaqua spoke of the journeys of his youth, of the desert places, the crumbling cities, painted treasures, the mountains he climbed, the lands of ice, and the tombs of their ancestors.

"Desperate, I drank from our lakes,
        And found them bitter with the gifts of the white man.
I searched for the Hurons,
        found only their shadows!
I sought the Ojibway, the Abnakis, the Ottawa,
        they live in the white man's house!
Where are the people of Tahiawagi?
Maybe the mighty Iroquois have the drink?
I sought the Mohawk, the Oneida, the Onondaga,
        found them wearing the white man's clothes,
        their bodies infected with his poisonous sores.
I asked the white man if he had such a drink.
And, indeed, he did!
I drank it.
        But it was bitter poison.
        And caused me to wander without purpose!
I searched for my people,
        and found the Erigh...not at all."

At the mention of the Erigh, hooting, both fearful and angry, erupted from many. A few of the elders recognized this holy man was, in fact, the great sorcerer Chittaqua. The clan was in danger!

Another explosion from the fires silenced the room. With a flick of his fingers, Chittaqua tossed the second of the plant-filled pouches into the nearest fire pit. Atop the blazing hot coals, a smoky incense spewed into the air as if from a large pipe. Chittaqua spun several times in a circle with his arms wide to disperse the sweet-smelling smoke around the roundhouse. It moved in spirals toward the walls and the men sitting there.

The Andrototekan spoke again.

"O people of the Wolf,
  my doom brings me to you.
I have cast aside the white man's clothing,
  his weapons,
  his pots made of metal.
I stay not at his house and eat not of his food.
I war not on his people.
I shun his poisons, his drinks.
I no longer suffer his diseases
  that eat at the face and body so
  even the carrion birds shrink away in fear.
And as I cast aside these evils, my heart was mended,
  my spirit soared like His messenger.
Oho!
I found a secret place in my heart,
  and the drink was there, pure, golden with life,
  healing in its gaze!
But I drank not one drop, despite the trials I endured,
  because having cast aside
  all the evil things consuming my spirit
  and cleansing the bitterness from my heart,
My desire for the drink, was gone!"

The room was hushed. Some elders suspected the shaman was finished. A few imagined a hex was coming. But no one wanted to be the first to challenge the Andrototekan's powerful magic. Embers from the fires swirled above their heads, a bee-like swarm of glowing red lights. Dizziness abounded. Hallucinations became pronounced. A buzzing sound was heard. A man became fascinated by a spider climbing his arm. Another man stepped forward and urinated into one of the fires, then collapsed unconscious. Some vomited. Others began singing and dancing nonsensically.

Again, Chittaqua spun in a circle, swinging his totem stick above his head, creating broad wide eddies in the air. He spoke in a voice rising slowly in strength and condemnation.

"O people of the Wolf, you are in peril.

The end with no purpose approaches!
Cast out the white man's poison!
*Or your totems will cease to exist...*forever!*"*

Everyone was profoundly affected by the sweet smoke permeating the room. Many had stopped watching the apparition entirely, already lost in a dreamlike world of their own. Only Piqua and a few of the elders still listened, though most of them were starting to see strange things and were afraid.

The skull of a wolf above Piqua began swaying back and forth, swinging in larger and larger arcs until it flew through the air and into the fires. A fountain of sparks burst upward. The skull was engulfed in flames.

"*Queee! Queee! Queee!*"

Distressed hooting erupted from all sides of the great room. Warriors pointed across the room at others, shouting blame and accusations. Some began to dance. One warrior threw off his cloak and tried to mount a man sitting next to him.

Piqua was blinking rapidly at the strange sights and sounds surrounding him.

"There is wisdom in these words," a warrior shouted.

Sauquita shook his head to dispel his dizziness and struggled to his feet.

"I do not believe this," he screamed above the babbling voices of the others. "These are false dreams! The smoke has poisons!"

Chittaqua was satisfied few had heard the hot-tempered youth. The Seneca's fear was at its highest. But now Chittaqua also began to feel the effect of the smoke and knew he must get outside soon before he was overwhelmed. He pointed his totem stick at Piqua.

"*You* allowed death into your village!"

Piqua recoiled.

"I sense the presence of a white man. Evil comes if he remains. Evil that will suck the eyes from the Wolf and feast on its heart."

Another skull above Piqua's head began to sway. The clan chief's head was throbbing. He looked at Ootego in desperation.

"What must we do?"

The clan was close to panic. Ootego felt an urge to laugh. Everything he now beheld seemed wildly funny. But a stronger surge of fear kept his attention focused, the fear he would be blamed for the results of this night.

Chittaqua pointed his totem stick at each of the wolf skulls, which were now all swinging back and forth. The Seneca had never seen these hallowed totems react like this before.

"Your totems see this danger!" Chittaqua continued. He pointed the tip of his staff at Piqua's chest. "I see evil moving on the lands outside. It is coming!"

"What must we do?"

Ootego stood between Chittaqua and Piqua and raised his hands to try and calm the room.

"The white man must leave our village," Ootego shouted.

Piqua saw skulls dancing all over the room. He became agitated. His mouth moved but no words came out.

The walls of the roundhouse began to heave. Ootego knew he must find a way clear of this situation, and fast.

"Oh, Ghost Dancer," Ootego entreated loudly. "Will *you* remove the evil from our village?"

"I will do this," Chittaqua replied. "I will remove the evil and the red skull. But the evil will lurk until the sun rises. All must remain here."

"Nooo!" Sauquita screamed, suspecting a trick. He threw himself at Chittaqua, reaching out to strangle the shaman's throat. He was stopped by Ootego and two of the elders.

"Take the white man from my village, Ghost Dancer," Ootego implored. "Remove this curse."

Many heads around the room nodded vigorously.

Sauquita glared at Chittaqua. "Nooo! He is lying!"

The veins on his neck and head bulged with fury. Breaking free of the others, the young warrior lunged at the painted shaman again. But with this sudden movement, Piqua's tolerance of his son ended. He rapped Sauquita sharply on the temple with his stone war club, knocking him senseless to the ground. The room went instantly quiet. The elders looked at Sauquita's inert body with astonishment. Piqua scowled and looked around to see if there were any more dissenters.

"We will stay until the sun rises," Piqua proclaimed. Then the clan chief squatted down and inexplicably began to defecate.

His movements followed by anxious eyes, the Andrototekan left the room. Once outside, Chittaqua took several deep breaths of the clean night air. He moved quickly to where Snow Hair was restrained.

In the moonlight, Chittaqua examined Philippe's injuries as best he could. Philippe hung limp in the tethers, legs slack, dried blood crusted down his arms from the bite of the leather binding his wrists. Gripped by fever, his body twitched and trembled. His skin was dry and hot to the touch, his breathing labored. A bitter, foul odor exuded from him.

The shaman strapped his ghost mask and totem stick over his back. He lifted Philippe onto his shoulder and cut the bindings free. The *coureur de bois* moaned softly but made no other movement. Snow Hair was heavy, but danger compelled Chittaqua to move quickly. He didn't think the Seneca would remain inside the roundhouse all night. The village looked deserted as he walked toward the main gate carrying his heavy load. The sentries on the walls were gone. The gate was the last obstacle. To his surprise, no one was there either.

Philippe moaned loudly each time he was jostled. Chittaqua carried him down the path leading to the stream, hoping he would remain asleep. In his delirium, the *coureur de bois* might try to resist, which would slow the escape.

The totem stick kept poking Chittaqua painfully in the back. He laid Philippe on the ground and stabbed the ornately carved totem stick into the center of the path and hung the mask at the top. If the Seneca followed, the mask of prophecy might dissuade them for a while.

Once across the shallow stream, the shaman proceeded to a place about a mile beyond the cornfield. He lowered Philippe to the ground, untied a rope strapped around a tree, and lowered the clothing and provisions he'd suspended from a branch further up. He took a heavy beaver-skin cloak and covered Philippe, then washed much of the itchy paint from his face and body. Discarding the soiled loincloth, he dressed again in traveling clothes. He slipped Philippe's ring back on the *coureur de bois'* hand.

Under the moonlight, Snow Hair's eyes flickered.

Good, Chittaqua thought.

The shaman discarded all of his supplies with the exception of weapons and his medicine bag. Hoisting Philippe back over his shoulder with a grunt, he started walking again in a northerly direction. He intended to walk through the night, to travel as far as possible before morning, or until he was exhausted. The Seneca brave who had tried to attack him would soon follow, he was certain of that.

Philippe's weight slowly sapped Chittaqua's strength. After two hours of continuous march, he was forced to rest. Under the moonlight, he used the rest time to examine Philippe's injuries more closely. There were numerous superficial welts and cuts all over the body. He saw deep, scabbed-over lacerations on the wrists. He cleaned and bandaged those. A small piece of Philippe's scalp was missing, but the wound had been cauterized, probably with hot coals from a fire. Chittaqua also saw long sinuous burns on his arms and legs, where someone had dragged a burning stick.

Moving carefully, he squeezed along the flesh of the arms and legs, searching for the hard swollenness of fractures. Fortunately, none of the bones were broken. Chittaqua prepared some medicines and carefully coaxed Philippe into swallowing a mixture of water and his most powerful healing herbs. For himself, the shaman took a copious amount of another medicine that would keep him awake and increase his strength to help him to run further. Within minutes, his heart began pounding. Chittaqua lifted Snow Hair, who now seemed lighter, back upon his shoulder. But the false sense of strength would not last for long.

His instincts urged him to hurry.

CHAPTER 14
RIVIÈRE AUX BOEUFS
AUGUST 1754
Louie Hawkfeeder and Michel Langlois

By the time Pierre Dunemoore and his men reached Fort Machault, Chittaqua had already rescued Philippe from the Seneca and was making his way east toward the Allegheny River.

With only a vague idea what the *shérif* looked like, the Scotsman entered the fort with his men, posing as another group of *coureurs de bois* traders. If Gaspard de Propei was there, they planned to kill him at the first opportunity. But after much questioning, they determined no one resembling the *shérif* had been seen there. Pierre sent Michel and Louie to collect his *coureurs de bois* and went to see Captain Daniel Joncaire, the fort commandant.

"Monsieur Dunemoore! It's good to see you again. War creates odd coincidences, does it not? Before present circumstances, I saw you twice in three years. Then, all at once, I see you four times in three weeks." The officer shook Pierre's hand vigorously.

Daniel Joncaire was a curious army officer, in Pierre's opinion. He was an aristocrat and extremely wealthy. Purportedly, he'd chosen to become a soldier because he found the uniforms appealing. Outwardly, he projected the appearance of a fop. But Pierre knew the officer to be a fearless, almost reckless fighter. A man who had been wounded more than once in violent wilderness skirmishes, which stood in stark contrast to his eccentricities and fastidiousness. The commandant was attired in an impeccably clean white-and-gray dress uniform.

"And where are you bound this time, Monsieur?"

"I'm looking for Shérif Gaspard de Propei. Deeya' know him?"

The commandant leaned back in his chair. The smile disappeared.

"Yes. I met him on my way here. Detestable human being. Filthy as horse dung." Joncaire sniffed. "In fact, he smells like horse dung…no, on more reflection, horse dung is a perfume compared to him."

"Nice tah' know ya' like him too. He's pursuing Philippe Gerrard."

"I know."

"Deeya' know where he is?"

"I expect he's at Fort Le Boeuf, where I saw him last."

Pierre frowned. "Tha's too bad."

"What do you mean?"

Pierre related the whole story concerning Philippe, Michelle, Henri, Maltoc, Piqua, and Chittaqua.

Captain Joncaire listened carefully. His frown deepened. "How may I help you?"

"I'm goin' tah' the Wolf clan village tah' get Philippe. I will bring him here."

"Do you need troops?"

"No. The Seneca are in a rage aboot Fort Duquesne. They're scouting the army continuously. My *coureurs de bois* leaving this fort will be ignored. And we can move faster without bein' seen."

"Do you need any supplies?"

"A bit o' food and as much powder and shot as we kin carry would be welcome. I expect a bloody brawl before this next leg is over."

Ootego remained awake through the disconcerting night. The room resonated with snores and heavy breathing. The dancing had lasted only a few more hours before most of the men and boys fell asleep from exhaustion. The smoky opiate in the air dissipated as the fires burned low, but the apprehensive elders continued to ask Ootego question after question to interpret the Andrototekan's prophecies. One message was clear, Ootego emphasized, they were to rid themselves of the white man's poisonous ways, whiskey included. This had not been welcome news to Piqua. He'd already sent his wife to bring him a half-full jug and was sipping at it during the discussions. He flatly refused any suggestion to give up his whiskey. Eventually, Piqua became too drunk to argue and fell asleep.

When the first rays of morning light were seen above the trees, Ootego breathed a great sigh of relief. He cut the leather bindings restraining Sauquita. The brave jumped to his feet and shoved past Ootego. The angry man ran to the hanging posts and screamed with rage upon seeing his enemy gone. Enraged, the young brave went to his lodge to collect his weapons.

"I will kill Snow Hair myself," he vowed. He also planned to capture and drag the famous Erigh medicine man back to the village. Then he would personally torture the shaman to prove Chittaqua possessed no magic, and his prophecies were nothing but lies.

As Sauquita walked determinedly to the main gate, he was joined by two dozen, eager, younger braves. Drawn by Sauquita's warrior ways, his hatred for the white man, and his fearsome defiance of the elders, Ootego, and even the legendary Andrototekan, they were anxious for his leadership and ready to fight. Bolstered by the raw courage of the young warriors, Sauquita suddenly recognized this pursuit could establish something legendary.

I will become war chief after this, he thought smugly.

As Philippe Gerrard became more coherent, he also became more sensitive to his pain and had begun to moan weakly. The shaman slipped the woodsman from his shoulder and laid him beneath a pine tree on a bed of needles.

Philippe gazed up in surprise. "Chittaqua?" He attempted to sit up but was overcome with dizziness. He rolled to his side and retched.

Chittaqua quickly mixed an herbal remedy from his medicine bag in a wooden bowl of water.

Philippe flopped over on his back. "I don't understand. Where...how?"

"Drink this," the shaman urged, helping Philippe to a sitting position.

It tasted bitter. Philippe gagged.

"Do not spit it out! The medicine will ease the pain in your head and make you strong enough to walk. When did you last eat?"

"Eat? I don't...Chittaqua? How...what did you...where ...?"

"I brought you from Piqua's camp," Chittaqua said quickly. "But the Seneca will come for us soon. Can you stand?"

"I want water."

Philippe swallowed huge draughts of the cool, sweet liquid. The water temporarily quenched the burning cramps in his stomach. He drank until he was panting for air.

"You came to Piqua's camp alone?"

"Yes. Drink more."

"But how did you...wait! Where is Michelle?"

"Animal Scalp has taken her to the fort on the Buffalo River," Chittaqua assured. "She is safe."

Philippe rested his head in his hands. "Thank God."

Chittaqua touched his hand. "Your totem."

"What?"

Chittaqua pointed at the ring. "It has made you stronger."

Philippe held up his hand and looked at the ring in surprise. "I gave this ring to Pierre …"

"I met him on the river.'

Philippe looked around dully. "Is he here too?"

"No. But he is coming."

Philippe looked into the shaman's intense dark eyes. "I thought…I worried I might not see you again."

Chittaqua regarded Philippe steadily. "Why? You are protected."

Philippe smiled weakly and shook his head at the shaman's enduring stubbornness.

"Help me stand."

He was seized by dizziness, which subsided after a few seconds. He took some unsteady steps, holding out his arms for balance. He rolled his neck and twisted at the waist to see if anything was sprained. Hardened scabs from dozens of minor flesh wounds split and started oozing from his movement.

"Christ, my skin feels like it's being stung by hornets!" Philippe shivered. "I am cold." He was naked from the waist up.

Chittaqua pulled some clothing from his bag. "Wear this."

Philippe slipped on the deerskin and instantly felt warmer. His heart was pounding inside his chest.

"What did you give me?"

"Walking medicine. Drink more," Chittaqua urged. It was his most powerful stimulant, and he had given half a pouch to Philippe.

Philippe swallowed as much as he could of the bitter fluid. Chittaqua drank the remainder.

"Good. Now we go," Chittaqua said firmly. He repacked his medicine bag.

"Where?"

"To the fort at Venango."

Chittaqua started walking; Philippe limped along beside him. The shaman slowly increased his pace and carefully monitored Philippe's ability to keep up. He wanted to drive the *coureur de bois* but not beyond the ability of his weakened body.

"I want to go to Fort Le Boeuf," Philippe said between breaths.

"First we go to Venango."

Chittaqua stopped suddenly and turned.

Philippe halted next to him and crouched, peering in every direction, looking for danger.

"What's wrong?"

Chittaqua grabbed Philippe's shoulders.

"Your son is at the fort on the lake," the shaman said proudly. "The one you call Presque Isle."

"You found him?"

Chittaqua nodded.

"You blessed, blessed man! They are both safe!"

"No," Chittaqua warned. "The evil one searches for them. And the Seneca are not far behind us."

Yet another branch slapped Louie Hawkfeeder across his face. It was too dark.

"*Merde*! Pierre, I cannot see where I am going."

"Aye," Pierre agreed. "It's hard for me too. But we must go on."

"The forest is too thick. There's not enough moonlight to light our trail."

"All right. We'll make torches."

"What? Every Seneca scout in these hills will know exactly where we are. We might as well shoot each other."

"I know! But we kinnah' stop! This is wha' we'll dah'. I'll carry the torches. You and the others trail back aboot twenty paces to stay out o' the light."

Michel Langlois shook his head and smiled. "Then we'll have to listen to you brag forever about your bravery. We'll take turns holding the torch."

Pierre smiled. "Good! Now we kin' make bets on which o' us will draw the first arrow."

Only Michel, Louie, and Pierre thought the prospect funny.

It was getting difficult to see Chittaqua's tracks, but now Sauquita saw two sets of footprints.

"Look, the devil shaman no longer carries Snow Hair." Sauquita tried to match the pace of the tracks by stepping in them. "You see. They have started to run. We must run too."

Sauquita called his braves back to the main trail. He didn't want to lose any of his men in the darkness.

"We move in a line," he told them.

They walked single file, holding the shoulder of the man in front, using only the dim moonlight shining through the trees to see their path.

When they reached a point where the trail split, Sauquita dropped to the ground and felt the earth with his fingers, attempting to feel the tracks of his quarry. But it was hopeless.

"What's wrong?" one of the braves asked.

"This trail leads up the hill. The other goes around."

The younger brave was tired and didn't relish the thought of climbing a small mountain in the dark. "Snow Hair was sick and weak from torture," he argued. "He would not climb this hill at night."

Sauquita grunted. "Maybe the devil shaman will make him fly," he said sarcastically.

"They *will* have trouble walking in the night like us," another brave added. "They may not be far ahead."

"And we may also go by them while they hide," Sauquita said.

He debated silently what to do. He was determined to have his revenge. They could keep going down the trail or they could camp and take up chase again at first light. *Or*, they could turn and go up the hill.

"Pierre," the man carrying the torch called anxiously.

No one wanted to carry the torch for long. Only Louie carried it for as long as Pierre did, but Pierre didn't blame the others over this. If they encountered an enemy, whoever was carrying the torch was certain to be among the first killed.

The Scotsman walked forward and accepted the torch from the other woodsman. It was burning out. The other man avoided his eyes.

"I need another shirt," Pierre announced. They were using their clothing as fuel.

"I can hear the legend being told years from now," Louie said. "Five naked white men emerged from the night forest, frightening the Seneca into flight when the Indians saw the size of their cocks."

"They will more likely die from laughter after seeing yours," Michel said.

Pierre grinned. "Remember nah' tah' fire right away, even if I'm shot. It will only give away your position."

"No one is going to attack us, Pierre. The Seneca actually *sleep* at night," Louie Hawkfeeder joked.

"I hope you're right," Pierre said under his breath.

"Only a white man is stupid enough to march around in the dark with a torch for everyone to see," Louie continued.

Pierre found the hunting trail leading from the Allegheny River surprisingly easy to follow in the wavering torchlight. The ground had been depressed by the feet of thousands of Indian hunters over centuries of time. The night was eerie and quiet as he moved between the shadows of the ancient trees. The only sounds the Scotsman heard, other than an occasional clank of metal behind him, was the lick-snap of the torch as it slowly consumed another linen shirt.

Pierre walked as fast as he dared. Though the trail was well worn, there were plenty of protruding rocks and snagging tree roots. If he tripped, he might accidentally extinguish his makeshift torch. Louie had gotten powder burns on his hands helping Pierre light the first torch. It had not been that dark yet, and they could still see. But this deep into the forest, it was black like the inside of a cave.

To ease his nervousness, the Scotsman hummed a nautical ditty his father used to sing. Pierre wasn't worried about being overheard. An enemy would see the light long before they heard his voice. Occasionally, the canopy of the trees above him cleared enough to see the starry sky. The ground began to slope upward.

We're at the foothills, he thought.

"Oho!"

A voice boomed unexpectedly from the darkness in front of Pierre. His whole body jerked. The hairs stood up on his neck.

"Merciful God," the Scotsman said softly. "I'm dead."

But he wasn't dead. If it *had* been Seneca, he knew they would have killed him immediately. *That's a French voice.* Pierre held the torch higher and squinted into the blackness.

"Who's there?"

Pierre could hear swearing and stumbling behind him as his terrified men cocked their muskets and ducked behind trees to either side of the trail.

"I want to meet the white man brave enough to travel a Seneca hunting trail at night carrying a torch," said the voice from somewhere up ahead.

"Philippe!"

Two men stepped into the small circle of his torchlight. Chittaqua was supporting the *coureur de bois* under one shoulder and carried his pack and weapons in the other hand. Philippe was limping badly at the shaman's side.

"Philippe!" Pierre shouted, delighted.

The Scotsman hugged them both. "My God, laddie." He wiped some tears from his eyes. "Ya' great blond-haired fool. I thought I'd find ya' dead! Dinnah' ya' ever dah' anything tha' daft again! Deeya' hear me, laddie? And dinnah' ever, ever, *scare* me like tha' again. I'll be walking back with my pants full o' shit."

The other *coureurs de bois* joined the happy reunion.

"Michelle?" Philippe asked anxiously.

"She's safe, laddie. And Henri too. Chittaqua must have told ya'. Both are safe inside a fort protected by French cannon and soldiers!"

Now that he'd found Philippe, Pierre wanted to make camp and sleep until morning.

Chittaqua turned suddenly, his attention on the darkness behind them. "Quiet!"

"Wha'?"

"They're coming," the shaman warned.

"The Seneca," Philippe added.

Pierre squinted. "In the dark? Are they using a torch?"

"No torch. They *see* yours. This is *their* trail."

Pierre did not like the idea of fighting at night. "How far away?"

The shaman gazed into the darkness.

"Not close." He looked at Pierre. "But even without a torch, they run this trail faster than you."

"Then we are goin' back tonight," Pierre declared. "Give me another shirt! Louie, Michel. Help Philippe. I'll lead the way. This time, stay close."

The *coureurs de bois* slipped their arms under Philippe's shoulders.

Pierre led them back down the trail at a fast walk. Half an hour later, the trail split and Pierre took the one leading north.

"Wait! That's the wrong way," Philippe said. "The river's that way."

"But we're nah goin' tah' the river. We're going tah' Venango, tah' Fort Machault."

"The river will be faster."

"Nah' if you have tah' swim. We dinnah' have any canoes. We walked from Fort Machault."

Though the trail to Venango was straight, Philippe knew the safety of the fort was still about five more hours away. "The Seneca are likely to catch up with us before we get there."

The exhaustion the men felt moments before melted away at the thought of being in a fight with the Seneca. The *coureurs de bois* would sprint if Philippe had been able to run.

"Then there's no time tah' lose. Keep the pace, lads. It's a deadly race we run," Pierre said.

The air of the forest had the odor of rotting vegetation as the hunting trail passed through a place where the small streams coming down from the hills created a marshy area. The earth beneath the decaying pine needles and dead leaves was soft and moist.

Sauquita hissed for everyone to stop. He dropped to his knees in the gooey mud and passed his fingertips lightly over the bumps and ruts in the ground. He could feel faint indentations where men had walked and could trace the outlines of feet. But it would be almost impossible in this wet dark place to determine how many men had passed this way or to guess at the age of the tracks. Still, Sauquita was a master hunter, and he moved his fingers methodically from left to right, gently examining each mark he determined to be made by a man. It took patience, but none of the prints he found exhibited the distinctive drag of Snow Hair's left foot.

Sauquita stood and grumbled with frustration. He gazed into the darkness all around them, hoping his desire for revenge would give him insight into where they might be hiding. But it was useless.

Again, he has eluded me, he thought bitterly. *But not for long. Snow Hair's wounds will slow them, and he will get weaker.*

Sauquita concentrated and tried to recall the most difficult parts of the trail, the ravines, wet shale hillsides, and the depth of the streams they would have to ford. He tried to picture the degree of effort it would take for the devil shaman to help the much bigger and injured man.

Chittaqua will be tired. But neither of them will rest. They must take advantage of the darkness. But Sauquita knew it might be long after sunrise before they could close the distance between them.

"Snow Hair's wounds will slow them. We will walk this trail in the dark all night. Make leather straps. Tie them to the man in front of you. If you lose your grip, cry out, and we will stop."

Taking the lead, Sauquita did his best to move at a steady pace up the trail, pulling at the man behind him. The ancient hunting trail twisted and turned randomly through the trees. He had hunted and traveled this path hundreds of times since he was a boy, but never at night. The younger braves stumbled, bumped into the trees, and ran into one another. Sauquita heard their labored breathing and cursing as roots, rocks, and overhanging branches snagged at their bodies.

Sauquita was never going to stop. He must have a victory, and Snow Hair carried great status in the eyes of all the tribes. Chittaqua too. Killing them both together would be legendary. He kept his arms outstretched and up in front of his face. Each time he touched the trunk of a tree, he glanced up through the canopy of leaves at the stars, gauging the distance between the trees before deciding to pass it to his left or right. Occasionally, he would stop and search the ground in front of him, feeling for the edge of the rut they walked, to be certain they were still in it.

The trail suddenly veered sharply to the left.

Sauquita smiled. The worst was over. The hunting trail was broad and straight from this point forward.

"Ho!"

He called out each warrior's name and someone answered. No one had been lost.

"We must move with the quiet speed of the lynx. The land slopes down from here and the trail becomes straighter."

Reaching the lower bluffs of the hill, a breeze rose around them as the trees thinned. Sauquita stopped at the top of a rise. He could see much of the valley below them. The stars showed the boundary between the sky and the tree tops. When he saw the orange flicker of light far ahead in the distance near the valley floor, a smile spread across his face.

A torch, he gloated. *A mistake*. His decision to march all night had been a good one. The trail Snow Hair took led to Venango…and the new French fort. If his enemies reached there first, they would be safe.

"There!" Sauquita marshaled his men. "There is Snow Hair! See his light? Who makes fire in the open at night for everyone to see?" Sauquita said loudly to bolster their spirits. "Men who will soon lose their *scalps*!"

Pierre's pace had been relentless. The *coureurs de bois* had all taken turns supporting Philippe, but he was breathing heavily.

"Pierre, I cannot walk so fast."

The invigorating effect of Chittaqua's medicines had totally worn off. Exhaustion lay on him like a blanket of rocks.

"All right. We'll rest for a bit."

The Scotsman leaned his back against a tree and watched Chittaqua help Philippe drink some water. He lifted his eyes to the sky and was pleased to see the first pink-and-gold hues of sunrise. But in the forest, it would be another hour before they could travel without using the torch. He turned his head and peered back at the hill tops. He felt grim. If the Seneca were on this side of the hills, they knew exactly where they were.

Chittaqua gave Philippe a bowl of ground willow tree bark mixed in water. The *coureur de bois* gagged but forced himself to drink it.

"It's nah' much further, laddie," Pierre consoled. "We kinnah' stop for very long."

"I know. But I can hardly stand," Philippe said, disgusted with his weakness. "Maybe it would be better to hide me somewhere off the trail and bring back soldiers from Venango."

"*No*, laddie. We are *nah*' goin' tah' leave *anyone* behind."

"Pierre," said Louie, "I can carry him on my back if someone else will carry my pack and musket."

With a grunt, the giant *coureur de bois* hoisted Philippe to his shoulders and nodded at Pierre. "Let *me* set the pace."

Louie Hawkfeeder's pace was slower than before, but it was steady. In another hour, the trail narrowed to a cliff-side path running along the high embankment of the Allegheny River. The latest torch in Pierre's hand sputtered out. He tossed it aside. All the men were shirtless now, but they wouldn't need the torch anymore. It was light enough to see.

"Woo hoo! We've reached the river!"

The river meant the fort was close. The men were anxious to move faster. Louie Hawkfeeder groaned and wheezed under his heavy load. Philippe's head lolled back and forth, his body limp; he had lapsed into a stupor an hour earlier.

"It's nah' much farther, lads."

"There!" Sauquita pointed. "Seven of them. Not enough to win against us," Sauquita gloated. "And they carry Snow Hair on their shoulders!"

The Seneca began to hoot and scream, their weariness evaporating with the expectation of an easy and bloody victory. Several braves broke free and sprinted ahead of Sauquita, hoping to strike the first blow.

Sauquita didn't try to restrain them now. The *coureurs de bois* were certain to turn and fire their muskets.

One of the *coureur de bois* heard a noise coming from behind them.

"Seneca!"

Everyone turned.

The war party was trotting along the embankment trail several hundred paces behind them. The *coureurs de bois* looked to Pierre for a decision.

They'll catch us in minutes, Pierre thought. He quickly counted the ones he could see. *At least a dozen! Probably more.*

"They're too many. If we sprint we kin' beat them tah' the fort. It's less than a mile away." Pierre turned. "Louie?"

The panting *coureur de bois* wearily shook his head. "I cannot run with him."

"Then some will stay behind with me and slow them. The others carry on tah' the fort. Bring back the soldiers."

"I'll stay," Louie declared. "It will be faster if two men carry Philippe. I am too tired to run, anyway."

"Chittaqua, go with Philippe. Who stays with me?"

They all volunteered.

Pierre smiled. "I love every one o' ya'."

The hooting war cries of the Seneca got louder.

"Michel, my friend, you're the best shot. The rest of you, leave all your muskets but one. We'll make our stand right there."

Pierre smoothed the blood-and-sweat matted hair away from Philippe's forehead.

"Well, laddie," he said softly. "I guess you'll beat me to Venango after all." He touched his head to Philippe's and kissed his friend's cheek.

"*Adieu, mon ami*," the Scotsman whispered.

Two *coureurs de bois* grabbed Philippe by his shoulders. Chittaqua took his feet. They began to trot down the path.

Pierre pulled his porcupine scalp from his pack and slipped it on his head. He grinned at Louie and Michel.

"You look pretty," Louie said.

"All right, spread out among the rocks. Michel, show these heathens wha' a marvelous shot ya' are."

Steadying his musket's long barrel on a rock, Michel dropped the lead warrior, placing a slug in the center of his chest. The brave straightened then tumbled once before rolling off the embankment into the river.

Sauquita saw three of the *coureurs de bois* take cover among the rocks. He let a few more braves run by. He knew what was coming next.

The entire war party hesitated as the first warrior fell. The next two musket shots splattered off the stones.

Normally, Sauquita would have his men charge without slowing, knowing it would take time to reload a musket. But the distance and accuracy of the first musket shot surprised them. The *coureurs de bois* were bound to have extra weapons. He could not afford to lose too many of his men.

"Use the cover of rocks and trees to move up the trail," Sauquita shouted to his braves.

The *coureurs de bois* carrying Philippe were happy to see the embankment trail drop as it became level with the river. The trail turned sharply inland toward Fort Machault. The forest gave way to a freshly cut road amid the stumps leading to the fort.

Philippe awakened when the first sporadic musket shots rang out. "Stop!" Recognizing the sounds of battle, he struggled to stand on unsteady legs. "What's happening?" Philippe staggered around in confusion looking for the battle. "Where's Pierre?" he asked Chittaqua hoarsely.

Chittaqua pointed in the direction of the gunfire. "The Seneca."

Philippe's head was throbbing with pain. "What is…why are we …?"

"Pierre ordered us to take you to the fort," one of the men said.

Philippe grabbed the last musket. "No!" he told them. "Give me your powder horn and shot!"

"We have no other weapons."

"Go the fort! Bring the soldiers," Philippe said, gasping for breath.

He'd taken only a few steps before he began swaying drunkenly, barely able to keep his balance. He felt a strong arm slip beneath a shoulder.

"We go," Chittaqua said.

Michel Langlois' fire had been deadly accurate. Four shots, four dead Seneca. Louie could claim two hits, but those braves were only wounded.

"Aha!" Pierre shouted. His third shot had wounded a brave in the shoulder. But they were getting closer. He could see the leader pointing and giving orders to the others. The man had a familiar look. He stopped loading and concentrated on the brave's face.

"Move back!" Pierre shouted to the others.

The three men scrambled down the trail to another group of rocks.

"It's Sauquita," he told Louie and Michel.

"Sauquita," Louie repeated, his face hardened. Up to this point, they had not been too worried about the outcome. Most of these skirmishes usually ended if the attackers lost more than half of their warriors. But that was now unlikely. Piqua's son was a fearless and ferocious fighter.

Less than thirty paces separated the combatants. The Seneca had already fired the few muskets they carried and did not bother to reload, reverting to their faster shooting bows. They were becoming more careful about stepping into the open. Michel stopped firing and spent a minute reloading three muskets.

"Here," he shouted to Pierre and Louie, tossing them each a loaded weapon. "They'll be on us before we load again. We should fire in volley."

The Scotsman pulled the thick leather cover off his war ax. He glanced around the boulder he crouched behind. There were more than a dozen of them left.

Sauquita signaled for his men to charge.

Rising from their cover, the *coureurs de bois* fired the three-shot volley. Three Seneca fell dead.

Sauquita knew he couldn't afford to let them reload again. Holding up his war club, he screamed, and the remaining Seneca boiled forward almost tripping over one another to close the few remaining yards.

Pierre struggled to reload his musket one more time. In his haste, the ramrod slipped out of his hand and fell between some rocks. A screaming brave leaped at him.

Pierre barely had time to wield his ax.

Michel had reloaded and discharged his musket directly into the face of the charging warrior. The man's head exploded. Two other braves slammed into the marksman, knocking him backwards, driving tomahawks into his chest. Michel screamed, mortally wounded, but managed to disembowel one of them with his skinning knife before he died.

Upon seeing the death of his lifelong friend, Louie bellowed in anguish. "*Nooo!*"

Louie raised his tomahawk and knife. Pierre his pistol and war ax.

The rest of the Seneca were only steps away.

"*Adieu*, Pierre!" Louie shouted.

"Send them to hell, Louie!"

Each screaming their own war cries, Louie Hawkfeeder and Pierre Dunemoore charged the attacking Seneca.

Pierre aimed at Sauquita and shot his pistol. It missed.

Louie split the skull of a brave directly in front of him, as another speared him in the side. Yelling with agony, Louie slashed his skinning knife sideways, knocking the spear clear of his broken ribs. Blood spewed from his side. He swung wildly with his tomahawk and knife at anyone who came near, slicing open the chest of another warrior. One of the braves who'd killed Michel fell on Louie from behind, driving a knife into the *coureur de bois'* spine.

Louie screamed briefly before falling forward, dead before he hit the ground.

The triumphant brave turned, only to see the flash of Pierre's war ax as it bit into his throat.

A head flew in a bloody arc above the decapitated body.

Back-swinging the powerful ax, Pierre sliced through the elbow of the man with the chest wound, cutting deep into the brave's side rupturing internal organs, killing him instantly.

Sauquita was bumped as he pulled the trigger of the dragoon pistol he carried. The shot struck Pierre in his left thigh.

The Scotsman dropped his ax. He screamed at the blistering hot pain and fell to one knee.

"Sweet Jesus!"

Two more braves dove toward Pierre, knives and tomahawks raised above their heads. He retrieved his war ax, but they were already too close. He used the haft as a club, slamming it viciously into the groin of the first man before lifting it further to deflect the downward strike of the other's oncoming tomahawk. The first brave screamed and fell into the path of the other attacker. The second warrior shoved the first out of the way over the river. He grabbed Pierre's hair and was startled to see the scalp lift easily from the white man's head.

Whipping the ax handle back to the right, Pierre pushed the razor sharp head into the soft exposed belly of the second man, burying it to his wrists. The man fell backward with a gurgling scream, clutching his guts in one hand. The dying brave managed a glancing blow to Pierre's head with his tomahawk. Pierre experienced a shower of painful sparks. He was stunned instantly. The war ax dropped from his numbed fingers. He collapsed to a seated position. He shook his head, desperate to clear his blurry vision.

I'm dead! The final blow could come at any moment.

Only three attackers remained upright. Sauquita and two other braves, one was wounded in the shoulder by Pierre's ax.

The battle had been more costly than Sauquita had foreseen. He'd won, but most of his men were dead, the rest were wounded. And Snow Hair was not among the dead. He was being carried away by others. The warrior knew the fort was close. He retrieved a dropped spear and turned his attention back to Animal Scalp.

Pierre's vision cleared enough to see Sauquita advancing on him. The Scotsman felt a palm-sized sharp rock beneath one hand. Reacting quickly, he chucked it forcefully at the warrior.

The rock struck Sauquita's mouth. Blood spurted from lacerated lips and broken teeth. He howled and heaved his spear. It entered Pierre's chest at an angle. The Scotsman flew backward as if yanked by some large imaginary hand.

Pierre pulled the spearhead free and weakly clutched his side. He managed to smile at the Seneca brave.

Sauquita spit out a broken piece of tooth. He cursed and pulled out his steel tomahawk, intent on driving it into the Scotsman's smiling face.

"Pierre!"

Sauquita and Pierre looked to see two men coming back up the trail. The person in the lead was stumbling, almost falling over with each step.

"Snow Hair," Sauquita said with excitement.

Philippe lifted his weapon and fired, aiming for Sauquita's chest. But the trembling of his arms upset his aim. The shot hit Sauquita's steel ax head instead, snapping the haft in two.

His fingers stinging, Sauquita dropped the now useless weapon.

Philippe's last bit of energy gone. He collapsed.

Chittaqua knelt at Philippe's side.

When Sauquita saw Snow Hair and Chittaqua on the ground less than twenty paces away, and one of them helpless, he hooted triumphantly and charged. Two wounded braves followed their leader each wanting to be the first to reach Snow Hair. They ran past Pierre's prostrate body, thinking him dead.

Pierre had seen Philippe fall clumsily to the ground. He heard Sauquita's cry of triumph as he and his two remaining braves ran by. Pierre pushed himself to his knees, quickly grabbed his war ax, and, with one last effort, hurled the heavy weapon at the three Indians. It spun end over end and buried itself in the center of one wounded brave's back. The warrior screamed hideously and fell dead with the ax protruding from his body.

The assault from behind caught Sauquita by surprise, stopping his charge. Snarling, he turned and ran toward the Scotsman intent on slitting his throat.

But before Sauquita could reach him, Pierre rolled off the embankment and into the river. He gasped as cold water sucked at his remaining strength. His wound would prevent him from swimming, but at least he had denied the Seneca the pleasure of killing him.

Animal Scalp was out of reach!

Sauquita howled with fury. He turned again. "Snow Hair!" he screamed.

The two remaining warriors yelled battle cries and started running toward Chittaqua, waving their tomahawks above their heads.

Chittaqua crouched with his tomahawk in one hand and a knife in the other, ready to spring and kill whoever reached him first. But before the Seneca had covered half the distance, ball slugs from a volley of musket fire whined angrily past their heads, splattering bits of rock in the air as they plowed into the shale.

The Seneca stopped. Scores of shouting soldiers were running up the embankment trail, their *baïonnettes* gleaming in the sunlight.

Sauquita realized he could not reach Snow Hair with this new threat, and he did not plan to die this day.

"We go!" he shouted.

Sauquita paused long enough to rip Pierre's beautiful war ax from a dead brave's back. Gripping the heavy blood-covered weapon with one hand, he sensed its power. It was perfectly balanced. As he ran back toward his wounded warriors, Sauquita swung the war ax in a circle above his head to indicate a retreat.

The musket fire was coming dangerously close.

"I am Sauquita," he shouted at the charging soldiers. "Remember my name!" The defeated warrior then turned to lead the remnants of his decimated war party to safety.

Chittaqua saw the fighting was over. After he had convinced himself Snow Hair's wounds were not fatal, he sprinted toward Pierre. Jumping down the embankment into waist-high water, he was gripped by the muscle-cramping cold.

I am too weak to swim to him, he finally admitted to himself.

The shaman watched helplessly as Pierre Dunemoore thrashed the water with one arm, struggling to stay afloat. Each time Pierre's head submerged before reappearing long seconds later, Chittaqua heard Pierre wheezing and sputtering for air. Chittaqua slogged his way downstream in the shallows to stay even with the drowning man, holding out a hand. He prayed frantically for his totems to help the white man. He saw two canoes full of soldiers paralleling the troops advancing along the embankment.

Chittaqua yelled and waved his arms.

The soldiers heard his shouts. Chittaqua pointed at Pierre. The soldiers took aim and muskets balls began splashing in the water around him. The shaman ducked beneath the paralyzing, cold water.

"Hold your fire!" Captain Joncaire yelled angrily, waving his sword in the air. "He's not the enemy!"

Chittaqua held his breath as long as possible before cautiously raising his head above the surface. When he was convinced the soldiers were not going to shoot a second time, he continued shouting and pointing at Pierre.

The Scotsman had stopped his struggles and was now floating on his back in the water. The current had carried the body to the center of the stream.

A sergeant in the lead canoe yelled an order. The craft moved swiftly to intercept.

Chittaqua was overcome by a dark foreboding. He had not foreseen Pierre's death in his dreams. This should not have happened.

This is not right, he thought. *What else have I not seen?*

CHAPTER 15
RIVIÈRE AUX BOEUFS
AUGUST 1754
"...they are not safe!"

Seven muskets fired into the air. A salute of honor. The French lieutenant in charge of the detachment whipped his sword from his nose to his side.

In a small and sparsely furnished room, situated against the south wall of the fort, Philippe Gerrard jerked to a sitting position at the sound of reverberating gunfire. He looked around in bewilderment, hands trembling, worried he was under attack, unable to comprehend where he was. To his amazement, he found himself in a bed with a mattress, covered in white linens and blankets.

"What the ...?"

Philippe's head throbbed. His hands moved to his temples. The stabbing ache made him dizzy, disoriented. He pulled himself to one side of the bed, grabbed a polished wooden bedpost, wondered a moment about that, then slipped his aching legs from underneath the folds of clean linen and heavy wool. A breeze flooding through an open window wafted across his naked body making him shiver. More bolts of pain blossomed from other places on his body. He tightened his grip on the bedpost and closed his eyes. The room stopped spinning. Clenching his teeth, Philippe forced himself to stand. Another rush of nausea swept over him. When he opened his eyes, he was looking at his hands. They were bruised and chaffed, two fingernails were missing, but the skin was amazingly pink. The scratches looked like they'd been scrubbed clean.

He examined the rest of his body and saw swaths of bandages wrapped in different places. With his balance restored, he staggered on unsteady legs to a large mirror standing in one corner of the room and wonderingly stared at the gaunt, exhausted, unfamiliar face and body of a stranger. A large padded dressing was wrapped around his head. The gray scar on his cheek, old in comparison to his other wounds, glistened against the pale yellow skin of his drawn features. He saw numerous scabs and abrasions on his torso and arms. The bow in his left leg looked...he winced and stopped looking at it.

"My God," he uttered softly.

Though the morning's cool air flowed over his nakedness, this small amount of exertion had now made him sweat. He held his pounding head with one hand and staggered further to the window. There appeared to be a tall palisade of new timbers everywhere he looked. He was in a fort.

Machault?

On the mustering grounds, fifty paces in front of him, were four orderly rows of soldiers. They stood at attention, muskets held in front of their chests. A seven-man squad stood at right angles to the rest, flanked by three gold-braided officers. A crowd of *coureurs de bois* and other civilians in various forms of dress were aligned to the other side. Their hats were removed and heads were bowed respectfully in a ceremony of some sort.

Philippe vaguely recalled being awakened by an extraordinarily violent storm in the black of night. But the morning seemed unusually serene. Even the breeze moved noiselessly, its presence betrayed only by the occasional snap of the flags and pennants among the companies of soldiers.

An officer shouted an order. Out on the mustering grounds, another detail of soldiers walked forward to lift two long wooden boxes atop their shoulders. He had a sinking feeling.

Horrific images of the river battle came rushing back. Philippe groaned and extended a hand toward the coffins.

"No!" he growled in a choked voice. "God! *No!*" His shivering worsened. *I've got to get out there!*

He looked around for his clothes. The room was empty. Philippe turned and pulled a blanket from the bed to cover his nakedness. He opened the bedroom door and entered a smaller square room.

Startled by the angry looking *coureur de bois'* sudden appearance, a soldier jumped to his feet from behind a rough wooden table.

"Where am I?" Philippe demanded in a hoarse voice. "Where are my clothes?"

"Fort Machault, Monsieur. There,"—the corporal pointed to a chair—"your clothes."

A clean, folded pile of clothes were neatly stacked on a chair next to the door. New, polished boots had been placed on top.

Philippe gathered the bundle in one arm and turned back toward the bedroom.

"Captain Joncaire ordered me to call him the moment you were awake."

Philippe nodded. "How long was I asleep?"

"Over a day, Monsieur."

"Over a day?!"

"*Oui.*"

"The...funeral?"

Nervous, the corporal hesitated. "Uh...it's for some of the men who were with you when the Indians attacked. Captain Joncaire hoped to delay the ceremonies until you awakened, but..."

Philippe went numb. The nausea came back again. His breathing heavy with anxiety, he went into the bedroom, shut the door behind him, and dropped the clothes on the bed as a fresh wave of dizziness descended.

"*No. No. No.*" He grimaced, held onto the post, and stared miserably at the floor.

Get dressed, some distant part of himself urged. *Hurry.*

He stretched his arms and legs in every direction, stiff joints popped, some of the brittle scabs cracked and oozed.

Crowd noises from outside drew his attention again to the window. Coffins were being carried outside the gates. The soldiers on the mustering grounds had been dismissed and were milling about. The ceremony appeared over.

Hurrying now, Philippe painfully slipped on his cleaned leather trousers still stiff from drying in the sun. Grunting, he pulled on the new boots, which fit perfectly. They looked like ones Captain Joncaire would fancy.

Pierre would be envious, he thought suddenly. The thought of his partner made him clutch his stomach and bend over in misery.

"I'm such a fool."

"I always thought so," came loud agreement from the window. Pierre's face and shoulders loomed above the sill. A cloud of blue smoke swirled up from his pipe.

Philippe blinked. He stumbled to the window and grabbed his partner's shoulders.

"*Oww!* Oww! Easy, laddie. Kinnah' ya' see I'm wounded?" The Scotsman steadied his balance with a crutch.

"I thought you were *dead*!" Philippe said in a voice that betrayed his emotions.

"I should be, considering how long I had tah' hold my breath in tha' river."

Philippe wiped his eyes. "But the funeral?"

Pierre's lips tightened. "Louie and Michel."

"Oh, God…*nooo*…" He grabbed hold of the sill, sank to his knees, buried his face in his arms. A lifetime of memories, laughter, shared perils, and trust that could not be measured had abruptly and painfully ended. He would not see the likes of those two men again.

Pierre had already shed so many tears for these close friends, he had no tears left. It was hard to imagine anything being the same without them. They were the heart of the company's *coureurs de bois*.

After awhile, Pierre cleared his throat. "It was Sauquita who attacked us."

Philippe cleared his throat, wiped his eyes. "He's dead, I hope."

Pierre tapped his pipe bowl on the side of the window sill. "He got away. We killed almost his entire war party, all except Sauquita and a few wounded. Sauquita managed tah' steal my ax too," he added glumly.

"It should have been me, Pierre. Not Louie, not Michel. If I died back in Piqua's village, none of this would have happened."

"Now dinnah' be talking like tha'! If things were reversed you'd given your life for them. They both knew tha'."

"They came to rescue me."

"And *you* saved them on more than one occasion. It was their time, laddie. I'll miss them too…but it was just their time."

Philippe noticed a bandage on Pierre's head. "You're hurt?"

The Scotsman scoffed. "Aw, a few ball holes, a spear wound tah' the side, and a bash on the head. I've been tended tah' nicely. Captain Joncaire's surgeon actually seems tah' be a real doctor."

"A *few* holes?"

"There's one here in my leg. Nothin' broken. The ball passed straight through. Sauquita was carrying some bloody over-powdered English pistol. Two wounds for the price o' one ball! A bargain. The surgeon says they will heal clean."

Pierre stuck a hand inside his jersey and wiggled a finger through a hole in his shirt.

"The spear hit here. Shattered my best pipe and tobacco pouch. Bruised a rib beneath it. It only cut the flesh."

Philippe shook his head. "I remember the Seneca firing on you…I saw you fall…I thought …"

"Now dinnah' go on aboot it. Look," the Scotsman held up his new pipe, "Captain Joncaire gave me this. It comes all the way from one of his fiefdoms in France. His choice of tobacco is lousy, o' course, but the pipe is seasoned and draws smooth."

A breeze pushed through the window. Philippe shivered.

"Chittaqua?"

"Aw, he's all right. He's fuckin' cursed and hexed nearly everybody. The soldiers haven't shit right since. The fish floated tah' the surface after he waded in tah' save me. He and the fort Jesuit have been casting spells at one another…when they're not arguing."

"Arguing? About what?"

"I dinnah' know exactly. Aboot God, I guess. He must be pretty convincing. Yesterday, Chittaqua was tattooing something on the chaplain's arm."

Philippe grimaced. "My head feels like someone pounded on it with a rock." He continued dressing, then suddenly paused and looked up. "Michelle?"

Pierre frowned. He didn't want to talk about Fort Le Boeuf yet.

Philippe sensed Pierre's reservation. He stopped lacing his jersey and stared at Pierre intently.

"What?"

"Michelle is at Fort Le Boeuf."

"And?"

"Camille Prideaux is commandant there. He's takin' good care o' her."

There was more. Philippe frowned.

"Now dinnah' get all worked up."

There *was* more! "And?"

Pierre sighed. "Okeanneh is at Fort Le Boeuf."

"Okeanneh?"

"She's been hurt. But she's okay," he added quickly.

"Hurt?!" Another icy shiver. "Jesus Christ! What the fuck do you mean she's hurt? Why is Okeanneh at Fort Le Boeuf? What happened to her?"

"She came there looking for you, I suspect."

"What happened to her?"

It has to be now, I guess. Pierre took a deep breath and exhaled.

"Okeanneh was clubbed in the head by Gaspard de Propei."

"Clubbed in the head?" Philippe repeated, outraged. "Okeanneh? Jesus God!" he screamed angrily at the ceiling.

Pierre continued with emphasis. "Okeanneh's all right, laddie! Michelle too! Really! Camille Prideaux and his surgeon are tending to their needs. They're guarded by soldiers day and night. They're alive, safe, and waiting for us."

Pierre decided not to mention that Okeanneh couldn't talk.

Philippe's legs began trembling. He sat down and finished dressing in silence. He carefully removed the bandage beneath his chin that wrapped around his head wound. He looked in the mirror again. There was a six-inch long laceration stitched neatly shut. The blond hair surrounding the wound was clipped short but matted and scabbed.

"Wha' are ya' doing?" Pierre asked, alarmed. "The cut will infect."

Philippe didn't care. "Where are my weapons?" he said looking around. "Why?"

"Why?! Because I am going to Fort Le Boeuf! That's why!"

"Dinnah' be daft, laddie! You're …"

Before Pierre could protest further, Philippe staggered out of the room. "*Merde*! Damn!"

The Scotsman hobbled to the front door of the headquarters in time to see Philippe walk unsteadily out of the building and stumble to the main gate. There was a small military graveyard on the right, already dotted with crude crosses. A few soldiers were digging holes. Philippe staggered over to the two coffins awaiting burial. He fell heavily on his knees between them and laid an arm over the top of both the wooden boxes.

There had never been better men, good men, tested men. No braver or better friends existed.

"*Adieu, mon amis*," he whispered, a sob caught in his throat. "I promise, I will avenge you."

Philippe stood and addressed the soldiers. "Please make certain the holes are deep."

He turned and went back through the gate, deciding the orderly outside the bedroom would know where his pack and weapons might be kept. Pierre caught up with him. He didn't stop.

"Philippe! Wait!"

The *coureur de bois* turned.

"I want my weapons, Pierre. And I need supplies. How many days has it been?"

"I thin' you should—"

"Philippe! You handsome peasant! I was told you were awake. Did you find my bed comfortable?"

Captain Joncaire grabbed Philippe's shoulders and kissed each cheek. His entourage of immaculately dressed staff officers beamed and smiled from behind him.

"Captain," Philippe began. "I must leave at once for Fort Le Boeuf—"

"Nonsense!" the commandant bellowed. "You can barely stand! You are going to eat and rest another day, at least, before you go anywhere. I order it."

"I cannot," Philippe replied.

"Philippe, my friend, I sent ten soldiers to Fort Le Boeuf with specific orders to guard Sister Michelle until you arrive. Captain Prideaux will also protect her. Now, allow me the honor of dining with a man of legend. The Iroquois are singing night and day about your escape from the Wolf clan and the battle on the river."

"Good men died because of me. I did nothing,"

"You, sir, are a modest liar. You are a *hero*, and I have standing orders any passing hero must dine with me."

"Listen tah' him, laddie. I know ya' think you're strong enough, but ya' will nah' get two miles before ya' collapse, if tha' far. How much good will ya' be tah' Okeanneh and Michelle if tha' happens?"

Philippe could feel his legs trembling again.

"And how far can ya' get with a loaded pack?"

Pierre was right...as usual.

"All right... But I am leaving tomorrow, at first light," he stated, determined.

"Splendid," Joncaire shouted. The commandant looked at his expensive vest watch. "It's early, but my table's always set." He turned to his aide. "Lieutenant, decant the best of the Beaujolais. Have the cook prepare some spiced venison. Philippe, *s'il vous plaît*, attend me awhile. I must prepare my daily dispatch to Colonel Contrecoeur, and you may have valuable information."

As the commandant turned to enter his headquarters, Philippe spotted Chittaqua standing off to one side. Philippe walked unsteadily to the shaman and placed a hand on Chittaqua's shoulder.

"I find myself in your debt again, old friend."

"As we are bound forever," Chittaqua shrugged. "Our debts are the same."

"I am going to Fort Le Boeuf in the morning," Philippe said. "Okeanneh is hurt."

Chittaqua nodded. "She is safe…for now."

"Did you see her? Did you see the man who hurt her?"

"He was not at the fort when I came. But I see him in my dreams."

"Where is he now?" Philippe demanded.

Chittaqua stared off into the distance. "The evil one goes to the white man's great village on the river."

"Montréal?"

Chittaqua nodded. In his dreams of the previous night, the shaman had come face to face with the red-eyed spirit seeking Snow Hair's life. He'd spread his arms and chanted spells to stop the demon's advance on his friend who was asleep on the ground behind him, unaware of the monster's approach. It had slashed out with its claws and knocked the shaman aside. The pain had been so real, Chittaqua awakened and anxiously searched his body for wounds he did not find.

"I see much now, much more than ever before."

A corporal approached them warily and cleared his voice. "Captain Joncaire is waiting for you, Monsieur."

Philippe nodded and limped up the steps to the headquarters. Pierre and Chittaqua watched his labored walk.

"You should convince him tah' rest another day or two," Pierre said.

"No. Snow Hair must not rest!"

The Scotsman looked at him, surprised. "Why? Another day will nah' matter. Sister Michelle and Okeanneh are both safe. Ya' said so yerself. And he can barely walk."

Chittaqua looked at the Scotsman and shook his head. "They are *not* safe. And Snow Hair must *not* wait beyond tomorrow's sunrise."

Pierre grumbled with resignation. "Well, my *wizardly* friend...ya'd better bandage up my bloody leg real good and give me some o' your magic herbs so I can walk without this damnable crutch. Because I'm bloody well goin' with ya'!"

Sauquita was the only one among his braves free of any wounds. And there were only six of them left. He had nothing to show for this clash, other than the great war ax. The weapon was beautiful but it was a personal prize. It was not enough. With so many dead, he would be expelled from the tribe, be he Piqua's son or not. The only way to change that was to bring back the scalp of Chittaqua, Snow Hair's too, if possible. So Sauquita sent the wounded men back to his village while he stayed behind, lingering near the Venango fort, talking with the Mohawk spies, watching the fort, hoping for a new opportunity.

And an opportunity arose four days after the battle by the river, when a Mohawk scout told him the one called Snow Hair was seen in a canoe going up the Rivière aux Boeufs.

Sauquita did not hesitate. But traveling by canoe would be too dangerous, so he began trotting up the trail on the western bank of the river. Eventually, Snow Hair would have to make camp. *And if Snow Hair makes camp on this side of the river ...*

On foot, it would take Sauquita five days to reach Fort Le Boeuf, even if he ran most of the way. The trail was predominantly flat, and the western trail less traveled by soldiers and French *voyageurs*, who preferred river travel by bateaux. He wondered how much he could do alone against Snow Hair, who was certain to have other men with him. But five days later, Sauquita would encounter an ally who hated Chittaqua and Snow Hair with a passion that rivaled his own.

CHAPTER 16
MONTRÉAL
AUGUST 1754
"Never, never again."

Corrinne de Chanaye had crafted a new plan. But it was a plan easily compromised by the fickleness of men, and there were several whom she must persuade. If any one of them failed her, the plan would fail with grave consequences for many people. In the end, she must rely on the promises and representations of these men. It was risky. She did not like relying on anyone, particularly powerful men. But if the risk was great, she regarded the reward as greater, thus worth the risk. Corrinne decided to start with the Governor. His personal contribution to the grand design… validation…would be the most important. Governor Duquesne, however, was very accessible and easily given to making promises, and this in itself was a problem. For if promises from the Governor were readily obtained, he was also the most fickle.

Therefore, my persuasions, she resolved, *must be strong and memorable.*

This latest rendezvous was in her city house.

"I am surrounded by corruption, Mademoiselle," the Governor bellowed. "The English colonialists do not have to wage war to defeat us. Given enough time, we will *starve* our troops to death for them."

Completely naked, Duquesne slumped dejectedly on one of Lady de Chanaye's overstuffed, cushioned chairs covered in expensive silk. Several missives from Colonel Contrecoeur's dispatch pouch lay scattered at his feet.

Corrinne de Chanaye gazed fondly at the ranting Governor-General. Her boudoir was lit only by the sinuous light of a single candle and the glowing embers of the fireplace. While Governor Duquesne thundered on about the incompetence of his officers and the scandalous designs of Intendant Bigôt, she was lying naked on the bed memorizing everything he said.

Disgusted, he tossed the dispatch on the floor with the others. Corrinne glanced at them with envy, hoping he would forget to collect them when he left, at least long enough for her to transcribe the most important pieces of information.

"You worry too much, my lion. You have the upper hand. Did not Coulon de Villiers defeat Washington and get revenge for the slaying of his brother?"

Duquesne gazed at her appraisingly. "I must say, you are surprisingly well informed."

Corrinne smiled. "I am only trying to ease your anxious mind. Your military genius has been confirmed, has it not?"

Duquesne moved to the bed and lay back on the pillow. "Well, true. But there are those in King Louie's court who will lay claim to my strategy."

Corrinne's fingers moved slowly down his chest. "I've heard it said further," she cooed, "that the English have no more presence west of the Allegheny River." She went to work on him and listened intently.

Duquesne closed his eyes and enjoyed her wonderful caressing touch.

"Yes," he agreed, his breathing heavy with pleasure, "with the powerful fortress at the forks of the Ohio, we now control the fur trade. This should stop the English expansion. And if the English begin to war, I will make them regret waging it on our frontiers." He sighed. "God that feels wonderful."

She stopped massaging him. "Then you have won! The English will probably seek a treaty, yes?"

He guided her hands back to his erection. "No, this war will go on for some time. We can beat them in the forests. After their recent defeat, most of the Iroquois favor us now, except for the Mohawks."

Corrine lowered her head, kissing the tip of his member, and stopped again. "Then why would the war go on?"

"Madam, you are vexing me," he gasped.

"I am trying to understand. There is not much profit in war, and I thought you said we won?"

"The English navy," he replied as if the answer was obvious.

"Navy?"

"They can easily blockade the river and strangle us. We've not enough ships to stop them. Now, may we concentrate on the...*battle* at hand, uh, in your hand?"

She replied by surrounding him with her mouth. She proceeded slowly with her lips and tongue. She gauged his signs pleasure, and abruptly stopped again.

"What?" Duquesne asked with exasperation.

"I think the Governor of New France is preoccupied with wars and navies. There are other matters equally important…matters important to *me*. I am very distressed. There is a murderer among us."

Duquesne snorted. "New France is full of murderers of various persuasions."

"This murderer is different."

The Governor's brow furrowed. He propped himself up on an elbow and gazed down at her while his other hand guided her fingers back, again, to his groin.

"Someone has threatened you?"

"A high official," she said. Again she stopped.

Duquesne became interested. *A high official?* He groped for her hand. "A threat to *you*? Who?"

Corrinne hesitated. "Gaspard de Propei has recently returned to Montréal." She began kissing his stomach, a promise of things to come, then stopped.

"Oh…him." The Governor cared little for the man. His expression turned curious. "And what's your interest in the King's obnoxious *shérif*?"

Corrinne moved out of Duquesne's reach.

"Gaspard de Propei seeks to arrest Philippe Gerrard."

Oh, so that's the Philippe whose name you shout in ecstasy.

"Indeed," he said. "The list Monsieur Propei carries has many names. And the *shérif* seems most interested in our *coureur de bois* mapmaker. His name is at the top. But, who cares?"

Corrinne leaned forward and breathed hotly into the hair of his groin. Duquesne gasped at the fluttering heat. His hands moved toward her head. She avoided the motion, sat up, and fixed her green eyes directly on his. One of her hands moved back to his hardness and massaged him.

"I care," she revealed. "And I ask you for a favor. Will you intercede in Monsieur Gerrard's behalf if it becomes necessary? Will you do this for me?"

Duquesne was impressed by her apparent sincerity.

"You are concerned about this *coureur de bois'* welfare? I should be jealous," he joked. "I was not aware you had a…predilection for commoners."

"Please do not mock me. I have *never* asked you for a favor before."

True, Duquesne reflected. "But *why* should I intercede on your behalf? Or in Monsieur Gerrard's behalf, I should say."

"We can call it chivalry," Corrinne suggested, knowing Duquesne harbored an idealistic view of himself, "because you cannot help yourself. You are a chivalrous gallant." She bent and kissed his nose. "And because I ask this *one* favor of you. And because I will be *very* grateful."

"But this is a…a clerical matter, not an affair of state. My slightest inquiry will only draw more attention to the Monsieur Gerrard. I would make it worse for him, not better. You must have other avenues of influence? Intendant Bigôt's gendarmes perhaps?"

"Philippe Gerrard is important to me," Corrinne admitted. "I would not ask you otherwise." She went back to massaging him with both her hands.

Duquesne's eyes closed. *God, that feels so, absolutely, wonderful.*

"Please?"

Duquesne sighed, resigned. "Very well. What would you have me do?"

"I will prepare the documents for you."

His eyes widened. "Documents? What documents?"

She drew back the coverlet, further exposing his erection and started kissing the Governor's chest again.

"It's the only way to remedy this. It must be official."

"What documents?" *God! Go lower! Please!*

She sucked at his nipples and felt them stiffen.

"The *shérif* has the support and endorsement of Intendant Bigôt. There is undoubtedly corruption between them."

Bigôt? Duquesne found the mention of the corrupt intendant's name annoying and immensely distracting to his immediate circumstance.

"François Bigôt is vermin. If he is a villain in this, I will not allow him to succeed."

Corrinne beamed. *It's almost like playing a harpsichord*, she mused. *Maybe a deeper melody is in order.* As her kisses reached the hair of his groin, she paused.

"What now?" Duquesne's expression was almost desperate.

"The favor I ask of you requires your signature on some documents. But not now, sometime in the future."

"Now I must *sign* something? What nefarious intrigue are you designing?"

He didn't say no, Corrinne noted. Her hands slipped around him again. "I would never do anything to harm or embarrass you. You know that," she said tenderly.

Alternating between pleasure and frustration was maddening. Dreamily, Duquesne wished it could go on forever. "Against *whom* will my signature be employed?" he asked.

"François Bigôt, of course."

"Bigôt again?" Duquesne repeated the name with loathing. "My lady, you have *gripped* me with your conspiracy."

It was time. "Then I have your word?"

"Yes."

Corrinne had not expected the Governor would cooperate so easily. *Remember, he can be fickle.* She lifted her head and looked directly into his eyes.

"I *truly* have your word?"

"Yes! You *truly* have my word. I will help you. Why, I don't know, but I will help you. Now, *please*, may we continue?"

Corrinne saw no duplicity in his eyes. She was flooded with a sense of relief. Her emerald green eyes sparkled, luminous with unshed tears. "I have been lied to before," she said in her most vulnerable tone of voice, one she had rehearsed prior to their assignation.

Duquesne smiled fondly, caressed her cheek, suddenly wet with a tear. He held her chin.

"You have my word," he repeated.

"Thank you," Lady de Chanaye whispered. She turned her attention to the Governor's erection and smiled. Her lips descended. And this time she did not stop.

Mon Dieu! the Governor thought, before all thought became impossible. *How does anyone ever say no to this woman?*

Corrinne sipped tea while Archbishop Nicolet read the contents of the letters from her agents. She gazed out the window to enjoy the comforting street traffic of Montréal and thought of Governor Duquesne's comment about the English navy blockading the river.

The French navy already has a warrant to board the Falcon Queen, she thought. *And the English navy will sink or seize it as a prize of war.*

The Ile Royal *is equally in danger. This will go on for years! And without my trading ships ...?*

"Are you listening?"

Corrinne returned her attention to the archbishop.

"Apologies, Eminence."

"You have asked for my help, so first we must locate the document. Where do you think Monsieur de Propei safeguards it, Quebec or Montréal?"

"Eminence, the question to ask is not *where* but with *whom*? Gaspard de Propei had letters of credit for an enormous sum of money."

"And?" he prompted.

"So the question is *who* could Monsieur de Propei bribe with enough money to ensure his new *birthright* remained safeguarded? Who would establish the letters of credit for funds in Quebec City and Montréal? And *who* would later collaborate with him on the certificates of death?"

Nicolet knew at once. "François Bigôt."

"Of course."

Archbishop Nicolet looked out his window and watched the routine movements of the carriages, carts, wagons, and pedestrians on the street below.

"If Intendant Bigôt even thinks I am interested in that document ..." He paused. "You will have to get it."

"M-me?" she stammered. "Certainly you have the authority—"

"It is not a public document of New France. The intendant undoubtedly has it hidden. I cannot coerce him to turn it over. There is no law that says he must. Surely you can buy it from him?"

Corinne's expression turned stony. "Buy it?"

"Mademoiselle, I cannot help Philippe Gerrard while that document exists," he said evenly. "Declarations by the Governor carry no weight against royal decrees."

An awkward silence ensued. She found getting anywhere near François Bigôt repugnant. But Lady de Chanaye knew it was probably the surest way to obtain the document in the time available to her. *Probably the only way*, she thought and resigned herself.

"Money may not be enough." She did not meet his eyes as she spoke. "My influence over Intendant Bigôt tends to be constrained to one specific area of interest."

Archbishop Nicolet realized what she was implying. "I-I did not mean... We will find another ..."

Corrinne shook her head and acquiesced. "No...you are right. There is no other way."

This could not wait. The fate of Philippe Gerrard was not an issue of great consequence to the Society of Jesus or the government of New France when there was a war beginning. Archbishop Nicolet's generosity would have limits, both in time and attention, whether he knew that now or not.

"I will ask for a meeting ..."

Corrinne shook her head more strongly. "Eminence, remember the story you told me about your early years of missionary work. How once you killed an Ottawa brave who attacked the children in your mission."

The archbishop said nothing for a long moment. "Yes," he finally said, his eyes turning sad. She had touched a wound in his heart that had never healed.

Lady de Chanaye stood and walked over to the cleric and kissed him lightly on the forehead. Then she lifted his chin so she could see into his eyes.

"God knows you to be a decent and courageous man André Nicolet," she said. "So let me ask you...if you had to defend those children, again... would you?"

"I took a life." The archbishop looked down at the floor. "It was a grievous sin for a priest."

"And you saved the life of innocents. If you had to do it again...would you?"

Archbishop Nicolet stared at her. Lady de Chanaye saw the answer in his eyes and turned before he felt compelled to say anything in reply. In a flurry of rustling silk, she swept out of the room to do what must be done.

Lady de Chanaye's request to Intendant Bigôt received a reply in less than an hour. She read the expected response and nodded.

"My lady. That man is evil." Mathilde's face was filled with dread and worry.

"I've dealt with the intendant many times before. He holds no surprises for me. Come, I must dress quickly. The intendant awaits my call."

Mathilde went to a closet brimming with clothes and came back with a demure, high-collar day gown.

"No, Mathilde. My attire for this meeting must be special."

Lady de Chanaye opened the drawer where she kept her special undergarments.

Mathilde's eyebrows rose in surprise. "My lady?"

Corrinne held them up in front of her. Her expression resolute.

"We will start with these."

Intendant François Bigôt canceled his afternoon appointments when he learned of Lady de Chanaye's request for a meeting at his earliest convenience. He had not been truly alone with her in four years. *She must want something badly*, he thought. *But what?* He had sent word back with the same messenger. He could see her immediately.

Less than an hour later, she arrived.

"The Lady Corrinne de Chanaye," the intendant's swarthy secretary announced.

Corrinne brushed past the Corsican and into the room before the secretary had finished his introduction.

François Bigôt looked up from a document he had only been pretending to read. He inhaled deeply at the sight of the woman's provocative beauty.

She wore a lavish velvet dress of royal purple. It was cut very low across her breasts, barely covering the nipples, which were hidden by translucent gauze of purple lace cinched from the brassiere and shoulders to her neck. These frilly supports were joined to an ivory peacock cameo suspended by purple ribbons around her shoulders. A three-carat ruby centered in three long raven feathers adorned a luxuriant black wig. The headpiece contrasted sharply with liberal amounts of cheek rouge and a luminous red lip coloring. The long-sleeved gown flared across her hips, petticoats spreading and flattening the front of her figure in the latest Parisian style. Black lace gloves covered her hands to her elbows. She carried a black-trimmed ornamental parasol and a matching purse.

The intendant had never seen her with black hair before. She was magnificent. He licked his dry lips and gestured with his hand.

"Dismissed," he told his indignant secretary. "Do not interrupt me unless I call you. Is that clear?"

The red-faced functionary nodded and quietly closed the door behind him.

François Bigôt arose, walked to the door, and bolted it. He leaned back against the jamb. His lips spread in a leering smile.

"Your perfume is lovely."

Lady de Chanaye casually inspected the office decor. "Well, François, I see your taste in furnishings still resembles a warden's."

The intendant pulled on both sides of his waistcoat to smooth it over his obesity.

"No doubt due to a lack of contact with someone of your exemplary social graces," he replied.

Corrinne swept across the room and took a seat on a sedan to one side of the gilded desk. Her clothing had a crisp sound when she moved.

The intendant was transfixed.

François wanted to hide his corpulence behind his desk, but she had taken a seat in a place where he would have to turn his chair to face her. So, instead, he walked to his shelf of books and randomly selected a volume of poetry.

"Have you read any of the works of Voltaire? He is quite popular in Paris."

"François, you know I am not here to discuss poetry." Her practiced eye noticed one of his legs was trembling. *He's already excited.*

He laid the book on his desk and gave her his attention.

"Mademoiselle?"

Lady de Chanaye recalled how rapidly her influence and commercial power had grown because of this man. Initially, he'd been most helpful and polite. The sex he demanded in return was not enjoyable in any way, though she had not let him know that. But as her public popularity grew so did his need to abase her in private. She found his perverse desires and coarse body odor repulsive. And when she had amassed enough friends among his enemies, she rebuffed any further advances from him. There were a few ugly public incidents when he tested her politics and resolve. Eventually, one of his private footmen was slain, the body left sitting in the intendant's official carriage, a sword held in a lifeless hand. It was rumored the footman was challenged and slain by an unknown *coureur de bois*. To François Bigôt, the meaning was clear. The risks associated with contests of influence would extend beyond official channels. After that, he interacted with Lady de Chanaye only at governmental affairs or soirees, where she remained polite but aloof.

His face had grown puffy and red since she last saw him in private. Too many goblets of strong spirits, she concluded.

"I understand you act as counsel for Shérif Gaspard de Propei."

He looked at her quizzically. "I am afraid I do not understand your comment."

And so it begins.

She smiled. "François. We have known one another for a long time. Let's not trifle with one another."

The intendant's waxed mustache wriggled nervously above his protruding lips. The ends were twisted to fine points two inches to either side of his long, pointed nose. It gave him the look of a rodent in Corrinne's eyes. *Appropriate enough.* The *coiffure* curls of his mediocre brown wig shook as he talked.

"Let me say it differently then. *I am afraid*," he emphasized, "that I do not understand what you mean."

She gave him a reproving look. He twitched.

"The *Shérif* Gaspard de Propei registered with you upon his arrival. Your offices established a letter of credit with the bankers in Quebec and Montréal for the amount of three hundred thousand livres. This letter of credit was guaranteed by the signature of the Intendant of New France, François Bigôt. Gaspard de Propei attended your offices for two days prior to his journey into the wilderness. He undoubtedly received schooling only someone like you could provide."

The Intendant smiled indulgently. He walked over to his liquor cabinet. "Some brandy perhaps?"

"Yes, that would be agreeable."

Serving her allowed him to get closer to the heady but subtle aroma of her intoxicating perfume. He inhaled deeply then took a seat in a chair to the right of the sedan. One of his legs continued to tremble.

She left the brandy untouched.

"'Giving him counsel' unfairly characterizes the relationship. We are merely business associates…of a sort."

She persisted. "His papers are registered with your office, are they not?"

He shrugged but didn't answer.

"There is a document I want."

François Bigôt smirked. The trembling stopped.

"Yes?"

"Actually, there are two documents I would like."

"Only two?" he asked, content to play this game for however long it lasted.

"I am prepared to pay you for them."

"Oh, yes, my lady"—he chuckled—"to be certain! You have not visited these offices in years and have levied uncounted financial misfortunes upon my estate. You publicly snub me and privately induce gossip concerning my, uh, masculinity."

Corrinne spoke patiently, as if to a child. "François, your business suffers its setbacks no worse than mine and under the same set of rules. If we are somehow competing, it is because you choose to do so. The rest of what you say is a fabrication. I certainly have nothing to gain in engaging in such slander."

It was a lie, but an effective lie. She'd spent a lot of time inducing gossip about him. It was one of her favorite pastimes.

His face became pained. "Why did you stop seeing me?"

"You wanted things from me I could no longer afford to give."

"I only wanted your company," he whined.

She eyed him sharply. "You wanted *much* more than that, François."

The intendant leaned back in his chair.

A silence ensued. He sipped his brandy and studied her expressionless face over the top of his glass. His mustache continued to wave and wriggle.

"What is it you want?"

"I have already told you—two documents."

"Go on."

"The first is the warrant for the arrest of Philippe Malthais."

He smiled wryly and shook his head. "Still protecting your woodsman, I see."

She ignored the comment. "The second document is the certificate for the transition of the marquisates of the House of Propei, the *lettres patentes.*"

Bigôt was openly stunned. *How does she learn about these things?* He cleared his throat.

"I am afraid…I think you are misinformed …"

"François, Governor-General Duquesne, Archbishop Nicolet, and most of the aristocracy in Montréal and Quebec are aware the document exists. There are some in the Church who consider it disingenuous. The Bishop of Paris will oppose the endorsement of Gaspard de Propei as a Marquis or even a *seigneur*."

She paused.

François Bigôt stared at her and said nothing. Lady de Chanaye had mentioned the names of his most powerful enemies.

"I find your remarks extraordinary. No such document exists, certainly not in my possession."

Corrinne smiled. "You think I speculate? Let me tell you what the document states."

To his astonishment, she recited it almost verbatim, as if she'd seen a copy. But that was impossible. The original was safely retained in the false bottom compartment of his desk drawer. His price for collaborating with Gaspard de Propei was two hundred thousand livres, two thirds of the *Shérif*'s credit. But that left one hundred thousand. Bigôt planned to get the rest of the money somehow.

"Interesting story. I don't understand what this has to do with me."

Corrinne did not appreciate his play at ignorance.

"François, someone must sign the certificates of death to authenticate Monsieur de Propei's claim to the marquisate. There are only *three* such men in New France vested with such authority. Two of them would rather see him dead. That leaves you."

His expression turned serious. "So?"

She leaned toward him. "I know you have made a bargain with this man. If you conspire with him in this, you will be *destroyed*."

Intendant Bigôt knew when it came to business, Lady de Chanaye never made idle threats. The idea of being destroyed was not appealing.

"*Destroyed?*" he bellowed. "Don't presume to threaten me you...you *whore!*"

Corrinne laughed lightly. "Oh, François, I am not here to threaten you at all. Gaspard de Propei's reprehensible plans will simply never succeed. Many oppose him already. If you are in league with this man, the association will certainly do you harm."

The intendant regarded her bitterly. "It occurs to me, Mademoiselle, others have reason to promote misfortune for me."

"That may be true. But as you so shrewdly recognized, this matter is of a personal nature to me. So...I believe we may have reason to cooperate, if only temporarily."

Corrinne saw his eyes glance up at the ceiling. She knew the sign. He was calculating something.

*If he hints at money...*she hoped.

François Bigôt rationalized he really could care less about Gaspard de Propei's hereditary claims. The only significant characteristic of the man was his menacing presence. Beyond that, the intendant considered him a pathetic pretender. But two hundred thousand livres was not something to be dismissed lightly.

"I will match whatever sum he has offered you."

She is reading my mind!

"He offers three hundred thousand livres."

Corrinne knew it was a lie.

"Done," she answered promptly. "I will have the draft of transfer presented to your financiers tomorrow. Please have the documents ready."

In a sweeping motion, she rose from her seat and walked swiftly toward the office door.

He was not ready to see her go. "Unless," he said, interrupting her exit, "you prefer to have the documents now?"

Lady de Chanaye stopped but did not turn around.

Ahhh, he thought with pleasure. *She wants them very badly.*

Corrinne sighed. Before she came to his office, she'd resigned herself something more disagreeable than a financial transaction might have to take place

It will be the last time, she promised herself. *Ever*!

She inhaled deeply and spun to face him with a smile.

"Yes, I would prefer to have the documents now."

"Then I assume we can proceed to more...cordial matters..."

"No, no, Monsieur," she chided. "Business first. We must seal this bargain."

"What do you mean? The money transaction will occur tomorrow. You said so yourself."

"And it most certainly will," she agreed. "But you have just made me a new offer. My terms are these. I will not transfer any money to your accounts, and I must first receive both documents. In return, I am...at your disposal for the remainder of the afternoon."

She prayed he would take the money.

François Bigôt hesitated. He wanted to reconsider giving her the papers tomorrow, or perhaps not at all. And whether she paid him or not, he would get Monsieur de Propei's two hundred thousand livres, he had already plotted for that. He could even arrest the *shérif* on some charge if he chose.

"That is not possible. The documents are not here."

"François, François, certainly you remember I have been in these offices when you have opened the false bottom of your desk. Please. This could become a *very* pleasant afternoon for the two of us," she lied. "Do not spoil it."

"The word 'pleasant' has many definitions."

Lady de Chanaye could see the weasel's imagination working. She walked to the divan and dropped her parasol and purse. Her hands moved behind her waist to the tiny silk laces holding the gown together. The purple lace tumbled down and the beautiful dress slipped halfway down her arms. She stopped its descent and held it up by crossing her arms and pushing up with her wrists to make the breasts bulge outward.

Bigôt was transfixed.

"Well?" she asked, waiting.

Bigôt licked his lips and stepped behind his desk, his mustache twitching constantly. He ripped out the drawer and turned the contents upside down. Papers, quills, money, jewelry, and other small articles scattered noisily to the floor. The oak bottom slid away easily, revealing a two-inch high space. Several documents were exposed. He picked out two, broke the wax seals, and scanned them briefly. He nodded and held them up in both hands for Corrinne to see.

"You for the afternoon *and* two hundred thousand livres."

"Done."

"Then I believe these are what you are looking for."

She reached out with one hand, but the intendant quickly withdrew them.

"François?"

Several feet behind his desk was a floor-to-ceiling bookcase. He walked quickly to the bookcase and pressed something on one side. There was a click. The entire bookcase swung open to reveal a dimly illuminated bed chamber.

Corrinne glanced inside and squinted. Someone was already in the bed, another woman who sat up when the door opened. She was young. She was naked. Several items dangled from a rack on the walls, much of it leather, some made of metal chains.

"I believe it was your idea to seal the transaction," he said. "I will bring these," he shook the papers, "into the room with us."

Corrinne approached within inches of the trembling aristocrat. Her left breast was now totally exposed. Bigôt raised a hand to touch the pale bodice, holding the papers behind him in the other. His face was mottled, flushed. His breathing heavy. He briefly caressed the creamy surface of her breast. Then she pulled away and circled to the front of his desk.

"What…what is wrong?" he gasped.

"I will have the documents *now*," she demanded, then allowed the dress and bodice to fall to the floor, exposing her black undergarments. Straps supported her breasts from underneath. Tight black briefs could be seen under the lace of the half-slip of the same color. She still wore her gloves and shoes.

He had only ever *dreamed* of seeing her dressed like this.

"Now, François!"

The intendant moved closer. He handed over the papers and started pawing hungrily at her breasts.

Her expression one of disgust, Corrinne scanned the papers quickly to make certain they were authentic. Quickly, she strode to the office door, unlocked it, and held out the documents. The strong arm of her footman grasped the paperwork and slammed the door shut.

"What trick is this?" Bigôt shouted.

"Calm yourself," she soothed and relocked the door. "It was my body-guard. He will take care of the papers."

Returning to him, she reached down and began to rub the bulge in his satin trousers. The excited intendant began licking and slobbering on her chest. His hands tore at the lace slip.

Lady de Chanaye escorted him to the bed chamber where the other woman waited. François Bigôt began whining like a small child. He did not notice the tears wetting Corrinne's cheeks. She glanced back toward the light of the other room before the bookcase door took it away, leaving her in shadowed darkness. The door closed behind them with a loud click.

Mathilde followed Lady de Chanaye to the boudoir. Once there, Corrinne threw off her cloak.

"I want a bath. Immediately!"

"Yes, Mistress. Oh—what has happened to you?"

The purple velvet dress was ripped down the side. Only by holding up the front with one arm did she hide the nakedness of her breasts. Her heavily rouged cheeks were stained by spidery black streaks running from her puffy eyes. Her lips were red and swollen. One sleeve was missing from the gown. The undergarments were missing. She carried a ruby-decorated black wig in her other hand along with some documents. Her blond hair was greasy and soiled. There was an odor.

"Fill the tub with hot water," Mathilde told the servant girls.

The Indian servant women looked at Lady de Chanaye with curiosity, but pulled the boudoir door shut behind them.

Corrinne threw herself onto the bed. "You will pay dearly for this, you bastard!" She let the wig and documents fall to the floor.

"Here, Mistress, drink some water," Mathilde offered, her own eyes full of tears.

Corrinne rolled over, sat up, and drank the cool water greedily. The torn dress fell away to her waist.

The maid winced and gasped. "*Mon Dieu*! Oh, my dearest love!" She hugged Corrinne.

Corrinne's breasts, torso, and back were covered with bruises. There were also pink welts, as if she'd been lashed repeatedly. In dozens of places, she saw teeth marks. Someone had bitten the skin…hard.

Corrinne patted Mathilde's hand. "Bring me a large *douche* with Queen Anne's lace and all the salves."

Never, never again, Corrinne vowed to herself. *Never again.*

CHAPTER 17
FORT LE BOEUF
AUGUST 1754
"...she carries his child!"

After Michelle's arrival, it wasn't until the morning of the second day that Okeanneh discovered the white woman's identity. The nervous fort commandant had come to inspect her condition and whispered her name as he knelt beside her bed. Michelle remained deeply asleep.

Sister Michelle! Okeanneh had been stunned by the revelation. The name echoed repeatedly in her head. For hours afterward, she could only sit on the opposite side of the room and stare malevolently at this rival, her enemy, contemplating ways to kill her.

The next two nights, Okeanneh crept silently across the space between them and drew her knife. She had but to draw the sharp blade across the sleeping woman's throat and it would be done. Being blamed for the woman's death did not frighten her. She could claim the white woman attacked her in the middle of a bad dream. But in fact, she didn't care what anyone thought.

To her own surprise, however, both nights she hesitated. Something stayed her hand.

Days later, Okeanneh still could not explain why she did not kill the Sister, except that the woman did not seem a threat, and the things Philippe had said about her appeared to be true. Okeanneh expected the white woman to react with similar hostility. But during the brief periods when Sister Michelle was awake, she barely acknowledged Okeanneh's presence. When she ate, propped up on an elbow, she only picked at the food. When she moved to make her toilette, she was terribly weak and needed constant support. She would whisper *merci* to Okeanneh for any kindness and return to bed. At night, the white woman was tormented by bad dreams. Sometimes she'd awake breathless and sweating, as if fighting with someone.

But most of the time, Michelle would stare listlessly at the roof, her eyes glazed and emotionless.

It was almost another week before Michelle was finally able to sit up and eat, but her knotted disheveled hair kept getting in the way. Asking the beautiful Indian woman for help, she'd washed and braided the hair into a long tail for convenience. Her hair no longer in her face, Michelle's pinched expression, hollow cheeks, dark circles, and grayish skin pallor all gave her the haunted, melancholy look of someone whose spirit was badly damaged.

Michelle was retching a lot. She wondered if she would ever get over the endless bouts of sickness she suffered. But, as if in answer to her prayers, the following morning was sunny, and she did feel much better. But within a few hours, she was again overcome by more nausea and more retching. It did not make sense.

"Oh, blessed Mother, help me understand this malady." Almost instantly, a disturbing explanation came to mind. "*No*," she whispered, not wanting it to be true. "I…I am carrying a child."

Michelle quickly counted the days. If true, the child belonged to the disgusting Englishman, the one the Seneca called Iron Pots. *Mother of God!* Michelle looked at the beautiful Indian woman who occasionally helped her. Large amber eyes stared back, the expression unfriendly. *She knows*, Michelle thought.

While she waited for Philippe, Okeanneh remained attentive to the white woman. There was little else to do, and the soldiers would not let her out of the fort. Not that it would be hard to escape if she really had wanted to. It would be easy to sneak over the partially finished palisade during the night. But Okeanneh could not walk more than twenty paces before the pounding pain in her head would force her to lie down again. It was getting worse every day. And even if she could walk, she was convinced Philippe would come here. *The white woman is here. And the white woman carries his child!* Philippe was going to make a choice, that thought repeated over and over inside her mind. *The white woman carries his child. He will choose her.*

The next morning, the air resounded constantly with clanging and banging sounds as more defenses were added to the walls. The twenty-foot-tall palisade was higher than anything Okeanneh had seen in her life, though anything the white man built tended to be large and ugly.

She was sitting on a short round stool, her back against the open doorway of Captain Prideaux's quarters, her face slightly lifted toward the sun, feeling its warmth. Her long skinning knife was in its sheath lying next to her, in case she felt the urge to pull out the blade and end the pathetic white woman's life, or so she told herself.

Skrieee!

It was the cry of an eagle. She shifted her gaze. Squinting, she thought she saw a flash of white among the tree tops but could not be sure. If she lifted her chin for long, the punishing ache in her head would pound harder. This morning that pain seemed tolerable, so she stooped, searching the sky.

Okeanneh dropped her gaze and twisted on the stool to look back into the room at the sleeping figure of Sister Michelle. She glowered. *If you were from my tribe, I would fight you for the right to be Philippe's only wife.* But laws of her tribe could not settle this. This was a white woman. It would be Philippe's choice and the white man's laws. *And she carries his child!* There it was again.

Philippe would send Okeanneh away in shame. His eyes would no longer gleam with desire for her. He would no longer want to touch her. The horrible image of Philippe pointing his hand at the fort's gate made her inhale sharply.

Okeanneh scowled at the tiny, spiritless white woman.

Puny bird! You cannot care for him. You will only bring him to his death! You will not fight his enemies. You lie there, ready to die, even now, even as he searches for you! You do not care if his enemies may kill him.

Wind whistled through the numerous unfilled chinks in the wall planks and through the open doorway, blowing Okeanneh's long black hair distractingly across her face. The air had a sweet smell in comparison to the rancid, muddy odors rising from beneath the birch log flooring.

Okeanneh felt a sudden craving for salt. She placed the stool inside and closed the door gently behind her. Standing, she went to her pack dangling from one of the heavy iron stud nails driven into the overhead joists, intending to retrieve a piece of salt jerky.

Michelle groaned and coughed.

Okeanneh glanced over at the white woman. Her hands slowly dropped away from the pack. *You do not know who I am, do you?* The pain in her head pulsed strongly. She winced and sat down on the stool again, panting quietly. *What will you do when you find out who I am?* Okeanneh wondered.

A gust of air rushed through the doorway. It smelled wonderfully fresh. *Something good will happen today.*

Michelle came wide-awake in the shadowy room. The good thoughts vanished. *Oh, no, not yet!* She tried to force herself back into dreamless oblivion. But, no, her mind was active. The daily agony of remembering past torments would begin anew. First, a journey from the austere safety of a convent, to the primitive savagery of an unexplored wilderness. Two different lives by two different people.

And now, I am with child! She was being punished by God for her sins. There was no other explanation. *Not this! Think of something else! Anything else!*

Memories came to her randomly. It was hard to focus. Try as she might, Michelle could not remember her rescue, could not remember Philippe's face, or what he had said to her. She dwelled on how he looked at Fort Niagara. He had changed so much from the handsome boy she knew in Rouen some thirteen years earlier. He'd become this intimidating forest man, bearded, covered in leather, huge hands, loud, bellowing laughter, lined and scarred, all sinew and quick movement. Foreign. But, oh, how Henri adored him. She had worried the stories she'd told Henri about his father were over embellished. But Philippe turned out to be a larger, more imposing figure than any bedtime fiction. Virile, strong, respected, and feared. There were other rumors certain people made sure she heard, as if she would be proud.

Philippe Gerrard has killed many men in duels, they said.

Duels? With who? Why? And then the stories about the Indian woman called Okeanneh, Philippe's wife.

Philippe deserves a wife, she thought. *A good wife.* She prayed Okeanneh was a good wife.

More recent, more painful memories burgeoned. Tears began to well in the corners of her eyes. She was unclean, a failure. A cruel, brutal man, the one called Curtiss, had raped and abused her at the Seneca village. *And now I carry his child! And the Seneca have Philippe! If only I had the courage to take my life before Philippe returns. Save him from all this. What will he think when he finds me with child?*

Michelle swallowed. Her throat was sore. *Water*, she decided. She sat up and saw the Indian nurse sitting pensively on a stool illuminated by beams of sunlight shining through the cracks in the door. Michelle smiled and nodded at the woman. But the woman made no response. She sat there, quietly, staring at her with those golden eyes so full of mystery, intelligence…and suspicion?

How could people capable of such cruelty, produce a woman of such extraordinary beauty?

The Indian woman had not spoken a word since they'd met. Michelle assumed she could not speak French. Then it occurred to her, the woman hadn't uttered any sounds at all, not even Indian words. She would vigorously pantomime what she wanted.

She cannot talk!

Okeanneh shifted nervously under Michelle's steady gaze. The gold medallion of Saint Denis hanging around her neck caught the sun and reflected light across the walls in the room.

The light sparkled across Michelle's face. She raised her hand to shade her eyes. She'd not noticed this necklace before. She leaned forward to view it more closely. It looked oddly familiar. *Where have I seen this?*

Okeanneh followed Michelle's eyes and quickly slipped the necklace back inside her dress.

"Please…may I have some water?"

Grimacing with pain, Okeanneh stood, retrieved the water bladder, filled a wooden mug on the table, then knelt beside the cot and assisted Michelle in drinking.

She doesn't speak, but she clearly understands me. Michelle swallowed the wonderfully cool liquid. Her eyes were drawn again to the necklace.

"*Merci.* May I see that?"

With apprehension, Okeanneh drew the medal from its hiding place.

Michelle gently touched the warm engraved gold surface.

"How can this be?" she whispered. It was the medal she'd given Philippe the night he fled from Rouen that first time, so long ago, when he had killed a man who had tried to rape her. "*For your safety,*" she had told Philippe, pressing it into his palm.

"But how did you get ...?" Michelle's eyes widened. She pushed herself into a fully seated position on the cot and leaned back against the wall.

"Blessed Mother...*Okeanneh?*"

Okeanneh put away the necklace and moved back to the stool near the door. Her head was pounding.

For a few moments, the two women stared, taking each other's measure. Michelle could see the angry challenge in the woman's eyes. But Michelle had many questions.

Where did you come from? Why have you been so kind to me?

"How you must hate me," Michelle said instead.

Okeanneh's head tilted. She did not feel *hate* for this woman. There was another emotion—jealousy. But it was just as strong and just as hot.

You do not belong here, Okeanneh signed.

The hand gestures meant nothing to Michelle. "Do you understand French at all?"

Okeanneh gently nodded her head. Her nostrils flared.

"Philippe is your husband?"

Okeanneh nodded once, and then she had to lie down again. The throbbing pressure in her head was relieved instantly.

Michelle was overwhelmed. The medallion she'd given Philippe in France over twelve years ago had somehow found its way to a place over the heart of this beautiful woman; its presence revealed to her *now* in the middle of this wilderness. It seemed preordained.

All these days you helped me, Michelle thought, wondering why Okeanneh would bother. *You must think Philippe loves me instead. And you know I am with child ...*

"Oh, no...Y-you must think this child is Philippe's," she whispered.

Michelle forced herself to rise and moved on unsteady legs next to Okeanneh's bed. She knelt, and took hold of the Indian woman's hand. She pressed it against her stomach.

"This is *not* Philippe's child," she stated. "*Not* Philippe's."

CHAPTER 18
FORT PRESQUE ISLE
SEPTEMBER 1754
The Portage Stone

The Presque Isle villagers looked out across the lake, wondering if the storm was coming this way. It lingered on the northern horizon. Tall mountainous clouds were illuminated like lanterns each time lightning exploded inside them. There was an eerie stillness to the air, a humidity making one's skin feel oily.

Standing on the shore, Henri could feel the warmer air from the land gliding past his fingers as it rushed toward the storm. No hills or trees to block his view, he'd never seen a storm so completely exposed like this. It was magnificent and unsettling.

"Anamosa," he called. She'd been making sand piles. The sun had set. It would get dark quickly. "Come. It's time to eat."

Henri took her hand. They went to Juniata's lodge.

Two hours later, a drenching downpour started. The main force of the storm roiled in from the lake with a droning howl, accompanied by hail and lightning exploding from the clouds in deafening, flashing booms.

Anamosa trembled beneath her blanket. When one bolt exploded close by, she cried out. Lightning storms had always terrified her.

"*Shhh*, Anamosa! Come over here," Henri called.

The little girl quickly crawled over and snuggled into his protective arms.

"It's okay. It's only a storm," he said, wrapping the army blanket around them.

She was trembling and sniffling. Henri was nervous too, but holding Anamosa somehow made him feel safer.

The storm grew stronger and frozen rain began bouncing off the stiff leather hides and birch bark covering the lodge, making snapping, popping sounds. Flashes of lightning created momentary fingers of light between the seams. They heard a rumble, like a stampede of animals, only much louder.

But above the thunder came an angry howl. It rose in intensity.

"Ahh-ree!"

"I got you, Anna! Don't worry!"

There was nothing to do but pray. Henri hugged her more tightly when the support poles of the lodge started rattling, as if shaken by a giant's hand. The hides bulged in and out, like a blacksmith's bellows. The entire lodge swayed, creaked. The timbers strained against the trusses lashed with thick leather and rope around the joints. Another brilliant flash burst beneath the door flap, illuminating the interior. There was an instantaneous clap of thunder. The ground vibrated.

Henri's skin felt prickly. A strange burning odor permeated the air.

That was close, he thought, his heart pounding out a fast rhythm. The storm was as exhilarating as it was frightening.

"Ahh-ree!"

"It's all right, Anna. I'm right here."

Ten minutes later, the worst had passed and the storm moved on, walking on legs of light and sound until its rumbles became muted, distant, almost melodic. In its wake, the rain pattered gently on the hides and bark of the lodge.

Henri rose on one elbow. In the dim firelight, he could make out Anamosa's blue eyes, wide and nervous. He looked over to see if Juniata was awake. The older woman was lying on her back with the blanket pulled close to her chin, snoring softly, oblivious to the whole ordeal.

"You see, I told you it would be all right."

Anamosa smiled, shiny white teeth gleaming. To Henri's delight, she lifted her head and rubbed her nose on his. It made them both giggle.

As the night grew quiet, he expected Anamosa to crawl back to her pallet of skins and blankets. Instead, she pulled his arm under her head and curled up contentedly into a ball. Henri stroked her soft black hair and allowed the rain's patter to send him into a dreamless slumber.

Henri emerged from the lodge before sunrise. He stretched lazily and walked around the encampment to check for damage. There was a cool, wet, clean breeze blowing briskly from the lake. It carried a hint of snow. Among the green of the forest, he saw a scattering of leaves tinged with the red-and-yellow colors of the autumn.

The morning seemed so peaceful compared to the violence of the night before. The winds had swept the entire village clean of anything not tied down. The entire refuse pile was gone! But to his amazement, none of the well-anchored lodges had been damaged or blown over by the storm.

A few dim stars were still visible above the deep, golden pink of the sun's emergence, including one very bright light.

"It is the war bird of the Great Spirit," Chittaqua had told him one morning. "It is a guide. Observe it each night, and you will see it move. That one talks to me," he said, pointing to a particularly bright light above the horizon. "It is His messenger. On nights with no moon, you can see four lesser eagles flying with it."

Henri liked Chittaqua's story better than Captain LaTour's, who had called the bright light *Jupiter*. As usual Henri squinted, but he had yet to perceive those eagles. He gazed at Chittaqua's star reproachfully.

"You should have taken me with you," he admonished in a whisper, as if the star were directly connected to the shaman. "It was not fair to use one of my father's promises to make me stay."

But the other villagers were grateful for Henri's presence. He and Chesanin had become the main hunters for the village, surprising even the most experienced men with their luck and cunning. They had discovered a valley with steep slopes and a blind at one end. The ground at the beginning of the valley was dotted with bulging salt licks. They turned it into a natural trap, refining a tactic where one of them would flush their quarry from the brine-rich ravine, chasing them back to the blind side, where the other hunter waited with a deadly bow. It worked well. Every day, they brought home enough fresh game to feed most of the families, earning the praise and admiration of everyone. In appreciation, the soldiers living in the village gave the boys muskets, plus powder and lead. Henri and Chesanin were delighted and practiced the complicated technique for loading, aiming, and firing the powerful weapons all at a run. The range and killing superiority of the smoothbores was conspicuous. The next day, they made major kills on a six-point buck and a wolverine, animals of speed and agility, nearly impossible to get close to for a bow shot. In addition, shooting an aggressive wolverine, which often attacked the hunter, was an exceedingly dangerous thing to do.

This supply of food greatly relieved the pressure on the new village elders to provide for the women and children. One of the Huron scouts was so impressed, he tattooed arrows on one of Chesanin's arms and spears on the other, in recognition of his prowess. Henri rubbed his arms thoughtfully in the cool morning air as he walked along the beach, wondering whether he should have allowed the Huron to give him a similar tattoo.

But Henri had tired of hunting. Even the unique excitement of using a musket had lost some of its allure. He was now preoccupied with the desire to travel south, on the Fort Le Boeuf portage.

"Maybe I'll visit Fort Presque Isle today." Then he recalled the suspicious looks the priests had given him the last time he visited and decided against it.

"Or maybe I will talk with the people on the portage coming from Fort Le Boeuf."

A great portage milestone had been set at the crossroads three days earlier by the soldiers of Presque Isle. The stone indicated the name, direction, and distance to the next marker of its kind. He could sit there all day watching the road traffic and asking questions of anyone coming north from Fort Le Boeuf.

Yes, he thought. *That's what I will do.*

The young *coureur de bois* sprinted back to the village. Chesanin was outside his lodge, tightening some lashings loosened by the storm.

"The rain has awakened all the animals in the forest. We will have a good hunt today," Chesanin said, excited at the prospect.

Henri had moved out of his lodge and back in with Juniata when Tamaqua's incessant demands became too painfully reminiscent of his experience at the Hawk clan village. Chesanin was living in a lodge with a Seneca girl.

"I do not hunt today," Henri said. "I am going to sit by the portage stone."

Chesanin looked puzzled. It seemed a great waste of hunting daylight. "Why?"

"To talk with people. You don't need me anyway."

Henri ducked inside the lodge before Chesanin could protest further. Juniata was combing Anamosa's hair. He tickled Anamosa's sides until she giggled, then proceeded to collect a skin of water, a round loaf of fresh bread, hard army cheese, and salted meat.

"Where are you going?" Juniata asked.

"To sit by the portage stone."

"You're not going to hunt?"

"No," he answered, feeling guilty.

Carrying his new musket over one shoulder, he quickly walked the half mile to the crossroads. He climbed on top of the three-foot-tall square piece of granite and sat down to wait. To pass time, he pretended to shoot at the hovering sea birds with his musket. It was very early in the morning. By the time he saw anyone, Henri had killed flocks of imaginary gulls.

CHAPTER 19
FORT PRESQUE ISLE
SEPTEMBER 1754
"You will watch Him swallow hope."

"For God's sake, Philippe! Kin' ya' slow the pace just a little!"

The crutch Pierre had devised for himself was heavily wrapped in rags but had chaffed his underarm raw, nevertheless.

Philippe looked back over his shoulder. Pierre was panting heavily. Even Chittaqua looked wearied by the intensity of the march. The *coureur de bois* nodded to the shaman. They carefully lowered the canoe they were carrying. Pierre struggled to catch up.

Philippe's body ached everywhere. In hindsight, it'd been a blessing Pierre and Captain Joncaire had persuaded him to rest for another night. The hot meals and additional sleep had physically revitalized him. It had been three days of hard travel up the Rivière aux Boeufs from sunrise to sunset. They had been lucky. The recent heavy rains had raised the water level of the river above its normal flow for this time of year. It allowed more than half of their journey to be made in the canoe instead of carrying it over the shallows.

"Animal Scalp must rest longer," Chittaqua cautioned. "His wounds are bleeding."

Philippe agreed reluctantly.

"We'll rest here and eat," he shouted back to Pierre.

Pierre shuffled the last few yards and balanced himself on his crutch.

Chittaqua pulled a water bladder from the canoe. He handed it over, and Pierre took several long swallows.

"Sit. Show me your leg."

The Scotsman grunted his way to a boulder, unlaced his leather breeches, and let them drop to his feet.

Tiny streams of dried blood had spiraled around the trader's leg from his thigh to his boot. The skin above the knee was swollen and mottled with green and purple bruises. But the skin's appearance did not concern the shaman. He was more interested in signs of infection.

Chittaqua unwrapped the blood-soiled cloth bandages. He carefully lifted the leg and examined the oozing bullet wounds. He frowned at what he saw and prodded the area around each hole with his fingers to see if he could make it pus.

"Ow! Ow! Be careful ya' bloody heathen!"

"You cry like a white man."

Blood seeped over and around the scabs. Chittaqua sniffed. The leg had a bad smell. But the wounds weren't infected…not yet. Chittaqua dipped some clean rags in the river and washed the leg, ignoring Pierre's howls of pain. The wounds were raw. The exit wound looked worse. The inflammation had spread in a scarlet star-shaped pattern two inches in length.

Chittaqua pulverized and sprinkled pieces of a dried tree root on the injuries, which would promote scabbing. Then he prepared a poultice full of healing herbs and soaked it with river water."

Pierre sighed loudly as the shaman placed the soothing emollient directly over the sores.

"Egad, that feels good!"

After wrapping the leg in clean bandages, Chittaqua washed his hands in the river.

"Well," Pierre remarked, trying to sound lighthearted, "am I goin' tah' live?"

"You need rest for two suns. Your wounds will not start to heal unless you stop walking. But I found no evil spirits."

Pierre winked at Philippe. "Well tha' is certainly good tah' know. Would nah' want any nasty evil spirits swimming aboot inside me."

Philippe had gathered some deadwood. He ignored the banter and started a fire, staking some salted venison over the flames to warm the meat.

"We are less than a half a day from Fort Le Boeuf," Philippe said to Chittaqua. "Is Pierre strong enough?"

The Scotsman became indignant. "Dinnah' start talkin' around me as if I kinnah' hear ya'. And dinnah' worry aboot me keeping up. I once walked for a month on a broken…"

Philippe exhaled, sagging wearily in front of the fire. "I don't want to argue."

"Laddie…Chittaqua's wrapped my leg tight. I kin' walk. Let me sit here for a while and we can move on. I'd rather spend my time resting at Fort Le Boeuf anyway. They might actually have real beds."

"*You* must eat and rest," Chittaqua told Philippe.

Philippe shrugged off the concern. "I must get to the fort."

Chittaqua's body jerked, as if struck by something. An unnatural chill crawled over his flesh. He closed his eyes.

Philippe and Pierre reacted, instantly alert. "Are you all right?"

The shaman saw the image of a standing stone falling over into the river. Only one stone remained standing, and it was leaning perilously. He sensed the presence of the demon from his dreams.

"He is here," Chittaqua whispered. His voice was filled with anxiety.

"Who's here?" Philippe asked urgently. He saw fear spread across the medicine man's face.

Philippe and Pierre cocked their muskets. Chittaqua blinked several times. He stood and staggered backwards. The medicine bag slipped from his fingers.

Philippe moved toward him. "Chittaqua?"

The shaman's body went rigid. His fists balled at his sides and his head tilted backward.

"Catch him, laddie! He's havin' a bloody seizure!"

Philippe caught the shaman and propped him up.

"Dinnah' lay him down or he might swallow his tongue!"

Chittaqua's head snapped forward. His eyes rolled until only the whites were showing. He looked directly at Pierre and spoke in unaccented French. But his tone of voice was guttural.

> *"It has fallen,*
> > *It is free!*
> *Hear me, hear the doom,*
> > *Of He that comes to devour your spirit.*
> *All light has left your homes,*
> > *You will watch Him swallow hope.*
> *Your wounds will never heal,*
> > *Creatures of fear will share your bed.*
> *He waits for you now, in the dark,*

He knows you will come.
Receive His gifts of agony and sadness.
　　Beware!"

Chittaqua's head lolled forward. He drooled on his chest. His body went limp. Philippe gently laid him on the ground. The shaman's breathing was ragged. His lips moved queerly, muttering, but there was no sound.

"Well...tha' certainly was encouraging!"

Philippe replied with irritation, "Can't you see he's sick?"

"I dinnah' mean tah' mock him!" The Scotsman clambered over to the medicine man and felt his forehead. "No fever. It was just a seizure, laddie."

"What do you mean *just* a seizure?"

"I mean, he's nah' dyin'. I've seen this before. These shaman are forever swallowing all kinds of poisonous herbs, frogs, and roots. It's a wonder they can speak any sense at all. They kin' slip into hysterics whenever they want. I once saw one o' 'em in a trance like this, walk through a waist-high fire without singeing a single hair. O' course, none o' 'em had a tendency tah' babble like Chittaqua. *Swallowing hopeless fear creatures?* Isn't tha' wha' he said? Wha' the bloody hell does tha' mean?"

"I don't know." Philippe listened to the shaman's chest. "His heart beat is strong. What should we do?"

"Throw a blanket over him and wait."

"Wait? For what? For how long?"

"Kinnah' say. He could wake up a minute from now or in a few hours. Best we just finish eatin'."

"How can you think of eating now?" Philippe accused.

"Because I'm bloody tired and bloody hungry. Chittaqua's goin' tah' be fine. Cover him up and leave him be."

Philippe slipped the medicine bag under the shaman's head and covered him with a blanket. He settled back with Pierre, who was already tearing into the venison. Now and then Chittaqua would mumble something unintelligible but otherwise remained motionless.

"Here, eat this."

Philippe chewed the meat mechanically as he watched Chittaqua's breathing.

Pierre watched too. "Did ya' see his eyes roll over white? Reminds me o'—"

"Jesus, Pierre!"

Philippe woke after a few hours of fitful rest. Pierre was snoring. Chittaqua was sitting up, staring trance-like at the fire.

"Chittaqua?"

"We must go," Chittaqua replied. The shaman reached over and shook Pierre's shoulder.

"Wha' ...?"

The Erigh clan chief had never experienced so potent a vision without the help of his medicines. A powerful demon had spoken. It had declared Snow Hair and his clan would die. This ancient evil was getting stronger. They must defeat it before the last of the standing stones fell. Despite the vision, he still felt one stone was standing.

Chittaqua helped Pierre to his feet. The Scotsman groaned loudly.

"Bloody hell! How could resting make my pain *worse*?"

Chittaqua looked at Philippe. "Your doom approaches." He looked at Pierre. "And yours."

"Wha' the bloody hell are ya' talkin' aboot?"

"We've faced this evil before," Chittaqua said. "All of us. Together. Now we face it again." He pointed at Philippe and Pierre. "As one."

Philippe was baffled too.

"Aha! Evil. He must mean Major Péan," Pierre offered, pleased with the comparison.

Chittaqua shook his head, disappointment on his face. He collected the muskets and powder horns without explaining further.

Pierre grinned. "I think our friend has swallowed too much o' his magic fungus, laddie."

Philippe scowled at the Scotsman.

"Well, dinnah' get mad at me! *He*'s the one havin' seizures and seein' demons!"

Philippe slung water bladders over his shoulders and belted the pistols. Together, with Chittaqua, they hoisted the empty canoe above their heads to portage around the next set of rapids.

"Leave the other supplies. We should be at the fort in another four or five hours."

CHAPTER 20
FORT LE BOEUF
SEPTEMBER 1754
"Sometimes dreams are just that...only dreams."

Portaging around the frequent rapids required Pierre Dunemoore to carry a heavy pack and hobble along behind Philippe and Chittaqua, who carried the canoe above their heads. Getting in and out of the canoe was a painful process. The scabbing on his leg wounds cracked and bled constantly. Anytime the water flowed smoothly on the Rivière aux Boeufs, the Scotsman prayed it would last until they reached the river landing at the fort. Finally, it did.

"Thank God," Pierre muttered.

They saw small parties of soldiers moving about near the bank of the river, some covered in bandages, some wearing arm slings. They limped between the lunettes of the fort and carried the rotting remains of month-old dead Seneca braves to a huge funeral pyre. An oily black pillar of smoke spiraled above the flames. Another detachment of soldiers were digging graves. Only two sentries were posted at the main gate.

The soldiers carrying the dead Seneca spotted the canoe. Chittaqua sat in the bow. His native dress was obvious. The shout of alarm stopped all work. Within moments, numerous muskets were aimed at them.

"Ho! Hold fire," Philippe hailed loudly from the canoe. "We are French!"

They pulled on their oars and paddled quickly toward the tiny dock. As they neared, some of the soldiers recognized Philippe and began to relax. A scowling few who had lost friends in battle kept their weapons trained on Chittaqua.

Pierre limped toward the gate, balanced between his crutch and Philippe's shoulder.

The muskets of the soldiers followed Chittaqua as he passed by. One made a show of cocking his weapon.

"Captain Prideaux!" Pierre shouted.

The fatigued army officer turned and was startled to see the Scotsman leaning on a crutch and Philippe Gerrard. The hawkish features of Chittaqua loomed over the traders' shoulders. The Erigh shaman stood with his musket cradled in his arms. He nodded once in greeting.

"Pierre! Philippe! Where have you come from?"

"Fort Machault. Where are Sister Michelle and Okeanneh?"

"My quarters," Prideaux said, his voice subdued. He pointed toward a building at the center of the fort. Two soldiers stood guard at its entrance. Looped around one shoulder of their uniforms was the distinctive blue-and-red braid of Captain Joncaire's regiment.

"I've done what I could to make them comfortable."

Philippe nodded to the guards and pushed on the door. It creaked open. The room had two beds. Both were occupied.

"Hello," he called softly.

The nearest body moved slightly. A head turned in his direction. "Philippe?"

His eyes adjusted. He knelt between the two beds.

"Philippe!" Michelle sat up and hugged him, sobbing his name over and over.

The medallion of Saint Denis around Okeanneh's neck reflected the intruding light, drawing his eyes. She stretched out an arm and touched Philippe.

Philippe released Michelle and leaned over Okeanneh. He smoothed tear-wet hairs away from her face.

"*Cou ti si mah*," Philippe whispered to her. He kissed her tenderly. "*Cou ti si mah.*"

She smiled with great joy and strained to reply. Her lips moved soundlessly. She signed she loved him.

Philippe saw her struggle. "Why don't you speak?" He caressed her cheek.

Okeanneh kissed his hand. Tears wet his fingers.

"She cannot speak," Michelle said quietly. "The surgeon claims it's because of the injury to her head. And it's hard for her to sit up for very long without her head aching terribly."

Philippe swallowed, struggling to control the hot rage that surged in his chest. *Save it for the shérif.*

Okeanneh attempted to sit up, only to be overcome by a painful dizziness that made her gag.

Philippe gently eased her back down.

"It's all right. It's all right." He kissed her forehead and cheek. "All this is my fault," he confessed to them. He held Okeanneh's hands as he talked. "I should have told you where I was going," he said to Okeanneh. He looked at Michelle. "I should have never left you and Henri alone."

"I didn't think I would ever see you or Henri again." Tears fell from Michelle's eyes.

Philippe and Michelle conversed for almost an hour, sharing information about what had happened to each of them since they'd seen each other last. Philippe kept repeating it was his fault. Michelle kept telling him it was not. Michelle did not mention being raped by the English trader, Pemberton Curtiss. Philippe did not tell her the extent of the Seneca's torture or about the deaths of Louie and Michel. As they talked, Philippe stayed by Okeanneh, caressing her face and hair.

Okeanneh signed how Henri was taking care of Anamosa and that Henri and Anamosa were at Fort Presque Isle.

"Henri? At Fort Presque Isle? Right. That is where we are going next." Philippe stood. "I will be right back," he assured.

The *coureur de bois* walked outside into the sunlight. He looked around and saw a group of men, including Chittaqua, congregated near the commandant.

Captain Prideaux shifted anxiously as Philippe approached.

"Monsieur, I am sorry ..."

"Captain, I need a wagon to transport the women."

"A wagon? But of course." The officer gestured to his sergeant to fulfill the request.

Pierre sagged wearily on his crutch. "I take it we're nah' staying for supper then."

"I want to retrieve Henri and Anamosa from Fort Presque Isle and get back to Fort Niagara as soon as possible." He turned back to the commandant and spoke in a low voice, his expression dark. "Where can I find this *shérif?*"

Captain Prideaux swallowed. "I...I thought he'd fled to Fort Presque Isle," the officer stammered, feeling somehow guilty for the man's actions and subsequent escape. "I sent the majority of Captain Joncaire's men in pursuit. But two days ago, a dispatch arrived from Captain Pouchot at Fort Niagara. Among other things, it said the *shérif* passed through Fort Niagara some weeks ago without being seen. He was disguised as a voyageur on his way back to Montréal."

Chittaqua was pleased to hear this. *Ahhhh! Now Snow Hair must go to the great village. He will see Picture Maker there.*

"Montréal." *So be it,* Philippe thought. "I will be heading up the portage with Sister Michelle and Okeanneh as soon as the wagon is ready."

Two half-breed army scouts standing nearby glanced at each other. The famous *coureur de bois* was one of the survivors of the *French humiliation of the Seneca,* on the Rivière aux Boeufs, as the Iroquois had come to call the series of Seneca defeats. Snow Hair's sudden appearance at Fort Le Boeuf was significant. That he was going to Fort Presque Isle might suggest a new wave of retaliation by the French soldiers. Within an hour, the scouts casually left the fort to hunt. Instead, they rendezvoused and relayed this new information to Maltoc's spies lingering in the woods.

Pierre Dunemoore and Philippe exchanged angry words. The Scotsman insisted they remain at Fort Le Boeuf the rest of the day and through the night. "One more day will nah' matter!" Philippe eventually gave in but never stopped working, loading the wagon with extra weapons, food, blankets, and bedding for the women and Pierre. Captain Prideaux volunteered two dispatch horses for use as the team. Before Philippe lay down that night, everything was ready except for harnessing the horses. He barely slept at all and was up and about with the dawn.

The morning found Fort Le Boeuf peaceful and calm, save for the stoic march of the sentries back and forth along the walls. Philippe's tongue felt thick, his mouth sticky. He was thirsty. Pierre's soft snoring reminded him most people were still asleep. He looked for Chittaqua but didn't see him anywhere. The shaman's weapons and backpack were also missing.

Philippe stood up slowly, letting his joints snap and pop as he stretched his limbs. The noise and movement startled Pierre awake. The Scotsman sat up, ready to fight, a skinning knife gripped in one hand.

"Philippe!" Pierre swung the knife around, confused. "Wha'…? Oh…

Fort Le Boeuf." He exhaled, relieved. "I'm thirsty."

Philippe grabbed one of the waterskins hanging on a peg by the door. He drank for a long time and brought the bag back to Pierre, supporting the bag while Pierre quenched his thirst.

"Help me stand." Pierre began to move and stretch. "Christ…I feel like I just crawled from a grave!"

"Did you know he pissed on her, Pierre?" Philippe said suddenly. The *coureur de bois'* voice had a manic edge to it. "After he bashed her unconscious, he cut open her dress with a knife and pissed all over her." Philippe was shaking. "He did it to taunt *me.* He knew I would learn of it. And he was right. I will gut that bastard if I have to follow him back to France!"

Philippe's eyes darted wildly around the room, his hands fisted.

"Laddie! Laddie!" Pierre gripped Philippe's shoulders, refusing to let go until he made eye contact with his partner. "Calm yourself! We've still a journey tah' make. I'm with ya'. But I need ya' tah' think aboot the trail ahead. Dinnah' worry, we'll get the *shérif.* We'll get him!"

Philippe left the water bag with Pierre and limped outside toward a cooking fire surrounded by some soldiers, one of many inside the fort that sparked to life every morning. Following behind him, Pierre noticed Philippe's injured leg had healed with a permanent bow. He gave the soldiers a silver livre then wolfed down a bowl of food scooped from the cook pot, a gluey mix of beaver meat, fish, roots, and fresh bread.

"Monsieur Gerrard?" It was Captain Prideaux. "Monsieur, I cannot spare any men from this garrison, but I will send Captain Joncaire's four guards with you as escort."

"Thank you, Captain."

"This man keeps stilettos hidden up his sleeves," Prideaux said. "The *shérif* that is…except I don't think he's a *shérif.* I think he's just a common murderer."

"He is a dead man."

Philippe bought a smaller, empty pot from the soldiers and added enough food to fill several bowls for the women to eat in the wagon.

While soldiers harnessed the horses, Philippe went to Captain Prideaux's quarters. Michelle was already dressed and had collected a small pack of things to take with her. She'd already vomited once that morning and prayed it would not happen in Philippe's presence.

"We're leaving," Philippe said in greeting.

"I'm ready."

Philippe carefully lifted Okeanneh from her bed along with the blankets. He kissed her tenderly before lowering her gently on the new bedding in the back of the wagon. Then He kissed her again. Okeanneh glanced at Michelle to see the woman's reaction to this display of affection. But Michelle took little notice of the kiss.

Helping one another, Michelle and Pierre climbed in next to Okeanneh. "Let me know if you need anything," Michelle whispered as she placed a rolled blanket beneath Okeanneh's head to make her more comfortable.

"Where's Chittaqua?" Pierre asked Philippe.

"He was up and gone before me. His pack and weapons are gone too. He might be scouting the portage."

"Trouble?"

Pierre's question gave Philippe pause. He'd been so focused on Gaspard de Propei, he'd not considered the usual dangers.

"Have there been any skirmishes on the portage?" he asked Prideaux.

"Not a single incident since the Seneca attacked us. They suffered heavy losses. Only a handful escaped."

"And Maltoc?"

"My scouts see no sign of him at all. We're not sure he's alive."

That's why Chittaqua is scouting, Philippe thought. *To look for Maltoc.*

Maltoc's men had indeed been slaughtered in the cross fire between the lunettes of Fort Le Boeuf. Many had died without striking a blow, a direct result of Maltoc's flawed plan. And the battle had been over quickly.

It's the white man's cowardly way of fighting, the sachem thought sullenly.

Nevertheless, Maltoc knew he was now regarded as a renegade in the eyes of the French, the English, *and* his Iroquois brothers. A renegade war chief with only *three* followers!

The last time he'd eaten inside a lodge seemed like many moons ago. Much had happened since then. Yet, it had been little more than a moon. Still a long time, but Painted Snake and two other braves followed him dutifully.

Another two survivors of the attack he'd sent scouting or spying on the forts. They'd all lost their families in the Erigh attack on their village. But Maltoc was still chief of the Hawk clan.

Maltoc knew the soldiers had suffered as well, and they were still suffering. There was sickness among them. They'd made no attempt to pursue him. For weeks after the attack, Maltoc debated what to do next. They'd ambushed a group of six *coureurs de bois* marching to Fort Presque Isle from the west. Killed them all. Stripped the dead of anything valuable, food, weapons, clothing, and left the furs they'd carried to rot. They could continue to ambush and kill the French as opportunities arose. *But for how long?* The nights were getting colder. If Maltoc and his men were to survive the winter, they needed food. They needed shelter and protection. Most of all they *needed* a village. They heard that the French had sent men to help rebuild the Hawk clan village palisade.

"It's a trap to kill us, should we come back to see," Maltoc told his remaining warriors. "Let them rebuild it. We've no one to left to do it ourselves."

Voices raged inside Maltoc's head: *Go to the sunset, to the tribes of the plains. You are a chief. A Seneca. A member of the council of five hands. You fought bravely! Tell them about your battle with the French.*

Then what?

Without a clan and home, you are renegade.

Maltoc reflected there were still crops to be harvested in the field next to his old village. The problem was, he needed more men...and women! Women were important for harvesting the squash, beans, and corn. But women would not return to a clan that could not provide shelter and protection. Of course, the French were rebuilding shelters too. Men might come for that. But he needed warriors. And to draw warriors to his leadership, Maltoc needed to rub away the stain of his failure at Fort Le Boeuf. He needed a victory. But now they were too few in number to achieve a victory of any consequence. And simply ambushing *coureurs de bois* marching the forests would not produce winter tales of Maltoc's courage.

He considered marching south to visit the other clans. There were always young warriors, hot with anger, wanting to prove themselves in battle, seeking a strong war chief to lead them. But that would mean leading them to another battle, *if* they would follow him. And who would they fight? Where would they fight? How would they win? The outcome of such a battle would be as uncertain as the one he just lost. Moreover, the other Seneca clan chiefs would vigorously oppose his challenge to their clan loyalty. Nevertheless, it could be done. But if this task could not be completed before the snows were upon them ...?

Then what?

Across the fire, Painted Snake observed the wrinkled, pained expression of his leader. They'd solved their temporary needs for survival, food, weapons, and shelter. But even Painted Snake could not think of the next action to take. That meant Maltoc was equally troubled. Painted Snake glanced at the other two braves. They were quiet—too quiet.

The French have a reason for rebuilding our village, Painted Snake concluded. *This was an act of peace. We could accept it and save what's left of the Hawk clan, or...or die.*

Maltoc could feel the eyes of the Hawk clan braves watching him. They expected a new plan, but he had no reasonable plan to announce. After a few more days, the warriors' restlessness would compel them to abandon their chief. Maltoc brooded miserably on this prospect.

And after that?

There seemed no way out. But to the sachem's utter astonishment, the solution to his dilemma marched boldly into the camp.

"Oho, Maltoc!" Sauquita greeted the chief.

Sauquita had learned where Maltoc and his braves were camping from the Mohawk. He felt Maltoc would be a willing ally for what he had in mind.

The Seneca jumped to their feet, weapons ready, eyes looking left and right, expecting an ambush from the trees.

"This weapon once belonged to Animal Scalp," Sauquita continued as if his welcome had been warm. "It now belongs to me." He held out the war ax for admiration. "I took it from Animal Scalp in battle."

When no one else appeared, Maltoc tentatively took hold of the battle ax, his distrust persisting. He ran his hand over the shiny head and touched the purple stone imbedded in the metal. He handed the weapon back and regarded Sauquita suspiciously.

"From where have you come?"

"From the Wolf clan village."

"And why are you here?"

"To kill Snow Hair," Sauquita boasted. "He is at the French fort on the

River of Buffalo. Animal Scalp and Chittaqua are with him too."

Maltoc's mood lifted at this revelation. "*Chittaqua* is there?"

"*And* Snow Hair and Animal Scalp!" Sauquita repeated. "I've come to help the Hawk clan avenge the attack on its village."

"*You?* You are alone?"

"Yes." Sauquita was not going to mention his recent losses.

Though possession of the great war ax was impressive, Maltoc doubted Sauquita's sincerity, if not his sanity. *What can one more man do?*

"The French fort is too strong," Maltoc said bluntly, deciding not to mention the cost to his clan for their reckless attack. "And my men are scattered...searching for the Erigh."

Sauquita smiled and offered his most valuable piece of information.

"Tomorrow they will not be in the fort. In the morning, Snow Hair, Animal Scalp, and Chittaqua will be traveling the portage road together."

Chittaqua's dreams the night before were the most disturbing they had ever been. They brought him fully awake long before the sun was up, sweating profusely and breathing as if he had been held underwater to the point of blacking out. He'd seen faceless people screaming in agony. Everywhere he'd flown while joined with the white eagle it had been the same. Violent death. But what awoke him was the death face of the only person he recognized. It was his own reflection in the pool of water. And then nothing.

Chittaqua brooded darkly as he trotted up the hunting trails north of Fort Le Boeuf. He knew these trails well enough to see the path in the darkness.

Sometimes dreams are just that...only dreams.

How many times in his life had he appeased the fears of apprentice shamans with those words? And behind this comforting encouragement, he'd never believed what he said. Dreams should never be ignored. And yet, he had to ignore his dreams; the amount of death he had seen in his night visions was simply too severe, too painful, too close.

Chittaqua expected an attack by Maltoc. After he'd learned the *loyal* army scouts were actually confiding to the Mohawk, he assumed the Seneca would learn Snow Hair had reached the fort. Maltoc's losses in the attack on Fort Le Boeuf had been very, very heavy. Though no one knew the strength in numbers of the surviving Seneca, even if Maltoc was the only one left in his clan, the opportunity to ambush all of his enemies at the same time would be too tempting to disregard.

These were Seneca lands. If Maltoc's mortal enemy was near, Maltoc would come. The only questions were *where* and *when*.

The march to Fort Presque Isle would take two days, three at most, and Snow Hair would hurry the travel. There would also be soldiers moving in both directions. Chittaqua had run halfway up the portage to Presque Isle by midmorning. He knew of four places for an effective ambush. He'd scouted three of them already and found no sign of the Seneca. There was one more to scout further up the flatlands, but it was much closer to the lake fort and the chance of even more soldiers would make it less favored. By midafternoon, Snow Hair would reach the place where he stood right now. And the *coureur de bois* would be on guard.

If I were Maltoc, Chittaqua weighed. *I would make my attack on the French road to Niagara...where it would not be expected.*

CHAPTER 21
THE PRESQUE ISLE PORTAGE
SEPTEMBER 1754
The Stalking

As they advanced along the bateaux portage between Fort Le Boeuf and Fort Presque Isle, Philippe studied the terrain and woodlands, calling upon his hard-learned forest knowledge. This rutted road had been widened by the French engineers to create easier passage for heavily loaded ox-drawn wagons carrying larger river craft. He thought about ambush, trying to anticipate the likely places where it might occur. Here, the features of land travel were not friendly, even for those who preferred to walk. The hills were not that high, but wagons travel best on flat ground. Driving a wagon back and forth along the narrow switchbacks of even a small hill was precarious and slow, with frequent stops, and would unbalance loads. An ideal place for a surprise attack.

Fortunately, there were not many hills. Upon reaching the last hilltop before the flatlands, he stopped to scrutinize the forested landscape in front of them while the horses rested. The likelihood of trouble once on this higher ground was low, due to a clear view of the approaches. But the long road through the flatlands ahead also contained numerous places to stage an attack. Indeed, the entire portage was thick with trees on both sides; an attack could come from almost anywhere. But only a few places had intersecting hunting trails, which would allow an attacker to make a quick retreat if things went badly, or well, if captives were taken.

If it's going to happen, Philippe thought, looking over the sea of green, *it will happen down there, and sooner rather than later.*

Pierre Dunemoore took a large swallow of water and handed the bag down to Philippe, who was standing by the wagon. "Wha' deeya' think?"

Philippe took a drink and handed the bag over to the soldiers. "We should be all right until we reach the bottom…I only wish Chittaqua would come back from wherever the hell he went."

"I think heeda' warned us already if there was trouble ahead."

Unless trouble has already found him, Philippe thought moodily. He walked to the back of the wagon to check on the women. Gently, he touched Okeanneh on the forehead and cheek. She kissed his palm and smiled before her expression returned to one of pain from her terrible headaches. The bumpy ride had only made it worse.

Save for willow bark tea, Philippe was at a loss what to do for her, except get her to the small hospital at Fort Niagara as quickly as possible.

"How long will it take to reach Fort Presque Isle from here?" Michelle asked.

"We can push the team pretty hard on the flatlands, at least until darkness makes the road too difficult to see. I'd rather not use any torches. A day or so, depending on our speed. But even if we have to camp tonight, we'll arrive well before midday tomorrow."

"It seems so beautiful," Michelle said wistfully as she stared out at the tree tops.

"What does?"

"The trees...I've never seen the top of a forest spread out like a huge green quilt."

Philippe stared at the seemingly endless expanse and frowned. "Yes... the trees are beautiful, but if you wanted to pick a spot to hide, a place from where you could notch an arrow and let it fly before we even knew you were there, which of those trees would you choose?"

Philippe instantly regretted his words. "Forgive me. That was a careless thing to say."

"It's true though, isn't it?" Michelle gave her attention to the trees again, her forehead creased with worry.

"So we're going tah' play a *voyageur* game?" Pierre rolled his eyes. "Then, I'd choose *tha'* tree, laddie. Oops, no, tha' tall pine there looks better...then again, maybe tha' oak...no, tha' big chestnut over there. A dozen bloody murderers could hide behind tha' one....tha's definitely the one...no, no, look there! It has tah' be—"

"Christ, Pierre! Enough!" Philippe said, frowning. "I'm sorry, Michelle. After all that's happened...I...well ..."

"Dinnah' worry, Michelle. This is a French army road. And as ya' may have noticed, Philippe's usually wrong *all* of the time."

Giving Pierre a sharp look, Philippe smacked one of the horses on the rump and the wagon lurched forward. Okeanneh groaned. He regretted doing that too.

As the wagon progressed along the short downhill switchback, the road curved sharply back in a westerly direction. On foot, Philippe could usually slide straight down the looser stones of this hillside on his boots. It would take him only a few minutes. The portage road ran west along a shallow ridgeline face for a quarter mile, following a gentle downward slope, intentionally made by the French road engineers to permit easier but slower wagon travel. It made another sharp switchback back to the right, coming halfway back along the ridgeline while dropping the remaining altitude. The road's final turn was to the left and proceeded directly northwest on level ground for miles until it intersected with the Niagara portage road. After reaching that junction marked by the portage stone, it was a straight one-mile trek to reach Fort Presque Isle.

Before leaving Fort Le Boeuf, Philippe had asked Joncaire's soldiers to change from their usual gray-white uniforms, which now lay folded inside a tied bundle in the back of the wagon. They donned traditional *coureur de bois* dress to be less conspicuous.

"The Indians are more wary of *coureurs de bois* than soldiers, no offense. And you can see your gray-white uniforms a long way off."

The corporal and three privates were happy to comply.

The courier horses did not like the harness and were sweating heavily, stumbling, and kicking back at the wagon. Reaching the bottom of the hill, Philippe rested the team again.

"Corporal, bring your men together for me."

He picked a spot far enough in front of the wagon not to be overheard and spoke to them in a low voice.

"If there's going to be trouble, it will happen anytime between here and Fort Presque Isle," he warned grimly. "Be on guard. If there is an attack, they will come at us from all sides. Do not stand your ground. Fall back to the wagon right away. Don't lie in front or behind the wheels. The horses may rise up or bolt. I will get up in the bed to protect the women. Pierre will drop back over the seat to the bed as well and hold the reins. If the horses bolt, move as a group to whichever side of the road gives you the best cover. Remember, you have greater strength in acting together. And don't bother to surrender; they will only torture you to death later. And don't run; they would only cut you down one by one."

The corporal swallowed hard. "But we have a chance of winning too... don't we?"

"Of course," he lied. "Pierre and I have bows and you have pistols, knives, and tomahawks. Aim carefully with your muskets. Make that first shot count. Pace your shots. You are better at defense than they are at attacking." His second lie. "Corporal, make promises to one another now that you will not panic. Plan what each of you will do. Try to fire one at a time if possible. One man should hold his fire to give cover when others reload."

"Oho! Wha' now?" Pierre shouted from the wagon.

"Just giving some advice to our companions. There's only four hours of daylight left. With luck, we may get in another mile or two before having to make camp. If you're going to eat," he addressed this to everyone, "do it now. There'll be no fires tonight if we camp in the open."

The soldiers started talking among themselves as Philippe walked away.

Michelle helped Okeanneh into the trees to make their toilet while Philippe stood guard nearby. Pierre spread food on a blanket on the back of the wagon. Everyone ate and drank their fill.

Philippe loaded the extra muskets and dragoon pistols and placed them between the women.

"I'm not sure how to use these," Michelle said as the wagon lurched forward.

Okeanneh touched Michelle's hand and gathered the weapons close to her. She then proceeded to show Michelle how to load a pistol.

Michelle smiled and placed her hand on Okeanneh's arm. "Thank you."

It was a simple touch, but Okeanneh's head lifted in surprise. The way they related to one another had evolved rapidly. With Philippe's return and his constant displays of affection to Okeanneh in front of the white woman, her rival's complete lack of concern over that had assuaged Okeanneh's anxiety. She no longer considered Michelle a threat. In fact, Michelle's frequent acts of kindness toward her were the actions of a friend.

For the first time, Okeanneh smiled back at Michelle. Okeanneh had missed her moon blood again; now by two moons. That morning, she woke up sick and it wasn't the pain in her head. She could barely contain her joy, but she wanted to be certain before telling Philippe. Impulsively, she took hold of Michelle's hand and placed it flat on her stomach.

Michelle's eyes widened. *Okeanneh's pregnant, too!*

Before Michelle could speak, Okeanneh quickly placed her fingers over Michelle's mouth and slowly shook her head. Michelle nodded.

"I understand. It's your secret," she whispered.

They touched foreheads in solidarity.

Philippe positioned one soldier in front of the wagon, one to each side, with the corporal bringing up the rear.

"Keep your eyes on the trees in back of us, Corporal."

Pierre continued to drive the team at a slow walk. Philippe bounded ahead on the trail, searching the trees left and right for signs of danger. It was slow going, but they had to be sure it was safe. Even a few seconds of warning against an attack could mean the difference between life and death.

Maltoc began to feel uneasy and decided to stop and rest. They'd been heading toward another hunting trail that crossed the portage road, planning to reach that spot hours before the wagon. But, ever since the white man's road was finished, soldiers daily moved in both directions, and although they had not seen anyone else on the portage that particular day, their pace was cautious.

Painted Snake was uneasy too and became suspicious first. "We are being followed," he told Maltoc.

The Seneca abruptly turned. Maltoc experienced a deep tingling sensation in his abdomen. Painted Snake was right. They *were* being followed. And this person was close enough to catch up to them easily if he chose to do so, yet he hadn't.

A traitorous scout? Maltoc voiced his opinion to Painted Snake.

"Maybe. Should I circle back?"

"No. He sees us. Our numbers are too great for him to attack. We must draw him closer."

They had been moving parallel with Snow Hair's wagon a half-mile distant, after having watched it slowly come down the hillside. Maltoc had ventured close enough to count six *coureurs de bois*, including Snow Hair. He'd studied how the men were arranged and formulated his plan of ambush. He could not afford to lose any more men, not even one. The only way to do that was by complete surprise.

Animal Scalp was driving the wagon and he saw at least one woman riding in the back.

"That's her," Maltoc said. "Snow Hair's woman."

"Snow Hair's woman is mine," Sauquita announced.

"She's yours *only* if we have victory!"

The rewards for winning this battle could be greater than Maltoc had first thought. The woman would be an unexpected benefit if they took her captive again. However, there was no sign of Chittaqua. That bothered Maltoc the most. *Was he the one following them?*

One of Maltoc's braves had just returned from scouting Fort Presque Isle with the report that another wagon and ten soldiers had started down the portage from the lake fort. That meant they would meet with Snow Hair's wagon before dark and might make camp with them. Their combined numbers would be far too large for an attack, even at night. They would have to wait until they separated again. And whoever was trailing them might still warn Snow Hair.

Painted Snake began to think this was not a good time to attack. And he could sense Maltoc's growing uncertainty. "Snow Hair will not stop at the lake fort," he told the sachem. "He will take his woman back to Niagara where we took her captive. There is a better place for ambush on that river portage. And many more crossing trails to make an escape afterwards."

"Where?"

"Just after the Cattaraugus River. What better place to take our vengeance than near the Erigh's last village? We might even find Chittaqua there."

Maltoc found this idea compelling. And, afterwards, they could travel one of several hunting trails directly to the Allegheny River and canoe the rest of the way back to Logstown.

"And if it is Chittaqua who follows us?" asked one of his braves.

Maltoc sneered. "He is only a man. And I will kill him. If Chittaqua follows us," Maltoc told Painted Snake, "leading him away from the wagon will make it easier to draw him into an ambush."

The other warrior nodded.

The sachem assigned one brave to follow the wagon's movement until it reached the lake fort.

"Stay with them for at least a day to learn of their intentions."

The rest of them headed east to the Cattaraugus lands.

Chittaqua had been trying to determine the Seneca numbers. He'd seen only five so far, too many for him to attack by himself in the daylight. To his great surprise, one of the Seneca turned out to be Sauquita! Could anymore of the Wolf clan be involved in this? After trailing for several hours, the Seneca were joined by one more.

Six, he decided. *Snow Hair's numbers are the same. Just barely enough for an ambush to work, but they must have total surprise.*

Chittaqua was about to warn the *coureurs de bois* when he saw the Seneca pause and turn around. He ducked behind a tree, notched an arrow, and listened for their approach.

They know someone follows, he decided.

Chittaqua immediately chose a direction in which to flee. If they pursued, he would draw them away from the wagon. To his surprise, the Seneca didn't pursue. After a short pause, they went in a different direction, moving away from the portage. If they thought someone trailed them, they did not appear to care.

Where are they going?

Chittaqua debated whether to follow the Seneca further, or rendezvous with Snow Hair and warn him. Snow Hair already expected an ambush. What Snow Hair didn't know was *where* the ambush would take place. Chittaqua didn't know either. But the Seneca may still be joined by others warriors.

The shaman decided to keep following them.

CHAPTER 22
THE PRESQUE ISLE PORTAGE
SEPTEMBER 1754
Anamosa's Dolls

Henri Gerrard collected his hunting weapons early that morning and hurried out to follow Chesanin. Ten paces from the lodge, he found old Tamaqua crouched over on the ground, struggling with some animal she'd apparently caught with her bare hands. She raised her knife to strike a killing blow when Henri heard a loud bark and yelp.

Horrified, he yelled at her. "Noooo!"

Tamaqua stopped and frowned at him. "*Eeeyaaa!*"

"*Eeeyaaa* yourself," Henri replied hotly. "I told you before. We. Do. Not. Eat. Dogs!"

Tamaqua released the terrified mongrel, which scampered off into the nearest stand of trees. The old woman sat down on the ground. She pointed at her empty cooking pot, folded her arms across her chest, and scowled.

Henri shook his bow at her. "I will bring you something to eat! No dogs!"

As he walked away, he heard her muttering more *eeeyaas* and other Seneca words he assumed were obscene insults of some kind. Seeing Chesanin waiting ahead, he trotted toward him. Just as he reached him, another voice called from behind.

"Ahh-ree! Ahh-ree!"

The hunters turned. It was Anamosa. They waited for her to catch up. She was panting heavily.

"Ahh-ree! Anamosa go," she pleaded.

Chesanin frowned and said something under his breath.

Henri sighed. He had been looking forward to a hunt, his first in almost three days.

Anamosa stopped short of them by several feet and regarded the frowning face of Chesanin with uncertainty. Her blue eyes shifted to Henri and sparkled.

Henri smiled and knelt to let the happy little girl run into his arms. He hugged her tightly and tickled her sides until she squealed with laughter.

"Anamosa must go back to Juniata," Chesanin protested, irritated at this disruption.

"No!" Anamosa made a face at Chesanin.

"Anna," Henri said, "we are going to hunt a big animal."

"Anamosa go too," she countered in a hopeful voice.

She touched his face and hair lightly. As usual, Henri found her affection irresistible. He surrendered as tiny arms snaked around his neck. She pulled on him tightly.

"Take me, Ahh-ree. Play with me."

Chesanin was exasperated. "Wolf-Bear! Come! We go. Women should not interfere with the hunt. Especially, the little ones."

"You go on ahead, Chesanin. I will find you."

Chesanin's frown deepened.

Anamosa laid her head on Henri's shoulder and gave the frowning brave a gloating smile.

"I will hunt in Rock Valley," Chesanin said.

It had become Henri and Chesanin's favorite place. They named it that because it contained plenty of enormous boulders to hide behind, and the deer always came to drink at the small streams winding through the valley.

Henri nodded. "Go. I will follow soon."

Chesanin glared at Anamosa. She stuck out her tongue at him and buried her face in Henri's neck. Chesanin trotted off.

Anamosa's smile broadened.

Henri watched his friend with envy until he had disappeared among the trees. Then he laid Anamosa on the ground and tickled her more.

"See what you did?"

Anamosa burst into peals of laughter.

I'll stay just for a little while, Henri thought.

Anamosa stood and began to sing an Ottawa song, spinning happily with her arms above her head. Henri knew she was lonely. There were no other children in the Presque Isle village her age. Juniata gave her motherly kindness, but Anamosa was forever trying to hug him and rub noses. Not that he minded all that much.

"I love Ahh-ree. I love Ahh-ree," she sang, switching to French.

Anamosa's adoration had grown steadily ever since Henri had defended her from the older boys at Fort Niagara. She would sulk on the days he went off to hunt and would run to his arms with joy when he returned.

Henri was equally charmed by her. He lifted her atop his shoulders. Anamosa entwined her fingers in the blond hair she found so beautiful. "Let's walk to the portage stone and see if anyone interesting passes by," he suggested, glancing up at her face. "What say you?"

"*Oui!*"

Anamosa's shiny white teeth gleamed. She'd learned some French and understood about half of what Henri said normally. But that didn't matter, as long as she was near him.

It was unusually quiet at the crossroads for being midmorning. Henri set her down. She continued to sing, pick flowers, and dance around on the weedy grasses. Henri recalled the column of men and supplies that had left the day before, going to the relief of Fort Le Boeuf. The column had passed in a long parade. He'd ached to go with them and had remained at the crossroads for a long time after they disappeared in the distance.

Anamosa was carrying her wooden doll. It had been crudely carved from a piece of dry oak. The facial features were sharp and angular, with eyes blackened with fire soot. No arms. And it was dressed with a stained piece of doeskin that had become dirty and frayed from being tucked beneath the girl's chin when she slept at night.

She needs a new doll, Henri thought.

"Anna, come here."

Henri lifted her onto the edge of the portage stone. She was now at eye level. He pointed at the doll.

"What's her name?"

Anamosa held up the doll. "Kee-ko."

"*Bonjour,* Kee-ko. I think Kee-ko would like a friend, eh? Stay here."

Henri searched nearby until he found a dry dead branch not infested by insects. He used his skinning knife to cut a foot-long cylindrical piece, about as thick as his wrist, and placed it atop the portage stone. The skinning knife was too large for whittling, so he switched to the smaller one he used for cutting bones from fish.

"Here we go."

Anamosa watched Henri's work with a look of wonder. The wood was hard and whittling turned out to be more difficult than he expected. He would've quit except for the look on her face. In half an hour, he managed to whittle something that was shaped a little like Kee-ko, though his doll had a thicker neck and less curves.

"Well, what do you think?" he asked her. Her smile was dazzling. "Maybe it needs clothes."

Henri decided to use the lower arm of his leather jersey. He had some decorative beadwork on the sleeve. It would make the doll more colorful. He slipped off his jersey and cut out a small square piece containing the beads from the end of one sleeve.

"Hold the knife like this."

Anamosa held the long skinning knife erect while he carefully pulled one edge past the razor-sharp blade, creating short, thin pieces of leather cord. After punching a line of small holes in the remainder with the tip of the knife, he stitched the tiny coat together making sure the beadwork was in the front.

Henri inspected the new doll. It looked foolish. The top of the head was flat and the coat was cinched at the neck. He carved the top of the doll to create a roundness to the head. Then, suddenly inspired, he cut crisscross indentations on the top until the surface was rough with snags. He reached up and cut a lock of his hair, laid the hair across the snags, and tied a thin piece of leather around it like a headband. The hair was loose and would eventually fall out, but when they returned to the village, he would find something to hold it more securely. It would do for now.

The finished creation looked totally ridiculous. Henri laughed. "Sorry, Anna. It's the best I can do."

Anamosa cradled the new doll in awe. She gently stroked the magic hair and looked at Henri with even greater affection.

"You're happy, yes? Maybe *now* I can go hunting?"

Holding the dolls in one arm, Anamosa leaned forward and rubbed her nose on his.

Henri touched the new doll on the chest. "What's the doll's name?"

"Ahh-ree!" she answered.

"Ohhh?" Henri smiled. "Ahh-ree?"

She nodded. "Ahh-ree."

Henri took Anamosa in his arms. She giggled as he spun her round and round until they were both dizzy and collapsed to the ground. She suddenly stopped laughing. Something beyond Henri's shoulder catching her attention.

Henri rolled to his feet. He saw a soldier coming up the portage in front of a wagon pulled by a team of horses. Moving quickly, he scooped Anamosa up and set her down behind the portage stone.

"Stay down," he said firmly.

Henri climbed on top of the stone to better see the road.

Pierre Dunemoore thought it fortunate they met the column of soldiers coming down the portage in the late afternoon the day before. Both groups had planned to travel further in the last few hours before sunset, but seeing the women, the sergeant in charge of the soldiers decided to camp for the night at the spot where they met, to provide them some extra protection.

The result was good food, a full night's rest for everyone, and an early start on a promising new day. Philippe made good progress before they stopped to rest and water the horses.

"We were lucky, laddie. Those soldiers probably drove away any danger lurking around us, yes? It kinnah' be but a few more hours till we reach the junction."

"Maybe. I will lag behind to make certain no one follows us while you drive on. Corporal! Have one of your men take the lead."

The high wagon seat permitted Pierre to see the furthest down the portage. A hundred paces or more ahead, he saw what looked like a young brave standing on top of the square, slab-like portage stone. He craned his neck further and cautiously took hold of his musket in case of ambush. The person looked oddly familiar. He squinted and shaded his eyes. The blond hair was unmistakable.

My God, the Scotsman thought. *That looks like Henri!*

Dressed in leather, feathers dangling from his hair, Henri cradled a musket across one arm, facing the advancing wagon in a spread-legged stance, almost like a sentry, as if the wagon would have to stop and explain the reason for its passage.

Pierre smiled and decided to hold his tongue. *Best let Philippe notice this on his own. Amazing. The lad even stands like him.* He looked behind the wagon to where Philippe trailed by about thirty paces, walking backward most of the time, his eyes carefully scanning the forest for signs of movement. As they'd gotten closer to the fort, the greater danger lay behind them.

Looking ahead again, Pierre saw the palisade wall of Fort Presque Isle looming east of the water inlet of the peninsula. He halted the wagon ten paces short of the portage stone.

"*Bonjour,* laddie," he greeted.

Henri was incredulous. "Monsieur Dunemoore?" He jumped down from the stone.

Hearing the familiar voice, Michelle sat up, peering at the road ahead. When she saw Henri, she screamed with joy and rolled off the back of the wagon.

"Henri!"

"Mama!"

They flew into each other's arms in front of the horses. Michelle was trembling so hard she sagged to her knees. "Oh, my baby! My baby!" She clung to her son, sobbing uncontrollably.

Hearing Michelle's sudden scream, Philippe spun around to see the wagon stopped and Michelle running toward the front. Thinking an attack in progress, the *coureur de bois* swore, cocked his musket, and sprinted past the wagon, only to find Michelle kneeling on the ground, embracing what looked like a young brave.

Philippe stopped by the wagon. "My God. Is that Henri?" he said in a whisper.

"Aye, laddie," Pierre responded, his face split by a massive grin. "And he's never looked better."

With his mother sobbing in his arms, Henri looked up and saw his father approach. At least he thought it was his father. The man he saw limped forward. Philippe had lost over thirty pounds, looked exhausted, and was covered in grime. His face was lined from worry. His clothing was ragged, torn, bloodstained in many places, but it was *his* voice. The voice Henri heard spoke in familiar, strong, reassuring tones.

"Oho, Henri!"

Henri called to him. "Oho, Monsieur," his voice thickened with emotion.

Philippe knelt and circled his arms around them both, laying his head on the back of Michelle's shoulder.

"Forgive me," Philippe said softly. "Forgive me."

Henri tried to choke back his tears, but they came anyway.

Pierre Dunemoore could barely contain his own sniffling. He got down from the wagon and used his crutch to hobble next to them. Not knowing what else to do, he simply patted Philippe's back.

"Well done, laddie. Well done."

Hearing Henri's name, Okeanneh had pulled herself up and peered over the seat.

Peeking around the portage stone, Anamosa saw her mother's face.

"Mama!"

It was a little girl's voice. Philippe saw Anamosa. When she neared, Philippe picked her up and lifted her into the wagon where Okeanneh waited with outstretched arms.

"I love you," Philippe said to reassure Okeanneh again, knowing she had seen his reunion with Henri.

Alerted by an advance soldier, people from the lake village came running forward to investigate the commotion at the crossroads. Juniata was leading the women and spotted Okeanneh in the back of the wagon.

Before the crowd reached them, a horse-mounted soldier rode up. He asked Pierre Dunemoore who was in the party and the status of their condition.

People started bringing food and water to the wagon. Philippe waved away the gifts. He already felt a gnawing weariness begin to descend. *Can't sleep yet*, he thought and shook off the feeling. He saw a soldier approach leading two hardy farm horses drawing a wagon behind them from Fort Presque Isle.

"They're sending us a new wagon," Pierre shouted over the noise.

"Good, we'll swap wagons," Philippe said.

Pierre's shoulders sagged. "Laddie, ya' *kinnah'* be serious aboot traveling more today?"

Philippe responded in a low urgent voice. "We won't be safe until we reach Fort Niagara. Look at this place, Pierre." He waved his arm expansively. "Half the Indians camped here may be renegade…or might already be hired to hunt for us."

Pierre's voice became insistent. "Laddie, we all need tah' rest.

Particularly the women. Michelle's still nah' well! And Okeanneh? She kin' barely stand! We can surround them with guards and volunteers for one night of rest, at least."

Philippe was pensive. In addition to the disorganized village, there were dozens of tents and pathetic lean-tos in the distance, closer to the fort. He turned and looked warily at the nearby forests. It would take less than a minute to cover that distance at a run. And standing about them on the road, armed men in mixed forms of dress had collected. They were staring at them dispassionately. Still…Pierre was right.

"All right. We'll camp in the village for one night…but we're leaving at sunrise in the morning, Pierre. Once we reach Fort Niagara, we'll rest a week or so and let you heal. Then after that, I'm going on to Montréal to find that *shérif*. He can flee to Montréal or Quebec, but he won't gain passage on any ship back to France. Corrinne will see to that."

"Laddie, tha' man is nah' fleeing tah' anywhere. From what I kin' gather, he is *waiting* for ya'."

In the morning, Juniata approached the bigger wagon with two sacks full of supplies. She pushed it on the back and got up on the seat next to Pierre. Since no one knew where Chittaqua was, she was determined to go with them. Chesanin came next, carrying three muskets and other weapons.

Pierre saw Henri approaching. "Damn! The lad's already packed," he said to Philippe, with a jerk of his chin.

Henri was carrying a huge pack of supplies above his head, plus pistols tucked in his belt, two muskets, knives, a war bow decorated with feathers, and a quiver full of arrows. Anamosa danced along behind him, hopping and spinning, clutching a pair of dolls to her chest.

"He's carrying a bloody arsenal!" Pierre noticed something hairy dangling from Henri's belt. "Bloody hell! Is tha' a scalp?"

"Oho!"

They turned to see a horse-drawn cart pulling up.

"The commandant sent me to fetch you both," announced the driver.

"Well, how thoughtful o' him. Tell the commandant we'll be along later."

He looked at Philippe as the messenger left. "I'll nah' be getting waylaid in this fort by one o' Major Péan's lackeys."

CHAPTER 23
THE NIAGARA PORTAGE
SEPTEMBER 1754
"All our totems are here!"

After five days of difficult woodland travel, the Seneca reached the deserted, charred remains of the Cattaraugus village. They walked around it silently without stopping to relish or celebrate the sight of their earlier victory against the Erigh in the spring of last year. Painted Snake pointed out a feathered hex sign dangling from a tall stick, swaying in the breeze at the main entrance, meant as a warning to anyone intent on desecrating the dead further that spirits guarded this place.

After surviving countless battles and skirmishes in his life, Maltoc had aged with much less respect for *ghosts*. The sachem pulled the hex from the ground and to the shocked expressions of his braves, threw the stick as far as he could.

"So what if it *is* Chittaqua who follows us?" Maltoc sneered.

Painted Snake stiffened. That particular shaman was not someone to challenge lightly. Chittaqua knew many ways to afflict someone. *He is probably listening to us right now.* Whoever it was had trailed them persistently ever since they'd left the French road. Never too close, but never too far behind. Three times, Painted Snake had swung back in a wide circle to confront the man. He'd found tracks but never the stalker himself. The tracks were not those of a white man, however.

"But the shaman does not attack us. What would be his purpose?"

Maltoc deliberated. If it was a detestable army scout, he was there to spy on them. He would not attack. If it was Chittaqua, by now he would have broken trail to warn Snow Hair, else he would have attacked. Or so Maltoc reasoned. He shared this logic with Painted Snake. The warrior grunted in agreement.

"Then it's a scout. I should lie in wait for him instead of circling. He is too clever."

"No. Let him see our ambush, so he can tell others of our victory," Maltoc said. "We go."

The sachem continued at a trot to a place where the Niagara portage road narrowed as it passed between a series of huge granite boulders. Maltoc scouted all sides of the road before deciding this was a good place.

They retreated two hundred paces south and stopped to eat the squirrels they'd randomly killed along their march. Maltoc's braves listened to his plan carefully as they ate, anxious by the prospect of battle.

"Once the wagon is between the two largest stones, we will attack."

Painted Snake, Sauquita, and one other brave would attack from behind. Maltoc and his other two men from the front. Maltoc would initiate the attack by killing one of the horses, effectively stopping the wagon. When the *coureurs de bois* retreated to the back of the wagon, Painted Snake would fire on them from behind. They would have them pinned between the boulders.

"Do not harm the woman," Maltoc cautioned. "As long as she lives, Snow Hair will remain with her. She will prevent his escape."

Maltoc had them pile dry wood and dead bushes among the smaller boulders on either side of the road. Before their attack, he planned to dust the piles liberally with their extra gun powder. During the battle, he would fire into the piles of kindling, setting them ablaze. Hopefully, the smoke would drive the survivors into the open. Each of the Seneca carried a musket and a pistol in addition to their bows, tomahawks, and knives, plus several horns full of powder, the spoils from their previous ambushes. Maltoc carried two muskets and two pistols. Before nightfall on the fifth day, the Seneca scout following Snow Hair's wagon rejoined with them.

"They stayed at the fort for only one night. They are coming up the portage quickly. They will be here at midday tomorrow."

Chittaqua waited patiently in his tree perch where he'd slept the night before. For most of the morning, he watched the forest trail. The repeated attempts by a Seneca brave circling back to find who trailed their party had forced the shaman to proceed with greater caution. Because of that, Chittaqua had fallen half a day behind the Seneca.

Their persistent travel parallel to the portage and toward the Niagara fort was still puzzling. No one else had joined them. Their numbers were too small for anything more than an ambush of opportunity. And by now, Snow Hair had arrived safely at the lake fort and would likely rest for several days before traveling again. The Seneca knew someone was following them but continued without slowing, despite their repeated attempts to circle and capture him. So what was Maltoc's new purpose?

Later in the day, Chittaqua arrived at the Cattaraugus village. The hex sign he'd placed long ago was gone. He peered carefully through some burned timbers and viewed the village interior. Scavengers had ravaged the dead that had been buried in shallow graves, but there was no other movement inside.

The Seneca trail now turned directly toward the portage. He pondered this decision for a while and suddenly their intent became clear to him. *Ambush*, he decided. *And Snow Hair will be less cautious traveling this close to the Niagara fort.* The well-used portage made wagon travel easy. If Snow Hair rested only one night …?

He could be close to Cattaraugus even now!

Philippe had not relaxed his guard of the road even along the busy Niagara portage. They'd already passed by three dangerous places for an ambush; two places where the trees crowded the road closely and the other, the slow crossing at the shallows of the Cattaraugus River. When they reached the other side, he let everyone rest.

He'd seen no people coming from either direction. That alone was unusual.

"We'll rest the animals here for a while. Defend the wagon in a half circle," he told the soldiers. "Keep the river at your back." He turned to Pierre. "I will sweep the woods to either side of the road to the east before we continue."

"We're only aboot three days out o' the fort, depending on our speed. With the Cattaraugus at our backs, we should be safe now. The French army dominates these northern lands. Besides, we've only seen friendly faces since we left Fort Le Boeuf."

Philippe shrugged. "Other than the single column from Presque Isle, we've not seen many faces at all for that matter. And that makes me wonder where all the scowling faces are hiding. I'd feel a lot better if I knew what happened to Chittaqua."

"Maybe he went on tah' Fort Niagara?"

Philippe frowned. He squinted at the thick forest line ahead of them and shook his head. "Not without coming back to us first. He would have found a way to send us a message by now. I don't like it."

Philippe finished another wide sweep of the woods to the north and east. Every step brought them closer to Fort Niagara and safety. Was it possible the threat of ambush had indeed lessened? But some instinct told him to beware. After circling back to the wagon without incident, he decided to change plans.

"We'll stop and make camp in another hour or two…sooner if we spot a defensible location. It will still take three more days of travel, whether we hurry or not."

"Amen," Pierre agreed. "Hey, I remember a good spot! The road passes between some large boulders three or four miles up ahead. Two wagon lengths' at least. We could create log and bramble barriers on both ends and post guards front and back through the night. Wha' deeya' think?"

Philippe nodded. "I know the place. You're right. Good spot. That's where we'll camp."

When the Seneca scout returned from the French lake fort near the portage, Maltoc learned that Snow Hair was already coming down the Niagara road. There were now three women in the wagon, and a young girl too. Two younger boys had also joined them. But with great excitement, the scout said he had much more to tell Maltoc.

"More soldiers?"

"No, there are only four soldiers, all dressed like *coureurs de bois*. Animal Scalp drives the wagon. Snow Hair scouts in front, Snow Hair's *woman* rides in the wagon. Snow Hair's *son*, the one who escaped from our village, walks to one side. Chittaqua's *woman* is in the wagon. And Chittaqua's *son* is on the other side!"

Maltoc gawked at the warrior. This unexpected good fortune was astonishing! "All of them?! They are all together?"

"Yes. And some of our friends camped by the fort claim the women are sick."

Maltoc slowly looked from one warrior's face to the next.

"This is not just good fortune. All our totems are here! My *totem* is involved in this. *Your totems* are involved in this," he stated, his voice solemn. "The white man's *god* is involved in this. For many seasons to come, all of the lake and river tribes will sing songs of our victory today, and each of your names will be mentioned."

Painted Snake was less enthusiastic. *Has Maltoc forgotten Fort Le Boeuf already? The outcome of any battle is uncertain, until it is over.* But these thoughts he did not say. Instead, he stated something more obvious.

"Chittaqua is not with them. He *must* be the one following us."

At the mention of Chittaqua's name, Maltoc's expression turned mocking.

"*Eeyaaa*! Say it is Chittaqua who follows us"—the sachem smiled grimly—"then the great Andrototekan will be drawn to the screams of his woman," he boasted, "and to his death! So, I ask, which of you will be the one to take the sorcerer's scalp?"

The warriors began hooting but Maltoc quieted them right away, lest they be heard at a distance. But he knew this victory would be great indeed, maybe the greatest of Maltoc's life.

"Today, our women and children will be avenged. Today, the Erigh will be utterly defeated. Today, the Hawk clan's hated enemies will all be killed in a single battle. What other clan of the Iroquois has ever made such a claim?"

Philippe listened to the creaking sounds of the wagon moving slowly behind him a hundred paces back. He cautiously searched the woods to either side and examined the footprints in the road. There were hundreds of animal hooves, boots, and moccasin prints in the dirt, some old, some not so old. But too many to make much sense of any threat.

Maltoc placed Snow Hair in his musket sight when the *coureur de bois* first appeared at the front of the boulders.

Ah. There you are!

It took great restraint not to fire on his enemy. But this victory needed to be complete and overwhelming to be considered great. All of Snow Hair's men must die and lose their scalps. The women must die or be taken captive.

Wait for me, Maltoc hand-signaled his men as a reminder. *The horse first.*

The other braves had been instructed to hold their fire until Maltoc shot a horse. The sachem held his breath as the blond-haired woodsman approached to within thirty paces of where he lay concealed. Maltoc was a fairly good shot with a musket, but at this distance he might miss.

Patience, he cautioned himself. *Snow Hair's death awaits him.*

The *coureur de bois* looked and listened carefully before turning around to sprint back between the boulders.

Philippe trotted back to the wagon to wave it forward when he heard the sound of a woodpecker to his left. He knew that signal!

Chittaqua!

"Well?" Pierre Dunemoore asked expectantly. He had heard the bird too, but paid no attention to it. "Do we go forward?"

"A minute more," Philippe said, before disappearing into the trees to one side of the wagon.

Chittaqua was hiding about thirty paces in. He stepped into the open when Philippe approached. They spoke in hurried hand signals.

Ambush, ahead, beyond the rocks, the shaman signaled. *Maltoc.*

How many? Philippe responded, alarmed he'd not seen any evidence of their presence.

The shaman's hands moved in a flurry. *Six Seneca.*

Philippe deliberated what to do. They were already in place, waiting! Chittaqua's warning had come almost too late.

Painted Snake saw Snow Hair return from scouting the rocks. He'd expected the wagon to rumble forward into the trap and was surprised when it did not move at all. He also heard the sound of the woodpecker and saw Snow Hair move quickly into the woods.

The devil shaman is here, Painted Snake decided. *Chittaqua will warn them.*

No time to tell Maltoc. The *coureurs de bois* would soon start hunting the hunters. The ambush would fail, unless Painted Snake did something.

To Sauquita's surprise, Painted Snake signaled the other brave and together, they raised their muskets and fired, killing the nearest soldier.

Assuming an ambush was coming from behind them, Pierre Dunemoore didn't hesitate.

"*Heeeyaaa!*"

Pierre snapped the reins on the horses' rumps. The animals' front legs reared slightly and the wagon surged forward toward the rocks, leaving behind the other three soldiers who fired a volley toward the spot in the woods from where the attack had originated.

"Henri! Protect the women!" Pierre shouted.

As the moving wagon came rumbling by, Henri and Chesanin grabbed hold of the sides and swung themselves up into the back.

Henri pushed Anamosa into the arms of Juniata and quickly placed supply packs between them and the side of the wagon. Michelle was clutching a pistol, which he tried to take from her, but she refused to let go of it.

"Lie down by Juniata," Henri told her sternly.

"Pierre! *Wait*!"

Philippe and Chittaqua started sprinting. Philippe understood the tactics of the ambush now. *They'd heard Chittaqua's call and saw me react. Others are waiting beyond the rocks!*

The corporal and his remaining two men drew pistols and fired another volley into the trees. One of the Seneca grunted loudly and fell dead. Painted Snake and Sauquita fired two more muskets. Another soldier fell, mortally wounded. Thinking their companions dead, the corporal and his remaining soldier scrambled to catch up with the wagon.

Pierre had slowed the wagon to safely negotiate the boulders when more shots rang out; this time from in front! One of the horses whinnied in agony and collapsed to its knees. Seconds later, it rolled over dead. The other horse, a minor flesh wound to its shoulder, began bucking and pitching wildly to get free from the harness.

The Scotsman rolled backward over the seat and picked up a weapon lying next to Okeanneh, who was already aiming a musket of her own.

Henri and Chesanin fired together at a sign of movement nearby in the trees. They heard a man scream.

Maltoc knew there were many muskets now pointed in his direction. Killing the other horse made no sense. The animal was creating more havoc with its panic. Instead, the sachem fired at the powder-laden bushes. It took two shots until one pile exploded in a roar of sparks, flame, and thick smoke. The horse neighed, turned, and tried to run backwards, slamming into the side of the wagon so hard it toppled over. Everyone in the back of the wagon tumbled out. The women began screaming.

Maltoc yelled his war cry and surged forward with his two braves. *Speed brings victory*, he thought.

Thirty paces back. Philippe heard Michelle's scream.

"*Noo!*"

Snow Hair reentered the road only a few paces in front of Painted Snake. The *coureur de bois'* attention was completely fixed on the wagon. Painted Snake lifted his musket.

Chittaqua had already aimed his musket at the Seneca warrior aiming at Philippe when he sensed a presence close behind him. Startled, he jerked, which spoiled his aim. The ball seared across Painted Snake's hairline and caused a fracture to his skull. Painted Snake's musket fired randomly as he pitched forward into unconsciousness. A ball missed Philippe but struck one of the soldiers in the foot.

Sauquita fired his musket as Chittaqua was turning, striking the shaman in the gut, rupturing and tearing holes through his intestines before exiting out his right side.

Philippe finally made it to the wagon. He'd not seen Chittaqua fall. His only objective was to pull the women away from the wagon, which was already catching fire. Pierre had hit his head hard on a boulder when the wagon rolled and was struggling to rise to his knees.

"Henri, help your mother!"

Michelle was dragged toward the back of the closest rock. Chesanin helped Juniata and Anamosa. Philippe was about to retrieve Okeanneh when a wounded Seneca brave leaped over the top of the wagon brandishing a tomahawk. He fell upon Philippe, and the two of them started rolling and wrestling on the ground.

After seeing Chittaqua fall and not move, Sauquita assumed he'd killed the famous shaman. He whooped, tossed aside his musket, and unshouldered the beautiful, deadly war ax. Seeing Snow Hair struggling up ahead with another brave, he elevated the ax and ran forward to kill the *coureur de bois*.

First Chittaqua, now Snow Hair, he thought, eager for the next kill. *Songs about me will be sung for countless winters.*

Philippe was lying flat on his back, hands restraining the wrists of his attacker, holding back the thrust of a tomahawk and a skinning knife, when he saw another Seneca brave appear to his right, a huge war ax elevated and ready to strike.

Before Sauquita began his downward swing, Henri flew at him, plunging a skinning knife into Sauquita's shoulder. The warrior's fingers went numb. The ax dropped harmlessly behind Sauquita's back to fall directly in front of Pierre Dunemoore.

Sauquita staggered backward one step.

But Michelle suddenly stepped forward and pointed the barrel of a heavy dragoon pistol at Sauquita's chest. She pulled the trigger.

For a moment, Pierre Dunemoore marveled at this miracle of his war ax appearing before his eyes when he heard Maltoc's distinctive ululating war cry. The sachem was charging around the other side of the wagon and would reach them in seconds. The Scotsman's hands moved in a blur as he grabbed and heaved the ax in a sidearm toss. It made one clockwise rotation before burying its head in Maltoc's neck, nearly decapitating the war chief.

Okeanneh aimed the muzzle of her musket into the armpit of the brave perched above Philippe and fired. The warrior's body was violently flung sideways from the blast into one of the boulders.

The remaining Seneca warrior, now standing atop the overturned wagon, saw his chief and the other braves were dead. He quickly turned to retreat into the woods but Chesanin was there waiting with a drawn bow.

Philippe jumped to his feet, a knife in each hand and spun around. He saw no more attackers. The *coureur de bois* checked on Michelle, Okeanneh, and Juniata, who all nodded they were unhurt.

"Ahh-ree!"

Henri lifted Anamosa into his arms. She was sobbing and shaking violently. He carried her to Okeanneh, but Anamosa refused to let him go.

Chesanin returned whooping and waving a fresh bloody scalp over his head.

Pierre Dunemoore stood unsteadily, arms outstretched to maintain his balance. He was sporting a large red lump on his forehead but was smiling with grim satisfaction.

Like so many other times after a battle, it became strangely quiet. The ambush was over.

"Tend to the remaining horse," he told the corporal. He used an empty musket to beat away the burning brambles and poured his canteen water on the minor fire started on the wagon's seat. The flames were quickly extinguished.

Pierre was chuckling as he retrieved his ax. He bent over and cut away Maltoc's scalp and bone ornaments from his nose and ears.

"These'll bring a pretty price at the fort."

Philippe allowed himself a momentary pause of relief, before a spike of concern took his breath away.

Chittaqua?

He looked back down the road. A familiar body lay half on the path to one side, near where the other soldiers had fallen.

"No! No! *NO!*"

Looking back down the road and seeing the reason for Philippe's sudden cry, Pierre slumped.

"Oh, hell! Please God! Please…not him too …"

Then everyone looked back down the portage. Juniata starting screaming and followed Philippe at a run. Chesanin was right behind her.

Henri panicked. "Is that Chittaqua?!"

"No! Laddie, stop! Stay here with the soldiers and guard the women. Reload the muskets and pistols! This may nah' be over!"

Reaching his friend, Philippe lifted the shaman to a seated position.

Chittaqua moaned.

Juniata arrived, crying, and touched Chittaqua's face.

Philippe laid him back down. "Juniata, put your hands here and here, and press down hard to stop the bleeding." Then he ran into the woods to find Chittaqua's medicine bag.

Michelle came next and knelt beside the prone body. Chittaqua's face was twisted with pain. She quickly examined his wounds and pressed some cloth bandages she'd brought with her to the front and back, then wound one bandage tightly around the shaman's waist.

When the bandages were tied, Juniata lifted her husband and started rocking him mournfully in her arms, low murmuring groans escaping from her lips.

"The ball passed straight through," Michelle told Pierre when he finally hobbled up. "But it entered through his stomach."

Pierre winced. A wound to the gut was almost always fatal. There was no way to treat it. And there were no words to describe the pain. If lucky, the unfortunate victim died quickly. But Pierre had seen more than one hardy *coureur de bois* take days to succumb to the inevitable fever and bloating infection. In the end, many begged their friends to end the suffering. Often they did.

Chittaqua forced Juniata to stop the rocking motion. He moaned loudly, lay back on the ground on his wounded side, and pulled his knees up around the pain.

Chesanin knelt and cradled his father's head. "I'm here, Father. Tell me what to do."

Philippe returned with the medicine bag. "One of the soldiers lying on the road back there is wounded badly," he told Pierre. He turned his attention to Michelle. "How bad is it?"

Michelle shook her head. "It's a stomach wound. We need a surgeon."

Philippe and Pierre traded gloomy looks.

"We are three days out from Fort Niagara with only one horse," Philippe began. "We'll have to travel through the night. Bandage him tight, Michelle. Stay here with Chesanin. I'll get the wagon ready and bring it back."

With the soldiers' help, Philippe pushed the wagon upright and cut away the harness of the dead horse. He calmed the remaining animal and turned to the wounded soldier.

"Fill a water bucket for the horse to drink. Corporal, one of your men lies wounded in the road back there. Tend to him, and I will bring back the wagon."

Philippe gently lifted Okeanneh into the back of the wagon and convinced Anamosa to let go of Henri. They reloaded the scattered supplies.

"Climb up on the seat and hold the reins so there is little slack," Philippe told his son.

"I've never done this—"

"It doesn't matter. Just keep hold of the reins, don't pull on them. I will get the horse to back the wagon through the rocks and use the bit to turn it around."

The wounded soldier in the road bled to death before he could be saved. They decided to bury the dead soldiers in shallow graves by the side of the portage and marked them with crosses made of branches. The army would have to retrieve them later for a proper burial.

As the sun was setting, Philippe made up a dozen torches. The soldier with a wounded foot sat at the back of the wagon and held up one torch.

Philippe would lead them carrying another. The corporal and Chesanin followed the wagon on foot.

Juniata, Anamosa, and Okeanneh crowded around Chittaqua, with Michelle tending to him. Pierre drove the wagon, staying close to Philippe's circle of torchlight. The progress was slow but steady. Henri walked alongside his father. Not much was said.

"I think I've staunched the bleeding," Michelle told Pierre and Juniata after a few hours.

But not the poison, the Scotsman thought without responding. Pierre felt a hard tug on his boot.

"What the …! Whoa!" He stopped the wagon.

Chittaqua motioned for Pierre to hand down his medicine bag. Groaning painfully, the shaman pushed himself up on one elbow. He searched with his free hand and withdrew a dozen small leather pouches from the bag. He opened each one and carefully examined the herbal contents until he found the one to deaden his pain.

"Water," the shaman gasped.

From up ahead, Philippe shouted. "Why did you stop?"

"Philippe! Ya' better get back here."

Following Chittaqua's directions, Michelle mixed the contents of the pouch in a metal cup. It had a powerful pungent odor.

Philippe arrived panting heavily. "What's wrong?"

"He's going tah' drink some o' his magic roots, I suspect. And I'm nah' sure tha's wise with a gut wound."

"Well, he knows more about medicine than any doctor I've ever met. Sure as hell more than you." Philippe climbed into the wagon and helped Chittaqua drink. When finished, the shaman grabbed Philippe's hand with surprising strength. He pressed another pouch into Philippe's hand.

"Keep this for me. I will need it soon. You must take me…take me to the great falls," Chittaqua said, gasping with each word.

"The falls?"

The shaman's grip tightened. "You *must* take me ..."

"All right, I will! You rest."

The shaman lay back and exhaled with a cough.

Philippe and Pierre traded troubled looks. Chittaqua had a slight chance to live if they went directly to the fort. But a detour to the falls?

"How far?" Pierre asked.

"Hard to tell in the dark. But when we hear the roar of the water, it's usually less than an hour on foot. With a wagon, I don't know. But we'd better get moving. Give an extra torch to the private at the back of the wagon. Michelle needs to watch Chittaqua carefully. There's a rocky road ahead."

"Wolf-Bear!"

Henri heard Chittaqua's call and climbed into the back of the wagon.

"Yes."

Under the torchlight, Chittaqua searched his medicine bag and found another small pouch. He handed it to Henri then gripped the boy's hand tightly.

"Hang this around your neck."

"What is it?"

"Something to help you see...to see when evil darkness closes around you like a cloud."

"I don't understand."

"It can only be used *once*. Put what is in this pouch under your tongue. You will know when it is time. *Once! You will know* when it is the right time."

Henri, at a loss for words, nodded, taking the pouch from Chittaqua.

An hour later, the wagon suddenly lifted and came down hard as it rolled over a large tree root. Chittaqua groaned.

Pierre glanced back at the shaman. In the flickering torchlight, he could see the shaman's stomach was grotesquely swollen to twice its normal size. He cursed himself for not avoiding the obstacle.

"God...I'd be screaming without end," he said.

"It must be these herbs." Michelle picked through a pinch in the palm of her hand. "I wish he could tell me what this is," she added. She closely examined the mashed gray lumpy substance, holding it to her nose and sniffing. It had no odor. "Whatever it is, it has deadened most of his pain."

Michelle got to her knees and held onto the seat next to Pierre. She saw Philippe thirty paces ahead, crossing the road, moving relentlessly back and forth among the trees to either side. Henri carried his musket and was walking behind him in the center of the road. Anamosa was sleeping with Okeanneh. Michelle looked up and, through the canopy of leaves, she could see the stars twinkling and a full moon rising. The night had turned cold. She could see her breath now. She'd only managed short fits of sleep from sheer exhaustion, as the ride was bumpy. Juniata was hugging Chittaqua and grieving silently. Michelle's gaze returned to Philippe, sprinting way in front of them again, going from side to side, examining the road and the nearby trees.

"Does he ever get tired?"

"Actually, I dinnah' think Snow Hair likes tah' sleep. Tha's why he is always in such a foul mood when he gets wounded and is forced tah' rest." Pierre nodded toward Chittaqua. "I expect he's nah' rested much either?"

Michelle looked at the shaman and frowned. "How much farther to the falls?"

"We should arrive when the moon is high." He lowered his voice to a whisper. "Deeya' thin' he'll live?"

"To the falls? Well, possibly. After that?" Michelle shrugged and shook her head sadly.

Chittaqua reached out and touched Michelle's hand. He pointed at one of the herbal pouches. She nodded and mixed the contents in a cup of water.

Chittaqua raised himself to a sitting position, high enough to drink the potion with his own hands. He gulped the contents loudly, spilling some over his lips. Then he collapsed to his back, and began chanting quietly.

"What's he saying?" Michelle whispered.

Pierre had heard similar sounds from his friend often enough over the years, though he could only guess at what they meant.

"Magic, lassie. Chittaqua's making magic. And I thin' he'll need it all."

Philippe and Henri did not talk much beyond the conversation necessary to advance down the road. It was too hard for Henri to accept Chittaqua was dying. Even Juniata showed little emotion beyond the gentle care she gave her husband. Anamosa was the least affected and demanded hugs from Henri whenever she had a chance.

Thoughts about Anamosa and his sudden need to talk about something to break the gloom, if only temporarily, induced Henri to ask an overdue question.

"Monsieur?" Henri whispered.

Philippe looked at Henri. "Yes?"

"Is Anamosa my sister?"

Philippe paused, surprised by the question. He shook his head.

"No. Anamosa was with Okeanneh already when we met three years ago. Her real father was another *coureur de bois*. He was killed in a skirmish out here somewhere. But I love Anamosa as if she were mine. Why?

"Well, Louie once mentioned something about her father to Michel, and they weren't talking about you. I never asked anyone to explain this to me." Henri paused. He felt awkward. He looked at his father. "Well, she seems to like me—a lot. And I, well, I like her too."

Philippe smiled and ruffled Henri's hair. "Well, then look after her for me."

CHAPTER 24
NIAGARA FALLS
SEPTEMBER 1754
The Ghost Eagle

Juniata awoke at the rumbling sound of the great falling water in the distance.

Animal Scalp was driving the wagon and the half-asleep soldier behind him still held the torch. Another soldier was following on foot. Michelle had rested her head on a blanket roll on the seat next to Pierre. Chesanin was now out in front walking with Henri. Okeanneh lay motionless across from Juniata. Thinking Okeanneh too still, Juniata nudged her to be sure she was all right. Okeanneh growled with irritation and rolled over to her side.

The cold air smelled good and the stars overhead had never been so bright. *A perfect night*, she thought. Then crushing grief took control again, pinching her heart with sadness. She caressed Chittaqua's tattooed face and brow. His normal expression had become haggard and creased from so many years of war and disappointment. Juniata knew her husband would be pleased to spend his final moments near the falls. It was his favorite place to meditate. She felt fortunate she could share this time with him. Most wives never had such good fortune. Many husbands simply never came home.

Chittaqua moved, as if sensing her anguish.

Juniata put aside her own distress. She removed a hot wet cloth from his fevered brow and replaced it with a cool wet one from the pot of water. For hours, Juniata and Michelle had taken turns wiping his face and body with wet rags to quench the fire in his skin.

"I will do it," Michelle offered, once more taking over the bucket and rags. "What's that loud roar?"

"The falling waters."

Michelle stood on her knees and stretched her arms above her head to relieve the stiffness. With Juniata's help she changed Chittaqua's stained bandages. And at his request, they helped the shaman drink another potion of herbs for his pain. It seemed to help him. But the color and festering of the wound in the torchlight was purplish and more gruesome each time Michelle cleaned away the bubbling pus.

At least, I'm used to the smell. Michelle rolled up one of the cool wet rags and placed it under the shaman's chin to keep his head from lolling.

Okeanneh touched Michelle's arm and gestured for the water. Accidentally, some of the water splashed on the shaman's face.

Chittaqua reacted with a sound, this one different, not of pain, but more fearful.

"Yes, my husband," Juniata said softly. "I am here."

But in his dream, Chittaqua watched the last stone on the island topple into the water. From somewhere far away, a foul and terrible thing looked directly at him.

"It has fallen! The last stone has fallen!"

Eyes tightly shut, the shaman struggled to sit up, grunting and grimacing, searching out with his hands, attempting to grab the sides of the wagon.

"Chittaqua! No!"

"We cannot let him get up!" Michelle said urgently. "The bandages will burst. The bleeding will worsen!"

But the convulsions became stronger. Chittaqua pulled his hands from theirs, swinging wildly with his fists as if wrestling something unseen. The effort became too great in his weakened condition. Chittaqua fell back, mumbling something in a tone full of sadness and distress.

Reacting to the sudden commotion, Pierre halted the wagon. "What's wrong?"

"Bad dreams," Michelle answered.

Philippe and Henri ran back to the wagon. Anamosa was awake.

"What was he saying?" Michelle asked Juniata.

"He was shouting about *stones falling*...or something like that," Juniata replied.

Philippe saw the concern in Pierre's eyes. They both knew when the delirium began, death soon followed.

"Stay here with your mother and Anamosa," Philippe told Henri.

Philippe went forward and grasped the harness of the horse near the bridle.

"Chesanin, come hold the torch for me. Pierre, I'll lead the horse on foot. We'll make better time. You try to get some sleep."

The wagon lurched as Philippe got the horse moving again. Chittaqua continued to chant sporadically and made other eerie noises. Henri looked across at Anamosa. She held her dolls tightly and anxiously eyed the dying shaman.

Seeing her fear, Henri opened his arms, beckoning to her with his hands. She crawled to him. Chittaqua began chanting again, so Anamosa began singing a simple song as she stroked the heads of her dolls. Her voice had a high-pitched, sweet sound.

Angels must sound like this, Henri thought. *Maybe they are coming for Chittaqua.*

An hour later, Philippe stopped the horse.

Pierre could hear the falls clearly now. They had come to the trail branching to the left. Fortunately, it looked wide enough for the wagon's passage.

"We're very close now. This trail is short but very rocky."

Pierre took hold of the reins even as Philippe led the horse by its bridle.

The sound of the falls quickly grew to a rumbling roar. Stirred by the rising moisture, the air was misty and more turbulent. Sensing his destination was near, Chittaqua roused and started to sit up.

Walking beside the wagon, Chesanin noticed first.

"Father!"

Hailed by Pierre, Philippe walked back to the wagon and touched the shaman's shoulder.

"Water," Chittaqua said.

Juniata lifted the waterskin to his lips and the shaman sucked greedily at the wedge hole.

After several swallows, Chittaqua lay back panting. "There is no pain," he assured her.

Chittaqua also had no feeling below his waist, but he didn't tell them that. *The poisons have killed my legs*, he thought. The stronger medicines were gone, but soon he would have no need for medicine at all. It was all as he had foreseen. He was pleased the recent images of death concerned mostly enemies. Hopefully, only good visions would come now. He gestured for the waterskin again and allowed more of the cool water to splash over his face and chest.

"Let's get there," Philippe said.

A hundred paces further, the wagon emerged from the tree line. The splendor of the falls lay before them, an endless river of water thundering over the precipice, the foams and mists illuminated majestically by the light of the full moon. For a few minutes they all stared, entranced by the cascade's splendor. Philippe recalled something Chittaqua had said about the falls.

A powerful spirit dwells here. It was here long before our ancestors. It will be here long after our children's children have died. It is endless. It watches us and smiles at our foolishness. And it has great wisdom to share...if you will listen.

Chesanin climbed into the wagon next to Henri.

The shaman's wound reeked of dead flesh and fecal matter. Henri could hardly believe Chittaqua had endured long enough to reach this place.

Juniata pointed. "There. That is the place he likes to sit; over there, by that tree."

The spot was in the middle of a broad outcropping of land, just beyond the edge of the cascade. A towering chestnut tree with an enormous trunk stood at its center.

"Yes," Chittaqua confirmed in a coughing voice. "Carry me there."

Chesanin and Juniata carefully slid the frail body to the back edge of the wagon. Henri slipped an arm under the shaman's left knee and the other arm underneath the dying man's left shoulder. Philippe did the same for the right side. Chittaqua felt amazingly light. The heat from fever radiated from his skin.

The chestnut tree was huge and looked very old. Fungus-covered bark had fallen from the diseased trunk and lay piled at the base.

Philippe pointed at a place away from the bark. "Michelle, spread a blanket there."

"No! I must touch the tree," Chittaqua insisted hoarsely. "I must be able to see the mists. I must have my back against the tree."

Philippe relented. "Henri, clear a spot in front of the tree. Chesanin, unload all the blankets from the wagon."

The dead bark was cleared and the blanket positioned against the tree. Philippe lowered Chittaqua to a place where the shaman could rest his arms on some extended roots, as if he sat on a throne.

They would stay here the rest of the night. The exhausted soldiers tended to the horse, removing its harness. Michelle and Juniata tended to Chittaqua. Carrying one of the torches, Chesanin and Henri went into the woods to collect dry firewood. Pierre organized a fire pit with the wood laying nearby, starting it quickly with gunpowder and a flint.

Philippe placed Okeanneh on a blanket next to the fire and covered her with another. She hugged him and gestured she was all right. Philippe took another wool blanket, rolled it, and placed it behind Chittaqua's back. He covered the shaman with a second blanket.

Chittaqua pointed weakly. "I gave *you* the medicine."

From his pocket, Philippe pulled out the distinctive leather pouch the shaman had given him earlier.

Chittaqua fumbled with it and handed it back. "My fingers are stiff."

Philippe spread an empty pouch near one of Chittaqua's hands and poured the contents on top of it.

Chittaqua used his fingers to separate a small piece from the jumbled mass. It was powerful medicine. He wasn't certain how much to use in his weakened condition. Too little and he would not be able to communicate with the spirit of the falls. But too much would send him into the violent sleep of death. Throughout his life, Chittaqua noticed he needed consistently larger amounts to create and sustain the desired effect. For this night, he decided to use the usual amount. But it was too soon to swallow it; first, the full moon must rise to its highest point.

The shaman laid the empty leather pouch over the potent fungus to keep it dry and prevent it from blowing away. The fire was just close enough, he decided. He gestured for Philippe to come closer.

The *coureur de bois* leaned toward him.

"The spirit of the waters will speak to *you* this night," he said, his voice a faint whisper. "The evil I spoke of is in your great village. The stones have fallen. The evil is powerful now. Its hatred for you and Henri is great. You must find the Picture Maker."

Spirits talking? Falling stones? The picture maker? Philippe blinked at these nonsensical statements. But evil he understood. His expression tightened.

"The evil one? Where is he?"

Chittaqua's face became strained. "I...I cannot see him...see his face. But you must go to the great white village on the river. You must find the one called Picture Maker. He will know the face of evil. Promise me you will find him."

Philippe shook his head, thinking Chittaqua was near death and feeble-minded. He responded in a compassionate voice.

"Chittaqua, I do not know this man. How will—"

"You *must* find Picture Maker. He is at the great white village. Show him your ring."

Not this again, Philippe thought before relenting. Chittaqua was a shaman. He was his great friend. And he was dying.

"What about my ring?" he asked.

"The Picture Maker will tell you." Chittaqua saw doubt in Philippe's eyes and paused. "After all that's happened...you still do not believe me?"

"If this is what you want, then I promise...I promise I will find the picture maker and show him my ring."

"Tonight you will see a sign with your eyes, and *then* you will believe," he said with certainty.

Philippe was prepared to see whatever Chittaqua wanted him to see, if it pleased his friend. He prayed God would permit this gentle soul, this courageous human being, to pass on peacefully.

"It's getting colder," Philippe said, to talk about something else.

"I'll make the fire larger," Pierre said.

Chittaqua rested his head on a root and closed his eyes.

A larger fire will help. Then he will see. They will all see.

Philippe had never seen a moon so full and brilliant as the one rising that night. There was an icy crispness to the air. He could see his breath. Thankfully, the winds had abated making the lower temperatures tolerable.

Henri shivered beneath his blanket as he huddled with the others around the fire. Juniata had spread her dew-covered blankets near Chittaqua, to lie by his legs, her head rested on a blanket roll. Anamosa was cradled in Okeanneh's arms. Michelle sat at her side. The soldiers lay on the side of the fire closest to the tethered horse. They were already asleep. The corporal was snoring.

Chesanin sat cross-legged across the fire from Henri.

A melancholy silence ensued as they kept vigil over Chittaqua and simply waited. Philippe cooked some corn mash and beans. They glanced awkwardly at one another while they ate. Little was said. Silence seemed more appropriate. Unnoticed at that moment, the shaman lifted his hand to his mouth and placed the potent medicine beneath his tongue.

Minutes later, a slab of limestone mantle, hundreds of years old, succumbed to the water's power at the top of the falls. It cracked at the crest of the cascade and broke free, crashing upon rocks at the bottom, rolling over them in a series of muffled booms.

Philippe and Pierre were instantly alert.

The corporal awoke. "That sounds like cannon fire."

The shaman was already feeling dizzy from the medicine under his tongue. He looked up at the moon then gestured for Chesanin and Henri to sit closer. The shaman sat up straighter and raised his arms above his head. He shut his eyes tight in concentration and began to chant. The others began watching him.

"Chittaqua?"

The shaman lowered his arms and pointed at the *coureur de bois'* ring. Chittaqua's eyes reflected the firelight, a wild yellow glint reflected in his pupils.

Philippe extended his hand in front of him. The purple stone in his ring seemed to be glowing brightly. "What the hell …? Is this a trick?"

"*Loh cai teem,*" Chittaqua said.

"*Loco wha'*…?" The Scotsman leaned forward and touched the stone in Philippe's ring with a finger. "It's cool to the touch. Maybe it's just the firelight?"

Pierre began to feel rather…*pleasant.*

Henri pointed at Pierre's ax. "Monsieur!"

The jewel in its metal head was also glowing.

"Bloody …" the Scotsman said softly. He cautiously pushed the weapon a few feet away from him.

"Why is it doing that?" Henri asked.

"I sure as hell dinnah' know!"

Chittaqua spoke in the Erigh tongue.

"*Four clans face One.*
Stone totems face all.

The demon trapped.
In the dark without bottom.
But the stones have fallen!
Beware!"

Chittaqua closed his eyes and repeated the same words over and over, his voice dropping steadily until it was inaudible against sounds of the falling water.

Philippe experienced a sudden queasiness, a dizziness. His mouth was dry. His skin began tingling.

"Should I do something for him?" Michelle asked.

"No," Philippe responded, though he really didn't know what to do. "He's just...he's praying."

Henri watched the shaman's lips move. "What's he saying?"

"He speaks in the Erigh tongue." Pierre repeated the words in French. He kept glancing down at his war ax, as if expecting the heavy weapon to start flying around at anytime.

"*Demon?*" Henri glanced at everyone nervously. "What does that mean?"

Pierre shook his head. "I dinnah' know, laddie. But dinnah' worry. Chittaqua usually has a herd o' good spirits tha' follow him around...for some reason."

"My husband speaks with *ghosts*," Juniata said with humble dignity.

"Well...ya'...there's usually some o' them around too." Pierre drew on his pipe. "He seems tah' be very popular with all the little gods...and my bloody ax is still bloody glowing!"

Michelle crossed herself and began to pray.

Anamosa started whimpering. She reached out for Henri. Okeanneh pulled her back into her arms.

Henri looked at Chesanin. But the young brave only watched his father intently and seemed undisturbed.

"*Loh cai teem,*" Chittaqua said again. "The Moon," he addressed Henri. "The Moon!" Chittaqua pointed at the moon. "*Mah han atakehsey. Ha teh ko ha sen kah.*" The ghost's lifting wind. One life. One light.

Philippe shook his head to dispel the strange dizzy sensation that was getting stronger.

"Aieeee! *Mah han atakehsey! Ha teh ko ha sen kah!*" Chittaqua pointed toward the canyon.

They all looked where Chittaqua was pointing. The usual roiling mists at the bottom of the falls began swelling, billowing upward in a thick white fog.

Pierre began to feel almost giddy. "Bloody hell," he said softly. "I need a drink. Did we bring any rum with us?" He looked at his pipe suspiciously. "Did tha' bloody shaman put somethin' in my tobacco?"

Long fingers of creamy white fog rolled over the edge of the cliff, moving sinuously to where they were sitting. It started swirling around them.

Pierre stood hastily and placed his hands over his crotch.

"Bloooody!"

"Monsieur ..." Alarmed, Henri looked to Philippe.

"Philippe?" Michelle said with more urgency.

How is he doing this? Philippe wondered. "It's all right." At least, Philippe hoped it was all right.

"Ho! My children!" Chittaqua's voice had become stronger. He looked from face to face. "Henri, Wolf-Bear,"—he gestured—"come to me! Chesanin, the Lion! Come to my side!"

Chesanin moved quickly to do as his father requested and took a seat on the shaman's left.

Henri looked at his father. Philippe nodded, his eyes darting back and forth from his glowing ring to the scene in front of him. Henri moved to sit on Chittaqua's right.

The eerie luminescent mist gathered no higher than a few inches above the ground. It was a shimmering blanket of moonlight. The shaman reached out and took the hand of each boy, clasping them together between his hands.

Chittaqua's voice rose and fell in harmony with his breathing. "Henri, my teacher. Chesanin, my hunter. My spirit sons," he said with pride. He closed his eyes and chanted soundlessly for a few more moments before his grip went limp. His hands fell from theirs. He sagged back against the tree and exhaled a loud rattling sigh. His eyes fluttered. He began to cough painfully.

Philippe reacted. "Henri, move over." Quickly, he took Henri's place next to the shaman. "Chesanin! The water!"

Philippe slipped his arm behind the shaman's shoulders and tilted the waterskin to Chittaqua's lips.

Chittaqua turned his head. The water dribbled off his cheek. He shook his head and smiled weakly. With great effort, the shaman reached out and rested a palm on Philippe's cheek.

"You and I...we have come far...together," he whispered proudly, amid shallow breaths.

Philippe's eyes were wet. "Shhhh. Don't talk."

Chittaqua dropped his hand to Philippe's ring, feeling the smooth facets of the stone. The jewel still glowed eerily in the moonlight, its purple hues as mysterious now as it had been the first time Chittaqua had seen it. The ring hailed from an ancient time, as did the evil they opposed. He understood the evil, its hatred and its relentless pursuit. But the shaman would never live to divine the legend or the reasons for this battle. He only knew his intuitions were right.

When I join with the ghosts I will know, he consoled himself. But Picture Maker has the answers. Snow Hair must find this man.

Chittaqua found it increasingly hard to breathe, as if heavy rocks were being placed on his chest with each passing moment.

"Snow Hair has...much farther...to go," he told Philippe between coughs. "The Picture Maker knows the secret...beware the evil." His coughing grew wet. Bloody spittle abruptly appeared on Chittaqua's lips. "The evil...seeks...your son."

Philippe rested his hand on Chittaqua's. A tear dripped upon their fingers.

"Remember your promise. Find the Picture Maker."

"I will remember," Philippe said past the thickness in his throat.

Chittaqua's fingers moved beneath the tears. "It's time," he whispered.

The shaman looked up at the moon. With a trembling finger, he pointed to a place over Philippe's shoulder.

Everyone turned in the direction of the falls.

"God!" Philippe whispered.

The mists over the canyon had billowed even higher, saturating the night air with moisture. The moon's brilliance mixed with the mists. Bands of colors suddenly arched across the canyon, ghostly reds, purples, and blues, a moonbow riding on the mist. The colors waxed and waned to reappear several times amid the swirls.

"You see," Chittaqua whispered, his voice beginning to fail. "The spirit of the falling waters speaks to you. That is his sign."

For a few minutes, the group was transfixed by the moonbow; its colors changing to new hues, blending together, swirling among the mists of the falls.

Chittaqua was suddenly filled with a great sense of calm. It was the most wonderful feeling he'd ever experienced. His pain completely disappeared. He felt drawn to join with the moon, which brightened and drew closer and closer to him. His body felt light. He was lifting.

Skrieee!

Philippe noticed his ring had stopped glowing. He touched it and twisted it around his finger to be certain it was back to normal. He turned back to Chittaqua. The shaman's head was tilted forward, his chin touching his chest at an unnatural angle.

Above Philippe, a presence began to move.

Reacting instinctively, the *coureur de bois* pulled his knife and rolled to his feet in a fluid motion. A shadow was coming down from the tree. It swooped toward him, leveling its dive several feet above Philippe's head, before gliding past. Illuminated by a few seconds of firelight, Philippe saw the body and wings of a great hunting bird. The eagle was pure white! Gliding away from the firelight, the eagle became a shadowy silhouette against the brilliant background of stars. It flew directly out across the canyon. With each powerful thrust of its wings, the mist curled, marking its passage. The warmer air from the land rushed to follow, pulling warm swirling eddies in the eagle's wake.

"Do you see that?" Philippe asked to no one in particular.

"Unfortunately, I do," Pierre replied. "And I thin' I've soiled my pants again."

This new wonder did not last. In a few moments, the ghost eagle's silhouette was obscured by the opaque churning mist. Then one by one, the haunting colors of the moonbow grew fainter and fainter.

And then it was gone.

CHAPTER 25
FORT NIAGARA
SEPTEMBER 1754
"...this is my friend, Roland."

Philippe Gerrard led the melancholy group of travelers to Fort Niagara, arriving without stopping on the morning of the twenty-eighth of September. Word of Chittaqua's death spread quickly. A great lament arose from the different tribal peoples still encamped around the fort's perimeter.

The Andrototekan, Shaman Who Wanders, was dead!

Chittaqua was lost to the wilderness, *forever*. No man would ever be so named again. Chittaqua was the last, some would claim the best, of these wise shamans; leaving legends and a legacy going back uncounted seasons, even before the beginning of their songs. The peoples' way of life had changed, permanently, and not for the better. Even enemies of the Erigh understood the terrible significance Chittaqua's passing represented. While many had strived against the Erigh, they had not foreseen the consequence of his sudden loss. Chittaqua was a holy man. This was not something they wanted. This was not something to celebrate.

The grieving quickly became a chorus.

Alarmed by the loud, mournful hooting, soldiers and civilians thronged to the new battle walls. As the wagon passed through the gate, Philippe was recognized. Claude Guillot ran from the store to greet his employer.

"Pierre! Monsieur Gerrard! Oh, what a happy day! Everyone said you'd been captured! Others claimed you were dead. And Henri is with you too! And Okeanneh! And Sister Michelle! Oh happy, happy day indeed!"

Except for a brief nod, Philippe did not return the enthusiasm. The *coureur de bois* scanned the faces of the people coming to the yard to greet him and those looking down from the wall. He'd never seen Gaspard de Propei before, but he was certain he would have no trouble recognizing an agent of the Marquis...if he was there.

Philippe moved the wagon across the marshalling grounds toward the store, keeping a careful watch on the faces in the crowd, some smiling, others weeping. He shifted his attention momentarily to the immense breastworks that had been constructed since he'd left the fort months earlier.

"Do we still have a trading post?"

"*Oui*. The same place. Over there." Claude Guillot pointed. "It only looks smaller. Have you ever seen so many cannon? Heh, heh! And look at all the soldiers. They buy from us in crowds every day. The company is making great profits!"

Pierre's smile was grim. "Well, profits at least sound good, eh? There's been damn little profit in anything we've done in the last few months."

Claude Guillot noticed other people start to crowd around their wagon, many of them in Huron dress, grumbling about the *body*.

"Body? Monsieur! Whose body is in the wagon?"

"Chittaqua's," he replied in a flat voice.

"Chittaqua?!"

Philippe ached all over. He was tired and did not feel like answering Claude's endless questions.

Philippe helped Michelle from the back of the wagon. She eyed the chapel. "I want to get out of this deerskin." Her leather dress was filthy, foul, torn, and bloody. "I'm going to my quarters if Farther Beauharnois permits."

Claude Guillot spoke and then regretted it immediately. "Monseigneur Beauharnois is not here. He is missing."

Everyone stopped and looked at him.

"What do you mean?" Philippe asked. "Missing?"

"He left the fort weeks ago to find you."

"*Alone?*"

"Yes, he planned to take the short trail to Fort Le Boeuf. He had a map. But we've heard nothing from or about him since. Unless you saw him? Did you? See him?"

Pierre and Philippe traded somber, knowing looks.

They had not seen any sign of Father Antoine. And if the priest had ventured alone into Maltoc's lands …!

"No," Philippe finally said. "We've not seen him."

"Monseigneur Cortelaine has taken his place," Claude said, then added in a reproving tone: "He's new."

Pierre Dunemoore climbed down from the wagon seat, grimacing and favoring his leg.

"Claude, place some o' our *coureurs de bois* around this wagon tah' guard it. I do nah' want Chittaqua's body disturbed. And close tha' store until tomorrow."

"*Oui*, Monsieur."

When Claude was far enough away, Pierre spoke again. "I'm sorry, Michelle. If he's been wandering tha' wilderness alone, I'm afraid, we'll nah' be seeing Father Antoine again."

Philippe hugged her tightly for a moment.

"I know," Michelle said. "But I have no more tears to shed on any of this. I...I killed Sauquita. And I do not regret it. I would do it again. But with his death, my old life is gone...forever."

Philippe had no words for her. Too many good people had died. He certainly did not regret Sauquita's death. But he saw Michelle was in pain, and his expression showed his sympathy.

Michelle kissed both of Philippe's cheeks, and his lips, as if in farewell, and walked away.

Philippe turned back to the wagon and carefully picked up Okeanneh. "Henri, stay by the wagon."

He carried his wife into the store and carefully placed her on their bed. He kissed her. "Rest now. I will be back soon."

As Philippe came back outside, Pierre diverted his attention to a commotion at the front gates. A dozen Indians pushed their way through the crowd and walked directly toward the wagon.

"*Merde*! Well...it looks like our day is only beginnin'."

Claude Guillot ran over to them. "They've been waiting in the broader camp outside the walls for over a day," he told them. "No one knows why."

What now? Philippe thought wearily. Their expressions did not look friendly.

They stopped in front of him. Philippe recognized their dress as Ottawa, Huron, and even a few Oneida. The rest were of mixed blood. But the four elders of the group bore the distinctive tattoos, charms, and bone ornaments of tribal medicine men. The man in front, a wrinkled old Huron shaman, heavily decorated with bone necklaces, extended a piece of skeleton, the bones of a human hand. He pointed it at the wagon.

"I am White Crow Foot. We come for Shaman Who Wanders," he

declared in heavily accented French.

Nearby, a platoon of nervous soldiers held their muskets at the ready. A harried French officer Philippe had never seen before pushed his way to the front.

"You men! Shoulder those weapons!" The officer turned to Philippe and gave a short nod of greeting. "What do these savages want?"

Philippe eyed the officer with distaste. "First of all, start by never referring to them as savages again. Most of them are important shamans, and all of them understand French. They came to ask for Chittaqua's body."

"Who?"

Philippe was tired and had no patience. "*S'il vous plaît.* Stand over there, shut up, and listen for a while."

Philippe switched to an Indian tongue. "Shaman Who Wanders is my friend," he told the elder. "I want to bury him."

"No," insisted the old shaman. "You do not know the proper way. Shaman Who Wanders was the Andrototekan and the last high shaman of the Erigh. We will create a burial mound for him, in the way of the *Aerie* people. "

"I do not want his body …" He looked at Pierre. "Is there a word for *desecrated*?"

"Careful, laddie," Pierre cautioned. "Would ya' agree tah' let them bury Michelle if they had her body?"

Philippe knew Pierre was right. He announced that he would turn over Chittaqua's body so long as he could join with the decision on where to locate the mound, deciding this was one way that would keep him involved.

The shaman elders whispered together. There was agreement.

With great ceremony, Chittaqua's body was carried on the shoulders of the elders to the old Erigh encampment outside the fort's walls. Juniata and Chesanin went with them.

"What happens now?" Henri asked. He still carried Anamosa on his shoulders.

Philippe shook his head. "I really don't know." The *coureur de bois'* head started to spin from exhaustion. He staggered to his bed.

"Monsieur Gerrard?" a voice whispered. A hand touched his shoulder. "Monsieur. Wake up."

Philippe blinked a few times. The speaker's face was shadowed by the light streaming through the window behind him.

"Claude?"

"*Oui*. Commandant Pouchot is here to see you."

"The commandant?"

Philippe rolled his tongue around his dry mouth and lips, wondering how long he'd been asleep; couldn't be that long. He checked on Okeanneh who was sleeping peacefully at his side. *She is sleeping more and more*, he thought. He wasn't sure if that was bad or good.

Philippe swung his legs out of bed and limped to the main trading room to find the commandant and the lieutenant waiting for him.

"*Bonjour*," Pouchot greeted. He was stunned by Philippe's haggard appearance but hid his reaction.

Philippe nodded. "Captain."

"I have much to learn from you; news from Colonel Contrecoeur a priority. But I can see your exhaustion. For the time being I would ask your assistance on one matter only."

"Yes?"

"Work on the battlements has stopped altogether. The majority of my native laborers are occupied with a funeral for Chittaqua."

"You've met Chittaqua."

"I have indeed, Monsieur. I deeply respect the shaman. I understand the natives' need to honor his memory. However, the completion of this fort's battlements is of utmost importance. This fortress will be the main stronghold against the English. But as it is incomplete, it is quite vulnerable and easily overrun. I am sure you understand the urgency to finish it. I've been told you have influence with these people. Therefore, I'm asking your help in entreating them to return to work."

Philippe gestured for the officer to sit and asked Claude to bring some water. He took several long swallows before speaking.

"There may not be much I can do. Chittaqua was no ordinary shaman to the tribes. He was revered, much like we revere the Pope. And I mean *revered*—even by his enemies."

Captain Pouchot frowned. "I see. Well, obviously the army cannot force them back to work. But that does not change the need for progress. Surely there's something you can do?"

"They intend to create a mound grave," Philippe said. "That means carrying many baskets of dirt. It's likely to take four or five days."

"Four or five days!"

"Commandant, even if I was very convincing, only a handful would return to work. Let me suggest a different approach. Offer some of your soldiers to help them build the burial mound."

Captain Pouchot bridged his hands in front of his face, lips pursed in thought. The *coureur de bois* seemed to be speaking honestly. The army needed the voluntary cooperation of all these half-breed laborers. Sighing loudly, Pouchot stood.

"Very well. The army must defer to your experienced counsel. I will consider this."

Philippe heard the edge in the officer's tone, but didn't care. He changed from his soiled clothes into something clean and left the store. He proceeded outside the fort gates. The shaman elders had already selected a site for the grave mound. It was a clearing at the edge of the old Erigh village about a half mile away. As Philippe walked, he constantly examined the faces of strangers, looking with the sullen glare of a potential enemy. Upon reaching the burial spot, he was surprised to find a circular hollow in the ground had already been dug. The grass, weeds, and surface dirt had been removed to a depth of about one foot. Philippe estimated the mound's diameter at its base would be ten to fifteen paces.

Curious *coureurs de bois*, *voyageurs*, and residents from Fort Niagara gathered about to watch the work. Philippe nodded to familiar faces. To his surprise, twenty soldiers from the fort approached. The corporal in charge announced they were the commandant's volunteers, sent to help with the grave. The soldiers did not look too pleased about this. Philippe hailed the group of shamans and pointed toward the men, explaining the soldiers were sent by the commandant to honor Chittaqua's memory by helping with the grave. As Philippe expected, the astonished shamans were perplexed but greatly impressed. After much mumbling discussion, the eldest of the shaman politely refused the army's assistance.

The Church was not so easily persuaded this was a harmless activity. Monseigneur Cortelaine considered it a pagan ritual. With many of the half-breed *coureurs de bois* and *voyageurs* participating with the mound's construction, he spread word anyone participating in this "devil's altar" could be excommunicated. When this threat was largely ignored, the monsignor began railing at Captain Pouchot. *The heathen are building a pagan altar less than a mile from our chapel! I cannot permit this!* But to everyone's surprise, Captain Pouchot sent his soldiers out to volunteer a second time in response to the monsignor's protest.

The shaman refused them again.

The soldiers were in good spirits about this decision.

At noon on the second day, Chittaqua was carried ceremoniously to the center of the small excavation. He had been dressed in the finest robes, feathers, and bone jewelry available. The enigmatic tattoos on his face and body had been enhanced with fresh stain. He was propped in a sitting position directly in the center of the burial ground. The mound would be created around and on top of him. Arrayed around the Erigh high shaman were his most powerful charms, totems, weapons, and other possessions to signify his importance to the spirits of his ancestors. Philippe did not want them to bury Chittaqua's medicine bag or his spirit cloak, particularly Chittaqua's silver talisman, and had kept them hidden inside the forge room's vault.

The shaman elders divided the workers into two groups, some dedicated to carrying baskets of dirt, and an equal number tasked with tamping down the loose earth with their bare feet. They worked from the outside of the circle by torchlight through the night. The level of ground rose steadily.

On the morning of the third day, the shaman elders permitted Pierre Dunemoore to approach the grave. The Scotsman carried with him his precious porcupine headdress that he'd had for almost twenty years. He stroked the quills fondly. They were soft, despite the spiky appearance presented when he wore it. He knelt and placed his coveted porcupine war bonnet near Chittaqua's head, now the only part of the shaman's body still exposed. He bowed his head. With moist eyes, he leaned close to the shaman's ear and whispered.

"Fare thee well, old friend. Go with God...or your gods...or whoever the proper heathen totems should be. I will miss ya'."

Amid the crowd of onlookers, Henri groaned and turned away as they finished covering Chittaqua's head with dark, moist earth. Philippe placed an arm around his son's shoulder.

"This mound is an enormous honor for Chittaqua."

The line of men carrying baskets of dirt seemed endless. The final work on the mound proceeded methodically and was completed by the end of the next day. It was a remarkable sight to the white men of Fort Niagara. Many had come out to watch the construction with interest. A burial like this had never been seen before and would likely not be seen again. Some of the carters made wagers on the final height. The finished mound was a fifteen-foot-tall cone of compressed earth, with a gentle rounded top.

A large crowd of native onlookers had collected at the mound on the side opposite to where the people from the fort had gathered. One of them bore the markings and dress of a Seneca warrior. He had a shallow head wound, a musket ball crease at his hairline. It had been crudely bandaged. Crusted blood and stains could be seen on his clothing. His identity was unknown. His angry scowl was frightening to behold. But since he showed no signs of being violent, his presence at the ceremony was ignored or tolerated. There were many such Iroquois and Huron present.

Painted Snake was wearing two scalps in his belt, both taken from the soldiers' bodies he had dug up from the shallow graves along the portage. He wanted to see the end of Chittaqua, the burial of the great shaman. He planned to take credit for this kill as well. He would use this to build his fame. There were now a great many clanless Seneca and men of mixed blood living in and around the French lake forts…and even more women. If he acted quickly, he could assert himself as chief of the Hawk clan village and attract a survivable clan. Certainly, there were many braves unhappy with their dishonor in the squalor where they lived. True, the Hawk clan village was still being rebuilt, but there were ripe crops in the field that had not been harvested, ample food for a small clan, enough to survive a winter.

And he planned to build on that, until the Hawk clan was strong again, strong enough to take revenge on the French.

As the rich golden reds of sunset became visible, White Crow Foot, the shaman who demanded Chittaqua's body, walked to the top of the mound and cried loudly as if in great pain. The old and wrinkled man had painted his entire body black, painted over again with white to create the look of a skeleton. The sockets of his eyes were dyed red. He began the ritual by

facing the sunset, as Chittaqua had taught to him to do long ago. Four huge
fires were lit around the mound before darkness gathered. The women and
older children carried armloads of wood to the flames. Drums began beating
in unison. Led by other tribal shaman, hundreds of men began a rhythmic
singing, their deep voices resonating with great sorrow. When the waning
moon appeared above the horizon in its ascent, White Crow Foot howled
again. The men began to dance in a circle around the mound to the feral
rum-thumping of the drums. When the moon reached its zenith, the shaman
dancer cried out a third time.

On the walls of Fort Niagara, the sentries nervously walked their posts as
the kettle-like drumbeat grew stronger and stronger. Monseigneur Cortelaine
was unnerved as well and stood atop the highest palisade above the gates
and sang a Latin hymn celebrating the passion of Christ over and over, as
a way to dispel the sounds of the devil worship in the distance.

Then, all at once, the drums and dancing stopped. Loud hissing sounds
followed as jugs of water were poured onto the ritual fires. In silence, the
people retreated from the mound to their lodges and tents.

Henri Gerrard had quietly watched the entire ceremony from the darkness of nearby trees.

Later, when the area seemed abandoned and quiet, he walked over to
the base of the mound and dropped to his knees. Shivering in the chill night
air, he cut a hole with his skinning knife into the side of the mound, as deep
as he could, about the length of his arm. He removed the leather thong from
his neck that had long tufts of Roland's hair tied to it. He carefully separated
several long strands of white hair from the others and placed them deep
inside the hole. Then he packed in dirt to seal it.

Rising to his knees, Henri crossed himself, bowed his head, and spoke
in choking whispers. "Chittaqua, this is my friend, Roland. He...he likes
to lick your face...but only sometimes...and he is a good hunter...and he
will help keep you warm...he defended me against a bear and...and he is...
he is...very *brave* ..."

Henri barely uttered the last words before he had to press his face into
his sleeve. No one was near enough to hear the soft sobbing that continued
for a long time.

An unusual stillness and an absence of any natural noises settled upon Fort Niagara. It was a windless night, and the temperature dropped to freezing. Halfway to morning, in the darkest hours, the quiet was disturbed by the distant howl of a wolf. It had a lonely sound, the call of a soul lost in the wilderness. The mournful call permeated the lodges, tents, and even the stone buildings of the fort. It made the sentries on the wall apprehensive, another reminder this was not their home.

Sunrise revealed a raw burial site, high with dirt, surrounded by wet ashes. A dozen hex staffs dotted the perimeter. The ground was now consecrated. In less than one season, wild grasses and flowers would take root and cover it all in forest colors. As more time passed, sapling trees would appear. Eventually, the forests would obscure any evidence that someone important rested there.

But the people would remember and would sing heroic tales about Shaman Who Wanders around their winter night fires.

Only the white man ever dared to walk upon the grave of the Andrototekan.

CHAPTER 26
FORT NIAGARA
SEPTEMBER 1754
The Masquerade Ball

Helmut Colbért had expected a carriage to arrive at the farmhouse that morning to take him to see Intendant François Bigôt. By midmorning, when none arrived, he decided to walk to the city instead; something he was used to doing. He'd been staying at an isolated farmhouse belonging to Major Péan. It was situated beyond the swamp lands three miles to the northeast of Montréal's city walls. He could have demanded much better accommodations at one of the hotels or inns, but it was the assassin's nature to be secretive about where he slept. He'd been waiting over a month to make this kill. Waiting was something the assassin was not used to doing, unless it was lying in wait for his prey. That type of waiting he found exhilarating. And this kill involved three people.

"The woodsman should be here by now," he often grumbled. But his night visitor repeatedly promised the man was on his way.

Colbért wondered if Intendant Bigôt purposely did not send a carriage to make him late, as a petty attempt to embarrass him. As he began the three-mile walk from the farm, he mused on whether he should kill Intendant Bigôt before he departed. As a favor to France.

Colbért usually walked to the city each day to wander the streets and frequent the more rowdy taverns and eateries. He kept to himself, aloof, polite, saying little, watched, learned, studied the streets and alleys, desiring to know the rise and fall of every building, the stairways to the rooftops, the interior gardens, where certain people lived, how often guards were changed, and on what days and times the streets were the most deserted. He made acquaintances with some of the seamier citizens of the city. Most of them dwelled near the waterfront, living in hovels. Major Péan claimed the winter cold usually killed many of them. But like fresh mold, more would appear every spring from different parts of New France. They were half-breed outcasts, destitute citizens who'd worked their way across the ocean on a trading ship, wayward adventurers, bankrupt *voyageurs*, or infirmed *coureurs de bois*. Most of them were desperate to survive, hungry for food, drink, whores. Some were more than willing to slit a throat for a few pieces of silver. Colbért's kind of people. And after one of them foolishly challenged the better-dressed stranger with a knife, they quickly learned to give this man a wide berth. All in all, however, Montréal was tiny compared to Paris. Finding private space inside the walls was impossible, leaving few places to hide. And after exploring every corner of the city, Colbért had found little that interested him. Indeed, the waiting was so tedious he had even obtained some books to read.

The assassin was anxious to get back to France to start his new life as the Marquis de Propei. After all, that was the whole point of this endeavor. He was ready for the life of an aristocrat, a life beyond the gutter from which he came. But first, there were three killings to perform. Philippe Malthais, also known as *Gerrard*, would come to Montréal for vengeance. He'd bring the boy and the boy's mother with him. The night messenger of his dreams said this would happen soon. Colbért could almost sense the man's approach. He would take Malthais by surprise. It would not be disputed. He was, after all, a *shérif* of the crown. The boy and the mother would require more discretion. Their deaths in or around the city would likely cause an outrage considering the boy's new celebrity, and he had to kill them fast. So for the first time in his career, Colbért considered hiring another assassin for this work. Then he could slay that man when the job was done.

But the slayings were only half the objective, the easy part, from his point of view. When he returned to Rouen, the Marquis de Propei would insist on seeing their official death certificates before their bargain was sealed. Intendant François Bigôt would provide the certificates of death, for a fee, of course. Colbért also needed to arrange his passage back to France. Again, Bigôt. Again, for a price. Yet money was not a concern for Helmut Colbért. The biggest problem was *time*. He was running out of it. Winter was approaching. The river would soon start icing over. By the end of November, he'd been told, there would be no more ocean crossings until the spring. He had to kill Malthais, the boy, and the boy's mother, obtain the proper paperwork, and get downriver to Quebec City in time to take passage on a ship.

"*Bonjour,* Monsieur de Propei," a guard said as Colbért passed through the north gate into the city.

Helmut Colbért nodded politely. *Now for the worst part of the walk,* he thought. He walked east on the south side of the Rue Notre-Dame, passing between the Terrain des Jésuites and the large chapel across the street from it. Here was André Nicolet, the Jesuit Archbishop of Montréal, a man plotting against him. A minor nuisance, but any obstacle the Jesuit imposed, if it caused a delay, could now have a huge impact. Colbért could not hold back the winter. Back in Paris, he would simply slay the archbishop. But that was not possible in Montréal. Even François Bigôt would not tolerate an action so drastic. Fortunately, Intendant Bigôt hated the Jesuit Intendant. There had to be a way to use that malice.

This land teems with killings. All these people do is kill one another. Yet a simple murder is made complicated.

The assassin kept his eyes fixed on the front door of the Terrain des Jésuites as he walked by. He had told a few of his *employees* along the waterfront, he would give an ounce of gold to the first one bringing him news of Philippe Gerrard's appearance in the city. He knew some of them kept watch at the boat landing. He was certain the woodsman and the boy would arrive any day.

Helmut Colbért turned the corner at the end of the street. The Governor's house was busy with soldiers. He entered the first floor of Intendant Bigôt's mansion that stood across the street from the Governor's mansion. The gendarmes were used to seeing him now. One of them escorted Colbért upstairs to Intendant Bigôt's secretary.

The Corsican secretary looked up from his desk at the sound of approaching footsteps. He pointed to a chair, signaling he was to wait.

Colbért ignored the gesture and went to the window overlooking the street instead. More soldiers and a few cavalry mounts had gathered in front of the Governor's house, further signs New France was shifting to a war footing. Not that he cared.

At the sound of footsteps, he turned. One of the intendant's guards took a position outside the office door, so he could be called upon, if needed. The guard seemed more stupid than brave.

"All right," the Corsican said. "You may go in now."

Colbért found François Bigôt hunched over his desk, examining a sheath of documents.

"*Bonjour,* Monsieur Intendant," he said with mock flourish, doffing his hat.

"You may sit," Bigôt said, not bothering to look up. "You are here to make new arrangements?"

"I believe we already have an arrangement. You asked for this meeting, not me."

Intendant Bigôt leaned back in his chair, his hands in a steeple before his chest.

"Yes, I did. Complications have arisen. I've read the latest dispatches from the portage forts. Disturbing reports. Your name is mentioned often."

"What difference is that to us? I grew tired of the chase. I gave Philippe Malthais reason to come looking for me. He will soon arrive in Montréal."

"Nevertheless, there is now anticipation of his arrival and your meeting. And Monsieur Gerrard has friends. I presume your plans are discreet?"

"My *plans* have never changed. Philippe *Gerrard* and the boy will be executed within a day of each other."

"Executing the woodsman will not be challenged, you have the warrant. But it will cause fewer complications, *for you,* if you could dispose of the boy somewhere outside of the city. Some place not visible to the residents, eh?"

The intendant was right, of course. Once again, this was not Paris. But Colbért had already made plans for the boy's death. He wondered what *complications* Bigôt would foresee if he learned the nun would be killed too. It was the reason the assassin would employ someone else for the Sister.

"Kill the boy outside the city? So as not to bloody Montréal's streets unnecessarily?"

Bigôt sniffed, he did not care for the assassin's sarcasm and had no tolerance for any challenges to his authority.

"Do *we* have an understanding?"

Colbért leaned back in his chair, restraining himself.

"*We* have a bargain."

"Yes, we do. You've signed the necessary papers?"

"I shall hand them to you after I board a river sloop bound for Quebec. And after you hand me certificates of their deaths."

"Your letter of credit will grant me the balance of your funds in the bank in Quebec?"

"All of my remaining funds, three hundred thousand livres, less the pittance I've spent thus far."

"Very good." Intendant Bigôt gazed upward for a few moments.

"Archbishop Nicolet may pose a problem."

"Yes?"

"Unfortunately, the Jesuit is a confidante of Governor-General Duquesne." François Bigôt absentmindedly tapped a front tooth with his finger as he deliberated. "I think you should leave Montréal tomorrow."

"What? Leave Montréal before I have accomplished my purpose?"

"Yes, leave. Load your baggage on a river sloop for Quebec. Except, don't go to Quebec. As soon as you are out of sight, have the sloop put you ashore and circle back to Montréal. Afterwards, come into the city only at night or in a disguise during daylight hours. I recall you professing a knowledge of disguises, yes? My office will report you have departed for France. The government will not give much thought to your abrupt departure. A war is starting. Many people hurry arrangements to make the crossing before winter. Your disguise and discretion will make it easier for you to dispose of the *coureur de bois*. No one will anticipate your presence."

The amount of detail suggested Bigôt had been thinking about this new plan for more than a few minutes. Colbért liked refining plans, not changing them.

"I assume this idea is not a sudden inspiration?"

"Of course not. It's why I sent for you."

Move only at night? Wear disguises? He'd done that before, for a day at a time. But this plan was more complicated than Colbért preferred. And he would be abdicating the advantages of his *shérif*'s title. There were other uncertainties concerning the kill. Who would be where? And when?

"Why the need for a charade? Montréal is too small to walk around unnoticed for very long, even at night. My mission must be completed soon. I'm told the time approaches where the river may become bound by ice and the sloops will no longer transit to Quebec. I cannot sit outside the city and wait like a spider for the fly to enter my web by accident."

An appropriate analogy, Bigôt thought. "But removing that uncertainty is the reason for your departure."

"I do not understand."

"The woodsman is your main problem. Philippe Gerrard may hide among his friends when he reaches Montréal, though he obviously comes here to hunt *you*. Philippe Gerrard's dangerous reputation is well deserved. This *coureur de bois* is aggressive and quite fearless."

Colbért shrugged. "I do not intend to *duel* the man, nor do I plan to give him *any* advantage. If he gives me the opportunity, I will simply slash his neck as I walk by him on the street."

"Possibly, but as I indicated, killing him inside the walls may cause official complications, investigations could be ordered which could lead to delays. But my plan *guarantees* the woodsman will come to you alone, at a time and to a place of your choosing."

"I'm listening."

"The woodsman has an Achilles' heel."

"A what?"

"Philippe Gerrard has a *weakness*. There is a woman here in Montréal who is very important to him. First you abduct *her*, take her somewhere outside the city, then allow the woodsman to learn where. I assure you, he will come in haste and he will come *alone* with intentions for your death. I presume that is not a problem for you. I would hate to gamble with our agreement were some misfortune to befall you."

A woman? It had been a long time since Colbért had been with a woman. This plan might have merit.

"Who's the woman?"

Intendant Bigôt sighed. "Her name is Lady Corrinne de Chanaye." He provided information on her background and where she lived.

Helmut Colbért had doubts. "An abduction is far more complicated than a killing."

Intendant Bigôt dismissed the contention with a wave of his hand. "I will help to arrange it when the time comes."

"How?"

Bigôt explained, then added an extra inducement. "And while you wait, you can enjoy yourself with her."

Colbért experienced a sudden surge of pleasure in his loins. He nodded.

"After the woodsman is disposed of discreetly, you can return in disguise and take care of the boy. We can exchange the documents. You get certificates of death. I get your letter of credit as per our agreement. *Voila!* You are on your way back to France, *Monsieur le Marquis.* No official complications! But first you must make a visible departure."

"Where will I stay after tomorrow?"

"I own several farms. A few are not being worked. I will provide you with a map leading to one of them. I will choose one east of the swamps again but closer to the city road than Major Péan's farmhouse, so it will not be difficult to send messages between us. A wagon will deliver you plenty of food and drink. We'll use the old Indian, Singing Owl, as our messenger. Of course, after tomorrow, we can no longer be seen together. There is a fête honoring the Governor's departure tonight. A masquerade. You will be masked when I introduce you to Lady de Chanaye. We will use the ball to spread the news of your departure in the morning. This will initiate the ruse. What say you?"

Colbért was silent for a few moments. Sudden warmth crept up his neck. His face flushed. He gazed intently at the administrator's eyes looking for deceit. He saw many things, but the man spoke true. The warmth vanished.

"I will enjoy seeing the bait for the trap."

Intendant Bigôt smiled lewdly. "*Enjoy* seeing her? You will *indeed*." To indicate they were finished, he stood.

"Guard!"

A guard appeared immediately. "Yes, my lord."

"Escort Monsieur de Propei out." Intendant Bigôt came from behind his desk and extended his hand politely.

He requires a guard for a handshake? The assassin smiled at the aristocrat's nervousness.

"Until tonight then, Monsieur Intendant."

Intendant Bigôt sniffed once and retreated behind his desk. "Be sure to wear a mask…and maybe a bath is in order," he added with barely concealed disgust.

Colbért glared at the guard until the man wisely backed away. Without another word, he left the intendant's office.

Intendant Bigôt exhaled when the door closed. Gaspard de Propei's sudden return from the frontier had given Bigôt pause, particularly when he'd read the dispatch concerning the assault and defilement of Philippe Gerrard's Indian wife at Fort Le Boeuf. But the Marquis de Propei had enormous sums of money at his disposal. He reviewed his plan again looking for flaws. He saw none. Yet there was an opportunity to extort more profit from this new plan, and in an enjoyable way. When the time was right, he would meet with Lady de Chanaye and explain the threat to her woodsman.

What will she do, he wondered, *when I tell her Monsieur Gerrard will be arrested, imprisoned, executed*—he visualized the exhilarating power of that moment—*that only an order from* me *will stop it. What will she do then to protect her precious woodsman?*

Delicious images sprang to mind.

"The Lady Corrinne de Chanaye," the herald announced her entry.

Heads turned in her direction. There was a sharp intake of breath as she descended the eight marble steps leading to the large oval-shaped hall that was the Governor's ballroom. Corrinne wore a white gown with red sequins, cut low in the front, with a bone-reinforced bodice pushing up her ample breasts, accentuating her smooth, milky cleavage dusted with powder. A single three-carat teardrop-shaped diamond rested in the valley between her breasts at the end of a thin golden chain. Capturing the light of the immense candelabras hanging overhead, the flawless stone sparkled and shimmered casting a rainbow of colors. The gown was made of a tight silk mesh, the sequins arranged in the shape of dozens of small flowers. In contrast to the other women with heavily powdered faces, whose dresses were hooped at the waist with layers of petticoats underneath, Corrinne wore no cosmetics at all, save for some dark red lipstick. She had no blemishes to hide beneath powder. And she wore nothing at all beneath the dress. She had foregone the hoops that exaggerated the hips. Her dress draped over her waist all the way to the floor, showing every curve of her magnificent body. As she moved, the white silk material would flow back and forth over her naked skin. A red leather belt, Y shaped, cinched her waist with the tail hanging down between her legs. It had the effect of drawing the admirer's eyes to the juncture of her legs. If an onlooker watched her carefully as she moved about, the gown occasionally moved and the spaces in the mesh would expose tantalizing glimpses of her skin. The white silk dress covered her arms to her wrists, where she wore a lot of jewelry, much of it gifts from the men in the room, gold and diamond bracelets, large gemstone rings on several of her fingers. Her pure white hair was curled and tied high on her head, held in place with several strands of rubies and pearls. She carried a simple red sequin mask on a stick and had placed a beauty mole above and to the left of her lips.

Corrinne de Chanaye was gratified by the open-mouthed stares of the men and the jealous anger of their wives. She'd chosen her style of dress purposely. It wasn't often she was invited to official social functions. This was a masquerade party in the Governor's honor. It would be Governor Duquesne's last public appearance in Montréal before he left for Quebec to welcome the new Governor-General arriving from France. She needed an audience with him. With the war and so many affairs of government pressing, it had been hard to get past his secretary. Hopefully, she would draw him closer, enticing him with the chance of glimpsing her nakedness.

The room was forty paces long and thirty paces wide, surrounded by ceiling to floor length windows and doors. Small, round marble-topped tables each surrounded by two or three upholstered chairs were arrayed around the outside of the floor to make room for dancing. But the tables had been placed too close to the cold seeping in from the windows. As a consequence, most of the people thronged near the center of the floor. In the middle, to one side, the string quartet was playing music. But no formal dance was arranged as there was no room for it.

Corrinne walked directly across the center of the floor. She headed to the table full of sweet cakes and pastries at the other end of the room. Her eyes darted over the masked faces of the men and women in attendance.

The string quartet fumbled with the sheet music and played the most popular minuets, but the noise in the room was dominated by conversation. Corrinne reached the table, selected a small sugary cookie to nibble upon, stepped halfway back toward the middle of the room, and waited for the moths to approach. She expected the men to fawn and ogle. The women were more discreet. They would walk close behind her and speak in whispers. Men or women, it did not matter, much of what they said Lady de Chanaye had heard many times before.

My lady, you look exquisite ...
Mademoiselle, only angels reflect as much beauty ...
I am hoping you will share a dance with me ...
Whore!

Corrinne dazzled them all with her smile. The mask was cut with over-sized holes to showcase her eyes, eyes that could mesmerize the men lucky enough to draw her attention.

*You are too kind, Monsieur…My, how handsome you appear tonight…
Indeed you do look like a muscular soldier of Rome in that costume…We
must find time to share some words in private, Monsieur.*

But she glanced often at the Governor, costumed as an English corsair.
She watched for the opportunity to approach him. Duquesne caught her
glance, detected her intention, and with subtle steps moved closer to where
she was standing. When the Governor was close enough, she stepped away
from the others and interrupted his discussion with an army officer.

"Ahoy! A treasure-rich galleon approaches," he boomed. Duquesne
raised her delicate fingers to his lips. "Reef your sails and prepare to be
boarded."

"I willingly surrender to you, Captain. Explore and plunder whatever
you desire," she answered, holding her arms wide.

Duquesne inhaled her perfume. *God, what a glorious scent!* With a tiny
nod of his head, Duquesne dismissed the gawking officer and other men
closest to them so he could talk with her alone.

"My lady, I count myself lucky to have dwelled in a place and time
where I could know you."

The sincerity in his compliment was genuine and endearing. Corrinne
reached up to caress his cheek lightly with her fingers. "And I have touched
history. Scholars will study you centuries from now."

Duquesne smiled wryly. "Would that were true." He sighed.

"You've beaten the English to the three rivers," she reminded him.

"The fort bears your name."

"Well…*that* is true." Duquesne nodded and chuckled. "Of course, it has
my name because I *ordered* it so. But how long will it bear my name? *That*
is the more important question. Nevertheless, I have been recalled to France
for my reckless incompetence. As usual, my victories have a dozen sires,
but my defeats, if not orphans, are ignoble bastards attributed only to me."

"And I say, history will otherwise discover what I am already privileged
to know. Michel-Ange Duquesne de Menneville is a brilliant soldier, and
a loyal patriot of France." She glanced about before continuing. "He also
possesses the cock of a bull," she added.

Duquesne's deep, prolonged laughter echoed around the room. "My
lady, of all the people I've met in New France, I think I shall miss you the
most." He paused and smiled at her with genuine affection. "I would like

to do you some favor before I depart."

"Truly? Then you have read my mind," she stated, "for indeed there is a favor I would ask, in keeping with your promise when last we spoke."

"Oh dear, I had forgotten...well...what was it you would have me do?"

"I need only your signature."

"Indeed," he chuckled again. "Granting you my estates?"

She smiled. "No. But perhaps the estates of someone else."

"And what part of you...shall I sign...and with what instrument?" his voice had lowered.

Corrinne touched her lips with one finger. "I believe I made it clear you are most welcome to board my vessel in any manner you choose, Captain."

God! Duquesne cleared his throat. Then, suddenly noticing many others straining to overhear their conversation and others waiting to talk with him, he adopted his governor voice once again.

"I shall be leaving for Quebec by the end of the week. I will tell my secretary to grant you an appointment. Now, Mademoiselle, go that way,"—he pointed—"and we shall see how many of these men stay in line to flatter me."

"My Lord Governor." Corrinne curtsied gracefully and walked toward the windows. She glanced back. More than half of the men shuffled along behind her. The Governor gestured to her line of followers and shook his head.

The cool air near the window carried the odor of pomade with a hint of something more rancid. She recognized the smell, restrained her grimace, and turned to greet Intendant Bigôt. He was dressed as a fool of the court. He wore the mask of comedy with an outrageously long nose.

"François," she greeted, extending her hand. "What an appropriate costume."

"My lady, I see you have come dressed to do business."

Intendant Bigôt lifted his mask, grasped her fingertips, and brought them to his lips. Instead of a polite kiss, he used his tongue to lick at them. Corrinne drew her hand back sharply. Her expression hardened.

"Oh, have I offended you so soon? Please forgive me." François Bigôt could not resist goading her.

"I find little about you that is forgivable, Monsieur."

Before she could excuse herself, he gestured another man forward.

"Mademoiselle, may I present Gaspard de Propei, heir to the Marquis de Propei and *shérif* for the King."

Corrinne's heart began to pound so hard she was certain others could hear it. François Bigôt was amused by her obvious surprise and repugnance.

"Monsieur de Propei, may I present Lady Corrinne de Chanaye. That God became man is scripture," Bigôt said. "Yea, but behold the devil become woman!"

The man introduced as Helmut Colbért stepped forward and bowed his head slowly in greeting. She did not extend her hand.

"*Enchanté*, Mademoiselle."

He wore a suit of black silk. But for his mask and the silver buckles on his shoes and belt, everything he wore was black. Like her, he wore a red mask but one covering his entire face, a caricature of the frowning jester, the mask of tragedy, an expression of sorrow. But the eyes Corrinne saw in the round holes were opaque and black, eyes of a predator.

"It's unfortunate I am leaving for Quebec in two days to gain passage on a ship for France before the winter. I hear your name often mentioned in my conversation with others," Colbért told her, "which suggests we have common interests."

"You may be assured Monsieur de Propei, we have *nothing* in common."

"Can you be so certain? We've not had time to discuss our mutual… *passions.*"

Instead of responding, Corrinne turned and walked slowly toward the side door leading outside to where the carriages waited, brushing aside attempts by other men to gain her attention.

Intendant Bigôt pursed his thick lips, annoyed. He had wanted more interaction. Not this! This meant she was already scheming, devising new plots against him!

Helmut Colbért watched the woman move across the floor, his eyes following the natural, sensual sway of her hips. *I will have her*, the assassin thought. He decided to scout her city house. He grew hard at the thought of tying her hands and feet to bedposts. His pants bulged visibly.

"I thought you said she was dangerous."

François Bigôt's looked at him askance. "*That* woman is most dangerous when she appears to retreat."

Helmut Colbért snorted. "You make a joke, no?"

Outside the mansion, a soldier waved Corrinne's carriage forward. She was pensive and frightened. Gaspard de Propei evoked memories of nightmares she had as a little girl in the orphanage: the fear of clawed, crawly things lurking in the dark—feelings so strong, it became difficult to concentrate.

Think, she urged herself. *Think! What was the purpose of Bigôt's introduction?* Afforded her complete attention, the intendant would not be inclined to share Lady de Chanaye with anyone. *And why would the shérif inform me of his intentions to return to France?* She had already invented a rumor in this regard in her letter to Philippe, in an effort to spur him along. To find out it was true was, well, disconcerting! Why? This revelation bothered her most of all. *And Bigôt knows I will tell Philippe!*

"At least we all seem to want the same thing," she whispered, "Philippe's arrival in Montréal!"

The carriage pulled into the street for the short ride to her city house. The blast of cold air stimulating her thinking.

It didn't make any sense. *François Bigôt is a fool, but not that big a fool. The shérif's introduction to me was intentional! Why? All right, assume the shérif's departure is a facade, and he comes back to Montréal but remains in hiding. To what advantage is hiding? He is a* shérif. *Why hide at all? Philippe is the one who must hide.* She shook her head, frustrated.

The thought of Philippe induced a horde of connected questions, foremost of which started with, *Philippe, where the hell are you?* It was a question she asked repeatedly while looking toward the sunset nearly every day. The refitted *Falcon Queen* had already returned to New France. She hadn't seen it yet, but Captain LaTour sent overland letters describing the almost luxurious renovations that the Gloucester shipyard had added. Corrinne had elected to keep the *Falcon Queen*, the Dunemoore Company flagship, anchored near Quebec City, as opposed to bringing it upriver where Intendant Bigôt might seize it under some pretense. It carried no cargo from the English colonies, and she had secretly been sending numerous river sloops from Montréal with the more valuable of her personal possessions to load onto the *Falcon Queen*. She intended to sail from New France before the snows and ice of winter froze everyone else in place. She had already sent letters to be given to Philippe when he returned to Fort Niagara, asking him to make haste. Certainly, he'd suffered enough dangers to himself and his son that she could convince him to leave New France with her. Of course, *Sister* Michelle could pose a problem…then there was the biggest problem of all….Okeanneh!

I will worry more about that after I get him here…when I get him here.

As the carriage pulled up, Corrinne was tormented by endless questions. The unexpected introduction of Gaspard de Propei signaled the start of the end game. Plans were now reduced from spanning months to short weeks and before long to just days.

Philippe, where the hell are you?

Now Corrinne regretted doing Archbishop Nicolet the favor of providing temporary shelter for the ward, ostensibly a maiden of sixteen years, of a visiting former abbot.

I should have asked André for how long. And maiden? *That girl had spread her legs for many men long before her arrival*, she thought wryly. *She's probably been sleeping with the pious Father who brought her over from France.*

Not that Corrinne cared a wit about the girl's boudoir frolics. But she was also headstrong and tended to slip out of the house to walk around the city without taking one of Corrinne's footmen as an escort, as she'd been told to do.

That makes her vulnerable, which in turn makes me vulnerable!

Intendant Bigôt's pleasant introduction of Lady de Chanaye at the masquerade party for the Governor was an unexpected surprise to Colbért. She was even more stunning than Bigôt had described her to be. Colbért had sensed her immediate discomfort with his nearness. It was apparent she found him repulsive; therefore, he decided he must possess this captivating woman. And it was just as well that she fit into his plans for murder and assassination because raping and killing her was now at the top of his list. *Well, almost at the top…above fucking her, for certain*, he thought. He grimaced. *I'll probably pay a price for thinking that the next time I sleep.*

Colbért left the party soon after Lady de Chanaye's departure, and, after changing his clothes in the carriage stable, ventured out into the night and found a spot on a rooftop adjoining Lady de Chanaye's house, which provided him the perfect vantage point to see directly into her boudoir window. He waited patiently in the cold and was not disappointed when she finally entered the room to take a bath. With the help of her maidservant, she disrobed, revealing her exquisite naked beauty. The woman was about to step into the tub when she suddenly turned toward the balcony door, staring out the window at the place where he crouched in the darkness on the opposing rooftop. Colbért was certain she could not see him. It was too dark outside and her eyes would be affected by the light in the room. Seconds later, however, Lady de Chanaye slipped on her robe and backed slowly away from the window and from the room. Colbért imagined he heard the door locking. She obviously had finely honed instincts. Something he would do well to remember.

But I must do this again soon, he thought.

Charles VanderMeer had waited patiently in Archbishop Nicolet's ante-room for over an hour. It was late in the afternoon. The evening shadows were gathering, darkness coming early because of an overcast sky.

Father Tinian glanced again at the somewhat agitated artist. The man looked pale and frightened.

"I am sorry for the long wait, Monsieur, but the intendant usually does not accept visitors without an appointment."

The artist swallowed and gripped a canvas bag on his lap more tightly. To his side was a second canvas bag with two large books within. Gilded leather covers with worn corners could be seen edging above the top of the bag.

"*S'il vous plaît,* good Father. The archbishop *must* see me. It has to be today. You have to intercede. I will wait as long as it takes. The matter is most urgent—"

Father Tinian raised a hand. "All right, all right! I understand, Monsieur. But his day is ending. He has other duties of his office to attend to. When the archbishop is alone, I will ask…but if he refuses…you must also agree to leave without argument."

VanderMeer nodded rapidly. But once that door opened, he had no intention of leaving.

A few minutes later, from the other side of the door, there came the sounds of people making their farewells. The door opened, and a well-dressed monk appeared in the anteroom. A smiling young maiden with auburn hair followed him out of the office. They turned together to face the Jesuit Intendant.

"As always, Eminence, your wise counsel and support has made all the difference."

"Father Cortois, given your circumstances…you've only been in Montréal for what, two weeks? You will have to trust in my judgment. Your ward is safe. If Lady de Chanaye seems stern to you, she has good reasons. And, young miss, you should be grateful. Under the circumstances there are not many options for you, unless you want to take residence in one of the convents. No? I didn't think so. Nor should either of you be dissuaded by any disparaging remarks you may hear about Lady de Chanaye. I personally endorse she will provide safe, if only temporary, shelter until we can find someplace more permanent for you before winter arrives."

The young maiden bowed and kissed his ring "Thank you, Eminence. I am forever indebted to you."

Archbishop Nicolet noticed Charles VanderMeer in the anteroom and squinted at the man. When he spoke again to his visitors, his voice was hurried.

"I look forward to our next meeting. Now, if you will excuse my abruptness, I have another pressing appointment." The Jesuit gestured at Charles VanderMeer to enter his office.

The priest and the girl left.

"*Bonjour*, Master Artist. What an unexpected and pleasant surprise. Please come in. Father Tinian, more tea if you please."

Father Tinian cleared his throat. "Eminence, I should remind you that you have an evening Mass scheduled in one hour."

"Will this take long?" Nicolet asked the artist.

"Possibly, I'm afraid."

"Very well. Father Tinian, make arrangements for someone else to celebrate the Mass."

They sat by the window. Outside, the city's candle lamps were being lit.

"That should drive away some of the darkness, eh?"

VanderMeer gave a small, polite smile. "We can always hope." He set the heavy canvas bag on the table between them, the books to one side. When Father Tinian shut the office door, he began without prompting.

"Eminence, I am sorry to disturb you unannounced, but—"

"And what is this?" the archbishop asked, looking at the heavy sack with a questioning expression.

"If you would indulge me…something has happened I cannot explain."

Before the archbishop could ask any questions, the artist pulled a polished wooden box from the bag.

"The contents of this box were given to me by an Indian shaman at Fort Niagara who is called *Chittaqua*."

"Chittaqua? I am familiar with this name. He is Erigh and has an extraordinary reputation."

The door opened and Father Tinian brought in a tray of tea. Seeing the table between them occupied by a box, he glanced reprovingly at the artist.

"Over there." The archbishop waved a hand.

The secretary set the tray on a corner of the archbishop's desk. "Eminence, I will leave the office for the day to attend to the other arrangements."

"Of course. Good night, Father. Please continue, Monsieur VanderMeer."

VanderMeer nodded. "Your awareness of Chittaqua's reputation may help. Forgive me, what I am about to tell you may sound preposterous. This box has been on an upper shelf of my studio since I returned from Fort Niagara a week ago. I promised to discuss the contents with Philippe Gerrard upon his return to Montréal—"

"Philippe Gerrard?" the Jesuit interrupted. "What does he have to do with this?"

"Eminence, I am equally bewildered, forgive my impertinence for continuing. Since I plan to leave Montréal for France before the winter sets in, and given that Monsieur Gerrard has not returned as yet, I was not sure what to do with this object. So I took it down from the shelf this morning to decide who I might leave it with…and how to get a message to Monsieur Gerrard …"

"You are repeating yourself. What is it?"

"It is better to show you." VanderMeer swallowed. "If I may, place your palm on the top of this box, like so."

The Jesuit indulged the artist. The lid felt unusually warm, like the surface of a warming oven. "And so …?"

"The heat is noticeable, yes?"

The artist unlocked the lid. Inside the box was a worn leather pouch filled with an odorous mixture of dirt and bone fragments. Lying on top of that was a hand-sized, engraved silver amulet with a beautiful emerald gemstone at its middle. The emerald jewel at the center of the amulet was glowing.

Archbishop Nicolet leaned forward to peer at it closely. "Very fascinating. A creation of yours, I presume?" He touched the amulet with one finger and withdrew it quickly. It was hot.

"Trickery?" He rubbed the tip of his finger with his thumb. Nothing blistered.

"No, Eminence, not trickery. Though I wish it were. I brought many books of my trade with me from France. Books chronicling the gem trade, origins of gemstones, the lineage of the more famous ones. There is a story in two of the books—I've brought them with me—of a legend concerning Normandie standing stones and the *sigilla* of four great houses distantly related to the markings on this amulet. There are four sigilla, and one is a Celtic cross," he said, his eyes glancing momentarily at the crucifix the archbishop wore. "I'd hoped to share this information with Monsieur Gerrard. It seems that he possesses a ring with exactly the same engravings."

André Nicolet felt the beginnings of a bad headache forming, which sometimes arose for no apparent reason. He rubbed his temples. "Well, Monsieur VanderMeer, this is all very interesting but it's likely some sort of elaborate coincidence."

"No coincidence that I can believe, let alone comprehend, Eminence." His voice began to rise. "But I was hoping to borrow from your knowledge of history on the meaning of the *sigilla* from this legend in my book. Or maybe a scientific explanation for the heat or the stones because the more occult suggestions in this legend are very…disturbing."

Charles VanderMeer was clearly upset and visibly shaken. Nicolet placed a hand on the man's shoulder.

"Calm yourself, Master Artist. It could be alchemy, a substance reaction, as those knowledgeable in such things would describe it."

"No, Eminence. Please forgive my impudence." He pointed a trembling finger at the Celtic crucifix hanging from the beads attached to the intendant's robes. The center purple jewel of the cross was also glowing.

"Neither is that trickery, I fear. And if you find that intriguing, then look further at the back of your crucifix and you will see the same four engravings match the ones on this amulet and the ones on Monsieur Gerrard's ring."

The information was coming too quickly for André Nicolet to properly digest. It all seemed too theatrical, contrived, even a ruse to him, except that he knew this man to be a renowned artist of the King. Nevertheless, it was late, and he was tired.

The archbishop arose and poured them both a cup of tea while he decided whether to listen to any more of this. *Maybe tomorrow*, he thought, *when I am better rested.*

"Have some tea, Monsieur VanderMeer," Nicolet said, taking his seat again. "I've always found that tea tends to calm frayed sensibilities. And while the stone on my crucifix is, indeed, glowing very oddly, I confess I have witnessed this optical illusion on other occasions, usually when I am overtired."

The artist smiled sadly. He'd witnessed such patronizing dismissals before; rejection because of class by arrogant royals. Not that the archbishop was a family royal, but he was a royal of a sort for the Church. Vander-Meer was tired too. Weary from the arduous travel back from Fort Niagara. Tired from fitful nights of sleep. Terrified that this…slashing *thing*…would suddenly reappear. He politely took a large swallow of tea. He would not give up just yet.

"If I may be permitted to intrude further, Eminence. Have you recently suffered from any unexplainable bouts of raw pain? Something that seemed to occur spontaneously…that came upon you as if you were attacked by something invisible? And then, just as suddenly, it stopped? Your subsequent investigations, and that of your physicians, could find no wounds, no bruises, indeed no reason of any kind to explain this pain. And it has not occurred since?"

As the artist spoke, André Nicolet straightened in his chair. His tolerant expression vanished, replaced by one of anger.

"Who have you been talking to?"

"Chittaqua, Eminence. I have been talking to an indigenous medicine man whom I have never met before in my life. And he introduced me to this." He pointed at the pouch with one finger. He ran his finger through the dirt until the human jawbone and teeth were visible. "According to this shaman…*this* is what attacked you. And if it helps my credibility, it attacked me too, slashing both of my hands, causing incredible pain that only stopped when the amulet you see here was placed atop this bag of dirt and bones. Dirt and human bones that came from some ancient grave in the wilderness…or so Chittaqua claimed."

Archbishop Nicolet pushed back his chair and stood up. "Get out! Take your magic trickery and your obscene fairy stories and leave my presence. Now!"

The artist, though exhausted by everything that had led up to this moment, did not move.

"We are out of time, Eminence. According to Chittaqua, the stones have probably fallen over by now."

These were unnerving, cryptic words. The archbishop thought the man might be insane. And if he was carrying weapons …?

"*Get out!*"

Charles VanderMeer understood now why the shaman did what he had done in the forge at Fort Niagara. How else do you explain something like this to a man of the natural sciences? "Very well." He stood, picked up the amulet. "You may want to back away from this table."

"*What—?*"

Holding the talisman before him like a shield, as Chittaqua had instructed, VanderMeer slowly stepped away from the table, his gaze fixed on the bag.

"Stop this…stop…whatever you are doing!" Instinctively, Nicolet backed away from the table too. He shouted for his secretary, "Father Tinian!"

It did not take many steps before several creamy-white strands of smoke oozed out of the pouch and reformed into something resembling long talons. Moments later, Archbishop André Nicolet, Jesuit Intendant of New France, was lying on the floor of his office, gripping his right leg, screaming in agony. VanderMeer quickly placed the talisman back atop the pouch and helped the groaning man rise up off the floor.

"Is it gone?" the archbishop asked in a voice filled with panic.

"No." VanderMeer thought the question was absurd. He pointed a trembling finger. "No, Eminence. That *thing* is right over there! I apologize for letting it loose, but you *must* listen to me."

The archbishop was panting. "Don't ever do that to me again—"

"Pardon me, Eminence. *I* did not do that to you. *It* did. And I have been carrying that thing with me for weeks! From what I have read in these histories concerning this legend, if I were a hundred miles away from you, and if somehow that talisman is ever moved too far away from these human remains, if that is what they are, this attack on you will happen again.

"Chittaqua said he disturbed the original grave months ago. I expect that would explain the night of the attack on your person. You are involved with this...*curse*, for lack of another word, whether you like it or not... and now so am I."

Curse? Nicolet was not prepared to discuss anything like this. But that horrible pain was as real as the first time it had struck; gone again in an instant, just like the first time. He spoke in a tense, frightened voice.

"What do you want?"

"Please, sit down." The artist opened his bag of books and withdrew two volumes and laid them on Nicolet's desk. He opened them to places kept by ribbon markers and turned the books so the pages faced the priest.

"Eminence, I am the bastard of a Dutch nobleman, who was kind to me and saw that I received the best possible education. I have been blessed with artistic skills, obviously, but I am also a man of the natural sciences, philosophy, and mathematics. Some of what is written in these books is Frankish history, mixed with legends and Celtic mythology, recorded in several languages. I have been able to translate much of it. There are Latin passages...but it is very old Latin. You may be able to help me with that. What Chittaqua shared with me at Fort Niagara is the other half of the story in these books. If I had not seen that thing with my own eyes...As I said, I am a Christian and a man of science, but the thing in that pouch has made me challenge all those beliefs. And I must tell you this whole story because...we need to help each other."

Archbishop Nicolet gazed at the artist, measuring the veracity of the man. VanderMeer's gaze did not waver. The Jesuit tentatively sat back down.

Father Tinian burst into the room. "Eminence, are you all right? Someone claimed they heard screams coming from your office." The secretary looked at the artist warily.

The archbishop frowned. He glanced at the books with the diagrams and foreign script. *One way or the other, I must hear this story.* He resigned himself.

"I am fine, Father. Bring us a larger pot of tea. Monsieur VanderMeer and I will be talking for a while."

CHAPTER 27
FORT NIAGARA
SEPTEMBER 1754
The Heartbroken Song

From many people in the fort, Philippe confirmed the *shérif* had not stopped but continued to Montrèal with a group of *voyageurs,* followed shortly after by Major Péan and his escort. Philippe was anxious to start the same journey.

"The sooner the better," he told Pierre two days after Chittaqua's burial while breaking their fast. "I'll hire *voyageurs* and buy two or three bateaux today."

Pierre replied but with less enthusiasm. "It is October. If we're going, we need tah' go before the snows begin. And wha' aboot Okeanneh?"

"What about her?" Philippe's jaw clenched. "I'll carry her all the way there myself if I have to. I'm not leaving Okeanneh at Fort Niagara."

The Scotsman held up his palms. "I'm nah' saying we should. But she kinnah' stand for very long without bending over in agony. Tha' journey is nah' exactly a carriage ride."

"She'll be lying down in the bateaux most of the way," Philippe replied. "We'll take a stretcher too. At least she's not getting any worse."

But she is not getting any better, Pierre left unsaid between them.

Philippe avoided his eyes.

It wasn't just Okeanneh Pierre was worried about. The *shérif* had been looking for Philippe when he nearly killed Okeanneh. Philippe blamed himself. And if Okeanneh died during the journey, Pierre worried his partner would not be able to handle the loss. Not after Chittaqua, and Louie, and Michel. And Pierre didn't feel physically strong enough to cope with the potential outcomes.

Not out there, he thought.

The near argument had fomented an awkward silence. Philippe did not finish eating. He made up an excuse to leave the trading post and went out to the boat landing to locate the bateaux. During the negotiations, he asked the *voyageurs* if they recalled seeing anyone like the *shérif*. They shook their heads, but one of the nearby sentries overheard his question.

"I saw a man traveling with some *voyageurs*," the corporal provided. "But he didn't look like them."

"What'd he look like?" Philippe asked.

"Tall, black hair, and beard. Played with his mustache a lot. Kept his chin low and his eyes were always on the move, looking left and right, like he was on guard. Clothes were filthy and splattered everywhere with bloodstains. And he smelled *bad*, rotten, like something dead." The soldier wrinkled his nose at the memory. "It was the second time he'd passed through Fort Niagara. The first time, some Oneida came here to the fort after he had left. They were looking for him."

"Oneida?"

"Yes, an Oneida chief. And his blood was up. There was almost a skirmish right here on the boat landing. He complained some white man had killed his daughter. And the only white man seen coming from the east along the south shore of the lake was that *shérif*."

"What was the chief's name?"

"Don't really remember. *Tree Mountain*, or some name like that. You'd have to ask Captain Pouchot."

Philippe did just that.

"Yes," Pouchot said, after consulting his diary. "The Oneida chief was called Tall Mountain Among Trees. He claimed to be from a village near the English Oswego fort." The commandant explained the rest of the story and the accusations made. "In hindsight, maybe I should have detained the *shérif* when he passed through."

Philippe was disgusted. "You didn't try to stop him?!"

Pouchot stiffened. "Not that I owe you any kind of explanation, Monsieur, but my main responsibility is seeing to the construction of this fort. At that time, the *shérif*'s assault on your Indian wife had not yet occurred."

Philippe glared at the officer. "My *Indian* wife?"

The commandant did not care for the *coureur de bois'* insolent expression. "I think it's time you go about your business, Monsieur," he said, his voice flat, "before we start saying things to one another we might both regret, yes?"

Before Philippe responded Sergeant Major Gabriel abruptly pushed through the office door carrying three bulging canvas bags containing mail and dispatches.

"These just arrived, Commandant," the sergeant said. His smile faded as he sensed the tension in the room.

Captain Pouchot gestured curtly for Philippe to depart.

With the *coureur de bois'* departure, Sergeant Major Gabriel broke the seals on the bag of official government dispatches. "This one is overloaded," he said with appreciation after dumping the contents on the table. "Whew! You would think there is a war on. The other two contain the usual mail and letters. They still need to be sorted for the other forts."

Remaining incensed by the attitude of the civilian fur trader, the commandant nodded absently. Sergeant Gabriel placed the empty government pouch next to the commandant's desk and moved to take the civilian mail to another room for sorting.

"I will bring you the tallies after the count."

"Wait, Sergeant." Captain Pouchot opened a side drawer on his desk and withdrew two wax-sealed letters. "These letters were included in the last government dispatch pouch. I presume it was an error. I've been keeping them safe. Add them to the fort's civilian mail we just received."

"Yes, sir."

Sergeant Gabriel accepted the missives and had turned to leave when he noticed the names on the outside. "Captain, one of these is addressed to Philippe Gerrard and the other...the other is to his *son*, Henri."

"Very observant, Sergeant. Is there a problem?"

"Well, these are old. I should carry them to him immediately, yes?"

When the work stopped on the fort because of Chittaqua's burial, Pouchot had decided to withhold the *coureurs de bois'* mail until work resumed, lest he need a way to encourage Philippe Gerrard's assistance. That precaution turned out to be unnecessary, but with all that had happened concerning the shaman's burial, Captain Pouchot had simply forgotten he still retained the letters. And giving them to Philippe Gerrard today, after their words, could provoke more unpleasantness he'd rather avoid.

The commandant leaned forward and spoke firmly. "Sergeant, add these letters to the mail received today and have it distributed to the proper people *tomorrow*. As far as anyone else is concerned, all of these missives just arrived. And you are *not* to clarify this otherwise. Are my orders clear enough for you?"

"Absolutely, sir." Sergeant Gabriel had no intention of obeying him.

"Where the hell did you march off to?" Pierre complained when Philippe came into the trading post. "I sent Henri down to the boat landing looking for you."

"You already know. I went to the boat landing to see if any bateaux were available. I've arranged for four of them. Then I visited Captain Pouchot for a morning chat…managed to do it without coming to blows. New mail arrived this morning, by the way."

Pierre regarded him somberly. "Okeanneh's been moaning for you for over an hour. Juniata is with her."

Philippe immediately went into the bedroom. Juniata left. He slipped his arms around Okeanneh lying in the bed. She hugged him tightly. Tears streamed down her face. Then she pushed him back and pounded on his chest.

You left me again, she signed angrily. *Why? Why?*

"But I didn't leave you!" Philippe told her what he'd been doing. "I was here all night. I am never leaving you again." He tenderly showered her face with kisses. "And we are leaving the fort soon. We are going to Montrèal. There are better doctors in Montrèal. We're not spending the winter here."

When?

"Tomorrow, probably, but no later than the next day."

When Philippe reentered the trading room, Pierre was still sitting at the table smoking his pipe. The Scotsman grinned and waved a letter in the air.

"Sergeant Gabriel brought this for ya' while ya' were out. Said he was supposed tah' wait until tomorrow. Asked tha' we keep his charity tah' ourselves."

"For me? From who?"

"Now who deeya' think? Corrinne. It was mixed in with the government pouch."

Philippe accepted it from Pierre. "Did *you* read it?"

"O' course I read it," he replied. "She's my partner too. Besides, I never get letters from anyone."

Philippe opened the folded missive. It was short.

Philippe,

    I pray this letter finds its way to you with the greatest possible speed.

    The fall months are upon us. Shipping will soon be interrupted. Our common enemy threatens us, though some say he plans to make a crossing to France before November. I will try to frustrate him and keep him here. Please come to Montréal without delay. There are other serious reasons for this that I will not dwell upon here, but which are equally important. I would say more but I am concerned this mail could be intercepted. I will send another soon.

    Please come with all speed.

    All my love,

    Corrinne

Furious, Philippe crushed the missive in his hand. "Now the *shérif* threatens Corrinne!"

"I know. And Corrinne loves you too! How aboot tha'? No one seems tah' love me. When do we leave?"

"Are we ready?"

"We only need tah' load the boats."

"Tomorrow then," Philippe said. He paused before continuing. "Okeanneh said her headaches are getting worse. It hurts whether she sits up or lies down. Sometimes she sleeps in a chair. I'm hoping the doctors in Montréal can do something for her."

Pierre shook his head slowly, drew on his pipe, and exhaled a long plume. "Let's pray they're better than the doctors out here." Pierre didn't think so, but he kept that to himself.

One effect of Okeanneh's condition Philippe had not mentioned to anyone. Okeanneh had been unable to make love since the attack, though she was more distressed by this than he was. The one time they had tried since coming to Fort Niagara, the rocking movement made the pain in her head unendurable within seconds. She had squeezed her temples between her fists, gasping and panting. He'd told her over and over it was all right. She was mending. He could wait. But Philippe could see her humiliation and shame.

"If it hurts so bad tah' move," Pierre continued guardedly. "How kin' ya' expect Okeanneh tah' travel on the lake?"

"The fort surgeon gave me something for her pain."

Pierre stopped smoking. He did not trust army surgeons at all. "Wha' kind o' something?"

Philippe related a discussion he had with the surgeon a few days earlier.

The veteran surgeon had first said plainly there was little he could do to speed up the healing process.

"I have received some new opiates from the Orient. But even so, it could be so potent it may cause her to become morbid. And the relief would only be temporary. The wound on the outside of her head has healed completely. As for the loss of her voice, this too may pass," the sympathetic surgeon had added. "Injuries to the inside of the head, however, result in very unusual behavior. I'm afraid we know too little how to treat such maladies. But take heart, Monsieur. I have seen soldiers return from the battlefield afflicted with wounds to their skulls even more grievous, some of them blind, some unable to walk, some with no memory of who they are, yet, weeks later, find themselves miraculously healed. Tomorrow morning, your wife may awaken completely healed."

"Let me have some for her."

"This is *not* a medicine, Monsieur. It will only lessen her pain. And that could be dangerous. We need our pain. It is a warning from our bodies to be heeded."

Philippe had asked for the drug anyway. The surgeon frowned with indecision then gave him two small pouches of the opiate.

"Only a pinch or two under her tongue, Monsieur. I have not given any of this to our soldiers yet. I do not know the proper dosage or what effects to expect. Use it sparingly."

Pierre spit on the floor after hearing the story. "You're gonna' give Okeanneh some type of Chinese opium?"

"She's in pain," he replied evenly. "And I will not leave her behind!"

Pierre drew on his pipe and stared directly at Philippe's brooding face. *He wants my approval*, Pierre thought. The Scotsman would not give it;

he did not think Okeanneh would survive the winter. In fact, Pierre did not think she would survive another month. Her pain seemed to be steadily worsening. He'd seen slow, agonizing death before. Men eaten by the flesh rot, or delirious with fever, puking and shitting themselves into a stupor, or overwhelmed by violent convulsions. And beautiful Okeanneh wasn't even able to give a voice to her pain. To Pierre, the choices were simple and equally gloomy. *We kin' wait for her to die here and get trapped by the snows for the winter, or we kin' leave and risk the chance she'll die before we get to Montréal.*

And since Philippe intended to give her opium, Pierre decided it must be said.

"I say it with regret, laddie, opium or nah', Okeanneh might die anyway," he spoke quietly and kindly. "Whether we go tah' Montrèal or nah', Okeanneh's very sick. And I'm sorry, laddie. I dinnah' thin' she'll recover."

"I know," Philippe said, his voice thick. "That's why I—"

Pierre continued without letting him finish. "So if we do this, laddie, this march tah' Montrèal…I want your *word* ya'll nah' let her death get the best o' you out there, in the forests, or out on the lake. If we're gonna' take Sister Michelle, Okeanneh, Henri, and Anamosa with us and something bad happens…it'll take both o' us tah' lead this journey. Even if I was nah' so crippled up—*which I am*—I kinnah' have ya' flopping around out there wailing like a baby."

"When have I *ever* acted like that?!"

"Never. Nah' once. But Okeanneh's different. If she's dies out there …"

"She's *not* going to die!"

"You see, laddie? Tha's wha' I mean. You kinnah' deal with the thought o' it! But if she dies, then we bury her…like we buried Michel and Louie—and then, we move on. Or we might as well nah' go in the first place, and we stay here for the winter."

Philippe finally lifted his eyes from the floor to Pierre, his face tight. "Don't worry about me, partner."

"Well, I am worried aboot ya'! Because it's gonna' take all o' us tah' work the oars and the sails. And who knows wha' else might 'appen?"

"Three other *voyageurs* elected to go with us. And Henri will help."

"And thank God for Henri," Pierre agreed. "But ya' better think aboot wha' I said. Wha' aboot Juniata?"

"I'm going to let Juniata and Chesanin live here at the store. I see no reason to bring them with us. They've suffered enough. I've already told Claude."

Pierre finally nodded in agreement. "All right, then it's best we leave tomorrow. The weather could turn dangerous cold at anytime."

The door to the trading post opened. Henri entered carrying two full buckets of water. He, of course, was followed by Anamosa.

"Oho! Anna! My little lassie! Come give your Uncle Pierre a hug!"

Anamosa scrambled onto Pierre's lap so he could tickle her.

Pierre looked at Philippe and tilted his head toward Anamosa. *Remember*, his eyes communicated silently. *She's going too.*

"The *voyageurs* told me we're going to Montréal!" Henri said after setting the buckets over by the hearth.

"Yes, tomorrow."

"Tomorrow?"

On impulse, Philippe went to the wall of the trading post and took down a brand new musket from a rack of three. He held it out to Henri.

"Here. This is yours. It is a new French design. There are probably less than a hundred in the world. And a bag of grooved ball shot."

Henri accepted the weapon with a look of awe.

Pierre smiled. "There's nah' a better one made anywhere in the world," he told the boy. "Nah' even the English ones. But dinnah' run out o' that shot, or the musket just becomes an expensive club."

Henri looked at his father. He didn't know what to say.

"No need tah' look so humble," Pierre added. "You've earned it."

"You're a *coureur de bois* now. Go tell your mother we leave for Montréal in the morning. Okeanneh and Anamosa are going too."

"Juniata and Chesanin?"

"They'll stay here at the store. We'll see them again in the spring." Philippe felt strange as he said this, as if he somehow knew otherwise. "Stay here with Uncle Pierre. I'll be right back."

Henri frowned at the thought of leaving Chesanin behind. He stooped to hug Anamosa.

"*Coootseemaah*, Ahh-ree."

"*Coot-see-mah?*" Henri asked, puzzled.

"Tha's one o' Chittaqua's special words, lad," Pierre said. He tickled

Anamosa under the chin. "And you should be honored someone this beautiful said it to you."

"What does it mean?"

"I expect she'll tell ya' herself some day, in her own time."

Henri could not wait to fire his new musket and ran out to the main gate to do so. He waved at the sentries on the walls and held up the polished weapon for them to see.

"I'm going to try a shot."

They waved back.

He walked out a hundred paces and looked around. Finding a large bristle cone, he propped it atop a fallen tree nearby and retreated back to the front of the gate. He carefully loaded a ball with odd spiral grooves cut in it and sat down on the ground to balance the barrel over his knee. He took a deep breath, exhaled, aimed at the bristle cone, and fired.

The loud sound and the smoke was much more pronounced than that of anything he'd shot before. But the bristle cone flew into the air in pieces. The sentries on the wall cheered.

"*Woo hoo*!" Henri was elated. He was about to fire again when someone called his name.

Sergeant Gabriel was standing in the gateway with his hands on his hips. He looked irritated. "No more of that! You might trigger a call to arms. You men up there know better!" he shouted.

"I'm sorry, Sergeant. But it's my new musket. Did you see the range?"

"I did." The Sergeant held out a rolled document. "Here, occupy yourself with this. It's a missive addressed to you."

"A missive? From who? I don't know anybody."

The Sergeant gave him a look. "That's why it's sealed with wax. So no one can tell who it's from. You will be the first to know. But find a place to read this privately. Maybe out by the boat landing. You're not supposed to have it until tomorrow, and I don't want others in the fort seeing you reading a letter, yes?"

Henri accepted the roll, holding it carefully. It looked like it consisted of two pages. He smiled.

"Did you hear me? Read it privately. Yes?"

"Yes, Sergeant."

Three bateaux were loaded with supplies, covered and lashed with skins before nightfall. At Pierre's direction, the *voyageurs* filled half of one with some furs and other cargo as well. They'd need only to push off the next morning to be on their way. When hearing about Philippe Gerrard's intentions, Captain Pouchot volunteered his courier and one other soldier as oarsmen. The *coureurs de bois* gratefully accepted the commandant's offer. Pierre Dunemoore was particularly pleased for the extra help. Now they would have two or three men in each bateau for the rowing, or to help face what other trials they may encounter. With the prospect of sleeping for days on the cold ground, Captain Pouchot graciously offered Pierre Dunemoore a real bed inside the castle for his last night at Fort Niagara. Pierre accepted the invitation, deciding it would be better for Philippe and Okeanneh to be alone together during their last night in the fort. Who knew what lay ahead?

With final preparations complete, Philippe went back to the trading post. He stoked the fires and entered the bedroom. Anamosa was already asleep in her small bed. But to his surprise, he found Okeanneh sitting on the edge of his bed, drying herself with an extra linen sheet. She'd endured the pain of a bath.

Okeanneh smiled at seeing him. The pain she felt was throbbing and constant, like a bird pecking strongly inside of her head, as it had been for more than three days. Sitting up made it much worse. Fortunately, the hot bath in the forge room had relaxed her, somehow helping to diminish the pain, if only temporarily.

Philippe knelt down before Okeanneh and kissed her. "I love you."

Okeanneh smiled and stood, gesturing for Philippe to sit on the bed. Wrapped in the linen sheet knotted at her chest, she moved quietly to retrieve a chair from the other side of the room. She set it down before the fireplace. Returning to stand in front of Philippe, Okeanneh smiled and pulled Philippe's head close to her stomach. He clutched her tightly, his arms circling her waist. Philippe sobbed abruptly. Okeanneh did not comprehend the reason for his persistent sadness, but she was determined to give Philippe pleasure at least once before they began this long journey to the great white village on the river. There would be no time for pleasuring during the travel.

Tonight I will make you forget about everything but me, she promised him silently.

Okeanneh lifted his chin and kissed him deeply. Even that slight bend to her head made the throbbing ache intensify. She hid the pain. Her eyes spoke of her intentions to make love.

No, Okeanneh, Philippe thought. He didn't want to cause her more pain or humiliation.

But Okeanneh's expression was determined. She gestured for Philippe to sit in the chair. She went to the fire and placed a new log on top of the coals. The flames licked hungrily at the dry wood.

Philippe knew Okeanneh intended to make love sitting up in the chair as a way to minimize the pain. *This is not going to work*, Philippe thought. *We've tried this!*

"Wait, Okeanneh." She frowned as Philippe got up. He searched his coat and retrieved the small pouches of opiate powder the surgeon had given him.

"It is for the pain," he whispered to her. He opened one of the pouches, showing her the yellowish powder. He wet his finger as the surgeon told him to do. Curious, Okeanneh wet her finger too.

"Stick your finger in the pouch until the powder sticks to it and then put your finger in your mouth under your tongue."

Okeanneh did so, noticing the powder had a very bitter taste. But then again, all medicine tasted bitter. Impulsively, she wet her finger and sucked at the powder two more times before Philippe grew worried and stopped her.

"That's enough. Now we wait," he said.

Philippe kissed her and pulled her to his lap. She sat sideways and rested her head against his shoulder. Together, they watched the flames build in the hearth, the warmth radiating through the room's coolness, pushing back the night chill. He held her gently in his arms, the smoothness of her cheek nestled against his neck, one of her arms draped up and around the back of his head, the other already moving mischievously in his lap. He kissed her forehead, the scent of her long hair reminding him of her stronger more compelling aromas further down. Okeanneh's fingers became more persistent. He felt himself harden and swell. His hips began to move in response. It was inevitable now. They were going to try.

God, he prayed. *Please don't let this hurt her.*

Yes, she smiled with satisfaction as he became aroused. *Yes. Now we will make pleasure.*

All of a sudden, Okeanneh felt a little dizzy. But to her surprise, the ache in her head was almost completely gone. The medicine was powerful indeed. She sat straighter and gazed into Philippe's eyes, seeing his desire. She kissed him again, inserting her tongue deep in his mouth.

Yes, she thought. *Yes!*

She untied the laces of Philippe's jersey and helped pull it over his head. In the soft light of the candles and fire, the scars on his face, chest, and arms looked pink and ropey. Okeanneh got up from his lap and knelt in front of him. She slipped off his boots and, upon her urging, Philippe lifted his hips so she could drag down his leather leggings, leaving him completely naked.

Philippe asked with concern. "Does it hurt?"

Okeanneh experimented by tilting her head slowly back and forth. *No pain*, she signed. In this moment, she was happy and carefree. She grasped him in both hands and moved them up and down, enjoying the sounds he made.

Standing, she unknotted and threw off the linen sheet. Philippe was completely awed by the sight of her naked beauty.

Breathing harder, he reached out to grasp her breasts, feeling the heavy, hanging roundness, the skin hot, the flesh yielding to his fingers, the nipples stiffening to hard knots.

Okeanneh moved back from his grasp and smiled at seeing his hardness pulse and throb. He was ready. But she wanted to go slow, to pleasure him as long as she could. This was their love. *I am yours and you are mine.*

Okeanneh found she was curiously dizzy, and that it was getting stronger, and then there was a new, floating sensation. Her skin tingled. The flame of the candles guttered slowly.

Philippe could not recall Okeanneh looking more beautiful than she did at that moment. He could see the desire in her half-lidded eyes.

She began to rub the luxurious mound of hair between her legs with one hand, moaning softly at the pleasure this induced. Her head tilted forward. Long black hair hung past her shoulders to drape on either side of her breasts. The light from the candles and fire gave Okeanneh's skin a sheen.

She seemed thinner than Philippe remembered, and her breasts seemed much larger. As her hands moved, her body shuddered with expanding pleasure, the muscles beneath her golden skin moved and rippled sensuously.

Okeanneh lifted her chin as this amazing floating sensation grew stronger. It felt so…so wonderful! She gazed at Philippe, stepping close to him.

He leaned forward, moved her hand out of the way, and took hold of her hips. She caught her breath as he buried his face in that special spot, that place where every pleasure expanded at his slightest touch. She wondered if he could taste the waves of pleasures he was making in her. It was an odd question. She must remember to ask him later. She closed her eyes, gently pressed on the back of his head, and concentrated on the liquid sensation, the warmth and wet movement of his tongue sliding so wonderfully back and forth, and up and down.

Philippe's sense of smell was completed saturated. He moved his nose, lips, and tongue over and back through her curly hair and wetness, immersed in the hot, spicy aroma, a quick, incense-like smell that made the blood in his head rush and pound. He matched his movements to the sounds she made, attempting to give as much pleasure as possible lest she experience any pain.

Cou ti si mah, she thought. *Oh yes. Oh yes.*

A short burst of pain flashed in the healed wound at the side of her head, quickly followed by another sharp pulse near the back. But the spikes of pain were gone almost as soon as they had begun, overwhelmed by the intense pleasure she was experiencing. Her right arm suddenly went numb.

The dizziness intensified. Okeanneh began losing her sense of balance.

But that was all right. *Maybe I will swim in the lake tomorrow*, she thought. *Swim?* Such an odd idea when she really meant to collect wood. *Wood? Why am I thinking of these things?*

Okeanneh gently pulled away and crawled atop his body, straddled his legs with her own, held onto his shoulders, and lowered her wetness over his hardness until they were one, a river one with the land, flowing, moving, twisting.

Philippe helped Okeanneh move ever so slowly up then down. Holding her hips with his hands, she would grind deliciously into his lap, uttering deep guttural groans of pleasure.

It was like a dream. Okeanneh felt herself floating, dizzy, riding up and down, a canoe rocking on the gentle swells of a lake, tingling bursts of pleasures surging upward higher and higher with every thrust. She opened her eyes to look into Philippe's, one of her hands slipping down between their bodies so she could touch the wetness where they were joined and bring the taste up to their lips. They both kissed the taste, tongues overlapping at her fingers. The smell, taste, and touch made it complete, she pressed down and rolled her hips away then forward, and away again. Her arms and legs began to tremble. The tingling gushed upward, overflowed, spiraling higher, rushing madly back and forth like a canyon in flood from a heavy rain.

Now, she thought. *Now!*

Okeanneh pressed down with her feet, tightened the muscles of her stomach and thighs and pulled at Philippe with her sex, to bring him the wonderful pleasure she felt. A bright light flashed before her face. A new feeling of hotness rippled down her arms, now both arms were numb.

She ignored these new intrusive sensations and concentrated. She tensed the muscles in her groin and gripped Philippe tightly. He groaned.

"Philippe!" Okeanneh groaned loudly as her body suddenly rattled with waves of tingling pleasure. She bit into his salty, sweaty shoulder. They clung to each other.

Philippe pressed his hips upward, holding onto her back as he shuddered and pulsed, hoping not to shake her too passionately, saying her name over and over.

As the waves of pleasure calmed, they held one another tenderly. Their breathing slowed.

Did she say my name? Or did I imagine that? Philippe lifted his face to look into Okeanneh's eyes. They were huge, liquid, unfocused.

"Okeanneh," he whispered. "You said my name!"

Yes, Okeanneh thought, *Yes, you are mine.* The dizziness was strong. She stood up feeling him slide out from her.

"Sleep," she whispered, pointing at the bed limply with one hand.

"You *can* talk again," he said, excitement, joy, and relief bursting inside.

Okeanneh smiled and leaned over to kiss him. "*Cou ti si mah.*"

"*Cou ti si mah.*"

"Sleep," she repeated.

"Yes. Sleep."

He stood, lifted her in his arms, and lowered her gently to the mattress and pillows. She started to shiver. He got in beside her, pulled the blanket and soft furs over their nakedness, drawing her hips in tight to his groin to cup her body with his, wrapping his arms around her chest and shoulders.

Okeanneh sighed amid the embracing warmth of his body. She wriggled and pressed her buttocks against him, feeling him grow hard with excitement again. Lifting her leg, she grasped his flesh and slipped it inside her sex. The hardness felt good. She slowly ground her hips back and forth, slipping one hand between her legs to grasp and caress. In response, one of his hands came around her waist, his fingers pressing and rubbing her wet little spot of pleasure. She continued her grinding movement until he groaned again, this time the sound was long and slow. His hands pulled her hips tightly against him. She gently rolled and tugged at him with her fingers until his groaning subsided.

Okeanneh sighed happily and relaxed. *You are mine*, she thought, surrendering to this incredible, gentle floating. Now her arms had no feeling.

There was an unusual tingling in her left foot. But it was not unpleasant.

You are mine, she thought again. *And tomorrow I will tell of your child that I carry. And we will be one together and forever.*

Her breathing slowed. A comforting numbness rolled upward from her knees like a warm wave washing over her as if she lay on a summer lakeshore. Her last thoughts were of Anamosa's laughter.

The surgeon was right after all, Philippe thought blissfully. *She's talking again. She's going to get better.*

Philippe smoothed Okeanneh's long black hair away from her face and kissed her neck before closing his eyes. For the first time in months, he drifted off to sleep without being tortured by his dreams or awakened in the night by anxiety.

Henri heard the call of a tiny voice. He'd been sleeping in his new bed in a room added and constructed off the back of the forge. It didn't have a door yet and was lit by the reddish embers of the hearth within the trading post. But he could see the outline of a small shadow from the light coming through the trading room doorway.

"Huh?"

A little voice spoke in an excited whisper. "Ahh-ree?"

"Over here."

She carefully walked across the gritty floor until she stood next to him, her teeth chattering from the cold. He pulled back the blanket cover. She slipped off her shoes and crawled in. Her hands were chilled, so he tucked them against his neck. She was asleep within minutes.

Unfortunately, now he was wide-awake. He craned his head over hers and looked out through the doorway. The high window to the left of the hearth showed the barest hint of morning light. He preferred to get up, but didn't want to disturb Anamosa. He laid there for a while and let her sleep, dozing on and off, every slight noise or sound waking him up again. His thoughts naturally turned to the letter he received. He'd read it a dozen times already and had memorized every word. Reading it the first time out by the boat landing had brought tears to his eyes.

Amazingly, it was from Father Cortois.

The door from the trading store to the forge suddenly opened with a strong draft of air. Juniata entered, gathered food stuffs from the larder, and returned. Anamosa stirred right away and sat up. Seeing his chance, Henri slipped around her and pulled on his coat and boots.

"Morning, Anna."

She hugged his waist.

"Come, let's see what Juniata has to eat."

They went into the store and smelled many delicious aromas. When Juniata saw him, she pointed at the empty water buckets. Henri went out to the well, with Anamosa prancing along behind him. After bringing in the water, Juniata said it would still be awhile until the cornmeal bread was finished baking.

"I will be out at the boat landing. Anna, you stay with Juniata."

She frowned but took a seat at the long table.

By the time he reached the boat landing, Henri decided it would be a beautiful day. The four bateaux were completely loaded. The *voyageurs* were already inspecting the canvas covers and lashings. He figured they would leave before midday. Juniata and Chesanin had decided to come with them too, the result of Henri's convincing argument that they needed to see the white man's big village, and it would be a safer place to spend the winter. But the greater truth was that Henri simply did not want to say good-bye to these people. They were his family…his connection to Chittaqua. And until the letter from Father Cortois came, he had been undecided about whether to go to Montréal at all. After all, there was nothing there for him. Fort Niagara was his home now. But then, last night, his mother came to the store. She was no longer wearing the habit of a good Sister. She announced to everyone she was leaving the Sisterhood and returning to Montréal permanently. To the collective shock of all, she gave no explanation why and she would answer no questions.

Then the letter.

Henri took a seat on a rock where the morning sunlight could warm him as it rose. Sitting down made a hard lump in one of his deep pockets more noticeable. He reached in and, from among other clutter, pulled out a small stone figurine. It was the object he retrieved from Chittaqua's medicine bag when his father had dumped out the contents. He'd forgotten about it till now. In the sunlight, he looked at it more closely. It was dark, almost black, and oddly heavy, like it was made of metal rather than stone. It was an idol or pagan god of some kind. The head was triangular and where the mouth should be, there was a straight line with *X*s all across it.

Like stitches, he thought. He turned it over and around a few times. It felt warm for some reason. He remembered Chittaqua saying something about a picture man in Montréal. Then he shrugged and decided to keep it in his pocket for now.

Henri took the wrinkled letter from another pocket to read it again. It had been written in Latin, but he could read it. Father Cortois had taught him Latin long ago.

My dear Henri,

I have been told this letter to you can only be two pages long, as the volume of missives and dispatches being sent is usually very large, and it may take weeks for this letter to find you. You are no doubt surprised to get a letter from me, and even more surprised to learn I am now in Montréal. I arrived on a ship a week ago. I have been accepted to join Archbishop Nicolet's Jesuits. They are educated men of science, history, and letters, interests similar to mine. Like them, I will dedicate the rest of my life to spreading the word of Christ and converting the pagan populations of New France. Leaving Saint Ouen's was a difficult decision for me. But every day since has brought new wonders, new surprises. I can only imagine the joy in your heart at making the ocean crossing, at seeing those glorious stars, the raw, freshly built cities of Louisbourg, Quebec, and Montréal. The colorful, though sometimes frightening, peoples who inhabit this end-less forested land seem from our ancient histories. And yet, here we also find Frenchmen, noblemen to hardy commoners, all struggling together to create something new and special in this wilderness. Truly New *France is the proper name for this place.*

The stories Archbishop Nicolet has related to me about your capture, and Sister Michelle's too, by the wild tribesmen and the details of your escape and your trek through hundreds of miles of forests by yourself is beyond astonishing. It is something heroic, as if written by Homer. There is even a claim you fought with a bear? I stand in awe of you, Henri. And yet, I should not be surprised, yes? I have seen your courage and watched the yearning to explore grow inside you from an early age.

The archbishop tells me you and Philippe Malthais are expected in Montréal before the snows arrive, although no one can say when that will be. He encouraged me to write you this letter. I cannot wait to see you again, to hear about your adventures. I'm afraid my own exploits, albeit exciting to me, simply do not compare. In this regard, you have now become the teacher. In truth, you became my teacher even before you left Saint Ouen's monastery, when you reminded me of my failings, and the failings of the Church in protecting Sister Madeleine from her incestuous father. I am pleased to inform you I subsequently devised another intrigue and managed to bring Sister Madeleine with me; although she is no longer part of a Sisterhood. Of course, I was declared a kidnapper and an outlaw for what I did. Much like your father! Somehow I find this a rather romantic reputation, yes? And I am proud of what I did, even if I am only a priest.

Madeleine is living here in Montréal. She is very excited at the prospect of seeing you again someday, as am I. But now I am running out of paper. You can find me at the Terrain des Jésuites. In Christ's name, I will pray for you.

Rene Cortois

Oh, one more marvel I must mention. This morning, across the street, on a rooftop, I saw a great eagle with completely white feathers! It made me recall your visions of a large white raptor haunting Saint Ouen's spires. I'm told the natives call it a ghost eagle. *Can you imagine that? I trust you have seen them too?*

Henri smiled at reading those final words again. He knew something about that ghost eagle, something the Father might be hard pressed to believe. But the revelation about Madeleine…that she was in Montréal…was astonishing. He looked to the northeast, toward the sunrise. That was the direction she lived now. But she was from another life, another time, another place so far away it now seemed foreign, and the life he lived then seemed trivial in comparison. Yet he could still remember Madeleine's face…and her kiss. And any hesitation he had about going to Montréal had dissipated instantly upon learning she was there.

His stomach growling, Henri pocketed the letter, got up, and walked back inside the fort through the boat-landing gate. He saw Juniata by the well in the middle of the yard talking with Claude Guillot. Claude pointed in his direction. Juniata hurried toward him.

"You must come," she shouted, terrible panic on her face. "Come now!"

"What's wrong?"

"Okeanneh is not breathing!"

"What?"

A scream erupted from the Dunemoore Company front door.

"*Ahh-ree!*"

Henri started running as fast as he could.

Seconds later, the morning quiet was shattered further by the first of the many drawn-out, guttural howls that would issue from inside the trading post. Soldiers and traders, men prone to action when faced with any danger, were immediately drawn closer to the store, weapons at the ready, ready to offer help. And as the reason for Philippe Gerrard's cries spread, they felt utterly at a loss on what to do. *Okeanneh's dead*, they repeated to one another in disbelief. *Impossible!* The only thing to share now was Philippe's suffering, his shrieks of agony. But the keening howls were not from torture. Torture they'd heard before. *Torture* they understood.

At some point over the years, they'd all been captivated by Okeanneh's compelling allure, her large amber eyes, the gaze that made the most common man among them feel measured, important, and welcome. To many, she was the connection to the civilized part of their character, a reason to be polite. Some would joke that they trapped and nearly starved all winter long to experience her compliments and genuine appreciation of the furs they brought back to the store in that brief hour of appraisal, to hear her words of admiration, to see her smile, the expression of approval, an affirmation of their hunting prowess. Each one believing at the end of the season, he was the best among the *coureurs de bois*. If you dispute this, you only had to ask Okeanneh. That was the usual bluster. But no longer. She was gone from their lives, forever.

And Philippe's enormous capacity to love his wife was now exceeded by the painful shredding of his heart. Each piteous howl of sorrow the sign another piece of his soul had withered. And before the morning was over, even the most toughened *coureurs de bois'* hoped to quickly forget the sounds of the woodsman's anguish.

That would take a long, long time.

Peter Blue Jacket led a group of three hardened Oneida warriors, bypassing Fort Niagara, intent on intersecting another trail that led straight to Fort Le Boeuf. He had informed Tall Mountain Among Trees the white man he sought was at Fort Le Boeuf. Peter was sent back to capture the murderer and bring him back.

They were moving at a swift pace of travel, a trot short of a full run, the eyes of each man assigned to watch a different part of the trail, the sides and rear. As the leader, Peter watched straight ahead for any signs of strangers. They were not expecting too great a danger, but this was Seneca territory, Maltoc was warring, and you couldn't be certain what to expect.

Leaves were starting to fall, thinning and obscuring the density of the forest. The warrior watching to their right called out that he saw something at the bottom of a ravine, deep among the trees.

They stopped and walked off the trail toward the remains of a man who was suspended between two trees. The body had been ravaged by animals and insects. Little was left except for some shards of dried, blackened skin. The decomposing skull lay on the ground, the jaw askew. Any bones still hanging from the trees did so because the wrists and ankles had been pinned to the trunks with large iron spikes. Both of the long shin bones of the skeleton had been broken, probably by the large rock they saw nearby, which had stains of blood on it.

From several paces away, Peter Blue Jacket peered carefully at the remaining shreds of clothing, hair, and the contents of the backpack that had been spread all over the area. The red piping on the black robes was unmistakable.

"I know this man. He is the chief of the black robes at the French Niagara fort. His name is André Beauharnois."

The three Oneida braves accompanying Peter Blue Jacket were expert trackers. They approached the dead man dispassionately but warily, examining the surrounding ground carefully.

"The white man we seek did this," one of them said.

"How do you know?" Peter asked.

"I saw his boot print where he killed the daughter of Tall Mountain Among Trees. These are the same."

"He dragged this man down here from another trail," said the second tracker. "You can still see the marks made by the heels of the shoes."

"Those are the beads and cross of a priest," said the third.

"The white man was coming back from the Le Boeuf fort. He must be at Niagara," said the first.

Peter Blue Jacket was perplexed. Why would Gaspard de Propei torture and kill this important white shaman? He collected a handful of relics from the area, the crucifix, beads, parts of the black robes with the faded red trim.

"We go to the Niagara fort, to learn where the white man is hiding."

The arrival of four heavily armed Oneida warriors caused a great commotion at the fort. Peter Blue Jacket led them into the marshalling yard and was confronted by Captain Pouchot in the middle. He noticed the fort was surprisingly empty of people. He had expected more of them to be crowding his arrival by now.

"Oho, Captain."

The commandant nodded politely, but his expression was stern, unfriendly, suspicious, presuming these allies of the English were here to spy on the fort's construction. He was therefore upset they had gotten all the way to its center.

"I am called Peter Blue Jacket."

"I have heard of you."

"These are Oneida warriors. Tall Mountain Among Trees has sent us to find Gaspard de Propei."

"The *shérif* has gone on to Montréal."

Peter looked around again. Few people had gathered to them. He held forth the relics collected from Father Beauharnois and dropped them to the ground before the officer.

"We found these things at a place where a priest was killed by Gaspard de Propei. His trail led back to this fort."

Captain Pouchot's eyes widened. The red piping was unmistakable.

"These things belong to Monseigneur Beauharnois! What have you done to him?"

Muskets from the surrounding soldiers were elevated. Peter Blue Jacket held up his palms and turned slowly around.

"Oho! I am Peter Blue Jacket. I have visited here often. All of you know me. I would not have done this thing. This priest was killed many weeks ago."

Captain Pouchot eyed the brave suspiciously. "Where is the body?"

"It is two days from here. I can show you. But this was done by Gaspard de Propei. Now, maybe you will help us capture him."

"I told you, he has gone back to Montréal."

Peter glanced at the stone castle and frowned, thinking the commandant was lying to him. Their discussion was interrupted by a new commotion at the fort's main gate.

A stream of *coureurs de bois*, soldiers, and fort civilians began returning from the funeral for Okeanneh. She had been buried near Chittaqua's mound; the first of many graves that would later be made near the famous shaman, as people desired the spirits of their dead to be associated with the spirit of the great Andrototekan in the afterlife.

"Guard these men," Captain Pouchot told his soldiers when he saw Philippe Gerrard limping toward the Dunemoore store.

"Monsieur Gerrard!"

Philippe, Pierre, and Henri stopped to face the commandant who approached at a fast walk.

"My apologies for not attending the services, Monsieur. With so many people absent from the fort, I did not want to vacate my command."

Philippe did not respond. They all turned their backs to the officer.

"Monsieur, *s'il vous plaît*. There is an Indian here. You know him, I think. Peter Blue Jacket? He claims to have found Father Beauharnois' body in the bush. He further claims the priest was killed by Gaspard de Propei."

Philippe reacted instantly. He looked beyond the officer and saw the Mohawk and the Oneida standing in the middle of the yard.

"Henri, take Juniata and Anamosa into the store. Pierre, let's see what this Mohawk spy has to tell us."

Philippe and Pierre led the visitors to the more isolated boat landing. They had food and drink brought out from the store. They sat and talked with Peter Blue Jacket and the Oneida braves for a long time in their native tongue. Within the first minute, Commandant Pouchot grew tired of not understanding a word that was said. He asked to be informed what the *coureurs de bois* learned when they were finished talking.

Hours later, Philippe and Peter Blue Jacket solemnly shook hands. Philippe went back to the store. Pierre went to see Captain Pouchot.

"It was as Peter Blue Jacket described to ya', Captain. The Oneida found Father Beauharnois' body while tracking the *shérif*. He was tortured before he died. The *shérif* did it."

Pouchot spoke quickly. "How do you know they didn't do it?"

"He'd been crucified, Captain. Nailed tah' trees with iron spikes in his wrist and ankle bones. His shins were broken with a rock. Only a good Christian murderer would be familiar with the Roman way o' prolonging such a hideously painful death. Peter and the Oneida will lead ya' tah' collect the corpse when you're ready."

"Was that all he said after three hours?"

"Tha' was all tha's important for the army tah' know."

But much, much more was discussed. Pierre left the castle without revealing this. Two company *coureurs de bois* were sent that day by fast canoe to Montréal with a message for Corrinne. She would have notice of their arrival a week before it occurred.

Three days after Okeanneh's funeral, on an icy October morning, before the sun had fully broken above the horizon, the Dunemoore Company bateaux pushed away from the boat landing at Fort Niagara. Four *voyageurs*, the commandant's courier, and one other soldier from the fort were spread out among the boats along with Philippe, Henri, Pierre, Juniata, Chesanin, and Michelle, who held the weeping Anamosa in her arms. A large crowd had gathered at the shore to watch them leave. But no one was cheering; sporadic well-wishes for a safe journey were said quietly. A few hands waved slowly in a gloomy farewell.

Philippe Gerrard's expression was a hardened mask of anger and resentment, his eyes darted wildly, the whites visible around the iris. The *voyageurs* called it forest madness in their private whispers among themselves. For a few weeks, only the empathetic voices of Michelle and Pierre could reason with him.

Henri Gerrard sat in the middle of the lead bateau with his father at the front. For every stroke Henri pulled, it seemed his father pulled two. Sitting backwards, working his set of oars, he watched sadly as the stone castle of Fort Niagara slowly became obscured in the morning mists.

As the line of bateaux paralleled the Lake Ontario shoreline, moving quietly further and further across its placid waters, the forlorn howl of a wolf could be heard somewhere far in the distance.

Roland.

Henri swallowed hard at this thought and pulled at the oars more strongly, hoping the heavier exertion would curb the sudden surge of tears that threatened to spill over.

Adieu!

The heartbroken song did not last long, diminishing quickly with the distance. And when it finally faded, Henri was overcome with uneasiness; the feeling he would not be coming back.

Helmut Colbért walked by the harvested fields north of Montréal and entered the city through its farming gate in the late afternoon. From a trunk full of clothing and costumes purposely not transported with the bateaux, he'd chosen to wear drab, coarse, woolen pants, a gray linen shirt, a deerskin coat, boots, and a sock hat common to various laborers, ordinary attire worn by hundreds of men in Montréal.

The autumn days were getting shorter now, the sky overcast, so when dusk gathered, night came quickly, even before the city finished lighting its candle lamps, another reminder he was running out of time. Colbért had thoroughly memorized the streets on this side of Montréal and immediately walked toward the Rue Saint-Claude. Halfway down this road there was a narrow alley to the right, which ended in the garden area behind Lady de Chanaye's townhouse.

Since returning to Montréal, Colbért had been making daily forays into the city, mostly at night, learning the streets, avenues, buildings, houses, taverns, shops, walking the perimeter of the walls, observing the activities in the warehouse area belonging to the Dunemoore Company, gazing at the upper floors, knowing it was another place Lady de Chanaye would often stay. At times, he lingered quietly in the favorite haunts of the riverfront's thieves and murderers, listening to the gossip and rumors. He counted his steps everywhere he walked, sometimes closing his eyes, pacing his stride to see if he correctly estimated when to make a particular turn. Before long, walking anywhere within the city at night would be second nature; it wasn't very big anyway. And he'd come to the conclusion that compared to Paris, the walled city of Montréal was a shithole...smelled like one too. *Why would anyone want to live here?* In his mind, its only redeeming quality was that it was small.

As he slipped unseen down the alley, he was pleased to see no one about. Not much to do in the winter months of Montréal, he thought; too wet and too cold, but that was better for what he intended. He easily climbed the wall between Lady de Chanaye's house and the next property and went to that place on top of the low roof, an ideal spot that allowed him to gaze into her second-floor windows. This was the second time he'd scouted the room to learn her habits. If he decided the abduction would be done by breaking in through the balcony door, he wanted to have an idea of when she would bathe and how long she would tarry in the tub.

He crouched down and waited, patient and motionless, gargoyle-like for almost two hours before being rewarded when the first candle was lit in her boudoir. Then a second lamp was lit, and another set of tapers.

With each new candle and lamp, the room illuminated until he could clearly see the portly maidservant and discern the pale green color of her dress. He stifled his disappointment. He knew this meant the lady would be along soon enough. The maid was there to help with her dress...or *undress*. But when the maid began pouring buckets of steamy water into a bathtub, he knew the wait would be longer. She took several trips down and up the stairway until the tub was full. However frustrating the wait, it only heightened his expectation of what was to come.

"Ah, finally," he whispered, "the queen approaches."

The slender outline of a female in a thin white nightdress entered the room. Her nakedness beneath the gown was enticingly outlined by the candlelight.

Helmut glanced up the alley toward the Rue Saint-Claude. There was no one in sight and no shadowy movements while he'd waited. Same as last time. His plan began to take shape.

Enter and kill the maid. Wait for the queen. Choke her unconscious. Gag and tie her securely. Wrap her in blankets. Shoulder her over the balcony. Carry her to the wagon at the end of the alley. Drive out the east side gate. Should take no more than thirty minutes.

His gaze returned to the boudoir just as her nightdress dropped to the floor. The maid took one of her hands to help her into the tub. As she lifted a leg over the side, the entire front of her body could be seen clearly... and there she was, revealed to him again...except...except the hair of this woman was decidedly not white-blond.

It's not her!

Colbért slipped silently from his perch to the ground and quickly scaled the dividing wall, walking carefully along the extremely narrow top until he reached the wooden overhang of the balcony adjoining the boudoir. He'd planned to do this another time when the room was empty, to lessen the chance of being seen or heard, but he had to get closer to see who this new woman might be. If the wooden rail creaked too loudly, he would drop like a cat to the ground and wait to see if anyone appeared. But he was lucky; the balcony was solidly built of thickly cut, pegged hardwoods. In the cold, the wood was like stone. Moving spider-like up over the rounded rail, Colbért took a position to the side of the door leading into the room from the balcony. He peered through an opening at the edge of the lace curtains.

Only two paces away, the girl was standing in the tub, arms outstretched, while the maidservant soaped and washed her down with sponges. Her skin was pale white, untouched by the sun, her dark nipples erect from the cold. Her long curly hair glowed reddish-brown in the candlelight, the hair of her pubic area dripped with the soapy water. Eyes closed, the enjoyment on the girl's face to the maidservant's cleansing attentions was provocative.

"There! All clean," Mathilde said in a motherly tone as she poured a bucket over Madeleine's shoulders to rinse her off.

"It feels wonderful," Madeleine agreed emphatically.

Mathilde poured a long stream of a flowery aromatic fluid into the water from a cruet. "Now lie back down and relax in the water. I will return with more hot buckets of water to refresh the heat."

Madeleine lounged beneath the water up to her neck, its warmth penetrating deep into her muscles, drawing the tension from her back and shoulders. The immersion in the heat reminded her of lying naked, skin-to-skin with someone in bed. In the tub, she was surrounded by intoxicating heat. The sensation induced a long-denied craving too tempting to resist. One of her hands slipped between her legs and she started to pleasure herself.

I must hurry...before Mathilde returns.

Colbért saw what she was doing. It angered him. He'd spent his childhood in a brothel, peering through a hinge in the door of the standing closet in his mother's room, where she would confine him most nights while she pleasured the numerous men who visited her.

The maidservant was gone. It would be a simple task to ease silently through the door. He could choke her unconscious, gag and take her with him, wrapped in a blanket. There were plenty of handholds on the building to carry her down over his shoulder.

But this is not Paris, he reminded himself. It would be a simple abduction, yes. But even on a cold night like this, he'd likely be seen by someone. He did not have a wagon at the end of the alley. Then there was getting her through the gate over his shoulder... He would probably have to kill a sentry. And Lady de Chanaye would search for her relentlessly.

It could be done...but it is too risky, he decided.

The girl's body arched, explicit with orgasm, the expression on her face unmistakable.

His anger spiked again. The Night Butcher reached out and quietly tried the door handle. It didn't move. It was bolted from the inside. He could break it easily with just a shove, but then the maidservant returned, and behind her entered Lady de Chanaye. And *she* was carrying a small *pistol* in one hand!

He sidled back from the door and flattened himself against the side of the house. Heavier curtains were abruptly drawn across all the windows and the balcony door. Some heavy thing was shoved against the door with a thump. And while this was occurring, the room was filled with the sound of a female voice full of angry admonition.

Patience, he heard the voice from his dreams whisper. *And you can have them both at the same time.*

An appealing thought. But he still needed to learn who this girl was.

The next morning, Colbért entered the city through the east gate on the road from Quebec, disguised as a naval courier. The uniform gained him an immediate audience with Intendant Bigôt, who was *not* pleased by the military disguise and the unplanned appointment and said so when they were alone.

"Are you *mad*? Coming directly to my office dressed like a military courier! And without my permission? Taking the chance of being recognized! You could be hung for that disguise."

Colbért shrugged. "My disguise did not raise a single eyebrow, not even from your snide little Corsican sitting outside. I need information that cannot wait."

Bigôt saw a chance for recompense. "What type of information?"

"An identity. There is a young maiden staying with Lady de Chanaye. She may complicate my plans...*our* plans. I am confident you know who she is, yes?"

Intendant Bigôt squinted at the odd question. "The girl's name is Madeleine Louvet. She is sixteen and crossed in mid-September accompanied by"—Bigôt checked a document—"...accompanied by a René Cortois, a Benedictine monk, who is joining the Jesuit order here in Montréal. They are from Rouen. Your relatives, maybe?"

Colbért knew the name.

"Cortois, you say?" He leaned forward in his chair. "Why does the girl stay with Lady de Chanaye?"

Intendant Bigôt was irritated and dismissed the question with a wave of his hand.

"The girl likely comes from a family of influence who wish to see to her well-being. I'm sure Corrinne de Chanaye will attend to all her needs, in *all* things, and will expand the girl's education accordingly. Now, please tell me that's not all you wanted...that you did not chance ruining our plans just to learn a girl's name?"

"A family of influence? Then how did she end up living with Lady de Chanaye?"

"Archbishop Nicolet arranged for her to stay with our most famous courtesan."

"Archbishop Nicolet?" Colbért said, mildly surprised.

Intendant Bigôt suddenly sat up straight, as if the idea had just occurred to him. "Would it be possible for you to arrange for the archbishop's demise?"

For a moment Colbért stared at the man in disbelief. "Maybe you would have me slay the Governor too."

The sarcasm was lost on Bigôt, who squinted, pursed his lips, and looked up at the ceiling to consider.

"Uh...no," he answered after a thoughtful few seconds. "He's leaving soon. No advantage to it. But the archbishop is now accusing me publically of corruption with the army. It's becoming a great nuisance. So, it is possible, yes?"

You are *fucking corrupt*, Colbért thought. *And why should I care?*

He closed his eyes and massaged the top of his nose with a thumb and forefinger to try and suppress the headache gathering there. *People here contemplate murders like eating morning biscuits. I guess I should be pleased.*

"I will pay you, of course."

"No, Monsieur Intendant. It is not possible. Surely you have other confederates to employ in this regard."

"I need discretion. Someone like *you*."

"Like *me*?"

It occurred to Colbért what the intendant really wanted: a way of covering up their association by blaming him for the murder of the archbishop, which would also provide a convenient reason for the intendant to order his death. "Well, Monsieur Intendant, I have put *your* name back on the list," he said quickly and without thinking.

"What list?"

Colbért stood up to leave and shook his aching head wearily.

"I have made lists. I have too much to do and not much time."

CHAPTER 29
MONTRÉAL
OCTOBER 1754
The Favorite Bastard

Corrinne read the dossier on Charles VanderMeer while sitting in her carriage at the back of the Terrain des Jésuites. She was early for her appointment with Archbishop Nicolet and was now contemplating an alternate plan to prevent Intendant Bigôt from seizing any of her ships. It was Financier Machault's idea added at the end of his final letter concerning the Marquis de Propei. He recommended she talk with this artist, without explanation, except for the subject.

About ships, of all topics?

But if Machault thought this a prudent discussion, that was good enough for her.

Every year, Lady de Chanaye received dozens of dossiers, from paid agents in France, on visiting members of the aristocracy, high-ranking military officers, wealthy merchants or other persons of influence. It detailed their proclivities for vice, social status, wealth, and abilities for influence, which she studied to assess potential *opportunities*. Some dossiers arrived on the same ship with the person, some many months later. The dossier on the Dutch artist was delivered in a standard pouch of missives the day he arrived in New France. She had not read it before simply because she did not think he was that important. He was just a painter for the royal court; a maker of portraits. As she read the information on this man, she realized what a mistake that presumption had been.

Another excellent example of the many poor decisions I've made this year.

Not only was Charles VanderMeer important, he was *very* important... important enough to build an even better strategy around, as Financier Machault hinted in his recent letter. If the artist would cooperate, of course. That might be a challenge based on what she was reading.

I cannot believe he never flaunts who he is, she thought after reading the first few lines of information. *He is a bastard, but still.*

CHARLES VANDERMEER

LINEAGE:

FATHER: *Louis Ernest of Brunswick-Lüneburg-Bevern, the Duke of Brunswick-Wolfenbüttel.*
Captain-General of the Netherland armies.
Primary advisor to Anne, Queen Mother to the next King, William V, and the solitary Queen Regent of the Netherlands until her son comes of age, a boy who purportedly considers Louis Ernest his second father. If anything happens to the Queen Regent, it is anticipated Louis Ernest will become the next Regent of the Netherlands.

MOTHER: *Unknown*

OTHER CHARACTERISTICS: *He has no distinctive vices, prefers women, but does not pursue them vigorously, and remains unmarried. Considered to be the favorite bastard of all Louis Ernest's bastards, ostensibly because he never presses his father for any favors, writes him regularly and reports on rumors he overhears concerning the court of King Louie. You may antici-pate he will write the Duke of Brunswick whenever he learns something of interest about New France, and certainly about you.*

He is not considered ambitious…is scholarly, pedantic, educated in all the sciences, philosophy, and astronomy. … He is a reputable gem mer-chant and designer, highly respected, and an accomplished painter, which appears to be his passion. Has amassed dozens of books on history and the chronicles of disposition for family crown jewels, dating back almost to the Roman Empire. He takes these valuable tomes with him everywhere he goes, so anticipate he will set up a library of sorts somewhere. … He is genuinely polite, does not flatter dishonestly, and is in great demand by the various crown families for painting portraits, and, of course, his current commission is making paintings of New France for King Louie.

"Extraordinary," she whispered.

With this summary, several new ideas rushed to Corrinne's mind. She now understood exactly what Financier Machault was suggesting. From discussions with Archbishop Nicolet and the Governor, she knew the Netherlands would remain neutral in the coming war between France and England. There was great profit in neutrality during times of war. And the enormous wealth of the Dutch East India Company, ergo the banks, made the Dutch the most powerful bankers in the world. And they had a global-trading fleet, with many more ships than the English, possibly twice as many, or so contended her smuggling partners in Boston and New York.

From them, Corrinne learned that real wealth was directly related to the number of ships a trading company owned, much more than the preferred cargo they transported, which varied in value.

Intendant Bigôt was scheming to seize her ships. He would probably try to do it when the Governor went back to Quebec for the winter months. So she'd left them anchored in Quebec to await their final cargoes of the year, instead of bringing them upriver. But even that precaution provided only temporary safety.

Monsieur VanderMeer could offer a perfect solution to that problem.

He may not be corruptible by sex, she mused further. *But he is educated. We must have something in common, some way to influence him. André Nicolet has made use of him in the past. Maybe he can suggest something.*

Minutes later, she stood before Father Tinian's desk, carrying the flat banking valise she'd pulled from a secret underground vault beneath the Dunemoore warehouse outside the city. She stared invitingly at the priest, who grew uncomfortable under her gaze. He was sweating.

"My lady, would you care to sit down?" He coughed lightly then gestured. "The archbishop should be available soon."

Corrinne did as he suggested and began thinking of other ways to tease him when he coughed again. His cough sounded wet. Concerned, she rose from her chair, went over, and placed her hand on his forehead. His skin was very, very hot.

"What are you—?"

"Father Tinian, how long have you been sick like this?"

"A few days, my lady. It's nothing."

"Vomiting? Running bowels? Tell me!"

"Well, yes. But I can still—"

"Nonsense. You are very ill. Do you know Doctor La Galissonière?"

"He is the physician to Governor Duquesne …?"

"Yes, well, he is also my physician."

She took his scribing pen, inkwell, and a blank piece of paper, wrote half a page, signed and folded it up.

"Take this, go down to my carriage. Tell the driver I want him to escort you to see Doctor La Galissonière at the Hotel Dieu."

"But, my lady, I have duties …"

"Do it now, Father, or I will invent a story to the archbishop that you opened the front of my dress." She began to unbutton it as she talked. "Doctor La Galissonière will give you medicine. Then go to bed." Impulsively, she took his hand and pushed it inside her dress against her naked breast and found that the warmth of his hand actually felt rather pleasant. "There, that should give you something to dream about at least. Now go!"

Minutes later, André Nicolet opened his office door when Father Tinian did not answer his call and found the anteroom empty except for a smiling Lady de Chanaye.

"Umm, hello…where is Father Tinian?"

"He was coughing and sick with fever. He worried he may infect you too and asked me if I thought you would mind if he left. I told him absolutely not. That he should go to bed directly. That was the right thing to do, yes?"

Archbishop Nicolet tilted his head and smiled wryly. "I must presume it was." He gestured for her to enter. "You were in a hurry for this meeting."

She entered and seated herself before his desk, instead of taking a chair by the window.

"I gather this is to be something official?"

Lady de Chanaye gazed fondly around the office, at the shelf upon shelf of books she loved so much. Her countenance softened as she looked at him.

"This is my favorite room in the entire city," she said wistfully.

The Jesuit's brow wrinkled. "Is something wrong?"

"Do you mind if I call you André? Just for today? As my surrogate father, my mentor, and confidante?"

"Oh, no," the archbishop groaned. "There *is* something wrong."

She took a deep breath. "I will be leaving New France soon, before November, if it's possible. And I will not be returning."

"What? What do you mean? Would this be permanent?"

"I have several things to reveal to you." She opened the valise and pulled out some scrolled papers. "Some information concerning my past. Some things dear to me I want you to have as a gift. Some things I beseech you to sign. Some new documents to share. And other private matters, which I will explain further."

She paused, to give him a chance to say something, her expression somber.

"My God...you *are* serious!"

Their discussion lasted most of that morning.

Colbért's dreams steadily worsened, becoming more vivid, with his sleep at night interrupted so often he'd taken to sleeping more during the day. From the beginning, any visit from the *voice* had been terrifying, but now the punishing, daily occurrence had a certain consistency. He had gotten used to its presence and knew what to expect. He could deal with it. After all, he was still alive and physically unharmed. But he did not dismiss its fearsome menace. Somehow, the *voice* could create intense pain in his head, and he was not sure how far that could be taken. The very notion of this other-world spirit had been hard for him to accept as real, but Colbért's world was already a perverse and twisted place of pain and misery. And in that vein, this *voice,* this *messenger,* had not taught him anything new. But the *thing* had changed well beyond its original presence of scratchy whispers, evolving into a shapeless black form that would press to within inches of his face, a sooty cloud, emitting heat, as if he stood in front of an open door to a kiln. He would usually bolt awake with that experience, covered in sweat and exhausted. The message itself had also changed since his return to Montréal, becoming enigmatic, more insistent: *Find the box… kill the boy*! And this was repeated over and over. The boy, he assumed, was Henri Gerrard, but the box was something new. What *box*?

All during the day, he suffered from dull, persistent headaches. Bearable, but he could not get used to them; the pain sometimes pulsing, moving to different areas of his head, as if someone were stabbing him randomly with a pointed object. He sought relief from the few physicians Montréal could offer, but they did little more than heat a watery mix of gritty powders made from pulverized tree barks for him to drink, which never worked. And these reputed medicines were concoctions of the local savages, no less!

Waiting for Philippe Gerrard to arrive in Montréal was worse than when he waited for him at Fort Le Boeuf. Singing Owl had provided another girl at his request, but she was too young and died too quickly, leaving him more restless and unsatisfied than before.

One morning, Intendant Bigôt sent a message to attend his office. The weasel-looking official had nothing new to offer regarding Philippe Gerrard, except that Snow Hair, as the Indians referred to him, had finally arrived at Fort Niagara with his Indian wife and was planning to come to Montréal without delay.

Good. He's taken the bait.

Then to Colbért's surprise, the intendant handed over a letter clearly addressed to Gaspard de Propei that had arrived in the latest dispatch pouch. It was from the Marquis de Propei. Of course, the thick wax seal on the letter had been broken, something the Marquis had told Gaspard to expect.

Colbért unfolded the three-page missive. His mustache curled above his smile. "It must have proved intriguing reading for someone."

The pages were nothing more than a long series of numbers, a cipher.

"Why would the Marquis use such a secretive device to send you a communication, when hostilities with the English become more blatant and deadly with every passing day? Shall I treat you as a spy, Monsieur?"

Colbért smirked at Bigôt's irritated tone and shrugged. "I am as surprised as you. I had no anticipation of this."

"But you can decipher it, yes?"

"I don't know," he replied in a rare moment of honesty. "But I promise to tell you what it says…if I can figure out what it says."

Before he had left France, Colbért had been given an obscure book from the Marquis' library, one of two that existed. Colbért had brought it with him to New France in his costume trunks without ever planning to use it. The Marquis retained the other. It was expressly provided for the purpose of deciphering coded missives. But the person must have the correct book.

"Well…if I have to rely on your natural intelligence to break a cipher, then you may leave." The frustrated intendant made an annoyed sweeping gesture with his hand.

Many men had their throats cut instantly for lesser insults. Colbért pondered whether there might be any advantage gained in puncturing one or both of the snide intendant's lungs with his stiletto and allowing the man to drown in his own blood while he watched. But he knew that would only provide a temporary amusement. And the repercussions might distract him from his greater goal. *I will let you live*, he thought, admiring his self-restraint. *A gesture of mercy! How noble of me. I am becoming more worthy of my new title.*

Sitting on a hardwood chair at a peasant table in his isolated farmhouse, the deceptively simple deciphering turned out to be more laborious than he would ever have guessed. It was easy to get the sequenced three-digit numbers confused; page number, word number, letter number, repeat. Many headaches later, he was done. And once finished, Colbért took further time to fashion a separate fiction with some plausible questions of business to give back to the intendant, if he was pressed about the contents again.

The first page of the letter contained a list of names of people he should kill; Philippe Malthais, Michelle, Henri, Archbishop Nicolet, the artist known as VanderMeer, the priest called René Cortois, and a woman named Madeleine.

Seven people? Including the girl living with Lady de Chanaye? The Marquis must think I employ assistants.

The reason for the last two names was a mystery to him until he finished deciphering the rest of the letter. It recounted Madeleine's escape from Rouen assisted by Father Cortois, who was further assisted by Archbishop Nicolet, and explained a certain relationship Madeleine allegedly had with Philippe Malthais' son, Henri. It was too many people to kill. Too much risk and too little time to make his retreat, all while having to locate a ship for a winter crossing back to France. He decided to contain his attention to Philippe and Henri first, then Michelle, if presented the opportunity. They would be his priority, since, at the beginning of this business, the Marquis claimed that would be enough to eliminate any threat to him as the legitimate heir to the marquisate. The last part of the letter added more information about Charles VanderMeer, that this artist possessed an object of extraordinary value, and he should do whatever was possible to obtain it and bring it with him back to France.

"What! Fucking! Object!" he shouted at the letter after decoding that sentence. *Wait...maybe it's the box the voice is always ranting about?* But then again—"What! Fucking! Box!" Even if these objects were the same, he would have to break into the artist's loft, locate some kind of *box*, probably do it all in the dark, and kill the artist too. It might get messy. *And it's not as if there are no magistrates at all here in New France.* And what size was the box? Hopefully it wasn't a coffin. He would have to make an escape plan after all of these killings, one which would get him to Quebec the fastest way possible. And it was still too many people. *I cannot eliminate all of them in one day!* Because of the *voice*'s obsession with a certain box that he now suspected the artist to hold, Colbért decided to make killing VanderMeer the third task, behind the deaths of Philippe and Henri...*Or should it be the fourth, after Michelle? Or should VanderMeer have the greater focus?*

And it suddenly occurred to him, the *voice* gave no indication that the continuation of his own life was of any importance after he had completed these tasks.

His head ached.

CHAPTER 31
MONTRÉAL
OCTOBER 1754
Daeniel's Curse

Henri had found the two-week journey from Fort Niagara exhausting, physically and emotionally. Okeanneh's death had depressed his spirit before the march began. Bad as he felt, his pain could not compare with that of his father's. The terrible sound of Philippe's wails and screams of anguish was something Henri would never forget. They'd buried Okeanneh the next morning, to the south of the fort, beneath the shade of a chestnut tree near Chittaqua's mound. Nearly everyone from the fort, save for a few soldiers on the walls, was present. The next day, his father's sobbing anger from the day before was replaced by a sullen, dull-eyed silence. When they pushed out on the bateaux from Fort Niagara, he wasn't much better; a movement of muscle, driven in one direction. During the first six days, Philippe did only what Pierre or Michelle asked him to do and not much else.

"He just stares. What can I do for him?" Henri asked his mother.

"Sit by him when he sits. His soul draws comfort when you and Anamosa are near. Don't bother him with any questions, and don't expect him to talk to you."

"Philippe blames himself for Okeanneh's death," Pierre added.

"But it's not his fault," Henri argued.

"He loved Okeanneh. His sadness is deep," his mother replied.

"I don't understand."

"A harsh judge lives inside your father, laddie."

"I am praying for him, that God will heal his spirit," Michelle said.

Pierre frowned. When Michelle was out of earshot, he whispered to Henri. "Your father will be healed when the bastard responsible for Okeanneh's death has paid for it with his life. And ya' and I are going to help him find the *shérif*."

The Scotsman was almost taken aback by the hard expression that came so quickly and easily to Henri's face.

"And I will take his scalp."

"Amen, laddie. We'll dah' it together. But dinnah' talk aboot this with your mother. She might nah' understand the need for this type o' justice."

During the journey, when they'd camp at night, Henri often heard his father cry out or weep in his sleep. And each time, his mother would rise from her blankets and cradle Philippe's head in her arms and speak to him in whispers, consoling him until the nightmares passed.

With the exception of a few words of direction, Philippe Gerrard's silence lasted the entire journey to Montréal, from canoe, to wagon, and now on foot. The journey to Montréal was almost over. The familiar sights and sounds of the Lachine portage appeared to intrude on Philippe's depression in a positive way.

He'd had another dream about Okeanneh the night before, as he did almost every night. But this time, the dream was not one of the nightmares where Okeanneh was killed by an evil, faceless, dark creature, and cruelly so, before Philippe could save her, and after being mutilated, dying broken and bleeding in his arms, saying his name over and over. The guilt Philippe would feel at that point was so overwhelming he'd cry out and wake up. But freedom of sleep gave him no relief. He would lie awake the rest of the night, reliving each brutal image again and again.

But the dream of the night before was different. It started as he lay on his back, waiting for sleep, gazing up at the stars on the cold, moonless night. The stars were spread like powder across the night sky; some large, some small, but a large quantity directly above him seemed to sparkle more than the others, drawing his eyes. The longer he stared at them, the more familiar they became; a shape he recognized. All at once the face and body of a woman took form in his mind.

"Okeanneh," he whispered with ache and longing.

The formation of stars descended slowly to settle upon him like an eerie blanket. His entire body tingled beneath the sparkling sensations. He reached out to the lights with his arms. They swirled around him like a gentle wind. His senses were saturated with the memory of her smell, her taste, the light fluttering touch of her fingers. They made love like they always made love, and this time when he cried out, it was from pleasure. He awoke abruptly to see a faint image hanging in the air above him, outlined by stars.

"Okeanneh," he sobbed in a whisper. He wanted it to be true.

A morning fog was burgeoning. The stars were slowly becoming obscured.

Cou ti si mah, it said with a smile.

"No. Don't go!" Philippe reached up to touch her. His hands tingled, but he grasped only cold, wet air. "I miss you so," he whispered.

Take care of Anamosa, it said. *Promise me.*

"I promise."

The image shimmered, slowly fading among the morning mists.

"Please…please don't go!"

Remember your promise. Cou ti si mah.

And the dream was gone. He lay awake in the dark of the early morning, desperately trying to remember everything, to make it real, to make it last. The fog hid the stars from his sight, there was nothing to reinforce what he had seen. The more he tried to remember, the more the dream dissipated. Doubt began to intrude, pushing back the wondrous images, the sensations. It was after all, just a dream. Eventually all he could remember were the words of the promise.

Cou ti si mah. Take care of Anamosa.

"That was real," he assured himself with a whisper.

It was the final mile before they entered the warehouse area adjoining Montréal's boat landing on the Saint Lawrence River, almost midday. Carrying backpacks, Philippe, Henri, and Anamosa walked among the carters and *voyageurs,* which were driving six wagonloads of Dunemoore Company furs. Pierre Dunemoore and Michelle shared the back of the lead wagon. The great quantity of furs they were carrying made Pierre happy. The threat of war aside, and although their personal losses had been great and painful, it had been a good season for their business, maybe the best one yet. This would be the final load delivered to Montréal for the year. Collected from fur traders in every part of New France, the furs were carried by canoe, wagon, or by foot to the Lachine rapids collection camp for final wagon transport to Montréal. Once in the company warehouse, the furs would quickly be sorted for quality, cleansed of any vermin, trimmed, and baled for transport to France, carried by cargo sloop to Quebec where the *Ile Royale* and the

Falcon Queen were anchored, waiting to be loaded.

"We beat tha' snows. At least the winter cooperated."

From the back of the lead fur wagon Pierre Dunemoore winked at Henri who was walking behind it on foot. "We'll reach the warehouses anytime now, laddie."

Henri smiled weakly. He was holding Anamosa's hand. Since her mother's death, she rarely strayed more than a few paces from him.

As more familiar sights came into view, Philippe recalled the beautiful apparition of his dead wife and the promise he'd made. And he had to think more about Michelle and Henri's safety too.

There is much to do before they are truly safe, he thought. *Many in Montréal will work against me. I must act with speed and find the shérif.*

Philippe inhaled deeply as if he'd not smelled the fresh air since leaving Fort Niagara. He saw a shadow moving rapidly across the ground toward him. He looked up in time to see it.

Skrieeee!

The huge bird swooped by them only a few feet above their heads.

"Look, Pierre!" Henri shouted. "It's Chittaqua's eagle!"

The caravan of wagons and walkers came to a halt to watch the beautiful animal soar and dive back and forth between the river and the trees. Its wingspan was six feet.

"Bloody...I thin' ya' are right," Pierre remarked, smiling a little.

The bird turned and glided toward the caravan again. The carters cheered. Henri thought the eagle looked directly at him as it flew overhead to disappear above the trees.

Henri had seen this bird at the great falls. *If Chittaqua's spirit is with us, then maybe Roland's is too.* Henri felt better than he had in weeks. He turned to say something to Pierre when he noticed his father watching the white eagle, a far-away stare in his eyes.

"It's the ghost eagle," Philippe said, feeling rejuvenated at the sight. "Don't stop! Keep moving," he shouted to the drivers. "These wagons have to be unloaded at the warehouse before nightfall."

"Well, helloo' tah' ya', laddie!" Pierre said after he had finished gaping. "It's nice tah' see ya' takin' an interest."

"I think the leaves will finish changing color within the week."

"Are we tah' have an actual conversation then?"

Philippe noticed the looks of happy surprise on the faces of Michelle, Henri, and Pierre and shrugged. It was one of those blue-sky days that seemed to guarantee nothing could go wrong, except Philippe knew better.

"It's the air. It smells sweet. Unusual for October."

"Aye, laddie, tha' it does."

The wagons began to move more quickly.

"Have you seen the ghost eagle before?" Henri asked.

"Yes, at the falls. Don't you remember?'

"Yes, but I mean before the falls."

"I've seen it four or five times." Philippe noticed Michelle watching him carefully. Her face was pale. "You seem to be having trouble keeping down your food. Are you sick?"

Michelle stiffened, desperate to keep her condition a secret from Philippe. She stammered an answer. "Y-yes, I am...I'm not sleeping well and...and my stomach is roiled from the camp food."

"No one else is sick. Maybe we should have a doctor in Montréal—"

"No, no doctors will be necessary," Michelle interjected quickly. "I will feel better once I enter a, uh, convent...as soon as we get to the city."

"Oh, so we are back tah' a convent then?"

Pierre Dunemoore had also noticed Michelle's sickness, which seemed to him to be worse in the morning. He had his suspicions about what this boded, but certainly didn't want Philippe to start speculating. Not now. Not after everything else that had happened. He would change the subject.

"Philippe, since we're gonna' arrive soon, wha' aboot Corrinne's warning?"

A missive from Corrinne de Chanaye had been delivered to Philippe and Pierre the night before in a wax-sealed envelope. She implored them, without much explanation, not to come within the walls of Montréal.

Philippe.

Intendant Bigôt intends to arrest you if you enter Montréal. It is imperative you, Pierre, and I confer in secrecy. I will come to the warehouse after dark.

Corrinne

It was her beautiful script, but it had been written in haste. Philippe expected that the warrant for his arrest was to be used against him. No matter. He could elude the city gendarmerie without too much effort. Maybe his conspicuous arrival might help to draw Gaspard de Propei into the open.

"Let's see what happens once we reach the warehouse."

As the train of wagons entered the street in front of the Dunemoore Company warehouse, Philippe watched carefully but did not see any city guards lingering nearby. He turned his attention to the bridge and city gate at the end of the street. The sentries were posted but were resting, bored with their watch. The usual flow of commerce passed back and forth through the gate. He counted seventeen river sloops at anchor in the harbor, waiting to transport the final shipments of furs and people to Quebec before winter.

The wagons stopped in front of the main doors of the company warehouse. Laborers amassed as the warehouse cargo masters began shouting orders.

"Monsieur?"

Philippe looked back at Henri.

"Where will Anamosa and I be staying?"

"Pierre?"

The Scotsman jerked a thumb at the inn behind them. "I assume the Palais de Voyageur."

Philippe noticed two men outside of the inn's front door. They stood in the street watching the wagons. Upon seeing Philippe's sudden interest in them, they walked off toward the city gates in a hurry.

"Did you see those two?"

"Aye. What now?" Pierre said.

People exited the Palais de Voyageur and lounged against the building, idly observing the burgeoning activity around the wagons with interest.

"We'll go to Corrinne's city house," Philippe said. "It'll be safer there."

"*Inside* the walls?" Pierre responded with surprise.

"Michelle, Henri, and Anamosa, at least. And then I'll escort Michelle to a convent. Might as well do it right away before word spreads too far. Juniata and Chesanin can stay with you. They are unknown to Intendant Bigôt and safer here."

Corrinne's house? Henri gripped Anamosa's hand and smiled at her reassuringly.

"Pierre, it might be better if you stay here too. I'll bring Corrinne back with me later. We can then sort out the news of the day and decide what to do next. What do you think?"

"Aye, but keep your eyes moving aboot ya' in the city, laddie," Pierre warned. "I'll collect the company's *coureurs de bois* here at the warehouse in case ya' need help."

The warehouse senior clerk approached.

"Monsieur Dunemoore! Monsieur Gerrard! Welcome home."

"I am going into the city."

"A carriage?"

"No. I prefer my whereabouts remain confidential. Monsieur Dunemoore can answer all your questions."

Philippe helped Michelle down from the wagon. He decided they would walk across the city to Corrinne's house. It would only take thirty minutes and would be much less conspicuous than a wagon or carriage. He gestured Michelle and Henri to the side of the street opposite the warehouse and quickly described Montréal's two main streets and the direction they were going once inside the gates and the location of Corrinne's city house.

"Follow close behind me," he told them. "But not close enough to give the impression we're together. If I am challenged by anyone, do *not* stop. I will probably run to avoid them and draw them away from you. Go directly to Lady de Chanaye's house. Michelle, if I cannot do it, Corrinne will see you safely to a convent. Henri, stay at the house with Anamosa until Pierre comes. All right? Don't worry too much. It's me they want and they will not catch me," he smiled briefly to reassure them. "You'll be safe. This is just a precaution. Chances are nothing will happen."

Philippe led them by the lethargic sentries at the river gate who did not bother to look at them. It was now late in October, and the citizens of Montréal were in a hurry to complete their business in preparation for winter before the snows descended. The city streets were jammed with people, farmers, *coureurs de bois*, traders, *voyageurs*, carters, buyers and sellers of every kind, all jostling one another, each making some type of noise.

They turned right on the Rue Saint-Paul. This street teemed with additional stone masons and carpenters hard at work all along the walls. The breastworks had been augmented with more stone and mortar. Dozens of

new cannon were being hoisted with block and tackle to the recently rein-
forced gun emplacements. Street vendors promoted their wares, hailing the
laborers and passersby, selling hot tea, sausages, salted cod, fresh-baked
bread, and confections. A pair of gendarmes walked leisurely among the
people, noise, and bustle. Wagons full of farm produce headed down the
street, in the opposite direction, toward the market square. Philippe did not
pause. As he expected, the citizens of Montréal paid little heed to them as
they walked.

But to Anamosa, the sights and sounds of the white man's village were
overwhelming. Her huge blue eyes gawked at all the wonders. She gripped
Henri's hand tightly.

"*Ahh-ree?*" she said in a nervous voice.

Henri swung her up and placed her on his shoulders. "It's all right.
I've got you."

The crowds began to thin as they moved beyond the artisan district to
the eastern end of the city where the larger homes and apartments began.
Philippe waited till they'd passed the Hotel Dieu, a hospital, before crossing the street to the other side. Upon reaching Corrinne's house, Philippe
gestured for them to wait on the street. He paused at the door.

The chamberlain heard repeated loud taps of the front door's brass
clapper. *The knock of a man in a hurry,* the old gentleman presumed. He
hurried from the *cuisine* and opened the door to see the weathered face of
a *coureur de bois*.

"May I help you, Monsieur?"

The weary traveler smiled weakly. "Have I changed so much?"

The chamberlain blinked at hearing the familiar voice. "Monsieur Gerrard?" He opened the door further. "Monsieur Gerrard!"

"*Bonjour,* master chamberlain."

The chamberlain looked with amazement as Philippe Gerrard moved
into the foyer, followed closely by a woman, a young lad, and a very young
girl. There was not much room to stand after he shut the door behind them.
The area was already crowded with wooden crates and trunks.

"Lady de Chanaye is not here. She had appointments. But I expect her
back at any time." The chamberlain recovered from the shock of seeing the
woodsman. "It is so *good* to see you, Monsieur Gerrard," he said, genuinely
pleased. "The lady will be delighted …"

"Who's there?" A maid stood at the bottom of the stairs. "Philippe?" she asked cautiously.

Philippe gave a courtly bow. "Mistress Mathilde."

Mathilde gasped. She had recognized the voice. *But the face?*

"Monsieur Gerrard?"

"*Oui*, Mademoiselle. In the flesh."

"Philippe!" She beamed and bounded into his arms, kissing his cheeks again and again. He felt hard, sinewy, callused. "Oh, Monsieur." She lightly touched his hair, beard, and scars with concern. She turned to the others. "And who do we have here?"

Philippe put his arm around Michelle. "This is Michelle. And this is her son—our son, Henri. And this pretty one is Anamosa. She is Okeanneh's daughter," he added the last somberly.

"*Bonjour*, Sister Michelle, Henri. Welcome, all of you, to Montréal."

Mathilde gazed at Henri as if he were a grandchild of hers. Already, there was a hint of the man Henri would become in his eyes, his posture, his serious, direct gaze. And she was transfixed by the little girl's blue eyes peeking at her from behind Henri's waist.

Mathilde stooped and smiled warmly. "Oh, my little *chéri*. Come to me." She held out her arms.

Anamosa looked up at Henri. He smiled and nodded. She stepped forward cautiously and allowed the big white woman to hug her. *She smells good*, Anamosa thought.

Philippe turned to the chamberlain. "I must leave them here with you. I am taking Michelle to the convent, and then I've appointments of my own to keep. Monsieur Dunemoore is staying for now at the warehouse."

"But of course everyone can stay, Monsieur," the chamberlain responded without hesitation.

"Philippe," Michelle interjected.

"What?"

"I've changed my mind…I'm not going to a convent. I would prefer to stay here, if I may?" She avoided Philippe's gaze and looked at Mathilde, who nodded.

"*Mais bien sûr, Mademoiselle.*"

Philippe was surprised, but decided this would make things much easier.

"As you wish. You will be safe here until I come back."

"Where do you go?" Henri asked. He did not want to be alone in this strange place.

There were men Philippe knew, men who lived on the waterfront and the edges of the city, men who were friends to no one but themselves. But information and loyalty could be bought for the right price. If Gaspard de Propei was lurking somewhere close, as Philippe suspected, such men would know of it. And some of these men owed him life debts. He was anxious to talk with Corrinne too, but she wasn't here and he couldn't wait. He'd been seen. Once the hunt began, there would be little time for anything else; his prey would be hunting too.

"I'm keeping my promise to Chittaqua."

"But what if something happens? What if you do not come back for some reason?"

"It will be all right, young sir," the chamberlain assured quickly. "Mathilde can show you to a large room where all of you can rest from your journey. I will arrange for some food and drink."

Philippe nodded at Michelle and Henri. "See? This is good. This house is well guarded. If something happens, the chamberlain will help get you back to the warehouse. But for now, this is the safest place for all of you. It will be all right. I will not be gone long."

"This way, please." The chamberlain gestured.

"Come. The library is warm and has comfortable chairs." Mathilde ushered them down the hallway.

Philippe spoke to chamberlain in a quiet voice. "We were seen arriving at the warehouse. The intendant will be alerted soon, if not already. We came into the city on foot. I think unnoticed. Are Lady de Chanaye's footmen nearby?"

"*Oui,* Monsieur. Three of them stay in the next apartment by the garden."

Philippe knew these bodyguards; they were well-paid swords and very capable.

"Have them posted near the entrances. Be wary, sir, of *any* strangers who come to the door. There are people about the city who wish us harm. Arrange an escape for them in case the gendarmes come. And the warehouse will *not* be the safest place."

The chamberlain nodded solemnly. "I know a safe haven for them not too far away."

"Do you know an artist in the city named Charles VanderMeer, and where he lives?"

"Yes, Monsieur, I've met the man once, but I do not know exactly where he keeps his studio. The Rue Notre-Dame, I presume. But Lady de Chanaye will know the artist's whereabouts. You should wait ..."

"I cannot wait."

Philippe left Corrinne's house and walked back down the Rue Saint-Paul. He asked the nearest stonemasons working on the walls if they could direct him to the dwelling of Charles VanderMeer, presuming the artisans knew one another. They did. He went back to the river gate, turned right, and walked past the open city market. The delicious smells and aromas from braziers sizzling with so many different foods made his stomach growl, a reminder he'd not eaten anything since the night before. But he did not stop. He turned right again on the Rue Notre-Dame, crossed one more street, and started counting buildings.

One, two, three.

Philippe paused in front of a doorway. On the street, he saw two armed soldiers lounging against a wagon that was being loaded with wood shipping crates of various sizes. Many of the boxes were three to four feet per side and only six inches thick. The work crew stacking the crates in the wagon handled them very carefully.

Philippe and the soldiers regarded each other.

"Why soldiers?" Philippe asked.

One of the soldiers frowned. "Does that bother you?"

"No."

A scowling army sergeant stepped out of the open door to the apartment. The sergeant eyed the *coureur de bois'* grimy clothing. "Who are you, Monsieur?"

"Claude Guillot of les Négociants Dunemoore. I am here to call on Monsieur VanderMeer."

"Is he expecting you?"

Philippe shook his head. "No. I've just returned from scouting duties for Colonel Contrecoeur and the army at Fort Duquesne."

The sergeant understood the implication. "You know Colonel Contrecoeur, eh? Well, we are Governor Duquesne's personal guard. Very well, Monsieur. Enter and make your call."

"What's in these crates?"

"Paintings and portraits bound for King Louie. My orders are to guard the King's property, as you might suspect. We can't have the savages stealing the King's pictures and hanging them in their round lodges, can we? I trust you're not here to have your portrait done? Monsieur VanderMeer is bound for France soon."

Philippe shook his head again. He stepped around the workers and entered the foyer of the building. He found three men standing over another, who was head down inside a trunk arranging the things inside.

"Pardon me."

The man straightened and turned.

Seeing Philippe, the man greeted politely, "Monsieur, a moment please. Yes, this one is ready," he told the soldiers gathered around. "Please try to be more careful." The artist wiped his brow with the back of one hand. He wondered if any of the crude laborers could appreciate how precious this cargo was. "Sergeant," he called.

The unhappy soldier stuck his head inside the door.

"When that trunk is loaded, you can order this wagon's cargo taken out to one of the Governor's sloops. The remaining items here are personal, and amount to only half a load. We can finish that the day I sail."

The sergeant smiled with relief.

"Very good, Monsieur."

VanderMeer turned to address the stranger properly. "Excuse my rudeness, Monsieur …?"

"Philippe Gerrard."

"Monsieur Gerrard!" VanderMeer's mouth opened wide with surprise. He eyes glanced down at the man's hands for a moment, taking note of the infamous ring. "You're the *coureur de bois* from Fort Niagara! The one Chittaqua talked about. He said you would come…and here you are! Remarkable man, Chittaqua."

"You *knew* Chittaqua?"

The artist's expression turned grave. "Come, come up to my studio. I've much to share with you, and I'm not certain where to begin."

The room above the ground floor bedroom and *cuisine* was at the top of a long, steep stairway. It was one large room with three tall windows that permitted plenty of sunlight. It was now fairly empty of the artist's work. In the middle, there stood a six-foot round table splotched liberally with different colored paints and four equally splattered wooden chairs. A conspicuous cushioned chair was off in one corner with a table next to it. Every flat surface in the room had candles with the remains of melted wax gluing down the holders.

The artist threw a large square of clean, white canvas over the table and quickly wiped down the wooden chair seats.

"They are all dry. Please. Sit."

A maid appeared at the top of the stair.

"Ah, good. Bring us a pot of tea, cups, and some bread and cheese if there's any left." He turned to Philippe. "Chittaqua will be interested to hear about what I've learned. You too, for that matter. Very extraordinary. But extremely…disturbing, I'm afraid."

Before the artist could continue, Philippe said shortly, "I am sorry to tell you, Chittaqua is dead. I buried him at Fort Niagara."

The artist's face showed heartfelt regret. He sat down in a chair, took off his spectacles, and massaged the bridge of his nose.

"I am very, very sorry to hear that. May I ask how he died?"

"Shot in a skirmish while saving another man's life."

"Then please, forgive my impertinence in asking you more questions."

"Chittaqua is the reason I am here. I made him a promise to find you. Something to do with my ring." Philippe held up his hand, showing his ring. "Ask as many questions as you like."

VanderMeer pulled a small jeweler's loupe from his pocket.

"May I hold it?"

Shortly after midday, Lady de Chanaye returned from the Terrain de Jésuites. Her chamberlain met her in the foyer.

"Monsieur Gerrard has arrived," he said, then added with less enthusiasm. "But he left again, leaving Michelle, Henri, and a young Indian girl with us, even though I implored him to wait here until you returned."

Corrinne frowned at this, another of Philippe's many frustrating, impulsive decisions. Adding to that, Philippe had left his family here in her house. She was delighted they were safe, but meeting them would now have to wait. She had to find Philippe right away.

Archbishop Nicolet had agreed to help with all her plans. But that placed many events in motion, events that could not be stopped. Her planning had collapsed from weeks into days. There was much at risk.

No, everything *is at risk! Why did you not wait for me?* she fumed silently.

"Where did he go?"

"I think to see Monsieur VanderMeer."

She brightened. "Monsieur VanderMeer? The artist?"

The chamberlain nodded.

"Well, that's fortuitous, at least. I need to speak with this artist too." She didn't bother to go inside. "I will be back."

"But Mademoiselle? What do I tell the others?"

"Tell them I went to find Philippe."

Still clutching the banker's valise, Corrinne walked directly back to the carriage house a street away, her two footmen padding along behind her.

She pointed at one of them as she climbed back into the carriage. "Wait for me at the house. Follow the chamberlain's directions. And guard the doors!" The other climbed on the back of the carriage.

The coach clattered up a narrow side street and turned left on the broader thoroughfare of the Rue Notre-Dame.

Minutes later, the artist's loft resounded with the sounds of clopping hooves and the rattling harness of a horse and carriage coming to a stop on the street below.

Concerned the noise hinted at something more threatening, Philippe edged over to the window and looked down. A familiar figure was being helped down from a carriage.

"*Corrinne.*"

VanderMeer's head snapped up from his books. He had been comparing Philippe's ring to the images there.

"Corrinne de Chanaye? Lady de Chanaye is coming up here? To see me?"

They heard the quick tapping of shoes from someone hurrying up the stairs. Corrinne de Chanaye rushed into the studio loft with a flourish. Her anxious expression softened as soon as she saw Philippe. But her smile lasted only a moment; her happiness replaced by shock at seeing Philippe's gaunt figure and scarred face.

"Philippe?" she said in a hushed voice, full of concern. "God! Look at you!"

And then she ran to him. "Oh, thank you, thank you …" She hugged him tightly. She could smell the sweat and grime from his journey, an odor quick, rank, but oh, so wonderful. "You're really here…really, really here."

They clung to each other hungrily in a way they had not before. So much had changed in the last six months. There were no more pretenses between them. Philippe needed Corrinne's strength now as much as she had ever needed his. They were rooted together in New France. They'd shared an escape from Le Havre, endured the crossing, survived the dangers of assassination in this new world. Two allies, surrounded by enemies. And here they were again in a life-saving embrace. Their unswerving dependence and loyalty to one another was never stronger, or more evident to them both, than at this moment. No matter the threat or the danger, they had *this*. And whatever *this* was, it was palpable and binding.

They loosened their grip on each other enough to allow Corrinne a closer look at his sunburned face. "Oh, Philippe, what has the world done to you?" Her cool fingers tenderly traced his ropey white scars. She kissed his cheeks and forehead, and then his lips, lingering there.

When the storm of emotion passed, their practical natures took over. They separated a step, still holding hands, their expressions turning serious.

"Do you know where he is?" Philippe asked evenly.

Corrinne cleared her throat.

"He left the city more than two weeks ago in a river sloop bound for Quebec. I sent men after him. They all turned up dead on the river road with their genitals cut off and stuffed in their mouths. One of my clerks arrived yesterday from Quebec. The *shérif* never arrived. I've solicited my usual sources on the waterfront but no one admits to seeing him anywhere."

"He's still here." Philippe gestured. "He's hiding in or near the city somewhere. He's waiting for me."

Corrinne nodded slowly. "He's in league with Intendant Bigôt. If the intendant's gendarmes see you, you'll be arrested at once, maybe even shot. I'm certain he knows you've arrived. His spies have been lurking near the Palais de Voyageur for weeks. But I have eyes and ears too. If the *shérif* is within a mile of the city, someone will see him."

"If they haven't already, I'm not sure they will. He is an assassin first, beyond all other charades. He knows the art of disguise." He paused. "Bigôt's men saw me when the wagons pulled up to the warehouse today."

"Did you not get my warning?" His expression answered her question. "You were supposed to wait for me!" she scolded. "We have too many villains at large in Montréal and—" Seeing a tiny grin forming on his lips, her anger boiled further. "So I've said something funny?"

Philippe shook his head.

"No. You are magnificent. And I'm just glad we are on the same side. I left Michelle, Henri, and Anamosa at your house. I didn't want—"

A throat cleared loudly.

They turned.

Charles VanderMeer looked abashed at his interruption.

"Forgive me, my lady, Monsieur Gerrard," he spoke apologetically. "I should not be intruding on your privacy, but there is nowhere else for me to go."

"Monsieur VanderMeer," Corrinne greeted him warmly extending her hand. "You've given no offense."

"Mademoiselle." He bowed and touched his lips to her fingers. "I am honored by your visit, but a little bewildered. Why are you here?"

"Actually, Archbishop Nicolet told me to see you." This was not exactly true, so Corrinne quickly added, "But I was also seeking Philippe."

"Then, of course, I am delighted you came. But the archbishop? Why did he suggest you see me?"

Corrinne hesitated. It was a topic she'd rather not talk about in front of Philippe, not until she had a chance to explain it all to Pierre first. "It concerns a matter of commerce."

The artist looked befuddled. "Commerce?"

Philippe was impatient. "Corrinne, Monsieur VanderMeer is telling me a story about my family ring. This was a promise I made to Chittaqua before he died. I want to do it now, before we are assailed by other surprises."

"Please, sit, my lady," VanderMeer said. "You may find this history most compelling."

On a shelf near the hearth, a sturdy-looking pendulum clock announced the hour of one.

"That was made by Julien Le Roy, clockmaker for King Louie. A gift to me from the King. It's been cumbersome to pack and ship such a delicate instrument, and it took me a week to get it operating properly again once I arrived, but it has a marvelous movement and sound, does it not?"

"Master artist, I do not mean to be rude, but your clock has reminded me, that after you share the history of Philippe's ring, I am pressed to share your time to discuss another matter."

"Ah, yes. Well. I should finish discussing Philippe's ring, and then I will tell you about some writings in these two books. But first, Monsieur Gerrard, let me start by asking you a strange question I posed to Archbishop Nicolet several weeks ago. This question will sound eccentric, but I put it to you sincerely. In the last three months, have you suffered a pain-filled experience? One that probably happened at night and came upon you without warning, like you were attacked by someone using something sharp, a knife or a metal spike, but without any visible evidence of a perpetrator, and if there were witnesses present, they saw nothing. And did the sensation of this pain vanish instantly as long as that spot on your person was not touched in any manner?"

Philippe and Corrinne did not respond. They sat stunned by this question that described their experiences so precisely.

"Before you answer, let me share that this experience happened to me, only much more recently. In my case, it was my hands." VanderMeer held up his palms. "And afterwards, there were no wounds, no scars, and no crippling effects."

Philippe was about to admit that he had had such pains when Corrinne spoke first.

"I-I had that exact experience. I felt attacked one night, as if someone were stabbing me over and over in my neck and shoulders. It was the most frightening thing I've ever endured."

Philippe looked at Corrinne.

"You! This happened to you too? Three months ago, on the Niagara portage, on my way to Fort Presque Isle, I also had an intense stabbing sensation in the freshly healed wound of my broken leg." He looked at VanderMeer. "And like you said, the next day, it was like it had never happened at all. The army surgeon told me it was all a war memory. A deceit of the mind. But I assure you, this was no war memory. This was real."

"Monsieur Gerrard, in truth, I expected you to confess to this occurrence. But, my lady, I am totally perplexed this could have happened to you."

From what the artist had read in the histories, those with some connection to the four Great Houses from the legend were so inclined to be afflicted. Philippe had his ring connecting him to this dark mystery, the archbishop his crucifix...*but, Lady de Chanaye? Could she be connected to the woman Maive mentioned in the legends?*

"Oh, but it did," Corrinne affirmed.

"What are you not telling us?" Philippe pressed, suddenly suspicious.

"Monsieur, I am about to tell you more mystifying things, disturbing things. First, let me say Archbishop Nicolet has suffered the same experience of pain. And yes, my lady. I see the doubt on your face. But he *did*, and he will admit it to you...though privately, I suspect. And Monsieur Gerrard, I am a man of the natural sciences, mathematics, and philosophy, with a strong faith in God. I told Archbishop Nicolet the same thing before telling him what I am about to tell you, starting with the history of your ring. Look at the sigils on these pages. These are the coats of arms of four great houses, lords, and royal families who lived in northern France back in the tenth century."

Gong!

It was half past the hour of two.

VanderMeer was gratified. Fortunately, this man and women were both highly intelligent. Their discussion of almost two hours had been detailed, intense, and full of questions.

For every question Philippe asked, Corrinne asked at least three. And to VanderMeer's great surprise, she could read Latin fluently, the antiquated Frankish text, and even many of the Celtic phrases. What she could not read she would deduce a translation for him. And she could pronounce all of the words with a delightful accent.

No wonder Archbishop Nicolet spoke so highly of this lady, he thought. *And here I had presumed it was her redeeming physical qualities.*

"Philippe, if this is all true, I'm at a loss what to say. How can we be related to these old families? Well, you have a ring, but what of me? And what do we do now with that smelly pouch of dirt and bones?"

It was sitting nearby. She glanced at it nervously.

Philippe wasn't sure what to make of any of this. And, moreover, while greatly intriguing, he did not have time to discuss it.

"Monsieur VanderMeer, since Archbishop Nicolet trusts you, I will trust you to do what you think is best. There is a man here in the city, who intends to kill me, my family, likely Corrinne too. His name is Gaspard de Propei—"

"But I know this man," the artist interjected. "He is detestable. I painted his portrait for Archbishop Nicolet." He hurried across the room and searched through a pile of discarded flat canvases until he found the portrait from six months earlier. He held it before them; an arrogant, evil-looking personality in outlandish red clothing stared back.

Corrinne shuddered. "I only saw him behind a mask at a masquerade. But I remember those eyes. The entire face is worse than I imagined."

Philippe stared intently, committing every facial feature to memory.

"I was going to burn this, but you may take it to show others if it helps. As to your other question, my lady, what do we do with the bones? These relics must be sealed again in a tomb of some fashion. According to the legend, of which Bishop Brevelaer writes, the exact words of these rune texts must be repeated, and the bones entombed under the standing stone sigils of these great houses."

As far as he was concerned, Philippe had fulfilled Chittaqua's promise of finding and talking with Picture Maker. His thinking was back on the present.

"Master artist, this has all been fascinating, but I—we—have dangerous enemies who may walk up those stairs at any moment. So, the need for erecting standing stones is not prominent in my thinking."

VanderMeer brightened. "Oh, but I have already created a tomb of sorts, with the necessary standing stones."

Philippe paused. "What—?"

The artist went over to a large wooden box and, with some effort, dragged it away from the wall to the center of the loft. He lifted the heavy lid.

"There, you see? The carpenters who made this for me said they use this type of wood for cannon mounts. It is dense, cured oak, and strong. The seams in the box have been sealed with sailor's pitch. It is lined and sealed further with stone, granite on the bottom and limestone on the sides, each piece of which is carved with an image of a sigil from a Great House. I'm afraid I'm only an adequate sculptor, but I think the images are exact enough for our purpose."

"What are you proposing?" Corrinne asked. She, too, needed to return to more pressing matters. Namely, an issue of commerce, which also needed to be resolved today. But she felt grateful at having found the possible cause of that ghastly attack on her person months ago. This legend and its possible connection to Philippe and to herself had some hold on her, which she could not otherwise explain.

"We must place the relics in this box and pronounce the sealing… words." He decided not to say *hex*. "And I propose we do this tonight."

"Tonight? That's not possible. I will likely be involved in deadly affairs tonight, Monsieur. And these affairs are much more important than any of this…occult history. Besides, what you propose sounds like some sort of devil's ceremony."

Philippe rose from his chair.

"Wait, Philippe!" Corrinne urged and grabbed his hand. "Please!" She felt this to be very important.

VanderMeer sighed and removed his spectacles.

"Monsieur Gerrard, my skepticism about this was no less than yours, and no less than that of the archbishop's. But the archbishop has already agreed to conduct this, *ritual*, for lack of a better word, as soon as I am ready. It must be done after sunset. Today, that will occur at half past the hour of six. So I suggest we gather here in my loft, at the hour of seven. This can all be done in less than thirty minutes, I think."

Philippe frowned. "Archbishop Nicolet agreed to this?"

The archbishop had not mentioned any of what the artist had revealed. But Corrinne kept that to herself.

"Archbishop Nicolet encouraged me to see Monsieur VanderMeer with great urgency." Which had only been after she had convinced the Jesuit of the necessity of doing so in regards to another matter. She kept this to herself as well.

VanderMeer looked at her quizzically. "He did? About this?"

"Well, I've described it as a matter of commerce, to be discreet, of course. And I still have further to discuss with you, Monsieur VanderMeer, if I might presume. And then I will carry the message of the meeting time back to the archbishop."

She smiled beguilingly at the artist, softening the fact that she had not given him a straight answer.

VanderMeer looked at Corrinne de Chanaye with great respect. *She is absolutely marvelous...and as devious as Julien's clock is complex.*

"Ah. Well, my lady, if we can all agree to meet at the hour of seven tonight, then you and I still have time to conduct further discussions."

Philippe looked at the clock and frowned. In the wilderness, he knew instinctively the length of the day and where he stood in it, sensing its passing, feeling the waxing and waning light between sunrise and sunset on his face. But these devices that spoke of hours in the day were now carried as pocket pieces by those who could afford them, usually people of business, creating rules and breaking the day into tiny little pieces. He never liked clocks, but he knew how to use them.

"That's only four hours from now. Adverse things are caused by hurried decisions...and mistakes."

Corrinne's brow lifted. "Oh? Of course, *you* never make impulsive decisions, do you? Clock or no clock."

Philippe ignored the comment. "Master artist, you said four people must represent the Great Houses. There is not enough time to find four willing people."

"Ah, yes. I have thought on the matter. I will represent the house of Daeniel the Druid, the moon sigil. Of course, Archbishop Nicolet will stand in for Bishop Brevelaer, the cross. You, I think, Lord Adaelric...then we only need someone to represent the ax sigil ..."

"Wait! Bring Pierre!" Corrinne suggested. "It's perfect. The three of us need to discuss other affairs afterwards. It will be safer to do that here, rather than at the warehouse or my city house."

"No, no," Philippe groaned. He had already thought of that. He didn't want to get Pierre involved with this foolishness too! "Pierre is skeptical of anything superstitious, and it makes him very nervous. He will refuse."

"Then don't tell him," Corrinne replied. "The archbishop will be here. Nothing bad is going to happen. We just say these...what, Monsieur, these sealing prayers, yes?"

"Essentially...yes," VanderMeer answered after only a moment's pause.

"See? And then we are done with this. Philippe, we needed to get together anyway."

VanderMeer brightened. "I presume Monsieur Pierre has an ax?"

Philippe nodded reluctantly. "Yes, he does."

"He possesses an amazing ax," Corrinne added enthusiastically. "I think you will find it most appropriate. It's as big as I am tall…well almost. Pierre will do this, Philippe. He will do this for me."

"Dinnah' be too sure aboot tha'."

Corrinne ignored Philippe's mockery. "He will do this!" Corrinne told the artist firmly.

VanderMeer rose. "Well, then until the hour of seven."

Philippe stood, hesitated, and then hugged Corrinne again, though less passionately.

"I will go back to your city house and comfort Michelle and Henri, tell them of our plans…well, most of them. Then I will either go back to the warehouse, or get a message to Pierre to rendezvous with me somewhere. We will try to learn more of the *shérif*'s whereabouts before we meet you back here."

Corrinne took hold of his shoulders. "Philippe, this will all turn out right. You will see. After what we have learned here today…*this* is important, Philippe. Somehow, there is fate in this. And *we*…you and I…we will face this together." She kissed him. "Now go. I will become more acquainted with Monsieur VanderMeer. And do not tell Pierre too much about any of this. You will only confuse him."

"*Commerce*, my lady?" VanderMeer asked after Philippe left.

Corrinne set her valise on the table. "Master artist, I too have a long story to tell you. And there is a type of fate involved with this one as well. But first, in the interest of establishing trust between us, here is a dossier on you. I paid an agent in France to collect these facts and send it to me. It's my fervent hope most of this is true. Here is a similar dossier on me, one which happens to be a copy of the same report given to Governor Duquesne. I will sip some more of your delicious tea while you study these."

VanderMeer gazed at the two documents lying on the table in front of him. Instinctively, he knew once he crossed this Rubicon, there would be no going back.

"Do I have a choice in this?"

"I feel this is meant to be," Corrinne stated. She touched his hand. "But I am already fond of you, Charles. May I call you Charles? I think we are going to be great friends."

He gazed at the slender fingers resting on the back of his hand and wondered how such a simple gesture could feel so pleasant.

"Well, Mademoiselle ..."

"Corrinne."

"Yes. Well, *Corrinne*. Before we proceed to matters of commerce, I have two paintings I would like to show you, if you please. I am supposed to give these to Philippe, or show them to him, at least. But based on his terrible personal tragedy, only recently revealed to me, I would like your advice on what to do with them."

CHAPTER 32
MONTRÉAL
OCTOBER 1754
"...impulsive, willful, and apparently fearless!"

When Philippe left VanderMeer's house, the first thing he noticed was the prevailing presence of the gendarmes. He saw three pairs within fifty paces of VanderMeer's studio, walking the Rue Notre-Dame. They were stopping people at random, asking questions.

Looking for me.

Philippe took out a sock hat he carried and pulled it down over his head to cover his blond hair. His beard still showed, but he would shave that off later. For now, this would have to do. He used the maze-like, less-traveled collection of streets and alleyways on the city's west end known as the *rue ménagerie*. As he approached, he saw more gendarmes on the Rue Saint-Paul and two more posted near the front door of Corrinne's house.

Damn!

Philippe quickly moved up a side street and took the servants' alley to the gardens behind the house, scaled over the wall, and pressed his ear against the back door. He could hear no noise inside. Holding his breath, he knocked softly and listened carefully. Someone approached. It would take only three steps for him to be back over the wall if he had to flee.

The door opened a crack. An eye peered out at him. There came a whisper. "Monsieur Gerrard?"

"Yes," he whispered back.

The door opened further until the chamberlain's face was visible. "The gendarmes are here, Monsieur! In the library. Madeleine is with them."

"Where are Michelle and Henri and Anamosa?"

"They are safe, Monsieur. At my mother's house. Near the market. They have been there almost since you left. Go to the market. I will send one of the servant girls to meet you there. She will wear a blue ribbon around her neck. Look for her soon, and she will guide you the rest of the way.

Monsieur Dunemoore intends to meet you there too."

They both heard the sound of heavier footsteps on the stairs.

"I must go!"

Philippe was over the wall in moments and moving toward the markets in the city's west end. He got there quickly, smelled food, and purchased a brazier of meat and vegetables to eat while he watched for a woman wearing a blue ribbon. Gendarmes milled through the crowded market square. But they did not seem too intent on questioning, showing more interest in the numerous girls carrying food baskets. Nevertheless, Philippe eyed them carefully and moved opposite of them to keep a safe distance away while he waited.

Finally, he saw an Indian girl with a blue ribbon waiting on Rue Saint-Pierre, on the east side of the market, holding a basket. She was staring directly at him. As soon as she was certain he understood to follow, she turned and began walking slowly toward the *rue ménagerie* intersections. Philippe followed quickly, but not close enough to be noticed. She paused in front of a door at a group of two-story houses, glanced once at him, then went in without knocking. After making sure he'd not been followed, Philippe entered without knocking. The small home was full of people, Michelle, Henri, Anamosa, the chamberlain's wife, and Pierre, who had shaved, bathed, and was wearing fresh clothing.

"Laddie! Took ya' long enough!"

Philippe thanked the chamberlain's wife, who handed him a mug of hot spiced wine. The warm flavorful liquid soothed his parched throat. He explained how the city gendarmes were continuously looking for him. "We cannot stay in Montréal. The Governor may leave for Quebec by tomorrow, and only he can help me," he lied. "We need to go downriver."

"I don't want to stay in Montréal at all," Michelle announced. "I would prefer to live in Quebec. They must have a hospital there too. I have renounced my vows. I will be a nurse instead. There is a war...nurses will be of use."

Pierre recognized what Philippe was trying to do.

"Captain LaTour has two river sloops at anchor, being loaded," the Scotsman volunteered.

"We need to get everyone on a sloop, ready to leave for Quebec. Pierre will stay with me for now."

"I want to stay with you," Henri said immediately. He learned that Madeleine was staying at Corrinne's city house. He wanted to see her before he left.

Philippe shook his head. "Too dangerous. And I need you to stay with your mother and Anamosa and Juniata."

Henri frowned. He had no desire and no intention of staying with the women.

Pierre explained he had men and boats waiting to transport people out to a sloop immediately. "We can make a second trip to the warehouse and retrieve Juniata and Chesanin too."

"Can you get through the gates?"

Pierre laughed. "No one is lookin' for anyone clean and shaven like me. They are lookin' for someone smelly, dirty, and blond, like you! But we should go soon. The city guards will watch the gates more closely when it gets darker. There are mobs o' people goin' in and out right now, so it will be easier tah' pass. But the company warehouse is well guarded and so is Corrinne's city house, I'm told."

"I was just there. The gendarmes are already inside."

Before Pierre led them out to the streets, Philippe pulled him into the *cuisine* and quietly explained about the meeting at VanderMeer's studio, leaving out the details about a potential *ritual*.

"Archbishop Nicolet and Corrinne will be there. We need you too."

"Why?"

"Everyplace else is being watched. Among other topics, we will be discussing the *shérif* and Intendant Bigôt. And make sure you bring your ax with you."

"My ax? Bloody… why? It's nah' an easy thing tah' hide."

"So wear a long coat and strap it inside. VanderMeer wants to see it. It's a courtesy to him. Oh, and in my trunk you will find Chittaqua's talisman. Can you bring that with you too?"

"Kinnah' do tha'."

"Why?"

"I gave the bloody thing tah' Henri tah' wear on the way here—dinnah' look at me like tha'—you were mumbling tah' yourself and having bad dreams, so I could nah' ask ya'. Henri wanted it. And if it has all the magic Chittaqua claims it does, the lad needs it more than ya' do anyway."

Philippe looked around the corner of the *cuisine* into the other room. Henri glanced at him expectantly.

"O' course, ya' kin' go take it from him right now. Tha' would likely go well, eh?"

Before Philippe could reply, Pierre handed him a stack of fresh clothes.

"Here. Ya' may want tah' wash off some o' the marching stink, at least out o' respect for the chamberlain's wife and home. And it might make ya' a wee bit more tolerable in a small studio loft too."

Within the hour, Henri sat in the harbor launch with his mother, holding a sleepy Anamosa in his arms, while Pierre walked the shoreline to the warehouse to fetch Juniata and Chesanin. Once they reached the sloop, he was pleasantly surprised to see the first mate of the *Falcon Queen*.

"*Mon Dieu!* Henri! Look at you! You've become a *coureur de bois*! Wait till the others see you."

Henri smiled and gave Anamosa over to his mother. "I'm going back with the boat to get Juniata and Chesanin," he told her.

Michelle was too tired to argue. An equally exhausted Anamosa frowned but did not protest.

As soon as the harbor launch pushed ashore on the riverfront behind the warehouse, Henri sprinted for the warehouse backdoor and slipped inside. It didn't take long for him to find Pierre shouting orders at some of the workers.

"Henri! Wha' are ya' doin' here?"

"I'm going to Corrinne's house. I just wanted you to know. My mother and Anamosa are safe on the sloop."

"Corrinne's? There are gendarmes at that house!"

"Madeleine should be back from her tutors by now. And I am *not* going to Quebec without seeing her first. You are not going to stop me, Pierre. So please don't try. I just wanted you to know. I'll come to Quebec with my father tomorrow."

"Madeleine? Who the *fuck* is Madeleine?"

"A girl I knew in Rouen."

"Rouen? A *girl*? Are ya' daft?!"

"I'm going to see her, Pierre!"

Without waiting for further argument, Henri ran out the back of the warehouse, pulling a sock hat over his hair. Walking straight to the gate road, as if he'd just gotten off the launch, he moved calmly toward the boat-landing gate. He intentionally did not try to avoid the guards, passing directly next to one of them. The guard eyed his face and determined it was only a boy, no beard, and much too young to be the woodsman they had been warned about. The guard acknowledged the boy's passing with a nod.

Henri proceeded up the Rue Saint-Paul till he reached the street before Corrinne's house, going up the side street, then down the servants' alley, and over the wall to the backdoor, simply retracing the same path they had used to escape the house earlier. He decided to hide his rifle, bow, and quiver of arrows beneath the back steps. He covered them with fallen leaves. Then, taking a deep breath, he moved quietly to the back door, pressed an ear to it, and listened for a moment. Hearing no sounds, he knocked softly.

The door opened a few inches, and the chamberlain looked out. "What are *you* doing here?" he whispered harshly.

"I came to see Madeleine."

"Madeleine? She's with the gendarmes in the library."

Henri glanced toward the balcony above his head. "I will wait for her up there," he whispered.

"No!" the chamberlain whispered in horror before making other nonsensical choking sounds as Henri began climbing up to the balcony.

The door to the boudoir was locked, so Henri sat down to wait, frequently looking up and down the servant alleys. It would be easy to see anyone coming. He could collect his weapons and be away in seconds.

The minutes passed slowly, but, suddenly, he heard movement inside the room, sounds of something being shoved aside, then the lock turning.

And there she was. *Madeleine.* Henri was speechless.

She was smiling. In a long blue dress. A gold link necklace with a cross. Curly auburn hair. A sprinkle of freckles across her nose. And absolute joy on her face.

"Henri!"

Before he could reply, she grabbed the front of his leather jersey, pulled him inside the room, and kissed him deeply, her tongue delving into his mouth.

Henri was stunned. He did not know how to react, did not know what to do with his hands, did not shut his eyes, did not resist. Finally, she stopped and spoke to him, rushed and breathless.

"Henri, I have missed you! Look at you! You are already taller than me! You've certainly had some birthdays since I saw you last." Her nose wrinkled. "But you don't smell too good. Do you not bathe?"

"Uh, I...hello, Madeleine."

"*Hello*?" She pulled him close and kissed him again. Her hands began moving all over his body.

They were abruptly yanked apart by the strong arms of Mathilde. "Stop this, *now*," the maid whispered in a harsh voice. But it was clear she was speaking directly to Madeleine, whose expression turned defiant and sullen.

"Henri? What are you doing back here? There are four gendarmes waiting downstairs! Why are you not with your father?"

Henri told them all that had happened. Mathilde looked out the window and thought about what to do.

The maid went to Corrinne's writing desk, took a piece of parchment, and drew a crude sketch of Montréal.

"Henri, look at this. We are here. Go north of the markets to Rue Notre-Dame. Lady de Chanaye went to see an artist named VanderMeer." She circled a spot. "He lives somewhere near this corner. You will have to ask someone when you get close. Maybe one of the artisans working on the walls. If you find her, tell her the gendarmes are here in the house. I do not know their intentions, except they claim she is helping Philippe. Tell her we are in no danger and they are not mistreating us. But I'm not sure she should return home right now. Then tell her everything else you just told me." She touched his cheek affectionately and smiled. "I cannot believe how much you look like him. Now, go—the way you came in!"

Henri hugged Madeleine. She kissed his cheeks.

"Don't worry. We will be able to sit and talk with each other soon, I'm sure. Like we did before."

There was an odd tremble in her voice that Henri did not understand.

Suddenly, they heard footsteps coming up the stairs.

"Go!" Mathilde urged.

Henri went over the balcony, collected his weapons, and vaulted the garden wall in less than thirty seconds. He'd learned the direction of the markets when they went to the chamberlain's house. They had even gotten close enough to smell the aromas of food emanating from the area.

He pulled the sock hat further down over his head and moved at a fast walk. The crude map Mathilde had made proved to be accurate. He went by the chamberlain's house, further down the street to the marketplace, stopping for a few seconds to stare at the menagerie of people in different styles of dress, some tribal peoples, soldiers, all crowding and moving back and forth in every direction amid delicious smells and a din of noisy shouting. His mouth started watering, but he went north all the way to the wall and asked a stone cutter about a Monsieur VanderMeer, taking time to mention he'd cut stone for Saint Ouen's Church. The man seemed pleased with that revelation. They talked about types of saws and chisel cuts before he personally led him to the door of the artist's loft.

Henri knocked lightly, and, when no one answered, he stepped inside the small foyer and quietly said *hello*. Still no one. He heard voices coming from the top of the stairway.

It must be them, he decided. Instinct warned him to be cautious.

Not wanting to shout out, he moved up the stairs and stopped at the upper step, his thick leather moccasins making the climb soundless. He saw a man and woman leaning over a table at the center of a large room, going over some documents together.

Henri removed his sock hat. "Hello."

The woman made a gasping noise and turned quickly. The older man removed his spectacles and stared.

"I know this boy," Charles VanderMeer said with amazement. "It's Henri Gerrard."

"Henri?!" Lady Corrinne de Chanaye quickly crossed the room to stand before him. She touched his face and hair. "My God, you look just like him!"

Henri gawked.

"You're like a flower," he said with wonder, and then a blush came over his face. "A-apologies, Mademoiselle," he stammered.

"Oh, *Henri*. Oh, I think I'm going to like you," she replied, embracing him and kissing his cheeks. He even smelled a little rank, like Philippe.

"Come, come." VanderMeer gestured at the table. "Come and sit."

Henri laid his weapons aside. Corrine poured him some tea, which he did not drink.

"How did you come to be here?" she asked.

Henri told her everything, from the time they arrived at her house, to the retreat across the city, to Philippe's conversation at the chamberlain's house, to moving his mother and Anamosa to the sloop, going to the warehouse, his words with Pierre, and his return to Corrinne's house, but less about Madeleine, and finally what Mathilde had said about the gendarmes.

"But Philippe said for you to stay on the sloop?"

"I wanted to see Madeleine."

Of course, thought Corrinne. He was impulsive, willful, and apparently fearless. *Remember, this is someone who kills bears.*

"A moment, Henri." Corrinne turned to the artist. "Monsieur Vander-Meer, do we have an agreement?"

"Yes, I think we do, my lady." But VanderMeer was staring intently at Henri's chest, where a glimpse of a silver amulet could be seen above the top of the boy's leather shirt. He pointed. "Is that the talisman?"

Henri placed a hand over the amulet. "This is mine."

"I understand. It belonged to Chittaqua, yes? May I see it?"

Henri slipped it out of his shirt but did not take it from around his neck.

The artist glanced at Corrinne and pointed at the sigils engraved in the silver.

"You see? As I told you, Chittaqua made this." There was a tuft of long white hair tied where the leather necklace strap ran through a hole in the amulet. "What are these strands?"

Henri's expression became stiff. "They are Roland's."

VanderMeer sensed he should not ask more. He nodded appreciatively and stepped away.

"Thank you."

Much as Corrinne wanted to hear of Henri's adventures from his own lips, she glanced at the clock and considered what to do now, based upon what Henri had shared.

"I will have these witnessed and signed by Archbishop Nicolet and Governor Duquesne before I return them to you," she said, collecting all the documents on the table, being careful with the two new ones she'd penned together with VanderMeer.

VanderMeer regarded her admiringly. "You can do that in the next few days?"

"I will."

"Then our lives are entwined forever, I think."

"I will hope that remains true."

"What now?"

"I will go to Archbishop Nicolet and bring him back with me." Corrinne looked at Henri. "Henri should stay here with you. Will that be all right?"

"I would be honored. We can share stories of Chittaqua while we wait for your father."

"Are you coming back?" Henri asked Corrinne.

"Of course, as will Philippe and Pierre *and* the archbishop of Montréal."

CHAPTER 33
MONTRÉAL
OCTOBER 1754
The Great Houses

The chamberlain's wife set up a bathing area in the garden outside the back of her house. She draped blankets over some ropes for privacy and, with Philippe's help, carried out a huge kettle of hot water, soap, and towels. It was windy that day and even with the hot water, he was shivering heavily the whole time. By the time he was done, she brought a second, smaller kettle of hot water with some bitter-smelling herbs added to it, and helped him scrub and soap away the lice and dirt from his hair and beard.

"I'd forgotten what it was like," he told her when he was back inside and dressed in fresh clothes.

The fifty-five-year-old gray-haired woman smiled thinly and with some amusement. "I'd forgotten too. Shall I burn these other clothes or try to wash them?"

"I'll need the jacket, gloves, boots, and weapons. A clean sock hat would be helpful...some foot socks too? Everything else is probably too foul to clean."

"Well, at least half of the stink is gone. Try not to wear that coat for too long or none of your fresh clothing will make a difference." She handed him a missive. "This was delivered while you were washing. I read it in case it was urgent. I know the place, if you don't."

The square piece of parchment had Pierre's name at the bottom. Above that, "Voyageurs' Crotch," the name of the grittiest tavern on the south wall of the city, located between the two boat-landing gates. The desperate men who went there looked for any kind of work. At least one death a week occurred there in the summer months.

"I know it."

Philippe tried to give her a gold piece for the trouble.

She waved it away. "Seeing you naked was payment enough."

Philippe carried a pistol and three knives under his wilderness coat. He wasn't worried about who might be in the tavern. He'd been there numerous times over the years. But it was right next to the gendarmerie barracks on the city's west end. The city soldiers rarely entered the tavern, except when they were looking for someone…*like they were now.* Pierre knew this too. He must have selected it for a good reason.

There were soldiers all over this street, so he marched down the middle, making no attempt to try and hide. The gendarmes' attention was more on the gate traffic streaming in and out. Among the crowds of people on the street, he was little noticed. It was still light out when he entered the tavern, and it took a minute for his eyes to adjust to the candlelight inside. There were no windows here. One way in, and one way out.

Philippe moved toward an empty table nearest to the doorway and sat so he could see the door and a view of the room. The tavern served warm ale or black rum in unwashed clay cups. He paid silver for a dram of rum and sipped it sparingly. As his vision improved, he could see that the room held less than a dozen men at the tables and four leaning against the bar, one of whom was looking at him directly. The man's face was shadowed, and it wasn't Pierre. Philippe returned the stare. If the man was one of Intendant Bigôt's spies, he would soon make a move for the door. Philippe would kill him before he made it outside, then make his own retreat.

As expected, the man lifted his arms from the bar and began walking in his direction. Philippe slipped a long, slender boning knife from his belt and held it ready under the table. To his surprise, the man did not go to the door. Instead, he veered directly to Philippe and stopped a few paces away.

"I think you know me," the man said.

Philippe still could not see the man's face because of the shadows, but he knew the Mohawk accent. It was Peter Blue Jacket.

"Sit."

Peter sat down. They spoke in low whispers.

"Snow Hair is famous among many tribes and peoples. Most hope to kill you. If you were Mohawk, we would celebrate you as a hero for so many enemies."

"How did you come to be here?"

"Animal Scalp said to meet here."

"When?"

"Today. Now. Soon. Later. I am glad you came. Now you can pay for the rum I buy."

The door opened and the room was filled with afternoon sunlight. A man entered and stopped just inside the doorway to allow his eyes to adjust. Then he walked directly to Philippe's table. It was Pierre. He took the remaining seat.

"No one leaves before us now, until we leave first," Philippe whispered in Mohawk.

"No wonder everyone comes here at night. Ya' kinnah' see anyone in the daytime." Philippe and Peter said nothing. "Oh, I know, I know, in Mohawk."

"Are you ready?" Philippe asked Peter.

"We wait at the small pier downriver. When do you come?"

"Maybe tonight, maybe tomorrow. But we will come."

"Do this, and one less tribe will seek to kill you," Peter said.

Philippe knew it was said in humor. He placed two silver pieces on the table. "Pierre and I will leave now. You should wait longer, I think. This silver is to pay for the rum you drink while you wait."

Peter Blue Jacket nodded.

Pierre leaned over to Philippe and whispered the word *market* in his ear. Philippe left first. A few minutes later, Pierre reached over and drank Peter Blue Jacket's dram of rum. The taste made him cough, but he nodded approvingly. He thanked the half-breed, gave him another piece of silver, and followed after his partner.

VanderMeer was showing Henri the writings and pictures in his book when they both heard a loud knock at the door.

"Gendarmes," his maid called as loudly as she dared from the bottom of the stairs.

Minutes after searching the first floor, the two soldiers made their way to the top of the stair. They lowered their muskets seeing the studio room was empty except for the artist in residence. VanderMeer was behind an easel, wearing a gray, paint-spotted cloak. On the easel was a canvas painting.

The artist set aside his palette and wiped his hands on a rag.

"*Messieurs*? May I be of service?"

The soldiers scanned the room closely, but it was empty, except for a few piles on the floor and a square trunk. Opening the trunk, the corporal peered closely at the pouch of dirt and noticed the glint of metal beneath the edge of the flap.

"This stinks."

"It is night soil," VanderMeer said quickly.

The man straightened, disgusted. "Can't afford a clay pot?"

"I am an artist."

The other soldier looked out the tall windows, glancing left and right. The roof was steep to either side and it was a two-story drop to the servants' alley. "No one here," he told the corporal.

"Lady de Chanaye was seen leaving this building. Why was she here?"

"I was painting her, of course."

The soldiers moved to see the painting. VanderMeer held his hands wide to block their approach.

"*S'il vous plaît*, Messieurs. It is not complete!"

The corporal pushed him out of the way and stared at the highly detailed nude.

"So, this is how she looks," he remarked, licking his lips.

"Her cunny has no hair," the other soldier said with surprise. "The whore shaves it, eh?"

But the nude was incomplete.

The corporal's eyes shifted to the painter. "Where's the head?"

VanderMeer shrugged. "I was about to paint that next when she abruptly had to leave."

"To where?"

"She did not say."

"When will she be back?"

VanderMeer shrugged again. "She's a royal. She will arrive when she is inclined to do so, I presume."

"A royal?" The corporal snorted derisively. His expression turned threatening. "We are watching you, artist."

"How comforting."

The soldier backhanded him across the face, hard enough to make a point.

VanderMeer tasted blood in his mouth. His eyes narrowed and he rubbed his sore chin. But he did not react.

The corporal kicked over the easel and the two gendarmes went down the stairs.

VanderMeer went to the window overlooking the street to see which way they walked. Satisfied they were not coming back, he went to one of the tall windows and pushed up a vertical slide-lock on its frame. The window swung inward.

"Henri! It is safe to come back in."

Shivering from the wind and cold, Henri carefully stepped around the corner of the two-foot fascia-gutter and around the frame into the room.

"You are brave. It must have been terrifying, balancing on that tiny ledge."

"It was cold. But I was not afraid. Chittaqua was with me, sitting atop the next roof."

"*Chittaqua?*"

Henri pointed out the window.

VanderMeer saw the form of a large white bird soaring away to the right. He looked again at Henri. *If believing that made the difference, so be it.*

VanderMeer handed him the half-full pot of tea to hold for warmth.

"The gendarmes are gone…for now, at least."

Henri saw the nude lying on the floor. VanderMeer followed his eyes and smiled. He picked up the painting and showed it to him proudly.

"Do not be embarrassed to look at this. As an artist, I consider the female form to be second in beauty only to the face of the Creator, which I have never seen, of course. This woman was a Saxony Duchess. Her husband had her beheaded for adultery. Hence, this work remains unfinished. Now, make yourself comfortable while I straighten up the room for the visitors that will come soon."

Lady de Chanaye told her driver to stop at the Hotel Dieu. She went inside the hospital and spoke to Doctor La Galissonière, and was directed to the bed where Father Tinian lay sweating, his breathing labored. There was a bowl of cool water and rags on the table next to him. She wet one of the rags and laid it upon his brow.

The priest's eyes fluttered open. "I am in heaven," he whispered upon seeing her face.

"I am flattered. How are you feeling?"

"Worse, I think."

"The doctor claims if you were going to die, you would already be dead. But he said you will be here for a week at least before you are well."

For the past two years, Lady de Chanaye had made a point to flirt with the archbishop's secretary, in preparation for a favor she would ask someday, although, at the time, she had no idea what that favor might be. As the months went by, she watched with amusement as the priest struggled to suppress his natural inclinations. It became a test of his willpower and self control. She found herself slowly charmed by both the strength of his restraint and his loyalty to Archbishop Nicolet.

"Why are you here, my lady? I do not feel disposed toward our contest, I am sorry to say."

"Our contest? I am offended. You make our delightfully wicked relationship sound inferior!" Corrinne smiled and her voice softened. "I came to say good-bye to you, Father Tinian."

"Good-bye," he croaked. "But...but why?"

"I am leaving Montréal. Don't look so glum. I plan to write to you from the place I live next."

"Where are you going?"

"On a ship, I suppose."

"When?"

"Soon. But I have a favor to ask of you. I told you long ago, I would ask a favor of you someday, yes? Promise me to look after the archbishop. He does not have many friends. I count myself fortunate to be one of them. But after I leave, and Governor Duquesne returns to France...well, loneliness can be as destructive to a person's well-being as any disease. So promise to write me about his mood and condition, so I may write back to him with the proper words of cheer."

The priest looked stricken by her words. "You speak true then? You are leaving?"

"I speak the truth. Now promise me."

"I promise."

"Good!"

She wet another rag and wiped off his face and lips. Then she leaned over and kissed him lightly. Her other hand briefly massaged his groin.

"My parting gift to you. There, you see? You are feeling better already, no?"

"Mademoiselle, I fear you have placed me in the confessional for the rest of my life."

"Well, I certainly hope so. I worked hard to please you. You resisted me more than any man I know…well, save one." Her expression saddened. "I shall miss you, Father Tinian. Truly. Now pray for me. My life and the lives of others I love are in great danger right now. In the next few days, I will need all your prayers."

"I think my heart is breaking."

"*Adieu*, good sir." She squeezed his hand.

Corrinne stopped to see Doctor La Galissonière on her way out. To her surprise, the physician held up his palms to stop her approach.

"Did you touch the priest?"

"Pardon?"

"He is sick. Some of us are certain his sickness can be spread by touch. If you touched him, wash your hands in this bowl." From a wine bottle, the doctor poured a clear liquid into a metal basin. "This is a condensed distillate vapor of rum. Many of my equals suspect it purifies the skin."

Corrinne did as he directed, then took a fresh linen square, dipped it in the distillate, and meticulously wiped her mouth and face. There was a stinging sensation on her lips.

"I kissed his forehead," she explained, upon seeing the doctor's slight smirk. "Will he get better?"

"I think so. He lives a disciplined life. He has the strength. Half of the others will die."

"I will be going downriver tomorrow."

"As will I," the doctor replied. "The Governor left for Quebec today instead of tomorrow as planned."

Corrinne fumed silently. *He promised!* She had managed to arrange a meeting with Duquesne for the next morning, and now his early departure changed her plans, again!

"To the house," she told the driver as she climbed into the carriage.

When she saw gendarmes still posted outside her front door, she told him not to stop. "Take me to the Terrain des Jésuites." The carriage turned, left, and clattered up the Rue Saint-Claude directly to the garden behind

Archbishop Nicolet's domicile.

Seeing the gendarmes made her realize it was now dangerous to carry the valise and all its documents around with her. *If I were suddenly arrested …*

Corrinne hugged the valise tightly to her chest. Her home no longer seemed a safe place.

I must get the archbishop to hold these for me.

Pierre joined Philippe at the back of the market, at a place they had rendezvoused for years, near the entrance to the tiny Récollet chapel. The market was thinning of people with the approach of sunset. They saw only two gendarmes, who seemed intent on cajoling food from the carts of the remaining street hawkers.

Pierre, speaking quietly, told him about Henri showing up at the warehouse and announcing his plan to see Madeleine.

Philippe halted mid-stride, incredulous. "And you didn't stop him?!"

"Whoa! First o' all, it's clear he is *your* son! Second, he dinnah' wait for my opinion before running—let me repeat tha'—*running* out the door. The last I saw o' him, he was walking directly past the boat-landing gate gendarmes who barely looked at him."

"So he's here now? Somewhere inside the walls?"

"Safe tah' say. But steady, laddie. Henri's smart. He knows the gendarmes are in Corrinne's house. If he could no' find a way tah' say hello tah' Madeleine, whoever the hell she is, my guess is he went back tah' the chamberlain's house. It's the only other place he knows. No one is looking for a boy. He doesn't know the city, and he knows we'll come lookin' for him. And we kinnah' go running all over the streets just now. We need tah' stay out o' sight until it's dark."

Philippe was furious, but mostly at himself. "All right. What now?"

Pierre glanced warily at the two soldiers. He gestured at the door to the chapel. "Supposedly, a friend waits for us inside."

The interior was candle lit and heavily shadowed. They took off their sock hats. When their eyes adjusted, they saw the chapel was empty except for a small figure hunched over on a pew resting against a side wall. Whoever it was had watched them enter and was looking at them now.

Pierre pointed. "There."

Philippe had one hand on his knife as they approached the seated person.

He sidestepped his way keeping one eye on the door.

"Oho, Singing Owl," Pierre said quietly. "It's been a long time."

The old Indian gazed around Pierre and saw Philippe.

"Oho, Snow Hair."

"Oho, Singing Owl."

Pierre and Philippe sat on the floor. Singing Owl joined them. Pierre gave the man a small sack of tobacco and confectioneries he'd pilfered from the warehouse. Next, he gave him a Louis d'or.

"Where is he?" Pierre asked without further pleasantries.

Singing Owl whispered in the Huron tongue. "By day, he sleeps in a white man's house just beyond the swamps on the river road to Quebec. After the first village, a path leads into the forests. All the homes but one in that place have collapsed or were burned many seasons ago. The bite of the flying ants is terrible there, and mountain lions prowl those lands. But at night, the one you seek is here, inside the walls. He wears dark clothes and many different hats. He moves around the streets. He likes high places and sometimes sits on roofs, still, like a hunter, and looks in windows."

"Is he here now?" Philippe asked urgently.

"I have not seen him. But the sun is setting. He will be here."

"Where?"

Singing Owl shook his head. "If you stay in the same spot all night, he will eventually walk by you. He is looking for you, Snow Hair. I have told him you are coming."

Pierre frowned. "Why would ya' do that?"

The Indian shrugged. "He pays me for what I know. He offers me money to find you for him. But you have paid me first. And you have always treated me with respect."

"Which gate will he come through?" Philippe asked.

"He uses them all. But now he knows you are here, I think he will use the river-road gate. It is the fastest way."

"I am going to kill him," Philippe told the Indian as a warning he should not get in the way.

For a few moments, the old man made no reply. Once a shaman for a Huron tribe, before it was slaughtered, he gazed deeply into Snow Hair's eyes.

"Snow Hair is brave. But Snow Hair is foolish. You think your totem *strong*? This white man is possessed by an evil that is not of the people. Not of this land. It does not fight like you. It will use magic. Chittaqua is no more. You need someone who knows magic. Instead, you speak bravely, and threaten an old man. You should be running away now, I think. But instead, this evil uses your bravery to bring you closer. Every step you take this night, will be taking you to the evil one. Step left or right, go ahead or turn around. It does not matter. All the paths you take will be the same, because you cannot *see* the path of magic. At the end of *your* path waits death. And the people will sing of you around the winter fires and say, Snow Hair was brave, but Snow Hair is gone. And they will sing of you no more. That is all I have to say."

Singing Owl got up and left the chapel by its back door.

"I thin' tha' went well, eh, laddie?"

"Now we know where the *shérif* is, Pierre."

"Did ya' even listen tah' him, laddie? Singing Owl was once a powerful shaman. He was givin' ya' a warning."

"I know about magic." Philippe said, thinking of the strange story he had heard that day. He stood and gestured to Pierre. "Let's go to the chamberlain's house."

Corrinne sat by the window in the archbishop's office.

The Jesuit wondered why she was clutching the valise to her chest with both arms.

She began telling him of the day's events: of Philippe's return, her meeting with VanderMeer, the successful negotiations and agreements. But she hesitated briefly before relating the revelations made by VanderMeer.

The archbishop could tell there was more. "What?"

"He asked if we had any recent pain-filled experiences. And told us about his. He showed us pictures in his books and related the legend of the Great Houses."

Archbishop Nicolet frowned uncomfortably. He didn't want to talk about these things. He'd been struggling with what had happened and what it portended. Since the meeting with the artist in his office, his skepticism had returned, and he was half convinced the artist had somehow created an illusion of trickery. It was simply easier to believe this than any other explanation.

"He said you had been affected too? That this happened to you? Did it?"

"I don't know what happened," his voice hinting at denial. "It could have been just a painful cramp in the muscles of my leg."

Corrinne saw fear in his eyes. She had been terrified by the attack. But now she had a reason to explain it, bizarre as it was.

"It happened to Philippe and to me," she replied calmly. "It was not an illusion. It was definitely not my imagination. It hurt me terribly. It scared me so badly I lost control of my bowels. For a long time afterwards, I worried I was losing my sanity. I have not been able to even talk about this until today. And to learn this artist and Philippe and even *you* have experienced the same thing. André, this was not from our imagination. This is not coincidence."

For the first time ever, the archbishop avoided her eyes.

He does not want to accept this, she thought. *He does not want to face this. Well, neither do I. But we* are *going to face this.*

Corrinne saw the darkness gathering outside the window. The sun had set. She continued talking.

"Monsieur VanderMeer has fashioned a *châsse* of wood and stone to use as a sepulcher of sorts. He has researched the proper words—"

"It is blasphemous," the Jesuit blurted.

"It's no more blasphemous than *exorcism*," she responded, her voice rising. "The Church provides for that, yes? Except we are not casting *out* a demon, we are sealing one, imprisoning one. And we cannot do this without you! A cross is on one of the sigils. You know this to be true. The sigils are on the back of the crucifix you wear."

The archbishop's hand took hold of the cross reflexively as he looked out the window, again avoiding her gaze.

"What the artist intends goes against every facet of my faith in God and the Holy Trinity."

"Eminence. Sometime tomorrow, Philippe and I will have to deal with all the deceits planned by the *shérif* and Intendant Bigôt. We have to do this tonight. Philippe and Pierre are waiting for us right now at VanderMeer's loft to perform this…ritual. Henri Gerrard is there too. The artist will place the pouch in the *châsse* and say the words. It will not take long. VanderMeer claimed you've already agreed to this. That is why I came here. To get you."

To her surprise, she saw an expression of wide-eyed distress on the Jesuit's face. "Henri Gerrard?! Philippe's son?"

"Yes."

"He is only a *boy*! He is with VanderMeer? Right now?

"Yes."

"With that…*thing*…in the same room?!"

"Yes."

"*Yes?* If he were your child, would you agree so blindly?!"

For the first time, Corrinne spoke to the archbishop in an angry voice.

"Do you presume I want to do this? Eminence, I did not ask for this trial. But from what Charles VanderMeer has found in the histories, this… *evil thing*…associates with families. Our families! And Henri Gerrard is Philippe's *son*. It will attack him as it has attacked you, and me, and Philippe. And only we can stop it. Do you offer an alternative?"

The archbishop abruptly arose and moved to leave. Corrinne barely had time to place the valise atop one of his bookshelves before following him out the door.

Philippe and Pierre took separate routes to the chamberlain's house. As dusk turned to darkness, the *rue ménagerie* alleyways filled with people going to their homes.

Philippe did not knock. The main room was dark when he entered. There was candlelight in the *cuisine*. It was too quiet. Philippe pulled out his dragoon pistol, cocked it, and glanced briefly around the corner into the *cuisine*. The chamberlain and his wife were waiting at a table. The older man had an arm around her. He smiled with relief at seeing Philippe's face, exhaled, and stood to greet him.

"Monsieur Gerrard! I am so glad you are here. We worried it might not be you."

Philippe lowered the hammer of the weapon. "Apologies. Pierre Dunemoore is not far behind me."

Even as he said this, the front door opened again. It was Pierre.

The chamberlain explained to them that the four gendarmes had not left Lady de Chanaye's house. Mathilde and Madeleine remained under watch, waiting for Corrinne's return. All the other servants had been dismissed.

"I presume they consider me unimportant. I slipped out the back door and over the wall. They are waiting for my mistress, Monsieur. I suspect to arrest her."

Pierre spoke. "Are ya' ready tah' leave Montréal?"

The chamberlain looked at his wife and shook his head. "This is our home, Monsieur Dunemoore. But Mathilde is ready, and Madeleine as well. Madeleine has no one else but Lady de Chanaye to sponsor her. All the household things of any value have been moved to the river sloops."

"Then go to the Dunemoore Company warehouse in the morning."

Pierre told him the names of senior clerks at the warehouse who would see Mathilde and Madeleine safely aboard the sloop.

"They can leave tomorrow, if necessary?" the chamberlain questioned.

"It *will* be necessary. Ya' will see them in the morning?"

"In truth, I am going back to the house to stay the night. I only came here to warn you, and tell you about Henri."

"What about Henri?" Philippe prepared himself for something bad.

"Henri is a brave but reckless young man. Climbed up the balcony above the garden just to say hello to Madeleine. Mathilde chased him out seconds before the gendarmes would have…well, I'm not sure what they would have done, but Henri was armed, so it may not have ended well. Before he left, Mathilde had enough time to draw him a map of the city and told him to go to the home of the artist called VanderMeer."

Pierre and Philippe looked at one another in alarm. Quickly, they said their good-byes and hurried out the front door.

At the center of the *rue ménagerie*, they split up once again to be less conspicuous, but it was unnecessary. They saw no gendarmes patrolling the Rue Notre-Dame either way they looked. The night candles were being lit. And a carriage was stopped on the street facing east in front of VanderMeer's studio. Two men were standing by it. Corrinne's men.

"Is she in there?" Philippe asked.

"Yes. She arrived with Archbishop Nicolet less than an hour ago. We've not seen her since. She told us not to come up for any reason. But I am nervous, Monsieur. It's not like her. And it's too quiet."

"Do as she has told you. I am going up and if there are problems, you will probably hear some pistol shots."

Philippe looked around the streets once more, searching for something out of the ordinary, someone lingering in a doorway. An hour earlier, there were gendarmes walking in pairs in every part of the city. Now, Philippe did not see a single one; for that matter, there were almost no people. A suspicion honed from years of detecting ambush began to stir.

Philippe hand signaled to Pierre as he approached from the other direction. He quickly whispered what the footmen had told him. They entered the house together, dragoon pistols drawn. It was quiet. The bottom floor was dark. The loft was illuminated. Philippe went up the stairs first.

"It's Philippe," he called out at the halfway point.

A woman's voice made a sound of relief. Corrinne appeared at the top of the stairs.

"Philippe! And Pierre too! You see, Eminence. Now we are all here!"

The *coureurs de bois* entered the studio to see Archbishop Nicolet's decidedly unhappy face. Henri stood next to him, by the table and chairs. VanderMeer stood by the large wooden *châsse*, which the artist had moved to the center of the room. There were four lanterns atop shelves in each corner.

Philippe ignored the others. "Henri, why are you not with your mother?"

"Captain LaTour's first mate is in charge of the river sloop. Mother is safe. I can do more good being here."

Pierre grinned at the resolve he saw in Henri's eyes. *That boy is not going anywhere he doesn't want to go. He even sounds like Philippe.*

"I would like to get this over with," the archbishop announced tersely.

"Get wha' over with?" Pierre asked, realizing something unknown to him was about to occur.

VanderMeer spotted Pierre's ax hanging from the shoulder strap beneath the Scotsman's long coat. It had a gemstone in its metal head that he wanted to examine immediately, but, instead, he began talking, knowing he must hold everyone's attention.

"Monsieur Dunemoore, I have spoken to everyone, save you, regarding the sigils on Philippe's ring, which match the engravings on Chittaqua's talisman,"—the artist gestured to Henri, and Henri pulled the amulet from his shirt—"and the engraved symbols on the back of Archbishop Nicolet's crucifix."

André Nicolet's cross was hanging straight along the front of his black robes. The Jesuit frowned and gave no support for the artist's words.

"Seeing your ax, Monsieur, I suspect there are some engravings or sigil impressions somewhere on its metal head."

There *were* some faint impressions in the metal head. The Scotsman felt a queasiness in his gut.

"Wha' the hell is he talkin' aboot? What are we all doin' here?"

"Let him speak, Pierre," Corrinne urged. She slipped her arm around his.

"For your benefit, Monsieur Dunemoore, I have a story to tell you. Everyone else has heard this, so I will try to be brief."

VanderMeer explained the history, the legend, pointing at various pages in his books when necessary, asking Philippe to hold up his ring for inspection. He quietly explained his interactions with Chittaqua and what the wise shaman said to him about the island of stones, the history and legends of his people.

Pierre snuck glances at the others while the artist spun his tale. To his surprise, they did not seem disbelieving.

"Well...tha's a nice winter tale, Master Artist. Now, will someone tell me wha' we are doin' here?"

Corrinne sensed Pierre was ready to leave. She tightened her hold on his arm.

VanderMeer continued bluntly.

"According to these ancient writings, they were called *vulnax* in the old Celtic tongue. A *scarring wraith*. This wraith attacks in our *shadow* dreams—a place before deep sleep, where malspirits perchance dwell at the same time. It was written"—he pointed at the books—"that once the wraith finds you, it returns over and over to slash and mark your flesh, leaving scars that never heal. But these scars are not visible. You cannot see them. They only hurt if you touch them. Once is merely a nuisance, like a painful bruise. But if the wraith comes in your dark dreams every time you sleep, your body becomes infested with such scars. The Druids write that those afflicted soon become too frightened to close their eyes. But when you become exhausted enough, all of us sleep, yes? In fact, you collapse and sleep even longer. Because of that, soon there is not a place on your skin that does not ache."

VanderMeer turned to the other book on his table to read another passage directly. He touched the Celtic words with his finger and spoke slowly.

"'A few survived the ritual to cast out the scars, yea, but struggled afterwards to call themselves fortunate. Of the others...it is said that some took refuge in opiates ever stronger, while the rest descended into a naked, absurd...shrieking...grotesque...madness. You cannot run. You cannot escape. Life itself becomes the reason for your agony. And then…even the strongest among us will seek a way to die.'"

"Bloody…," Pierre said loudly, glancing around at everyone's rapt attention and shaking off Corrinne's grip. "Enough o' this offal! Philippe! Wha' are we doin'? Why are we listening to this nonsense? We are supposed to be hunting the *shérif!* Am I the only one—?"

VanderMeer decided Pierre and the others must be reminded again. They must be shown. He took hold of the silver amulet with the emerald stone, removing it from the pouch of dirt. Holding it before him with one hand, he stepped backwards, carefully testing the distance. He wanted to let the wraith emerge as it did at Fort Niagara, but only enough to be seen by the others.

But he stepped too far.

In an instant, a creamy smokiness oozed over the sides of the *châsse*. The candles in the lanterns began to flicker. There was a faint buzzing noise. A foul odor permeated the air.

Simultaneously, Corrinne, Philippe, Pierre and the archbishop flinched. The pain was not strong enough to be disabling, but it hurt!

The Jesuit gasped at the sharp stab in the back of his right thigh and collapsed backward into a chair.

Philippe, Pierre, and Corrinne had never seen the wraith before. This was not something explainable by any of their life experiences. They were overcome with childlike terror before instinctual preservation took control. They all reacted at the same time.

Philippe grunted and hunched forward to grip the scar on his left leg. He drew his skinning knife and stepped forward to attack the creamy smoke. The pain increased tenfold with a single step. He screamed, the knife slipped from his fingers, and he fell to the floor gripping his injured leg.

At the same time Pierre bent over from the wrenching pain in his gut. "Blooody…!" Still clutching his stomach, Pierre raised his ax to strike at something. But what? *It must be the bloody box*, he thought. The Scotsman raised his ax and stepped forward to chop the box into pieces. The pain increased so rapidly, he could only inhale before the ax slipped from his hands.

Corrinne's hand flew to her neck. She groaned loudly in terror. "No! No! No!"

VanderMeer was equally affected. His hands felt on fire, the amulet began slipping from his numb fingers. *If I drop it and it rolls too far away ...!*

Henri was gripping Chittaqua's talisman. The center gemstone was glowing. Seeing his father lying on his side, the archbishop unable to stand, Corrinne in obvious pain, and Pierre prostrate, the great war ax useless, Henri began to panic. He raised his musket toward the box, when, out of the corner of his eye, he glimpsed a white form hovering outside the tall window. Henri knew that shape, moved quickly, pushed up on the vertical slide-lock and allowed the window to swing inward.

The white eagle fluttered to a landing and perched on the sill.

The lantern light recovered.

The pain everyone felt lessened almost completely, but it did not disappear. VanderMeer could now hold his amulet firmly and quickly began reading the first rune from the book in a Celtic tongue.

The others looked on with disbelief.

"Who that dares seal a wraith, crafts a doorway to hell.
That door must have a lock. That lock a key.
A door thus locked, can be unlocked.
And thrice stronger the wraith emerges,
To impart hellish torment on his oppressors.
Those who dare to seal a wraith, thus seal their doom.
Beware!"

"The next verse is in a Frankish dialect," VanderMeer said and, without stopping, continued reading the hex.

The artist heard his own voice become unintentionally more resonant. And as VanderMeer spoke, everyone in the room could sense the attention of something invisible and pitiless.

"In the marsh he laid with the crone,
Among the stinkweed and slime.
The crone farrowed there,
And spewed forth the dark one's brood.
From that get rose one,
Vaelblez.

And his house sharked with the moon,
And glut their maw with the flesh of men.
From thence a veil draped the sun,
A tarnish to the moon.
Until four Great Houses joined,
The ax with the lion, the cross with the moon.
And cast into the pit,
He will rot beneath their signs."

The buzzing noise stopped, replaced by low rumblings that intruded from every direction. The air felt hot and prickly.

Corrinne could feel the hairs on her arms straightening.

"The last verse is in Roman Latin," VanderMeer said. "It must be said in a single breath. But it is too difficult for me to read." He looked toward the Jesuit. "Eminence, can you help me?"

Help you do what? Perform an act of devil worship? Distraught and rattled by these occult events, André Nicolet sat wide-eyed, breathing heavily, his faith and sensibilities jolted as if he'd been struck in the head by a heavy stone. At the honorary address, and seeing the frightened eyes of everyone, he struggled to find the strength to react as the senior prelate of New France. But there was no precedence for any of this.

Nicolet attempted to stand, but his legs buckled, and he sank back in the chair. "No! I will not help you! And we will *not* be using the holy tongue. This blasphemy must stop! Enough of this—"

Unexpectedly, the Julien Le Roy clock made its first gong as the hour of eight was reached. Corrinne, Philippe, Pierre, the archbishop, and VanderMeer all winced from a brief spike of pain that occurred. Before the clock gonged a second time, abruptly, the elegant time device shattered into pieces. Shards of glass and metal tumbled through the air to bounce and rattle across the floor. No one was hurt, but the room was filled with a shocked silence.

"Wha' the...hell," Pierre said timorously. He managed to stand up. "Philippe! We need tah' leave—"

"I will read it," Corrinne said loudly and stepped forward, trembling heavily.

Over the protest of the archbishop, she looked at the place where

VanderMeer pointed in the book. She took a deep breath, and began to read the Roman Latin.

"A bane on the house of Vaelblez!
Malus spiritus be condemned to shadow!
Sealed forever beneath the stone crests!
And as these four houses stand,
So shall it be!"

In an instant, the creamy apparition was gone. The sensation of heat left the room, replaced by a gust of chill night air coming through the open window. The white eagle was gone too.

The pain everyone experienced vanished.

Still holding his silver talisman, VanderMeer slowly stepped back three paces from the *châsse*. The apparition did not return. *Maybe we've done it*, he thought. But he stepped back a few paces more to be certain.

As the others awaited another bizarre turn to occur, the artist silently reread the next paragraph of the history concerning the blood in the grave. Without pause, he poured some water into a cup. Pulling a palette pin from his sleeve, he pricked his finger. A drop of blood appeared. He dipped his finger into the water.

"Eminence, give me your hand."

The artist took hold of the archbishop's small finger and pricked it with the pin. The Jesuit recoiled.

"What are you doing?!"

"Dip your finger in the water. It will feel better."

The rattled priest did as he was told.

VanderMeer moved to Corrinne next. "It's written in the legend," he told her.

She complied immediately.

"I will nah'—" Pierre protested.

"Just do this, Pierre!" Corrinne pleaded, gripping his arm. "Please!"

Philippe was next. He had stood up again, baffled as he'd never been in his life. He could not make sense of any of this. It all happened too fast. Without a learned or instinctive reaction to provoke a response, he stood ready to strike at something he could not see, or fight, or run from. Yet, here was Corrinne, gliding around the room, assisting the artist like she knew exactly what was happening.

She touched Philippe's wild-eyed face, smiled weakly, and nodded. "I am here, my love. I am with you," she said. "We can do this."

Philippe hardly felt the needle's stab.

VanderMeer carried the cup to the *châsse* when he noticed Henri standing quietly next to the window.

Henri? He is present. The runes claim that all present must be included in the ritual.

VanderMeer approached the boy. Henri held out his hand. A drop of his blood was added to the others.

In silence, they watched the artist pour the pink-tinged water into the open pouch of dirt and bones.

"*Bloody...!*" Pierre grimaced and held an arm in front of his face, expecting the box to explode, or something even stranger and violent to occur.

VanderMeer stooped to pick up a square piece of limestone lying nearby on the floor and showed it to everyone.

"You see? The sigils of the four Great Houses are carved in its face. They are also carved into flat stones lining each side of the box, and a duplicate of this one lies on the bottom. I will place this piece on top of the pouch before I seal it all under a lid."

The limestone perfectly matched the square shape of the box and fit snugly over the pouch.

"Now, we all must throw something in the box on top of this. It can be anything as long as it's thrown in by your hand."

"It is like a funeral."

Hearing Corrine's words, VanderMeer reflected on this.

"Yes. That is what it was...originally. The ceremony in 988 began as the burial of Lord Vaelblez."

One by one, they picked up parts and pieces of the shattered clock. Metal and glass popped, snapped, and bounced on the stone as they landed in the box.

VanderMeer lifted the heavy wooden lid and pushed it over the top. There was a hole at each corner. Retrieving a mallet, chisel, and wooden pegs from a shelf, he hammered the lid shut with the pegs and chiseled flat any excess from the dowels.

"There. It is done." The artist exhaled, relieved. He looked around the room, unsure what else to say.

For a moment, they were all too shocked to move or talk.

"Well, wha' the *fuck* dah' we dah' now? Sit on it? I need something tah' drink."

Archbishop Nicolet recovered his composure and with it his sense of office. His outrage swelled over what he had just participated in doing. He stood up and pointed.

"I want that *thing* removed from the city by tomorrow!"

"To where?" the artist asked, feeling his part in this had been completed.

"*Out* of New France! Throw it into the sea!"

"Wait!" Philippe raised a hand. "If throwing this *thing* into the sea was a good idea…someone long before us would have done that a long time ago. I'm not sure how to explain any of this. Or why this only concerns us… but whatever we decide, we better be in agreement and be certain it's the right thing to do. Chittaqua said this thing was buried in the ground, yes?"

"As I explained, he told me this was interred in the ground beneath four standing stones engraved with the four sigils," VanderMeer responded. "That's why I carved the sigils into the new *sealing* stones I made. Based on what we just saw…I believe it was definitely the right thing to do."

Corrinne had been thinking through all the recent events and the details relayed in VanderMeer's books. "Yes—*no*—I mean, I believe it must be buried *deep* in the earth, which is why it is attacking us now. The legend claims the original grave was hidden, buried in a stone crypt, deep under-ground. And when it was plundered by mercenaries in 988, or whenever that was, the heavy stones were broken apart with metal bars and levers. That tomb had been sealed so as not to be opened, and hidden so as not to be found," she added with emphasis.

Corrinne paused at saying that. Her expression changed to one of sur-prise. "That's it!"

"Tha's *it*?" Pierre asked in a tone of utter bafflement. "I've no idea wha' the fuck any o' ya' are talking aboot! If we need to bury it, let's take it outside and dig a hole! And be done with this, before—"

"That's what Chittaqua said to me one night," Henri interjected.

They all looked at him. The boy was calm, surprisingly so, considering all that had occurred.

"What did Chittaqua tell you?" VanderMeer asked.

"He told me about an island in the middle of a river that had standing stones with symbols, like the ones on my father's ring. He asked if I had ever heard of such things. We were talking about all sorts of things that night, mostly about books and how to make letters in the sand. He considered books to be, well, magical. Anyway, I told him there were lots of standing stones back in France and in other countries. Then he said the ones on this river had been hidden beneath a mound of earth, but that the river had washed away all of the dirt. He said he found bones at the center and the stones were falling over. So he took them. He said the bones must be buried again. But he was not sure how to do this. I tried to look at them once, and he got very angry with me. Said to never touch the pouch. And he never talked to me about it again."

Corrinne spoke with certainty. "Someone brought these relics across the ocean from Francia to bury them here, because the grave in Francia was known to everyone! Someone would plunder it again. So they came over here and buried the relics in a place so foreign and so remote, no one could find them. And the secret lasted almost eight hundred years. They brought the relic here on purpose! And tonight we saw why. Who would do something so remarkable?"

"Apparently, a very terrified Druid priest called Daeniel," Archbishop Nicolet replied. He glanced warily at the box, still wishing he was not in this room, that he had not participated. "It's all written there"—he pointed with annoyance—"in Monsieur VanderMeer's books of *pagan* folklore. This Druid priest named Daeniel performed the original ceremony. A Catholic bishop named Brevelaer, banished him afterwards...*imagine that*? *I wonder why*? But it was written in this tale that the Druid took some of the bones from the body of Lord Vaelblez and sailed off into the western seas with the Northmen. He never returned or was heard from again. Ever heard a story like that before." The sarcasm apparent.

"So you still don't believe *any* of this?" Philippe asked with amazement. "How can you dismiss what just happened?"

"I am an archbishop of the Catholic Church. I am the Jesuit Intendant of New France. My mission here is to spread the word of Christ to the peoples in this new land. I *believe* in God the creator, I *believe* in his only son, Jesus Christ, and I *believe* in the Holy Ghost. That's what I believe."

"Well, wha' aboot the huge white fuckin…beggin' your pardon…huge white bird tha' just perched in the window a little while ago? How do ya' explain tha'?"

"I *cannot* explain that," the archbishop proclaimed angrily, "anymore than I can explain anything else that happened here tonight…or why I am inexplicably attacked by something I cannot see. But if we *sealed* that thing, as Monsieur VanderMeer claims we did, according to how it was done in his devil's book, and if burying it someplace far away and deep underground will bring us all peace of mind, then I can accept that as our path."

"And I believe that as long as we place this box in a safe place where it will remain undisturbed," VanderMeer offered, "this *thing* will remain undisturbed, like it was for centuries until it got free again. The question is, as Monsieur Dunemoore so eloquently posed it, what do we do with it now?"

Corrinne answered without hesitation. "I will take it," she stated with finality. She was convinced. This had to be done right, and she did not trust anyone else in the room to ensure that it would, indeed, be done right. She must bear this burden. She turned to the artist.

"I want this box sent to the *Falcon Queen*'s river sloop, along with the paintings you showed to me today, and anything else you want transported. I will send a wagon and men to you tonight."

They exited the loft as a group, leaving the nervous VanderMeer alone to deal with the aftermath.

Corrinne's driver and footman were hovering by the front door. She had given them explicit orders not to come into the house or up to the studio loft no matter what they heard. After hearing the screams, however, they were inclined to disobey her wishes. They were about to ascend the stairs when people started coming down to the foyer.

Her footman spoke first. "Gendarmes are approaching."

Archbishop Nicolet looked around the coachmen into the streets. "People have come out of their homes?"

"Everyone heard the shouts and screams," the carriage driver explained.

Philippe and Pierre slipped on their sock hats and started whispering about the next place to rendezvous.

"The Terrain des Jésuites?" Corrinne suggested.

The archbishop, having recovered his composure enough to deal with this new problem, frowned but agreed.

"Get in the carriage, but let me answer any questions. Philippe, Pierre, on the back as footmen. Henri, in the carriage with Corrinne. Pretend she is your mother."

"I'm to be his *mother*?!"

They positioned themselves in the carriage just as a gendarmerie sergeant approached.

"Good evening, Eminence. People here indicate they heard screaming and crying."

Corrinne cradled Henri close, as if he were weeping. Her head bowed over his, she kissed his forehead gently and made soothing sounds.

"Yes, a funeral ceremony," Nicolet stated. "We are returning to the Jesuit chapel."

"Who is with you?"

"The widow. Her son. These are my footmen." He wanted to avoid more questions. "Driver, proceed."

The horse clopped down the street heading to the back of the gardens at the Terrain des Jésuites.

When Henri sat straight again, he gazed at Corrinne's chest in awe. "You are wonderful."

The courage of a grown man but the innocence of a boy, Corrinne thought.

"We will discuss wonderful things at another time."

Chapter 34
Montréal
October 1754
Abdication

Near midday, Singing Owl told Colbért that Philippe Gerrard had arrived and was moving around the city.

"Where is he?"

"He does not stop. He is hunting you," the old Indian told him. "Snow Hair is a good hunter. He has many friends. Many more than you. He has hidden the boy and the mother someplace in the city. Maybe at the lodge of the *Falcon Queen*."

But Singing Owl was not certain about this and claimed it would take more time to learn where.

Colbért knew this could not proceed as a hunting duel. The assassin must take control and force the *coureur de bois* into the open. The cleverness of Major Péan's original plan was still evident.

Draw the woodsman to your ground. Do something to make him angry and careless.

"Find the boy and his mother," he told Singing Owl. He gave the Indian another piece of silver. "Bring the information to me at the farmhouse. And take this missive to Intendant Bigôt."

He handed the Huron a folded piece of parchment.

It said, *All is ready. I will act this night.*

In the late afternoon, Singing Owl came again to the cabin near the swamp.

"Snow Hair's woman and the boy were seen being carried to a large river bateau at anchor. There are three hands of such bateaux waiting on the river. It is said most of these will go to Quebec in the morning."

In a way, this made things simpler. *I can kill the woman and boy in Quebec if I get there first*, he decided. It was perfect. Their deaths could be certified by government lackeys. *But first, the woodsman.*

He handed more silver to the Indian. "Find me a fast canoe and men to take me to Quebec. Have the canoe and men ready for me by the river road by sunset."

As dusk approached, Helmut Colbért started from the cabin in a wagon he'd stocked and prepared days earlier. He decided to check on the courier canoe that would carry him to Quebec. Where the road from the farmhouse connected with the one running alongside the river, he turned left instead of right. The long, sleek vessel was securely moored to a tree a short distance downstream, well camouflaged with branches, not easily seen unless you were looking for it. As directed, Signing Owl had supplied two half-breeds to paddle and guide the boat. They were waiting at the side of the road, sitting under a tree. They had the look of killers. He stopped.

"Stay out of sight. I will be coming back later tonight or before sunrise in the morning. At first light, or sooner, we will start downriver."

Satisfied that this first step in his escape from Montréal and New France was in order, he turned the wagon around and headed toward the river gate at the city's east end. He was only a quarter mile away when the enormous spike of pain struck. It was so intense he gripped his head and fell off the driver's seat, out of the wagon, thrashing around on the ground for a long, long time. It was excruciating. No voice. No message. Just repeated stabs that robbed him of his ability to walk or do anything except moan loudly, shouting, "What do you want?" and groaning for it to stop. He rolled around so violently, he ended up halfway down an oily black slope of mud to within a few feet of the city's privy ditch full of swamp water and sewage.

Then the pain vanished, as mysteriously as it started. Gone, leaving him sweating and panting. It was now past sunset and dark. He crawled to the top of the ditch, sat up, propped his head in his hands, elbows on his knees, and waited for another burst of pain. There was none. He rose to his knees, paused, then pushed himself to his feet and walked unsteadily to the wagon. He held on to the side for a while. Fortunately, the dim-witted horse had not bolted when he fell. He felt around in the back where some torches lay, selected one, dropped it to the ground behind the wagon, and ignited it with flint and gunpowder.

Now that he could see where he was going, he gathered the reins and climbed back onto the seat. Still no pain. Not even the usual dull ache! Such soothing relief felt odd after so many months of prickly aggravation. Yet, he could still sense the sinister presence, as if it were resting listlessly nearby.

"Good. Stay asleep. I need a clear head."

He snapped the reins and held the torch while the horse proceeded more rapidly along the road. In the back of the simple cargo wagon was loose straw and a long wooden box filled with more straw. It was the size of a coffin and he planned on using it as such, except the person going into it that night would still be alive. He'd also brought a large sheet of sail canvas, plus plenty of linen rags and rope.

Just behind the tops of the trees, he caught a glimpse of the full moon beginning to rise. It was going to be bright on such a clear, cold night.

Might not need a torch later.

He stopped the wagon at the river gate, which slowly opened far enough to allow two men to come out. One sentry aimed his musket, while the corporal approached the wagon.

"The city gate is closed until morning. State your name and business, Monsieur."

"My name is Gaspard de Propei. My business is mine own." The assassin held out two gold pieces, one for each guard, as Bigôt had directed. "There will be two more of these when I return later."

The gate opened wide.

While Montréal settled down to rest for the night, Intendant Bigôt remained in his office, as he had since early morning, receiving constant reports from his gendarmes. The exact whereabouts of Philippe Gerrard still eluded him. There were possible sightings of the woodsman all day long in different parts of the city, but Gerrard never stayed anywhere long enough for the intendant's men to act upon. Six different men were arrested and released. The city was crowded during the day, with much more activity now that the government was officially moving downriver to Quebec for the winter.

The merchant traders were filling the river sloops with their cargo for transport back to France. The large sea-going trading frigates lay at anchor in Quebec waiting for them. Two of those ships belonged to Lady de Chanaye. Bigôt planned to seize them after they were fully loaded with cargo. He relished the thought of what he might find aboard those vessels. If she harbored Philippe Gerrard, even for an hour, that would be enough to declare her a traitor-abettor. It was also likely she would be smuggling something. Even a foreign-made weapon would be enough to order a seizure. After she was arrested, Governor Duquesne would be required to sign over the ships to the government of New France so they could sail for France before the cargo spoiled. And, unknown to the Governor, the government of New France would sell them for a pittance to François Bigôt as soon as the paper could be signed and witnessed. Plenty of clerks in Quebec to perform that transaction. And the ships would start the winter crossing immediately. The profits would be enormous! He could hardly calculate the extent of the fortune until the ships were unloaded!

Best of all, with the Governor already gone from Montréal, Intendant Bigôt was now the ultimate authority; civilians, the government, and even the army must answer to him until Governor Duquesne sent his deputy military marshal upriver from Quebec. That would take a week at the minimum; ample time to do what he planned.

He'd received the message from Gaspard de Propei in the early afternoon. The *shérif* would abduct Lady de Chanaye that night. The woodsman would reveal himself in a reckless rescue attempt. And *voilà!* The timing could not be more perfect.

The two-foot-tall timepiece on his library shelf *tinged* a small bell once. It was half past the hour of eight. Fifteen minutes later, there was a knock on his office door. The Corsican entered followed by Major Péan.

"Well? Did you find him?"

"Lady de Chanaye's carriage just pulled into the gardens behind the Terrain des Jésuites. In addition to her, it carried a young boy dressed like a half-breed. It also carried Archbishop Nicolet, and three footmen, two of whom were dressed like *coureurs de bois*."

"That's them!" Francois Bigôt stood, agitated, ready to act. "Did you stop them?"

The major exhaled, annoyed. "No, Monsieur. We had only time enough to see them as they passed by. But it does not matter. My gendarmes are surrounding the Jesuit missionary quarters now. They aren't going anywhere."

The intendant began tapping his lips thoughtfully with a finger. *If the shérif lies in wait for the courtesan,* he thought, *he will abduct her as soon as she gets back to her city house and take her out the river gate. If we*

*capture the woodsman alive and jail him, she will pay any ransom I ask for
him! I can prepare documents for her to sign while I wait!*

"Oh, this is a most fortunate circumstance. Pull your gendarmes back
from the Terrain des Jésuites into positions where they will be unobserved.
But make certain when the woodman appears, you can close ranks on him
immediately. And make certain your men know we want him taken *alive*.
And withdraw your guards from Lady de Chanaye's house. Deploy them
far enough away where they can watch for any suspicious movement. If
Lady de Chanaye leaves the Terrain des Jésuites, do not detain her. If they
see *anything* out of the ordinary at her city house, have it reported to you.
They are *not* to interfere for any reason."

"What would be happening at Lady de Chanaye's city house?"

Bigôt dismissed the question with an irritated wave of his hand. "It's
just a precaution. If Philippe Gerrard eludes your men, he will run to ground
within the city knowing he is hunted. He cannot get out of the gates, so I
suspect he will sprint to the courtesan's house. I want him to settle in. And
you can then surround the smaller place more easily."

Major Péan knew the insufferable twit was lying, but he did not see
anything wrong with the order. He saluted.

"Yes, sir."

From his scouting forays, Colbért knew he would use the garden
entrance, go up the balcony, but, this time, into the house to wait. He would
kill whoever he must and abduct Lady de Chanaye after rendering her
unconscious. The image of her naked, splayed facedown, and tied hand
and foot to a bed was arousing. He licked his lips.

Colbért stopped his wagon on the Rue Saint-Claude at the end of the
servants' alley leading into the gardens behind Lady de Chanaye's house.
He saw a vagrant huddled in a nearby doorway and paid him a silver livre
to watch the wagon, promising two more when he returned. He walked
down the street to the Rue Saint-Paul. Two gendarmes were standing sentry
outside the whore queen's house. A street carter trundled by, on his way
home from selling bread at the market. Seeing an opportunity, he purchased
a loaf of still warm bread, wrapped in linen from the baker, and casually
approached the two soldiers.

"You both look cold. Here, I have some bread leftover. It's still warm and I ate the other one."

"Very kind of you, sir," the corporal said.

The gendarme tore into the savory loaf.

Colbért stretched his arms wide in a friendly way and looked at the sky. "Beautiful night, isn't it? Who has you standing watch when you should be drinking, the Governor?"

The corporal snorted. "No. The Governor is halfway to Quebec by now. No one's inside except servants. This is Lady de Chanaye's house. She's not here. Probably cavorting tonight, fucking somebody important."

They all laughed.

"Then what are you doing here?"

"Just following more senseless orders. We are to detain the good lady when she gets back from her humping and inform our superior."

"Probably his turn," Colbért replied lewdly. "He gets her ass!"

They all laughed again.

Leaving the soldiers, Colbért circled around on the next street and came back down the servants' alley from the opposite direction. The gendarmerie's presence was unexpected, but at least he knew she was not home. Kicking the vagrant awake again, he decided to loiter in a doorway near the corner of Rue Saint-Paul and keep watch on the front of the house. When she finally approached in her carriage, he could sprint up the street, down the alley, and get up into her boudoir long before she even started up the inside stairway. If he did this right, the soldiers would not know she was gone until it was too late.

Archbishop Nicolet was met at the back entrance to the Terrain des Jésuites by Father Cortois, who he had selected only that afternoon to take Father Tinian's place until the secretary was better.

"*Eminence.*" The Father dropped to one knee to kiss the archbishop's ring.

"Do *not* do that again," Nicolet said wearily. "This is not Rome and I am not the Pope."

Henri followed next. There was a pause while a joyous, one-sided reunion took place between Henri and the Father. Henri's face was apprehensive, preoccupied. His reaction greatly subdued.

"Ahh, and Philippe Malthais too! It is almost impossible to believe we are all meeting again on the other side of the world, yes?"

Father Cortois went to embrace the *coureur de bois*, but Philippe pushed him away brusquely with one hand; his expression that of someone who had just witnessed something terrible.

"Another time, Father, if you please."

Corrinne turned to her footman and driver and spoke to them tersely.

"Here are six pieces of gold to bribe the guards at the boat-landing gate. Go to the Dunemoore warehouse. Tell the senior clerk to send a wagon to Monsieur VanderMeer's studio and retrieve his remaining cargo. I want this done *now, tonight*," she emphasized. "Tell the clerk to have the artist's cargo loaded on the *Falcon Queen*'s river sloop. When this is done, return and bring all the other footmen with you. If you hurry, you may keep whatever gold you do not use to bribe the guards, and I will give you each another piece."

At the top of the stairs, they shuffled into the archbishop's office.

"Father Cortois, bring us wine," Nicolet said curtly before he shut the door and took a seat at his desk.

The others took various seats around the room as were available.

While they waited for Father Cortois to return, an awkward silence descended; the trauma of what had happened in the artist's loft still resonated in their thoughts.

Pierre rationalized in a practical way. *Okay, there are ghostly monsters in the world. How do we deal with them? Evidently, you seal them in a box lined with stone and move on. Simple enough.*

The archbishop was deeply troubled. He needed to frame what occurred somehow. It had to tie into something he knew to be true. It had to reconcile with his knowledge of science, his strong faith, his logic. Otherwise it challenged his foundational beliefs in science, faith, and logic—the very basis of how he approached his life. Explanations about what happened and why were debatable; less debatable was how something like that could happen. If he accepted that it did happen, he would have to answer how? And he could not.

Corrinne had an answer, however implausible, to the pain she'd experienced, and a way to control it permanently. She had other priorities in her immediate life much more immediate and dangerous. She was ready to move on. But they had to reach an agreement in order to restore the harmony among themselves.

Henri saw this through Chittaqua's eyes. The Ghost Eagle was real to him and it was there specifically to counter this evil. It was not going away. He was used to others being skeptical.

Philippe looked at the faces in the room and understood their reluctance to speak. *Where do we begin?* He spoke first.

"Well, I will start then. I feel we must reach some conclusion on what occurred. I have never been an overtly religious man, maybe I should have been. But neither was I ever a believer in things of a mystical or occult nature. Like Pierre, I am a wilderness man, a *coureur de bois*. In the wilderness, my life and survival depends on my knowledge of forest lore and the support of my friends. This so-called *wraith* is from some ancient time. It has no place in my life, our lives, our time. So, what is common to us? We are all friends after a fashion, but something different, something unusual, has tied us together. Chittaqua knew what it was. I never believed him."

Philippe took off his ring and laid it on the desk.

"Pierre, your ax."

Pierre was going to argue but didn't. He placed his heavy ax on the desk, the jeweled head toward the center. Philippe's ring was dwarfed next to it.

"Eminence, your crucifix…please."

André Nicolet held up a hand. "I will only say this once: I am forced to concede what happened to us was no coincidence. My logic tells me this was supposed to happen. And if we follow the example of our ancestors seven hundred years ago, we can put this evil thing out of our lives again. And by that logic alone I will do this, and that is what I support."

The archbishop set his jeweled crucifix on the table, turning it over so the sigil engravings could be clearly seen.

Philippe looked to his son. "Henri. The talisman."

Henri lifted the amulet from around his neck and laid it among the other objects. "This is what Chittaqua predicted would happen when we met the picture maker, Monsieur VanderMeer. A message would be revealed. He knew this before anyone else. At least that is what I believe. And the Ghost Eagle is part of the legend. For me, at least. I saw it from the spires of Saint Ouen's Church in Rouen, as early as I can remember. No one else could see it but me. Father Cortois knows this to be true."

At that moment, Father Cortois pushed through the unlocked door carrying a serving tray holding two bottles of wine and a platter of bread and cheese. The tension eased with the appearance of food and drink.

Pierre poured a cup of wine and drank it in one gulp. "I thin' we'll be needin' more of this," he told the priest.

After Father Cortois left the room, Philippe continued, pointing at the sigils and the objects as he talked.

"These symbols. These things are the connection…as I see it. The connection from our past to what happened today. At some point, when there is more time, I think we need to make a record of what has happened. We can bury this *thing*, but it will endure I think, and who can say to what purpose? Eminence?"

The archbishop contemplated Philippe's words for a few moments before he replied.

"The Church can take no part in creating a record. No acknowledgement, no witness, no approval. I will write nothing in my hand or name. But since, according to VanderMeer's histories, the legacy of this evil will continue, even to our progeny, it may prove beneficial to compose our version of what happened today, and our counsel. If the rest of you are so inclined to do this, I will not try to dissuade you."

"Then I will do this," Corrinne announced. "With Monsieur Vander-Meer's assistance, I will create a record and make copies for each of us to keep."

There was a consensus. Everyone nodded. This was the right thing to do.

"So be it," the archbishop certified, rapping his knuckles on the desk.

The declaration produced an immediate, if odd, sense of relief. It would never be possible to forget what occurred, but the archbishop's statement sanctioned a common resolution. It was over…at least for now. The objects were withdrawn.

They would not speak of it again as a group.

Philippe welcomed the opportunity to refocus on his existing objective: another evil, this one flesh and blood. And it moved among them and against them right now. He was anxious to get at this.

"I saw at least a dozen gendarmes on the street outside, and it looked like more were gathering."

Nicolet stiffened. "They will not dare enter the Terrain des Jésuites."

"I need to present some other things concerning—" Corrinne rose from her chair to collect her valise still sitting on the bookshelf. "Eminence, if you please, with your permission, I would like to complete the matters we discussed early this morning, though it seems like days have passed since we talked."

With the bizarre imagery of an hour earlier still dancing in his memory, the archbishop slowly nodded his head. "I'm sorry. You were saying?"

"Should I continue?"

"Yes."

Corrinne proceeded in a somber voice, as if she were discussing some-one's last will and testament.

"I declare the partners of les Négociants Dunemoore to be present before you. Since the Governor has already departed for Quebec, and Intendant Bigôt would probably make this…difficult, I am requesting your signature, Eminence, as a witness."

"I agree to be witness." The archbishop exhaled wearily. "Do Messieurs Dunemoore and Gerrard know about these transactions?"

"No. They do not. There's been no time. Certainly not today, obviously. But if we do not do this now, well, I am not sure what tomorrow will bring."

Pierre finished downing another cup of wine. "Know aboot wha' transactions?"

Lady de Chanaye turned slightly in her chair toward her partners. But she spoke mainly to Pierre.

"I have made some decisions this year, many of them recent, many of them personal, some you may have expected, others will be new. I would ask your indulgence to allow me to explain all of them to you first, before you start *shouting*."

"Shouting?" Philippe touched her arm gently. "Why would we shout at you at all?"

Pierre just stared at her.

"Pierre?"

"Wha'?"

"Will you let me finish explaining all of it first?"

"Why are ya' only askin' *me* tha'?"

"I…I don't have the strength to deal with any more confrontation."

Philippe slipped his arm around her shoulders. "Go on."

"Very well. First, I have decided to leave New France. I will sail with the *Falcon Queen* when she leaves Quebec. It will be sailing to Boston."

"Boston?!"

Corrinne's lower lip trembled. "You see! Can you wait until I'm finished?"

Philippe glared angrily at Pierre.

"All right! I'm sorry, lassie. I'm sorry."

Corrinne went on to explain her reasons, the changing government, the war, her expectation that Intendant Bigôt was on the verge of seizing all of her possessions including her ships, that the corrupt intendant could also gain control of the Dunemoore Company since she owned fifty-one percent.

"Therefore, I have sold my ownership in the company to Archbishop Nicolet."

"Bloody...!" Pierre caught himself. He held up a hand and bowed his head in apology.

"The archbishop, as agent, and therefore the Church, will become the majority owner, preventing anyone in the government of New France from seizing the company. But this ownership percentage applies only to transfers in title. Pierre, I am giving *all* my shares in profit to you. That *gives* you a seventy-six percent share in what means the most to you...the money, yes?"

"Why would ya' dah' tha'?"

"If I may continue," Corrinne said in an emotionless voice. "I also recommend Philippe transfer all his remaining shares in ownership and profit to Henri. Henri has not been declared a traitor to the crown and potentially subject to losing all his property." She looked at him for his reaction.

Philippe's face was impassive. "I'm just listening."

Henri had many questions, but wisely decided to wait.

"Pierre, I have further decided to sell my city houses in Montréal and Quebec to you for one thousand livres. The only stipulation being that you retain all the servants in both houses for as long as they desire, most importantly, the chamberlain and his wife. Mathilde will come with me. The deed of sale will indicate you have paid me the one thousand livres weeks ago, which I am certain you have, in some fashion, at some time in the past. In fact, all of these documents are dated weeks ago. And it will be so witnessed."

Pierre continued to glug his wine and chew bread as he listened.

Philippe brooded. He sensed she had more serious matters to reveal.

"The documents that require your signatures are all complete." She carefully slid a stack of documents from the valise. "I should finish my explanation before we sign them."

"Ya' mean there is more?"

Corrinne turned to Henri.

"Henri, this next document concerns you. You must understand what this portends. Ask questions if something is unclear. *This* transaction will require the Governor's signature when we reach Quebec."

"Wait!" Philippe said, suddenly looking alarmed. "Why should Henri be exposed to any of this?"

"Let Corrinne finish," the Jesuit said, "then decide."

"I recently received a missive from Financier d'Arnouville, Jean-Baptiste de Machault. The crown of France has declared the Marquis de Propei to be insane; his wealth forfeit. By now he is confined to an asylum. The Marquis has no recognized heir except for Gaspard de Propei, whose dubious legitimacy is being challenged by the Church. *If* the Church's challenge is upheld by the crown, the marquisate title falls to Michelle de Propei, whose vows are permanently recorded at Saint Ouen's Church in Rouen. Because of those recorded vows, her claim to title would be forfeit. Therefore, the marquisate would fall to Henri. I will explain why."

She paused to collect her breath.

"Before the current Marquis was declared insane by the King, he had averred Henri to be Michelle's bastard, with no connection to the Propei family. But the Church will now be supporting a claim for Henri to have the hereditary title as the Marquis' son and heir."

Philippe suddenly crossed his arms. "How is this so?" There was an edge in his tone.

"Since Michelle was not the Marquis' natural daughter, the Church will assert Michelle was actually the Marquis' *wife*. If this assertion is not refused by the King, the Church can, and will, declare Henri to be the natural son of the Marquis de Propei."

Now Philippe spoke loudly. "Everyone in Rouen knows Henri is my son! Including the Church! Most importantly the Church, who gave him Holy Sanctuary!" Philippe shot a disapproving glance at Corrinne. "Why would you contrive to do this? To Henri?"

When Corrinne saw Philippe's expression of betrayal directed at her, she trembled even more. "No, Philippe!" She reached out to him, then dropped her arms, hugging them tightly around herself. "Please! Philippe! There was no time to tell you until now! Wait—"

"Monsieur Gerrard," the archbishop said strongly. "*I* also took a part in this at Corrinne's request. And if you are fortunate, I hope you learn one day how often Lady de Chanaye has acted for your benefit. Over the last several years it was multiple times, usually placing herself at considerable risk. So allow her to finish!"

Corrinne recovered her composure, though Philippe remained sullen. She pointed to an ornate parchment lying beneath the others.

"That particular document was prepared by the Church in Paris. It states that Henri is declared to be the hereditary heir of the Marquis de Propei, and *if* he abdicates, then title to the lands and wealth of the House of Propei will pass back to Michelle de Propei. And because of her recorded vows of poverty in the Sisterhood, it further passes to the Church. In consequence, the House of Propei, by title or land, in its present form, will cease to exist. And *that* is the purpose of these contrived events…to destroy the House of Propei."

Corrinne stopped and placed her face in her hands for a moment. *I am not strong enough to face all this alone*, she thought. *Not without Philippe.* She took a long swallow of wine and set down her goblet. Taking a deep breath, she spoke again.

"Since none of you knew about any of this before tonight, I want to give Henri the courtesy of asking questions about the marquisate, because, in the same breath he is also being asked to abdicate."

The plan was brilliant. And Philippe could plainly see Corrinne's distress, and worse, her gathering sadness all because of his words. *She does not deserve any criticism from anybody, and least of all from me.*

"Corrinne." Philippe took hold of her hands and looked into her eyes. "I will never doubt you again. And I should not have doubted you now."

Then he kissed her.

Corrinne was elated just from his kiss!

The archbishop raised his hand. "If you please. May we dispense with the kissing?"

"Yes, Eminence. Henri? You must have questions."

"Yes, my lady, I do. Does what you explained mean that I *am* the Marquis de Propei once we sign these things? Right now?"

"The hereditary title must pass to someone. It could be Gaspard de Propei or another distant relative. But the Church wants *you* to have this title, and so they declared this title should come to you."

"But they want that I abdicate too." Henri looked up at the ceiling for a moment. "I *think* the Church wants me to abdicate this title so it might have the lands and wealth of the marquisate."

"I believe that is one underlying motive, yes," Corrinne agreed. "But they also seek to have the House of Propei disbanded permanently."

Pierre noticed a look of fatherly pride on Philippe's face. "He obviously gets tha' logical ability from his mother," Pierre said quietly.

Corrinne watched Henri thinking. She prodded. "Henri? Questions?"

"The Marquis de Propei kept my mother prisoner at Saint Ouen's Church. The Marquis' hired swords hurt a lot of people. They stabbed me in the thigh with a rapier and almost paralyzed my friend, Brother Daniel. They tried to kill my father."

Henri turned to Archbishop Nicolet.

"Eminence, if I sign this document to abdicate, will this cause the House of Propei harm?"

"Potentially. Of course, Gaspard de Propei has a documentary claim of hereditary title, which applies only if it is proven your mother is dead and that you are dead. And you should understand that *all of this petty argument concerning hereditary claim*, can be dismissed by King Louie…*with a simple wave of his hand*…vacating anything we decide or sign here tonight."

Henri nodded. He understood.

"But no matter what the Church, or any document might state otherwise—nothing can ever dismiss Philippe Malthais as my real father, or Sister Michelle as my real mother, or that Captain LaTour taught me the secrets of the sea and the stars, or that Pierre Dunemoore is my friend, and so were Louie Hawkfeeder and Michel Langlois, or that Roland died for me," he said in a choking voice. "And that Chittaqua died for me too, or that Anamosa loves me…and I think Corrinne who I never met before today loves me too. And that *all* of you stood with me, and before me, to defy a *demon*! Even a King cannot dismiss any of these things, yes? Because all of us know the truth of these things. So if he takes away a title that I never had and do not want, what have I lost?"

"Nothing." Corrinne's hands went to her lips as tears spilled from her eyes.

Archbishop Nicolet nodded. "As she says…nothing. And the rest of us have gained the privilege and honor of knowing *you*," he responded, wondering at such wisdom in a boy so young.

"Then I will sign what you ask."

The signing proceeded quietly and anticlimactically. Pens and inkpots were passed among themselves. Henri's heartfelt words had made all other discussion and opinion seem trivial for the moment. To the archbishop's surprise, Corrinne, most of all, remained silent. She would only shake her head or nod when asked a question.

Almost two hours had elapsed since their arrival when they were finished.

Corrinne collected all the signed documents into the valise and handed it to the archbishop. "Can you keep this for me, until we reach Quebec? They need to be recorded officially, of course. And I don't know what the rest of this night portends. I'm worried if I were arrested—"

"Of course."

Father Cortois knocked and opened the door.

"Pardon, Eminence. My lady, there is a carriage come for you. It is waiting out back."

"And the gendarmes?"

"There are still a few walking the streets, but not so many as before."

She looked at Philippe and Pierre. "What now?"

"Back tah' the warehouse?" Pierre suggested.

"No," Archbishop Nicolet said. "The intendant and Major Péan probably know you are here. We are all tired. You need to rest. Henri needs rest. We have plenty of beds. The night belongs to your enemies, but you are safe here. We can begin this again tomorrow—in the light of day. Maybe you can disguise yourselves as Jesuits, eh?"

Philippe recalled doing something like that before. "Corrinne needs to be escorted to her house."

"Nonsense," she interjected. "I have three well-armed footmen. And if I still feel threatened, I will pick up stray gendarmes along the way to join me. And did I mention…they are even *inside* my house? Or, I should say, your house, Pierre. I will be fine."

CHAPTER 35
MONTRÉAL
OCTOBER 1754
The Dull, Black-Eyed Gaze of a Hunter

The hour was late and still the whore queen had not arrived. An hour earlier, gendarmerie sentries were pulled from the front door and were followed by two more from inside the house. They proceeded east on Rue Saint-Paul almost halfway to the Governor's palace before they stopped to lean upon a building on the other side of the street.

Colbért thought the withdrawal meant her approach, but no.

"Patience," he told himself. "She will come."

An hour later, the noises and shouts from the nearby taverns increased as the scum of Montréal got drunk and began brawling among themselves. Colbért watched two men, down by the soldiers, begin circling one another in the middle of the street. Knives flashed out. They swung at each other clumsily. Suddenly, a carriage came round the corner, disrupting the fight.

It's her!

The Night Butcher did not wait. He ran up the street, removed the hobble from his horse, and tied off the reins to a storefront door handle. He found the vagrant asleep for the third time. *Stupid ass!* He cut the man's throat and took back his money.

Sprinting down the servants' alley, he gathered up the sail canvas, linen strips, and ropes he'd left beneath the back porch and scaled up to the balcony. The boudoir room was dark and empty. He pushed on the door, breaking the flimsy bolt lock, shoving back the heavy piece of furniture enough to permit him entry. Once inside, he picked up the furniture and quietly moved it out of the way. He took a position to the side of the door so when it opened it would block any view of him. If the person that entered next was not the whore queen, he would muffle her mouth, cut her throat, and lay her soundlessly on the floor behind him, then shut the door and wait for the next person. He'd killed six servants this way one night in Paris, before his intended victim came into the room. The floor there had been marble. It had gotten very slippery with blood.

He reminded himself to lay the bodies on rugs this time.

"My lady, we were all so worried," said the chamberlain.

Mathilde could see the weariness in Corrinne's eyes. "We are so glad you are back."

"Where are the gendarmes?" Corrinne asked.

The chamberlain shook his head. "Along with the guards at the door, they suddenly left, over an hour ago. They left without saying why, or if they would be coming back. We worried something terrible might have happened to you or Monsieur Gerrard."

"Messieurs Gerrard and Dunemoore are safe for the night at the Terrain des Jésuites. Henri Gerrard too. What an absolutely marvelous young man," she told them, the tiredness in her voice giving way to affection. "I've never seen such courage, intelligence, and maturity in someone so young. He may have stolen my heart." Corrinne looked around the foyer. "Is this the remainder of the baggage?"

"Yes, Mistress," Mathilde replied. "Except for a trunk in your boudoir, and a few items I've kept separate."

Corrinne turned to the chamberlain. "And you are certain I cannot change your mind?"

The old man smiled. "Pleased as I am to serve you, my lady, I am too old to start a new life somewhere else. Montréal is my home. And I must presume Monsieur Dunemoore will have need of a good chamberlain?"

"Indeed, he will. And he's already agreed to keep you on as long as you want to be here."

"So we are truly leaving?"

"Yes, Mathilde. You and Madeleine should be ready in the morning to go. Where is Madeleine?"

"Once the gendarmes left, she went up to her room. Do you want something to eat? Or to drink, perhaps?"

"No. I would like to take a hot bath and go to bed. Master chamberlain, have a footman posted at the door throughout the night. Tell them to stay armed."

Mathilde went into the *cuisine* to heat bath water. The chamberlain went outside to organize the footmen.

Corrinne trudged up the stairs, arranging her thoughts toward the sequence of the next day's events. Suddenly, a question intruded again. *Why would the gendarmes abandon the watch on my house?* She paused at the top of the stair. Something was not right.

No one else but Intendant Bigôt would have given that order! Why? He knows I've been loading my household to the sloop. If he is going to act on me, he must keep track of me. The gendarmes were doing that for him. So why did he order them to stop? And at night, when it would be even easier for me to slip away from Montréal unnoticed?

Pondering these thoughts, she slowly walked a few more steps down the hallway toward the door to her boudoir. *I am overtired.* She paused again. She reversed direction and went quickly down the hall to the other room, quietly opening the door.

The room was completely dark. No candles were lit.

"Madeleine," she called out softly.

The bedding rustled. "Uh, yes, my lady. Is that you?"

Corrinne exhaled. "Yes. I just returned. I wanted to see that you are all right."

Madeleine yawned. "The gendarmes were tedious and crude. So when they left, I decided not to wait up for you. Was that wrong?"

Corrinne yawned too. "Of course not. I'm sorry I woke you. Go back to sleep. Tomorrow we will—"

"Did you see Henri?"

Corrinne heard excitement and hope in the girl's voice. "Yes…I did. But we can talk about that tomorrow."

She closed the bedroom door. There was something about Madeleine that Corrinne did not trust. Madeleine had suffered a terribly abusive childhood to be sure, subject to the sexual whims of men, and worse, her father, which could certainly twist one's character, and Corrinne was highly empathetic to that history. It was the main reason why she agreed to Archbishop Nicolet's personal request to foster the girl temporarily. But Madeleine's nature seemed strangely predatory. Corrinne noticed how overtly flirtatious she acted with any of the younger boys *and* girls she had occasion to meet. And Madeleine's intense interest in Henri only made Corrinne's misgivings deepen.

But, the gendarmes' departure had nothing to do with Madeleine, she thought as she returned to the door of her boudoir. She hesitated again as the uneasy feeling persisted. Unbuttoning her dress from the top, she began searching for that *something* to become clear. She usually did such acute problem solving in front of a mirror; looking down to ask the question, looking at her reflection for the contrasting points of view. Except this seemed urgent to think about, *now.* That was odd too.

Maybe the gendarmes left because they know Philippe is in the Jesuits' compound. Nothing more complicated than that. But that was over an hour ago, wasn't it? It should not matter, yes? But why didn't the gendarmes stop me when I left Archbishop Nicolet? At least to ask me questions? Moreover, there were no gendarmes on the street, where, earlier, several dozen gathered near or around the Jesuit quarters. Does that not seem odd? Maybe they went to bed. That seems plausible. Corrinne shook her head to clear her thoughts.

"Bed. Sleep. That's what I should do," she whispered to no one. "I think too much."

She opened the door to the room, stepped inside, and saw it immediately. The balcony door was ajar. She felt the door handle slip away from her grip as it shut. Her head snapped to the right and met the dull, black-eyed gaze of a hunter, millimeters from its prey.

Those eyes!

Corrinne de Chanaye did not have time to scream.

The hunter slammed the haft of his stiletto accurately, striking her head above the temple.

Her head jerked sharply. Blackness descended.

The Night Butcher caught her before she fell to the floor. Moving quickly, he laid her in the center of the sail canvas, stuffed a wad of linen in her mouth, tied more in a blindfold and gag around her head, pulled off her shoes, noosed rope several times around her ankles, rolled her over, cinched her wrists together behind her back, rolled her over again, and searched her clothes for any hidden weapons.

He slipped a hand inside her unbuttoned dress and pinched a nipple hard and watched for a reaction. She did not move.

Good.

Colbért rolled her again, this time within the folds of the sail canvas, tied off the top and bottom, effectively making it a cocoon. Hoisting her up over his shoulder—she was surprisingly light—he had stepped through the balcony door when a terrified scream erupted behind him. He glanced back. It was the girl, Madeleine. She screamed again and ran.

Colbért climbed down the balcony and sprinted down the servants' alley. He laid the body in the back of the wagon, climbed up, unlatched and opened the coffin, laid the body inside, added more straw, closed and latched it again. He went to the front to gather the reins and was confronted by two footmen running out of the alley, their swords drawn.

With a shrug of his elbows, the stilettos dropped quickly from the scabbards into his hands. They attacked. Grunts and yells echoed off the buildings. He parried the sword thrust of the closest man with one stiletto, stabbing the other long blade into the man's eye. He shoved the dead body into the second man's sword thrust, diverting that attack. An instant later, he sliced the throat and groin of the second attacker simultaneously. The entire fight was over in seconds.

Taking some linen rags, Colbért quickly cleaned his knives and hands, and shoved the weapons back up his sleeves into the scabbards. Vaulting to the driver's seat, he snapped the reins. The horse reared slightly then moved off at a trot. Before he reached the Rue Saint-Paul, another man came running around the corner and up the Rue Saint-Claude directly at him. He steered the wagon to run the man down, but the runner jumped out of the way.

The chamberlain picked himself up off the street, ran back to the corner, committing the wagon to memory. A farm wagon, single horse, one driver. A wooden box in the back of the wagon, bouncing around. He was horrified to realize that Lady Corrinne was inside that box. She might be alive, but for how long? The wagon would pass the turn for the boat yard gate first, then it was a straight path to the river-road gate. He must get help! Messieurs Philippe and Pierre were at the Terrain des Jésuites. They would know what to do.

He turned again and started running as fast as he could up the Rue Saint-Claude.

The four shivering gendarmes were actually pleased to hear screams coming from the general direction of Lady de Chanaye's house.

"Was that suspicious enough to report," one of the men asked the corporal.

"Maybe, maybe not. Let's move closer."

Next, they saw a man burst from the front door of Lady de Chanaye's house and run up the Rue Saint-Claude.

"Something's happened," one of the soldiers said.

"We are not to interfere, only to report."

Then a wagon came rolling around the corner at a fast trot and clattered past. The soldiers parted to stay out of its way.

"Report now?"

"Yes!"

The corporal marched his men up Rue Bonsecours to find Major Péan.

Major Péan stood in front of Intendant Bigôt's desk, breathing heavily.

"Something important to report for once?"

"Lady de Chanaye has been abducted!"

The French officer saw the intendant's satisfied smile.

"You *knew* about this?"

"Of course not, Major. And watch your tone with me! But what this means is when word of the abduction reaches the woodsman, he will burst from cover. Your gendarmes are attending to all the exits from the Jesuit quarters?"

"I've already given those orders. Then you know who has taken her?"

"No, but I assume it was Gaspard de Propei. He said he was going to devise a plan to bring the woodsman to him. In fact, he mentioned this plan was your suggestion, yes?"

Major Péan sneered, disgusted. "You will not be blaming me for what happens this night."

Intendant Bigôt stood up. "We shall evaluate your performance to duty tonight, in the light of day tomorrow."

"The man is an animal."

"No doubt. He has assaulted other women…the woodman's Indian wife at Fort Le Boeuf, I think? I believe the troops there were under your command at the time, yes?"

Major Péan's face reddened. "Where did he take her?"

Intendant Bigôt took his time answering. "Let's see, it could be that swamp cabin east of the city. Some of our scouts spotted a person looking like him out there. But let's be sure. Send your best native scout to that cabin, and have Gaspard de Propei informed that Philippe Gerrard is under arrest. And *if* he has abducted Lady de Chanaye, she should not be harmed, but returned to your protection as soon as possible."

"He has tortured and killed other women, native girls, since he's been in Montréal. He is a killer. And you know this."

Intendant Bigôt shouted for his Corsican secretary to come into the room. "Yes, Monsieur?"

"Major Péan has just informed me that Gaspard de Propei has tortured and killed native women in a cabin east of the city. He will be sending scouts there tonight to see if he has abducted someone recently. Write a missive about this to send downriver to Governor Duquesne tomorrow."

"Yes, Monsieur."

Major Péan straightened, trembling with anger. "You are a coward. And when this is over, we will talk again. I will go to the cabin myself."

"No, I don't think you will. I am ordering *you* to arrest Philippe Gerrard tonight, alive, and incarcerate him in the Couteau du Fort." He looked at the secretary. "Make note of this order in the missive to the Governor."

"Yes, Monsieur."

"Now, Major, I *order* you to inform the Jesuits, preferably Archbishop Nicolet, that you suspect Lady de Chanaye was abducted by Gaspard de Propei, and that you have taken actions to confirm this, and if it's true, you will arrange for her rescue…*in the morning*."

A cold, calm look dropped over Major Péan's face. He saluted slowly. "Yes, sir. And I look forward to discussing this night with you in the future."

Intendant Bigôt struggled for something to retort, but the major had already left the office.

He went to his window on the Rue Notre-Dame, overlooking the Terrain Des Jésuites. The Corsican waited patiently to see if he was dismissed.

"Time to balance our accounts," Bigôt announced. "Enjoy yourself tonight, Monsieur de Propei."

His gratified smile vanished at a disturbing thought.

He wouldn't really kill her, would he?

The intendant thought more about it. He didn't want Lady de Chanaye killed. *Abused*, fine, but not *murdered*. He had plans for her. Personal plans. François Bigôt pondered the ramifications of what the *shérif* might do to her. He decided the worst that could happen was the usual abuse whores suffered. But that meant only bruises, maybe bleeding, puffy lips. And she had survived bruises before. Bigôt knew this because he'd personally given her breasts and ass several large purple bruises with his teeth. *Of course, he might cut her up a little with those deadly stilettos.* He shook his head at the image. *No*, Bigôt decided. He pulled the curtains over the window shutters.

"There's no reason for him to kill her," he argued aloud. "She's a whore! Only a deranged idiot would kill her. Monsieur de Propei is not stupid. He won't risk losing everything."

Bigôt noticed the Corsican's appraising expression. "You have something to say? If I lose, you will lose much more."

"Of that, I have no doubt. But, if I may, is there any value to you in her survival? You can still seize her ships for a variety of reasons now. You already have proof of her smuggling. If Gaspard de Propei kills her and is captured doing it, then this could be advantageous to you in several ways, eliminating him as a stray thread on this tapestry. If he does not, she can be persuasive and dangerous even from a jail, no? And there is the Governor and Archbishop Nicolet, who will both assist her."

Intendant Bigôt bestowed the Corsican with a patronizing look.

"You really must improve the creativity in your thinking. If she remains alive, I will send word to her that she can secure the woodsman's release, but she must come here to pay his...*bail*. The woodsman is her single greatest weakness. She is planning to flee New France, maybe even tomorrow. Both of her ships have been loading cargo in Quebec all this week. We will seize them once they are loaded, or I can make her sell them to me outright."

The intendant pulled open a desk drawer and lifted out freshly inked documents.

"I've already prepared the bill of sale for her to sign in anticipation of this negotiation. And this next document has her selling her ownership in les Négociants Dunemoore as well. And we can probably get her to pay a large sum of Louis d'ors, which she has sequestered somewhere, be certain of that. *Voilà!* All of this is possible, probably tonight. She becomes irrational where the woodman is concerned. We can strip her as she stands here in my office. She'd walk naked through the Sulpician seminary if I asked her to, and would probably enjoy it for that matter."

The Corsican's eyebrows rose at this last comment from the intendant.

"Actually, why not ask her to fulfill some of our personal needs for enjoyment tonight as well. You may take your pleasure with her in any fashion you like. All of her orifices will be available and compliant. We will call it a gift for your good work this year."

The Corsican bowed. "I am deeply grateful for your generosity, Monsieur."

"Now, we only need Philippe Gerrard arrested alive and jailed. And Lady de Chanaye returned to me tonight to secure his…ransom."

"And if he accidentally kills her?"

Bigôt scowled. "Well…that would be tragic. But if he does, we still seize her company and her ships, and Gaspard, le Marquis de Propei, will pay a ransom to secure Philippe Gerrard's execution. Then we will keep Gaspard de Propei in the Couteau du Fort and demand a second ransom to avoid his own death for murdering Lady de Chanaye. And while we are talking about this, see if you can locate Sister Michelle and Henri Gerrard. Some say they were seen on a *Falcon Queen* river sloop, others are not so sure. There was a boy in the carriage going to the Terrain des Jésuites earlier. The *shérif* also has *my* spies looking for them. It's been alleged his marquisate is in jeopardy if they remain alive. How, I am not sure, but there could be more money to earn in that regard."

The Corsican made a short bow and turned to leave.

"And try not to be so pessimistic! You are depressing my mood."

His fury unabated, Major Péan stomped back out onto the Rue Bonsecours and gathered together his three lieutenants and senior sergeants. Everyone was tired, and this night was not close to being over.

"Philippe Gerrard will be emerging from the Jesuit barracks soon. Position your men on alert. I want this *coureurs de bois* captured alive! Fix *baïonnettes* on your muskets. There will be no firing unless I order it! Is that clear? Double the guard at all the gates. No one leaves or enters this city without my permission."

Péan's seconds rushed to redeploy the troops of tired soldiers half-asleep in doorways or crouched behind shrubs and bushes on every side of the Jesuit compound. The Montréal gendarmes were composed of two companies of men assigned by the army, around two hundred, usually the malcontents. They were surly and less disciplined than the regular army counterparts, but if you paid them well and paid them on time, they would do whatever they were told, without question. Intendant Bigôt kept them well paid.

Left with his personal platoon of regular army soldiers, Major Péan sent his best half-breed scout to the swamp cabin with instructions to tell the *shérif* that Philippe Gerrard was in jail and to bring the women he had captive back to the city.

"Tell him this order comes directly from Intendant Bigôt."

Major Péan watched the scout run off toward the east city gate. He then walked slowly toward the atrium entrance of the Terrain de Jésuites, but stopped halfway and gave new orders to put men on the wall directly above them and at every intersection and street leading to the compound and particularly close to the entrances. At that moment, he saw a man coming secretively up the Rue Saint-Claude, slinking along the shadowed doorways of the street. The man stopped at the corner when seeing all the soldiers.

"Corporal, seize that man!"

The man made no attempt to escape and slouched unhappily, looking at the ground.

"Who are you sir? And what is your business?"

"I am house chamberlain for Lady de Chanaye."

For a moment, Major Péan was at a loss for words.

"What are you doing scurrying around here like a rat?"

"I was…going to the Terrain des Jésuites."

"Why?"

The chamberlain could not contain himself. "My lady was abducted from her house tonight by a man who placed her in a *box* and took her away in a wagon! He killed two of her footman. The wagon was heading toward the east city gate."

"And the Jesuits?"

"I wanted to inform…inform Archbishop Nicolet…t-to ask him for help."

"And that's because the archbishop is known to be so much better at policing the city than the gendarmes?"

The chamberlain looked helplessly at the ground.

"Well, do not be fearful. You may proceed to the Jesuits and so inform the archbishop."

The chamberlain was shocked. "*Merci*, good sir."

Major Péan watched the man hasten away.

"All right, Sergeant, alert the officers in charge at the other entrances. We should see activity at any time now. Remind them again I want the *coureur de bois* taken alive!"

He will try to get out the east city gate, Péan thought. *That's what I would do.*

The major decided to wait with his personal platoon of professionals at the point of the garden at the north end of Rue Bonsecours. He glanced up at the second-floor office of Intendant Bigôt. The lanterns were still burning, but he saw no shadow at the windows. The discussion with the intendant left him sick and disgusted that his own corruption had placed him in moral proximity with that man. That Gaspard de Propei had abducted Lady de Chanaye was so repugnant to him, he wanted to lead a company of gendarmes to find her.

I will follow my orders tonight, but I will also find a way to mitigate this.

"There are gendarmes everywhere outside," the chamberlain told them.

Philippe, Pierre, and Henri were already strapping on their weapons. Archbishop Nicolet was thinking about the surrounding compound and the best way out. Father Cortois hurried into the large foyer carrying water bladders and small sacks of food.

"We'll only need water," Philippe said tersely.

"There is a lieutenant of the gendarmerie at the garden door," Father Cortois told the archbishop anxiously. "He was alone. He asked for you, Eminence."

Philippe and Pierre made a move toward the garden area.

"Wait! I know who this is," the Jesuit told them. "You may stand nearby to hear what he says, but I want no violence here."

The garden door was actually two doors separated by a small mud room. Philippe, Pierre, and Henri waited beyond the second door, which the archbishop left open.

"Lieutenant?"

The officer dropped to one knee and kissed the archbishop's ring before rising again.

"Eminence, the Terrain des Jésuites is completely surrounded by the gendarmes. Our orders are to arrest Philippe Gerrard and anyone with him. Major Péan said there is to be no musket fire except by his order. But they have fixed their baïonnettes and will use them, I am afraid. We know the *coureurs de bois* are in here with you. There is no way to leave without a confrontation. There are extra guards at the gates and more men on the walls above this compound. My ability to intervene for you will be greatly diminished. I will have to follow my orders."

The archbishop nodded and smiled at the young officer. "Go with God, Lieutenant."

After the man left, Pierre spoke first. "We kin' rush out the front, directly across tha' street into tha' Jesuit chapel. Go out its back door into tha' gardens. Get around them and across tha' Rue Saint-Paul and over tha' riverside walls. I know several places tha' are unguarded."

Philippe frowned. "It would take too long. And the gendarmes will surge toward the river as soon as they see us move in that direction."

"Then we'll take a bateau into tha' river."

"In the dark?"

"I have a better idea," Archbishop Nicolet said.

Withdrawing closer toward the east gate, Major Péan had just sat down on a lower step of the sweeping stairway leading into the Governor's palace when he heard the sound of a musket being fired, followed by shouts of men in the gardens of the Terrain des Jésuites. He cursed loudly that his orders were being disobeyed. The next day he would learn the musket was fired in the air by a certain Father Cortois.

"Someone fired a musket in the atrium of the compound," the sergeant shouted.

Gendarmes from all directions began converging toward that place. Torches were lit everywhere.

A minute later, Major Péan heard a horse-drawn carriage galloping toward him from the Jesuit gardens.

"The musket shot was a diversion," the major shouted. "Fall back to the east gate! Quick time!"

The carriage plunged between his soldiers, who barely had time to jump out of the way. The side door bore the shield of Oñaz-Loyola, the family crest of Ignatius, founder of the Society of Jesus, and the symbol of the Jesuit Intendant of New France.

The archbishop's plan was to use the carriage to hurtle through the surrounding troops. Then use the authority of his office to force the guards to open the east gate and allow his carriage to pass. If they refused, Philippe and Pierre would overpower them by surprise.

"Without bloodshed," the archbishop told them sternly.

"Well, Eminence, it's unlikely I will nah' bleed if they start sticking me with a fucking *baïonnette*. Pardon. And if they do, they are goin' tah' bleed too."

As the carriage approached the eastern gate, it was completely dark. Even with the rising full moonlight, the interior side of the gate was covered by the shadow of the walls. The carriage driver was forced to slow and halt the wagon. The archbishop stuck his head out the window.

"This is Archbishop Nicolet. Open the gate and let my carriage pass."

"Eminence, I cannot do that," said the corporal in charge.

André Nicolet got out of the carriage. "My business is urgent. Peoples' lives are in danger. I order you to open this gate immediately!"

"Stay here," Philippe whispered to Henri, before he and Pierre slipped out the other door.

An enormous flash of gunpowder almost blinded Philippe and Pierre, not four paces from the carriage.

The corporal's torch burned brightly. Philippe saw he was surrounded by soldiers.

"Don't move, Monsieur!"

Panting from running, Major Péan stepped toward Philippe. The *coureur de bois* pulled out his skinning knife, sizing up which of the soldiers he could feint his way by first. The muskets tipped. Long *baïonnettes* gleamed sharply. The soldiers held their ground.

"You are under arrest, Monsieur Gerrard," the major said curtly. "Put down your weapon!"

Pierre Dunemoore waited until the major was within a few feet before throwing his first punch. But the major ducked away in time.

Out of the corner of his eye, Philippe saw Henri look out the carriage window. *If this becomes a fight …*

"Pierre, get Peter Blue Jacket's help," he whispered. Then he dropped his skinning knife on the ground.

"Very sensible, Monsieur," Major Péan said. The officer gestured to his corporal.

The soldier approached Philippe from behind and smashed the brass butt of his musket into the back of Philippe's head. The *coureur de bois* dropped to his knees and collapsed forward onto the street. He pushed up on his arms, groaned once, and lapsed into unconsciousness.

"Now tie his hands and feet securely. We'll carry him to the jail."

Pierre took another swing. "Ya' fucking *turd*!"

More gendarmes arrived at the gate. The *baïonnettes* were now directed at the Scotsman.

"Monsieur Dunemoore! This is not helping," the Jesuit Intendant said loudly. "Major, I demand Philippe Gerrard be released to me. I will take responsibility for him. Are you aware that Lady de Chanaye has been abducted?"

"Yes, Intendant Bigôt so informed me an hour ago. Then he ordered me to surround the Terrain de Jésuites and arrest Philippe Gerrard. Unfortunately, he is my military commander. I have orders from the Governor to obey *him*."

Pierre Dunemoore spit at the officer. "You corrupt fucking bastard!"

Major Péan pointed a finger at Pierre Dunemoore. "Sergeant! Arrest that man."

"Sergeant, I speak for General Duquesne," Archbishop Nicolet shouted, his voice becoming hoarse. "You will disregard Major Péan's orders and release Philippe Gerrard!"

From inside the carriage, Henri could see the heated argument escalate. Too long a delay could mean Lady de Chanaye's death. Where was she being held? Someone had said something about a swamp cabin east of the village.

The arguing quickly turned personal, each side trying to intimidate the other with threats of official reprisal. Out of the corner of his eye, Henri noticed all the guards had been drawn away from the gate toward the confrontation, leaving the small sentry doorway ajar and unguarded.

Henri got out of the other side of the carriage and stepped quietly to the ground, taking his rifle and bow with him. The gate sentries had gathered in a semicircle around the sergeant of the guard, Major Péan, Pierre Dunemoore, and Archbishop Nicolet. If the soldiers were highly uncertain about whose orders should be obeyed first, they all seemed to be immensely enjoying the spectacle of clashing egos, kicking, spitting, and shouted threats.

The open sentry door in the thick oaken gate beckoned to Henri. He took a deep breath and sprinted the final ten paces, going through the door just as one of the guards turned his head.

"Hey! You! Come back here!"

The sentry followed through the gate but stopped a few paces outside. He was more interested in the unprecedented shouting match between Major Péan, Pierre Dunemoore, and the Jesuit Intendant of New France, chuckling each time the Scotsman kicked out at the French officer.

Seeing no one running after him, Henri slowed to catch his breath. The village was supposed to be a mile or so down the road in front of him, near a swamp. But without a torch, even in the moonlight, the road would be heavily shadowed. Then he remembered the small pouch he carried, full of something with an earthy smell. Chittaqua had given it to him before they reached the great falls, before he died.

Something to help you see…to see when evil darkness closes around you like a cloud, the shaman had told him solemnly. *It can only be used* once. *Put what is in this pouch under your tongue. You will know when it is time.* Once*! You will know when the time is right!*

He searched his pockets and found the leather pouch. He opened and smelled the insides. His nose wrinkled at the strong, spicy pungency. He pinched the contents with two fingers. *Once*, he thought. *Under your tongue.* He sat down on the road. Tilting back his head, he placed the medicine under his tongue. It was incredibly bitter. He forced himself not to gag. His mouth started to water heavily. Soon the bitterness became tolerable. He thought about drinking water, but did not recall Chittaqua doing that.

It must have to stay under the tongue, he decided.

After a few minutes, Henri stood, expecting to feel nauseous but was surprised. He did not even feel dizzy. He actually felt more vigorous than before. His heart was beating rapidly. So he kept going, being careful where he stepped, watching for holes in the road. He did not want to sprain any-thing in a fall.

Gradually, the road surface became visible, enough to allow a fast walk, and then even a trot. But after trotting a hundred more paces, Henri noticed a brightening, an eerie glow begin to blossom all around him. Everywhere he looked, he saw a strange light. Huge boulders, small rocks, even the stony gravel imbedded in the hard dirt of the swamp road all glowed with a soft purple light. It wasn't much light but enough to outline the road.

Without wondering more about it, Henri began running at a steady pace. He wasn't sure what he would do when he got to the village by the swamp. All he hoped was that someone there had seen the *shérif* come by with the wagon and would be willing to point the way to the cabin.

CHAPTER 36
MONTRÉAL
OCTOBER 31, 1754
All Hallows E'en

The entire abduction went smoothly, Colbért decided. He even got to kill a few hired swords for practice, though it wasn't much of a match. But as the wagon neared the swamp village, three men blocked his way forward on the road. They had the look of killers for the sake of killing, or for money, and it would not matter which if they were also drunk. Since they stood just outside the tavern, he presumed the latter was true.

Colbért pulled back the hammer on the dragoon pistol lying on the seat beside him and slowed to a stop.

One of the men took hold of the horse's bridle. The other two slowly approached on either side of the wagon, stopping at the horse's rear haunches.

They've done this before, Colbért quickly assessed. *They will use the same tactics. And it will have a flaw.*

"What do you want? Or should I bother to ask?"

"Askin' is good," said the man on Colbért's right.

Several moves came to mind; two of these men were dead for certain. But to kill all three, he saw only one move that would produce that result. It was elegant and would require a bit of luck.

The one on the left stared. *He's the one,* Colbért decided.

Colbért lifted the large dragoon pistol on the seat to his right to show them he was armed. He adopted the local accent, adding a splash of dumbness for good measure.

"Well, thar's only one shot in this thing, and I'm not a good shot anyway. So I'm hopin' I'm lucky. Sold my crop. Got drunk. Too drunk, really. Spent most of it. I've a few money pieces left after leaving Montreal, seven for certain, maybe some larger silver if the last whore didn't dip her hand into my pocket too deeply when she was sucking my cock."

The assassin watched for his opening.

They laughed. The one on the left took his eyes off Colbért for a second as he shared his amusement with the one on the right.

It happened fast. The man on the right was still laughing when his head exploded, the heavy dragoon ball passing through his forehead. Colbért shot the pistol with his right hand and simultaneously snapped the reins hard with his left. The horse surged forward, ran down the man in front, and quickly pulled the wagon wheels over him. He let go of the reins and sprang the stiletto from its scabbard into his left hand. Using the force of the forward movement of the wagon, the assassin pushed off the seat with his feet to fling himself at the man on the left, who was just drawing his pistol. The assassin slammed into the man's chest, drove the stiletto into his gut, and shoved the razor sharp blade straight up into the man's heart.

They were all dead in seconds.

Blood and gore lay everywhere. Colbért pulled the loaded pistols from the belts of the two lying closest to him, plus the throwing knives they carried, and waited for any concerned citizens who might come through the animal skin hanging over the tavern entrance. He moved a few steps closer to the hovel to keep any such persons crowded together before they rushed him. The precaution would prove unnecessary.

Four men, one of them the proprietor, stepped out and looked around in confusion.

"They try to rob you?" the owner asked.

I'll let you live, Colbért thought. He nodded his head and watched the eyes and reflexes of the other three.

"Did you clean them out?" another spoke.

"Just their weapons," Colbért replied.

"Do you mind if we go over them?"

Colbért moved to make way for them. All three hurried past.

"Throw them bodies in the river or you're not coming back in here," the owner warned in a loud voice. Then he shrugged at Colbért and went back inside.

With one eye on the scavengers, Colbért moved toward the wagon, which had not gone twenty paces before the walking-averse horse stopped in the middle of the road. On the way, he paused by the third dead robber, whose head had been crushed by a wheel. The assassin pulled another dragoon pistol and a throwing knife from that man's belt. He placed the extra weapons in the back with the coffin and shoved the box farther into the bed. He gathered up the loose reins, got up in the wagon, and continued down the road. The blood on his hands was sticky.

Before he made the left toward the farm, he rode farther until he found Singing Owl's men by the canoe. They had made a tiny fire to keep warm. It was in a pit and hard to see, but he was looking for it.

"I will still be coming here tonight. And I could see your fire a quarter mile back. In case that worries you."

"Thanks. It doesn't," one of Singing Owl's men replied.

Colbért got down from the wagon and kneeled at the edge of the water. He washed his hands and cleaned his knives.

"Trouble?" one of the men asked.

"Not anymore."

Skriee!

"Uhhhh!"

The white eagle swooped a few feet above Henri's head and flew up the road a hundred paces before rising again into the night sky. In the bright moonlight, its white feathers gleamed against a backdrop of stars.

Henri watched in fascination as the bird soared in circles above his head. Henri's eye caught the glow of Chittaqua's moonstone hanging around his neck. The amulet had shaken free from his jersey as he was running. He took hold of the talisman and the lock of Roland's hair, immediately sensing their spirit presence. They were with him.

Show me the way.

Henri wondered what he would actually *do* when he found the *shérif*, the man who murdered Okeanneh. He was not afraid. He didn't need more weapons. He carried his loaded musket in one hand, his bow and quiver full of arrows over one shoulder, plus he had his knives. But the man he hunted was said to be a skilled killer. He could not beat him in a close fight, he reasoned, no more than he could beat a bear up close. He had to win from a distance. *How* would depend on what he found at the cabin by the swamp. But no matter what happened, Henri resolved to bring Lady de Chanaye back from wherever the *shérif* held her captive. That is what his father would do.

Despite the lightheadedness he experienced from Chittaqua's medicine, he could see things in the dark as if it were twilight. And he had a sense that he could run forever if he wanted. Nevertheless, it seemed a long time before he saw the first glimmers of torchlight through the trees somewhere up ahead. As he neared, he began to make out the shadowy shapes of buildings, some with the rounded roofs of traditional Indian lodges. Soon, he was moving among the structures situated to either side of the road. Most of the buildings were dark and appeared deserted. But at the far end of the village, he heard noises and laughter coming from one of the larger-cut log structures, a torch burned atop a pole near its entrance. He pushed aside the canvas covering the doorway and stepped inside. The room reeked of vomit, sweat, mud, smoke, and spoiled food.

Henri held his rifle across his chest and gazed around the heavily shadowed room. He detected six tables, some broken chairs and stools, a serving bar illuminated by two dim lanterns, and a small fire burning in a hearth to one side. Two men were leaning against the serving bar. He counted seven others spread out among the tables. Four of the men at the tables had Indian women sitting on their laps. One of the women was naked to the waist and was being groped by another man. The entire room went silent when he entered.

Henri took a deep breath. "*Bonsoir, messieurs.* I am looking for a *shérif* called Gaspard de Propei," he announced. It was too dark to discern their expressions or measure their reactions to that name.

"'*Bonsoir*'? Where the hell did you come from?" someone slurred.

"Montréal," Henri responded, trying to be friendly. "I was told you might help me."

"Help you?" the voice repeated. "*Help* you?"

Others in the room laughed derisively.

"I'm trying to find a man named Gaspard de Propei."

Heads twisted to one another in amused disbelief.

"And I'm looking to get *fucked*," replied a different voice, someone standing at the bar. "Maybe we can *help* each other, boy. What kind of ass do you have?"

Loud laughter erupted. Henri knew he'd made a serious mistake. The eyes of the faces about the room flickered red and yellow, reflecting the firelight in the dark room. Without saying anything else, he backed out of the building onto the road, stepping slowly backwards, not taking his eyes off the doorway. Seconds later, several men emerged in pursuit and spread out in front of him.

"Don't leave, *boy*," one said mockingly. "Stay and have a drink with us."

Henri leveled his rifle at the one he thought was speaking and cocked the hammer.

"Now what do you plan to do with that, *boy*?" asked another. "You've got only one shot. There are seven of us. You'd better put that musket down if you want to live through this night."

Skriee!

The eagle's talons raked across the heads of the men, sweeping and clawing. Most of the men dove to the ground swearing, two were injured and screamed. Henri didn't wait. He uncocked the hammer of his rifle and ran out of the village. He ran until he no longer heard any shouting from where he had come from. He leaned on the rifle stock to catch his breath, panting and shivering in the cold of the night, uncertain what to do next.

After this, I shall be rich, titled, and powerful. And my biggest dilemma in all this, the assassin mused, *is whether to enjoy her before or after I dispose of the woodsman.*

As he continued down the rutted road leading to the abandoned shack, his hand unconsciously massaged his groin. Colbért decided he wasn't going to wait.

Why deny what's due me? I'll see the woodsman's torch long before he gets here, he convinced himself. He licked his lips. *Then I'll spread his blood over her body and enjoy her again.*

Of course, the long delay at the swamp village had not been expected. That meant the time before the woodsman's arrival may not be long.

Well, maybe there's time enough to taste a few of her appetizers, to titillate my palate for the main course.

After arriving at the one-room cabin, Colbért strapped the semiconscious woman facedown across the bed and tied each of her hands and feet to the bed's corner legs. While she lay moaning and confused, he used a stiletto to cut away all her clothes. Her white nakedness was more exciting than he had imagined it would be. Her body was perfect and pure, completely unspoiled. He could not see a single blemish anywhere except for the lump on the side of her head where he'd clubbed her with the butt of his knife.

Now, he almost regretted doing that.

"Welcome to what awaits you," he whispered in her ear with relish. He gripped her between the legs, sliding his fingers in as far as they would go, and shook the lower half of her body in his hand to get her attention.

Corrinne moaned louder. "*Stoooop*," she pleaded, her voice sluggish.

He did and frowned. "Wake up, whore!" He slapped her hard on the ass a few times, leaving red handprints. "You're no good to me like this."

He went to a tub of fresh water and dipped a large ladle into it. He took several long swallows before refilling it, and then he poured it slowly over the side of her face. Parched, she caught a few drops with her tongue, and then sucked at the moisture on the filthy linens.

"You must be thirsty. Drink, drink! Make your mouth wet. We are just getting to know one another."

He checked the tightness of her bindings one more time and slipped out of his pants. He laid more wood on the fire and stripped off the rest of his clothes. He was hard and erect, throbbing with anticipation. But she was not fully conscious. And he wanted her *wide-awake*! Hoping to provoke some kind of reaction, he braced his knees on the side of the bed and thrust his erection between her cheek and the mattress, making sure to push himself across her lips. She moaned listlessly in response.

He slapped her hard on the side of her face. Again. And again. "I said wake up! Use your lips, whore!"

He had split her upper lip, which started to bleed, and bruised her right eye. Corrinne sluggishly tried to comply, but she was nearly knocked unconscious again by his next blow.

Disappointed, he retrieved his leather belt and lashed her four times, once on her legs, once on her back, and twice on her rump, but she barely stirred.

"You'd rather pretend you are asleep, yes? Well, I know a way to wake you up for certain."

The Night Butcher went over to the fire and speared a hot coal with the tip of a stiletto. Returning to the bed, he touched the coal to the bottom of one of her feet. The skin sizzled and smoked. A burning smell filled the air. The first scream she emitted was so exquisite, he ejaculated immediately on the floor. Her head twisted in his direction. Colbért finally saw the terror he desired in her eyes. He touched her other foot with the hot coal. Screams even more acute followed and then the begging and pleading Colbért wanted. He brought his hardness close to her face.

"Now, whore! Clean it!"

Henri felt the ghost eagle's presence again. The great bird swooped over his head and circled above the trees. He watched its flight, and his eyes fell on a path to his left, its stones illuminated in the moonlit forest. He moved off the road and followed the new path.

Henri lost sight of the eagle as he trotted along beneath the canopy of trees, but he could hear its comforting call somewhere above. For the next few minutes, he walked briskly or ran as quietly as he could, uncertain where the trail was taking him. From time to time, the road was flooded over with marsh water, but it was shallow enough to cross. When the trees ended, he found himself standing at the edge of a broad field of withered cornstalks and weeds. But it was the obvious beginnings of a farm, or possibly an Indian village.

If there's a farm, the farmhouse will be nearby.

He felt a gust of wind as the eagle swooped down from the trees over his head once more. He watched its direction of flight and walked the same way. The walking was more difficult on the rutted dirt, slick with dew. More than once, he stumbled and almost fell. When he was halfway to the other side of the field, he heard a woman scream in pain.

The sound was chilling. *It has to be her*, Henri thought. His panic rose! It had to be Lady de Chanaye!

"*Nooo!*" he shouted. His voice was absorbed in the dense cold night air.

He ran, stumbled, tried to hurry. Her next scream was prolonged and steadily became louder, more desperate, more terrifying.

He's going to kill her!

Henri impulsively stopped and fired his musket in the air. The explosion shattered the stillness of the night. The noise would warn the *shérif*, but maybe it would draw his attention away from her.

The screaming stopped.

Maisson Cloudwalker had not been pleased with Major Péan's order. He was a warrior, not a messenger. He should be paid more silver for doing this. Still, the major paid him well for his scouting work, and he was acclaimed as first scout among all the others, a position of trust, which also permitted him first choice in any spoils from battle. So he did as he was told, without complaint.

After leaving the city's east gate, the half-breed Ottawa avoided the more frequently traveled river road to go north of the deep water wetlands, east of the city, to get to the cabin. He knew exactly where it was, but this particular Frenchman was dangerous and easily triggered to violence. He wanted to see him clearly, from a distance, before making his own presence known. The man would likely be watching the road leading up from the river. So approaching from the other direction was safer.

The travel across the shallower northern marshes turned out to be more difficult than he had expected. The bright moonlight helped, and he never felt lost, but there were frequent sinkholes he had to avoid, so progress was slow.

Light from the cabin suddenly appeared off to his right. It was bright enough that he should have seen it long before this.

This shérif must have just arrived, he thought.

The cabin was still a half mile away and the light would serve as a beacon. He moved toward it carefully. The dangers of hidden hazards beneath the marsh waters were still the same.

As land beneath his feet finally become dry and solid, he heard the first scream. He was almost in shouting distance of the cabin. The white man was supposed to have a woman captive. It was part of the message he was to deliver: bring this woman back to the city. He walked a little closer. She screamed a second time, louder and longer. *Torture.* But Maisson Cloud-walker had not expected the explosive sound of a musket firing. That startled him! It was close! He threw himself to the ground.

Snow Hair?

Henri panted from exertion as he reached the other side of the field. He pushed through a line of trees and came upon a small clearing. He could see the shadows of two buildings, the larger one appeared collapsed, and the other had a window glowing with light.

Henri paused and held his breath. From the lighted window issued the faint sobbing of a woman. Carrying the musket now made no sense. It would take too much time for him to reload in the dark. The bow was faster. He set the heavy weapon down and took up his bow. He toed one end, bent the seasoned wood, and eased the line into the notch. He crouched and carefully scanned the surrounding area, watching for signs of movement in the shadows. Seeing none, he moved cautiously five or six paces, crouched, and watched again. He could hear sobbing.

At least she's not screaming. But where is he now?

"More, whore! My pleasure or your pain," the Night Butcher told her, relishing the revulsion he saw in her eyes. "Make your choice. Show me how—"

A not-so-distant musket blast pierced the air.

Colbért blew out the candles, leaving only the small fire to illuminate the room. He was dressed again in less than a minute.

"If you warn him," Colbért whispered harshly, "the pain you feel now will seem like the tickle of a feather when I come for you again."

Corrinne de Chanaye turned her head to muffle her sobbing. But beneath her tears and fear, rage surged hot within her. *I'm not going to die like this,* she vowed.

Colbért slipped quietly out the door and moved away from the house, selecting a spot among some trees where he could watch both the road and the front door from a prone position.

Lying flat on the ground, he carefully searched for signs of movement. It did not take long for his eyes to adjust to the dark. His instincts told him the musket shot had not been an accident. There was no one living in any of the swamplands' crumbled hovels who would care. It had to be the woodsman.

He heard her screams, Colbért thought. *The fool foregoes the advantage of surprise to ease her pain.* The assassin was intimate with killing from an ambush position in the dark. The ground to him did not matter. *All right, woodsman, it's time for our dance.*

Colbért smirked. The assassin visualized the woodsman growing more anxious and concerned. The *coureur de bois* would approach the house cautiously. He will glance through the single window and see her lying on the bed, lashed to the posts, naked, helpless, and in pain. His worry for her will increase, but he will steel himself and search further to locate his enemy. *But I will lay here quiet and unmoving, even if he comes close.* Thinking his enemy fled, the woodsman—tortured by her desperate sobbing—will discard his caution and hurtle into the shack to rescue her. *How brave, how fearless, how noble. How stupid!* The hero will comfort her. He will cut her bindings and say soothing words. *I will move next to the door and wait again.* Realizing her feet are injured, the woodsman will pick her up in his arms to carry her to safety. Sobbing, she will cling to her hero tightly. His arms will be restrained as he steps through the door.

And then I will strike!

The method of attack formed in the Night Butcher's mind as a series of blood-spattered images. As the woodsman stepped unsuspectingly through the door, he visualized grabbing the woman's arm. The images were wonderful. The whore queen would scream. The woodsman would turn to shield her body from any attack. He would thrust the stiletto upward, cutting into the woodsman's neck deeply, beneath the jaw, severing the large blood channels there. Then quickly stabbing his chest to puncture the lungs. The woodsman's arms would go numb. The screaming whore queen would flop to the ground. Blood would spurt and spray in every direction from the fatal wounds. The woodsman would cry out in agony, but she would hear only gurgles. He would stagger, his hands clutching at his throat. *And still, his concern would be only for her.* He would try to call to her, tell her to run, but she would hear only wet sputtering as his lungs emptied air though the wound before filling with blood.

But I won't finish him, Colbért thought. *I'll let her try to save him and become covered with his blood. And he will choke and die slowly. She will see her last hope of rescue die in her arms.* He smiled greedily. *And then, I will drag her by the hair back to the bed. And the whore queen's more earnest begging will begin.*

Colbért gloated at the prospect of fulfilling both his destiny and his deepest carnal desires.

BEWARE THE BOY!

The sudden thought made Colbért's body flinch. It was the grating whisper of the night messenger. The previous night, in a dream, the messenger had spoken the same words—*beware the boy*—but with less intensity.

It's the boy *who approaches? Impossible.*

It was too ridiculous to believe, but after so many warnings and predictions coming true, Colbért had learned not to question the *voice*. But Philippe Gerrard had arrived in Montréal! It had to be him. Yet, the woodsman had heard people screaming before. *He would never betray his presence by firing the musket,* the assassin reconsidered. Maybe it *was* the boy…and he had panicked at hearing her screams.

Beware the boy, Colbért thought mockingly. *Slaying the blond-haired nit will be the most fun of all. So easy a kill.* He visualized other things the boy could do. *Or, maybe I can capture him instead, and persuade him with a stiletto to join in the festivities with the whore queen.*

Out of the quiet emptiness of the night, a high-pitched eagle's call punctured the silence.

The assassin's head swiveled violently.

Henri had crawled to within five paces of the lighted window on the backside of the cabin. The eagle's cry came from the right, drawing his eyes toward the road leading to the farmhouse. He detected movement among the trees near the road, low to the ground. Henri held his breath and watched intently. The shadowed movements were much more subtle after that, but he saw them.

It's him, Henri thought. *He's watching the door. Waiting.*

Henri wondered what kind of weapons the *shérif* was carrying.

Knives probably. They say he likes knives. It's too dark to aim accurately, even with my bow, he reminded himself.

Henri's eyes shifted to the window. It was low enough. He could slip inside the house that way. But could he get in and back out without making noise? Henri frowned. He didn't think so.

Skriee!

This time, the shadow's movement between the trees was easily discernible.

The eagle called again.

Henri slowly slid on his belly to his left, until he was completely hidden by the house. He notched an arrow and waited, listening intently, hoping the *shérif* remained distracted by the eagle.

Colbért rolled to his back and glared at the outline of the winged creature he saw circling above the tree tops.

Come on down here, you feathered fuck!

He had both of his stilettos drawn, but the bird wouldn't stoop close enough while he lay beneath the trees. The bird soared out of sight again. But the sudden appearance of the animal had unnerved the assassin. He rolled to his stomach, certain the boy was only paces away somewhere. Colbért had memorized most of the shadows. Another careful search with his eyes yielded nothing.

He's searching for me too, he decided. *But she will cause him to move first.*

Maisson watched the person who fired the musket approach the cabin. He was good. His speed did not change, and he listened a long time between movements. But to his surprise, the *shérif* was good too. He was on the opposite side of the cabin. They could not see each other, but the scout could see them both. He could assist one or the other. But the repeated cry of the diving ghost eagle was another matter. This was a high totem. There was big magic here. He decided to do nothing, except observe.

Inside the house, Corrinne heard the cry of the eagle. Then she heard it again.

Someone's coming, she decided. *That's why the bastard stopped.*

Fully awake, Corrinne's rage overpowered any fear she'd felt. He might hurt her, but she was not going to lie meekly and accept it. *If he brings that cock near my mouth again, I will rip it off with my teeth*, she promised. *I don't care if he sets me on fire.* She started pulling at her leather bindings angrily. If she could get just *one* hand free. In the darkness, the fingers of her right hand touched something pointed and sharp. She explored it tentatively. The tip of a nail was sticking through the bedpost. Excited, instead of pulling at the strap, she pushed forward with her hand, an easier movement. The thong stretched enough to reach the tip of the nail. Then she started working it back and forth, making sure she kept up her sobbing sounds so the *shérif* would not become suspicious. While she sawed away, she deliberated what to use as a weapon; she needed something that could kill him when he returned.

There must be something next to the hearth? A poker. An ax. Something? Please, God, let there be something!

Henri peeked above the bottom of the window. *It's her!* Lady de Chanaye was face down on the bed. Naked. Her hands and feet were tied. He wanted to call to her but didn't dare lest the *shérif* hear. He could see her right hand pushing back and forth against the bed post in the dim light of the fire. *What is she doing?* No matter, he was going in. He hoped she would not cry out. He slipped his bow over his head, said a prayer, placed his hands flat on the window sill, and pushed.

Don't see me yet, Mademoiselle, he prayed. *Don't turn your head!*

Henri swung one leg over the sill, moving slowly till he felt his foot touch the floor, then repeated the move with the other. Corrinne was pushing and pulling her hand back and forth more frantically. She groaned and strained. There was a snapping sound. The leather binding parted.

Outside, Helmut Colbért had closed his eyes, listening to the sounds of the night, reaching out with his senses. Somewhere, far away, he thought he heard the sound of hooves. But his concentration was disturbed by the whore queen's short scream of surprise.

He's gone in through the window!

The assassin crept back to the house, right next to the door. He could feel the delicious excitement before the kill coursing through his veins. From inside, there came hurried whispering, a woman's voice.

The assassin scratched on the door with his knife to draw their attention, wanting to make them think he was about to come in. The whispering stopped. He moved silently around to the back and peeked into the window. What he saw made his excitement treble. The whore queen was no longer in the bed. She was standing wrapped in a blanket. And standing next to her was…

KILL HIM!

The Night Butcher was overcome by a powerful tingling pulsing up from his legs, expanding into his chest and arms to become a roar in his head. He bit his lip to restrain the urge to yell he felt building, but was unsuccessful. A guttural growl burst through his clenched teeth.

Corrinne and Henri saw a shadowy black form climbing into the room, eyes red and gleaming.

Henri moved in front of Corrinne. "Get back!" He notched an arrow, aimed, and loosed a shot. Incredibly, the black form twisted. The arrow missed.

"Run!" Henri shouted.

Corrinne had already thrown open the door and was running down the road, ignoring the terrible spiking pain from the burns on the bottoms of her feet. Henri followed close behind her, notching a second arrow as he ran. He could hear the growling, heavy breathing coming closer. He spun to draw and shoot, but the black form was right *there*, already jumping at him, a knife elevated to strike.

The eagle slammed into the Night Butcher, knocking him sideways. Henri was so startled, he released the arrow without aiming. Another shot missed. He turned and ran after Corrinne again. In another ten paces, they had run free of the trees surrounding the house as the access road crossed the fallow cornfield. Behind him, the eagle screamed several more times, each scream matched by a ferocious, animal-like growling. He'd never heard sounds like that before, not even from the bear inside the cave.

"Keep running, Mademoiselle!"

He notched another arrow to loose, stopped, and turned. He sighted the center of the roiling shadow, waiting until the eagle rose up from a dive, and released. This time, he heard a scream.

Henri yelled from his success. "*Hooo-keee-yi-yi-yi!*"

Behind him Corrinne screamed. She'd stumbled and fallen. "Merde! Merde! *Merde!*"

Henri was at her side in seconds, pulling her to her feet. "Hurry!"

"Owww! No! Wait! I can't! I've twisted it," she said, angry, frustrated. "Give me your knife!"

Corrinne's hands started fumbling at Henri's belt for the skinning knife. Henri notched a fourth arrow. He *wanted* to fight this man, to wound him with another arrow, then get close enough to hurt him, before he killed him. But first, he had to make sure Lady de Chanaye was out of danger.

Henri squinted at the darkness. It had become quiet. Too quiet.

"Do you see him?"

Corrinne squinted too. "No," she answered and grimaced when she accidentally put too much weight on her twisted ankle. "*Merde!* No, I can't see him! Where are you? You bastard!"

"Mademoiselle! No! Don't call to him!"

"Don't call to him? He already knows where we are!"

She waved the long skinning knife in the air above her head and shouted again.

"Come and get me, you coward!"

But the *shérif* was gone.

And the night sky was still.

The confrontation by the city gate had moved to the Couteau du Fort, where Philippe was carried unconscious into a jail cell, still in shackles. After a long impasse and various, repeated threats of reprisal, the arguments were irrelevant. Major Péan would not relent.

The archbishop changed his tack to one of reason and common sense.

"Major, you know very well, the Governor would support my request without hesitation."

"Eminence, I would wager money that your assertion is correct. But that does not make *any difference* in the military chain of command. Like it or not, Philippe Gerrard was declared a criminal by royal decree. He was to be arrested on sight. And I have followed that order. When the Governor is in Quebec, I take orders from his deputy military marshal, and absent a sitting marshal, I report directly to Intendant Bigôt, which he knows. This vacancy in leadership will only last a few days, a week at most, and I would rather take orders from a lizard, but this is the natural order of authority in this city right now. So, one last time…Monsieur Gerrard can only be released by a direct, *written* order from Intendant Bigôt!" He pointed toward Bigôt's office. "He is still awake. Present your demands to him. Bring me a written release and I will have the *coureur de bois* carried out on the shoulders of my men, as if he were on parade."

"We've wasted too much time here," Pierre told the archbishop. "We'll come back for him later. Corrinne's life is in danger. Philippe would agree."

The Jesuit nodded. "Major Péan. Give the east gate an order to let my carriage pass."

"With pleasure, Eminence. Although getting back through the gate before sunrise could be a problem."

"It should not. You can certainly manage to arrange that without Bigôt's permission."

They walked quickly back to where the carriage sat idle with its Jesuit driver. Henri was nowhere to be seen.

"Sergeant! Did you see the boy?"

"I saw him," said one of the guards. "He ran out the gate."

"*Wha…*? When?"

"An hour ago. When you were trying to kick poor Major Péan in the balls!"

The guards laughed.

Pierre started stomping his foot. "He's just…like…his bloody…father!"

"Come. We'll catch him with the carriage," André Nicolet said.

During the ride toward the swamp village, Pierre pondered how to locate the correct farmhouse. The moon was full and bright, but he'd only been this way once before. Maybe he should employ one of the cutthroats sure to be skulking among the hovels in the village? Although they'd more likely cut *his* throat than not. Fortunately, the night's first bit of good luck occurred when the carriage overtook another wagon emerging from a road leading up from the river. It was Peter Blue Jacket. They quickly traded information. Peter Blue Jacket had come to assist Pierre and Philippe as agreed.

"I know the way to the lodge you seek," the Mohawk said and described the way. But seeing the chief of the black robes in the carriage, he said nothing about what his wagon carried.

The two wagons rumbled down the road, the Jesuit's carriage leading the way. Now that Pierre knew where to go, he decided the Jesuit in the flimsy nightshirt simply wasn't driving fast enough. He opened the door and climbed up to the driver's perch.

"Here," Pierre Dunemoore shouted over the din of the horses. He handed the man a blanket and placed his ax beneath the seat. "Give me those!" Sitting in the driver's seat, Pierre took the reins. The Jesuit pointed the steering lantern at the road ahead.

The Scotsman snapped the whip repeatedly over the heads of the team. They started galloping wildly. Inside the violently swaying coach, Archbishop Nicolet hung tightly to the hand loops so he would not be tossed headlong out a window. The second wagon, driven by Peter Blue Jacket, with six men hidden beneath blankets in the back, followed close behind. The wheeled procession charged through the swamp village without slowing. No one emerged from any of the hovels.

Peter had told Pierre the road would fork about a mile past the village.

They were to go left. Less than a half mile after that, it would fork again. Again, left. The Scotsman cursed under his breath each time one of the city horses balked at a shadow, requiring his whip.

The archbishop prayed the entire way. *Please let us arrive in time!* Corrinne's life in danger was bad enough, but Henri's too?

The wagon reached the first fork. Pierre steered the team left but had to slow as the road narrowed sharply. They had seen no sign of Henri.

"How much farther?" Nicolet shouted up from a window.

"I dinnah' know. No more than a mile, I think."

Nicolet grunted.

There was a musket shot.

Pierre Dunemoore's heart sank. "Oh, bloody hell!"

The Scotsman snapped the whip. As the horses started to gallop, he was quickly forced to slow them again. The overhanging tree branches were so low he might get brained if he did not allow time to duck his head as the carriage went underneath. It became agonizingly slow. At the second fork, he steered left again, then slowed the horses to a walk. He had no choice. They had to walk. Swamp water lay over the road in places, and Pierre didn't want to slip a wheel into a hole and throw over the top-heavy carriage.

Finally, the carriage passed clear of the marsh and trees. They entered an untilled cornfield gone to weeds. Less than a quarter mile ahead on his left, Pierre saw a light flickering from a house window.

"Aha!"

He snapped the whip. The horses had barely begun their gallop when the shivering Jesuit seated next to him shouted.

"Watch out, Monsieur!"

The steering lantern illuminated two people standing on the road ahead, one covered with a blanket supported around the shoulders by the other. Pierre reined the horses to a stop as they came alongside. The Scotsman's jaw slackened.

"Bloody..."

"Corrinne!" Nicolet threw open the carriage door. She hobbled to his arms. He hugged her tightly.

"André!"

"Thank God! Are you injured?"

Corrinne clung to the priest, unsuccessfully trying to stifle her sobs.

"He lashed me to a bed and…and did awful things…burned my feet with coals…Then Henri climbed through the window and freed me!"

"Where's the *shérif?*"

Corrinne shook her head.

"Pierre!" Henri said. "We've no time to lose—the *shérif* is out there! He's in the trees ahead. I think I wounded him with an arrow."

"Ya' wounded him?" Pierre asked, incredulous over this, as well as all the boy had accomplished alone.

Peter Blue Jacket and six other men suddenly crowded to the front of the carriage. Pierre swung the steering lantern. The archbishop gaped. These were not common ruffians. They wore the traditional clothing, weapons, and war paint of Oneida warriors. Their faces wore the tribe's traditional fearsome scowl.

In the light of the carriage lanterns, the Oneida looked suspiciously at the white men. The leader's face was covered with endless lines of tattoos. His forehead painted red, his hair brushed straight up and cropped flat. Bone ornaments hung from his nose and earlobes. He carried a four-foot-long war club. One end of it bulged with a foot-wide knot of oak, a two-foot keel spike pounded through it, the point of which protruded wickedly out the other side.

"Torches!" Peter Blue Jacket shouted in the Mohawk tongue. Seconds later, three hand-held torches were lit from the carriage lamps.

"Do nah' be concerned, Eminence. These are Oneida braves," Pierre said cautiously. "And they're a long, *long* way from home."

The Scotsman stepped down from the wagon and greeted the war chief formally in Mohawk.

"Oneida?" the Jesuit said with surprise.

"Eminence, this is Tall Mountain Among Trees, high chief of the Oswego Oneida."

"What are the Oswego Oneida doing this far north?"

"I brought them here," Peter Blue Jacket explained. "A promise to Snow Hair."

Pierre continued. "We wanted Indian trackers we could trust tah' help find the *shérif*. People who would be ruthless in pursuit. People he could nah' bribe. In spring, when Gaspard de Propei came down from Montréal, he tortured and murdered a young Oneida woman, her husband, and their infant child. Tall Mountain Among Trees is tha' woman's father. These men are her brothers. They've come for justice."

The Oneida chief began to sign vigorously, his hands slapping and moving forcefully.

"He wants tah' know where tah' find tha' *shérif*," Pierre said.

"Tell the Oneida we want to capture the *shérif* alive." After being tortured, Corrinne wanted some revenge of her own.

Pierre looked at her doubtfully. "They will *nah'* let us keep him. The Oneida plan tah' take him back across the river."

Archbishop Nicolet knew that meant torture. "I cannot permit—"

"The Oneida do not respect the words of the Black Robes," Peter Blue Jacket interrupted. "The Oneida will take him, and *you* cannot stop the Oneida when they walk the path of revenge. No good will come from this if you try. This is justice by *your* laws too. If the *shérif* killed her,"—he pointed at Corrinne—"what would you say? Think carefully before you answer, Black Robe. I say, use this night to create an opportunity for a new alliance within the council of the Iroquois. And I will carry the message for you."

Driven back to the cabin by the eagle's attack, Helmut Colbért heated the tip of the stiletto in the fire to cut the arrow head out of his right thigh. He clenched his teeth, popped the sharp flint free of the sinew, and cauterized the wound. Blood from the scalp lacerations cut by the eagle's talons kept dribbling into his eyes. He sliced long strips of blanket, tied one tightly around his thigh to staunch the bleeding, then wrapped a second strip around his head.

Bird or no fucking bird, he was going after them. The whore queen's feet were injured. The two of them would not get far. And after disposing of the nit, he would sodomize and strangle her quickly.

Others will be coming. Killing the boy will only intensify the woodsman's resolve to find me. I'll set a trap somewhere else.

The assassin saw a wooden rake lying in one corner. He held the handle and stomped down on the end to break off the tongs. It would make an effective spear to keep the aggressive bird at bay. Unfortunately, he no longer felt the tingling sensation, the unbridled strength that had made his reflexes so instantaneous. But he wouldn't need it to finish the boy.

Colbért limped out of the house and trotted up the road to the edge of the trees. He stopped at seeing a carriage and wagon. *They've come already.* In the light of the dim carriage lamps, he counted shadows…at least six…too many for him now. But they'd come to the cabin next looking for him, that was certain. The whore queen and the boy would stay behind. He decided on a new strategy.

Circle around to the trees on the opposite side of the field. Come at them from behind, when they are distracted.

He made a quick search of the night sky and moved furtively to the right. The moon was now behind a cloud. It would be too dark to see very far. He should almost be invisible at this distance. But that would not last for long. He passed by the carriage and wagon on his left at fifty paces, close enough to hear the concern in their voices. He could dimly make out the robes of an archbishop.

Well, old man, if there is time, I will make you pay dearly for getting involved. And Intendant Bigôt will toss me a purse of gold for doing so!

Colbért entered the trees on the other side of the field, panting from the exertion. The bandage on his thigh had already soaked through with blood. His leg was pulsing with pain. He wrung out and tightened the blanket strip, leaving only enough slack for the leg to flex.

Skriieee!

He frowned.

The bird's cry was distant but loud enough to turn everyone's head.

"He's coming," Henri said.

Peter Blue Jacket spoke quickly to the Oneida. Without taking any torches, the Indians fanned out across the empty field to the left and right.

Better be cautious, Pierre decided. "Time tah' turn the carriage around and head back tah' Montréal. Let the Oneida find him. We kin' come back tomorrow—"

"No," Henri said immediately. "He'll get away if I don't stay. He wants me *dead*. The archbishop said so himself."

"Laddie! Ya' are nah'—"

"I'm staying too," said Corrinne. "I want to be here when they catch that bastard."

"Eminence, talk some sense—"

"If Lady de Chanaye chooses to stay, I am staying as well."

The Jesuit driver looked depressed but didn't say anything.

"Am I tha' only one here who is nah', bloody, daft?!"

In the darkness, the Oneida hooted to one another. Henri took back his skinning knife from Corrinne and went across the field at an angle. Peter Blue Jacket and Tall Mountain Among Trees ran down the center of the road toward the house carrying torches, knowing their visibility might draw the *shérif*'s attention away from the flanking attackers.

"Stay inside the carriage," Pierre told Corrinne. "There are more blankets under the cushions."

Pierre climbed up to the carriage seat, handing another one of the spare blankets to the shivering driver. "Put one over your legs." He took up his war ax from beneath the seat. He'd been standing on it to keep it from flying out during the gallop. He laid the heavy ax across his lap, stroking the curved metal head, feeling much more comfortable with the weapon close at hand.

How odd, he thought. The gemstone in the ax head seemed to be glowing. *Nooo! I do not want tah' start seeing this nonsense again!*

Inside the carriage, Archbishop Nicolet felt warmth at his belt. The stone in his crucifix had started to glow. He rubbed it with his thumb.

"Do you see this?" he asked tentatively.

"Yes," Corrinne answered. "Much has happened this night that I…I do not understand…" She thought of the ritual in the artist's loft, now seeming a lifetime ago, of the unnatural red eyes of the Marquis' heir, of that eagle that had somehow followed Henri from the artist's loft. "Yet I cannot deny any of what has occurred."

The archbishop grunted and did not reply.

The glow from all the tiny rocks in the field faded. Henri stopped advancing. But he saw them again, this time in a long narrow band pointing toward the trees behind the carriage on the other side of the field. Henri hurried back to the wagon.

"Pierre," he called softly.

The Scotsman grabbed the torch from the shivering Jesuit, who was using it to keep warm.

"Laddie?"

"The *shérif* is in the trees. Behind us."

"Get in the wagon! We'll drive tah' the house and get the others!"

"No! He'll get away. Come on. He came for me once, he'll do it again. Come down and stand with me."

Hearing the whispering, Nicolet stuck his head out the window. "What's wrong?"

Henri explained. The archbishop saw the other torches moving around the house and trees up ahead, but when he looked back toward the trees by the road, he saw only blackness. "Put out that torch," he told his driver.

"Wha—?"

"He's marking us clearly, but we cannot see him. He might have a musket."

"Bloody…!" Pierre had not thought of that. Alarmed, he grabbed the torch and threw it as far away as he could.

Pierre climbed down from the seat.

"There," Henri said, pointing at the spot where the farm road entered the woods. "He's right there!"

"Ya' can see him?"

"Sort of."

At her request, Henri gave Corrinne his boning blade. Gazing intently into the darkness, somehow he knew.

"There's no time. He's coming this way. He is coming now."

Henri notched an arrow and stepped away from the wagon, watching the path of luminescence move with him. Pierre trudged along behind him.

"Where're ya' going?"

"Moving away from the lady. He wants me, Pierre."

From somewhere far away, the lonely howl of a wolf carried across the night. Henri smiled. "Good boy," he whispered. "Good boy."

The other end of the path began to shorten. But Henri was not afraid.

"Here he comes," Henri said grimly.

Pierre gripped his ax. "Where? I kinnah' see a fuckin' thing. I kinnah' make a bloody ax throw if I kinnah' see him!"

The assassin saw the torch arc away from the wagon, taking away the light, except for the dimmer carriage lanterns. *Good*, he thought. He saw the boy's shadow perfectly now. He watched him move away from the carriage and out into the field. *Better!* One hand gripped a deadly stiletto, the other his wooden spear. He started moving directly toward the boy. *By the time the nit sees me, it will be over.*

The Night Butcher planned a quick, clean kill. He moved cautiously, watching the sky; the moon was still tucked behind hazy clouds. He glanced at the torches moving near the cabin. When the distance closed to thirty paces, he let the rake handle drop silently and took up his other stiletto. At twenty paces, he noticed there was another shadow standing by the boy. He stooped to a crouch and held his breath. *The boy's walking directly toward me*, he thought. Fifteen paces. Ten!

Skriiee!

Again, the great bird swooped to the ground next to Henri. The cornfield became illuminated by a soft, eerie starlight. And crouching right there before them was a misshapen figure with angry red eyes.

"Bloody hell," Pierre whispered. He raised his ax for a throw.

Henri loosed an arrow. The Night Butcher screamed as the sharp head pierced his shoulder, knocking him backward. Henri notched another, stepped closer, and shot again. This arrow sank into the Night Butcher's wounded leg.

Colbért howled with rage.

Henri felt something whisk by his face. He loosed another arrow, hitting the assassin's other leg. He reached back for another arrow, but found the quiver was empty. He pulled out his skinning knife and kept advancing.

"Get out of the way!" Pierre shouted.

They were suddenly overtaken by the shrieking war hoots of the Oneida. Two Indians ran by Henri to pounce on the shadow. One of them collapsed to the ground holding his chest. Tall Mountain Among Trees swung his club sideways and knocked Colbért senseless.

Henri stood next to the Oneida as they stripped the *shérif*'s body of its clothes. He saw where his arrows had hit. Tall Mountain Among Trees pulled off the wrist scabbards. Henri held out his hand.

The Oneida chief looked at Henri appraisingly, realizing he was the bowman. He slipped one of the stilettos into the scabbard and handed it to the boy with a nod of approval.

Silence followed. And like a candle being extinguished, the eerie light bathing the ground vanished.

Maisson Cloudwalker had chanced to move closer to the cabin. He now regretted that decision. He saw the shadows of many other hunters moving across the open fields. They moved like Indian warriors. But who do they look for? The *shérif* had already crossed the other way, much farther to the right. They were going to converge on the cabin from all sides.

The Ottawa scout turned around and ran back the way he had come.

One of the Oneida braves spotted the man's shadow, ran after him in pursuit, but stopped when he heard the sounds of fighting behind him. The man now ran swiftly in the other direction.

Maisson stopped too. *They have captured someone*, he thought. *But who? The major will want to know.* He trotted carefully back toward the fight and planned to remain unobserved until he learned the truth.

CHAPTER 37
MONTRÉAL
NOVEMBER 1, 1754
All Hallows Morning

Henri plodded wearily toward the carriage. His eyes lifted to search the sky for the eagle. But it was gone, and the comforting light with it.

"Henri, ride up here with me," Pierre said. He told the Jesuit driver to ride in the cabin with Archbishop Nicolet and Corrinne.

Out of arrows, Henri bent his bow to slacken the pull and slung it over his shoulder. He climbed up next to the Scotsman, who patted his knee, then gruffly fixed his attention on the road.

The Scotsman carefully turned the carriage around in the bumpy corn-field and proceeded back down the road.

"Ya' did your father proud, laddie. But it was also a *daft, reckless* thing to dah'. I dinnah' think ya' will be so lucky next time."

Henri smiled weakly, tired and drained of emotion. He felt empty in a way he did not comprehend.

"I left my new rifle somewhere by the cabin," he said glumly.

Pierre chuckled. "Lady de Chanaye will buy ya' the best one in Montréal after tonight. And if she does nah', I will. Hold the steering lantern for me."

Stripped of all his clothes, gagged, hands and feet bound tightly with leather cords, Helmut Colbért writhed with pain and anger as he was tossed into the flat wooden bed of the second wagon. The others climbed aboard. One of the Oneida was dead. Tall Mountain Among Trees held a bloody rag over the knife wound in his shoulder.

Peter Blue Jacket turned the wagon and followed the archbishop's carriage. As they moved along the road, the Oneida clan chief put a foot on Colbert's chest, bent over, and snapped off the shafts of the arrows. Using the flat of his hand, he pressed down on the arrowheads forcing them deeper into the wounds to increase the white man's pain.

Colbért inhaled sharply but did not groan aloud. He didn't want the primitives to think him weak. He knew they respected strength. He caught the glint of a stiletto in the belt of the wounded Indian. If the wagon hit a deep rut, he would use the upset in movement to roll toward the wounded man and retrieve his blade.

If I get hold of my knife, things will be different.

Fortunately, the arrows had all hit muscle. Even with his hands tied, at such close quarters he could kill all three of them.

The pain is bad, but my chance will come. It always does.

Tall Mountain Among Trees held a torch close to the white man's face and smiled at him cruelly. Torturing a white man was so much more satisfying than torturing one of their own. It took little effort to inflict great pain in them. And unlike true warriors, they could not send their spirits over to the other side. White men tended to live a long time, robbed of all other feelings except pain. Tall Mountain Among Trees sensed this white man was strong, made stronger still by the rage and hatred he saw in his eyes. The clan chief touched his torch to the man's naked stomach for a few moments.

Colbert's back arched in agony. When the torch lifted, he threw his head forward and butted the Oneida chief on the nose, driving him backwards. His sons held him down again and looked to their father to strike back.

The chief rubbed his broken nose. But he shook his head. There would be plenty of time later to make the white man beg for death, after they crossed over the river to Oneida lands.

The sons smiled at their father, amused by his mistake.

"Father, it was you who said, 'Even when the honey smells sweet, never put your nose too close to the hive,'" the wounded son taunted.

Tall Mountain Among Trees had loved his daughter as much as he loved his sons. Snow Hair and Animal Scalp had made it possible to take revenge for his daughter's torture and death. He would never forget that.

The Scotsman's hearing, ever alert for sharp noises, made him look around quickly. He tilted his head and listened, but only heard the plodding hooves of the tired horses.

"Did you hear a scream?" he asked Henri.

Henri answered dully, "No."

Pierre twisted in his seat and looked back at Peter Blue Jacket's wagon.

It was still following. There did not appear to be any sort of commotion. The Scotsman shrugged.

"I'm seeing things, hearing things. Too much bloody excitement."

"What now?"

Pierre steered to the right at the river road. Unnoticed, Peter Blue Jacket's wagon went to the left.

"We'll deliver Lady de Chanaye to her city house, and then retrieve your father from jail."

"What about the *shérif?*"

Pierre's reasoning wavered. "Good question. He's a royal. Much as your father wants tah', we kinnah' just kill him now that he's been captured."

"But I thought you wanted to?"

"We'll have tah' see."

"We can't let him go, Pierre!"

"I…I know."

The swamp village was dark except for the standing torch burning outside the log saloon as they wheeled through. Henri noticed the canvas pulled back from the open door. Inside, all was black, and no one emerged. Fifteen minutes later, they saw the sentry lanterns above the east gate of the city. Pierre reined the horses to a stop a few paces short of the heavy doors.

"Open the gate!"

The sentry on the wall of Montréal challenged them.

"Open it!" Pierre shouted back. "It's Archbishop Nicolet!"

The gates opened immediately. Pierre twisted in his seat. Peter Blue Jacket's wagon was no longer behind them.

"*Merde!*"

"What's wrong?" Henri said, alarmed, twisting in his seat.

"The other wagon's gone! I wanted the guards tah' see the *shérif* was still alive before the Oneida took him across the river."

Pierre stood up on the seat and pointed the steering lantern back down the road. It was deserted.

"You may advance, Monsieur Dunemoore," announced the sergeant of the guard.

Pierre sat down and snapped the reins. "Well, this should be interesting." He steered the carriage inside the gate and stopped to let the sergeant inspect the occupants.

"Everything all right, Eminence?"

"Yes, Sergeant. Where is Major Péan?"

"At his quarters. My captain said to tell you, the major is at your convenience, should you return tonight."

"You may jail the man tied up in the wagon—"

"Uh, Eminence," Pierre interjected.

Nicolet turned his head.

"Eminence, I believe Peter Blue Jacket took his wagon in a *different* direction."

Archbishop Nicolet pushed open the coach door and glanced down the road behind them. He frowned.

"Monsieur Dunemoore, please continue to Lady de Chanaye's house."

Pierre didn't hesitate. He snapped his whip.

In a few minutes, the carriage pulled up in front of Lady de Chanaye's house. There were no soldiers on guard. As soon as the carriage stopped, the front door flew open, and the chamberlain hurried down the steps, followed by a teary-eyed Mathilde.

Pierre handed the reins to the Jesuit priest. "Hold these until we sort this out." He lifted Corrinne out of the carriage.

"We are not finished yet," she stated tersely. "Eminence, I have one last need of your carriage tonight."

"Why?"

"I am calling on Intendant Bigôt."

"Bigôt?" The archbishop was incredulous.

"François Bigôt will give me Philippe's written release from the Couteau du Fort."

"Nah', lassie. Not tonight. We are nah' letting you dah' this now."

"*I will* see Intendant Bigôt," Archbishop Nicolet said. "No need for you to do anything but rest."

"I will go with you, Mademoiselle," said Henri.

At Henri's words, Corrinne hunched over and let out a painful sob, pent-up emotions from all that had happened spilling over. Tears gathered and dripped from her eyes. With effort, she collected herself, took a deep breath and placed a palm on Henri's cheek.

"Oh, Henri. I know you would. I hope someday you realize what a hero you are to me. But no. Not this time. It won't be necessary. Wait here with

Pierre and Nicolet."

Corrinne faced Pierre and the archbishop. "Do you both not see me? Do you see how I look? He *crippled me*! The intendant had a role in this! He *will* give me a written release! And I'm not asking either of you for permission. But I do need your help. Now, please…wait for me here, just for a few minutes."

Pierre handed her over to the chamberlain. As the man went up the steps, Pierre turned to the archbishop.

"Eminence, I'll be runnin' tah' my warehouse tah' bring back a few o' my *coureurs de bois* tah' help us. I think this night is far from over."

The chamberlain carried his blanket-covered mistress into the house, Mathilde following close behind. Corrinne had sliced a hole in the center of the blanket. She wore it over her head, cinched at the waist using Nicolet's rosary beads as a belt. The chamberlain set her down on top of the *cuisine* table then hurried from the room. In the light of the kitchen lanterns, the bloody, red, blistered bottoms of her feet were made visible. The wounds were foul with dirt and grime.

Mathilde brought over a bowl of cold water. She wet some towels and began to gently daub away the blood and filth.

Hisses of pain escaped from Corrinne's clenched her teeth.

Mathilde hesitated. "Should I stop?"

"No. Keep going. Scrub them completely clean." Eventually, Corrinne nodded. It was enough. "Make a bath for me, I wish to scour away all traces of …" Corrinne winced at the thought of what she had been through.

"*Oui,* Mistress. I will heat more water."

"No. Warm or cold, I have to do this fast. You can wash me down."

"*Oui,* Mistress."

Mathilde took a heavy kettle of hot water to mix with the large urn of fresh water she kept filled in the boudoir for daily ablutions. Taking a deep breath, she started up the stairs.

The chamberlain returned carrying a small brown jar containing a smelly, greasy salve.

"Is that it?" Corrinne asked dubiously.

"*Oui,* Mademoiselle. Opium paste. It's old, but I don't think it spoils."

"Well, go ahead."

The chamberlain dipped his finger in the paste and started smearing it over the burns on her feet. Corrinne inhaled sharply.

"Do you feel strong enough to carry me upstairs?"

The chamberlain smiled gravely. "Mademoiselle, it would allow me to feel like the man I was long, long ago. I will not drop you."

Mathilde had a chair set by the tub. The chamberlain carried Corrinne into the room and set her in the chair.

"I don't think you should get your feet wet until the salve dries."

"Master chamberlain, I need you to go to our stables and bring my carriage to the house with a full team. Bring an extra team of horses for the archbishop's carriage and have the stable master quarter and feed the others. Quickly, please. Everything we do tonight must be fast."

"*Oui*, Mademoiselle."

"I would like to heat one more kettle of water for you," Mathilde said after the chamberlain left. "It still feels very cold."

Corrinne shrugged off the blanket. The bruising on her body and the red welts from the lashing was horrible to see.

"Oh, Mistress! Merciful God!"

"Mathilde, please. You must help me into the tub. I will recline while I clean myself. Fortunately, he did not get the chance to rape me, but his fingers were deep into my sex. I am sore and bruised. I will need the Egyptian soap balms. And plenty of sponges. Hurry!"

Using the sponges, soft soaps, and rinses with the cold fresh water, Corrinne managed to clean her body, the formerly red welts taking on a pinkish hue. At least the grime was gone, and she thoroughly cleaned her sex and douched herself twice. But she did not touch the appearance of her face: the huge lump and bruise at the right temple, layers of black grime and who knew what else from the filthy linens around her mouth, her split bloody upper lip, and the purplish hues of the right eye. She wanted Intendant Bigôt to see this.

"Help me to the chair. I will balance on my heels. We will attend to my face later. What do I still have to wear?"

Mathilde was stunned. "You…you are not going to bed?"

"No. I need an old dress, something I can rip and tear and soil so it looks like I was in it when this occurred."

"Your trunks are on the river sloop, but I will give you one of my old ones, something that no longer fits me."

"Good. And we need to create some bandages for my feet."

In ten more minutes, she was ready.

"I will walk on my own downstairs. Do not help me. Where I am going, I must do this on my own. Get the chamberlain. Oh! And where is Madeleine?"

"You said to board a river sloop. So I sent her on ahead. I was worried she could be abducted next. I could not bring myself to leave, not without you."

Corrinne hugged her maid. "I would have waited for you too. Now, get the chamberlain for me."

Even with the opiate paste, walking on her burned, partially sprained feet was excruciating. But at the bottom of the stairs, over the protests of the chamberlain and Mathilde, she made herself walk unaided to the library and back.

"Is everything loaded on the sloop?" she asked, panting as she spoke.

They nodded.

"I will probably only be in Quebec City for two or three days, at most. So if there was something important we forgot, send it on in the morning."

"So you are not coming back tonight?"

"I am. But only to pick up Mathilde and whatever baggage that still remains that will fit into the carriage. Both carriages are outside?"

"*Oui*, Mademoiselle. Everything is as you wanted."

They all had tears in their eyes.

Corrinne hugged them both together. "You are both very dear and important to me. Wish me good luck. I will be back before another hour passes. I am going to get Philippe. And I will probably need a new dress when I return."

They took the archbishop's carriage to avoid any challenges to their passing. When they arrived at the front door of Intendant Bigôt's city mansion, she spotted a shadow standing at the third-floor window.

"I am going up alone. No, Pierre! You are *not* going with me. This will *not* work if you come."

"May we ask what it is you plan to *do*?" Archbishop Nicolet asked with grave concern.

"You may ask, Eminence." A weak smile briefly appeared on Corrinne's face. "With Intendant Bigôt, several things are possible. But I *will* return with a written release for Philippe Gerrard, signed by him, one that you can present to Major Péan. That, I promise you. After we get Philippe, I need only stop at my house once more to load my final baggage and my maid. Then I would ask for your help in transporting me down to the sloop wharf. One of the *Falcon Queen*'s cargo launches is anchored there."

"Bloody…tha's wha', six miles? Why nah' stay here tonight and get some sleep?"

"Pierre. Eminence. Henri. No matter what happens here, I *must* leave the city…tonight. *Philippe* must leave the city…tonight, yes?"

An awkward silence followed.

"Will I see you in Quebec?" the Jesuit asked.

"Eminence, I am not saying good-bye. And you will have my valise… and you will not forget to bring that, I hope."

"I will bring it."

Without saying more, André Nicolet got out of the carriage. Pierre followed next and lifted Corrinne to the ground.

"André, do you see that window up there?"

"Yes."

"Good. That is where I will be. Watch that window."

"Let me carry ya' tah' the door."

"No."

"Let me help you. Use my shoulder," Henri said.

They took the twenty steps toward the door slowly.

"Mademoiselle, I'm not leaving you here. If I hear anything wrong, I am coming up."

Corrinne shut her eyes tightly before turning to Henri. "I know what I am doing. I will be all right."

"Take this." Henri slipped something into her hand. It was a leather scabbard. "You know what this is?"

She recognized the feel of the object immediately.

"Yes."

Corrinne slipped it through one of the holes intentionally torn in the dress, positioning it inside the waist at the front, and shifted the dress over it. She took a deep breath to brace herself against the pain in her feet. She turned away from Henri and looked up.

There were six gendarmes at guard that night, three to each side of the double doors. One from each side opened a door for her.

She passed them and moved toward the long stairway. As she took the first step, she heard a voice shout from outside.

"I will be right here!"

At the top of the stairs, she almost fainted from the pain, but upon seeing the Corsican smiling sardonically, his arms folded across his chest, standing in front of the door to Bigôt's office, she stiffened.

"My, my! Lady de Chanaye! You look well, uh...*used*. You must have had an enjoyable night."

She took note of the small pistol in his belt. "Open the door."

Snorting once, the secretary allowed her entry, but he came into the room with her and leaned against the closed door.

"Lady de Chanaye! I have been expecting you. I see the rescue I ordered went well." He eyed her face critically. "Gaspard de Propei did not treat you too badly, I trust. The dirt and dried slime will wash off. I expect the bruising might take a week to go away. But you are used to such things."

Intendant Bigôt took a seat at his desk, his face full of confidence.

"You are here to plead for your woodsman's release from the Couteau du Fort, yes?"

Corrinne remained stoic. She nodded in reply.

"In anticipation of your visit, uh, which was much later than I expected— you were delayed? Yes? No? Well, no matter. I have prepared a full release, not his pardon, mind you. Only the King can do that. You presumably destroyed his warrant by now. But it was recorded in Quebec, so that does not matter either. Your woodsman is still wanted by the crown. But he can be released from the Couteau du Fort tonight, if you can pay his...bail."

"What do you want?"

He counted off on his fingers. "Your accommodation, your cooperation, perhaps your, um, prostration."

"Did you make a list? The order of things? Something for me to sign?"

Intendant Bigôt was pleasantly surprised. "So? It is to be that easy?"

"What is it you like to say so often, François? Time to balance accounts, yes? Well, it has been a long day and a longer night. Let's get the accounts balanced so I can leave. I am through fighting you. I only want one thing."

He smirked. "Your woodsman."

"May I see his release?"

He held it up for her.

She took a step closer, read it, and nodded. "So what do you want?"

His smile turned gloating. "This." He showed her a covenant of sale for all of Lady Corrinne de Chanaye's shares in les Négociants Dunemoore.

"Where do I sign?"

Intendant Bigôt glanced briefly at the Corsican, amazed at her quick acquiescence. "I have already signed it. There is where you sign. It has to be witnessed and recorded in Quebec, but I can do that when I go downriver tomorrow."

Corrinne noted his intent to go downriver. She rotated the document on the desk, picked up a quill, dipped it, and prepared to sign, then hesitated.

"What?"

"I want that release in my hands before I sign this."

"But I have *more* things for you to sign!"

"François, I will sign whatever you want. But I will have that release, *first*. You would say the same thing if the positions were reversed, would you not? You are not stupid. Your smelly little Corsican is guarding the door, and you could run to the Couteau du Fort and countermand any signed order you send down within minutes if I do not cooperate, yes?"

"As you say. Very well, here!"

Corrinne accepted the document. It was genuine. She walked slowly toward the lantern by the window, held the document up to its light, as if examining its quality. She paused, a half step away from the window and turned.

"This is not a forgery is it? Some kind of trick?"

"A forgery?" Intendant Bigôt looked affronted. "Of course not! How absurd."

With one quick movement, Corrinne opened the window and tossed out the document.

"How dare you!"

The Corsican moved toward her.

"Wait! I am still here. I will sign the documents just as we agreed."

Corrinne returned to the desk, picked up the quill, and signed the covenant of sale. "There. Satisfied? What is next?"

Intendant Bigôt could hardly believe how cooperative she was being. But her signature was authentic.

"Next, your city houses."

Henri captured the piece of parchment floating in the night air and brought it to Archbishop Nicolet.

The Jesuit and Pierre traded looks of amazement.

"Bloody hell. She's done it!"

"You stay here, Pierre. I will get Major Péan to release Philippe."

"Ya' will need my help. Philippe may nah' be able tah' walk, yes?"

The archbishop frowned.

"Henri kin' stay here. She may, uh, *nah'* be finished yet."

Henri nodded. He was staying either way.

"Pierre, I warn you, let me do the talking or…or I will excommunicate you," he said, half in jest.

"Oooh! Tha' is certainly a frightening prospect! Thank God I am a protestant."

A yawning Major Péan was strapping on his sword as he reached the heavy iron gate of the Couteau du Fort.

"Ahh, Eminence, Monsieur Dunemoore. Back so soon? And Lady de Chanaye?"

"She is back too," the archbishop said. "He tortured her, Major. Were you an accomplice to that rape? Be wary of lying to me."

"I swear to you, I learned of Lady de Chanaye's abduction just as you were learning of it. And I sent my chief scout to try and stop it."

"Well, we dinnah' see him. He must have gotten lost, eh? Nah' much o' a scout."

"Do you have something for me?"

The archbishop handed him the document.

"Deeya' see his signature? I kin' read it for ya' if ya' like."

"Pierre!"

"That won't be necessary, Monsieur. Eminence, do *you* swear this is genuine?"

The archbishop took hold of his crucifix. "I do."

"Sergeant. Take men to Philippe Gerrard's cell and release him. Bring him here to me. Double-quick, Sergeant."

Corrinne signed the third document for the house in Quebec. "I've dated this the fifteenth of November. After we go downriver, I will need a place to stay for a week." It was a lie, but it sounded good.

"Of course." Intendant Bigôt was feeling generous. "But you will be clear of your Montréal city house by tomorrow, plus a day?"

"As I have dated the document."

"Good. Excellent. Next your ships. Here is your choice. You can sell them to me, or I can seize them for smuggling. The government will then own them, and the government will sell them to me. The difference being, you will be hung for treason for smuggling if your ships are seized. So I presume you will prefer to sell them."

"Documents concerning the seizing of French ships will have to be signed by the Governor," she said tersely.

"Of course. He will be in Quebec too. You can try to dissuade him, but then the two French frigates at anchor in Quebec will board your ships and arrest you and the captains, and *voilà*, I will still own them in the end."

The intendant smiled with self satisfaction.

"Then we will sign them in Quebec. I expect a full pardon for Philippe Gerrard as well. I will ask and get the Governor to agree to that." A false request, but she knew he expected her to say something in protest.

"You will *not* convince the Governor to go against a declaration of the King. You are not *that* good. But, as you wish. Ask away. It makes no difference to me. And you and your woodsman can both sail away off into the sunrise together."

"Then everything is signed?"

"Yes."

Corrinne was satisfied this was all of his plans and strategies.

"I am defeated." Her voice was bitter, despondent. *A little overboard*, she thought. But Bigôt pounced on that too.

"Oh? And you are surprised it ended like this?"

"I was surprised by Gaspard de Propei's abduction. I did not think he was that...*creative*, in his strategies."

Bigôt snorted. "You are such a fool! The idea to abduct you was not his, it was *mine*! He is simple-minded, like you."

"François, he did not just abduct me, he tortured me with hot coals from a fire, beat me, lashed me, sodomized me over and over. Surely you did not expect he would be so cruel and disgusting …?"

Bigôt exulted! Her reaction to his words, the expression on her bruised and bleeding face! It was everything he wanted and so much more!

"Expect it? I *encouraged* him to indulge his every whim. Am I surprised? I am surprised you are not more disfigured. You are a *whore*!" he spat. "Did you really expect you would be treated differently?"

"I see. Then we are done?" Corrinne turned to leave.

"Mmm, not quite. I believe I mentioned *prostration*."

She paused before turning around and started to slowly unbutton her dress. "I am sure you will enjoy tasting Gaspard de Propei's essences?"

Bigôt sneered. "No, Mademoiselle. Not me. Him." He pointed to the Corsican.

A leering, repulsive smile spread across the Corsican's face. She walked to stand directly in front of him, gazing at him intently.

"Shall I begin here?" she asked and groped the bulge in his trousers with one hand.

"Oh…yes! Monsieur Bigôt, you offered your room?"

"Of course." Intendant Bigôt left his desk to open the hidden door.

"Lean against the wall." Corrinne urged the Corsican. She quickly opened the front of his trousers and withdrew his erection. "Now close your eyes," she whispered, "and you will enjoy this much more."

The Corsican obeyed. He was living a fantasy he had only dreamed about. He could feel her hand sliding up and down his member while she slid down his body. Any moment now, he would feel her lips. *I will probably ejaculate instantly*, he thought, *but then we move to the bedroom, and I can put her in shackles!*

Corrinne saw his eyes remain tightly closed as she slid down his body. She slowly massaged him with her left hand and withdrew Gaspard de Propei's stiletto from its scabbard inside her dress with her right. She heard the door to Bigôt's hidden room click open just as her knees touched the floor.

"Are you ready for this, Monsieur?" she asked, her voice suggestive.

"*Yeees*. Oh, yes!"

In one stroke, Corrinne sliced off his erection and plunged the stiletto up into his lower chest directly into his heart, stopping it instantly. The Corsican exhaled a whoosh of air, and fell to his knees supported only by her arms, a terrible grimace on his dead face.

Seeing the Corsican hunched over Corrinne, the intendant bragged, "*Bravo*! Well done, Corrinne! I told you she was good!"

Corrinne left the stiletto in the man's chest. She rose from the floor with blood all over the front of her dress and the Corsican's pistol in her hand. She turned.

Bigôt's eyes widened with horror as she cocked back the hammer and pointed it directly at his face.

"I am an expert shot with a pistol, François." Corrinne's smile was grim. "One of the many things you do not know about me. We've a few more accounts to *balance*. I just wanted to hear your full confession first, from your own lips, which was impressive. Even for your inflated ego."

"You will be hung, before the sun rises!" His face was red, his voice hoarse with anger.

"Maybe I will, but you won't live to see the sunrise unless you do exactly as I tell you. Since I have killed your secretary, killing you will only be for my great pleasure. I have nothing to lose, yes? You should know that I have *dreamed* about putting a ball in your head, and much worse. You can only hang me once. And as you like to say, live or die, it is now your choice. Let's see which choice you make. *Go* into the bedroom."

Corrinne made him take off all his clothes and shackled him naked to his bed. She pressed the mouth gag through his clenched lips, buckled it tightly behind his head. Slipping a thin linen noose around his scrotum, she threw the other end over a ring hanging from the ceiling, which had a small weight attached to it, enough to keep the line taut.

"There, there, François. All comfortable? No? I should remind you that if you struggle too much, this linen cinch will tighten. It's your ingenious design. Do you remember when you strung two of these around my breasts the first time to ensure my *maximum* cooperation, or so you claimed? I learned a lot from you. I could do so, so much more, but I have other appointments. Maybe another time. Now, try to sleep. I am sure someone will eventually come looking for you...perhaps by midday meal tomorrow? Feel free to soil your bed. You should be used to that by now."

While he watched with bulging, terrified eyes, Corrinne went to a closet full of various types of women's clothes and withdrew a simple front-buttoned dress. She threw her bloody dress onto the closet floor, put on the new one, looked in the mirror, and tore back the top of one side, so one breast could be seen completely. She also found a long, nautical coat hanging from a door hook.

Perfect, she thought.

Lady Corrinne de Chanaye paused at the hidden bedroom door and looked back at François Bigôt.

"I hope those tapers on the bedside tables burn cleanly. Try not to rock the bed and knock one of them over. It wouldn't do for a fire to start, would it? *Au revoir.*"

Corrinne shut the door until it clicked. It was the only entrance. Pressing her ear against the door, she could hear some muffled shouts, but only if she listened carefully. Satisfied, she examined the long coat and cut open the seams high on the inside lining. Then she stuffed every single document she could find in Bigôt's desk, including the secret drawers, and the documents she'd just signed, into the coat's double lining, using it like one giant pocket.

She searched and found the key to the office in the pocket of the dead Corsican's tailored waistcoat and placed the pistol back in his belt. She blew out all the candles in the room, leaving only the fire hearth for illumination.

Corrinne closed the door behind her, locked it, and put the key in her pocket. She took a decorative brass plaque and chain from the top drawer of the Corsican's desk in the hallway and hung it over the intendant's door handle.

Ne pas déranger. Do not disturb.

Corrinne hated to have Henri see her like this, but it could not be helped. Her injured feet were throbbing, the worst yet, as she left the mansion. The gendarmes ogled her breast and looked at nothing else as she walked through the doors.

"The intendant wishes not to be disturbed," she informed them as she limped past.

Henri dropped his gaze to the ground.

The gendarmes laughed and made numerous lewd remarks about her under their breaths. As soon as she felt far enough away, she buttoned up the long coat.

"Henri. I am safe now, but we must hurry. Where are they?"

"The Couteau du Fort."

She looked up the hill but could not see any carriages. Corrinne was concerned. She could not stay here, and she could not walk much farther. Certainly not up the tall hill to the Couteau du Fort.

She groaned. The pain was intense. "I don't know if I can stand up much longer."

Henri saw her grimace. "A moment, Mademoiselle." He went back to the guards and told them to tell the archbishop they were walking back to Lady de Chanaye's city house. He rushed back to her.

"Put your arms around my neck."

"What?"

"Put your arms around my neck," he insisted.

Henri picked Corrinne up in his arms and started walking down the Rue Bonsecours.

"Mademoiselle, you are not much heavier than a back pouch full of furs. And I've carried those for miles and miles."

She laid her head on his shoulder, feeling safe, as if carried by an angel.

When they reached Corrinne's city house, the chamberlain looked at Henri in awe.

"Mistress, are you hurt?" he asked.

"It's my feet. But I cannot stop weeping, so indulge me, please. And take this coat and guard it with your life. I must take it with me to Quebec. Make sure I do not forget!"

"*Oui*, Mademoiselle. Mathilde has heated you a full bath and soft towels and fresh clothes are laid out for you in your boudoir."

Philippe Gerrard was brought before the iron gate of the Couteau du Fort in shackles.

"Philippe!" Pierre waved wildly at him from the other side.

Major Péan stood a few paces in front of Philippe with ten of his regular army soldiers to either side.

"Monsieur Gerrard, before I remove your shackles I want you to know I was following orders when I arrested you. Not that you care about such things, but I do. I am also following orders for your release. It was a *written* order from Intendant Bigôt, and genuine, which I understand was secured by Lady de Chanaye. She is a resourceful woman. I was only made aware of Lady de Chanaye's abduction at the same time as you were, though you probably don't believe that. And I am pleased she has been rescued. Truly. Now, I expect that your temporary release from the fort will last until shortly after sunrise, so I urge you to use this time to go somewhere far away from Montréal, before I am ordered to pursue you, because I will do so with earnest. You can probably bribe the gendarmes, but my regulars"—he gestured to the men standing on either side of him—"I have ordered to shoot you if you commit any acts of violence while you are inside the city walls. Do you understand?"

"Yes. Gaspard de Propei?"

"Ah, yes. It seems Sieur Gaspard has been taken captive by some Oneida warriors who were on this side of the river. Very unusual. According to my chief scout, they were Oswego Oneida, no less. Still unconfirmed. But tomorrow I will send a search party to ascertain the truth of this. I am sure your Scottish friend can give you a much more colorful explanation. Now, I am going to have your shackles removed. Do not forget what I have told you. Sergeant!"

Major Péan gestured for the shackles' removal.

Philippe rubbed his ankles and wrists.

"Oh, yes. It may interest you to know that Coulon de Villiers, Ambassador Jumonville's brother? Well, Coulon destroyed the English forces under George Washington south of Fort Duquesne. Washington was released to return to the Virginia colony. With that action, it appears the war will now go quiet for the winter. So far, we are winning."

"The war is furthest thing from my mind right now, Major."

To Philippe's surprise, Major Péan extended his hand.

"I wish you *bon voyage* and *adieu*, Monsieur Gerrard. May you and Lady de Chanaye find peace somewhere."

Philippe shook his hand after a moment's pause. "You are actually a fine officer, Major, except for your singular flaw."

Major Péan laughed. "And what is that?"

"Money."

"Oh, that. Well, who doesn't love money? I have to pay for my own uniforms, you know."

During the ride back to Corrinne's city house, Pierre talked without pause about everything that had happened since Philippe's head was bashed with the butt of a musket.

At the first lull, Philippe asked, "Major Péan says the *shérif* is a captive of the Oneida?"

Pierre glanced at the archbishop. "Tha' is the rumor."

"And Henri and Corrinne?"

"Henri's fine. Corrinne is a little…well, she was tortured."

Philippe grimaced.

"Laddie, ya' kinnah' be like tha' with her right now. Ya' need tah' be strong for her."

Inside the front door, Philippe found Henri sitting, on guard, at the foot of the steps leading upstairs. He stood when he saw his father.

Philippe hugged him tightly. "I am proud of you, but that was a terribly dangerous thing you did."

"There was no one else to help her, Monsieur. And had I arrived any later, the *shérif* would have killed her."

"I know. But if you had been killed, what then would I do without you? And Anamosa?"

Henri was uncertain how to answer. But he frowned at the thought of Anamosa being sad.

Philippe touched Henri's shoulder with one hand. "It is not a question to be answered, Henri. It is just a question to think about, before you do anything like that again."

"Yes, Monsieur."

Philippe turned to Mathilde. "Where is she?"

"In her boudoir. She is resting. Waiting for you."

"Master chamberlain, I cannot promise this house will be a safe place for you tomorrow, or even a few days after that. The house indeed belongs to Pierre Dunemoore, but he will be going to Quebec for at least a week. We will send some company *coureurs de bois* to stay at the small apartments should you need assistance."

"I will be fine, Monsieur."

Philippe went upstairs and quietly slipped into the boudoir. Corrinne was sleeping. He took a chair and placed it near her bedside. There was water on the side table and a basin with more water and white cloths. The bruising, lumps, welts, and her swollen lips were not easy to look at. He laid his head next to her side and held her hand. The cleanliness of the linens, the bedding, her clothes, the aroma of her skin, everything smelled intoxicating. He was asleep a few seconds after he closed his eyes.

A short time later, Corrinne shifted her feet restlessly and the spike of pain roused her. In the dim light of the room, she saw Philippe's disheveled hair next to her and smiled with relief. She stroked his head softly and glanced out the window. It was still dark, but she knew it must be long past midnight.

We cannot tarry here much longer.

As her fingers slid through the thick, snarled blond hair, she discovered a huge lump on the back of Philippe's head.

"How did you get *this* one?" she whispered, so as not to wake him.

But it was loud enough. Philippe raised his head, blinking sleep from his eyes. Seeing her smile, he carefully climbed into bed next to her.

"Oho, Corrinne." His gaze was soft, affectionate.

"Oho, Snow Hair."

"Thank you for rescuing me."

"Well, I had some idle time on my hands, so …" She smiled. "Kiss me."

Their embrace was longer and deeper than any they had shared in the past. When they broke apart, she continued to caress the side of his face.

"We are certainly beat up this time."

Philippe kissed her hand. "But we are still here."

"Truly, but we need to be out of the city before the first hint of sunrise."

"I know. Major Péan told me the same thing."

"I have one of the *Falcon Queen*'s cargo sloops waiting for us at the river wharf. And the *shérif*?"

"I understand he belongs to the Oswego Oneida now. Some would pity the agony he will endure. I am not one of them."

"Neither am I."

"Henri?"

"He was standing guard on your stairway when I came in."

She began to weep.

"No, *mon chéri*, no. What's wrong?"

"By some miracle, Henri saved me. I love him so, but I cannot look at him or hardly think about him without crying, and I do not understand why."

She wiped at tears that would not stop.

"I told him how proud I was," Philippe said. "He claimed he only did what I would have done. I wish I had found a way over the wall instead. Henri could have been killed. And I don't know what I would have done if that happened."

Corrinne pressed her fingers to his lips. "You cannot save everyone. And you cannot blame yourself when someone you love dies."

Emotion rose. He licked his lips. He thought of all those he had lost. A tear dripped from one of his eyes.

Corrinne took his face in her hands and kissed away the tear and then each eye and finally his lips.

"Pierre keeps saying Henri is just like me."

"Henri is *too young* to be you. He is brave and courageous and wonderful, but emotionally he is still *twelve years old*! Do you not see that? Because of the trials he survived this last year, part of him has grown way beyond his years, and much too fast. You are a *god* to him. He *mimics* you! But if the boy in him does not have the time to finish growing, to give him perspective on right and wrong, what is foolhardy and what is wise…this burden may kill him. You want to save someone? Save Henri…save him before it's too late. Take him away from these lands, before the war erupts again next year. And save Anamosa too."

Philippe flinched at that last comment. "I promised Okeanneh I would take care of Anamosa."

Corrinne frowned, but only for an instant. "Okeanneh sounds like a wonderful woman and mother, so do it then for Okeanneh…and if you rescue them both, you will probably rescue yourself. And that is long overdue."

Philippe looked into her luminous green eyes. "You see things so clearly, long before I do. How did I ever earn having you in my life?"

Corrinne's eyes widened and her voice lifted in tone. "You are not alone, Philippe. I…I will help you."

Philippe touched Corrinne's hair and eyebrows, then her cheek and her lips. *And I almost lost you too*, he thought, looking into her eyes.

She could sense him thinking, weighing, deciding.

Just the notion of losing her caused a pain so sharp, it made Philippe stop breathing for a moment. It had only been a month since Okeanneh had died, yet here he was, surprised by how strongly he felt compelled to love again. But deep down, he had always loved Corrinne; they shared an unbreakable, unspoken devotion to one another. Yet, until recently, he had not realized the depth of her strength, or that her willingness to sacrifice for love was as strong...no, maybe even stronger than his own. She had the courage to confront the face of a *demon*! Then, only hours later, be abducted, beaten, crippled, and sexually tortured. And after her rescue, she had put herself in danger again, and in the face of more torture and humiliation, she still found a way to gain his release, and her first words when she saw him again were to urge him to rescue Henri and then himself.

Philippe knew he must leave New France. He stood at the edge of the rest of his life, facing some new place, a new culture, new unknowns. He had almost lost Corrinne three times in one day, and the painful enormity of that thought would have dropped him to his knees were he not already lying down. Corrinne's life was simply too precious, his every moment with her a gift. He loved Corrinne unconditionally. The memory of his love for Okeanneh would not be sullied by this.

He kissed her gently. He kissed her forehead, her cheek, her bruises, her neck, the top of her chest, finally, the palm of her hand.

"Well, that was nice," she whispered, a little nervous.

He stared intently into her eyes. "Whatever happens next, I don't want to do this alone. I love you."

Corrinne inhaled sharply. Joy filled her being. She swallowed.

"I love you *too*! I have always loved you. Ever since Le Havre. And the first time you—"

"Marry me, Corrinne."

She had not yet recovered from his admission of love. She was speechless. "Wha...what?"

"I said, I love you. Will you marry me?"

"M-marry you?!" Lady Corrinne de Chanaye began to sob.

Mathilde had been sitting in a chair in the hall in case she was needed, and, hearing sobs, rushed into the room.

"Did I say something wrong?" Philippe asked, confused.

"No! You idiot! Of course, I will marry you!"

Mathilde quickly backed out of the room before they noticed she was there.

CHAPTER 38
MONTRÉAL
NOVEMBER 1, 1754
The River to Cap Diamant

The chamberlain came up the stairs and pointed at the door.

Mathilde looked nervous and uncertain. "I think they want to be alone."

"Not possible. Monsieur Dunemoore said they need to leave right away. He did not say why."

Mathilde got up and knocked on the door. "Mistress, they are asking for you both downstairs," she said upon entering.

Corrinne sat up, smiling, and began rebuttoning the top of her dress. "We will be down directly. Is everything loaded?"

"Yes, my lady."

Corrinne turned to Philippe. "Can you wait for me downstairs unless I call for you?"

Philippe nodded, kissed her again, and left the room.

Mathilde looked at her expectantly.

Corrinne wiped the tears from her eyes. "There cannot be more contrast between two days as there has been between yesterday and today. From complete despair and horror to happiness and ecstasy, from demons to angels! And both completely unexpected."

Mathilde clasped her hands together. "I apologize, Mistress. I heard you crying and came into the room…but only briefly!"

"Then you know?"

"Oh, yes, yes, yes! I am so happy for you both!"

"Then help me get ready for a long day of travel."

Philippe walked outside to see many tired men waiting patiently. Pierre looked irritated.

"Kin' we go now, laddie? Before the gendarmes and our company *coureurs de bois* engage in a full skirmish?"

"Sorry, Pierre. I fell asleep."

"Ohh? Well…as long it was just tha'."

"How many men?"

"Six. Three tah' each carriage. And they are both fully loaded. I thought Henri and I kin' go in tha' archbishop's carriage. But as soon as we get through tha' gate, his Imperial Eminence is walking right back in. He plans to sail down the river this afternoon. I figure ya' and Corrinne and Mathilde kin' take her carriage. The plan is tah' go straight tah' the river wharf, load baggage, start sailing downriver at first light, and send tha' carriages back with our men."

Philippe nodded. "We need some men to stay in the footmen's apartments to protect your house. The *shérif* killed two of Corrinne's footmen. The other has not been heard from."

"They've already volunteered."

"The archbishop?"

"He's snoring away in his carriage."

Philippe climbed in and shook the man awake. The archbishop awoke with a start.

"Eminence, we are leaving."

The chamberlain looked at the folded, wax-sealed missive Lady de Chanaye had placed in his hand.

"Mistress?"

"This may be a little dangerous, so use an intermediary if you must, but it must be someone you trust. I want you to deliver this to Major Péan for me this morning, just before the noon hour. The wax seal must stay unbroken. Tell him I told you to do this. Tell him you do not know what it says. Tell him I am traveling to Quebec. That is all. Can you do this important thing for me?"

"It will be my honor, Mistress."

Henri was asleep on a couch in the library when the chamberlain carried Corrinne into the room. She regarded Henri warmly and put a finger to her lips, signing to the chamberlain to set her down next to him. She gestured for a chair, and mouthed, *Leave us*.

Corrinne stroked the sleeping boy's hair.

Henri mumbled, and his eyes opened. Seeing her, he sat up quickly, scanning the room for danger.

"It's all right, Henri. It is just us. We are alone."

Henri calmed. "Oh. Uh, what should we do?"

"I thought you might help me out to the carriage."

Henri jumped to his feet. "Just put your arms around my neck, Mademoiselle."

Henri carried Corrinne down the front steps of the house.

"Ohhhh! Tha's who she reminds me of," Pierre said, watching them approach. "She's like the story o' bloody Queen Cleopatra. Ya' know… carried around by somebody all o' the time…lots o' servants. Owns a navy. Though,"—he turned to Philippe—"I thin' she favors Henri more than ya', laddie."

"You'll get no argument from me. Why shouldn't she?"

Philippe accepted Corrinne from Henri's arms and placed her in the covered carriage. He followed by helping Mathilde into her seat and handed in a basket full of food, water, and wine. A second basket was delivered to the archbishop's carriage.

The chamberlain gave Corrinne the coat from Bigôt's office. "Your favorite coat, I presume?"

Corrinne handed it to Mathilde. "Do not misplace this, Mathilde."

She turned back and gripped the chamberlain's hands tightly.

"You will be in my heart and prayers. I will write to you."

"I will look forward to your letters, Mademoiselle, and to seeing you again someday, when the war ends, perhaps."

"I would like that."

She kissed his hand. "Do not forget to deliver the missive by the noon hour."

Philippe stood by the open carriage door. "You will have the lead all the way?" he asked Pierre.

"Aye. Henri and I will share tha' first coach."

Philippe looked back down the Rue Saint-Paul. He thought how he might not see it again. It was still too dark to see anything distinctly, but he did spot a few lanterns moving in the darkness on the city streets down near the markets. *The bakers*, he thought. *The bread always smells so good in the morning.*

"Let's go."

Archbishop Nicolet got out of the first carriage as soon as both were through the east gate. He walked back to see Corrinne, stepped up, and stuck his head through the carriage window.

"We will have dinner together in Quebec City this week."

"Eminence,"—she kissed his cheek—"thank you. For everything."

After they parted with the archbishop, the ride down the river road proceeded at an ambitious pace short of a gallop. Philippe held Corrinne in his arms. She lay against his shoulder and gazed out the window, looking at the stars flashing through the leaves in the thinning treetops and enjoyed the rocking movement.

Before a half hour passed, they'd reached the sloop wharf. There were two men waiting with a large flat raft tied at the end of a short wooden pier. Every year, the river ice would crush the wharf and snap the pilings. And every spring, the Dunemoore Company wharf would be rebuilt as soon as the ice cleared. They'd learned to do it in less than a day. A hauling line was already extended to the *Falcon Queen*'s cargo sloop anchored twenty meters away. The carriages were quickly unloaded.

Pierre gave final instructions to the *coureurs de bois* about returning the carriages. Philippe hugged each of these hardy men he had shared so many seasons in the wilderness with trapping furs among many other adventures.

"I will see you all again someday soon," Philippe told them.

Most suspected this was not true, but pretended it was. It made the farewells easier to say.

As the glimmer of sunrise appeared above the river, people and cargo were hauled over to the side of the sloop. As soon as everyone was aboard, the *coureurs de bois* retrieved the raft and secured it to the pier. After a few final waves, the first mate of the *Falcon Queen* began shouting orders.

"Hoist sail. Man the oars!"

"I want to stay on deck," Corrine said.

Philippe placed her among some soft cargo bundles of furs just aft of the helm.

Henri went immediately to the first mate. "What can I do?"

"From what I hear, you should rest for a few hours. Besides, a couple of female passengers down below are anxious to see you. A beautiful little someone will certainly be happy, and, I think, a little angry with you."

"Anamosa!"

He had barely uttered her name when someone, standing halfway out of the forward hatch, screamed.

"*Ahhh-reee!*"

Henri ran, scooped her up, spun her around, and kissed her tear-stained cheeks.

Michelle came next. Holding Anamosa in his arms, he hugged his mother, who was sobbing with relief. "Every time you go away, I think I will never see you again."

Striding to them, Philippe hugged them all.

"Is this finally all over?" Michelle asked him, her voice tinged with desperation.

"We will be in Quebec in a few days."

"And then what?"

"Then we have decisions to make."

"I wish to stay in Quebec."

"I know. Let's not talk about that right now. I would like you to meet Corrinne de Chanaye."

"The infamous one?"

"Not that infamous, I hope. She's been injured and could use someone to sit with while we sail downriver."

"Of course. It would be nice to have someone to talk with other than sailors and *coureurs de bois*."

Philippe took them back aft. "Corrinne, I told Michelle she could sit with you."

Underneath Corrinne's bruised and swollen face, Michelle could see beauty and a strength of will that had this lady smiling, when only a few hours earlier, horrible things had been done to her—or so she had heard it whispered.

"Philippe speaks fondly of you. We can share stories, if you like …?" Her eyebrows lifted. She tilted her head slightly toward Philippe.

Corrinne smiled broadly. "Oh, yes! We will get along especially well, I'm sure. And is this Anamosa?"

Anamosa had her head on Henri's shoulder. He knelt down. "She will probably want to stay with me for a while."

"Who wouldn't?" She touched Anamosa's face softly. "The blueness of your eyes! They are…startling, but beautiful."

Anamosa frowned suspiciously and turned her head away.

"She does not speak much French yet. She'll be friendlier after a few days," Henri explained. "I will sit with her up by the bow as we sail."

"If ya' ladies will excuse me. I think I'll find a place tah' collapse." Pierre went below to sleep.

Philippe had moved to the helm, questioning the first mate about Quebec.

Corrinne took hold of Michelle's hands. "Who should start? But first let me say that Henri is a wonderful, extraordinary young man. And I am sorry for these tears, but for some reason he has that effect on me. Perhaps it's because he saved me from being murdered last night."

"He is a child that has been severely scarred, burned by the world, yet does not complain. On the inside, he is still a child. I would cry if I had any tears left to shed. And now I know why Philippe loves you so much."

"Philippe? A month ago Philippe loved Okeanneh."

"Yes, he certainly did. But he's loved you since you met in Le Havre. He told me that on the crossing, when I asked him who paid for the rescue from Rouen. He said, 'Corrinne did. We love each other.' Forgive him. He is often confused and very frustrating."

"Yes. He certainly is." That Michelle knew this about Philippe, and Corrinne had only realized this now, caused her hurt. She pushed envious thoughts away. "Michelle, I will tell you anything you want to know, but you have told me more about him in a few sentences than he has in thirteen years. I pray you begin."

"Well, how to begin? I was sixteen when I met Philippe Malthais at Saint Ouen's Church in Rouen …"

Late the first day, one of the sailors spotted four bodies floating face down near the river's southern bank. The first mate changed course to investigate, but there were sandbars at this point, so he could only get to within twenty meters.

"Natives," the lookout called back after using the watch glass. "Feathers and red war paint. Dead and starting to bloat. They'll float by Quebec in another week if they don't get scavenged."

He decided it wasn't important enough to wake Lady de Chanaye or Messieurs Gerrard or Dunemoore. The mate steered to the center of the channel again. The winds were good and the current downriver felt strong today. In another hour, they would reach the company's next sloop wharf on the north bank. They would anchor there until morning.

For the next three days, Corrinne and Michelle sat side by side and enjoyed the glorious colors of the autumn leaves. Only on a few trees, the leaves were starting to brown and wither.

"I will miss this so. My favorite time of year," Corrinne said, her face wistful.

"And sailing so peacefully down this river," Michelle added, "is there a better way to enjoy this?"

They had both shared their life stories, telling each other everything they could recall. And at the end, each admired the strength, intelligence, and selflessness of the other. Their friendship was sealed.

At night, the sleeping areas were crowded, both down below and up on deck. The women slept separately down below for privacy, except for Anamosa, who refused to be more than an arm's length away from Henri. Henri did not seem to mind. They sat together on deck every night, bundled with blankets. He would point and tell her of the different stars. She liked hearing his voice.

"I'm pregnant," Michelle confided to Corrinne on the third day of their voyage. "The child's father is Pemberton Curtiss. He raped me in Piqua's village. It's really starting to show. I'm telling you so I don't have to tell anyone else, because I must tell someone. I think Pierre suspects I'm pregnant, but he's been polite and hasn't said anything. Juniata knows. I'm sure Okeanneh told her. But no one knows the name of the father, and I will always keep it that way for the child's sake. But I felt someone needed to know that too. I don't know why…perhaps, in case something should happen to me?"

"Michelle, your secret is safe with me."

"Well, here is another one for you to carry. Okeanneh was pregnant with Philippe's child when she died. I am certain Juniata knows. But Philippe doesn't know and never needs to know. At this point, it makes no difference.

And the guilt would overwhelm him, particularly right now. I am only telling you in case he finds out someday, because you will have to deal with any consequences of that."

Corrinne found that revelation unsettling, but she was glad to know of it now. It was a huge secret to share, so she returned Michelle's trust with a confidence of her own.

"I have two portraits, one of Okeanneh and one of Chittaqua. They are being carried on the next sloop with the artist, Charles VanderMeer. Other than the artist himself, I am the only one that knows the existence of these paintings. I've asked him not to tell Philippe and he has agreed to leave this up to me. But I really don't know what to do with them. I'd heard Okeanneh was beautiful. This painting shows that...and...and so much more. VanderMeer has captured her heart and her love through her eyes. I confess, I am jealous and fearful of Philippe seeing this right now, with her death an open wound in his memory."

Michelle thought on this awhile. "I would send them back upriver. Let them hang in the library of your city house in Montréal. Pierre will cherish them both. And if Philippe doesn't see them for several years, the time in between will cushion his surprise when he does, maybe even warm his heart with memories. It is better this way...I think."

It was an ideal solution. Corrinne had never really had a female friend in her life. She touched her head to Michelle's. "I feel so fortunate that I met you."

At this lull in their conversation, Anamosa came over to sit in Corrinne's lap. She had two wooden dolls with her.

Corrinne smiled broadly. "Well, hello to you too!"

"Kee-ko and Ahh-ree," Anamosa explained. She pointed and touched Corrinne's hair and then to the Ahh-ree doll's bald head.

"I am so flattered!" she told Anamosa.

With Michelle's help, they cut a lock of Corrinne's hair and fixed something permanent to the Ahh-ree doll. Michelle noticed a small red mark at the nape of Corrinne's neck, at the root of the hair.

"You have a red blemish on the skin back here?" Michelle touched it softly.

"Yes, I know. I have several. They are just birthmarks."

When they were finished, Anamosa put her arms around Corrinne's neck, laid her head on her shoulder, and went to sleep.

Corrinne placed her arms carefully around the little girl. "Oh, my. I feel honored."

Michelle smiled. "That's the way they are. Anamosa has decided to love you. And this is why we fall in love with her."

In the afternoon of the fourth day, a four-man courier canoe was spotted coming upriver with three men in it.

"Canoe!" the forward lookout shouted out.

This time, everyone was on deck. The canoe passed them on the port side. Philippe and Pierre waved, but the greeting was not returned. Two of the three men were Huron half-breeds and frowned as the two vessels passed one another. They knew the other man.

"Oho! Singing Owl!" Philippe hailed loudly, holding up his arm.

The old Huron shaman stopped paddling and stared ambivalently at Philippe. The canoe continued upriver.

Pierre and Philippe looked at one another, puzzled.

"Not even a wave? I have a bad feeling about this."

"Me too, laddie."

"When do we make Quebec?"

"If the winds stay strong behind us, soon, and well before nightfall," the first mate said. "We will tie alongside the *Falcon Queen*."

"We saw that man, Singing Owl, in Montréal, almost four days ago," Philippe explained to the first mate. "He should not be coming *back* from Quebec today unless he paddled fast all the way down, leaving on the same day we saw him ..."

"And *why* would he dah' tha'? Wha' was he carrying?"

A disturbing idea came to Philippe. He turned to the first mate. "Did you see any Oneida braves traveling on the river before we came aboard?"

The mate shook his head. "No. But we saw some bodies, dead Indians, floating along the south shore at the end of the first day."

"Describe them to us," Philippe asked, alarmed.

The first mate told them what he saw, and added he did not think it important enough to wake them. "We see dead bodies floating in this river all the time."

"Tha's Oneida war painting, laddie."

"I know," Philippe replied somberly. "We need to tell Corrinne."

They gathered in the back: Philippe, Pierre, Corrinne, with Michelle and Henri included.

"The bodies had the paint markings of the Oneida. That side of the river is Oneida land."

Corrinne churned over the information in her head. "Singing Owl has provided me with information for years in trade for silver. He will work for anyone who pays him. But he would not make a fast trip to Quebec unless he was paid a lot. He did not return your greeting, you say? Not even a wave?"

Philippe shook his head. "No. But our meeting with him in Montréal was not exactly friendly. He said he'd been talking with the *shérif.* But we did not part enemies. At least, I didn't think so."

"Gaspard de Propei was probably paying him for information on you. And Singing Owl hates the Oneida. They slaughtered his entire village long ago."

"Speaking of the *shérif,* he was wounded badly when tha' Oneida took him captive."

Henri spoke. "I hit him with four arrows. One in the shoulder. Two in the right thigh. One in the left."

It was the first time Philippe had heard that. "Four arrows?"

"Yes, Monsieur."

"But none o' them a mortal wound. And Tall Mountain Among Trees planned tah' take him back across the river, alive."

Philippe frowned as his suspicions grew stronger. "What are the chances that Singing Owl and his two partners ambushed and overpowered five armed Oneida warriors and paddled the *shérif* downriver to Quebec?"

"Chances do not matter," Corrinne said. "It is possible. That is what matters. And the *shérif* has a lot of money in Quebec to pay Singing Owl for helping him. So we must assume that is exactly what happened."

"He is heavily wounded," Philippe thought aloud. "He will look for a doctor. And he probably thinks we do not know about his escape. I mean how would he? He did not know our plans. And he probably left at night, hours before we did. There was a full moon. But he will not know we arrive in Quebec *today,* the same day he arrived."

Corrinne nodded. "That means he will stay out of sight, unless he hears otherwise. He must already have an ally there. That is his advantage. Word that he tried to torture and kill me will not be well received by Governor Duquesne. And Archbishop Nicolet will be here tomorrow. He will also tell the Governor all that's transpired."

"So?" Pierre asked. "Wha' do we do?"

"Either way, we have to complete our business. I have to meet with the Governor, along with Henri, probably you, Pierre, as escort, maybe Michelle as well. I've already told her everything about our earlier discussion. She agrees."

When they all looked at Michelle, she nodded.

"We need to act quickly in getting all of the agreements signed," Corrinne said. "But for that, we need the archbishop. He is bringing my valise, so let's pray he is not late."

The discussion stopped for now. Henri took Anamosa forward.

Corrinne touched Pierre and Philippe's arms. "Michelle, please stay. I have something more to tell all of you," she said somberly. "Henri does not need to hear this."

Pierre groaned. "I've heard tha' tone before. Tha' means we are nah' going tah' like this."

"It is something you all need to know. Some other things occurred when I was with Intendant Bigôt."

Corrinne appeared uncharacteristically nervous.

"Laddie, I think we should sit down."

Corrinne explained everything that happened, everything Bigôt admitted to her, the disgusting insults, the Corsican's death, but omitted the detail of his castration before she stabbed him in the heart with the *shérif*'s stiletto.

"But—"

"Wait. There's more."

Before Pierre could interrupt further, she continued, describing how she shackled Bigôt to the bed with a gag in his mouth and his scrotum cinched in a weighted noose.

No one said anything during these unpleasant revelations, though glances of alternating horror and amazement were traded between Pierre and Philippe.

"But there was a fortunate outcome in this—"

"No! Now ya' wait!" Pierre insisted. "Let me understand this! So ya' shackled the second most powerful man in New France, after the Governor, of course, tah' a bed, in a secret room, with a gag in his mouth, and his *balls* in a noose, and now we are going tah' 'hear' aboot tha' fortunate results of tha'? Oh, and I forgot aboot stabbing the Corsican!"

Corrinne's anger simmered short of a boil. "Pierre! Bigôt was in league with Gaspard de Propei, and they tortured, crippled, sodomized, and almost murdered me. I did what I had to do to get Philippe's release."

"I've no doubt aboot tha', lassie," Pierre said wearily. "But dah' ya' thin' he is still alive?"

"Someone went looking for him by the midday."

"Ya' mean ya' hope someone did."

"No. I mean I arranged for someone to come looking for Bigôt, and this person would not stop until Bigôt was freed. The man knew to look for a lock at the side of the intendant's liquor cabinet, that it opens a door behind the floor-to-ceiling bookcase."

"And who is tha' exactly?"

"Major Péan."

Pierre's mouth gaped open even further. "Sweet Jesus! And tha' is the *fortunate* result?"

"No." She explained how she'd emptied Bigôt's entire desk of documents. "I have them all with me, but I've not examined them yet."

Philippe had remained quiet through all of this.

Pierre looked at him again. "Well ...?"

"Well, what?"

The Scotsman could see it in his friend's face. Philippe would have killed both the intendant and the Corsican. So, in fact, it could have been much worse. He nodded.

"All right. All right. I guess we only need tah' worry if the little beaver turd shows up in Quebec over the next few days."

"I will not be going back to Montréal, Pierre," Corrinne said to assuage him. "And the crime is mine."

"Ya'...but I *will* be going back. And Bigôt hands out vengeance as welcome home gifts."

In another two hours, as the first mate predicted, Quebec City loomed atop the Cap Diamant prominence on the north side of the river.

"You will love Quebec," Corrinne told Michelle. "They call this the diamond cape. And the city is the crown jewel as far as I'm concerned. They once thought there were diamonds there. It turned out to be quartz. But it's the capital citadel of New France. We think it almost as sophisticated as Paris," she said proudly. "Though I am certain the Parisians would disagree."

"We passed the city coming over from France, but went on to Montréal. Why do you not live here?"

"My business was fur trading and Montréal was the center. I did live here in the beginning. But…well, Philippe was in Montréal. I did not admit it to myself then, but I followed my heart. I maintain a house in this city, though I am rarely there, except for some winters. We will stay there tonight, though. Hot baths and soft beds, like the Romans, yes?"

Michelle glowed at the thought. "A hot bath!"

Soon, they pulled into port, where the *Falcon Queen*, the *Ile Royale*, six other seaworthy merchant vessels, and two French navy frigates were at anchor in the Saint Lawrence beneath the guns of the great fortress. The ships were surrounded by dozens of cargo sloops, bateaux, and smaller craft.

"There she is!" Corrinne pointed, giddy with excitement. "The *Falcon Queen*! Oh, see how clean she looks now. Brand new sails too! Philippe look! Think of how black-stained, cannon-ravaged, fire-scarred, broken-sparred, and pitted she was when you brought her back to me from France last year."

Philippe frowned. "Does that suggest I have not apologized enough for that?"

Corrinne laid her head against his neck. "Oh, Philippe. You are so sympathetic. But no, my love. You have not apologized nearly enough. Maybe after another year of frequent apologies."

Captain LaTour spotted the company sloop. He scanned with his glass and saw Lady de Chanaye, Philippe Gerrard, Pierre Dunemoore and other passengers waving. He waved back.

"Step too it, bosun," he shouted. "All hands on deck! Her majesty is arriving!"

When Philippe carried Corrinne up the ladder to the *Falcon Queen*'s main deck, Captain LaTour was shocked at her bruised, swollen appearance.

"God's balls!"

"Such a heartfelt welcome." Corrinne smiled. "I've been traveling with Philippe, thank you! Now you know how I felt when I saw my ship last year."

"My lady, how did this happen to you?"

"Um, I think I will let Philippe tell you what happened. Oh, and both my feet have been burned. I cannot walk very well. But they will heal."

Captain LaTour saw the tense expression on Philippe's face and decided not to probe that topic further. "My…is that Henri? With feathers in his hair? He looks like a *coureur de bois*. Oho, Henri. Who are you carrying?"

Henri walked swiftly to the captain, beaming with delight. "This is Anamosa."

"Oh my goodness! I think I'm in love," the captain replied. "Look at the eyes on her! And Sister Michelle…your, uh, hair has gotten so long? And Pierre! I smelled you coming an hour ago!"

"Aye, Captain. The pleasure is mine. Why are ya' nah' flying your usual flag of bones from your mast?"

"The other sloop will be arriving tomorrow," Corrinne said. "Can you signal Captain Martin to come over? We need to talk immediately. And have a messenger sent to my city house. I want my arrival to remain a secret, but I plan to stay there tonight with Mathilde and my five guests."

"I will go with the messenger to begin the preparations," Mathilde said.

"Aye, Mademoiselle. Philippe, take her majesty below, so she can see the new *city house* the Gloucester shipwrights have created for her. We did not need that cargo space after all," he added with only a hint of sarcasm.

"There's room below for all of us then?"

"I think there's room for King Louie's court."

"Rum? Brandy? Wine?"

"Especially for you, Pierre. Ale too, from the Massachusetts' colony."

Captain Martin boated over from the *Ile Royale*. They collected around the opulent table that dropped over from one bulkhead. The other bulkhead held a six-foot double mattress. The seasoned seamen were aghast at such vanity, a waste of precious shipboard space, while Corrinne was delighted.

"I designed all of this!" Corrinne said, looking about proudly. "The eight chairs are cushioned and fold up to stow in the overhead too."

Captains LaTour and Martin sat at one end, Pierre and Philippe to the left, Corrinne at the head seat with Michelle on her right. A bright linen tablecloth was thrown over it. Pots of tea, mugs, a plate of hot sailor biscuits from the galley, and a clay pot of berry jam from a Quebec baker were laid on the table.

Lady de Chanaye was overjoyed to be sitting in these brand new accommodations aboard her rebuilt ship. Her smile was radiant, despite the bruises and swelling of her face.

"Thank you for indulging me. I have so looked forward to this. My captains, you are both very dear to me, but much has happened since I saw you last. This will come as an unfortunate surprise, but circumstances require that I leave New France as soon as possible. I would say permanently, but I hope to return again someday."

Captain Martin spoke first. "What? Why?"

Pierre interjected his answer before Corrinne could reply. "Let's just say it's unwise tah' ever make this lady angry."

Corrinne gave Pierre a sharp look. "There are several reasons. I've learned that Intendant Bigôt plans to seize and search the *Falcon Queen* and *Ile Royale* in the next few days, or at any time after he arrives in Quebec. No matter what he finds, he intends to declare us smugglers and will arrest the two of you, and me, and soon after that he will endeavor to hang us. I know this because he told me as much four days ago when he offered to buy the ships as an alternative, for a pittance of course. His offer was... disagreeable to me."

Upon hearing that understatement, Pierre choked on his tea. Philippe tried not to smile.

Corrinne stared at them both. "This is a serious discussion for these men."

"Apologies tah' all."

"The intendant will board and seize these ships under some pretense as soon as he can. There's more, but first, any questions?"

To Captain LaTour, there was no alternative. "Let's up anchor and sail...at first light."

Captain Martin nodded vigorously in agreement.

"I have found a better alternative that will frustrate the intendant's plans once and for all. I am going to sell my ships to the Dutch."

"Sell your ships to the Dutch!" Philippe was surprised. "You did not tell us that."

"I wanted my captains present when I did."

Captain Martin's face reddened. "We've no vote in this decision? After all these years?"

Captain LaTour looked betrayed. "My lady, I do not know what to say."

Corrine addressed her captains. "Please. Captain Martin. Captain LaTour. Please listen to everything I have to tell you first, my reasons, my rationale for doing this, your choices, and what the future portends. The buyer's name is Charles VanderMeer. Yes, the artist. He is also the son of the Duke of Brunswick, Louis Ernest, Captain-General of the Netherland armies, and counsel-advisor to the Queen Regent and William V, the future King of the Netherlands."

"The artist is a bloody royal?"

Corrinne ignored Pierre. "Charles VanderMeer carries his *lettres patentes*. He can authorize and sign for this transaction as if he were the Duke of Brunswick himself. My plan is to have this agreement signed and witnessed by Governor Duquesne, as soon as possible, after Charles VanderMeer arrives in Quebec. I expect him sometime tomorrow on our final cargo sloop. When our ships fly the flag of the Netherlands, Intendant Bigôt cannot board or seize them without committing an act of war. Charles VanderMeer will own fifty-one percent of both ships. I will owe forty-nine percent. The agreements I have in place with the two of you will remain inviolate. Your shares will remain the same, as well as those of your crew. And both of you will receive an additional ten percent of the profits for this next crossing, in respect of your captaincies and the precipitous way this has occurred. Charles VanderMeer has agreed to my management of any trading agreements in effect now, and going forward. Other than the flag, you will load and transport cargoes, but to many other ports of call."

Corrinne paused.

"You are resolved to this?" Captain Martin was not happy.

"I see no other way. The war between France and England will only worsen. The English *will* board and seize these ships while you fly the French flag. That will happen regardless of Intendant Bigôt's conceits. But the Netherlands will remain neutral during this war. There will be enormous profits to be made by a neutral country with trading ships during times of war. I estimate at least ten times the profits we realize now. You will both become rich."

"And the future?" Captain Martin asked, unconvinced.

Corrinne decided on an additional strategy. "When the war is over,

Charles VanderMeer will sell back his ships to me, for a profit, of course. And Captain Martin, I will *gift* you the *Ile Royale* as reward for your loyalty. It will be yours. Captain LaTour, I will not gift you the *Falcon Queen*, she is too dear to me. But, I intend to commission a new vessel to be built in Gloucester. You may have a hand in its design. Hopefully, it will be finished by the end of next year. You can take command under a Dutch flag, though the flag may change…we'll see at that time. But, like Captain Martin, regardless of the flag, when the war is over, she will be yours."

"And you will give me this in writing?" Captain Martin challenged.

"Is that the only issue? Do we have an agreement?"

Captain LaTour was already visualizing the lines of his new vessel. "You have agreement from me! Uh, the crews stay the same?"

"If they choose to stay. That is your decision in any case."

Captain Martin still did not like this. "I'll see it all in ink first, *s'il vous plaît*. Something we can sign."

Corrinne's tone changed slightly. "Captain Martin. You either have learned to trust my word, or you have not. I have never made any falsehoods to you. Unfortunately, you will not see this in ink first, before you make your decision. I can sell *my* ships if I choose to do so. You are an able captain for me. I do not want to lose you. But considering the speed at which I must complete this transaction, I need your answer tonight, before you go back to your ship."

"And if I say no?"

"Then I will have a new captain on the *Ile Royale* before the sun sets tomorrow."

"Now, let's not have this type of discussion," Captain LaTour protested quickly. "Captain Martin, let's each take a glass of this wonderful brandy and you and I go topside on the *Queen* to discuss all of this between ourselves."

After the captains left, Corrinne took a long swallow of cold tea. Philippe was looking admiringly at her, and Pierre was shaking his head.

"Dah' I still manage *my* company, or is there another revelation coming?"

Corrinne frowned, as if hurt.

"Now, lassie, tha's only a jibe! I love ya'."

The frown became a beaming smile. "You are too late. Someone has already said that to me." Corrinne felt almost lighthearted.

"But Henri is tah' young," Pierre teased back.

Corrinne looked at Michelle. "I am sorry for including you in this, if you found it tedious."

"No. I sat here dreaming about my bath."

Corrinne made another quick decision. "Pierre. I have given you my Quebec City home for a pittance. But I suspect you will not lodge there often, yes?"

"Probably never, if I kin' arrange tha'."

"Good. Then I suggest Michelle take primary residence over that household."

Michelle was bewildered. "What?"

"You need a place to stay in Quebec City. You can still work in the hospital, as you planned, or wherever else you choose, but you will have a full residence to call home."

Pierre pounded the table. "Splendid idea. Tha' calls for another drink."

Corrinne continued. "One other concession."

Pierre sagged and waited.

"Michelle, I would like Madeleine to stay with you. She cannot come with me in any case, and she has been fostered temporarily at the request of Archbishop Nicolet. I cannot send her back to Montréal alone. This will be a responsibility for you, so if you prefer not to do this, I'm sure Nicolet will help to make other arrangements."

Michelle thought about this for several seconds. She knew all about Madeleine and what had happened between the girl and Henri at Saint Ouen's Church. "Henri will be going with you?"

"Yes," Philippe said quickly.

"Well, that would give Henri two reasons to visit Quebec in the future, yes?" Michelle replied.

Corrinne hoped to dissuade him from seeing Madeleine at all, but she kept this to herself.

"Good. Then all we need to do now is wait for Captain Martin to tell me his decision, and we can all boat ashore to spend the night at my house... uh, or Pierre's house tomorrow, or Michelle's house the day after that."

Michelle and Pierre went up to the main deck to view the city lights, leaving Philippe and Corrinne alone in her stateroom. Philippe gazed at her with wonder.

"What?"

"How do you do this? Have so many things planned beforehand? And no matter the obstacle, you wave your hand and, *voilà,* solutions. You only now made up the idea to give your ships to the captains. And the Quebec house to Michelle."

"The house is not Michelle's. It belongs to Pierre."

"I think it belongs to the person living in it. And the ships?"

"Well, a lot could happen before the war is over, yes?"

Philippe smiled and wondered further. "Does anything about *me* seem remotely clever to you?"

Corrinne leaned in. "So now *you* are feeling neglected and forgotten. Painful, isn't it? As it happens, yes. I think it was *genius* for you to ask me to marry you. I am a wealthy woman, after all. Dozens of men have asked for my hand. I said no to all of them. I could have just as easily said no to you," she teased.

Philippe gently touched her hair, her cheek, and her lips. "I would love you anyway…even if you had said no."

Her heart melted.

"And *that* is your genius, Philippe Gerrard." Her green eyes warmed. "Your love has no conditions. And neither does mine."

They lingered over their kiss. Philippe's hand slipped inside the waist of her dress. He pushed it deeper, slowly passed her stomach, gliding, skimming, until he touched her wetness. Their mouths still joined, Corrinne moaned into his. Her hands began exploring inside Philippe's clothing.

The door opened abruptly. It was Captain LaTour. His nose was red from the brandy and the cold. He trudged into the room with a swagger.

"I have good news," Captain LaTour announced. His victorious smile vanished when he realized what he'd interrupted. "God's—! Forgive me. I should have knocked!"

Corrinne smiled. "Captain Martin?"

"He agreed! It only took me one extra cup of brandy."

As the twilight deepened, they went ashore for the night in the *Falcon Queen*'s harbor launch. Two carriages were waiting for them at the wharf. It was only a short ride to Corrinne's Quebec City house.

"Welcome! Welcome!" Mathilde greeted them. "There are hot baths waiting in all the bedrooms. And I have a full meal prepared to serve you an hour from now."

Neither Philippe nor Pierre had ever seen this house before. It was twice as large as the one in Montréal. Three bedrooms, each with its own bathing tub. A large dining room adjoining an equally large *cuisine*, attached servants' quarters, a library, a sitting room with cushioned chairs and a couch all arranged around a standing fire hearth.

"Bloooody…! Maybe I *should* stay in this house!"

CHAPTER 39
QUEBEC CITY
NOVEMBER 1754
Cap Diamant

Monsieur René Jordaine, forty-two, was a respected merchant in Quebec City. He lived in a proper two-story home in upper town. He had a wife, two small children, and was invited to most of the social soirées of the city; sometimes even to government celebrations usually reserved for those with royal connections. He owned a small upper-town restaurant, a bakery, and two taverns, one in upper town, the other by the waterfront. The tavern by the waterfront made him more money than the other three establishments combined and several times over.

In lower-town Quebec, Monsieur Jordaine was known by another name: *Rouge Piège*, Red Snare. And Rouge Piège was known for his ability to accomplish a variety of tasks for customers—as long as they had enough money. The city needed a man of his ingenuity to get questionable things done. He was discreet in his lower-town activities, and did not call attention to himself or embarrass the corrupt officials of government and ranking officers in the gendarmerie that supported him for protection. Murder, smuggling, sex, abduction, communications with his fraternal interests in the English colonies, there was little he would not do if the price was right. Rouge Piège was tolerated.

He had slept with Lady Corrinne de Chanaye frequently when she first arrived in New France. Quickly becoming infatuated with her, he had helped her validate credentials to distant, royal relations and establish her social position within Quebec. She had politely refused his proposal of marriage but remained one of his most trusted business allies. She was a partner in smuggling arms to and from various sellers and buyers over the years. Together, they had made a small fortune circumventing the government tariffs to sell valuable goods, both legal and illegal.

Rouge Piège's notoriety was well-known to associates in Paris.

Consequently, he had been named as the main contact in Quebec City for Gaspard de Propei when he first arrived. He had helped the future Marquis arrange accounts with a sympathetic local banker, subsequent accounts in Montréal, introductions to corrupt officials in government, including Intendant Bigôt. All for a large fee, of course. A lucrative, private, discreet arrangement. But he'd been relieved when this detestable human being went upriver earlier in the year.

When Singing Owl and his two men wheeled the wounded and bloodied Helmut Colbért in a pushcart, naked and wrapped in blankets, to the back of the waterfront tavern, Rouge Piège was not pleased with the prospect of dealing, again, with the unsavory *faux* heir to the Propei marquisate. But Monsieur de Propei offered to reimburse Rouge Piège at a rate of two-to-one for every piece of silver or gold he spent until he gained access to his remaining funds in Quebec. So he cooperated—for now. He had even arranged for a surgeon from one of the French frigates anchored in port to come ashore to the tavern and attend to the man's injuries. The officer was slightly drunk from the free brandy he was given as part of the fee for his services. He'd imbibed too early.

Rouge Piège was irritated. "No more brandy. And you can fuck as many of the whores as you like when you *finish* applying your healing skills to this man. If he dies, you get none of the money."

"That was not our agreement!"

"Since you drank too much, it is now. And since you protested, I will amend it further. I will allow you to *live* if he does not die under your knife."

The surgeon pulled aside the foul, rancid blankets and scowled at the swollen, pus-ridden wounds.

"I need boiled water, clean towels, sponges, and rum distillates. And I want some of your whores to scrub this man's body thoroughly from his head to his toes before I begin, including his lice-infested hair."

Three hours later, Gaspard de Propei was lying in a bed, the arrow heads removed, his shoulder and leg wounds cleaned, stitched, and bandaged.

Rouge Piège had stood to the side of the room the whole time, a per-fumed kerchief held to his nose, and watched the surgeon carefully. Drunk or not, the veteran doctor knew his trade well. When he finished, Rouge Piège counted out ten Louis d'ors into the surgeon's palm.

"The whores are yours until you tire."

The surgeon scoffed at the offer. "Those poor women are riddled with the pox." He glanced at the *shérif* now resting peacefully. "That man is lucky. He should be dead from lesion putrefaction after four days without treatment. The arrow penetrations were contained in the muscle and I saw no flesh rot at all. And I must say…I never had a man under the cut of my lancets who didn't scream at some point. Only an occasional hiss from this one. Almost like a snake, eh?"

You have no idea, Rouge Piège did not say aloud.

Mathilde introduced the six servants who were helping her. Four were natives who spoke French fluently, one of them was a cook, James, the chamberlain, and a carriage driver named Renard, who also acted as a footman when necessary.

Corrinne encouraged everyone to clean up before they gathered around the table to eat. She took the master boudoir, of course. Michelle took a second bedroom after coaxing Anamosa to come with her, and Philippe, Henri, and Pierre moved into the smallest bedroom.

"Ya' go first, Philippe. Henri and I can keep each other company in this library. Maybe I will learn something…or Henri kin' point out books tha' he's read."

In the bedrooms, they found stacks of clean clothing placed out in baskets for them. They sorted various pieces to find things that fit. There was nothing elaborate, mostly working clothes for the men, proper dresses for Michelle and Anamosa, but they were clean and would permit their other clothes to be washed.

In the relative privacy of the small bedroom, Philippe Gerrard stripped off all his clothes. Recalling Fort Machault, he closed his eyes before he stepped warily in front of an ornate, full-length dressing mirror. He'd expected to see scars and bruises, the loss of weight, the crooked appearance of his left leg. But the gaunt reflection of the man squinting back at him was some desperate stranger he'd never met before.

"My God," he whispered.

His face was lined and sunburned. He touched the chapped skin, the white creases in the corners of his eyes. With one finger, he traced the long angry scar running from his temple down the left side of his cheek into the scruffy beard on his chin. He covered the scar with one hand and turned his head sideways to see a glimpse of an earlier profile. He saw nothing very familiar. He pushed a hand through his matted, snarled hair and smoothed the whiskers on his face. Tilting his head, he spread the hair on his scalp to examine another scar. It was healed, but still looked tender and pink. He bent over to touch his right knee and let his callused fingers explore the coarse skin that healed over the knife cut on his thigh. He moved on to touch the dozens of cuts and burn scars on his chest and torso, Sauquita's legacy of torture. He stepped back to take in a fuller view. The outward bow in the shin of his left leg looked pronounced.

Philippe was almost ashamed. In disgust, he threw a robe over the mirror and stepped carefully into the oversized bathtub Mathilde had filled for him, allowing his head to slip beneath the steamy water. The soaking of his sore muscles was soothing beyond pleasure. He straightened his legs to push his head back above the surface.

"Ahh!"

The water felt silky from the salts Mathilde had added. On a side table, there was a soft bristle brush and brownish soap. He washed his hair first. Using the brush, he gently scrubbed away the layers of grime from his legs, arms, and torso. The water quickly turned reddish-brown and started to stink. Philippe got out and wrapped himself in a long white towel. At the foot of the tub was a two-foot-square shale door in the floor, which covered an ingenious sluice that ran outside to the gutters, then further down to the street. The tub had a broad lip on one end, much like a gravy tureen. He lifted the opposite end, emptied the tub completely into the sluice, pulled on the bell sash, and sat down on a wooden stool to wait for the servant women. It took three trips by each of them to refill the tub with hot fresh water. But they had numerous kettles bubbling downstairs.

He started with his hair again and scrubbed everything thoroughly one more time. He emptied the tub, pulled the bell sash, and picked through the basket of clothes and selected things to wear.

Pierre came in while the servant women were refilling the tub again.

"I dinnah' know your skin was white. And your hair is not brown after all," the Scotsman said, amazed at Philippe's clean appearance. "Henri is in the other bedroom. This house is a palace, eh?"

The food at dinner was delicious. But the hot baths had relaxed them, so much so, that, after talking about what might happen over the next few days, the conversation became subdued. Michelle impulsively said a prayer of thanks for their survival from all the ordeals they had suffered. Viewed in full, what they had all lived through was extraordinary; however, all of them had been scarred physically and mentally.

Corrinne tried to lighten the mood by holding out her hands until they joined with the others in a circle around the table.

"We are all still here. And we are all together."

Henri's eyes dropped. So did Philippe's. *Not everyone*, Henri thought.

Pierre was the first to yawn. "So, in tha' morning, or whenever the archbishop arrives, we will seek an audience with tha' Governor?"

Corrinne could see everyone's weariness. "Yes, but we can think about all that in the morning. I think sleeping would be the best remedy for us now."

"Amen to tha'."

"If it's all right, Anamosa and I will sleep on the floor in the library. She will be frightened if I'm not with her."

"Of course," Corrinne replied and nodded at Mathilde to arrange some bedding.

Thick wet fog moved fingerlike through the Quebec citadel and streets as the night grew darker, chilling the air, smelling of ice. The stars were hidden by the snow crystal-laden clouds coming down from the north.

Corrinne de Chanaye hobbled painfully to the window and pulled the curtains over the shutters. The cold air on her bare skin created goose bumps and made her shiver vigorously. Her teeth were chattering as she slipped again beneath the thick heavy quilt to press her nakedness hungrily against Philippe, nuzzling close enough to place her head on his shoulder. Philippe shifted drowsily. His arm moved. She reached back and took hold of it, pulling it around her neck, spreading his fingers so they lay fully on her breast. She'd not slept very deeply during the night, merely dozed, blissfully afloat on the strong beat of his heart and the deep, even breathing of his sleep. Tomorrow promised unforeseen trouble, though she knew not what it would be. But Corrinne could not recall a moment in her life when she'd felt such a sense of well-being. She wished the night would never end.

Alas, it will.

The reverie at dinner was short-lived. They were all thoroughly exhausted. The morning would bring more trials. After Corrinne had urged everyone to bed, Mathilde and the chamberlain helped steer the sleeping arrangements. And this time, Philippe didn't hesitate to undress and slide beneath the coverlets and blankets of Corrinne's bed. She guessed he'd not slept on a soft mattress in a long time. So great was his fatigue, he had fallen asleep before Mathilde assisted Corrinne into bed beside him. But Corrinne was content to lie next to him, to feel his warmth and his strength.

As the outdoor temperature dropped further, the house creaked as houses sometimes do. The noise disturbed Philippe's sleep. He rolled his body toward her, his chin now resting on the pillow above her head. As they faced one another fully, the air between their bodies grew warm. Corrinne's eyes shifted to the fire. It had almost burned out. That meant it was early morning, maybe a few hours before sunrise. Outside the window, she did not perceive an approaching dawn, but she knew, in another hour the household might begin to stir. Mathilde would be up, the servants would follow quickly.

Tomorrow? she pondered. *Anything* could happen on the morrow. *Deadly* things. Would they have another night together? She presumed so, but she was not going to let this night pass unfulfilled.

Corrinne moved a hand below Philippe's stomach and slipped her fingers around the long giving firmness she found there. His body jerked as the cooler skin of her hand enveloped his heat. He inhaled and started to awaken. Sensing his reaction, Corrinne's other hand joined the first, touching, cupping, massaging, the nails tickling.

"Corrinne," he whispered.

She lifted her face. They kissed, their tongues entwined, wet, and exploring.

Corrinne's hands continued to move, making longer strokes, pulling the hardness higher. In response, Philippe slid his left hand between her legs finding her wetness, which separated easily at his touch. His fingers caressed her, rolling the tiny spot of pleasure in small circles.

For the first time in her life, Corrinne allowed her passions, not her aims, to drive the lovemaking. She wanted to yield to Philippe utterly, no barriers, no illusions. She guided his hands purposely, encouraging him to do things she knew would bring her desire to the point of begging.

"I want you," she whispered. There was urgency in her voice. She slipped the covers down and began kissing him everywhere.

Philippe reveled under the flurry of her kisses and caresses. He gently pressed her panting body back against the pillows, moved his mouth lower, sucked on her nipples, inhaled her intoxicating perfume, kissed lower still, licked her navel, then lower down her abdomen. When he surrounded her core with his mouth, Corrinne's body arched. Avoiding the lump on his head, she pressed gently, urging more of his touch *there*.

Philippe's lips and tongue moved over her sex. He smelled and tasted her saltiness, an incredible, wonderful delight. He licked slowly up, then down.

"Yes," she moaned. "Oh, yes!"

Corrinne suddenly felt buoyant on a sea of tiny pleasure spirals, lifting and foaming, a swell before breaking as a wave. It was a warm, stretching, flowing sensation. It would be sooo easy to allow his lips to propel her to the end, but she wanted much more before that happened. Reluctantly, she reached down and lifted his face before she lost the ability to choose.

"Corrinne?"

"*Shhhh.*"

Corrinne pulled him back up next to her, then pushed gently on his chest to make him lie back.

"Shhhh."

She flicked her tongue playfully across his lips and sat up. She moved down his body, took hold of him with her hands, and swallowed his hardness. Her white-blond hair spread fan-like across his thighs.

"*Dieu,*" he moaned.

Philippe's hips lifted as the pulses of pleasure were exquisitely pulled, and pulled and pulled.

Corrinne listened to the sounds of his groaning, his breathing. When his legs began to tremble, she stopped.

When her mouth came away, he felt exposed, wet and cold. *No.*

Ignoring the pain in her feet, Corrinne moved to place her legs on either side of his waist, but Philippe rolled on top of her instead.

Corrinne felt a brief twinge of panic as Philippe's body completely overpowered her. She felt his muscled, sinewy legs between hers. His hands cupped her breasts. He kissed her nipples, chest, moved up her neck, and kissed her ears. Corrinne shivered as his hot breath washed over her puckered skin. He inserted his tongue between her lips. She sucked on it. And relaxed under his gentleness. Since she'd left France, Philippe was the first man she allowed to take her, willingly, this way.

"Oh, yes. *Yes*." She rolled her hips and joined with him in one enveloping movement, a silky, sliding movement of heat, filling her, expanding her.

They both gasped.

The tightness was incredible. A different tingling surged through Corrinne's stomach, chest, spreading across her shoulders, up her neck, into her face. She felt flush. Her chin lifted. It was going to happen too fast. She tried to slow it, but Philippe wasn't helping.

"Ohhhh, God!"

Corrinne's knees elevated in response. She reached around and between his legs to cup him gently with her fingers. Then she began to roll and grind against him, slow at first, centering, the need for release growing more urgent. Philippe was moving his lips and tongue over her lips, face, and neck.

She tried to hold herself back, to prolong the gratification, but the choice was no longer hers. Her ankles and arms locked behind his back. The edge of the waterfall was coming. She held on tight.

Philippe pushed with deep strokes, moving slowly, over and over. Their tongues met, mixing wetness with noises and groans, seized by sensations, wonderful, trembling, a sinking feeling, and then acceleration. The first shudder was a strong ripple. With the next, Corrinne's body shattered with a spasm of pleasure, then another, and another, each stronger than the one before. It swept aside all other thought.

"*I love you*!" Then only nonsensical words and sounds spilled from her lips, followed by a long stuttering series of sighs and gasps.

His release began as a small leak of pleasure at the onset, a relentless trickle from an overflowing dam, growing in strength, the prelude to the inevitable bursting. The pleasure pulsed out in a hot stream, melting his body into hers.

"Corrinne," he groaned in desperation and relief. His arms tightened their embrace. The muscles in Philippe's legs relaxed involuntarily.

She knew instantly what he felt, what he wanted. She wanted it too.

"I am here. I am here."

She sobbed softly as the tension eased and it was his turn to comfort her.

They had found one another amidst a world collapsing around them. And for a few moments, they experienced the glorious sense of oneness.

Like in the artist's loft in Montréal, only far, far more pleasurable, far, far more intense. Now, things would be all right. Whatever happened, they would face the future together. In the afterglow of bursting pleasure, *this* sublime feeling was almost better. Their bodies moved and clung to each other in the cold and dark of night. *This* was what they could rely upon. And it was everything.

Philippe eased half his body to one side. Corrinne slipped a leg over him, so he could feel her wetness and remain in his thoughts…just in case.

"*Well*," she said. "That was *very* nice …"

Philippe smiled in the darkness. "I was joined to you…it was different. Better."

"I felt it too." The lovemaking had been so right. So humbling. *So overdue*, she wanted to shout at him. *You magnificent fool, see what we've been missing?*

Corrinne rubbed her sex against him, nestled closer, and laid her hand upon his shrinking member. She nuzzled her head on his chest to hear the comforting sound of his heartbeat and the rise and fall of his breathing.

Philippe took a finger and pushed tendrils of silver blond hair away from her cheek. His hand moved down to hold her breast. He could barely see the outline of her face, the room was so shadowed.

"I love you."

Corrinne's smile of happiness was hidden by the darkness.

"I love you too," she whispered back. "Remember, I said it first."

Knocking. And then a whispered, "Mistress?"

Corrinne opened her eyes. Incredibly, she'd fallen asleep, again. She was wasting precious time. She sat up and stretched. Outside the window, the skies were dull gray. The wind was whistling.

The knock returned.

"Come in."

As soon as Mathilde entered, Corrinne pointed at Philippe with a finger to her lips.

"We are preparing food," the maid whispered. "Henri and Anamosa are sitting in the *cuisine*. The servants are pandering to them both. That beautiful little girl adores him."

"You noticed?"

"Do you need help dressing?"

"Stop whispering," Philippe said. He pushed himself up onto an elbow. "I'm awake. I will dress and leave so you can have the room."

"I will return in a few moments." Mathilde left.

Corrinne flung her arms around his neck. "I love you."

He pushed her on her back and kissed her. "I love you too." Without another word, his head moved between her legs and against her weakening protests, he pleasured her to an arching orgasm so strong, she covered her face with a pillow to muffle the sounds.

Philippe got up quickly, moved to a chair, and pulled on his pants and loose shirt.

"That's not proper," she said, reaching out with her arms. "Come closer to me. You know it's hard for me to walk."

"I was that good?" he mocked.

Socks were next, then his boots. Then he knelt next to the bed and kissed her deeply.

"There. Don't you taste wonderful? I think so."

She pretended shock.

"Well, Monsieur Gerrard, in all fairness, you must permit me to welcome your morning too."

When Philippe finally left the room, he saw Mathilde waiting patiently in the hallway. He hugged her until she groaned with laughter.

"It's a new day, Mathilde! Hopefully a good one."

He went downstairs to the room where Pierre was snoring. "Pierre! Get up!"

The Scotsman sprung from his bed, naked, with a knife in his hand. He squinted and blinked, seeing Philippe, he relaxed.

"Tha's nah' fucking funny!"

"Join me in the dining room."

The breakfast table was set with sizzling foods, butter and hot baked breads, cheeses, confectioneries, fresh cream, tea, ewers of water, bottles of wine. Anamosa had a circle of white frosting around her lips. She smiled. Philippe knelt and rubbed noses with her. She kissed his cheek. He took a seat. Henri came from the *cuisine*, followed by Michelle carrying plates.

Next came Pierre, his loud and welcoming voice booming about the room as he took a seat. He filled his plate with mounds of everything.

Noticing Corrinne absent, Philippe went back upstairs to see if she needed to be carried. He walked into the room to find her in the tub. He stared in wonder at her beauty. Mathilde was soaping her with a sponge. The maid nodded at him but did not stop. Seeing Corrinne like this made him want to put his hands on her again. Outside in the city, the gendarmes could be waiting for him on every corner, yet all he could think about was the way she looked.

Get your head on right, he warned himself.

Corrinne looked up at him, a suggestive smile playing at her lips. Feigning modesty, she covered herself with her hands.

"Monsieur Gerrard, I am not presentable!"

"Yes, it is what I like about you the most. I came to see if I could carry you downstairs," he said. With great effort, he looked for somewhere else to fix his gaze.

He went over to the window and threw back the shutters. The view she had of the anchorage before the citadel was exceptional, unobstructed by buildings or trees in either direction. He looked around near the window and found the watch glass he knew would be there somewhere. He raised it and peered upriver. He immediately counted at least ten river sloops appearing around the final turn. And while he looked, another appeared.

"It's only a few hours after sunrise, and they are arriving already," he observed, surprised.

"Who is arriving?"

"All of Montréal, I think."

"We are finished, Mathilde." Corrinne stepped out of the tub and sat on a chair. Mathilde dried her hair. Corrinne slipped on a towel robe. "Philippe, carry me to the window so I can see too."

He picked her up. She nuzzled his neck. Mathilde followed them with a chair, so he could sit and hold her.

Corrinne took the glass and quickly scanned the river.

Philippe pushed his nose into the damp hair behind her ear. She smelled of soap and water.

"They are not all cargo sloops," she said.

Philippe slipped his hand into the wet mound beneath her waist.

"You are distracting me!"

"I thought that was why you liked me?"

"Here. Pay attention. Look through the glass." She held it to his eye.

Philippe's hand kept moving between her legs.

Corrinne instructed him on what she'd determined. "See the two vessels in the middle? The first one belongs to the Jesuits. That has to be the archbishop's." Corrinne's hips began to move under the influence of Philippe's persuasive fingers. "B-but the other one is military. It's flying the *fleur-de-lis*."

"Maybe his escort?"

Corrinne frowned. She didn't think so. "Mathilde. Privacy please."

When the maid left the room, she shifted her legs to straddle and face him on the chair. She saw something white on the cheek near his lips.

"What is this?"

"Taste it. Anamosa was eating something covered with frosting. She kissed me."

Corrinne tapped him lightly on the chest. "So, you are untrue to me already?"

He pushed her robe open, bent his head, and took a nipple into his mouth. She sucked in her breath.

"They will all start docking within the hour," she said in a groan. "That is all the time we have before this day becomes controlled by others."

She lifted his face and fixed her warm green eyes on his. She untied the waist of his pants. "Since I cannot push with my feet, you will have to move me with your hands."

Philippe lifted his hips and she pulled the pants below the edge of the seat.

"Now this," she said as her hands began moving, stroking.

Philippe closed his eyes, pleasure overtaking him. "I am going to love loving you," he said softly.

"*Yeees*," her voice a breathy whisper as she slipped his hardness inside of her. "Oh, yes. You have been a great fool up until now...haven't you?"

He began slowly moving her hips with his hands. "Yes...I have."

Corrinne rested her head on his shoulder. Philippe did everything while she relaxed and allowed wave after wave of pleasure to wash over her.

Almost an hour later, Philippe carried a fully dressed Corrinne downstairs into the dining area. There was still hot food left. He set her in a chair. Henri was gobbling down buttered bread. Michelle was sipping tea.

Pierre was holding Anamosa in his lap, feeding her berry jam with a small silver spoon.

"Aha, *bonjour*. Been busy, lassie?"

Corrinne regally ignored his question.

"At least eleven river sloops entered the anchorage in the last hour. The archbishop is here. I saw him disembark. The Governor will send someone to request his prompt attendance. Nicolet will freshen up first. I need to go to the Jesuit compound and see him *before* he sees the Governor."

Michelle spoke up. "I am going to the Hotel Dieu here to find the physician."

"I can have Renard escort you there and back."

"His escort there will be enough."

"Pierre should take me to see the archbishop. Philippe, I do not know what's going to happen today. You have to stay inside, I think. You could be arrested if someone recognizes you."

"Like who?"

"For one, the troop of Montréal gendarmes that just disembarked from the sloop at the wharf. They carried someone in a stretcher."

Individually, they each speculated on who that might be. But Corrinne knew.

"Someone important in government, I would guess. So wha' are ya' going tah' dah' if someone recognizes the Lady Corrinne de Chanaye?"

"That's why we must act in haste."

They had all finished dining, with the exception of Corrinne and Philippe, and quickly made ready for the day. Presently, Philippe and Corrinne, Pierre, and Michelle gathered on the outside steps of the city house.

His face clouded with concern, Philippe kissed Corrinne.

"I'll take good care of her, laddie."

Pierre carried Corrinne to her two-wheeled *calèche*. She was carrying a heavy naval topcoat in her lap.

"Wha's tha'?"

"A present for the archbishop."

"Just give me tha' right directions." Pierre took up the reins and snapped the long crop.

Philippe and Michelle watched them drive away. He shrugged off his winter coat and placed it around Michelle's shoulders. "Here we are again."

Michelle smiled at him sadly, stood on her toes, held his face with her hands, and kissed him tenderly.

"I love you, Philippe. But this is God's plan, not yours. Though my path was difficult and dangerous, I am pleased that you brought me from Rouen. My heart is at peace. I will be happy here. I will do good things at this hospital. You will do good things for Henri, yes? And you will keep your promise to Okeanneh and care for Anamosa, yes?"

A tear ran down Philippe's cheek.

Michelle smoothed the tear away with her thumb. "Corrinne will kiss away all of your tears and your pain, and you will fill her desperate need for love for the rest of your lives. As it was planned for you to do from the day you met her in that waterfront tavern in Le Havre…of all places. She knew then. Didn't you?"

"I asked her to marry me."

"I know. She told me."

"She did?"

"We told each other *everything* on the river coming here. And French women prefer being married to the men they are sleeping with. Now, wish me good fortune as I start my next new life."

"Good fortune, Michelle."

She turned and waved back to him as she walked down the street on her way to the hospital with Corrinne's footman.

After Michelle disappeared around a corner, Philippe walked back upstairs to the viewing window in Corrinne's boudoir and took up the long glass.

He saw another sloop tied alongside the *Falcon Queen*. It was already being unloaded. He could just make out the figures of Charles VanderMeer and a young girl. *Madeleine*? He wondered where Juniata and Chesanin were.

Three days of huddling under the semi-putrid animal skins in the canoe on the river, followed by only a day and night of rest, did not provide

Colbért's wounds much benefit. He knew it would take at least a month for the deep gashes to heal. And, at best, he had only a couple days to act. But his luck seemed at its peak. His escape from the Indians was such a surprise, it could only have been predestined, he decided.

Singing Owl and his two men ambushed the Oneida as they were crossing the river. Colbért had been tightly bound and lying in the bottom of the bateau. The Hurons attacked quietly in the moonlight with their bows. They were fast, silent, deadly. One Oneida dove into the river and escaped in the darkness. They allowed the one called Peter Blue Jacket to swim to the other side.

"Peter Blue Jacket is my friend," Singing Owl had told Colbért.

They'd moved the assassin to the faster canoe and immediately started downriver.

"It was our agreement. You paid me already," Singing Owl explained when asked why they orchestrated this rescue. "And the Oneida are my enemies. Death awaits them on this side of the river. They know this again."

In another twist of fate, the voice in Colbért's dreams had been reduced to almost a whisper, and the messages had become distorted to a strange language of grunts, clicks, and snapping sounds. But that was all right, it allowed him to sleep more soundly.

That first morning in Quebec, after Colbért's wounds were attended to and bandaged, he awoke to find his arms and legs stiff. The steady pain in his shoulder and thighs was bad and made worse by the cold, drafty interior of the shack. But with a night of rest, the pain became his friend. It sharpened his thinking. He was now wide-awake. He spent the early morning twilight sitting in a chair by the door, waving at the passersby until he found a man willing to locate Rouge Piège for a promise of silver, of course, which his ally of convenience paid.

"Bring my banker to me and something to wear."

Amazingly, Singing Owl claimed Snow Hair, the boy, and the *Falcon Queen* were all traveling to Quebec, less than a day behind them. Colbért needed to complete his kills, have them validated by the gendarmerie, and arrange his escape. If they were coming to him, that made all of it possible.

There were trading frigates anchored in the river; he could easily purchase transport back to France on one of them. Before Rouge Piège returned with the banker, Colbért overheard the wharf laborers talking about the arrival of a large fleet of river sloops from Montréal. An hour later, in addition to the cargo they divulged, they would bring him news.

When Piège returned with the banker, Piège had him wait outside and brought Colbért a sack of clothing, the kind worn by day laborers and some others more refined. He would need both, but Colbért dressed as a laborer first. The shoes were too large, but he pulled on the socks.

Piège brought in the banker with three guards and three sacks of coin, two of gold, one of silver. The devious Québécois banker was aghast at seeing the physical state and living conditions of Gaspard de Propei, the heir to a marquisate, no less.

Gaspard de Propei explained his captivity by Indians, leaving out what had prompted the kidnapping. "I am staying here until I can make myself more presentable, as I obviously need to do." He offered to dine with the banker in another few days, perhaps with Intendant Bigôt himself. Lies wrapped in a flimsy story, but enough to last for a day. And the *shérif* was now enhanced by a *lot* of money; too much, unprotected money.

The banker thought so too. *It should be in a bank!*

Rouge Piège had noted the money. Colbért could see it in the man's eyes. But now the banker knew Gaspard de Propei was here, and word of his presence would eventually reach the ears of Intendant Bigôt. And *this* money, Bigôt considered to be his, a part of his commissions. He made sure to mention that to Piège.

"Find out the location of Lady de Chanaye and Philippe Gerrard. They are here in the city somewhere. Does she have a house? And have someone bring me food and drink."

Helmut Colbért shifted on his bed as Rouge Piège left the shack. He pulled the two blankets back over his shoulders. He expected Piège to return with some report that he could not find them. It would be a lie, of course. He rose from the bed with some silver coin and offered a wharf laborer money to bring him a length of rope, long leather strapping, and some light fishing wire. He broke apart one of the two chairs in the room to use its wood for a new purpose.

The room was square shaped. He paced it off; seven paces wide and long. He used the throwing knife to make scratch marks on the wall planks to his right, one for each pace, six in total, the single entry door occupied the last one. He had strength in his legs for one heavy lunge without resting. He took slats from beneath the bed mattress, put them on the floor, one end against the wall, giving him something to push off with his toes. Then he took a deep breath and threw himself forward as hard as he could. The spike of pain in his thighs was intense. He lay on the floor groaning, pounding with his fists until the pain subsided enough to allow him to sit up. The mark was four paces. Five would be better, but four was the mark.

He created a strong three-foot cutting noose with the wire, twisted the wire securely around the leather strapping, joined the strapping with the rope. He strung the makeshift garrote along the crossbeams supporting the roof and allowed the wire noose to hang at the five-pace mark. In the deep shadowed interior of the shack, the thin wire noose would be invisible, especially at night, unless a person was looking for it. He knew the woodsman would come for him with his long skinning knife; he preferred knives in a personal fight too. He aligned the open hang of the noose directly in the line of sight from the door to the place on the bed where he would sit. He wrapped the other end of the rope around the leg of the chair.

"The woodsman will slam open the door and rush me with his knife. In less than two steps, his head will be inside the wire noose. Pull it tight. He drops the knife. Pull him off the floor."

But he needed something to secure the rope.

He used his throwing knife to lift up a floorboard. He notched one of the cross logs on its bottom, enough to hold the chair leg and support the weight of the woodsman. "Pull to tighten, pull down enough to stand on the thick newel, push it into the floor notch with my feet and weight. The woodsman goes up, strangling…and then dies. Simple enough. Too bad I don't have more time to make it memorable for him."

Then just let him hang. And once word spread of the woodsman's death, the *boy* would come to find him.

"He likes to use a bow. I will need to be somewhere nearby, somewhere hidden but close enough to sight the door to this shack with a musket. Maybe two muskets, one for a second shot. Or maybe hire a second?"

Well, one step at a time.

Philippe found Henri and Anamosa in the library. Henri was sitting on the floor, his back to a couch, reading a book to her. Her head was resting on his shoulder. She was patting his chest softly with her fingers as she listened to his voice. They brightened at seeing him.

"It appears we have each other's companionship this morning."

Philippe browsed through the shelves of books, stopping when one with a worn leather cover and gilded pages caught his eye. *The Justice of King Harald.* He leafed through it. It was filled with sketches of how King Harald, in ancient times, would mete out punishment for crimes. Presented was a list of individual offenses or crimes, one per page, in alphabetical arrangement. The text noted it was not just the punishment, but the public display of the punishment after judgment that established the proper message. *If you do this type of wrong, here is what you can expect.* He took a seat in a cushioned chair and carefully translated the mix of Latin and old English as he read.

There was even a detailed punishment and death for an assassin. He found that page *very* interesting.

I guess it was important to write about this, he thought. *But who was it for? Most people back then could not read. Probably his enemies.*

The chamberlain appeared in the room.

"Monsieur Gerrard, there is a gentleman at the door who asked for you specifically."

"Asked for *me*? Do you know him?"

"Yes, Monsieur. His name is René Jordaine. He is a merchant here in Quebec. A respectable man, by reputation."

"A merchant?"

The chamberlain nodded.

Philippe wondered how this man knew to find him here. "Is he alone?"

"*Oui.*"

"Show him to the sitting room."

When the chamberlain left, Philippe gestured for Henri to follow him. They went into the bedroom Pierre used. Philippe strapped on his knives; Henri his knives and his bow.

"Listen to me. You are responsible for Anamosa, yes? Good." Philippe gave him a handful of coins. "Here's some silver to carry in your pocket. If something happens today and you find yourself alone with her and no one else, go to the waterfront and hire a boat launch to take you out to the *Falcon Queen.* That's where we may all be before this day is over anyway.

So you might as well get there first. Now, I am going to meet with this man. I don't know who he is or what he wants. You stay in the library like you've been doing. I don't want him to see you."

Philippe hugged Henri. "I am sorry this is starting again."

"Mother told me to tell you to stop saying you are sorry."

Philippe laughed. "I meant to say, please be safe."

"My totems are with me." Henri grasped the talisman that hung about his neck.

"Of course they are." He touched his hand to the silver amulet and bowed his head.

Philippe had not been in Quebec City in almost ten years. The name, René Jordaine, sounded vaguely familiar, but he could not recall why. He entered the sitting room quietly. The man was standing before the fire warming his hands, his back to him.

"Monsieur?" When he turned, Philippe recognized the man's face instantly and rested his hand on his skinning knife. "Rouge Piège."

"Please, Monsieur Gerrard. In upper town I prefer not to use my *nom de guerre*."

"What do you want? And how did you know I was here?"

"May we sit? This is private business. Completely confidential. I did not know you were here, but someone I know was *certain* you were, along with Lady de Chanaye. So, I thought I would check her house to see if this was true."

"All right. It's true. What do you want?"

"What we all want." He gestured expansively. "Justice, freedom, money. And oddly enough, I think you and I both want the same things. You are a fur trader, and I am a man of *business*. I have a business proposition for you that I know you will like."

"I'm listening."

He looked over Philippe's shoulder. "*Bonjour*, Mathilde. *Comment allez-vous*? It has been a long time, eh?"

"*Bonjour*," she answered tersely. "Monsieur Gerrard, may I bring you something?"

Philippe motioned toward Rouge Piège.

"*Merci*. Mathilde, do you happen to have some of that delicious coffee that has become so popular?"

They talked for almost two hours. Rouge Piège shook Philippe's hand at the door before he left. "Until then, Monsieur Gerrard."

Philippe checked on Henri and Anamosa in the library still reading books.

Henri looked up expectantly.

"Everything is fine."

Philippe retrieved *The Justice of King Harald* from the bookshelf and went over to Corrinne's writing desk. He searched the drawers and took out a large piece of rolled parchment. It was clean. There was a nearby blotter and a scratch parchment to test quill points. He experimented with the different tips until he found one he liked. He opened the book to the page titled *Assassins*, unrolled the parchment, weighted the corners, and began to make a careful transcription of the text in Latin, only modifying the last line. That, he wrote in French. When finished, he dusted the ink liberally, blew on it, and gently blotted it to be certain it was completely dry. Then he rolled it up and secured it with a ribbon.

It was midafternoon when people began returning to the city house. Corrinne and Pierre were first.

"Thank God," Philippe whispered when he opened the door to see Pierre holding her in his arms, a strained look on his face. "What can I do?"

"Take her. I've been carrying her up and down steps all day."

"With pleasure."

Corrinne wrapped her arms around his neck.

"To your room?"

"Please," she whispered, her voice held a tremble. As they reached the stairs, Mathilde met them halfway. "A bath, Mathilde."

"The water is already hot, Mistress. Leave her on the bed, Monsieur."

Philippe laid her gently on the quilts, feeling the tenseness in her.

"What's wrong?"

Corrinne looked at him. Her eyes were red. She touched his face and smiled wearily. "It's too much to tell all at once. But, we, that is, Pierre, me, Henri, Michelle, and Charles VanderMeer…we are to meet with Governor Duquesne and Archbishop Nicolet at the Governor's tower inside the citadel at sunrise, or just before, if the fog is not too thick and we can find our way.

Once there, we will sign everything…Henri's abdication…the sale of my ships to the Dutch. There is much, much more to tell you, but I don't have the strength right now. Let me bathe and refresh myself."

Philippe ran his strong hands over her legs, gently rolling the muscles of her calves and thighs, pressing his hands and fingers against her sides, moving them up and over the front of her dress, his fingertips pressing and circling. Finally he massaged her neck, shoulders, circling her temples, making long pressing strokes to her scalp.

Corrinne had closed her eyes, moaning with relief during the massage, but said nothing until he was done.

"That felt good," she whispered.

"I was worried." He looked at her searchingly. "I missed you."

"Good. Now all you need to do is say that a thousand more times and you will begin to understand how I felt when you would go off on one of your adventures."

Philippe found Pierre having brandy in the sitting room and staring moodily at the fire. He poured himself a glass and sat across from him.

"Well?"

"Well, wha'? Oh, ya' mean wha' happened when we first sat down with one angry archbishop o' tha' Church? Or wha' happened when Major Péan found Intendant Bigôt with his testicles trussed tah' tha' ceiling, and by then they were deep blue in color, and aboot the size o' one-pound cannon shot, according tah' tha' soldiers the major brought with him. When tha' major first found tha' dead secretary with one o' Gaspard de Propei's stilettos buried in his chest. Oh, and she forgot tah' tell us tha' she castrated tha' Corsican before she killed him. Tha' was quite a poetic weapon, eh? Where did she get tha', I wonder? She would nah' tell me—anyway, our major sent for a priest and a doctor…and they brought back, nah' just any priest, but his Imperial Eminence, and nah' just any doctor, but Governor Duquesne's personal physician, Doctor La Galissonière. And only then did tha' major push the hidden lever tha' opened the bookcase door, a clever mechanism tha' was, tah' reveal tha' Intendant of New France, tha' second most powerful man after tha' Governor—oh, I've said tha' before—with his bulging eyes, bright blue balls, a rather nasty bed full o' shit and piss, gagged, mind you, oh, and he evidently had tah' puke through his nose

a few times, he could o' choked tah' death. I reminded Corrinne o' tha'
during the ride back here, told her tah' remember tha' for when she takes
her revenge on another official o' government. But, Bigôt lived, so no harm
done in tha' regard, eh?

"Give me some more brandy, will ya' please. Anyway, tha' soldiers,
when ordered by our very own major, refused tah' touch any part o' tha'
rather disgusting intendant, instead they all looked tah' tha' Church for
assistance, and our Imperial Eminence stepped forward and ungagged,
untrussed, and unshackled tha' second most powerful man in New France,
who commenced tah' scream for wha' must have been a very long time for
one man tah' scream, according tah' the soldiers. O' course, all this screaming brought a long line o' Montréal's finest upper-town citizens tah' Bigôt's
office tah' see wha' happened. Oddly enough, the major ordered his soldiers
just tah' keep tha' line orderly while they paraded past tha' secret bedroom
door, looking in and commenting in horror while Doctor La Galissonière
applied cold towels tah' the crotch o' tha' second most powerful man in New
France. His Imperial Eminence made note that tha' interior o' the bedroom
was adorned with all sorts o' chains and hanging devices, various leather
straps, whips, some rather large wooden replicas o' tha' human phallus, and
other things he could only describe, when, behold, Corrinne in a fit o' tears,
told him tha' name and uses o' all these things, as she had been tortured
with them at one time or another by Bigôt over the years."

Philippe dropped his brandy on the side table and grimaced.

"It's all right, laddie. I almost cried too," Pierre said after taking another
generous swallow of brandy. "When the archbishop heard this confession,
he was no longer angry."

An awkward silence ensued.

"Go on."

"Are ya' sure?"

"Go on."

"Well, Corrinne was pretty spent from these explanations, so we stopped
tah' eat something, except we did nah' eat. When all o' a sudden, Corrinne
grabbed my boning knife, which sort o' scared me for a few seconds, and
sliced open this long coat she'd been carrying. It was loaded with documents, letters, and rolls o' parchment, all o' which came from Bigôt's desk.
The archbishop's eyes widened at reading just a few o' these. He asked

me tah' step out for a while, and he and Corrinne stayed in his office for another hour, at least, going over whatever was there. And whatever it was, it changed everything, according to his Eminence. Some o' tha' major's soldiers were outside, so I went out tah' talk with them awhile, and they pretty much confirmed everything Corrinne had told the archbishop, but in much more colorful language…they dinnah' seem tah' feel too sorry for tha' intendant. When I was invited back in, Nicolet was actually smiling. Corrinne too, only nah' as broadly. More brandy please. Wait, I've got tah' find a chamber pot."

Philippe considered going up to see Corrinne, but decided he better hear the rest first.

When Pierre came back, he was chewing on a baguette from the *cuisine*.

"I need to hear the rest. So Corrinne doesn't have to tell me."

"Well, I may nah' have the full story. And I am probably leaving a lot out o' it by my way o' telling this. Anyway, it seems tha' intendant was taken tah' tha' Hotel Dieu, the one in Montréal, and cleaned up. But he demanded tah' be placed on tha' government river sloop tah' Quebec tha' afternoon, accompanied by dozens of gendarmes, and our very own major, o' course. He arrived this morning with everyone else, but evidently he is so ill they took him tah' tha' Hotel Dieu here. But he's nah' so ill tha' it stopped him from issuing warrants for Corrinne's arrest, which tha' Governor suspended until he understands wha' she is being accused o' doing. I expect our very own Major Péan is providing him with a lot o' the details I've already given ya'. And wha' the major does nah' tell the Governor, the archbishop will. They are dining together tonight, I think."

"So now what?"

"Well, Nicolet left Corrinne and I alone for an hour or so tah' go see tha' Governor. And he took a lot o' documents from that coat with him. There were some Bigôt forced Corrinne to sign that she separated from the rest and burned in tha' fireplace. And when the archbishop came back, he said tha' Governor agreed tah' meet with all o' us tomorrow morning. Well, nah' you, o' course. The Governor is going tah' sign everything Corrinne needs him tah' sign."

Pierre took a long swallow of brandy.

"*Then*, Corrinne smiled a lot and started crying again, and her crying *really* upsets Nicolet—tha' man hovers over her like a father. There's more laddie, but I'm talked out for now. We need tah' worry aboot wha' Intendant Bigôt might do next, but I think the rest can wait until morning. And, like ya' said, probably better nah' tah' ask Corrine much more about any o' this. Let her tell ya' when she's ready. She doesn't need tah' relive it all again."

Philippe stared into the fire. "No. She doesn't."

Pierre went into the bedroom to nap for a while. Philippe went upstairs, sat on the top step, and waited until Mathilde came out.

"She's resting, Monsieur."

"All right. Come get me when she needs to be brought downstairs."

"It won't be long, I'm sure."

As Philippe came down the stairs, there was a knock on the door. The chamberlain reached for the handle.

"Wait!" Philippe said. "Find out who's there before you open the door."

"Who's there?" the chamberlain asked loudly.

"Charles VanderMeer."

Philippe pushed the chamberlain aside. He opened the door immediately. The artist and a young lady stood on the first step.

"Welcome, Monsieur VanderMeer! Come in. Come in."

"Monsieur Gerrard! I am so pleased to see you again!"

"The pleasure is mine, Monsieur VanderMeer. And you must be Madeleine."

"Madeleine Louvet," she answered, dropping into a pretty curtsey. "Is Henri here?"

"I am." Henri was standing at the head of the hallway leading to the library. He greeted her nervously, flushing slightly. "*Bonjour*, Madeleine."

"Henri!" She rushed to him and hugged him tightly, kissing both cheeks repeatedly. "I've missed you so!"

To everyone's shock, Anamosa, enraged at this attention given to Henri, rushed toward Madeleine, a breakfast knife gripped in her hand. Henri scooped her up quickly, but Anamosa swung the short blade in an arc and cut through the looser sleeve of Madeleine's dress.

Madeleine screamed and retreated backwards. Running, Pierre Dunemoore appeared, armed with a blade. Philippe stood in front of Madeleine. Charles VanderMeer and the chamberlain stood by, open-mouthed.

"What happened?" Corrinne shouted from the top of the stairs, where, despite the terrible pain in her feet, she had dashed upon hearing the screaming.

"I don't know yet," Philippe said. He ran up the stairs to her.

Mathilde rushed down the stairs to comfort Madeleine. Pierre rubbed his bald head wearily and looked around.

"Keep that animal away from me!" Madeleine shrieked.

Henri's face changed from bewilderment to anger.

"Don't ever call Anamosa that again!"

"But…but she tried to kill me!"

"Whoa. Everybody! Laddie! Calm yourselves. Henri, take Anamosa back tah' the library. Mathilde, take Madeleine into the dining room and have the servants bring her some wine tah' drink. Monsieur VanderMeer, uh, welcome. Come into tha' sitting room with me. There's brandy in there. We might as well finish drinkin' all o' it."

The foyer and hallway gradually emptied.

"Well, that could have gone better." Philippe held Corrinne tightly and spoke in a low voice, "I think I'll let Pierre handle this."

"I like Anamosa. She is protective about the one she loves. I might do the same if Madeleine ever tried to come between us."

Corrinne saw Philippe's expression turn somber. "What's wrong? I was making a jest."

"I need to tell you something. But not out here."

Philippe carried Corrinne into the boudoir. He was going to put her in the bed but saw the chair by the window. He carried her there, and she sat in his lap like before. She was so close; he could not help himself and kissed her tenderly.

"It's hard for me to keep my hands off you."

Corrinne looked amused. "Then don't. I will help you. Which part of me would you like to touch?"

His expression became troubled.

"What is wrong?" Now she grew worried.

"I assume you know Rouge Piège."

Corrinne's smile disappeared. "Yes."

Philippe nodded. "Well, so do I. But only briefly when I lived in Quebec, not long after we first arrived. I was looking for any kind of work back then. You remember. Anyway, he came to see me, here, today, at the house, after you left. He came to the door and asked for me specifically."

"How would he know you were here?"

"That was my first question to him. He said Gaspard de Propei told him."

Corrinne felt a gathering fear in the pit of her stomach. "So…he is still alive, as we suspected."

"Not by much. We went to the sitting room and talked for about two hours."

Philippe told her the entire conversation, leaving nothing out.

Corrinne's initial alarm dissipated quickly, replaced by a cold, hard emotion. And then she agreed with everything Philippe had planned.

"When?"

"Tonight. Considering Intendant Bigôt's arrival…and since Major Péan's with him too. Tomorrow might be too late."

"I love you," she whispered.

Philippe rocked her gently in his arms.

"Do you trust Rouge Piège?" he asked her.

Corrinne sat up in his lap and looked out the window, remembering.

"He was my lover in the early days. He helped me become…*accepted*. A year later, he asked to marry me. I refused. He married someone from upper town, but still wanted to bed me. I refused more strongly. But we became business partners of a sort, the smuggling kind. He was one of the reasons why I moved upriver to Montréal." Corrine paused and kissed him. "You were the main reason, of course. But the opportunities for our collaboration increased five times over the first year. Monsieur Jordaine has contacts in Boston, Albany, and New York, probably the same ones I do, but maybe not, we don't share that kind of information. He has never once betrayed me in a matter of business, nor I him. There is no profit in it. We agree on that. I have always evaluated what he would gain from any arrangement with me, made myself understand what was in it for him, asked myself if it was good business. Would I do it if the roles were reversed? The risk? Those kinds of questions. He is an honest thief, I think, or he would be dead by now. Do I trust him? Well, let me ask you, do you believe the story he told you?"

"His story of how the *shérif* got here fits with what we know. The timing. Singing Owl. The wounds. Piège wants nothing to do with the man, he claims. He is aware the *shérif* captured and tortured you. He seemed genuinely angry about that. Claims he wants the *shérif* dead, but does not want to do it himself. Said he could blame it on me later if he is pressed to do the deed himself. I should be gone soon, and he would only do that to save his own neck. But he wants the *shérif*'s money, a substantial amount, which he asserts will be in the room with Gaspard somewhere tonight. He knows I want the man dead. That I want anonymity. And I don't care about the money."

"What will he tell the *shérif*?"

"Nothing, Piège claims. Why alert him, he said. The man does not know we are here, only that if we were, we would be in this house. So he will say he checked, and the answer is, we were not here."

"But my ships are here. And the *shérif* must know about the arrival of the river sloops by now. He will assume you are in the city somewhere. He will expect you to come for him," Corrinne warned.

And with that thought, Corrinne knew she was right.

"*Oh, God*! The *shérif* wanted Rouge Piège to tell you where he was, to bring you to him." Her face became drawn. "He is waiting for you."

"He has been waiting for me for a long time. And you are tired." Philippe placed Corrinne back in bed. "Rest for now."

"Have Mathilde bring me willow bark tea."

Pierre lifted a glass in Philippe's direction. "Join us. I thin' I'm getting sotted."

"You may want to stop. I have something to tell you. No, Monsieur VanderMeer, please stay. You need to hear this too."

He quickly related to them what he had told Corrine.

"So it starts all over again," Pierre said, morose after learning about Rouge Piège's visit. He tossed the remainder of his brandy into the fire where it flamed and hissed. "Ya' know, I would really like tah' get back tah' fur trading at some time."

"As soon as it is dark, I will finish it."

Pierre scoffed. "Alone?"

"I can do this better alone, Pierre. You know that. Rouge Piège will help me, but only up to a point."

"What aboot all o' us?"

"Tomorrow, the Governor. Then, Monsieur VanderMeer, your ships. No matter what happens, all of this business *must* be done."

Charles VanderMeer had been listening patiently. Pierre Dunemoore had told him the horrifying story regarding Lady de Chanaye's abduction and torture, and the subsequent events with Intendant Bigôt. Now to learn the *shérif* had survived! Did anything he had to say, have any importance compared to the dangers these men were facing?

"Yes, the ships. Before I arrived here, I visited a seamstress I know in Quebec. She is creating several large flags for me…Dutch flags, of course. After the meeting with the Governor tomorrow, I plan to collect these flags and raise them, with your cooperation. The ships will then become property of the Duke of Brunswick, essentially Dutch territory. The French ostensibly cannot board them without challenging Dutch sovereignty. That might offer all of you some refuge of protection, yes?"

Philippe and Pierre had not thought of this advantage.

Corrinne already knows this, Philippe realized, a grin spreading across his face. He looked out the window. It was darkening. In another hour, it would be dark enough.

They heard the front door open. It was Michelle and the footman, just returned from the Hotel Dieu. She looked happy.

Philippe said quickly to Pierre and VanderMeer, "Let's not talk about this anymore, just for now."

Introductions were made. Madeleine appeared from a bedroom where she had been sleeping.

"Sister Michelle! I had no idea—"

"Madeleine! It is good to see you alive and well, here, on the other side of the world. And I have renounced my vows. I am no longer a Sister. I am now a nurse at the Hotel Dieu," she added proudly.

Philippe felt one small weight lift from him.

Henri came out from the library holding Anamosa. The girl had her arms around Henri's neck and stared at Madeleine as if she were a snake.

Mathilde rushed down the stairs and urged everyone to the dining area to eat. She touched Philippe's arm.

"She is asking for you again."

Philippe knew this would be a difficult good-bye. He climbed the stairs and then breathed deeply before entering the master bedroom.

Closing the door softly behind him, Philippe went and sat on the bed.

Corrinne sat up. "I need to be carried, of course. But before you do, I see that it is dark."

"They are gathered in the *cuisine*. I will take you down to sit with them. Then I will go out the front door. It will be better if I do it this way. Pierre knows, so does Monsieur VanderMeer, but not Henri or Michelle. Less questions. Tell them I went...tell them I went for a stroll."

"Now?"

"Now."

They stared into each others' eyes.

Abruptly, tears welled in Corrinne's eyes. "I am so scared for you, Philippe! He is so evil. He was possessed by something dark when he tortured me. I saw it! It was not human! You must come back to me. You cannot leave me. You are my life now. Promise me you will come back to me."

Philippe rocked her while she sobbed, until she calmed. Then he kissed her face.

"He is just a man, Corrinne. And he deserves justice. And I promise to come back to you."

In the small bedroom, Philippe collected his weapons and placed them in a back pouch, the kind the day laborers carried around with them. No pistols, just his skinning knife, two boning knives, a hood with holes cut for his eyes, should he need one, that he'd fashioned from the sleeve of a dark linen shirt, and the parchment roll from the library.

"Where are you going?"

It was Henri. He decided not to lie to him.

"The *shérif* is here. I am going to kill him."

"I will go with you!"

Philippe grasped his shoulders. "No. Not this time. You stay here. Protect Anamosa. That is your task now. And comfort Corrinne for me. She knows what I am doing. You can help her too."

"Mother?"

"Well, not yet. But if you think she should know…make sure Pierre is with you when you tell her."

"I love you, Father," Henri said for the first time, his voice thick. He started to sniff.

They gripped each other tightly. "I love you too, Henri. I love you too."

Henri took off his talisman. "Take this. Chittaqua and Roland will help you. They helped me."

Philippe slipped the silver amulet around his neck. "This is the first time I've ever worn this."

"Promise me you will hold it for a few moments when you get close to him."

"I promise." Philippe pulled on a sock hat. "Don't announce to everyone that I left. I will be back before long."

At the table, everyone heard a door close. Henri came back into the room. They saw the change in him. All in the room became quiet.

The wait began.

Philippe rendezvoused with Rouge Piège inside his waterfront tavern. They didn't stay but moved outside, far away from the buildings, so they could not be overheard. He'd brought a small steering lantern with him.

"Which building?"

"You will see it. It sits close behind the tavern. One door. He seems composed, waiting, almost on guard. I may have misled you, Monsieur. I think he *wanted* me to tell you he was here…so you would come for him."

"I am glad you told me this, but I already assumed that was his plan. Do you have the other things I wanted?"

"Over there, by the warehouse, near the gate leading out to the wharf."

The area was cold, dark, windy. An icy moisture hung in the air. A perfect place for an ambush. Philippe prepared himself. But Rouge Piège's word was good. Nothing happened. There were things leaning against the back of the warehouse. He struck a flint to light another small steering lantern. Barely enough light to see. Piège pointed out each object.

"I think I have all of it. I hope you can see this. A pike. Eight feet long. Steel pointed. Not an easy thing to find, I might add. A short war ax. A bucket. Several lengths of rope. A hammer and six spikes in the bucket. You presume to do a crucifixion?"

"No. The davit?"

"About twenty paces in that direction, on the right, where the pier begins. He pointed the lantern in that direction, but the dim light was absorbed by shadows. "Well, you'll see it when you get closer. It's permanent. Used to lift small boats or fish nets from the water. The lifting spar will swing and extends out over the water if that's your intention. Don't walk out on the pier too far. The boards are rotted near the end."

"The davit is roped?"

"Yes. Rope, pulleys, a lifting hook. They all work."

Philippe picked up one length of rope and placed it over his shoulder. "The pushcart?"

"Right next to the building he is in."

Philippe paused, considering whether he had missed anything. Rouge

Piège spoke first.

"Here. You will need this too."

It was a short, thick, heavy leather belt with two buckles. The top and bottom edges were fitted with short, curved metal gutter pieces.

"It's a fighting collar. He has a throwing knife, but he also obtained a garrote from someone. No pistols that I know of, the sound would only draw attention to him if used. But he may have obtained those kinds of weapons too. I don't know exactly."

Philippe put on the collar and buckled it tight on the back. It made his neck stiff.

"My thanks. This killer likes to use knives."

"Philippe, once this starts, I cannot help you, no matter what happens. And no one else will either. And we will not look to determine the victor until the morning, when it is light out."

"I understand. Just bar the door inside the tavern and don't let anyone out."

"On a night like this? There are only two others in there. And they will be given all the rum they can drink."

"And you?"

"I will be in there, but I will wait for the sun to rise as well. I don't think I will sleep much tonight, eh?"

"All right."

"Good fortune to you, Monsieur. I have not met many men with your courage."

Philippe approached the shack with great caution and a quiet step, both learned from his wilderness experience. He moved toward the door from its more shadowed side. There was a window, but it was covered tightly with a piece of leather. The leather flickered with light from a nearby candle inside.

The *coureur de bois* breathed deeply, calming himself. He steeled his thoughts on his purpose.

This man attacked, degraded, and killed Okeanneh. This man abducted, tortured, sodomized, and tried to kill Corrinne. This man tried to kill Pierre. This man tried to kill Henri. And I will bring justice to him.

The sounds of the night changed suddenly for no reason. *He is just outside the door*, Colbért thought. He readied to lunge. The noose was perfectly hung and perfectly still.

Philippe closed his eyes and took hold of the talisman as he promised Henri he would. When he opened his eyes, everything seemed brighter, as if bathed in moonlight. Except, there was no moon, no stars, only the numerous lantern lights from windows in the city proper. But the patina of light he saw was brighter than that, almost bluish in tone, enough that he could even discern the knots in the wood of the door.

Philippe took another deep breath, made the sign of the cross, and kicked in the door. It slammed open as he rushed in. The *shérif* was sitting at the side of a bed, smiling at him, almost lewdly. He was holding something. Philippe lunged, the skinning knife poised to strike, but he was stopped short when something dangling from the rafters looped around his head.

The *shérif* growled a welcome in a guttural voice and pulled down sharply on a rope.

A wire noose tightened around Philippe's neck so fast, he was lifted off the floor, his legs kicking and dangling in the air. Dropping his knife, his hands flew to his neck.

The assassin pushed the chair leg with his feet until it caught the notch in the floor. He picked up his throwing knife to cast it, but the woodsman's struggles became so desperate, he waited, enjoying the sight and sounds of the man's death. In a few more seconds, the woodsman's feet and hands ceased their frantic flailing and dropped to his sides, but they seemed to twitch spasmodically near his belt.

After the initial sounds of the door slamming open, there were sounds of a struggle…then silence. Rouge Piège decided one of them had died.

The strain from the full weight of Philippe's body on his neck was enormous. The wire noose pinched off his breathing even through the thick fighting collar. He was already dizzy.

Philippe finally got hold of the boning knife in his belt, reached up, and slashed frantically at the garrote line above his head. He dropped to the floor in a stooped position.

Colbért cast the knife straight at the woodsman's chest. But to his surprise, it struck metal and bounced off. *He wears armor!* The Night Butcher lunged, knocking Philippe backwards, turning Philippe's hand with the boning knife toward Philippe's face.

Philippe stopped the thrust within a few inches of his eye and a contest of strength began. The *shérif* was immensely strong and the blade point descended slowly, surely. Philippe only had moments to react. Instead of pushing back, he pushed sideways and rolled in the same direction.

The assassin's knife sunk into the soft muscle and flesh of Philippe's left shoulder. Philippe howled in pain.

Rouge Piège heard the scream inside the tavern. *But who screams?* He paced back and forth across the room.

Rolling slightly to the left allowed Philippe to pull his other boning knife free and he slammed the long, pointed blade through the *shérif*'s ribs into his heart. Or so he thought. But the man rolled away and stood up.

Philippe got to his feet, blood dripping down his left arm, the knife still protruding from his shoulder. He staggered backward and watched in amazement as the assassin pulled the boning knife free. A line of blood spewed forth. There was a glowing redness to his eyes.

"Do you think this is over, *Adaelric*? It will never be over, until you and your seed are all *dead*!"

Philippe had never heard a voice like that before. It startled him enough to pause.

Skrieee!

The sound came from outside.

The assassin lunged again. Philippe stooped backwards, grabbed his skinning knife from the floor, and met the attack, thrusting the heavy blade upwards, again toward the heart. The thrust was true and the blade penetrated, sticking out the man's back. But the razor sharp boning knife clutched in the assassin's hand slashed down toward his head. At the last instant, Philippe tilted his head to the right to avoid the slash. The blade caught his fighting collar. It was sharp enough to cut into the leather, but the assassin was already collapsing. The blade cut through only enough to slice Philippe's neck superficially.

Philippe heaved the dead body off to the left and crawled backward on his seat till his back was against the wall. He was panting heavily.

After a few moments, he got to his knees, and crawled over to a table in the corner. Standing, he grabbed some dirty linens off the top. Amazingly, there was a taper still burning in its holder on the wall behind the open door. He pushed the door closed. He took the taper and relit another on the opposite wall that had been extinguished in the fighting. Sitting in a chair at the table, he cut away his shirt around the boning knife. He took an empty bowl and held the candle-taper at an angle to melt the wax, until he had a pool he thought sufficient. Then, in one movement, he pulled the knife free, and poured the hot wax into the wound, screaming loudly at the pain, partially cauterizing and wax plugging the wound. He did it again. He wrapped the bloody linens around his shoulder, tying it off as best he could with his free hand and teeth. It was not perfect. He was still bleeding, but the wax and crude bandage might work as long as he did not lift his left arm too high.

He went outside and dragged the pushcart with one hand to the door. It took several clumsy heaves with one arm, but he got the *shérif*'s body onto the cart. He tied off the man's legs with cross-tied loops of rope from the ankles to the waist and chest, as he would a load of furs. It wasn't as tight as he wanted, but it would have to do. The loops would tighten like individual nooses when something hung from either end.

Philippe felt dizzy. Taking hold of the talisman, he closed his eyes for a few seconds. When he opened them, he could again see the strange bluish tinge highlighting everything he looked at. He looped more rope over his good shoulder, tied the ends to the lifting handles. Raising the feet of the cart, he pushed the two-wheeled wagon slowly toward the wharf and pier.

Nearly two hours later, in the midst of a freezing cold rain, Philippe Gerrard staggered through the *cuisine* door of Lady Corrinne de Chanaye's Quebec City home and collapsed on the floor in a pile of bloody clothing.

Amid the screams and cries of the women, Pierre Dunemoore quieted everyone. They quickly placed his body on the dining table and began to minister to his wounds.

The next morning, Rouge Piège, some fishermen, and the waterfront scum of Quebec were stunned to find the grisly remains of a man, dead and mutilated. The head had been cut off and placed on an old pike, the end of which was shoved between two planks of the pier to keep it erect. The body had been hung upside down by ropes tied around the legs and attached to a davit-lifting hook. The genitals were cut away and the man had been gutted. The viscera lay in a bloody pile beneath it. The hands and feet were also missing. Spikes had been driven into the head through the ears. The eyes were gouged, and the lips removed, exposing the teeth. The jaw sagging open revealed a missing tongue.

It presented a gruesome visage to anyone brave enough to stare at it too closely. Not many did. A piece of parchment had been nailed over the gaping hole in the torso. It was written in Latin, except for the heading and the last sentence, which were in French.

The heading read, *Assassin*.

The last line read, *Those who dare to touch the assassin in death, shall be judged like him in life.*

The body was not touched by anyone. The gendarmes eventually came, asked, and found no one who knew the man, or what had happened, nor anyone who could read the entire message.

But Monsieur Jordaine, a respected merchant from upper town, who happened to be *passing by*, stepped forward and tore the note from the body.

"A souvenir." The merchant shrugged at the aghast faces of the spectators. "The last sentence only says not to touch the body."

A gendarmerie officer swung the davit out over the river and slashed the rope attached to the hook with his sword. The body splashed into the water and began its long, decaying float to the great ocean. The same officer pulled up the pike, pointed it at the water, and shook it. The head slipped off, the weight of the heavy spikes pounded into the ears caused it to immediately sink to the bottom of the river.

CHAPTER 41
QUEBEC CITY
NOVEMBER 1754
William's Queen

Philippe awoke and held a hand to his eyes, squinting at the bright sunlight coming in through the window. He moved to sit up and was instantly discouraged from doing so by the shocking pain in his left shoulder.

Was he in Corrinne's boudoir?

He had almost no memory of coming back to the house during the night. He remembered falling on the hill steps at some point and lying back on the ground. Strong hands lifted him up...then nothing. He did recall a raging thirst for water, and there had been blood. Lots and lots of blood. In fact, his mouth right then was dry and tasted of blood.

I've got to get up, he thought.

It took inventive moves with his elbows and right arm to eventually sit on the side of the bed. Then his head began spinning. He grabbed a pillow, folded it in half, placed it on his knees, and leaned forward.

"Monsieur! What are you doing?"

Philippe squinted. "Mathilde?"

"You should not be sitting up. You will break all your stitches!"

"Stitches?"

He examined himself. He was naked. He immediately pulled the coverlet close. His left shoulder was heavily bandaged...and in a sling. No wonder it was so hard to sit up.

"I'm thirsty."

Mathilde filled a cup of water from an urn. Philippe took the urn from her and drained it.

"Thank you. Much better. Uh, clothes?"

Mathilde looked at him sternly. "I will get you some clothes to wear, Monsieur, but my mistress gave me explicit instructions you were not to be up and walking around."

"Clothes, please. But wait, where is your mistress?"

"They are all with the Governor since early this morning. Michelle is at the Hotel Dieu."

"Who is here?"

"Anamosa, Madeleine…"

"Not in the same room, I hope!"

"Madeleine is in the library, and Anamosa is in the *cuisine*."

"The time?"

"It is almost midday."

"*Merci*. Clothes, please. And if I do get up, it will only be to go down to the sitting room or the library, and I will go slow."

"She will be angry with me, you know?"

He threw back the covers. "I will go naked if I must."

Mathilde reddened and left the room.

Philippe got up slowly. There was some dizziness, so he got down on his knees and crawled over to the chair by the window. He wrapped himself with a towel placed on the chair and sat down. It was a hazy day. Most of the ships he saw yesterday were still there. The *Falcon Queen* had both of its river sloops tied up, one to each side. As did the *Ile Royale*. He tried to hold the watch glass with one hand, but it was too cumbersome to balance.

Mathilde came back into the room with a clean pile of clothes.

"What happened last night?"

"You came in the *cuisine* door, bloody from head to foot, and collapsed unconscious on the floor. We carried you into the dining room, cut away your clothes, and did our best to stop the bleeding from your shoulder. Monsieur VanderMeer ran out to find a doctor to bring back to you, which he did, of course. The man cleaned and stitched up the wound in your shoulder. He says it is deep. He said it would be two months before you have full use of your arm again."

"I have heard such things before."

Mathilde was not pleased with him. "I am sure of that."

"Is that all?"

"We scrubbed you down until you were completely clean of blood and put you to bed. You've been unconscious or asleep since then."

"What if I dress and sit with you in the *cuisine* and eat something? Will you forgive that?"

"I am willing to bring something for you to eat up here. Going downstairs will be against the wishes of my mistress. But you are a grown man, Monsieur."

Mathilde left the room.

Philippe dressed slowly. Pants first, knotted with a lacing. Because of the sling bandage, he could only drape the shirt over his left shoulder, leaving it half buttoned. Socks were difficult, but he managed. Shoes harder, so he did not wear any.

He was dizzy from loss of blood. He staggered from wall to wall, balancing on whatever flat surface he could find. He reached the top of the stair and sat down on the first step to dispel the growing vertigo and catch his breath. Vivid images from the unexpected vicious garrote, the knife fight, and death struggles began to flood back into his consciousness. He trembled, wondering if it was from these memories or his feebleness from the loss of blood.

Probably both, he decided.

But the most disturbing memory was the rasping, guttural voice…and the reddish glow that had come from the *shérif*.

Who was *Adaelric*?

Taking a deep breath, he descended the stairs by sitting on his rump, from step to step. Staggering into the cuisine, he saw the servants were busy making meals. All of them stopped to look at him in shocked surprise.

Mathilde turned and frowned.

Anamosa sat at a table with her two dolls, a glum expression on her face. Then she saw him.

"Fleep!" Anamosa said brightly upon seeing him. She hurried over.

"Oho, Anna! Let me sit! Let me sit down, first!"

She was patting his face gently, and trying to rub her face against his neck. He allowed her to sit on the right side of his lap.

With Anamosa's gentle, healing touch, Philippe's mood was suddenly buoyed, filled with a cheerfulness so welcome, he had to stifle the sob that almost burst from him in relief. The *shérif* was dead and gone. A great weight was lifted. But he also felt weary. *I just need more rest.*

"There," Philippe said to Mathilde. "You see? It's all good now."

"You are bleeding," she answered curtly.

He looked at his shoulder and noticed the stain spreading at the top of his shirt. "All right. Give me a towel to sop the blood and something to eat and drink, if you please."

Major Michel Péan had been standing before the bed of Intendant Bigôt at the Hotel Dieu for almost an hour. He was tired of answering the intendant's repetitive questions, almost the same ones, over and over.

The intendant's body twitched frequently and his eyes danced around, never resting in one spot for long. What happened to him in Montréal had affected him more than physically.

"As I said before, Monsieur, there are reports the *shérif* was taken captive by the Oneida. Reports he died in Montréal from arrow wounds. Reports he is actually here in Quebec as we speak. And finally a report he died in a knife fight on the riverfront here in Quebec, last night, as a matter of fact."

Bigôt shifted his waist. He waved at a nurse to change the cold towel on his crotch again.

"So which is it?"

Péan told him, *again*. "The Oneida cannot be approached. There were no dead bodies with arrow wounds lying around Montréal's walls, not before we left anyway. And the man from last night was beheaded and thrown into the river. So if he was the *shérif*, he is dead, and we will never know for certain."

Intendant Bigôt's balls throbbed constantly with pain. His sleep was sporadic. The doctors had told him the swelling and pain would eventually subside. The treatment was cold towels for an hour, followed by hot towels for an hour, which seemed ridiculous to the intendant, particularly the hot towels, which only made the pain worse.

"And if the *shérif* died, his money goes back to France!" He glared at the major. "You seem to have forgotten that. Part of it is your money too!"

"I have not forgotten, Monsieur." *I just don't care*, Péan didn't say.

"With the *shérif* presumed dead, now Nicolet will convince Governor Duquesne to intervene and allow the *coureur de bois* to go free. Then what?"

Major Péan knew Governor-General Duquesne was consumed with war plans. Bigôt's comment regarding the Governor's daily contemplations was absurd.

"Then what?" The major shrugged. "You said we will arrest Lady de Chanaye?"

"So you know where she is?"

"No. As I told you before, I do not. She is not at her house."

"Well, I will arrest her when I seize her ships tomorrow. Wait! Are the river sloops still tied alongside the *Queen* being unloaded?"

Major Péan moved back a step and gazed out the second-floor window. "Yes. I can still see them out there."

"The frigates have been ordered to intercept them if those ships make sail."

"They have been so ordered."

Why did the shérif have to die? Bigôt wondered sullenly. *Shot by a boy, no less!* A new idea seized him.

"Wait! The boy," he said to the major.

Major Péan squinted at him. "The boy?"

"You are certain it was Henri Gerrard who killed Gaspard de Propei?"

"Killed? No. According to my scout and the Jesuit carriage driver, the boy loosed at least three or four arrows into the man, but the *shérif* lived."

"Four arrows? And the *shérif* was only wounded? The boy's obviously not a very good bowman. But that is not what we will claim." François Bigôt smiled slyly. "We will say that according to your Jesuit informant, young Henri Gerrard shot a quiver full of arrows into one of King Louie's *shérifs*. You will take the gendarmes to Lady de Chanaye's house to locate and arrest Henri Gerrard for murder. And when you find he is not there, post bills around the city, offer a reward to anyone who will tell us where his is."

Major Péan gawked. "You're jesting! Arrest the *boy*? But he saved Lady de Chanaye's life!"

"I know! The meddlesome little maggot!"

The major shook his head. "Monsieur Intendant, the story of what the boy did to rescue Lady de Chanaye was carried downriver by the fleet of cargo sloops. You issue this order and the whole city will turn out against this and against you. Most of them want Gaspard de Propei arrested. They will more likely hail the boy as a hero!"

François Bigôt frowned at the major. "*I know that*! Why is such a simple plan so hard for you to appreciate? I want his father, the woodsman, to go *berserk* over this! And to keep him from doing something heroically stupid, Lady de Chanaye will be forced to negotiate with me *again*. *Voilà*!"

Major Péan knew the chances of Lady de Chanaye ever meeting with

Bigôt again, willingly, were nil. None of his ranting speculation made any sense.

Bigôt has lost his wits. This fool actually intends to do this. He will get one of his magistrate clerks to issue a warrant for the arrest of Henri Gerrard. Then he is going to order me *to do it. And he'll let* me *face the enmity of everyone in Quebec City and Montréal. Well…that's not going to happen!*

Philippe had finished eating a second plate of food when the chamberlain found him in the *cuisine*.

"Monsieur Gerrard, there is another man at the front door waiting to see you."

Philippe allowed Anamosa to slip down from his lap and stood up shakily. "Master chamberlain, you do understand, that we, all of us, including your mistress, we are trying to keep our presence here confidential."

The chamberlain seemed genuinely bewildered. "Oh. Then why do so many people come calling here looking for you?"

"Probably because *you* keep telling them I am here."

Philippe staggered to the small bedroom and found a boning knife, which he slipped into the waist of his pants beneath his shirt. He went to the front door, took a deep breath, and opened it slightly.

Good God!

Major Péan was standing at the door, his hat in hand. He was alone.

"Monsieur Gerrard? Uh, why would *you* answer this door?"

"I do not want trouble, Major."

"And I am not here to give you trouble. This is a personal call. May I come in?" He looked up and down the street. "It might be better if I am not seen standing in this doorway."

Philippe moved aside. The major entered.

"The sitting room is that way."

When they were seated, Mathilde brought them both coffee.

The major took a large swallow. "Marvelous. *Merci*."

"Major?"

"Were you in some kind of a fight, recently, Monsieur? Your shirt, there, is bloody?"

"Is that why you're here?"

"No." The major put down his coffee. "I just finished a long discussion with Intendant Bigôt at the Hotel Dieu. The man has lost his wits. He is ordering absurd warrants to be issued. I am here to tell you what he plans and when he plans to act. I am doing this as a private citizen. Tomorrow morning, he will send me out with the gendarmes. Under orders. And as I've told you before, I follow my orders."

"Continue."

Major Péan noticed the butt of a knife protruding from beneath Philippe's shirt. He pointed at it. "Before you decide to draw that weapon, please remember, it was my *personal* decision to warn you about this."

It was midafternoon when Corrinne, Pierre, Henri, and Charles Vander-Meer returned to the house. Corrinne was smiling as Pierre set her down on a chair in the sitting room. Philippe was sound asleep, sitting up in the middle of the couch, his head lolled back.

Mathilde came into the room and protested to Corrinne. "He refused to stay in bed!"

"Ahh-ree!" Anamosa jumped into Henri's arms.

Madeline appeared from the library where she had stayed the entire day. She was yawning. "*Bonjour.*"

Pierre and Charles VanderMeer took the other two chairs. Pierre sat down with a sigh.

"Uh, brandy for the two of us, Mathilde, if you please. And bring the bottle with you."

With some painful effort, Corrinne shifted over to the couch to sit on Philippe's right. She carefully brought his head down to her shoulder. He remained asleep. She stroked the side of his face and kissed his forehead before resting her head on his.

Pierre smiled and lifted his glass in a toast.

"Ya' should paint tha' two o' them sitting there like that," he whispered. "I can nah' think o' a more lovely sight after tha' last few weeks."

"Oh, but I can." The artist rose and retrieved his sketching pad from his baggage sitting off to one side of the room. Flipping to a clean page, he began to rapidly make a drawing. Madeleine sat in the chair vacated by Corrinne to watch him at work.

Two hours later, Philippe had not woken up, so Corrinne had a pillow put on the couch to allow him to lie down on the arm. She gathered everyone to a short dinner to explain the plans for tomorrow. Before she began, Mathilde whispered in her ear.

"Mistress, did Monsieur Gerrard mention Major Péan's visit to the house today."

"Major Péan! Here?! Today?! Why have you not told me this before now?"

"I presumed Monsieur Gerrard would tell you. He talked with the major for a long time and then the major left. The discussion seemed polite, but I do not know what they talked about."

Corrinne stood, excused herself from the table, and forced herself to walk into the sitting room. She sat down on Philippe's right and nuzzled his neck.

"Philippe," she whispered. "Wake uuup."

He groaned a little. His right hand groped her dress.

"Wake up, Philippe."

He blinked, saw her, and sat up too fast. A pained expression crossed his face. "Corrinne? When did you return? How long was I asleep?"

"In a moment. Was Major Péan here today?"

At the mention of Major Péan, Philippe came wide-awake.

"Yes. He was. To warn us. Intendant Bigôt is issuing a warrant for Henri's arrest."

"Henri?!"

"Yes! For the murder of the *shérif.*"

"That is absurd!"

"Yes. And Major Péan agrees. But he will be coming to this house to search for him tomorrow at the eleven o'clock hour. Also to arrest you, of course, for the murder of his secretary, and, I suppose, me as well. He recommended we go somewhere else, fast. He also said if we go out to the ship, Intendant Bigôt plans to come to the *Falcon Queen* personally with a boarding party. But that the intendant can barely stand, let alone walk, so that might not happen for a few days."

Corrinne was suspicious. "Why would Major Péan tell you this?"

"I don't know. He is a contradiction. But I do believe him when he says he will arrest us precisely at the eleven o'clock hour tomorrow morning."

"Well, we will be gone long before then, I am sure. Now, I have one more thing to tell you before you help me back to the table. I have been trying to walk a little…I want to be able to stand up tomorrow for something important. But I'm not sure it will happen just because I want it to."

"What you just said does not make any sense. Tell me this again."

Corrinne suddenly looked uncertain and vulnerable.

"What? What is it?"

Philippe took a seat next to Corrinne at the dining table.

Corrinne was beaming. "Fortunately, all of our business is complete," she announced. They noticed her eyes were glistening with unshed tears. "Charles VanderMeer owns my ships. A toast to Charles VanderMeer."

When the congratulations and clapping faded, Corrinne continued. "The *Falcon Queen* will be renamed *William's Queen* in honor of the Netherlands' next King. The *Ile Royale* will not be renamed for the time being. This transfer will occur as soon as Charles raises the Dutch flags, which he plans to do tomorrow afternoon, at the time of sunset. Philippe has told me Major Péan is coming in the morning to arrest most of us, so we need to be on the *Falcon Queen* as early as possible. And Henri Gerrard was heir apparent to the Propei marquisate for an hour today and then abdicated as witnessed by the Governor and Archbishop Nicolet. As a condition of her vows of poverty, Michelle's title, wealth, and lands for the House of Propei pass to the Church, as witnessed by Archbishop Nicolet and Governor Duquesne."

"Bloody marvelous! Tah' Lady Michelle! No finer woman has ever been a royal. And tah' Lord Henri! Marquis, if only for a day."

Glasses were raised. Henri's face reddened. Anamosa kissed his cheek.

"I have something to say," Michelle interjected. "I have requested a position for Madeleine as a nurse in training at the Hotel Dieu. Doctor La Galissonière has agreed. And Archbishop Nicolet subsequently assigned Madeleine Louvet as my ward, so she may live here permanently, while she chooses to do so, of course."

Madeleine did not react with any obvious signs of enthusiasm.

"Another thing to celebrate, Pierre has a new partner in les Négociants Dunemoore; Henri Gerrard owns twenty-five percent. And I have asked Pierre to give fifty-one percent of his ownership in this Quebec City house to Michelle. He agreed and it, too, was signed and witnessed by the archbishop."

"Here's to Pierre's diminishment," Philippe said, raising his glass.

"And one final announcement," Corrinne began.

Philippe touched her hand gently. "No. I will do this."

The *coureur de bois* got out of his chair and knelt before Corrinne de Chanaye, taking both of her hands in his.

"Corrinne. I am in love with you. Will you marry me, tomorrow, after we board the *Falcon Queen*?"

Lady Corrinne de Chanaye's smile was radiant, her eyes shone. But she was too choked up to reply.

Philippe was not sure what to say now.

Michelle touched Philippe on the shoulder. "That means *yes*, Philippe." Michelle continued, "Archbishop Nicolet has graciously offered to perform the ceremony tomorrow afternoon on the foredeck of the *Falcon Queen* just before sunset. And as we are all invited, we can therefore avoid having the entire wedding party arrested at the same time."

Philippe looked at Pierre. "I don't have a ring."

"Oh! I have rings!" VanderMeer said. "I have lots of rings! We can pick one out tomorrow."

Pierre Dunemoore raised his glass in another toast. This time he stood.

"To Philippe Gerrard, my dearest friend. And to Corrinne de Chanaye. I've never met or known a more amazing woman in my life. May you both enjoy the happiness you deserve."

Long before the sun rose, the city house was awake, packing and partaking of a light morning meal. Philippe came out of the small bedroom on the bottom floor where he had slept the night before, alone and having chaste thoughts about his future bride, as Michelle suggested was tradition for the groom-to-be the night before his wedding. As he lay alone, Philippe's thoughts were far from chaste.

As the sun broke over the horizon, the entire baggage load was gathered into the foyer area. It was clear there would be too much for a carriage, plus all the passengers, to carry. As they were discussing the need for two trips and how this should be done, there came a knock at the front door.

Philippe, Pierre, and Corrinne looked at each other in alarm. "It's too early," Corrinne said.

To everyone's distress, the chamberlain abruptly opened the front door. "May I help you sir?"

"*Merde!*" The Scotsman drew his pistol, holding it ready.

The chamberlain shifted to the side, and Corrinne looked around the corner of the door.

"Oh. It's you."

The man took off his hat and bowed. "At your service, my lady. And may I say, your beauty has attracted the sun to rise early in the sky."

"It is good to see you too, Monsieur Jordaine. What brings you to my door on this cold morning?"

"A little gray bird trimmed with gold has told me you may be in need of a wagon. Which I have, right here." He gestured toward a cargo wagon with a team of two horses.

"A wagon? Why would I need a wagon?"

"Because Major Péan will be calling on your residence at the nine o'clock hour. Two hours earlier than he reported. So he thought a wagon would help you make haste."

Philippe and Pierre stepped up to the doorway.

"Monsieur, if this is a trick," Philippe said, "you will pay within the hour."

"Monsieur Gerrard, if I wished to do you harm, I would not have carried you to your back steps last night."

"That was you?"

"I could not wait to see who prevailed. And you left a bloody trail that was easy to follow." The man withdrew something from a coat pocket. "Oh and here is the judgment you left on the body. A souvenir, perhaps, for Lady de Chanaye?" He handed it to her. "I saved it before the *shérif*'s body was cut down and dropped into the river. My Latin is not very good, but that was quite a declaration of punishment you wrote. And I think what I saw hanging captured the essence of the punishment and much more."

"It wasn't mine."

"Still, impressive and appropriate, I think. So, my friends, are you ready to load up? I've had someone signal the *Falcon Queen* to send over their launch."

"Why are you doing this, René?"

"My lady, let's just say, I find it is important to me that no further harm come to you…or to any of you for that matter. Many of my fellow Québécois feel the same. Intendant Bigôt is very unpopular. You have more friends than you know. And who knows what the future may bring as far as our mutual business is concerned, eh?"

And as the wagon was being loaded, Philippe took Michelle aside and told her she needed to hire a new chamberlain as soon as possible.

Captain LaTour hailed them in a booming voice. "I am so pleased to see you all safely back aboard. The rumors of what has occurred in the city have been disturbing. Monsieur Gerrard, it was heard said you were injured. They say it was your, uh, decoration hanging on the pier. And I see you wear a sling."

"A minor knife wound."

"I will have Victorio look at it right away. You can never trust a city doctor, eh? Pierre, my friend. The river sloop is loaded with fresh goods to sell in Montréal. You are leaving today, yes?"

"Uh, no. Tomorrow. I am attending a wedding today."

"Oh...not yours, I presume." He laughed. "Who would want to marry you?"

"Hers." Pierre pointed at Lady de Chanaye.

"God's—" the captain whispered. "Who is your fortunate paramour, my lady?"

"He is," she smiled and pointed at Philippe.

Surprise and happiness crossed Captain LaTour's face. He grabbed Philippe by both shoulders.

"Oh, glorious day, my friend! What a glorious day this is!"

Philippe winced and pointed at his shoulder. "Owww!"

"It will be here, on the foredeck, today," Corrinne said happily. "Archbishop Nicolet has agreed to perform the ceremony."

MICHEL-ANGE DUQUESNE DE MENNEVILLE, MARQUIS DUQUESNE
PERSONAL DIARY OF GOVERNOR-GENERAL DUQUESNE AS RECORDED BY HIS
ADJUTANT-CAPTAIN

At half past the hour of three, in the afternoon of the seventh day of November, 1754, Archbishop André Nicolet, Jesuit Intendant of New France, conducted a wedding Mass aboard the French trading frigate, *Falcon Queen*, celebrating the marriage of Monsieur Philippe Gerrard and Lady

Corrinne de Chanaye. Philippe Gerrard wore the uniform of a captain in the Troupes de la Marine, a commission ordered by Governor-General Duquesne in honor of Monsieur Gerrard's service in the war against the English transgressions. Lady Corrinne de Chanaye wore a gown of white silk and lace in honor of her chastity and virtue as publically affirmed by the Archbishop André Nicolet. Lady Michelle de Propei stood at Lady de Chanaye's left. Pierre Dunemoore, Managing-Director of les Négociants Dunemoore stood at Captain Gerrard's right. Captain Gerrard knelt on both knees and presented Lady de Chanaye with a ring of fine gold, set with a star of five diamonds, as designed by Charles VanderMeer, Master Artist for the court of King Louis XV. Captain Gerrard made a public vow of eternal love and devotion to the bride as he slipped the star of five diamonds on her finger. It was reported that Lady Corrinne de Chanaye wept copiously.

By order of Governor-General Duquesne, the French frigate, *Champion Mer*, fired a ten gun salute in honor of the nuptials.

At nine minutes past the hour of five, in the afternoon of the seventh day of November, 1754, the French flag of the *Falcon Queen* was lowered for the last time as a result of its sale. The Orange, White, and Blue, the Prince's flag of the Dutch Republic was raised, and the ship was renamed *William's Queen*, in honor of the Queen Anne, mother and regent to William V, the heir to the Dutch throne.

In a corresponding ceremony, the French trading frigate *Ile Royale* lowered its flag as a result of its sale. The Prince's flag of the Dutch Republic was raised. The *Ile Royale* retained its name, but in Dutch.

It was dark; the moon would not rise for several hours. The night sky was clear, the air icy cold, and the stars were brilliant. Corrinne claimed she'd seen some aurorae the night before and hoped to see them again this night. So Captain LaTour had arranged a place for them to watch the night sky in private, on the forward deck of the *Queen*.

Philippe was wearing his clean and pressed Troupes de la Marine uniform, Corrinne her wedding dress. Using some gold and silver coins given to her by Pierre, Michelle had purchased the dress from a specific Quebec dressmaker. She had brought it aboard with her in the early afternoon. The fit was perfect. Corrinne had been captivated by its beauty and did not want to take it off—not willingly.

They were lying amidst a pile of new, white sail canvas. Victorio, the sailmaker, planned to raise it in the morning to finish the dress of the foremast rigging. The heavy canvas was thick, yet giving, and it molded around their bodies like the nest of a bird. They could see their breath, but were warm under a lavish blanket of cured ermine fur skins. The furs, which Pierre had given to them as a wedding present, had an aromatic healthy scent that was comforting.

"This uniform hurts my shoulder," Philippe complained to Corrinne.

"Really? That is a *perfect* reason for me to loosen all your clothing, yes?"

She unbuttoned his waistcoat and the shirt underneath. Unbuckled the belt of his pants, and unbuttoned the front. She tugged the pants down to his knees leaving him naked and exposed. She caressed his hardness, up and down with both hands, then stopped. She lay back down on top of him and rocked her shoulders comfortably.

"What? Why? That's all?"

Corrinne replied, her voice coquettish. "I undressed you, Monsieur Gerrard. It is only fair for you to return my favor."

His left arm in a sling, Philippe started searching with his right hand to find a way to open the dress.

"Now don't tear anything! I want to save this dress."

"Then help me."

"As it is written, 'Great wonders await the intrepid surveyor when he explores the surface of an exotic new land with patient attention.'"

"I'm trying to get *back* to this *exotic new land*," he grumbled.

Philippe's right hand and fingers began roaming persistently over her dressed body. As he probed among the folds and seams to find the hidden buttons and ties to her dress, his fingertips tickled intimate places.

Corrinne lay with her head in the nook of his right arm and shoulder, her body across his stomach and lap, her right arm lifted, tucked around the back of their heads, her long fingernails lightly scratching through his hair, her lips barely touching his left cheek. She was enjoying this immensely. She would lick, blow, or chew gently on his ear when it moved close enough. Corrinne found his anxious frustration very sensual. She could feel his delicious, impatient hardness move beneath her now and then. She rocked her pelvis subtly to keep him that way. She preferred this exploration to continue for a while. But he stopped suddenly in one spot.

"Aha," Philippe said, jubilant. "There are loopy twists around each of these tiny pearls on the sides and the top."

"Please, be careful!"

Philippe was careful, and in several seconds he had the right side and shoulder of the pearl-embroidered bodice open, only to encounter a heavy silk undergarment, covering an enticingly pliant, warm, heavy breast. But at least he could touch it.

"*Yeess*! Finally. Does this pull up or down?"

Corrinne sighed loudly and contentedly. "I am sorry, Monsieur. I just...I just really don't know. I'm afraid it is much too complicated for me. Someone helped me dress."

"Well...Maybe this...?"

"*Don't tear it!* It's *silk*! It hangs all the way down to my ankles. You have to open the waist of the lower dress first. Then I can slip it off. There... that's the only clue I will provide." She rubbed her hips against him more strongly. "But hurry. I am starting to fall asleep."

Philippe began mumbling curses under his breath. "You know, I only have one hand to work with. The other was recently injured. Remember? Some people actually feel sorry for me. I was stabbed and wounded. Almost fatally, you know."

Corrinne feigned reluctance, smiled, and closed her eyes.

"Yes...I know. There is a belt, Philippe, with two *very* delicate clasps at each side. Be careful with them. It is not like opening your boots."

Within seconds, he found and opened the clasps. The cloth-covered lacings spread wider.

"Oh, that is very clever," he said. "This device could be used on fur packs."

"I am glad you are impressed. Would you like to study the mechanism further?"

"No."

The waist of the dress was loose. Corrinne now helped with her hands and slid the outer garment down over her knees and feet. She pulled it out from under the furs and set it to the right. Then she sat up and carefully slid the lace and pearl bodice around her left shoulder and arm and laid the piece upon the dress. Left on was the long, heavy silk from her ankles to her neck. Beneath that she was naked and hot.

And Philippe's hand surveyed that immediately.

She lay back against him again, closed her eyes, and enjoyed the luxurious, smooth feel of his hand gliding slowly over her silk-covered breasts, then down to circle her stomach, then further to linger and caress her sex.

When she opened her eyes again, the night had blossomed into waves of green light.

"Oh, Philippe, look!" She pointed, her wedding ring sparkling with ethereal light as she did so. "It's come back again! The aurorae! I love this. Isn't it beautiful?"

The sky shimmered and moved as the green drapes of light rippled back and forth.

Philippe stopped for a moment and answered in a mumble.

"Yes. Beautiful."

He began to tug carefully on the silk to pull it up her legs. She braced with her hands and lifted her pelvis. He yanked, and the silk rushed up to her waist, exposing her sex to his probing fingertips.

"Oh, yes," she whispered. "Right there."

Corrinne watched the wondrous flow of colors back and forth across the sky, imagining she was controlling the green shimmer of light with her hips, rocking them gently back and forth while his fingers slowly circled, over and over. Finally, she could no longer wait. She sat up on his lap and guided him until he was fully inside her. Then she rocked her pelvis on top of him while he continued to caress her with his fingers. When the foaming orgasm gusted through her like a storm, it was not the most powerful in her memory, but gazing at the aurorae at the same time certainly made it the most magical.

But Philippe was still not satisfied.

Corrinne turned over to face and straddle him. "Should I continue to be still, good sir? Or should I move?"

Philippe licked his thumbs. His hands groped beneath the silk to cup and hold her breasts, circling the nipples with his thumbs, feeling them stiffen.

"Oh, that feels good," she whispered. The side of her face was illuminated by the shimmering lights.

"Shhhh! I will move." His hands lifted her hips slightly. He held them still and began his own long steady thrusting. "Do you like this?" he asked in a whisper.

"Oh, yes. That is so much better," she replied in a strained voice. "So. Much. Better."

They kissed, then held each other tightly while shower after shower of pleasure from their loving ways surged through their bodies.

Several hours later, when the aurorae waned, Philippe helped Corrinne walk unsteadily down the main deck and up the short steps to the helm-deck. She was dressed in white silk, wrapped in the ermine fur blanket, and carrying her wedding dress. She gently shook Captain LaTour's shoulder. He'd been sleeping in a chair, ostensibly to prevent anyone from going out on deck and disturbing the newlyweds.

"Oh...I fell asleep on watch! I should be shot! Is everything all right?"

Corrinne touched his cheek. "Everything is wonderful, Captain." She bent and kissed him on the cheek. "Thank you for this day. And this night. It was a night of *perfection*. We are going below now."

CHAPTER 42
QUEBEC CITY
NOVEMBER 1754
Bon Voyage

The next morning, Philippe broke his fast with Pierre and Henri in the galley. He was still wearing part of his uniform.

"Ya' like tha' uniform, I see."

"They are the only clothes I had out. You will cast off today?"

"Tha's my plan. But only after ya' and I and Corrinne talk aboot our future dealings. Our fur-trading business, that thing ya' and I used tah' dah' together. I think it will snow today. So gettin' back upriver quickly is prudent."

"Where is Juniata and Chesanin?" Henri asked.

"They did nah' come down on tha' second cargo sloop. So I expect they changed their minds about going with ya'. The second mate claims they intended tah' stay near the warehouse somewhere. When I get back, I will find them."

"Chesanin…was my friend."

"He still is. But Fort Niagara was their home. Going tah' Montréal was far away for them, eh? But going further on a ship? No. I will write tah' ya' and let ya' know wha' I learn. I'll take care o' them, laddie. And dinnah' be so glum. You'll likely see them again, sooner than ya' think."

Captain LaTour barged into the galley.

"Morning, lads. Captain Martin is on his way over. I think the river sloops are loaded with goods for Montréal, and we are loaded with furs. So now all we need to do is have a talk with our owners, all of them, yes? And we can make sail when the time is right. Two of the other trading frigates have already weighed anchor."

Pierre, Philippe, Corrinne, Charles VanderMeer, and the captains all collected in the dining area of Corrinne's bedroom after the bed was raised

598

and the dining table was let down. Michelle and Madeleine had stayed onboard for the night after the wedding and were with Henri and Anamosa up on deck.

Corrinne did much of the talking.

"According to the figures provided by our clerks, it appears the Dunemoore Company has had another record year. I want to compliment Pierre and the hard work of the hundreds of *coureurs de bois* who succeeded in this business despite the challenges of war with the English and the skirmishes with various Iroquois tribes, not to forget the interference of our corrupt government. The information I have from my agents in France is that fur prices have tripled because of the expansion of war with the English. That's good news for all of us. However, the war will make the transporting of furs very uncertain next year. But thanks to the investment by his lordship and heir to the Duke of Brunswick—"

"Please—" VanderMeer interjected, flushing slightly.

"—our two great trading ships now fly the flag of a neutral country. So the *Ile Royale* and *William's Queen* can now exploit new ports of call and trade in more than just furs. I think this next year will be very lucrative for all of us."

"That's only *if* I kin' get the furs tah' tha' ships, yes?"

"I have ideas on that. But first…" Corrinne handed a valise to Captain Martin and a small book.

"You will carry your cargo to the port of Terneuzen, in the Dutch Republic. In the valise, among other things, you will find the name of an agent there. Go see this man. He is expecting you and will arrange for payment and will off-load your cargo. You will have sealed missives to deliver as usual. This man can be trusted to deliver them. New cargo will be brought for you to carry. Your next port of call will be given to you by this agent. He will speak for Charles VanderMeer and myself in this regard."

"Will I call on ports in France?"

"That is unlikely until the war is over. But you will probably still carry French goods. We will arrange for agents to come to you overland at first, or until we arrange for a free trade port where our ships can rendezvous and trade cargo. But not with this first crossing."

"The book?"

"Yes. You will have one, Captain LaTour will have one, and Charles

VanderMeer will have one. I will have the other. It will be used to pass ciphered missives among us. A simple cipher. Page, paragraph, word. You will notice the printing of the book will make this less laborious to cipher or decipher these missives."

"There is no title?"

"No title and no author. It is written in French."

Corrinne did not disclose she was the author of the tiny book of seventy-two pages. And there were five copies, not four. The other copy resided with Financier Jean-Baptiste de Machault d'Arnouville. She was not going to tell anyone that.

"Terneuzen only?" Captain Martin reflected. "If we cannot visit the French ports, I will begin losing my crew."

"Because of the war, Captain, that may be inevitable. But if you need to increase crew shares to keep your most important mates with you, make that decision on your own. But the increase will come out of your share. Your profits will be increasing dramatically, so doing so may be beneficial to you."

That was a veiled warning to Captain Martin. In matters of money and trading, Corrinne de Chanaye was a hardened banker. Pierre glanced at Philippe and winked.

Captain Martin went topside to return to his ship. Captain LaTour went with him to wish him fair sailing.

Pierre, Philippe, Charles VanderMeer, and Corrinne shifted to the topic of fur trading.

Pierre indicated he thought the trapping and collections would continue, unless the armed conflicts spread too far west of the Allegheny River.

"But, tha' will not be the problem. Tha' problem will be pulling all the collections tah' tha' company trading posts for curing, and tha' biggest problem will be transporting cured goods tah' a ship. Where will the ships be?"

Corrinne nodded. "The English will begin blockading ports and seizing French flags in the spring, so I have been told. The English have a larger fleet of warships and will be supported on land by conscripts and militias from the American colonies and their Iroquois allies."

"So no French ships, then?"

"If a French trading ship is seized or sunk, you would lose all your profit."

"Blooody…! So wha' then?"

Corrinne paused. "You may have to do something you won't like."

Pierre grimaced. "Here it comes."

"Don't trade east, trade west or south."

"West? With whom?" This time, Philippe asked the question.

"West to the traders that go downriver to New Orleans. South then east to Curtiss and Johnson."

"Bloody—! Why would I do tha'? Trade with our rivals?"

"If they pay you in silver and gold, twice what you get for furs today, would you trade?"

Philippe shook his head. He would still not want to do that. "There are other things to consider. Some people depend on knowing who *we* trade with, as a matter of trust, so we are predictable to them. Sorry, Pierre, I didn't mean to speak for you."

"No, laddie. Ya' are exactly right. And why would Curtiss and Johnson pay tha' outrageous price?"

Corrinne smiled. "Because they would get three times that price if they sell your furs in the colonies or four times that price if they can transport them to Terneuzen."

"On my Dutch ships," VanderMeer offered. "It makes good business sense."

"All right. All right," Pierre said, holding up his hands.

The others knew a counter argument was brewing.

"Wha' if Curtiss and Johnson will nah' buy our furs at twice the price, eh? What if they offer half our price, eh? Wha' then?"

Corrinne smiled. "Pierre, they *will* offer twice the price you ask and maybe even more the season after that. Pemberton Curtiss is dead."

Pierre squinted at her. "Pemberton Curtiss? I know he is dead, and I hope he roasts in hell. But so wha'?"

"Well, Pemberton Curtiss owned the majority of the stock in his company, Curtiss and Johnson, sixty percent to be exact. I happen to know by their rules of partnership that upon his death all his shares will be equally distributed among the remaining shareholders in Albany. There are three other majority shareholders registered in Albany. His dead brother's wife had ten percent. His partner, Johnson, sold his shares to others six seasons ago. Other than the wife, there are only two other partners, who each own fifteen percent. Once the distribution is made, twenty to each, the other two partners will each hold thirty-five percent and will be the majority holders. And they will make all the trading decisions."

Pierre rubbed his temples. "So?"

"The other two partners are actually trading companies, one in Albany and one in Boston, with managing-directors in their respective cities. And both of those trading companies are entirely owned by a third company, with an agent representing the owner who lives somewhere near Boston."

"All right," Pierre said with a sigh. "Who is the owner of this third company?"

"Official documents list the recorded name as *C. Chanaye*. It is all legal. Paid for with real gold or real silver."

Philippe tilted back his head and smiled at the overhead. "How I love this woman."

VanderMeer and Pierre stared at her in amazement.

"When did ya' dah' all tha'?"

"When Pemberton's brother ambushed Philippe and died in the attempt, Curtiss and Jonson's other investors in the colonies started to sell their shares. So my agents in Albany and Boston began buying them up. That was three years ago. I thought it a good risk back then, in case the war with England actually came about. It just turned out better than I anticipated."

VanderMeer took off his spectacles and cleaned them with a kerchief.

"I am so very pleased someone understands all of this. May I ask what *my* role will be? Aside from increasing in wealth through no merit of my own?"

"Oh, Charles! Your role is most important. You must help me determine the most lucrative trading routes beyond Terneuzen. I am assuming you can use your, um, family's suggestions? And there must be copious Dutch tax and trading laws we will be subject to for compliance, yes?"

The artist nodded. "Yes, Mademoiselle. There are certainly those. I am not, however, good at this kind of—"

"Please, Charles, never call me *Mademoiselle* again. It must be Corinne. And *I* am very good at this kind of thing. You simply need to expose me to it, inform me who I should talk with. And I will learn Dutch, German too, I suppose, in the next few months. I already speak English."

VanderMeer looked dazed.

"Ya', wha' your feeling is right. She is rather intimidating."

Corrinne frowned at Pierre and then continued.

"While the immediate transactions are being settled, and I get this new trading company in Boston properly represented and accepted, that will take three months, maybe six at most, Pierre, you will still be trapping and collecting and curing the catch. Once the new company is properly recorded and accepted, then C. Chanaye will sell out to this new trading company, the one that owns these ships, removing my name from the particulars, except as a shareholder. That means this new Dutch company, in addition to the ships, will own Curtiss and Johnson. So, Pierre, if the trade routes through Montréal and Quebec are blocked, you can arrange a confidential trade through Curtiss and Johnson, which will probably have changed its name by then. Les Négociants Dunemoore gets paid immediately, if you like. But you may want to create a company account somewhere else. The war will complicate everything, particularly the movement of monies. And I've talked with these colonial Americans. I think these colonies will prevail to independence no matter how the English fare in this war. So, friendly relationships to some extent with the colonial traders might be good business for you to consider. And we can all celebrate when the war is over."

An awkward silence punctuated the air. Corrinne waited for Pierre to speak.

The Scotsman looked from Philippe to Corrinne, opened his mouth, shut it, then bowed his head.

Philippe touched the Scotsman's arm. "What's wrong?"

"Ya' are leaving today. I'm leaving today." His voice was thick with emotion. "Dah' ya' think…we three…we three will survive this…this war?"

Corrinne's hand went to her throat, a lump lodging there. She climbed over Philippe, uncaring of appearances, to hug Pierre tightly. Then she hit him softly on the shoulder.

"Don't you *dare*…don't you *ever* say something like that again, Pierre Dunemoore! I refuse to let you dwell on such terrible, fatalistic thoughts. Of course we are all going to survive this. You are both the best friends of my life! No offense, Charles," she added with a sniffle.

The artist's eyes appeared misty. "I…I am honored to be sitting with all of you."

VanderMeer had never seen such a close bond between three unrelated people before. He'd read the history and legend behind the symbols and the rings and the amulets. Their resemblance to the characters of this history was remarkable beyond belief. And there was no denying the demon now boxed in one of the cargo squares down below. Now, here he was, sailing with this ship—*his* ship. Except, he had one thing he had not yet told Corrinne.

I better do that now, he thought. The silence had grown prolonged because of Corrinne's outburst, and Pierre's subsequent apologizing for his pessimism. "I have something to tell all of you, if I may."

"Well, I hope tah' God it is something happy."

"Possibly. You be the judge. But it is certainly something you must all know."

They waited.

"Very well. I will try to do this with one discourse."

He placed a hand on his chest. "I, Charles VanderMeer, am not a bastard after all. The *lettres patentes* I carry are not only genuine, they name me direct heir to Duke Louis Ernest of Brunswick-Lüneburg. My father was legally married to my mother. She was the youngest daughter of eight, a minor princess of a minor German baron. So much so, she was treated like a commoner by the other royal houses. My father was very young, and she was very young and very beautiful. They met, and married for love— uncommon for one of his station. All the royal families involved—and there were several, with many crossed lines by marriage, as usual—all these families were outraged. They sought to annul the union. But my mother became pregnant too quickly, I suspect she was pregnant before the wedding vows had been said, and before they could arrange the annulment. To the combined relief of my father's family, my mother died giving birth to me. My father offered to deny his marriage to her in trade for my life. But the record of this marriage still exists. When he gave me the *lettres patentes* at the age of sixteen, he said I could use them only once. I could choose the purpose, and he would support it, but on one condition. I must immediately abdicate as heir to his title, or it is likely I would be assassinated by at least a dozen other members of the Dutch royal family. So, I have written my father a missive that is now being carried by Captain Martin, telling him I bought these two ships as his direct heir. And I have asked for the Duke's permission and direction on how to abdicate so I do not embarrass or cause him, well, problems. I revealed my true lineage to the Governor, that I was not the *bastard* people presumed me to be, prior to our meeting with him, which might help explain why the Governor-General, Marquis Duquesne, was so immediately and graciously cooperative…with all due respect to you, Corrinne. Within six months this would be well-known to many others anyway; as I said, Captain Martin is delivering my missive. The Dutch Republic is neutral and the French would no doubt like to have the Dutch look favorably upon France while they are at war with the English, which I am sure the Governor-General saw as a strategic advantage, just now. But Governor Duquesne does *not* know of my agreement to abdicate. No one knows of this, except for my father, the Duke. And now the three of you. But you are my partners, and I will trust all of you to keep this secret. Hopefully, you will come to regard me with the same friendship and trust as the three of you have so generously permitted me to see. But henceforth, for probably the next year, until the flurry of missives my impulsive ship acquisition will no doubt engender, and I get direction from my father, I must permit people to acknowledge me as the legitimate heir to the Duke of Brunswick."

The artist observed their reactions to his revelations were not unlike if he had just revealed a third eye growing in the center of his chest.

"That's all I was going to say," he prodded.

Corrinne spoke first. "So you are *not* a bastard, whose father is going to grant him a favor. You are, in fact, the *direct heir,* whose father is going to endorse this transaction?"

Philippe spoke next. "Let me understand this clearly. If your father died for some reason, right now, *you* would officially be recognized as the Duke of Brunswick?"

"Well…God forbid that…and that thought had not occurred to me… and it is not something I wish to contemplate…but yes, I suppose I would."

"Bloody, bleedin', hell! Apologies, your lordship. But to think, my friend, Charles, tha' artist, *is* a real duke-tah-be! I am honored…just tah' drink with ya'! Which I have!"

Corrinne's eyes brightened. "And that makes the *Falcon Queen*, now *William's Queen*, of course, Charles' *flagship*! Isn't that marvelous? And we must introduce you as Lord VanderMeer, heir to the Duchy of Brunswick, when we get to Boston."

"Uhhhh, I'm not sure that is a good idea, Corrinne," VanderMeer protested.

Corrine de Chanaye's mind, however, was already churning with a flood of new possibilities.

Michelle watched the two veteran sea captains embrace before Captain Martin departed to boat back to the *Ile Royale*.

"Those two men see one another once a year, if they are lucky. But they appear to have strong respect and affection for each other. Strange breed of men. An unspoken sense of *fraternité* exists in their hearts, yes?"

Madeleine smiled politely, but did not respond.

Michelle could tell the girl was very unhappy about something. Even at the wedding, she had been very reserved. Michelle turned to her and took both of her hands.

"Madeleine, I am so happy you agreed to live with me in Quebec, or that house could end up being a very large and lonely place. But what is troubling you? Do you not want to live with me?"

"Oh, it is not that, Mademoiselle …"

"Stop! It's not *Sister* or *mademoiselle*, it will be Michelle. I want us to friends."

Madeleine took a deep breath then began. "I am afraid to tell you because it is about Henri."

"Never be afraid to talk with me about Henri. I know about what happened between the two of you at Saint Ouen's Church."

"You do?"

"Yes. And that might as well be a thousand years ago for all the things that have happened to Henri and me since leaving Rouen. He is not the innocent child hiding behind the altar anymore. Far from it. He has fought and had to kill grown men. He was abused and tortured. He walked across the wilderness with only a wolf as his friend. He fought and killed ferocious wild animals. But for all of that, deep inside, he is still Henri."

"But when that little girl attacked me…"

"Her name is Anamosa. Henri has saved her life on more than one occasion. Her mother died recently, and he has been taking care of her. And Anamosa loves him, obviously. The culture of these people is different from ours, in some ways hard to understand, in other ways better. She loves

Henri and considers him, well, her *property*. She sees you as a rival. It is ridiculous that a girl so young sees you like that, but that is their way. But, I assure you, Henri still remembers his time with you at Saint Ouen's. He's spoken to me of you. He had very few good memories of his time growing up there. You were the happiest."

Madeleine looked over her shoulder at Henri and Anamosa standing at the rail of the ship. Henri was pointing and talking of something he saw.

"At Saint Ouen's, Henri was my friend. He…he was my only friend. He cared about me. He *convinced* Father Cortois to rescue and bring me to New France! That was unbelievable! I could not wait for him to come to Montréal. I was so happy to see him. And he tried to see me too, before Corrinne was abducted. I only wanted to talk with him because I missed him terribly. He won't even look at me now. And today he will be sailing away forever. So…I am sad."

Michelle placed an arm around the girl's shoulders. "Listen, Madeleine. Two things. First, I am Henri's mother. And I will *definitely* be seeing him again and seeing him often. It may be difficult because of the war. According to Captain LaTour, sailing can take two weeks to get to Boston, depending on the weather. On a ship like the *Queen*, maybe faster by a week. Hard canoeing and portaging overland may take four to six weeks according to Philippe. But Henri can send letters by ship. Second, Henri will talk with you right now if you will approach him. Tell him you were scared when Anamosa came at you with a knife. He will understand. Say you're sorry for what you said about her. Then tell him everything you just told me about how you felt at Saint Ouen's Church. And be patient with his answers. He is growing from a boy into a man. He will seem naïve to you, and that's because he *is* naïve in many ways. Be patient with him. Ask him to write to you. And when he comes to visit *me*, you will be there too, *yes*?"

Madeleine looked over at Henri and Anamosa.

"She won't let me near him."

Michelle laughed. "I will occupy little Anamosa for a while. Wait here. When you see me go below deck with her, walk over to Henri and say hello. Go *slowly* with him. And everything will be fine. When you see me appear back on deck, say good-bye as if you will see him tomorrow. *Bientôt, oui*? Because you will."

Madeleine watched Michelle walk over and take Anamosa in her arms, nuzzling and cooing to the girl. They went down below.

Madeleine carefully approached Henri.

And then she did exactly what Michelle told her to do. It was one of the most wonderful experiences of her life…and his life too. When Michelle appeared back on deck, Madeleine smiled at Henri.

"It was so good to see you again. I will write to you, yes?"

"*Oui!*"

When Captain LaTour went below, he noticed Corrinne's eyes were red and teary.

"All right, what have I missed?"

"Nothing," Corrinne said. "We've just been discussing how to merge our fur-trading business with Dutch shipping laws, taxes, government regulations, things like that."

Captain LaTour sensed otherwise, but let it go.

"Such topics make me cry too. But we will be weighing anchor today to start our journey, and the start of a voyage is always a happy time for me, particularly this one, with my newly married guests, and Charles VanderMeer, the great artist."

"Tha' would be your lordship tah' us, common folk," Pierre added. "He's the bloody heir to the Duke o' Brunswick."

"God's balls!" La Tour's face split into a wide grin, and then he straightened. "Well…your lordship, I do have something to ask you. That heavy wooden box I stowed for you on centerline yesterday, in the second cargo square?"

The others traded quick glances.

"Yes, Captain? Is there something wrong?"

"Not exactly, but some in my crew are superstitious. They claim this *box* is making, well, strange noises."

"What kind of noises?" Corrinne asked evenly.

Captain LaTour scratched his head and looked uncomfortable. "My lady, they claim they hear grunting sounds, loud clicks, and snaps coming from it. But I went down early this morning. I did not hear anything unusual. And the hull of a ship will easily and frequently make all of those noises under the stresses and strains of the sea, though not often at anchor. But what I *did* notice, when investigating at the behest of my crew, was that this box is very warm to the touch. *Too warm.* So I feel I must ask, Monsieur VanderMeer, what is inside of it?"

Charles VanderMeer cleared his throat. "Captain, I will tell you, but I prefer to keep this confidential."

Corrinne began to protest, but Philippe touched her arm.

"The box is actually a coffin of sorts. I am moving the remains of someone at the request of others. It will leave your ship when we reach Boston. The box is probably warm in the way wet hay gets warm inside a barn. I will leave it to you to imagine why. But it is a common phenomena. I would hesitate to share this with your crew, as their superstitions might come to other conclusions. If you would like to make up some other story, I will support it."

The captain frowned. "A coffin, you say? With someone dead inside?"

"Yes," VanderMeer assured him.

"But it is very *square*. Was he blown up somehow; the body is in pieces?"

"Indeed, Captain. The body is in pieces. I apologize for this macabre inconvenience. But, it will be put ashore when we reach Boston."

"Was this from the war? Was he a soldier?"

"Not exactly a soldier as we know soldiers today. But the man was a warrior and died in battle."

Captain LaTour nodded. "So he is rotting inside that box right now. Is that what you are telling me?"

"Essentially, that is what I am telling you."

The captain looked at Pierre, Philippe, and Corrinne. "And all of you are aware of this?"

"All of us attended the funeral, Captain," Corrinne replied. "This person has relations in Boston. I intend to inter the body there."

"He must be someone important."

"*Very* important," Pierre agreed.

The captain exhaled deeply, coming to a decision. "All right. I will tell my crew, it is indeed the coffin of a man killed in battle, but blown to pieces. And that Lady de Chanaye is returning his remains to a family in Boston. And if they ask me why the box is warm, I will tell them the truth. His remains are rotting inside that box."

As the midday approached, the starboard-side river sloop cast off from the *Queen* to begin its journey back to Montréal. Pierre was still seeing to the last few items he would take on the portside sloop. In truth, the Scotsman was having trouble accepting he would be returning without Philippe or Corrinne, so he prolonged even simple tasks. With the first sloop on its way, the *Queen*'s harbor launch made ready to carry Michelle and Madeleine back to the Quebec City wharves.

Philippe and Corrinne waited, arm in arm, by the brow ladder for them to make their good-byes. Corrinne had some good wines from Bordeaux and a basket of fine cheeses that she gave to Michelle as a gift. Corrinne told Michelle she'd asked Monsieur Jordaine to establish an account for her at the bank.

"The account is under the name *Michelle de Propei*, with enough money to cover all the household expenses for at least a year. And next year, we'll see how you are faring."

Henri was on the foredeck with his bow, looking at the huge stacks of arrows from four different native tribes that Captain LaTour said would bring a high price no matter what port they stopped in. Henri had obtained his permission to loose a few of each off the bow to see how straight they flew and how far.

He noticed his mother looking at him. He set down his bow and came over to the brow, a look of worry and sadness on his face.

Michelle held her boy close and whispered to him. "Now, don't be too concerned, Henri. I will be in this nice house in Quebec City and you can come to see me as often as you can. I will be safe inside the great citadel and hospital. We can write letters to one another, yes? But you must go back to school as soon as you can. Philippe agrees with me on this, and Corrinne will find you excellent tutors, I am sure. You must learn to speak the English you've learned already, as if you were born there. You will see that I am right."

"I don't want to be parted from you," he said in a strained voice.

She placed her hands on his cheeks, cupping his face, and looked into his eyes. "We are not going to be that far from each other. Just a month of hard travel. That's all. And I want you to come see me, or I will come to see you. Now, no tears. The sailors are watching you, yes?"

Henri cleared his throat and nodded. They traded kisses. Michelle scooped up Anamosa to say good-bye and gave Henri a chance to do the same with Madeleine.

Madeleine took both his hands in hers. "I will wait for you to come see me again," Madeleine said. "Maybe on your next birthday? Or the one after that, yes? I will have a special present for you," she whispered in his ear. Then she chastely kissed both of his cheeks.

Henri blushed. "I will write you letters," was all he could think to say.

"*À bientôt*, Henri."

Madeleine walked down the brow and was helped into the launch. Henri watched her departure moodily.

Corrinne de Chanaye had taken note of their parting, and she was not smiling.

Michelle put Anamosa back down. Anamosa promptly took hold of Henri's hand and stuck her tongue out at Madeleine. Upon reaching the cargo launch, Madeleine stuck her tongue out at Anamosa in return, though this went unnoticed by those standing by.

Seeds were sown by those simple childish gestures that would manifest many years later.

Michelle was next. She caressed Philippe's face with both hands. "*You did well*, Snow Hair. I will be happy here. And I expect you to bring Henri to see me as often as possible."

"I promise."

"And I expect you to hold Corrinne when she cries and kiss away her tears and love her whenever she asks you to, yes?"

"I promise."

Corrinne had tears dripping down her cheeks. "I...I've never had a friend like you. I will always treasure our talks. And I will make sure Philippe keeps all of his promises, particularly the second one. And when this war business gets out of the way, you can come to see me, or I will come to see you. And I will make sure Henri studies hard, and Anamosa too. We can raise them together, perhaps? And perhaps Anamosa can live with you too for a time?"

"I would be overjoyed!"

"Then consider it a promise from me."

Corrinne and Michelle traded kisses, then Michelle stepped carefully down the brow, Corrinne's confidential mail in her bag.

With the passengers onboard, the launch cast off and the four crewmen began rowing toward the wharf. The passengers of each vessel waved at one another as the distance widened.

The first mate standing on the helmdeck was looking through his long glass. A naval launch had just undocked from the *Champion Mer*. The bow was pointed toward the *Queen*.

"Captain, the *Champion Mer* is sending someone over to us."

La Tour had been standing next to Charles VanderMeer watching the good-byes.

"What?" He walked up to the helmdeck and took the glass from the mate. What he saw made him frown. He kept the glass and went back amidships where Corrinne, Philippe, Pierre, and Charles VanderMeer were gathered.

"We may have a problem," he told them. He handed the glass to Philippe. "I'd hoped we would have sailed by now to avoid this, but there are three marines, an army officer, a naval lieutenant, and Intendant Bigôt aboard that launch, I am sorry to say. And the *Champion Mer* has hoisted its prepare-to-be-boarded pennant."

"Prepare to be boarded?" Charles VanderMeer stepped forward to the brow ladder. He spoke with an unexpected air of authority. "Captain, no one may board this ship without my permission."

Captain LaTour's eyes widened. "Uh, yes, your lordship." He turned to Philippe and Corrinne. "Maybe you should go below?"

"I will not!" Corrinne refused. "Intendant Bigôt is no threat to me or any of us, for that matter. Not anymore."

Philippe and Pierre looked at each other with uncertainly.

The Scotsman was standing next to Henri.

"Who is that?" Henri asked, curious.

"Tha' man in tha' middle seat is a vicious little turd named François Bigôt."

Unnoticed by Pierre, at hearing the name of the man who tortured Corrinne, Henri's expression changed dramatically, becoming hard and deadly. He gripped his bow and slowly notched an arrow.

The launch from the *Champion Mer* bumped gently against the brow platform. Securing lines were heaved to a crewman on *William's Queen*, who tied them off to a brow cleat.

Major Péan stepped onto the lower platform first. He came to attention and delivered a crisp salute.

"Request permission to come aboard."

"State your business," Captain LaTour replied.

"Intendant François Bigôt is here to deliver a message from Governor-General Duquesne of farewell and safe voyage to Lord VanderMeer."

The captain looked at VanderMeer for direction.

VanderMeer nodded.

"You may come aboard."

Major Péan came up the eight steps of the brow ladder first. He saluted the captain and made a short bow to Charles VanderMeer. "Your lordship."

The major turned and made a sweeping bow to Lady de Chanaye and Philippe Gerrard.

"My heartfelt congratulations to you both on your wedding," he said to them with sincerity. "I am very pleased for you. I wish I could have attended." He shook his head slightly and smiled. "What an extraordinary difference contained in a single day, eh?"

The next up the ladder was a marine, who moved slowly, one hand extended behind him to Intendant Bigôt, coming next, struggling on some crutches, with a small valise draped over one shoulder. The intendant refused any assistance as he labored over each step, a grimace on his face, until he reached the top. Another marine followed behind him but was constrained when the intendant stopped just in front of the top step.

Intendant Bigôt took a few moments to recover his breath. Then he straightened and made a deep bow to Charles VanderMeer.

"Your lordship, I am François Bigôt, Intendant of the Viceroyalty of New France. I bring written greetings from Governor-General, Marquis Duquesne."

"You may proceed," VanderMeer replied, his voice conveying annoyed aristocratic arrogance.

From eight paces away, Pierre gave an amused smirk to Philippe, who himself wondered why it seemed as if the artist had spoken this way for decades.

By happenstance, the participants were standing in a semicircle, in an almost ceremonial arrangement. The intendant faced Charles VanderMeer, separated by two paces. Captain LaTour stood at attention two paces to the intendant's left. Behind Charles VanderMeer, and to his right, stood Corrinne and Philippe, arm in arm. Major Péan stood stiffly at attention to the intendant's right with a marine at his side; the marine's musket held straight, in a present arms' position. The other marine was behind the intendant on the steps of the brow. He was, nevertheless, also standing at attention, his musket at present arms.

The intendant opened a side clasp and leather flap on the valise and withdrew a single roll of paper, which he unfurled. He cleared his throat and took a deep breath.

"To his Lordship Charles VanderMeer, from Michel-Ange Duquesne de Menneville, Marquis Duquesne. It is with great honor the Viceroyalty of New France has received your gracious visit. I found your company most enjoyable and our discussions productive. On behalf of King Louis XV, let me express the fervent wish of France to continue this dialogue of felicity and goodwill with the Dutch Republic. With humble optimism, please extend my best wishes to the Duke of Brunswick-Lüneburg in the hope a reciprocal visit may be granted to me upon my return to France next year.

"I will trust and pray for Lord VanderMeer's safe and pleasant deliverance to his next destination. May you enjoy great success in the coming year. In the name of King Louis, and with my deepest gratitude and appreciation. Michel-Ange Duquesne de Menneville, Marquis Duquesne, Governor-General, *vice-royauté de nouvelle-France*."

Intendant Bigôt made a slight bow and extended the parchment.

Charles VanderMeer accepted it. "You may tell the Marquis, I will see his missive delivered to my father and will mention his hospitality was both gracious and appropriate."

"*Merci*, your lordship." François Bigôt straightened. "I've been told that where I stand is as if I were standing on Dutch soil. Is that correct?"

Philippe, Pierre, and Henri reacted as if they had heard a predatory growl.

Major Péan turned toward the intendant, his expression one of shock.

Charles VanderMeer said nothing in reply, but his expression changed to one of insulted anger.

Unheedingly, Bigôt continued. "This very spot I stand is indeed the Dutch Republic? Well, then, as a private citizen outside of the land and laws of France, let me present my personal message." He reached into his valise and withdrew the same pistol Corrinne had pointed at him in his office in Montréal. He pointed it at her.

"My wedding present, *whore!*"

What occurred next happened in seconds.

Major Péan screamed *"No!"* and slammed his hand beneath Bigôt's pistol to foul his aim an instant before the pistol fired.

Henri Gerrard released an arrow at the intendant as the pistol discharged. It struck Bigôt at an angle on the chest. The flint arrowhead shattered and ricocheted harmlessly off the metal breastplate the intendant wore hidden beneath his shirt and waistcoat.

Philippe turned right to cover Corrinne with his body just before the pistol discharged. The ball struck his head. Corrinne shrieked wildly as they both fell back on the deck, Philippe's body limp atop hers, his hair burning and smoking from the ball.

The arrow had struck Bigôt at an angle, the force of it spinning the intendant sideways, to the left, and off balance. Henri's second arrow whizzed by Bigôt's right ear, missing it by millimeters as the intendant tumbled down the brow into the arms of the second marine who fell backward, both ending up in a pile at the bottom of the steps by the *Champion Mer*'s launch. The marine rolled the intendant into the bottom of the launch.

Major Péan struck down the musket of the other marine who had raised it toward Henri. It discharged into the deck. Then he spread his arms wide and started shouting.

"Stop! Stop! *Stop!*"

Captain LaTour, arms spread wide in front of Charles VanderMeer, yelling *"Stop!"* as well.

Pierre tackled Henri to the deck as he notched his third arrow, intent on firing at the intendant from the rail. It took all of Pierre's strength to restrain the boy.

Henri growled as anger surged within him. *"Get off of me!"*

Major Péan looked at Charles VanderMeer helplessly. "The intendant has lost his wits, your lordship! This was not intentional!"

"This was an act of *war*, Major! He has killed a guest of the Dutch

Republic!"

VanderMeer took the Governor's missive, shredded it, and threw it over the side. He pointed at Philippe being cradled and rocked in Corrinne's wailing arms.

"*This* is what I shall report to the Duke of Brunswick! Get *off* this ship."

A devastated Major Péan gestured to the other marine to go down the brow. He saluted Captain LaTour stiffly.

"This was not supposed to happen."

Captain LaTour spat the words in the officer's face, "Get off my ship!"

When Major Péan stepped into the launch, he pummeled Intendant Bigôt with his fists until the two marines restrained him. The naval lieutenant hurriedly cast off and had his rowers begin their return to the *Champion Mer.*

At the first sound of gunfire, Victorio threw down the piece of sail canvas he was sewing, grabbed his surgeon's bag, and laid topside through the forward hatch. He first went to Pierre and Henri, whom he spotted lying tangled on the forward deck.

Pierre shouted, pointing and waving. "We are fine! There! Back there!"

Victorio ran to Philippe Gerrard cradled in Lady de Chanaye's arms. She was wailing and crying, "*No!*" He saw a tiny wisp of smoke rise from the hair of the *coureur de bois.* Blood stained her fingers.

"Holy Madonna!" the surgeon whispered.

Victorio knelt at her side and carefully examined Philippe's head, pulling aside the heavily singed hair. The ball had only creased the skull, just barely, as it streaked past, the intendant's deadly aim spoiled by Major Péan's hand. Its speed and fire was enough to break the skin and burn through the hair, but it did not appear fatal. He quickly turned Philippe's head and opened an eyelid with his fingers. The pupils contracted.

"He is alive, Mademoiselle," he told her ardently. "He is alive! The wound is minor. Look. It is only a crease. Bloody, yes. Scalp wounds are always bloody. I think he is just knocked senseless. Let me have him. Someone bring me cold water and towels!"

"What?" Corrinne looked up at Pierre and Henri who had rushed forward to be with her. They had heard Victorio's words.

Pierre looked up and mouthed a prayer of thanks, and then he took Corrinne gently by her shoulders.

"Let Victorio have him, lassie. Let him go."

Corrinne let Pierre pull her back a few paces. Her sobbing diminished but did not stop. Agitated, her hands shook violently. Pierre hugged her.

"Philippe's going to be all right, lassie. Dinnah' worry! He will be all right. You heard Victorio."

But Corrinne remained terrified as she watched the surgeon, trembling all over, her teeth chattering, any further words she uttered gibberish.

"Bring some blankets!" Pierre shouted.

Victorio applied cold, wet towels to the wound on the top of Philippe's head, to staunch the bleeding, and wiped another cold towel around his neck and over his face, trying to rouse him back to consciousness. He listened to Philippe's heartbeat. It was steady and strong. Another good sign.

Suddenly, Philippe's eyes opened. He blinked once.

"Corrinne?" he rasped.

This time, her scream was one of joy as she threw herself over him and kissed his face repeatedly.

"Oh, my love! My love! My love."

Philippe replied to her kisses with repeated heavy groans until Corrinne realized she was pressing her elbow accidentally against the knife wound in his shoulder.

Philippe was taken below and put to bed, his wound cleaned, his head bandaged. Corrinne did not leave his side.

Later in the afternoon, Doctor La Galissonière boated out from the wharf to offer his services, which were refused. The doctor also delivered a personal apology to Charles VanderMeer from Governor Duquesne, conveying the Governor's shock and outrage over the actions of Intendant Bigôt, and his deepest apologies and sympathies to Lady Corrinne de Chanaye and Captain Gerrard.

"He intends to personally come out to you tomorrow morning to express this himself, if you will allow him to board."

Philippe spent the rest of the day and night in the caring arms of his wife, warm and secure, below decks in her stateroom. Mathilde doted on both of them.

Captain LaTour decided to wait one more day before weighing anchor to be certain Philippe's condition did not change. Pierre waited too, spending his time with Henri and Anamosa, calming them both.

Michelle boated out in the ship's launch to see Philippe. She went below without challenge, of course, to find Philippe lying in Corrinne's arms, his head heavily bandaged. They both smiled at her appearance.

She sat on the side of the bed and took Philippe's hand in hers.

"Oh my sweet, sweet Philippe," she said, shaking her head in sad sympathy. "Is there even one spot on your head anymore that does not have a wound or a scar of some kind?"

Philippe appeared to think about this. "Well, I think the right side, here, near the top." He pointed.

Michelle gaped at him. "That was not meant as a question, Philippe." She looked at Corrinne.

"He's all right, Michelle," Corrinne said with a smile of assurance. "That's just the general nonsensical confusion he seems to suffer from constantly."

Philippe frowned. "What?"

They continued talking for a short time before Michelle said her farewells again.

True to his word, Governor-General Duquesne came alongside *William's Queen* and was welcomed aboard by Charles VanderMeer, who thanked the Governor for his personal visit. He indicated that Lady de Chanaye sent her regards but preferred to stay below with her husband who was still in bed, healing from his head wound. The nature or seriousness of the wound was not disclosed.

Governor-General Duquesne gave Lord VanderMeer a new copy of his missive to the Duke of Brunswick with additional words of apology. He also mentioned he'd ordered the *Champion Mer* to escort *William's Queen* until they had cleared the river, just to be sure the transit was made safely.

Lord VanderMeer thanked the Governor for his personal attention and promised to deliver the new missive to his father.

"Much could be gained in the future by allowing the Marquis Duquesne to escape this gross embarrassment," Charles would later explain to Corrinne and Philippe.

Corrinne reluctantly admitted he was right.

Captain LaTour announced to everyone the ship would weigh anchor and start its journey precisely at midday.

Philippe rose from his bed and, with Corrinne at his side, bade an emotional farewell to Pierre.

"I will see you west of the Allegheny sometime in the spring," Philippe promised quietly.

"Doing wha'?"

"I don't know. But I will not sit around in an English city for very long, I promise you that."

"All right. Then I will be at Fort Duquesne before April. If ya' are nah' there, I will leave ya' a message at the store where ya' kin' find me."

Corrinne was next. Pierre embraced her.

"*Unng*! Pierre," Corrinne gasped, "you're squeezing too hard."

The Scotsman knelt down before her and took her hands.

"Lassie," he said softly, "God bestowed a great blessing on me, tha' I should have known ya'. And I kinnah' imagine wha' my world will be like without ya'. No cheer. No color. Much sadder, I think."

Corrinne kissed his cheeks, lips, his bald head, and hugged him again.

"I never imagined this would hurt so much, to say good-bye. I owe you my life, Pierre. I shall miss you terribly." She frowned. "Will you come to see us in Boston, or wherever we go? I will send a ship to bring you, if you like!"

"A ship?" He looked at Philippe. "I told ya'. Just like bloody Cleopatra." Pierre stood up. "Like ya' said. We will see each other when the war is over."

His voice still betrayed uncertainty over the future. Pierre gently grasped Philippe's right shoulder.

"Take good care o' her, laddie. Treat her like the royalty she is."

Pierre Dunemoore cast off the river sloop and started his journey back to Montréal.

Corrinne and Philippe held one another as the sloop raised sail and was soon out of sight. Pierre's words about surviving the war haunted them both.

At precisely noon, *William's Queen* weighed anchor. The new, brilliant white sails unfurled, heralding her departure.

Corrinne and Philippe stood on the bridge with Captain LaTour while he rang the ship's bell slowly, over and over, saying farewell to the people of Quebec City. In his heart, the veteran sea captain was not certain he would ever see Cap Diamant again.

By the Governor's order, Quebec City's church bells began tolling their farewell response.

Corrinne pressed her face into Philippe's neck.

The *Champion Mer* fired ten guns in salute to the famous trading frigate as it began its northeast transit. Then the French warship weighed anchor and followed behind the Dutch ship for three days until they were clear of the river.

"Come right and steer south-southeast," Captain LaTour ordered his helmsman.

"Come right, steer south-southeast! Aye, sir," Henri Gerrard answered.

The *Queen* turned swiftly and with the might of a northwest wind, her sails billowed. They seemed to fly across the waters.

Anamosa was standing next to Henri, one hand holding her dolls, the other gripping his belt. Cold sea spray sprinkling her smiling face. Up in the blue sky in front of the ship, she saw a large white eagle flying in the same direction.

"Ahh-ree! Look!"

END OF BOOK 2

EPILOGUE
ROUEN, FRANCE
NOVEMBER 1754
Manoir Saint-Yon

Liénard de la Montagne, Marquis de Propei crawled around the dank, filthy floor of the cell where he'd been confined in an asylum specifically created for aristocrats deemed *out of favor* with the King and further declared insane by the Church. He had lost an enormous amount of weight since his imprisonment, and so quickly, the skin on his body hung in folds like moldy sheets. He was weak from lack of food and water, but felt no real pain. In fact, except for his frailty, he felt better than he had in years.

As he did every day, he chewed into his arm and squeezed the cut to make it ooze blood. He was using a finger to renew the bloodstained symbols he'd drawn on all the walls. With a trembling hand, he moved an index finger as if it were a brush, daubing on the blood from his bleeding vein to the faded line on the wall. The nails of both his hands were shredded, bitten to the quick, though they had stopped bleeding weeks ago. Not enough blood flowed anymore.

But this was the only way to complete the preparation for his escape.

It must be tonight, the night messenger had told him. *The other one is dead.*

In the Marquis' dream of the previous night, the messenger revealed the demise of Helmut Colbért in that far away land, slain by the hand of descendant spawn from the house of Adaelric.

You must free your spirit while there is time, the messenger urged. *Choose another.*

From the first day he was incarcerated, the Marquis had methodically approached all of his jailers, wishing to befriend the one least likely to earn the others' suspicion. The various gruels he was given to eat were pushed into the cell though a slot at the bottom of the cell door, an iron slide covered the opening, little wider and higher than the dirty clay bowl passing through it. The routine was simple. The prisoner slid the old bowl out, and the guard pushed a new bowl in. No talking or one forfeited their meal. The Marquis had lost many meals experimenting with the guards, in order to learn which ones would talk, and who might be corruptible. Fortunately, the most talkative was also the most corruptible. His name was Joseph Laval, the bastard son of a scullery maid working at the asylum. Twenty-three, uneducated, but clever, Joseph learned early in his work that a guard could gather riches by passing messages to and from the cells of the wealthy prisoners. Week after week, the Marquis carefully gave Joseph rings from his hands and other coinage he had had on his person when he was first put into the cell, with the guise of obtaining better food, more deceitfully to gain his trust. Through Joseph, the Marquis quickly found out others outside of the asylum, with great wealth, were paying more to have his rations cut so low, he would starve to death.

So be it, he thought. *I'll escape another way. The way of the messenger.* And with the messenger, it was always about blood.

With the fresh blood applied to the most powerful symbol, the Marquis sagged wearily to the side of the cell door. It had not been opened since he was placed inside the ten-by-ten-foot square, twelve-foot-tall cell, the walls, ceiling, and floor thick stone. Other than the slot at the bottom of the bolted iron door, the only other openings were a hole in the center of the floor the size of a fist, long ago clogged and overflowing with offal. The other was a barred window near the ceiling in one corner, a foot square, just enough to allow air and swarms of biting insects passage. The Marquis didn't mind the insects. He found them as tasty as they found him.

It won't be long now, he thought.

The Marquis had been saving his sigil ring as the final enticement. It carried his coat of arms and was set with a bloodstone ruby gem. Joseph Laval had already asked about it.

The Marquis scratched at his gums to get them ready, to make them bleed, one of his rotting teeth coming loose in the process. He flicked the broken tooth across the cell, closed his eyes to rest, enjoying the taste of blood, and centered his remaining strength, waiting patiently with all the other prisoners for the guards to bring their supper.

Footsteps? The Marquis' eyes opened. *Yes!* He knew the sounds of Joseph's plodding walk.

A red glow began to emanate from the blood-painted symbols on the walls of his cell. Just enough light to see around the otherwise pitch-black interior.

The Marquis took off his ring and placed it on the floor, about a foot inside the slot. Then he got up on his knees and positioned his face above the slot hole. He heard the familiar scratchy shuffling and rattling as Joseph pushed food into the other cells and retrieved the used dishes. Finally, he stopped before the Marquis' door.

The iron sleeve slid open. Light poured in through the slot. A few seconds of silence followed.

"Monsieur le Marquis? Push out your bowl."

"Joseph? Is that you?" the Marquis whispered in a voice pretending at great sickness.

"*Oui*, Monsieur. Hurry. Your bowl."

"Joseph," he whispered. "I am dying. I do not want to eat anymore. But I want to give you a gift for all your kindness. Take my signet ring. You may have it. I've placed it on the floor in front of the door. Take it. It's yours."

The Marquis watched the intensity of the light coming through the slot dampen as the guard pressed his cheek against the floor to peer into the slot.

Yes, Joseph! There's the ring. Reach in and take it.

"I cannot reach it. Push it closer."

The Marquis de Propei did not respond. He braced himself.

Seconds passed. Joseph's arm snaked through the hole to seize the prize. But the Marquis had been waiting for this. He grabbed the guard's hand and arm, twisting it upward until more of the arm extended through the slot all the way to the elbow. He pressed a knee on Joseph's elbow near the slot so it could not be easily withdrawn.

Joseph Laval's screams of terror brought three other guards running. The other cells erupted in a cacophony of yelling and screaming, cell doors rattling.

Ahhh! Freedom, he thought stroking the smooth, white skin.

The Marquis knew he had less than a minute. He bent back the hand stretching the skin on the wrist and bit into the flesh and veins with his bleeding broken teeth, wrenching his mouth back and forth to make the lacerations deep, mixing the blood from his mouth with the blood spurting from the guard's wound. He could feel his spirit begin to invade the guard's body. It was a pleasurable feeling.

The guards tried yanking on Joseph's feet to pull the arm free.

"He's eating my arm!" Laval shrieked.

Joseph Laval's horrible howls of pain panicked the guards.

"Unlock the door," the *surveillant* of the asylum shouted.

One of them readied a truncheon. Another fumbled at the ring of keys at his waist. As the proper key was inserted into the rusted lock, Joseph Laval's arm was released. Despite what the Marquis had done to him, Joseph still clutched the signet ring in his palm. He quickly slipped it into a pocket. Then screaming, he held up the bloody limb.

"Christ! Look what he did! Oh, God, it hurts!"

The other guards recoiled in revulsion. The arm looked as if it had been chewed by a rabid animal. It dripped with blood, flecks of foam, and gluey saliva. Joseph wiped it on his clothes, and dislodged two rotted teeth from the cuts.

"Seal up the door," the *surveillant* ordered. "The Marquis just had his last meal."

After a week of depriving food and water, the Marquis' cell was unlocked. Six armed guards entered with torches. What they found on the floor and walls was so disturbing they fetched a priest, who ordered the cell burned out and sealed. Oil was poured in on the floor. A torch thrown in, and the cell's iron door locked and barricaded with bags of sand. The fire burned for two days, smoke billowing from the tiny vent, a smell so foul the occupants of the cells above and to either side died, strangled somehow.

When they finally entered the Marquis' cell again, no trace of the body remained.

Joseph Laval left Manoir Saint-Yon. He was seen later that day, his arm bandaged, dressed in traveling clothes, walking out the Rouen gate. The townspeople who saw him claimed Joseph's face had a haunted expression, his eyes unfriendly.

Understandable, the people told one another, for one who worked at *that* asylum.

In a new town, in a beggar's bed, beset with fever, the night visitor came to Joseph Laval's dreams and hissed.

You will serve me.

Glossary

This glossary of names is provided to assist the reader in the pronunciation as the author intended them to be pronounced. Some of the Indian names were invented by the author and have no root origin or meaning. Other names were found from reference materials. Those Indian names that were invented are marked with an asterisk; as the name is invented, so was the meaning. The pronunciation of all the names is shown phonetically. While there is debate as to the correct pronunciation of some of the names, the sound of the name depicted below is how the author "hears" them.

Chittaqua (Chi-tock´-qwah) • "one lost in the wilderness"

CHARACTERS FROM THE GHOST EAGLE

Prologue

Adaelric*	(Ah-del-rick) • Celtic Warlord of Normandie
Aermorgen*	(Air–morgan) • Danish warlord of Normandie
Brevelaer*	(Brev-lahr) • Catholic bishop of Normandie and Brittany
Daeniel	(Daniel) • high priest of the Druid sect in Normandie
Maive	(May-eve) • daughter of Lord Aermorgen, wife to Lord Adaelric
Vaelblez*	(Vall-blez) • warlord of Normandie and practitioner of the black arts

The Ghost Eagle

Achipan*	(Ahh-key´-pawn) • "diving hawk" • one of Chittaqua's twin sons who becomes a shaman
Allegheny River	(Al-lay-gay´-nee) • city, river, lake, county • origin unknown, possibly Delaware words *welhikwanna* and *oolikhanne* for "fine river" or "beautiful river," another interpretation is "laughing motion"
Anamosa	(Ah-nah-mho´-sah) • Sauk name meaning "white fawn" • Okeanneh's daughter by an unknown French fur trader (not Philippe)
Beauharnois, Antoine	(Awn-twan Bow-arn-wha) • Jesuit missionary and monsignor of the French fortifications on Lake Erie and Lake Ontario
Benoit, Jean-Claude	(Jon-clawed Ben-wha) • commandant of Fort Niagara, later Colonel Contrecoeur's second-in-command
Bigôt, Francois	The Intendant of New France. Second in power behind the Governor, in charge of all government administration, customs, tariffs taxes, control of trade. Title, essentially the chief administrator in charge of the bureaucracy under Governor-General Duquesne and appointed by the crown
Cattaraugus	(Cat-tah-raw-gus) • New York city, county, and creek • Iroquoian for "bad smelling shore"
Chanaye, Corrinne de	(Core-in deh Shah-nay) • wealthy and beautiful courtesan, aristocrat of Montreal; partner and owner of the Dunemoore Company

Chesanin*   (Kay´-zan-in) • "lion of the tree" • one of Chittaqua's twin sons, later Henri's best friend

Chittaqua   (Chi-tock´-qwah) • also Chautauqua • county and famous lake in New York • Iroquoian name believed to mean "place where one was lost" or "one lost in the wilderness"

Colbért, Helmut   (Hell´-moot Coal-bear) • assassin, murderer, serial killer, and all things bad and nasty

Contrecoeur, Pierre de (Con-treh-care) • Colonel, Governor-General Duquesne's chief of staff and eventual commander of French expeditionary forces south of the lakes

coureur de bois (coo-ruhr´ deh bwah) • "wood runner," "bush racer," "bush ranger," or "bush master" • name given to the famous French forest men of the 16th, 17th, and 18th centuries

Dinwiddie, Robert (Din-witty) • Governor of Virginia

Dunemoore, Pierre (Pierre Doon-neh-moor)

Duquesne, Marquis (Doo-kenz) • Duquesne de Menneville, Michel-Ange; Governor-General of New France 1752–1755

Erigh   (Ear-ee) • also Erie • the great lake of Ohio • tribal people known as "the cat people" also "the people of the panther"

Fort Frontenac   (fron-ten-nak) • named after Count Louis de Baude de Frontenac • wilderness fort located at the entrance to the Saint Lawrence River on Lake Ontario near Kingston, Ontario

Fort Le Boeuf   (lei-behf) • French word meaning "the beef" •

wilderness fort formerly located on present-day French Creek, near the town of Waterford, Pennsylvania

Fort Machault
(mah-sho) • named after financial wizard Jean-Baptiste de Machault, d'Arnouville • wilderness fort formerly located at the junction of French Creek and the Allegheny River, near the town of Franklin, Pennsylvania

Fort Niagara
located at the juncture of the Niagara River and Lake Ontario; it has been restored and accepts visitors daily

Fort Oswego
(osh-we-go) • Iroquoian meaning "the outpouring" • city • wilderness fort (English) located on Lake Ontario near the city of Oswego, New York

Gabriel,
Sergeant Major
(Gab´-ree-ell) • of the garrison at Fort Niagara advanced and second-in-command at Fort Le Beouf

Gerrard, Philippe
(Fill-leap´ Jurr-rard)

Gerrard, Henri
(Awn-ree´ Jurr-rard)

Huron
(Hyour´-ron) • lake and numerous counties derived from the French word *hure*, meaning "rough"; people believed to be a branch of the Wyandot tribe

intendant
title, essentially, chief administrator of any of the appointed postings in New France: Intendant Bigôt, in charge of the bureaucracy under Governor-General Duquesne and appointed by the crown; Jesuit Intendant André Nicolet, appointed by the Jesuit clergy, in charge of all missionary-related activities in New France

Iroquois	(Ear-row-kwoy´) • peak, national wildlife refuge, lake, and county • name given by Algonquians with French spelling meaning "real adders" • possibly from the Algonquian word *ierokwa* meaning "they who smoke" • probably the most successful native confederation in North America
Juniata	(Joon´-eeah-tah) • Chittaqua's wife • county in Pennsylvania • Iroquoian name
Lake Ontario	(On-tear´-ee-oh) • city and counties • from Iroquoian "sparkling waters"
LaTour, Captain	(Lah-toor´) • French merchant ship captain and smuggler for Lady de Chanaye
Machault, Jean-Baptiste d'Arnouville	(Ma-sho) • French financial wizard and statesman
machicolated	adjective applied to the stone castle of Fort Niagara, describing the numerous over-hanging dormers with gunports that allowed defenders on the third floor to shoot down at attackers outside the walls
Maltoc*	(Maul-tock´) • "walking eagle" • clan chief of the Hawk clan of the Seneca, his village was located near Conneaut lake in western Pennsylvania
Mohawk	(Moe-hawk) • New York river • possibly "wolf people" • Algonquian neighbors also named the "cannibals"
Monakaduto	(Mo-nack´-ah-doo-tow) • also called Half-King • "village chief" • high chief of the Seneca Indians, his village was located at Logstown near the city of Aliquippa, Pennsylvania

Monongahela River	(Mo-nan-ga-heel-ah) • rivers and national forest • from Delaware word *menaungehilla*, meaning "river with slippery banks"
Niagara fort and falls	• possibly Iroquoian "thunder of waters," also "point of land cut in two," or "thunder of waters resounding with a great noise"
Nicolet, André	(Awn-dray Ni-coh-leh) • Intendant General of the Society of Jesus in New France
Ohio River	also oheo • state, river, counties, municipalities • Iroquoian meaning "beautiful"
Okeanneh	(Oh-key´-ahh-nay) • or Okeana • city in Ohio • Iroquoian meaning "princess"
Oneida	(Oh-knee´-dah) • cities, lakes, counties • "stone people" • a tribe of the Iroquois confederation
Onondaga	(Oh-non-day-gah) • New York county • "hill people"
Ootego	(Oh-oh-tay-goh) • city • Iroquoian meaning "to have fire there" • shaman of the Wolf clan of the Seneca
Ottawa	(Awt-taw´-wah) • cities, counties, forests • Huron word meaning "he buys" or "to trade"
Péan, Major Michel	(Pay-awh) • second-in-command of the French expeditionary forces, later transferred to Montréal
Piqua	(Pee-qwah´) • cities • meaning "ashes" or "bear" • clan chief of the Wolf clan of the Seneca, his village was located at Slippery Rock lake near Portersville, Pennsylvania

Propei, Marquis de   (Pro-pay) • fictional Marquis of Rouen

Pouchot,   (Fran-swa Poo-sho) • commandant of Fort Niagara
Captain Francois   after Captain Benoit, responsible for the expansion
                          of the fort to its present size

Prideaux, Camille   (Pre-dō) • second-in-command of Fort Niagara
                          under Captain Benoit, later promoted to
                          commandant of Fort Le Beouf

Rivière aux Boeufs   (Ree-vee-ehr oh Buh) • "river of beef" or "buffalo
                          river" • known today as French Creek, traverses
                          western Pennsylvania until it merges with the
                          Allegheny River

Routier, Sergeant   (Roo´-tee-aa) • formerly Corporal Routier, a
                          member of the garrison of Fort Niagara under
                          Captain Benoit

Sauquita*   (Saw-kwee´-tah) • "black bull" • of the Wolf clan
                          Seneca, Piqua's son

Seneca   (Sen´-nick-kah) • county, lake, river, falls • possible
                          Mohegan given name meaning "stony place" • the
                          westernmost tribe of the Iroquois League

Tahiawagi   (Tah-heeya´-wah-gee) • Holder of the Heavens,
                          Iroquoian national deity

Tamaqua   (Tah-mock´-qwah) • city • Delaware name possibly
                          meaning "beaver women" • Seneca woman of the
                          Hawk clan

Tinian, Father   (Tin´-ee-ahn) • secretary to Archbishop André
                          Nicolet

| VanderMeer, Charles | (Van-der-mere´) • Dutchman and court artist to the crown of France, also a jeweler |
| *voyageurs* | (vwa-yaj-jars´) • travelers |

Characters from The Moon Promise
Note: Some of these entries are aliases of characters were first introduced in *The Ghost Eagle*.

Prologue

Red Moonglow	high priestess of the Chunkee people, sister to the Chunkee chief
Shengzong	emperor of Liao in Khitai (China)
Shou Yelu	from Khitai (China)

The Moon Promise

Cortelaine, Monseigneur	Fort Niagara missionary (ch.11)
de Villiers, Coulon	defeated Washington in revenge for the slaying of his Louis of Brunswick brother (ch.16)
Ernest, Louis	Duke of Brunswick-Lüneburg-Bevern, also of Louis of Brunswick Brunswick-Wolfenbüttel, father of fictitious character Charles VanderMeer (ch.29)
James	chamberlain of Lady Chanaye's Quebec City house (ch.39)
Joncaire, Captain Daniel	Fort Machault commandant (ch.14)
Jordaine, René	a respected merchant in Quebec City alias, Rouge Piège, Red Snare (ch.39)

La Galissonière — Montréal/Quebec doctor to Governor Duquesne and Corrinne de Chanaye, head of the Hotel Dieu in New France (ch.29)

Laval, Joseph — twenty-three, bastard son of a scullery maid working at the asylum (epil)

Le Roy, Julien — clockmaker for King Louie (ch.31)

Louvet, Madeleine — former Sister Novitiate and friend to Henri Gerrard at Saint Ouen's Church (ch.28)

Maisson Cloudwalker — half-breed Ottawa, first scout for Major Péan (ch.36)

Monakaduto — (Mo-nack´-ah-doo-tow) • also called Half-King,

Ootego — (Oh-oh-tay-goh) • Seneca Wolf clan shaman (ch.2)

Renard — a carriage driver of Lady Chanaye's Quebec City house (ch.39)

Tall Mountain Among Trees — high chief of the Oswego Oneida (ch.1)

Tiyanoga — (Tee yah oh ga) • Mohawk-Seneca council chief (ch.4)

Two Totem — one of Henri Gerrard's totem names, the other is Wolf-Bear (ch.9)

VanderMeer, Charles — fictitious artist and the direct heir to the Duke of Brunswick (ch.8)

Whiskey Man — Monakaduto's daughter's husband (ch.2), also brother to Pemberton Curtiss, and slain by Philippe Gerrard

White Crow Foot   Huron shaman (ch.25)

Wolf-Bear   Henri Gerrard totem name given to him
by Chittaqua in the Erigh naming ceremony (ch.9)

The Andrototekan holy words
All of these words are invented.

An dro to te kan   man of many tribes
Loh cai teem   guide to the truth
The deh roles   cools the burning grief
Bes mi on tig   gives rain to the earth
Soo anlo tamey   unite the weeping hearts
Mah han atakehsey   the ghosts lifting wind
Ha teh ko ha sen kah   one light, one life
Cou ti si mah   my spirit love

The Justice of King Harald

The Assassin
The assassin takes life without judgment, and gives death without mercy.
I therefore judge his death to reveal his life.
As he strangled his victims with his hands,
so shall his hands be taken in death.
As he kicked his victims,
so shall his feet be taken in death.
As he saw his victims die,
so shall his eyes be taken in death.
As he heard his victims scream,
so shall his ears be taken in death.
As he cursed his victims last breath
so shall his lips and tongue be taken in death.
As he drained blood from his victims,
so shall he be hung upside down and drained in death.
As his thoughts were of death
so shall his head be taken and spitted on a pike.
Those who dare to touch the assassin in death,
so shall they be judged like him in life.

References

I relied heavily on the list of references below to keep my imagination from straying too far from recorded history. *Wilderness Empire* by Allan W. Eckert (noted historian and seven-time Pulitzer Prize nominee), the second book in his *Winning of America* series, is an extraordinary read and was a primary resource of facts and information. I also relied heavily on *Opening the Gates of Eighteenth-Century Montréal* by Phyllis Lambert and Alan Stewart to give me the highly detailed, colorful background on this vibrant frontier city in 1753. Montréal is still an exciting place to visit for high culture, excellent food, and great people.

A huge amount of research for *The Ghost Eagle* as well as *The Moon Promise* was also obtained from standard Google searches and the extraordinary trove of information available from Wikipedia articles.

One new reference was added to the previous list, *Cahokia*, by Timothy Pauketat, Professor of Anthropology at the University of Illinois, Urbana-Champaign. He presents a well researched, insightful and excellently written description of the culture, religion and ruling practices of the native peoples who lived a thousand years ago on the Mississippi River near what is called St. Louis, Missouri today. They were an extraordinary Native American culture of astronomers and builders, avid sporting fans, traders, sophisticated farmers, with a strong, fairly peaceful government, which produced cities and packed-earth pyramids, including the Monks Mound, the third tallest pyramidal structure in North American history, rivaling the largest pyramids in Mexico and even Peru. You can still visit it today.

Eckert, Allan W. *Wilderness Empire*. Ashland, KY: Jesse Stuart Foundation, 2001.

Lambert, Phyllis and Alan Stewart. *Opening the Gates of Eighteenth-Century Montréal*. Montreal, QC: Canadian Centre for Architecture, 1992.

Dunnigan, Brian Leigh. *History and Development of Old Fort Niagara.* Youngstown, N.Y.: Old Fort Niagara Association, 1985.

————. *Glorious Old Relic.* Youngstown, N.Y.: Old Fort Niagara Association, 1987.

Snow, Dean. *The Iroquois.* Oxford: Wiley-Blackwell Publisher, 1996.

Grooms, Steve. *Return of the Wolf.* Minocqua, WI: NorthWord Press, 1999.

Eccles, W.J. *The Canadian Frontier.* Albuquerque: University of New Mexico Press, 1983.

Markale, Jean. *The Celts.* Rochester, VT: Inner Traditions International, 1993.

Graymont, Barbara. *The Iroquois.* New York: Chelsea House Publishers, 1988.

Dickenson, John A. and Brian Young. *A Short History of Quebec.* Toronto: Copp Clark Pitman Ltd., 1993.

Andrews, Ted. *Animal Speak.* St. Paul, MN: Llewellyn Publications, 1993.

Brandon, William. *Indian.* Boston: Houghton Mifflin Company, 1987.

Sun Bear and Wabun. *The Medicine Wheel.* New York: Simon & Schuster, 1980.

Hutchens, Alma R. *A Handbook of Native American Herbs.* Boston: Shambhala Publications, 1992.

Pauketat, R., Timothy. *Cahokia.* New York: Penguin Books, 2010.

About the Author

Quentin Grady was born in Hartford, Connecticut and raised in Cleveland, Ohio. Upon receiving a scholarship from the U.S. Navy in 1970, he graduated from the University of Utah in 1972 with degrees in computer science and mathematics. Subsequent to that he completed graduate studies in nuclear engineering. He served as a naval officer on nuclear submarines until 1980. After leaving the service, he held several senior management positions in the software industry for companies like Oracle, specializing in utility applications and engineering solutions. Passionate about fiction writing from an early age, he has devoted the last two years toward getting his first novel published with several more in production.

The Ghost Eagle was published in August 2013; *The Moon Promise*, December 2013.

The Falcon Queen, Book 3 of the *Ghost Eagle* series, is expected to be published by the summer of 2014.

These books can be found on the following sites:

www.amazon.com

www.ghosteaglepublishing.com

He lives in Lincoln, California near Sacramento with his wife, Brenda, an independent business woman and freelance artist.

www.ingramcontent.com/pod-product-compliance
Lightning Source LLC
Chambersburg PA
CBHW051927020726
47501CB00001B/12